# 100 DASTARDLY LITTLE DETECTIVE STORIES

# 100 DASTARDLY LITTLE DETECTIVE STORIES

Edited by
Robert Weinberg, Stefan Dziemianowicz,
and Martin H. Greenberg

BARNES
&NOBLE
BOOKS
NEW YORK

This edition published by Barnes & Noble, Inc.,
by arrangement with Martin H. Greenberg

1993 Barnes & Noble Books

Book design by Steve Morse

ISBN 1-56619-107-6

Printed and bound in the United States of America

M   9   8   7   6   5

# ACKNOWLEDGMENTS

"Better Hands" by Dale Clark, "The Cap'n Sleeps" by John Earl Davis, "Cop Maker" by Ronald Henderson, "Curtains for Kelly" by John Randolph Phillips, "Cut Glass" by Frederick Arnold Kummer, Jr., "The Dead Go Overboard" by Fenton W. Earnshaw, "Detective for a Day" by Walt Sheldon, "Die Before Bedtime" by Walt Sheldon, "Dust" by James W. Holden, "Extra Service" by John Mallory, "Eye-Witness" by Donald S. Aitken, "A Hand of Pinochle" by Theodore Tinsley, "Higher Education" by Sidney Waldo, "Hip and Thigh" by H. H. Matteson, "Ignorance of Art" by Vincent Hall, "Kansas City Connection" by Wayne McMillan, "Murderer's Handicap" by Alex Barber, "Old Calamity's Stick-up" by Joseph Fulling Fishman, "Old Guy" by Maitland Le-Roy Osborne, "Safety Deposit" by B. B. Fowler, "The Sign" by Tom Curry, "Smoke Sign" by Dale Clark, "Summer's End" by William Manners, and "A Tulip in the Snow" by John McCurnin copyright © 1934–1941 by The Frank A. Munsey Company. Copyright renewed © 1962–1969 and assigned to Argosy Communications Inc. All Rights Reserved. Reprinted by arrangement with Argosy Communications Inc.

"Anchor the Stiff!" by Dan Gordon, "An Axe to Grind" by Curt Hamlin, "Behind Murder's Eight-Ball" by Don James, "Calling Dr. Death" by C. William Harrison, "The Cop and the Lady" by Booton Herndon, "Duck Behind that Eight-Ball!" by Nick Spain, "A Friend of Davy Jones'" by Dan Gordon, "Heir-in-a-Hurry" by Morris Cooper, "Mrs. Belcourt Draws a Bier" by Alan Ritner Anderson, "Night Watch" by Scott O'Hara, "Packed House" by Robert Zacks, "Today's Special—Poison!" by V. E. Thiessen, "While the Cat's Away—" by Dorothy Dunn, "The Wire-Pullers" by Morris Cooper, "According to Plan" by Ray Darby, "Checkmated!" by Coretta Slavska, "Death Racket" by Frederick Arnold Kummer, Jr., "Knit One—Kill Two" by Fergus Truslow, "Three Men and a Corpse" by Victor K. Ray, "If the Body Fits—" by Larry Holden, "The Man Who Died Too Often" by David Crewe, and "A Shroud with a Silver Lining" by Marion Lineaweaver copyright © 1939–1952 by Popular Publications Inc. Copyright renewed © 1967–1980 and assigned to Argosy Communications Inc. All rights reserved. Reprinted by arrangement with Argosy Communications Inc.

"Affirmative Action" by Jon L. Breen—Copyright © 1990 by Jon L. Breen. Reprinted by permission of the author.

# CONTENTS

# INTRODUCTION

If the measure of a detective's capabilities is how fast he or she solves a crime, then 100 *Dastardly Little Detective Stories* is an introduction to some of the most formidable crimestoppers in all detective fiction: in each story, the detective unravels a mystery in several thousand words or less.

This is no mean feat—when you consider that the best-known detectives generally need at least three or four times that length, if not an entire novel, in which to prove their mettle. Nevertheless, the short-short detective story has a venerable tradition that extends back to the very origins of detective fiction. The earliest story in this volume, Abraham Lincoln's "The Trailor Murder Mystery," appeared in 1843, only a few years after Edgar Allan Poe introduced the first true detective of fiction, C. Auguste Dupin. In the century-and-a-half since, the short-short form has attracted the interest of some of the most distinguished names in literature, among them W. W. Jacobs (best known for his story "The Monkey's Paw"), novelists Charles Dickens, Jack London, Sir James M. Barrie, and short-story master O. Henry.

The single greatest influence on the stories collected here is Sir Arthur Conan Doyle's Sherlock Holmes. Doyle's master sleuth is emulated in the armchair detection of such stories as George Barton's "Adventure of the Baritone Singer," Rodrigues Ottolengui's "A Novel Forgery," and L. T. Meade and Robert Eustace's "The Outside Ledge," and his minimalist's technique is openly lampooned in a clutch of tales by O. Henry, Stephen Leacock, R. C. Lehmann, and R. K. Munkittrick. However, the short-short tale easily accommodates all detective fiction styles, including the hardboiled tradition of Theodore Tinsley's "A Hand of Pinochle" and B. B. Fowler's "Safety Deposit," the crime-suspense mode of Tom Curry's "The Sign" and John McCurnin's "A Tulip in the Snow," the police procedural form of Michael Black's "The Rosary" and Sidney Waldo's "Higher Education," the borderline horror of Larry Holden's "If the Body Fits," and the modern *noir* thriller elements of Wayne D. Dundee's "Harsh Light of Day" and Bill Pronzini's "Souls Burning."

Though brevity is the soul of the short-short detective story, there are no limits to the imagination of its practitioners. Detectives appear as professional investigators in Dick Donovan's "The Spell of the Black

Siren" and Larry Segriff's "A Point of Honor," policemen in Charles Dickens's "Artful Touch" and Gary Lovisi's "Dogs Know," cynical private eyes in Gerry Tollesfrud's "Night Work" and Fergus Truslow's "Knit One—Kill Two," savvy spouses in William Manner's "Summer's End" and Dorothy Dunn's "While the Cat's Away," maritime police in Dan Gordon's "Anchor the Stiff!" and "A Friend of Davy Jones'," crime reporters in Curt Hamlin's "An Axe to Grind" and Don James's "Behind Murder's Eight-Ball," doctors in David Crewe's "The Man Who Died Too Often," pullman conductors in Howard Finney's "Murder on the Limited," artists in Vincent Hall's "Ignorance of Art," and inventors in Maitland LeRoy Osborne's "Old Guy." Their adventures take places in locales as different as the highlands of Jamaica in Hugh B. Cave's "Naked in Darkness," the waterfront of Nagichak Island in H. H. Matteson's "Hip and Thigh," and the urban jungle of C. J. Henderson's "Bread Ahead." And they involve crimes ranging from homicide in Ray Darby's "According to Plan" to felonious impersonation in Donald S. Aitken's "Eye-Witness," a crime of passion in O. R. Dale's "The Bloodless Corpse," a prison breakout in Joseph Fulling Fishman's "Old Calamity's Stick-up," and grand larceny in Marcia Muller and Bill Pronzini's "Cache and Carry."

In the tales that follow, readers will find themselves collaborating with some of the most unlikely detectives in fiction to match wits with some of the most devious criminals. Not all of the solutions will come easily—but it is reassuring to know that they will come quickly!

—Stefan Dziemianowicz
1993

# According to Plan

*by Ray Darby*

It was after nine o'clock when Ben Wayne's taxi drew up at the corner, half a block from Doctor Ridgeway's white house in suburban Lynwood. Ben paid the driver, being careful to keep his face averted and the hat pulled low over his eyes. He mentally cursed that hat. It was quite a trick to keep it on his head at all, because it was at least two sizes too small.

As the taxi pulled away, Ben straightened his tie and smoothed the jacket of the double-breasted suit he had taken off the man in the jail corridor. The suit fitted him better than the hat, although Ben hated gray. He had always been a smart dresser, preferring browns or the darker tweeds. He hoped the guy in the corridor was still unconscious. If he came to and worked the gag off, he could raise a holler, and Ben's whole plan depended on getting at least a two-hour start.

It was a good plan. Ben had figured it all out after he'd got his brains unscrambled back there in Los Angeles County Jail. This had taken time, because when they brought Ben in he was raving. A man could go all to pieces over a woman.

It was a good plan, and yet, as he hurried down the street towards Doctor Ridgeway's house, Ben couldn't help thinking about all the things that could go wrong. The guy whose clothes he had taken might wake up and raise the alarm. The doctor might have changed his schedule. This would be fatal. It would leave Ben away out on the end of a limb, ruining his revenge and leaving him only the slim hope of hiding out somewhere in the city.

But luck was with him. The doctor's big black sedan was parked out in front of the house, and it was still only twenty minutes past nine. Ben made sure he was unobserved, and then he opened the back door of the car and squeezed in, doubling up his big body so that he was out of sight on the floor. It was cramped in there. The floor of the car was gritty against his hands and his cheek, but now that Ben was so close to success, minor discomforts didn't really bother him.

After five minutes of this his back and shoulder ached like fury. He

1

thought about Doctor Ridgeway, to get his mind off it. He wondered if the wound had left a scar on Doctor Ridgeway's face. The thought that he might have marred that handsome face permanently was pleasing to Ben. It was the next best thing to putting a bullet clean through his head, which Ben would have done if he hadn't had too many drinks in him at the time.

A door slammed up at the house. Ben froze. Hurrying footsteps approached the car. In spite of the tightness in his throat, Ben had a momentary feeling of satisfaction. Everything was working according to plan. The doctor was supposed to be at the hospital by ten o'clock, and he was right on schedule.

The front door of the car opened and he heard Ridgeway get in. The doctor was breathing heavily. He jammed his foot on the starter, slammed the car into gear and roared away from the curb with a spurt that ground Ben's cheek against the gritty floor.

Ben counted to twenty, slowly, before he got up. Then he raised himself just high enough to see the back of the doctor's head. Ridgeway was hatless. In the shifting light, Ben took note of the well-shaped head, the hair curling at the temples and beginning to gray. The doctor was handsome. There was no use denying it. A guy could hardly blame a girl like Louise for falling for him.

Ben was not handsome. He was just a big, ordinary guy, but Louise had loved him as no girl ever had—until she caught pneumonia and Doctor Ridgeway entered the picture. That was where they had both been wrong. Louise may have been everything they said she was at the preliminary hearing. Even a she-devil with the face of an angel. But she had belonged to Ben.

Ben reached into his pocket and took out the revolver. He pressed it gently against the back of Ridgeway's neck. "Don't turn around," he said softly. "Keep right on driving. Turn right when you get to Lakewood Boulevard."

The doctor's body went rigid. The car lurched, then straightened out again.

"Ben!"

"That's right, Doc. Ben. I told you I'd bust out."

"What do you want with me?"

"Plenty. You're going to help me get to Mexico."

"Help you?" The doctor's voice was scornful. "I wouldn't help you across the street!"

Ben pressed the gun harder against the back of his neck. "Sure you

2

will," he said. "I've come this far, and I'm going the rest of the way. They'll never put me in San Quentin."

You had to hand it to the doctor. He had guts. His neck muscles relaxed, and Ben knew that his quick brain was working. He felt a little uneasy. He would have felt really uneasy if he hadn't planned this thing so thoroughly.

"If they get you now," Ridgeway said reasonably, "they'll give you double the sentence. Look, Ben . . . let me out. Take my car and make a run for it. You've already tried to kill me once—"

"Shut up!" Ben snapped. "Turn here!"

The car swung into the heavier traffic of Lakewood Boulevard, heading south.

"One false move," Ben said, "and I'll let you have it."

"How do I know you won't anyway?"

"You don't. That's the gamble you're taking."

For a few minutes the car droned steadily on. Then the doctor tried a new approach. "Ben, if you're still sore about Louise, get over it. You would have lost her anyway." His voice grew bitter. "I lost her, too. She's fascinating—maddening. She drove you wild, and I don't blame you. But, Ben, she's as cold and calculating as a machine. Forget her, Ben."

"You can lay off the fancy talk," Ben said. "It's no use."

Just past Lakewood Village, near the airport, Ben said, "Turn here. To the right."

Doctor Ridgeway slowed the car. The road that branched off to the right was little more than a dark trail.

"Ben," the doctor said, and for the first time there was a note of fear in his voice. "You're not rational. Let me turn around. Let me talk to you. You're making a big mistake, Ben."

"The talking's all over with," Ben said. "Keep going."

"But you don't understand! Why risk your neck over Louise? She's not worth it! Listen to me, Ben—"

Ben swung the muzzle of his gun and cracked it smartly against the side of Doctor Ridgeway's head. "Keep going!"

The big sedan entered the shadowy canyon of the trees and was swallowed up.

At Signal Hill, Ben turned into Highway 101. The big car purred. The road lay ahead of him, all the way down to San Diego, and from there across the border into Mexico.

He felt the reassuring bulge in the pocket of the gray suit, where he had put Ridgeway's billfold with all his identification papers. He glanced at the automobile registration card that was clipped to the steering post of the car. There it was. Doctor Ridgeway. Ben smiled a tight smile and tried to feel as he ought to feel, being a doctor. He remembered, with a little flush of pleasure, that there *had* been a scar on Ridgeway's face from his first bullet. This time his gun had made more than a scar.

There were two State Police cars blocking the highway just after he cleared Long Beach. Ben took a deep breath and slowed down. He had been expecting this.

"Looking for someone, officer?" he asked the trooper who came over.

"That's right."

It was hard for Ben not to laugh out loud. He knew whom they were looking for. He knew they'd be looking twice as hard after they found Ridgeway's body, but by that time he would be lost in the wastes of Mexico.

"Your name?" the trooper asked him.

"Ridgeway," Ben answered calmly. "Doctor Emory Ridgeway. My card?"

The trooper took the proffered card and turned it over in his hand. Ben took out the doctor's driver's license and his insurance identification card, playing it to the hilt. The trooper glanced at these, too.

"Good enough?" Ben enquired.

The trooper nodded. "Fine, Doctor."

"Anything I can do to help?" Ben asked. "There hasn't been an accident, has there?"

"No," the trooper said. "Not yet."

Suddenly Ben found himself staring down the barrel of a big service revolver. He turned quickly, but another trooper was leaning in the opposite window of the car.

"What's the meaning of this?" Ben spluttered.

"End of the line, Doctor," the first trooper said grimly. "We figured you'd try to make a run for it. Get out of the car, with your hands up."

Ben's jaw hung slack with bewilderment. All this was away over his head.

The first trooper said, "We found the body of Louise Hilton at your house, just after you lit out. One of the neighbors heard her scream. That woman was no good, Doctor, but you shouldn't have killed her. Now come on out with your hands up."

# Adventure of the Baritone Singer

*by George Barton*

It was Kelly, the Chief of Detectives, who let Barnes into what afterwards came to be known as the "Mystery of the Baritone Singer." The old man was just considering the advisability of taking an extended vacation when the telephone rang and Kelly asked him to come down to a certain number on the avenue.

"I've got a case here," he said, "that threatens to develop into a first-class problem. I'd like you to take a look at it while all the evidence is fresh. I'm willing to divide honors with you."

Barnes accepted the invitation with alacrity and took Clancy along. The veteran had a sneaking admiration for Kelly and had cooperated with him in the solution of more than one big case. Kelly actually had ideas and was one of the few policemen in Barnes's acquaintance who was not as dull as he looked.

Kelly was waiting for them at the doorway of the house on the avenue, and acted as their escort, They passed through an elegantly furnished hallway and on to the stairway leading to the upper part of the house. At the landing, a frightened girl turned and opened the door of what seemed to be the living room of the house. The sight that met their astonished gaze caused Barnes to give a gasp of surprise. Stretched prostrate on the floor was an elderly man with his arms extended. On the carpet next to his right hand was a glass paper weight, as though it had just slipped from his grasp. A tiny pool of blood had trickled from a wound in his head.

The detective dropped down on his hands and knees and examined the prostrate body. It was rigid, and life was extinct. The old man turned to Kelly.

"You might as well have the body removed to the bedroom—then we can look around."

With the aid of the servants, Kelly succeeded in removing the corpse to the second-story front room. As soon as Kelly returned to the living room Barnes resumed his examination of the apartment. It

5

presented a scene of disorder. A costly velvet cloth had been torn from a massive walnut table in the center of the apartment. A half dozen books and magazines were scattered about the floor. Indeed, two of the books gaped with broken bindings as though they had been used as weapons. The shattered glass over a picture of George Washington on the wall indicated that the father of his country had been the unwilling target for one of the missiles. A pair of spectacles (also broken), an ash receiver, a Billiken, a spilled bottle of ink, and an overturned chair completed the wreck.

The master of the house was evidently a man of refinement who loved music. The room contained a piano, an organ, a harp, a phonograph and a mandolin. Bookcases lined the walls on one side of the apartment. An easel held an open dictionary, while on a couch lay the torn pages containing the words and music of "My Old Kentucky Home." There was a bay window in the rear of the room, but the chief noted that the sashes were tightly closed and fastened with iron clasps. At this stage of the inquiry the door opened timidly and Marie Hearne, a niece of the dead man, came into the room. She looked very white and very frightened.

"You are just in time, Miss Hearne," said Barnes gently. "I want to ask you a question."

She flung herself into a chair and began to rock to and fro nervously.

"I understand your feelings," said the detective, "but I want you to give me a plain story of all that has occurred in this house to-night."

"I can't!" she cried; "it is out of the question."

"But you will have to do so sooner or later. Please tell me now."

"You do not know what you ask," she shrieked; "it would kill me to say anything against Guy."

"Guy?" questioned Barnes, with upraised eyebrows.

"Oh, no," she corrected herself hastily. "I didn't mean that. Please don't mind what I say. You see that I am overwrought and not responsible for what I am saying."

"I have no desire to harass you," insinuated the detective in his caressing way; "indeed, I would like to help you if it is in my power."

The tears welled forth and relieved her from the strain under which she had been laboring. Indeed, she exhibited the common feminine appearance after a good cry. She seemed relieved. Barnes saw his opportunity and seized it.

"Now, Miss Hearne," he said, "I am prepared to hear your story."

She looked at Barnes apprehensively.

"I—I—that is, I fear publicity."

6

Kelly spoke up in the tone of one who has authority:

"You can depend absolutely upon his discretion. I vouch for Mr. Barnes and Mr. Clancy, too."

Miss Hearne seemed satisfied. She spoke slowly, as if trying to be accurate and fair in her statements.

"Uncle is a Southerner. He made a great deal of money in the iron business in Tennessee, but retired some years ago and settled in New York. We lived in apartments at first, but finally one of his friends, a lineal descendant of the early Dutch settlers, induced him to buy the house we are in now. I don't want to bore you with unimportant details, but you will see that all this is leading up to the affair of to-night."

"Go ahead, Miss Hearne," interjected Kelly.

"Well, the house is comfortable and roomy, as you notice," she continued, "but it did not seem to supply all that Uncle needed. He has never had any time for society as that term is generally understood, but he is a man with a very sociable disposition, being fond of company and passionately attached to music. Well, to shorten my story, we went to Steinway Hall one afternoon to attend a concert. One of the artists was Mr. Guy Avondale, a baritone of exceptional power. For an encore, he sang 'My Old Kentucky Home,' and he made a conquest of Uncle's heart.

"A few weeks after the concert Mr. Avondale was a guest at our house. For such a talented singer he was exceptionally modest. His manners were good, he made splendid company, and altogether we had every reason to be fond of him. He sang for us frequently, and it was Uncle's delight to get him in the living room to sing the dear old plantation songs of the South."

The young woman paused at this part of the recital, as if loath to say any more. But Barnes encouraged her in his friendly way:

"Go on, Miss Hearne, and remember that you have friendly listeners."

"I dislike to speak of my personal affairs," she said modestly, "but I must. I might say truthfully, that in the beginning I had no more than a passing interest in Guy Avondale. But before many weeks had gone by that interest became profound. You will understand my present position, gentlemen, when I tell you that I love him passionately.

"Events progressed so rapidly that a week ago he proposed to me, and I accepted, providing he could get Uncle's consent. He felt very confident of winning that, and so did I, but our hopes were destined to be shattered. Tonight was the time agreed upon when Guy should 'beard the lion in his den,' as he humorously phrased it.

7

"Just before the hour when Guy was to arrive, I ventured to broach the matter to Uncle, and he said he would never consent to the match. He went further than that, and accused Guy of being a fortune hunter. Incidentally, I want to say that I do not believe the charge. Guy is advancing rapidly in his profession. He is to sing in grand opera next season. I know that, because he showed me the five-year contract that he signed. And I firmly believe that in a few years he will be a great man."

"Please go on with your narrative," gently insisted the detective, fearing a never-ending rhapsody over the perfections of the singer.

"I'm going on," she said, with a self-willed toss of her little head, "but I've got to tell you all of it."

"What else did your uncle say?"

"He told me that he had hoped to marry me into one of the wealthy families of the town. He said that he had some one in view that was distantly related to the Astorbilts. Anyhow, I left the room weeping, and when I got downstairs I found Guy waiting for me in the parlor. He noticed that my eyes were red and insisted on knowing the cause. I told him all that Uncle had said and he was furious."

"What did he say?" asked Barnes.

"He said he was going upstairs to tell Uncle just what he thought of him. I begged him not to get into a quarrel for my sake."

"What else did he say?" persisted the detective.

"He—he said that love was the only excuse for marriage, and that if Uncle put money or position above love, he was not fit to live. He was very much wrought up and his wild talk distressed me. I told him that Uncle had forbidden me to see him any more, and I thought we should separate—at least, for the time being. He was sulky about it, but I said 'Good night' to him and came up in my room to throw myself on the bed and have a good cry. I left him standing in an irresolute way in the hallway."

"Then what happened?"

"I fell asleep crying. When I woke up I knew it must be quite late. Something prompted me to go downstairs, but no one was there. I came up slowly, and noticed that there was a light in the living room. The door was shut, but I could see the light streaming from one of the windows into the side yard. I knew by that Uncle was still awake, and I was filled with a desire to go in and throw myself at his feet and plead my cause. I knew that, after all, he could never refuse me any-thing that was necessary for my happiness. I had my hand on the knob of the door, when I was startled by a strong baritone voice breaking into song. It was Guy's voice. There can be no mistake about

8

that. I could tell it among ten million. He was singing 'My Old Kentucky Home.' The words rang out superbly. I stood there listening, enraptured, to the old refrain:

'The sun shines bright in my old Kentucky home,
In my old Kentucky home, far away.'

"It would not do to disturb them. I crept quietly to my room and waited. Surely, I thought, Guy must have pleaded successfully. Presently the singing ceased. I heard the front door close with a bang. Ten —fifteen minutes passed, and I determined to go down and hear my fate. I tapped on the door of the living room. No response came, and I turned the knob and walked in, and was horrified at the sight of my uncle's senseless body. I screamed. Aunt rushed a servant for the doctor and then telephoned for the police."

There was a long pause at the conclusion of the narrative. Finally Kelly said:

"What is the address of Guy Avondale?"

"Well," she said hesitatingly, "he has a flat on W. 110th St., but he is usually at a studio on E. 10th St. Besides that, he sings several times a week at the Church of the Golden Gates."

Barnes made a note of the addresses and said good-by to Miss Hearne. As they reached the front door the journalist turned to the servant girl.

"Susan," he said abruptly, but with easy familiarity, "did Mr. Guy Avondale go up to Mr. Fulton's room last night?"

"Yes, sir," she replied unthinkingly; then, with sudden terror, "I hope I haven't said anything wrong, sir."

"Not at all. You never go wrong in telling the truth, Susan. But how do you know that the young man went upstairs?"

"Because a messenger came here with a telegram for Mr. Avondale, and I delivered it to him personally. I supposed he was in the parlor and I called to him but the answer came from the head of the stairs, as though he had just come out of the living room."

"Thank you very much, Susan, and good-night."

As they reached the sidewalk, Kelly accosted the policeman on the beat:

"Well, Jake," he exclaimed cheerfully, "anything going on about here?"

"No, Mr. Kelly," responded the officer. "I saw Reddy Brown hanging around here earlier in the evening, but he's gone now."

"I thought he was in Sing Sing."

"Released this morning," replied the policeman.

"Do you think he's the fellow you're after?" asked Clancy, as they moved away.

"I'll know before daylight," said Barnes.

Before the three men separated Barnes asked Kelly to follow out a certain line of work and promised to meet him the next day. That night he sat smoking one stogie after another in his room and all the while thinking. At midnight, when he turned in, there was a smile of triumph on his face. The first thing in the morning he called at the Fulton home to make a second examination of the library, and when he finished the smile was actually expansive. A little later he met Kelly and Clancy.

"Well, boys," he cried, throwing away the stump of his weed and lighting a fresh one, "what luck?"

"Good and bad," said Kelly, taking the initiative in replying.

"Put it in plain English," suggested Barnes.

"Well," answered Kelly, "I went to Avondale's flat on W. 110th St., and found that he had left there at about six o'clock last night. He has not returned since."

"Sure he didn't return this morning?"

"Positive. The janitor assures me also that it is the first night that he has failed to return home since he rented the flat. He has won the reputation of being a man of very regular habits, and the janitor, who regards him as a friend and counselor, is very much disturbed over his absence."

"How about the studio on E. 10th St.?"

"He has not been there either. That is regarded as very singular, because he had a positive engagement at 3 o'clock this afternoon. He was to rehearse an opera in which he is to sing shortly."

"Well, son," said Barnes, turning to Clancy, "what have you to say for yourself?"

"I have to say that the bird has flown, and you might as well give up the chase?"

"How do you know?"

"Why, I went to the Church of the Golden Gates. He was to take part in a song service that began at seven o'clock. But he wasn't there. He has been singing at the church for two years and it is the first time he has ever been absent."

"What do you think about it?" asked Clancy, anxiously. "Was it the singer or the crook from Sing Sing?"

Barnes took a prolonged puff at his stogie. He ignored the last part of the question.

"I think your reports confirm my evidence," he said.

"What is that?"

"That Avondale is now in Boston."

"In Boston?" they cried in chorus.

"Yes, in Boston. I discovered that the telegram which was delivered to him last night was a summons to Boston. Who it was from I haven't learned, but I imagine he took the first train after leaving the Fulton house."

"What are you going to do about it?" asked Kelly.

"Simply wait for his return," was the calm reply. "He'll come back to New York. They always do. I was at the station tonight, but he did not arrive. I've got a man on my lookout now, but I won't anticipate any results tonight. From what I have learned of Avondale's tastes and habits, he'll travel on the Colonial Express. I want you two to be there tomorrow evening. Here's a description of the man and his photograph. If he comes in on that train, get him."

"You bet I'll get him!" retorted the detective.

At the same hour the following night a taxicab drove up to Barnes' apartments, and Kelly and Clancy alighted, followed by a tall, broad-shouldered, athletic fellow with curly hair and a slight blonde mustache.

"Barnes," said Kelly, "I want you to meet Mr. Guy Avondale."

"Charmed," responded the young fellow grasping the proffered hand, "although for the life of me I can't understand why I am given the pleasure."

"I want you to make a visit with me," said Barnes significantly, "a visit that may be of great importance to you."

"Go as far as you like," was the smiling rejoinder, and the four men climbed into the electric vehicle which was headed in the direction of the Fulton mansion. The journey was made rapidly and in silence. As the machine slowed up in front of the brownstone house, Barnes said carelessly:

"That was a sad thing about Mr. Fulton."

"What about him?"

"Knocked senseless in his library the night before last."

Avondale gasped.

"You amaze me! It's the first I've heard of it."

"Plays his part well," whispered Clancy to Kelly.

"Yes, he's a cool one, all right," was the muffled response.

In the parlor, Marie Hearne, white faced and stern, was awaiting them. The singer rushed over to greet the girl.

"Marie," he cried, "I'm amazed and shocked at the news I've just heard."

She shrank from him.

"You were in the room with Uncle."

"I?" he exclaimed, "you're terribly mistaken!"

"How can you deny it?" she cried, with a burst of indignation. "I heard you—I heard you singing."

Barnes held up his hands to stop the words that were on the lips of the young man.

"Tell me briefly what happened that night."

"There isn't much to tell," replied Avondale, with evident frankness, "I came here to speak to Mr. Fulton on a very personal matter. Something Marie—Miss Hearne—told me made me very indignant. I resolved to go upstairs and tell her uncle what I thought of him. She begged me not to do so. She bade me good night and left me standing in the hallway. I stood there irresolute for some time. Finally I went upstairs and had my hand on the knob of the door when I heard the voice of one of the servants calling my name. I came downstairs and Susan, the maid, gave me a telegram. It was from Boston, telling me that my brother was at the point of death. I decided to postpone seeing Mr. Fulton. I took the first train. Fortunately my brother rallied and is now on the road to recovery. I returned and here I am."

"My friends," exclaimed Barnes, as Avondale finished, "you have heard the truth. Mr. Avondale is perfectly innocent of any wrong. I have the real culprit in that room now."

They looked at him in perfect amazement.

"Come with me," commanded the veteran.

They followed him into the apartment. An object stood in the center of the table covered with a cloth.

"Here's the cause of all the trouble," cried Barnes.

With that, he threw off the cover, revealing a phonograph. He gave the lever of the machine a twist and immediately the apartment was filled with the strains of

> "The sun shines bright in my old Kentucky home,
> In my old Kentucky home, far away."

It was in Avondale's best voice. A cry of delight greeted the old song. Marie flew into the outstretched arms of the young singer.

"Can you ever forgive me?" she cried.

"I can and will," he said magnanimously, "but I'll never make another record for your uncle's phonograph."

12

"The thing's as plain as day," remarked Barnes, ignoring this flagrant exhibition of love. "Your uncle was suddenly seized by an attack of vertigo, and, in falling, he grasped the table cloth, throwing the books and papers all over the floor, and catapulting one missile straight into the picture on the wall. His head struck the fender and resulted in concussion of the brain. That was the real cause of his death, and it will be so certified by the coroner's physician."

"Will this mean a marriage?" queried Clancy, curiously, as they trudged down the avenue.

The old man chuckled softly.

"If I were as sure of Heaven as they are of matrimony, I'd be a happy man!"

# The Adventure of the Table Foot

*by Zero (Allan Ramsay)*

I called one morning—a crisp cold wintry December day—on my friend Thinlock Bones, for the purpose of keeping him company at breakfast, and, as usual about this time of the morning, I found him running over the agony columns of the different newspapers, quietly smiling at the egotistical private-detective advertisements. He looked up and greeted me as I entered.

"Ah, Whatsoname, how d'you do? You have not had breakfast yet. And you must be hungry. I suppose that is why you drove, and in a hansom too. Yet you had time to stay and look at your barometer. You look surprised. I can easily see—any fool would see it—that you've not breakfasted, as your teeth and mouth are absolutely clean, not a crumb about. I noticed it as you smiled on your entry. You drove—it's a muddy morning and your boots are quite clean. In a hansom—don't I know what time you rise? How then could you get here so quickly without doing it in a hansom? A bus or four-wheeler couldn't do it in the time. Oh! The barometer business. Why, it's as plain as a pikestaff. It's a glorious morning, yet you've brought an umbrella thinking that it would rain. And why should you think it would rain unless the barometer told you so? I see, too, some laborer pushed up against you as you came along. The mud on your shoulder, you know."

"It was a lamppost that did it," I answered.

"It was a laborer," quietly said Bones.

At that moment a young man was shown in. He was as pale as death and trembling in every limb. Thinlock Bones settled himself for business, and, as was the usual habit with him when he was about to think, he put his two long tapered hands to his nose.

"What can I do for you, sir?" asked Bones. "Surely a young swell like you, with plenty of money, a brougham, living in the fashionable part of the West End, and the son of a Peer, can't be in trouble."

"Good God, you're right, how do you know it all?" cried the youth.

"I deduct it," said Thinlock, "you tell me it all yourself. But proceed."

"My name is St. Timon—"

"Robert St. Timon," put in Bones.

"Yes, that is so, but—"

"I saw it in your hat," said Bones.

"I am Robert St. Timon, son of Lord St. Timon, of Grosvenor Square, and am—"

"Private Secretary to him," continued Thinlock. "I see a letter marked *Private and Confidential* addressed to your father sticking out of your pocket."

"Quite correct," went on St. Timon, "thus it was that in my confidential capacity I heard one day from my father of an attachment, an infatuation that someone had for him, an elderly—"

"Lady," said Thinlock Bones, from the depths of his chair, showing how keenly he was following the depths of the plot as it was unfolded to him by his peculiar habit of holding his bloodless hands to his nose.

"Right again," said the young man. "Mr. Bones, you are simply marvelous. How *do* you manage it?"

"It is very simple," Bones replied, "but I will not stop to explain. Whatsoname here understands my little methods quite well now. He will tell you by-and-by."

"It was an elderly and immensely wealthy lady, then," Robert St. Timon continued, "named the Honorable Mrs. Coran—"

"A widow," Bones interrupted.

"Wonderful," said St. Timon, "the Honorable Mrs. Coran, a widow. It was she who was simply head over ears in love with my father, Lord St. Timon. He, although a widower, cared little for her but—"

"A lot for her money," said the quick-witted detective.

14

"How do you divine these things? You guess my innermost thoughts, the words before they are out of my mouth. How did you know it?" St. Timon asked.

"I know the human race," Thinlock Bones answered.

"Well, if he could manage he wanted to inherit her money without marrying her. Would she leave him her riches if he did not propose, was the question? How to find out? He was a comparatively young man and did not unnecessarily wish to tie himself to an octogenarian, although a millionairess. But he mustn't lose her wealth. If when she died he was not her husband, would he get the money? If the worst came to the worst he must marry her sooner than let the gold slip out of his grasp. But he must not espouse the old lady needlessly. How was he to find out? A project struck him, and the means offered itself. We were both asked to a dinner party at the Countess Plein de Beer's where we knew the Honorable Mrs. Coran would be present, and—"

"You both accepted," interrupted Bones. "Oh," he went on before the other could ask the reasons of his swift and accurate deductions, "oh, it's very simple. I saw it in 'The Daily Telegraph's London Day by Day.'"

"Yes, we accepted," continued St. Timon, "and this was our plan of campaign: I was to take the old doting lady down to dinner and to insinuate myself into her confidence—aided by good wine, of which she was a devoted admirer—in a subtle fashion and thus to extract the secret out of her. I was to find out—by the time she had arrived at the Countess's old port—whether my father was her heir or not. Whether she had left him her money without being his wife. Time was short, and if she had not my father was to propose that very night after dinner. The signal agreed on between my father and me was that if he was her heir without being her husband I was to kick him under the table and he would *not* propose—otherwise he would. Oh! Mr. Bones," he sobbed, turning his piteous white face to Thinlock, "this is where I want your great intellect to help me, to aid me and explain this mystery.

"The plan worked admirably," he went on, "I gleaned every fact about the disposition of her money after her death from her when she was in her cups—or rather her wineglasses. My father was her absolute and sole heir, and I thanked the heavens with all my heart that I was spared such a stepmother. I kicked, as arranged, my father under the table, but oh! Mr. Bones, immediately after dinner my father went to her and asked her to be his wife and she has accepted him! What does it all mean, what does it all mean!!"

*"That you kicked the foot of the table instead!"* quietly replied the greatest detective of modern times as he unraveled the intricate plot and added another success to his brilliant career.

# The Adventure of the Two Collaborators

*by Sir James M. Barrie*

In bringing to a close the adventures of my friend Sherlock Holmes I am perforce reminded that he never, save on the occasion which, as you will now hear, brought his singular career to an end, consented to act in any mystery which was concerned with persons who made a livelihood by their pen. "I am not particular about the people I mix among for business purposes," he would say, "but at literary characters I draw the line."

We were in our rooms in Baker Street one evening. I was (I remember) by the centre table writing out *The Adventure of the Man without a Cork Leg* (which had so puzzled the Royal Society and all the other scientific bodies of Europe), and Holmes was amusing himself with a little revolver practice. It was his custom of a summer evening to fire round my head, just shaving my face, until he had made a photograph of me on the opposite wall, and it is a slight proof of his skill that many of these portraits in pistol shots are considered admirable likenesses.

I happened to look out of the window, and perceiving two gentlemen advancing rapidly along Baker Street asked him who they were. He immediately lit his pipe, and, twisting himself on a chair into the figure 8, replied:

"They are two collaborators in comic opera, and their play has not been a triumph."

I sprang from my chair to the ceiling in amazement, and he then explained:

"My dear Watson, they are obviously men who follow some low calling. That much even you should be able to read in their faces. Those little pieces of blue paper which they fling angrily from them

16

are Durrant's Press Notices. Of these they have obviously hundreds about their person (see how their pockets bulge). They would not dance on them if they were pleasant reading."

I again sprang to the ceiling (which is much dented), and shouted: "Amazing! But they may be mere authors."

"No," said Holmes, "for mere authors only get one press notice a week. Only criminals, dramatists and actors get them by the hundred."

"Then they may be actors."

"No, actors would come in a carriage."

"Can you tell me anything else about them?"

"A great deal. From the mud on the boots of the tall one I perceive that he comes from South Norwood. The other is as obviously a Scotch author."

"How can you tell that?"

"He is carrying in his pocket a book called (I clearly see) *Auld Licht Something*. Would anyone but the author be likely to carry about a book with such a title?"

I had to confess that this was improbable.

It was now evident that the two men (if such they can be called) were seeking our lodgings. I have said (often) that my friend Holmes seldom gave way to emotion of any kind, but he now turned livid with passion. Presently this gave place to a strange look of triumph.

"Watson," he said, "that big fellow has for years taken the credit for my most remarkable doings, but at last I have him—at last!"

Up I went to the ceiling, and when I returned the strangers were in the room.

"I perceive, gentlemen," said Mr. Sherlock Holmes, "that you are at present afflicted by an extraordinary novelty."

The handsomer of our visitors asked in amazement how he knew this, but the big one only scowled.

"You forget that you wear a ring on your fourth finger," replied Mr. Holmes calmly.

I was about to jump to the ceiling when the big brute interposed.

"That tommy-rot is all very well for the public, Holmes," said he, "but you can drop it before me. And, Watson, if you go up to the ceiling again I shall make you stay there."

Here I observed a curious phenomenon. My friend Sherlock Holmes *shrank*. He became small before my eyes. I looked longingly at the ceiling, but dared not.

"Let us cut the first four pages," said the big man, "and proceed to business. I want to know why—"

"Allow me," said Mr. Holmes, with some of his old courage. "You want to know why the public does not go to your opera."

"Exactly," said the other ironically, "as you perceive by my shirt stud." He added more gravely, "And as you can only find out in one way I must insist on your witnessing an entire performance of the piece."

It was an anxious moment for me. I shuddered, for I knew that if Holmes went I should have to go with him. But my friend had a heart of gold.

"Never," he cried fiercely, "I will do anything for you save that."

"Your continued existence depends on it," said the big man menacingly.

"I would rather melt into air," replied Holmes, proudly taking another chair. "But I can tell you why the public don't go to your piece without sitting the thing out myself."

"Why?"

"Because," replied Holmes calmly, "they prefer to stay away."

A dead silence followed that extraordinary remark. For a moment the two intruders gazed with awe upon the man who had unravelled their mystery so wonderfully. Then drawing their knives—

Holmes grew less and less, until nothing was left save a ring of smoke which slowly circled to the ceiling.

The last words of great men are often noteworthy. These were the last words of Sherlock Holmes: "Fool, fool! I have kept you in luxury for years. By my help you have ridden extensively in cabs, where no author was ever seen before. *Henceforth you will ride in buses!*"

The brute sunk into a chair aghast.

The other author did not turn a hair.

*To A. Conan Doyle,*
*from his friend*
*J. M. Barrie*

# The Adventures of
# Shamrock Jolnes

*by O. Henry*

I am so fortunate as to count Shamrock Jolnes, the great New York detective, among my muster of friends. Jolnes is what is called the "inside man" of the city detective force. He is an expert in the use of the typewriter, and it is his duty, whenever there is a "murder mystery" to be solved, to sit at a desk telephone at Headquarters and take down the messages of "cranks" who phone in their confessions to having committed the crime.

But on certain "off" days when confessions are coming in slowly and three or four newspapers have run to earth as many different guilty persons, Jolnes will knock about the town with me, exhibiting, to my great delight and instruction, his marvelous powers of observation and deduction.

The other day I dropped in at Headquarters and found the great detective gazing thoughtfully at a string that was tied tightly around his little finger.

"Good morning, Whatsup," he said, without turning his head. "I'm glad to notice that you've had your house fitted up with electric lights at last."

"Will you please tell me," I said, in surprise, "how you knew that? I am sure that I never mentioned the fact to anyone, and the wiring was a rush order not completed until this morning."

"Nothing easier," said Jolnes, genially. "As you came in I caught the odor of the cigar you are smoking. I know an expensive cigar; and I know that not more than three men in New York can afford to smoke cigars and pay gas bills too at the present time. That was an easy one. But I am working just now on a little problem of my own."

"Why have you that string on your finger?" I asked.

"That's the problem," said Jolnes. "My wife tied that on this morning to remind me of something I was to send up to the house. Sit down, Whatsup, and excuse me for a few moments."

19

The distinguished detective went to a wall telephone, and stood with the receiver to his ear for probably ten minutes.

"Were you listening to a confession?" I asked, when he had returned to his chair.

"Perhaps," said Jolnes, with a smile, "it might be called something of the sort. To be frank with you, Whatsup, I've cut out the dope. I've been increasing the quantity for so long that morphine doesn't have much effect on me any more. I've got to have something more powerful. That telephone I just went to is connected with a room in the Waldorf where there's an author's reading in progress. Now, to get at the solution of this string."

After five minutes of silent pondering, Jolnes looked at me, with a smile, and nodded his head.

"Wonderful man!" I exclaimed. "Already?"

"It is quite simple," he said, holding up his finger. "You see that knot? That is to prevent my forgetting. It is, therefore, a forget-me-knot. A forget-me-not is a flower. It was a sack of flour that I was to send home!"

"Beautiful!" I could not help crying out in admiration.

"Suppose we go out for a ramble," suggested Jolnes.

"There is only one case of importance on hand just now. Old man McCarty, one hundred and four years old, died from eating too many bananas. The evidence points so strongly to the Mafia that the police have surrounded the Second Avenue Katzenjammer Gambrinus Club No. 2, and the capture of the assassin is only the matter of a few hours. The detective force has not yet been called on for assistance."

Jolnes and I went out and up the street toward the corner, where we were to catch a surface car.

Halfway up the block we met Rheingelder, an acquaintance of ours, who held a City Hall position.

"Good morning, Rheingelder," said Jolnes, halting. "Nice breakfast that was you had this morning."

Always on the lookout for the detective's remarkable feats of deduction, I saw Jolnes's eyes flash for an instant upon a long yellow splash on the shirt bosom and a smaller one upon the chin of Rheingelder—both undoubtedly made by the yolk of an egg.

"Oh, dot is some of your detectiveness," said Rheingelder, shaking all over with a smile. "Vell, I pet you trinks und cigars all round dot you cannot tell vot I haf eaten for breakfast."

"Done," said Jolnes. "Sausage, pumpernickel and coffee."

Rheingelder admitted the correctness of the surmise and paid the bet. When we had proceeded on our way I said to Jolnes:

"I thought you looked at the egg spilled on his chin and shirt front."

"I did," said Jolnes. "That is where I began my deduction. Rheingelder is a very economical, saving man. Yesterday eggs dropped in the market to twenty-eight cents per dozen. Today they are quoted at forty-two. Rheingelder ate eggs yesterday, and today he went back to his usual fare. A little thing like this isn't anything, Whatsup; it belongs to the primary arithmetic class."

When we boarded the streetcar we found the seats all occupied—principally by ladies. Jolnes and I stood on the rear platform.

About the middle of the car there sat an elderly man with a short gray beard, who looked to be the typical well-dressed New Yorker. At successive corners other ladies climbed aboard, and soon three or four of them were standing over the man, clinging to straps and glaring meaningly at the man who occupied the coveted seat. But he resolutely retained his place.

"We New Yorkers," I remarked to Jolnes, "have about lost our manners, as far as the exercise of them in public goes."

"Perhaps so," said Jolnes, lightly, "but the man you evidently refer to happens to be a very chivalrous and courteous gentleman from Old Virginia. He is spending a few days in New York with his wife and two daughters, and he leaves for the South tonight."

"You know him, then?" I said, in amazement.

"I never saw him before we stepped on the car," declared the detective, smilingly.

"By the gold tooth of the Witch of Endor," I cried, "if you can construe all that from his appearance you are dealing in nothing else than black art."

"The habit of observation—nothing more," said Jolnes. "If the old gentleman gets off the car before we do, I think I can demonstrate to you the accuracy of my deduction."

Three blocks farther along the gentleman rose to leave the car. Jolnes addressed him at the door:

"Pardon me, sir, but are you not Colonel Hunter, of Norfolk, Virginia?"

"No, suh," was the extremely courteous answer. "My name, suh, is Ellison—Major Winfield R. Ellison, from Fairfax County, in the same state. I know a good many people, suh, in Norfolk—the Goodriches, the Tollivers, and the Crabtrees, suh, but I never had the pleasure of meeting yo' friend Colonel Hunter. I am happy to say, suh, that I am going back to Virginia tonight, after having spent a week in yo' city with my wife and three daughters. I shall be in Norfolk in about ten days, and if you will give me yo' name, suh, I will take pleasure in looking up Colonel Hunter and telling him that you inquired after him, suh."

"Thank you," said Jolnes. "Tell him that Reynolds sent his regards, if you will be so kind."

I glanced at the great New York detective and saw that a look of intense chagrin had come upon his clear-cut features. Failure in the slightest point always galled Shamrock Jolnes.

"Did you say your *three* daughters?" he asked of the Virginia gentleman.

"Yes, suh, my three daughters, all as fine girls as there are in Fairfax County," was the answer.

With that Major Ellison stopped the car and began to descend the step.

Shamrock Jolnes clutched his arm.

"One moment, sir—" he begged, in an urbane voice in which I alone detected the anxiety—"am I not right in believing that one of the young ladies is an *adopted* daughter?"

"You are, suh," admitted the major, from the ground, "but how the devil you knew it, suh, is mo' than I can tell."

"And mo' than I can tell, too," I said, as the car went on.

Jolnes was restored to his calm, observant serenity by having wrested victory from his apparent failure; so after we got off the car he invited me into a café, promising to reveal the process of his latest wonderful feat.

"In the first place," he began after we were comfortably seated, "I knew the gentleman was no New Yorker because he was flushed and uneasy and restless on account of the ladies that were standing, although he did not rise and give them his seat. I decided from his appearance that he was a Southerner rather than a Westerner.

"Next I began to figure out his reason for not relinquishing his seat to a lady when he evidently felt strongly, but not overpoweringly, impelled to do so. I very quickly decided upon that. I noticed that one of his eyes had received a severe jab in one corner, which was red and inflamed, and that all over his face were tiny round marks about the size of the end of an uncut lead pencil. Also upon both of his patent-leather shoes were a number of deep imprints shaped like ovals cut off square at one end.

"Now, there is only one district in New York City where a man is bound to receive scars and wounds and indentations of that sort—and that is along the sidewalks of Twenty-third Street and a portion of Sixth Avenue south of there. I knew from the imprints of trampling

French heels on his feet and the marks of countless jabs in the face from umbrellas and parasols carried by women in the shopping district that he had been in conflict with the Amazonian troops. And as he was a man of intelligent appearance, I knew he would not have braved such dangers unless he had been dragged thither by his own women-folk. Therefore, when he got on the car his anger at the treatment he had received was sufficient to make him keep his seat in spite of his traditions of Southern chivalry."

"That is all very well," I said, "but why did you insist upon daughters—and especially two daughters? Why couldn't a wife alone have taken him shopping?"

"There had to be daughters," said Jolnes, calmly. "If he had only a wife, and she near his own age, he could have bluffed her into going alone. If he had a young wife she would prefer to go alone. So there you are."

"I'll admit that," I said; "but, now, why two daughters? And how, in the name of all the prophets, did you guess that one was adopted when he told you he had three?"

"Don't say guess," said Jolnes, with a touch of pride in his air; "there is no such word in the lexicon of ratiocination. In Major Ellison's buttonhole there was a carnation and a rosebud backed by a geranium leaf. No woman ever combined a carnation and a rosebud into a boutonnière. Close your eyes, Whatsup, and give the logic of your imagination a chance. Cannot you see the lovely Adele fastening the carnation to the lapel so that Papa may be gay upon the street? And then the romping Edith May dancing up with sisterly jealousy to add her rosebud to the adornment?"

"And then," I cried, beginning to feel enthusiasm, "when he declared that he had three daughters—"

"I could see," said Jolnes, "one in the background who added no flower; and I knew that she must be—"

"Adopted!" I broke in. "I give you every credit; but how did you know he was leaving for the South tonight?"

"In his breast pocket," said the great detective, "something large and oval made a protuberance. Good liquor is scarce on trains, and it is a long journey from New York to Fairfax County."

"Again I must bow to you," I said. "And tell me this, so that my last shred of doubt will be cleared away; why did you decide that he was from Virginia?"

"It was very faint, I admit," answered Shamrock Jolnes, "but no trained observer could have failed to detect the odor of mint in the car."

23

# Affirmative Action

*by Jon L. Breen*

Eddie the gat had been with the Mob for a long time, far longer than most. He always thought he had lasted because he could cope with change, unlike a lot of guys who still had one foot stuck back in Prohibition. Times changed and the methods and practices of all big businesses changed and evolved as the years passed. Organized crime had to change, too. It stood to reason, though some didn't buy it.

Yeah, Eddie the Gat was flexible and cooperative as hell. But this latest instruction from the Boss had just about thrown him. Some in the Mob, Eddie the Gat among them, were seriously wondering about the Boss and whether he needed to be replaced. But for the moment at least, the Boss was still the Boss and, following instructions as always, Eddie found himself forty stories above the ground in a downtown office building, sitting across a neat, shiny desk from a snappily dressed but barely unpimpled kid who could have been his son.

"The Boss says I got to talk to you about—uh—hiring somebody to —uh . . ."

"It's all right," said the kid, "I know. You want to employ a qualified individual to eliminate a certain individual who has made his or her continued existence undesirable to the Mob."

"Uh, yeah, right. But why do I have to see you, kid? I never had to before. I don't mean no disrespect . . ."

"Certainly not. I understand."

". . . but I just was wondering. What the hell is an Affirmative Action Officer anyway?"

"Well, Eddie, my purpose is not to hinder your operation in any way. I am simply charged with making sure proper personnel practices are followed in the selection of your . . . what is the term applied to the position to be filled?"

"I guess, hitman."

"No, better make it hitperson. Or better yet, assassin. It avoids one of those 'person' words that always sound rather silly to me, don't they to you? Chairperson, foreperson, things like that?"

24

"Yeah, that sounds kind of silly, but assassin sounds kind of fancy. I mean, we ain't gonna hit the President or nothin'. And anyway, why does it matter what we call it?"

"For the job announcement."

"Yeah, well, you see, we never did it like that before. I mean, we were never so formal about it. Is this job announcement supposed to be in writing?"

"That is customary, yes."

"Well how can you advertise for a hitman—I mean, an assassin—in writing? It sort of spoils the element of surprise, don't it, if you send out an announcement that you're gonna bump a guy off?"

"How have you normally announced job openings in the past?"

"Well, it's been kind of word of mouth, you know? You sort of just let the word get around."

"I suppose that is advisable. Just so you make sure the announcement is made widely enough to attract the widest possible applicant pool without, of course, warning the potential victim or incurring the displeasure of law enforcement agencies."

"Uh, yeah. Whaddaya mean about the widest possible applicant pool?"

"To give a chance for all qualified candidates to apply. In the past, minorities and women have been sadly under-represented in many job classifications both within and outside the Mob. Are you aware of that?"

"Hey, we've always had women around."

"As secretaries and gun molls and camp followers, certainly, but not in positions of authority or responsibility. Have you ever seen a woman division chief in the Mob?"

"Well, no . . ."

"And as for minorities, most organized criminal organizations have confined their employees to members of a particular ethnic group— such as Italians, Irish, Jews, Blacks, or in the case of the present Mob . . ."

"We stick to people we can trust. If we spread the word about this hit far and wide, like you say, won't an awful lot of people know about our plans? We don't want the whole world to know who we're gonna knock over."

"You don't have to say *whom* you are planning to have killed."

"What do we do when police stoolies get the word? They will, you know, this way."

"Rumor is rumor. We deny it, that's all. And after all, the job only has to stay open two weeks."

"Two weeks? We want to hit the guy sooner than that!"

"No, I'm sorry, two weeks is the absolute minimum. Then we'll have to appoint a screening committee to go through the applications and arrange interviews."

"Hey, how long is *that* gonna take?"

"Once we get a procedure established, the screening, interviewing and hiring process shouldn't take long, Eddie."

"Are you telling me I have to hire a person just because he's black or he's a Mexican or he's a woman?"

"Certainly not. To do that would be to miss the whole point of affirmative action. You pick the most qualified candidate who applies, regardless of race, sex, or age. The purpose of affirmative action is to assure the widest possible applicant pool in order to give women and minority candidates the opportunity to apply and compete for the position. That is all."

"Oh." Eddie the Gat was silent for a moment. A voice in his head was telling him to move with the times, but the voice in his mouth said, "Is this really necessary, kid? I mean, who's gonna check up on us?"

"You never know, Eddie. But I for one would hate to see the Mob we've all worked so hard to build cited for unfair labor practices. And I would ask you this: do we abrogate our responsibility as good citizens simply because our business is crime?"

The kid walked to the window, raised it, and looked out at the crowded streets below.

"Look at that city, Eddie! The Mob has attained a position of importance, influence, and, yes, respect in this community. It has an obligation to protect its position and use it for good ends."

Eddie walked to the window and looked out, too. "Yeah, yeah, I can see that."

"I think the respect accorded us can grow only if people are aware that the Mob is an equal opportunity employer."

"How are people gonna apply for this job? I mean, we can't have a lot in writing."

"Give them a phone number they can call and give us their qualifications, suitably coded of course. At the same time, they can leave word where we can reach them if the screening committee selects them for interview."

"Sounds okay, I guess." Eddie thought a moment more. Then his eyes lit up suddenly. "Hey, kid, how'd you get this job anyway?"

The kid looked slightly embarrassed. "Well, actually, the Boss is my uncle. But that was the wrong way to do things, Eddie, and my goal is

26

to make sure no employee of the Mob is hired for reasons like that ever again."

"Still, it don't seem right," Eddie mumbled, under his breath.

The intercom line on the kid's telephone buzzed, and he walked to the desk to pick it up.

"It's for you," he said, handing the phone to Eddie.

"Yeah?"

"Eddie, this is Moe. We done the job on the Boss."

"Yeah?"

"It was time, Eddie. We couldn't wait no longer. We need new leadership. All the boys want you to take over, Eddie."

"Yeah?" Eddie saw that the kid had returned to the window and was looking out at the city. "Will you hold on a second, Moe?"

Eddie the Gat walked to the window, said in a soft and sincere voice, "Sorry, kid," and sent him forty stories with one good push. Then he returned to the phone.

"Moe, the first thing we gotta do is pick a new Affirmative Action Officer. And I want you to be on the screening committee."

# Anchor the Stiff!

*by Dan Gordon*

The bay was alive with pleasure craft. They crossed Lew Guyon's bow, sent clouds of warm spray flying over his tiny runabout, and in general threatened his life and health and played hell with his temper.

He cut the engine scant feet before he ran the schooner down. The *Sea Maid* was at anchor, and Sammy Sultan, her owner and skipper, was waiting at the rail when Lew slammed the speedboat into her side and swung himself aboard.

Sammy Sultan's dark face split in a welcoming grin. He said, "Hello, baby. Glad you could come."

"Troubles?" Lew Guyon said.

"Not yet. Very soon now, I think. Come. Let's go back to my cabin." Sammy's head moved significantly in the direction of the sailor who was making Lew's boat fast.

"New man?" Lew asked.

"Most of the crew. All new. The old gang tried it for a while with me when I married Sue and went legit. I do not think they liked it. A couple stayed. The others went back south."

Lew nodded, remembering the southern waters and the years when he and Sammy Sultan had spun the wild wheel of fortune, gambling, with little regard for the odds, on quick death or sudden wealth. It was strange to think of Sammy as married and settled down. Lew watched him pour rum into a cup, top it off with coffee. "Hey, Sammy," Lew said, "you joined the yacht club yet?"

"Not yet." Sammy's tone was sheepish. "Sue, she wants me to."

"Ducky," Lew said. "You can get you a new white hat, put a teak-wood deck on the schooner . . ." He paused and looked at Sammy. Sammy was trying to smile, but his heart wasn't in it. "I got your wire," Lew said in a different tone. "We were coming up the coast with the tug, and when they radioed your message I changed course and put in here."

"Yes. You remember Cipelli? You know he had a brother?"

"No," Lew said. "I didn't know." He remembered Cipelli, having blasted the retired gangster into permanent retirement less than a year before. Killing Cipelli had been legitimate enough. Lew Guyon, marine investigator, had been working on a case involving a series of holdups on the yachts here in Millionaire's Cove. Cipelli, having exhausted his retirement fund by purchasing one of the fabulous estates in this exclusive hideaway, had planned to regain firm financial footing. He had imported Sammy Sultan with his schooner and crew, and it had been Cipelli's intention to loot every luxury craft in the harbor, send the booty south on the schooner. Lew Guyon had stopped Cipelli with a tommy gun. Sue Brandon had stopped Sammy Sulton, had brought him to the side of law and order, using no weapon but her eyes.

Now, watching Sammy, Lew reflected that married life agreed with the little pirate. He had gained a little weight and looked very well except for the tiny worry wrinkles at the corners of his eyes. "What about the brother?" Lew asked. "He out to get you?"

"Worse than that. He's missing."

Lew's brows went up. "That's bad? Who cares if he never turns up?"

"I do. We had a mild beef when he first came here to live in his brother's house. A mean boy, but small-time. You know them, Louie. Guys like that, they'll kick dogs and play hell with women. But me, he would not mess with. This Gilbert Cipelli has not his brother's moxie. I could tell. He knew it, too, after we met just once."

28

"How's the local law?" Lew asked.

"Good. It is a man named Pryor. He has a deputy who is not much force, but Pryor is a good man. I think he knows about me and was willing to let it go. As you know, my record is clean in the States. Now, with Cipelli missing, this Pryor is looking at me."

"At you—or for you?"

"At me—now. He hasn't said anything, but I do not like his eyes. I am very happy here with Sue, and I say to myself, my friend is a big detective. He will know what should be done."

"Not so big," Lew said. "But I'll talk to Pryor. It shouldn't be too much trouble."

Lew was still feeling that way when, having left Sammy, he found the sheriff. He liked the man instantly. Pryor had the seasoned look, the calm face and alert eyes of an efficient peace officer. Formerly F.B.I., Lew decided. Lured to this quiet post by the glittering salary doubtless paid by the residents of the Cove.

Pryor was willing to concede that Sammy Sultan had become, to all outward appearances, a useful, substantial citizen.

"Then why not let him alone?" Lew pleaded. "You've got him worried to death."

"He has nothing to worry about," said Pryor, "as long as Cipelli's missing. The time for Sultan to worry is when Cipelli turns up dead."

"Would that make Sammy his killer?"

"Who else? Cipelli wasn't accepted in local society. He hung around in the cheap bars, drank with oyster dredgers and their women. Those boatmen are plenty tough, but inherently they have a lot of respect for the law. I doubt if Sultan has."

"Sammy's quit all that—"

"Surely. I know. I know. But his reformation is—recent, shall we say? Always, a man who has lived lawlessly, who has killed, has a different attitude. Mind you, I don't say your friend is guilty of anything. I say only that if Cipelli is dead, and I believe he is, I'll be sure to question Sultan."

"And bring up his former misdemeanors?"

"Naturally. They'd be pertinent."

Lew admired Pryor's calm, impersonal manner, and felt sorry for his friend. He left the little building with its carefully tended lawn, crossed the street when he saw Sammy Sultan in the car on the other side.

"Well?" Sammy said as Lew climbed in.

"Not good. If it comes up Cipelli's dead, Pryor puts his dough on you. He said Cipelli hung around with the oyster fishermen, but apparently that gang hasn't given him much trouble. He likes you best, Sammy boy."

"I love him too," said Sammy grimly. "Where do you want to go?"

"Let's look at those oyster boats. They don't work in the summer, do they?"

"Crabs. In the summer they fish for crabs. But some will be in, that's for sure."

They rode to the water's edge, left the car and walked out on a rickety pier. Several boats were tied up there, and Lew and Sammy stopped to talk with the owners who were working on deck. The only thing they learned about the missing Cipelli was that he had apparently had no friends.

"Imagine," said Sammy as they were climbing off one of the boats, "a louse like that, and he disappears, and it has to happen to me."

"You were always lucky," Lew answered. He was glad Sammy was taking it easy. Married life and quiet living had done a lot for the boy. Made him foresighted, careful. Sammy wasn't waiting for the law to grab him by the arm. He knew how things worked. Once the law made a grab, it had trouble relaxing its grip. Especially on the Sammy Sultans of the world. Lew brought his gaze back from the far horizon and focused his eyes on the girl.

She was poised on the top of a piling, and the soft breeze from off the water was fanning the hem of her brief white shorts. She was young, very young, and straight and slender. When she saw them watching her, something like panic crossed her childish face. She took off, went into an excellent dive, entered the water cleanly and swam away from the pier.

"Pretty," Lew said admiringly. "She'll be a doll, Sammy, give her a year or two."

"Somebody wouldn't give her a year."

Lew looked at him questioningly.

"The old story," Sammy said with a shrug. "She played around with the other kids. Only she's prettier than the others. Some monkey took her to town, doped her or got her drunk, left her lying beside the road, all battered up and scared to death. For a little while she was off her rocker."

"Looked all right to me," Lew said.

"She's coming around okay. But afraid of people. She knows me, and I know her father, but you see how she ran away." Sammy spread his hand, palm downward, and said in a lower tone, "Name's Jane Hartlett. This is her father's boat."

Lew eyed the trim ship approvingly. She was well kept, her bottom was clean, and from her lines and the height of her masts Lew judged she was plenty fast. He followed Sammy over the inclined board that served as a gangway.

Earl Hartlett, father of the girl they'd seen, met them at the rail and invited them below for a drink. He was a pleasant man with a peaceful face. His whiskey was excellent.

He said, in answer to Lew's question, "Y'might say I knew Cipelli by sight. Didn't know him personally. He hung out with some of the boys in the bars, but I do my drinking at home."

"You agree with the rest of the Cove—that he was a fourteen-karat heel?" Lew asked the question mechanically. He knew the answer by now.

The fisherman's head turned toward Sammy, noting Sammy's empty glass. "In the galley," Earl Hartlett said. "You know your way around here. Mix another one." Sammy passed through the small door out of sight, and Lew sat, hearing the sounds of cracking ice, waiting for Hartlett's answer.

Hartlett swung to face Lew. "Yes," he said. "I agree that he was useless . . . and evil. That's why I can't imagine you two caring whether he's missing or not."

"We don't," Lew said easily. "When Pryor, the sheriff, found out we were coming down this way, he told us to ask around."

Sammy came out of the galley, carrying a glass which contained some ice, a great deal of whiskey and very little water. Saluting his host with the glass, he said, "We'd better be going, Louie. I don't want my wife to worry."

"Any time," Lew answered. He watched Sammy toss off the drink, then tried to remember if he had ever before seen his friend take such a healthy slug of the stuff so early in the morning.

The alcohol seemed to have an immediate effect, for Sammy moved about uneasily until they left the schooner. He was preoccupied and somewhat irritable as Lew rode with him to his home.

"Lew," he said at last, "I don't want to hold you up. I know you were headed for another job when I sent that wire, and I'm sorry I brought you here for nothing. But—thanks for coming, Lew. I feel better about this thing now."

"Yeah," Lew said. "You look wonderful." He recognized the turn-off to Sammy's house and said, "Well, if you've got nothing to tell me, why not drop me at the boat landing? I'll go back to the tug."

Sammy opened his mouth, then closed it again. Several times, on the way to the boat landing, it seemed that he would speak. Lew sat, watching him quietly from the corner of his eye.

At the landing he got out and said, "So-long, Sammy. Sing out if you need me again."

"Sure. Sure, Lew. And—thanks." Sammy waved, gunned the motor and departed.

Lew Guyon went back to his tug.

Callao Johnson, his Panamanian mate, welcomed him aboard. "You are soon, sir," Callao said.

"Too soon," Lew answered. "So soon I don't even know what we're doing here. But, Callao, you remember that rig we used off Race Point?"

"To tow you under the ship?" Callao asked. And when Lew nodded, Callao shook his head emphatically. "Too dangerous," he said.

"Yeah, it's loony," Lew agreed. "But fast. We can cover a big slice of the harbor in a few days. Maybe find it this afternoon, if it's where I think I would put it."

Callao said with infinite patience, "Sir, what are we looking for?"

"Scenery," Lew said. "The water's clear and the sun's shining. It's a wonderful day for a ride."

"You get killed, sir," said Callao morosely, "that is your affair. But me, I am out of a job." He waved one huge hand at the crew members forward. Although he had not spoken to them, the men manned the anchor windlass, and the chain began clanking in.

Thirty minutes later the salvage tug was moving slowly over the calm surface of the bay.

Lew Guyon, in diving dress, was dangling at the end of a rope— eighty feet below the tug's keel. He was well aware of the danger inherent in this business of being towed beneath the bottom of a vessel under way. But the use of the method would enable him to search an enormous section of the bay's bottom. Walking or crawling, he might never locate Cipelli's body, or at best, the search would take days.

Now, as Lew rode along just above the bottom, the afternoon sun was striking the surface above him, sending green shafts of light through the clean water, illuminating the scene.

Lew's feet, in the lead-soled shoes, were riding six feet above the bottom. He had no sensation of motion, but the marine growth went sliding by beneath him. A man could build a house down there, if he could learn to breath water. Over there, by that stretch of shining pebbles. That would be a nice spot. Very nice, and—"Up!" Lew shouted suddenly.

Ahead of him, looming black through the light green water, he saw the boulder, huge and threatening. He felt the upward tug on his lines, and the rope sling pressed sharply against his legs as the worried men on deck heaved desperately to take him out of danger.

He had no control over his own movements, and the men on the tug were working blind except for his directions. If he failed to clear that boulder, he'd be smashed against it like a yo-yo swung on a string. His face plate would be bashed in, his lines and the air hose parted. He would die in a matter of seconds.

Lew Guyon knew all these things, yet all he said was, "Up!" again in that urgent tone. He felt his lines jerk more rapidly. His feet cleared the boulder by inches.

"Big rock," he said into the mouthpiece. "Lower me away." He went coasting down toward the bottom again as the men paid out on his lines. Then: "Hold it there," he said.

Riding about ten feet off the bottom, he dared not go any lower. A field of boulders stretched before him as far as he could see.

And it was between two of these that he found the thing he sought. The body of Gilbert Cipelli.

"On deck," Lew said. "Can you hold her where she is?"

"We'll try, sir," came Callao's voice.

The body appeared to be standing upright. It moved in the gentle current as if Cipelli were walking over the bottom. But as Lew worked his way closer, he saw why the man wouldn't walk away. Cipelli, if this were Cipelli, was wearing a harness of galvanized wire, well rigged and seaman-like. Bound securely at his feet was a fifty-pound mushroom anchor.

Lew went over the body carefully, disliking every moment of the grisly work. He found the wounds on the chest when he tore the shirt away.

Callao Johnson's voice came down from above: "You have find him yet, sir?"

Lew hesitated. Then: "Don't think so," he said. "Thought I had, for a minute. Take in the slack and haul me up." There'd be time enough to break the news after he'd thought things through. Cipelli wasn't going anywhere. Not with the rig he was wearing. Cipelli would be there for years. Maybe forever, for all Lew knew.

"Coming up," said Callao Johnson.

The men on deck laid back on the lines. Lew Guyon rose toward the surface. . . .

* * *

The first thing he saw when he entered Sammy Sultan's room was the knife in Sammy's hand. It was an oyster knife, a sturdy little implement designed to coax the tough-fibered bivalve out of its protecting shell. Moreover, the knife was clean and shining. Anyone, that is anyone except Lew Guyon, would have thought the knife was new. Sammy had been standing there, apparently balancing the knife in his hand, looking at it thoughtfully. When Lew came in, he laid it gently on the top of the desk.

Lew said, "What are you saving it for? You too cheap to throw the damned thing away?"

"They won't sink," Sammy told him. "Wooden handle would keep one bobbing right there on the surface."

"Cipelli won't bob," Lew said casually. "I was out to see him in the cove just now."

Sammy Sultan's eyebrows moved upward. "Yes?" he said. "How does he look?"

"Comfortable," Lew said. "He's spotted between a couple of boulders. They'll never get him by dragging for him. A grapnel hook would just go bouncing off the tops of those rocks. I found him by riding under the boat, but I doubt if they've got any boys around here who would work a search job that way."

He was talking, trying to convince Sammy—and himself—that their friendship was still the same. It wasn't, of course, and it would never be, not any more. Because Sammy had lied to him. Lew said, and his voice was harsh, "Why the song and dance? Why didn't you tell me you knocked the jerk off? You think I'd turn you in?"

"You don't understand," Sammy said mournfully. "It is not a simple thing, Lew."

"Then tell me about it. I'm a bright boy, Sammy. I'll understand what you say."

"I cannot," Sammy shook his head. "It is not mine to tell." He looked at the knife on the desk, then back at Lew. "When you brought Cipelli in, what did Pryor say?"

"I didn't bring him. Nobody knows he's out there but you and me." Lew's voice was tired. All the good years they'd had together were gone. Now they were playing it cagey, eying each other suspiciously, filled with doubt and mistrust.

"Louie, it is all right!" Sammy said. He smiled a delighted smile. "We leave the body there, get rid of the knife. Hartlett will be okay!"

"Hartlett?" Lew repeated. "Hartlett did it?"

"Him," said Sammy. "I guess," he added. "Today when I went into

34

his galley, I found three of these knives in a rack. Two of them used and dark colored. This one bright and shiny. A guy like him, he wouldn't know about blood stains. He'd think he could scrub the knife off." He winked at Lew. "Lew," he said, "a man should stick to his trade."

Remembering Hartlett's daughter in the sunlight on the pier, Lew said, "Then it would be Cipelli who kicked the Hartlett girl around?"

"Who else?" said Sammy. "It would take a thing like that to make Hartlett kill. He is not like you or me . . ." He broke off, for Lew was crossing the room, reaching for the phone.

Lew said, "What's Pryor's number?"

Sammy Sultan moved quickly and clamped one hand on the phone. "You can't do that, Lew. Cipelli had it coming. You can't turn Hartlett in."

"He murdered a man." Lew made his voice stern. "So we know he has to pay. Only question is—how much? Now, down there on his boat today I noticed a box of crabs on deck. Some were under the legal size. I figure we'll tell the fish-and-game boys. They'll fine him a hundred or two. . . ." He let his voice trail off and looked at Sammy questioningly.

Sammy took his hand from the phone. "Boy," he said, "you had me worried. I thought—"

"Maybe," Lew said thoughtfully, "Cipelli wasn't worth a hundred. But Hartlett's no better than any one else—and everything's high these days." He shrugged and picked up the phone.

# An Artful Touch

### by Charles Dickens

"One of the most *beautiful* things that ever was done, perhaps," said Inspector Wield, emphasising the adjective, as preparing us to expect dexterity or ingenuity rather than strong interest, "was a move of Sergeant Witchem's. It was a lovely idea!

"Witchem and me were down at Epsom one Derby Day, waiting at the station for the Swell Mob. As I mentioned, when we were talking about these things before, we are ready at the station when there's races, or an Agricultural Show, or a Chancellor sworn in for an university, or Jenny Lind, or any thing of that sort; and as the Swell Mob come down, we send 'em back again by the next train. But some of the Swell Mob, on the occasion of this Derby that I refer to, so far kiddied us as to hire a horse and shay; start away from London by Whitechapel, and miles round; come into Epsom from the opposite direction; and go to work, right and left, on the course, while we were waiting for 'em at the Rail. That, however, ain't the point of what I'm going to tell you.

"While Witchem and me were waiting at the station, there comes up one Mr. Tatt; a gentleman formerly in the public line, quite an amateur Detective in his way, and very much respected. 'Halloa, Charley Wield,' he says. 'What are you doing here? On the look out for some of your old friends?' 'Yes, the old move, Mr. Tatt.' 'Come along,' he says, 'you and Witchem, and have a glass of sherry.' 'We can't stir from the place,' says I, 'till the next train comes in; but after that, we will with pleasure.' Mr. Tatt waits, and the train comes in, and then Witchem and me go off with him to the Hotel. Mr. Tatt he's got up quite regardless of expense, for the occasion; and in his shirt-front there's a beautiful diamond prop, cost him fifteen or twenty pound—a very handsome pin indeed. We drink our sherry at the bar, and have our three or four glasses, when Witchem cries suddenly, 'Look out, Mr. Wield! stand fast!' and a dash is made into the place by the swell mob—four of 'em—that have come down as I tell you, and in a moment Mr. Tatt's prop is gone! Witchem, he cuts 'em off at the door, I lay about me as hard as I can, Mr. Tatt shows fight like a good 'un, and there we are, all down together, heads and heels, knocking about on the floor of the bar—perhaps you never see such a scene of confusion! However, we stick to our men (Mr. Tatt being as good as any officer), and we take 'em all, and carry 'em off to the station. The station's full of people, who have been took on the course; and it's a precious piece of work to get 'em secured. However, we do it at last, and we search 'em; but nothing's found upon 'em, and they're locked up; and a pretty state of heat we are in by that time, I assure you!

"I was very blank over it myself, to think that the prop had been passed away; and I said to Witchem, when we had set 'em to rights, and were cooling ourselves along with Mr. Tatt, 'We don't take much by *this* move, anyway, for nothing's found upon 'em, and it's only the braggadocia after all.' 'What do you mean, Mr. Wield,' says Witchem. 'Here's the diamond pin!' and in the palm of his hand there it was, safe and sound! 'Why, in the name of wonder,' says me and Mr. Tatt, in astonishment, 'how did you come by that?' 'I'll tell you how I come by

36

it,' says he. 'I saw which of 'em took it; and when we were all down on the floor together, knocking about, I just gave him a little touch on the back of his hand, as I knew his pal would; and he thought it WAS his pal; and gave it me!' It was beautiful, beau-ti-ful!

"Even that was hardly the best of the case, for that chap was tried at the Quarter Sessions at Guildford. You know what Quarter Sessions are, sir. Well, if you'll believe me, while them slow justices were looking over the Acts of Parliament to see what they could do to him, I'm blowed if he didn't cut out of the dock before their faces! He cut out of the dock, sir, then and there; swam across a river; and got up into a tree to dry himself. In the tree he was took—an old woman having seen him climb up—and Witchem's artful touch transported him!"


# An Axe to Grind

*by Curt Hamlin*

It was an axe murder.

It happened about midnight Saturday in one of those drab, down-at-the-eaves houses on lower Front Street. A man named Reik chopped his wife about thirty times on the head and back. He began hacking away on the second floor, followed her as she stumbled blindly down a narrow flight of stairs, finally finished her in the kitchen. The neighbors heard screaming and called the police. They found Reik squatting on the blood-slippery floor beside his wife's body, struggling to pull the wedding ring from her finger.

He wouldn't tell why he'd done it, but he admitted the kill. A denial wouldn't have done him much good. The two of them were alone in the house. His fingerprints were on the handle of the axe, and he was wet with her blood. They had this boarder, Ebert, but he was down at the corner tavern when it happened, drinking beer. The police were holding him as a material witness. It didn't look as if there was much of a story in the case, but if there was, Ebert could tell it. The city desk sent me down to get an interview.

He wasn't a bad-looking guy. About thirty. Big shoulders and a flat belly and lean hips. Blond hair cut in a stiff, brushy crop. A calm face. The features were heavy and immobile. He only smiled once the whole time I was there. His eyes were expressionless. Looking inward, with their backs turned. When I introduced myself he nodded without particular interest. I sat down on the cell cot beside him. He was in shirt sleeves, and his feet were pushed into a worn pair of bedroom slippers. I told him what I wanted.

He said, "Like I told the cops, I don't know nothing. I wasn't there. Joe done it to her about twelve. I left at maybe half-past eleven."

"Why?"

"I told the cops. I went to bed, only I couldn't sleep. I got dressed and went down for a beer. I guess you could say I got thirsty."

He said all this as though he'd told it before. Mechanically, with a flat inflection. I asked if that was all.

"Sure."

I waited. He wasn't the kind you could hurry. We sat close together, our shoulders almost touching. He smelled of sweat and sleep. After a little, when I thought he was ready, I asked how long he'd known the Reiks.

He said about four years. He said, "I lived with them for the last five–six months."

"I guess you thought you knew this Reik pretty well."

"Sure. As well as anybody."

"Only," I told him, "You didn't know him well enough to figure in advance that he was going to murder his wife."

I was trying to needle him. It worked. His face moved, like a mask slipping sideways, showing something behind the corners. A smug satisfaction. He said, and he said it slowly and deliberately so that I couldn't possibly miss the point. "I knew Joe was going to give it to her a month ago."

I didn't look at him. That would have been a mistake. He'd have shut off like a closed water tap. I said, putting a lot of sarcasm into my voice, "Sure. Sure you did. Maybe you even know why he did it."

"You think I don't?" The smugness was thick now. Thick as butter on farm bread. He shifted himself on the cot, getting comfortable. He said, "Look. Joe Reik's this kind of a guy. He likes to play around with the girls some and have his fun. Only he wants his own woman to stay at home and do the cooking and scrub floors. If he finds she's letting some other guy get to her he goes crazy mad. So he bats her with an axe."

"She was playing around with another man?"

"Didn't I just tell you?"

"So somebody tipped him off. You, maybe?"

He shook his head. "It ain't for me to tell him."

"Then how'd he find out?"

Ebert said, "I guess he just figured it. Maybe she got to giggling too much to herself, or wearing her hair different, or buying a lot of new dresses. You know how a dame is when she gets to cheating. She wants to tell, but she can't, so she's got a lot of ways of getting the idea across that she thinks her husband can't figure out. Joe did."

"Did he know who the man was?"

"He didn't figure that far."

"But you did?"

"Sure." He picked at his front teeth, looked at his thumb. He said, "Irma knew Joe was out to get her. A month ago. Like I did. That was her name. Irma."

"You told her?"

He said, "Nobody had to tell her. She knew like I knew. It was this night a month ago. I come home from work and Joe and Irma was out in the kitchen. Joe had a knife and he had Irma backed into a corner and he was holding this knife to her neck. I guess if he hadn't heard me come in he'd have done it to her right then. Only he heard me and he backed off and put the knife down on the drainboard. He giggled a little, and he said something like he was playing a game with her. Only he wasn't. He went upstairs for his hat and goes out and gets plastered. He didn't come home until two–three in the morning. I guess if he'd done that to you you'd've known he was out to get you, too."

I said I guessed I would.

"Sure you would."

I thought about it. The palms of my hands were too dry. They itched. After a while, I asked if this Irma was good-looking.

Ebert's heavy shoulders jerked noncommittally. "Not bad."

"Is that the only other time he tried to kill her?"

"I was going to tell you," Ebert said. "About a week ago, at night, I come downstairs to go out to a show. Joe and Irma was in the front room. Irma was lying down on the davenport and Joe had his hands on her throat and he was choking her. Her face was getting black and her eyes was sticking out a good inch. When he saw me watching he pretended like he was giving her a rub. A massage. And then he let her up."

He paused then, stared down reflectively at his beefy hands. "It was yesterday he bought the axe."

"Yesterday?"

"Sure. Yesterday was a Saturday. Me and Joe don't work on Saturday. Joe went out in the morning and got this axe. He brought it up and showed it to me. Nice axe, too. Double-bitted. I rent this room on the second floor and Joe brought the axe up there and then he took it down in the basement to sharpen it. We could hear him all day, working at the grindstone. He must've got it nice and sharp. It took him long enough."

I said, only because I couldn't think of anything else to say, "He must have hit her thirty times with it."

"That's what they tell me."

I waited.

Ebert said, "I figured I knew why he bought it."

I said it probably wasn't hard to figure. I took my handkerchief and wiped my face and rubbed my hands and put the handkerchief back in my pocket. I asked if he knew anything else.

"Not much else." He was polishing his slippers, first one and then the other, against the backs of his pant legs. He leaned over and studied them critically. They were old slippers, stained with white toothpaste spots and badly scuffed.

He said, "Last night, maybe a little after eleven, Irma come to my room. She was crying and shaking and so bad scared I could hardly understand what she was trying to tell me. She said Joe had this axe and he'd sharpened it and he was going to chop her up with it. She wanted me to do something. She come right in where I was in bed and told me. I don't know where Joe was. Maybe still down in the basement. I told her not to worry because Joe wouldn't do anything to her while I was in the house. He wouldn't've, either. Joe ain't so much for guts."

I said, and it was a long time before I could say anything because of the tightness in my throat, "But you went out. You got up and dressed and went out."

Ebert moved his big shoulders. "Sure. Like I told the cops."

Neither one of us spoke for a long time. A minute. I was sick at my stomach. My hands were shaking and I wanted something strong to drink. Something very strong. I offered him a cigarette. He pulled one from the pack, rolled it about idly between his thick fingers. I gave him a match. I said, "Of course, if you'd stayed, he might have killed you, too."

"There's that," Ebert said. He drew deeply on the cigarette, lay back across the cot, letting the smoke curl from the corners of his mouth. "Besides," he added, "I was damned tired of Irma."

It was then he smiled.

40

# Behind Murder's Eight-Ball

*by Don James*

In my one-room apartment there is a bookcase, and on the bookcase there is a pool ball mounted on a small block of walnut. It is a black eight-ball. The boys at the paper gave it to me at an annual press banquet where everyone shared in the gags.

On the wall above the eight-ball is a picture of Ed Tanner, the *Star's* city editor, making the presentation. I look like a short, fat, partially bald gangster in that picture. I look the same out of the picture.

Ed Tanner gave me the eight-ball and said, "I take honor in presenting to Stub Getchel, our ace news-photographer, this token that is symbolic of his past, present and future. The eight-ball. Stub is always behind it!"

Ed Tanner is one of the few men who really understands my bad luck. To a lot of people it's a joke, but to me it's a serious thing. I never get a break.

At least, I thought that until last Tuesday night.

It had been a typical day from the start when my sister, Martha, called to tell me that Timothy had appendicitis. Timothy is ten years old and one of Martha's six kids. He's named after me, only I hope he never gets the nickname of "Stub" and that he doesn't inherit my eight-ball.

Martha's husband has a job clerking and they're hard pressed for dough. The doctor had to be paid and there'd be a week at the hospital. Martha was on the verge of tears.

She made me a little sore. She didn't have to get weepy. You'd think she didn't have a friend or relative in the world. And with young Tim involved—well, it was a nice camera. It cost me over three hundred hard-to-find bucks.

Some day I'm going to slug that pawn shop pirate. Fifty bucks he offered me on the camera! I sold it to a rewrite man on the *Journal* for two hundred. I hope Tim's doctor and the hospital make good use of it.

Then, on the way to the *Star,* some jerk in a big convertible ran over a kid's dog on Seventh. It was lucky I was there. That kid was really in bad shape. So was the dog, but the vet put splints on him and he's going to be all right. He did a nice job for only twenty-five bucks. Fortunately I had that much left.

Anyhow, by the time I got to the *Star* I was plenty sore at the world and my luck. Nothing ever happens to anyone else. I was telling Pat Moharity, who covers police, about it when Tanner beckoned to me.

"Got a job for you, Stub," he said. "We're climbing on the band wagon with the sheets in other cities who are riding their cops to clean up the skid rows. Tonight you go down there and get plenty of pix showing what it's like. Bums on sidewalks, interiors of flop houses, maybe a drunk getting rolled—the works."

I decided I'd shoot most of the stuff infra-red. The bums wouldn't know I was getting them that way in the dark—no flash, and I could get some good candid stuff.

Tanner okayed ten bucks for expenses. I knew I'd need change to pass out among the bums. I always say you got to spend money to make money. Besides, a guy is more apt to let you take a few shots of him if you buy him a few drinks first, and those guys don't get too many, anyhow. To do it right, you buy them a bowl of soup and something to eat, too.

No one ever did that for me, but after all I'm the man on the other end. I'm doing the work.

Inasmuch as I was going to work that night, I took off the rest of the day and went out to the hospital. Tim had his appendix out with about as much trouble as I'd have having a tooth out and was feeling pretty good when I went home to dinner with Martha. When I finally got to skid row that night at about ten-thirty I'd lost four of that ten bucks to my brother-in-law playing rummy. I even get behind the eight-ball in a friendly game with my relatives. I got to lose.

Our skid row is like most skid rows. It's three or four streets of joints where you can get a shot for a dime, flop houses where you can sleep for fifteen cents. It's alive with petty crime and forgotten people. Life isn't worth much down there.

By midnight I had the job wrapped up. Tanner was going to be happy with what I had for him. The cops were going to be unhappy. I was going to be behind the eight-ball again, but I was all for Tanner on this deal. With my luck I'll probably end up on a skid row myself, and maybe Tanner and the *Star* could clean up ours a little for me before I get there.

I spotted an alley I hadn't covered and took a deep breath and edged into it. The place was as black as the inside of a darkroom. After a few moments I spotted a couple of winos dead to the world on the pavement. I got shots of them.

At the far end of the alley was a single, dim light over a doorway. I'd have ignored it if I hadn't spotted the car parked a few yards beyond.

It wasn't the kind of car you'd expect to find in a skid row alley. It was in the classy convertible class, only it was a sedan.

I eased up the alley and in the dark, behind a pole, I thought about it. What was a car like that doing there? Finally I had it figured. The building with the lighted back door was Barney Post's gambling joint and drinking dive on the fringe of skid row.

That explained it and I was about to call it a night when I spotted another man standing behind another pole less than twenty feet from me. I wouldn't have seen him if he hadn't dropped a cigarette, then by straining my eyes I could see his outline.

On a hunch I snapped one, not hoping for much, but he wasn't too far away. The infra-red might catch him. I wondered who he was and what he was doing there as I got ready to shoot another if anything showed up or happened as I left for home.

Before I got away from the pole something did happen.

The door beneath the bulb opened and I recognized Barney Post as he stepped out. He was alone. He turned toward the car and at that instant the other man behind the pole stepped toward him. He had a gun in his hand.

"I'll take it, Barney," he said.

Barney stopped and slowly turned. He looked at the man in the dim light from the bulb and said, "You'll take what?"

"The dough I lost in there tonight. One hundred bucks. I think your game was rigged."

"Look, punk, you can't get away with this."

"The gun in my hand says I can. I want that dough. I need it."

Barney hesitated and then shrugged. I snapped a picture fast and my heart began to thump. This was something for Ed. For Ed? It might be something for more than Ed! This might be for one of the national magazines, for the books! I saw bonuses and maybe some credit where credits count. I'd never had that kind of luck.

\* \* \*

By the time Barney had finished his shrug and a slow stare at the guy, I was ready for another picture. I watched Barney reach for an inside pocket.

"Okay," he said. "Take it easy. You can have your dough."

The other man stiffened. He looked young and his voice had sounded young.

I was ready for a quick snap of Barney handing over the money.

His hand came out, but not with a wallet. Light from the small bulb glinted on the black metal of a gun.

The kid saw it, too. He said, "Don't!" He sounded frightened. Barney struck down with his left hand toward the kid's gun arm.

The click of my camera was completely drowned by a gun shot. Barney staggered back and then stumbled toward the kid. He sprawled face down in the alley. For a full moment the kid was as motionless as I was—except for my hands. They were automatically busy. They responded even before the rest of me did. They held the camera that got a shot of the kid, face-on as he sprinted by me.

The rest of me came into action. I went after him.

Two men racing through skid row don't create too much excitement. The kid looked back at me and stepped up his speed. Once he slowed and I saw him throw the gun into a storm sewer drain. He was beginning to think.

He ducked into an alley. We dodged traffic crossing a street and I tried to spot a cop. There wasn't one in sight.

The kid rounded a corner and I put on a spurt of speed. Ahead of me tires screeched and something crashed.

Cars were stopping and a frightened driver was getting out of a sedan when I turned the corner. The kid was under the car and I've seen death too often not to know that it was hovering around there.

The kid was good looking, with blond hair. He probably was about twenty-six. He didn't look like a kid who would stick up Barney Post and murder him. He was breathing, but he was unconscious.

I got a picture of him under the car. I got one of the crowd, the driver, the cops who arrived, the ambulance crew at work, and then I faded out of the scene.

Hurrying to the dark-room at the *Star* was like watching the Derby when you've all your cash on the horse that's ahead by a nose. Maybe I had something. Maybe I didn't. You can't always be sure about infrared. If I did, I probably had the best news picture break of the last ten years.

Visions of bonuses and New York publishers' checks, and my name and a picture on slick paper were like shots from an Academy award movie.

Headlines were pleasant in my mind's eye. NEWS PHOTOGRAPHER NAILS MURDERER. I could almost hear that voice over long distance from New York asking me if I wanted a job. With any luck at all, the eight-ball had rolled away and I was on the road.

Then the eight-ball rolled back on the table. Maybe the pictures were no good. Maybe I'd missed.

I was sweating when I got to the dark-room—and it was a chilly night.

Those negatives were a newsman's dream of heaven. I had it! The whole story. Almost the whole story, I corrected myself.

I put on my poker face when I left the dark-room. This was for no one until I had it complete.

The girl on the switchboard at emergency hospital is a pal. She said to wait a moment and then she came back on the line.

"He's still alive, Stub, but it's only a matter of an hour or so."

"I'll be there!" I promised.

A taxi took the last buck I had. There was a little trouble with an intern. I explained that I'd caught the accident. I wanted a shot of the victim in the hospital bed.

"It's part of a traffic-safety campaign we're planning," I said. "Stuff like this makes people think."

He finally agreed. I got the picture.

When I finished he said, "His wife is downstairs. Maybe you'd like to see her."

I hadn't thought about his being married. "Yeah, maybe I would," I said.

She was alone in the waiting room. I'd expected the kind of girl you find not too far from the skid row. She wasn't. You could see that.

She put on a brave smile when I told her who I was and pulled the business about the safety campaign.

"You've—you've been up there?" she whispered.

I nodded.

"They said they'd call me if . . ." She couldn't finish, but she didn't break into sobs. She just turned away for a moment and then she looked at me again. Her lips were too tight.

I got her picture that way.

It startled her and anger flashed in her eyes.

"Why did you do that?" she demanded.

"Lady, I'm a news photographer. It's my job."

I could see her thinking about it and forcing the anger out of herself and trying to be calm.

"I suppose so," she said.

"They told me at the desk that his name is John Sabin. Where did —*does* he work?"

"He's out of a job right now. Today was his last day. They're cutting down at his plant. He's a guard."

That explained the gun. It explained quite a bit.

"Tough luck," I said.

She didn't answer. I watched her walk to a window and look out upon the street. Her body was young and slim, and very tense. She faced me again.

"I'm sorry," she said. "I guess I'm not very—I mean, well, waiting like this. I—I'm scared."

"Take it easy, Mrs. Sabin. All you can do is sweat it out."

"I had to leave Billy with the people in the next-door apartment. They don't like kids and—"

"Billy?"

"Our baby. He's two. He looks like Johnny. He hasn't been too well. He has to have an operation. I wanted to take him to the public clinic, but Johnny says that's charity. He said he'd get the three hundred dollars somewhere and—and now . . ."

She couldn't hold the sobs any longer. I put the camera down and suddenly—I don't know how—she was in my arms and sobbing against my chest. Like Martha did the night Ma died. I patted the back of her head and said, "Shh . . ."

When the intern came and said, "Mrs. Sabin . . ." I let her go. She saw it in his face, just as I did.

As they walked down the hallway I heard the intern saying the stock phrases: ". . . did everything we could, but there wasn't a chance, Mrs. Sabin."

I walked back to the *Star* because I'd spent my last buck on the taxi. I vizualized handing those pictures to Ed Tanner and the expression he'd have.

I went to the dark-room and made prints of the set. They were sweet jobs. Beautiful jobs. Sabin standing behind the pole, the stickup, the murder, the flight, the body under the car, the hospital deathbed.

They'd make a wonderful spread on slick paper in any of the big mags. Maybe my own picture would turn out better than usual. Maybe I could use a little makeup to hide the beard that stayed blue

46

under my skin, maybe wear a hat with the brim over one eye and some good lighting effects.

And the checks would be large and very welcome!

There was no picture of Billy, but I had his mother. It wouldn't take long to get a picture of the kid. Maybe in the apartment of the next-door neighbors.

That would tie up the series. A beautiful, wonderful sequence showing a man murdering a guy and getting killed, with shots of his wife and kid.

And some day someone would hand the mag to the kid and say, "Your old man, kid. This is what happened to him."

Ed Tanner really went overboard for the skid row stuff. He raved about it.

"These all of them?" he said.

"Yeah. All that turned out."

"Why? What else did you have?"

"On my way home there was a guy hit by a car. I thought I had a few good ones, but I must have had bum film. No dice. Blanks."

"Must have been the guy named Sabin. He was hit crossing a street a few blocks from the row."

"Yeah. Maybe it was. I didn't follow it up when I saw the negs were no good."

"The skid row stuff is a swell tie-in with Barney Post's murder. It's too bad you left down there just before he got it. Tough break, Stub —missing the murder and the accident shots, too."

"Sure," I said, remembering how my beautiful murder pictures flamed when I touched a match to them for a kid named Billy. "That's me. Always behind the eight-ball."

# Better Hands

*by Dale Clark*

Detective Lew Brady, in plainclothes, climbed the shabby rooming-house steps and applied his thick thumb to the landlady's green-painted push button. Plainclothes possibly wasn't the exact term for what Brady wore. He'd decked himself out in maroon, perforated footgear, noisy socks, ice-cream slacks, a tweed coat, with a crimson necktie, and an orange splash of handkerchief overflowing his breast pocket.

He thought he looked the picture of a cheap, flashy crook, and to further this impression he didn't lift his pork-pie hat when the white-haired woman opened the door.

"Morning, Missus Drummond."

"Good morning . . . I'm sorry." In the tiny interval, her blue eyes moved alertly up and down Brady's big, loudly clad figure. "I haven't a single vacancy just now . . ."

"Wait a minute, I ain't hunting a room. My name's Brady, and I'm lookin' for the kid."

Mrs. Drummond drew a quick breath. "Chuck's not in town at present."

"Sure, I'm wise to that, he's layin' low . . . Listen, it's okay, Steve Joppas sent me. We got a job for the kid, if you'll slip him the word."

"A job."

"Good money, too."

The white-haired woman nodded slowly, and said: "Maybe you'd better come inside, and tell me about it."

Brady followed her into the downstairs parlor.

She was smiling. "I guess you could stand a little drink, couldn't you?"

"I never turned one down yet," Brady said, a little surprised by the nature of her smile. It was almost sly, hinting at a secret knowledge of Chuck's activities.

Mrs. Drummond went out, and Brady made a quick tour of the room. One cigarette crushed in an ash tray, a crumpled newspaper—today's—opened to the sport's page. He wondered if the old girl smoked, if she followed the baseball news . . . Hearing footsteps, he lowered his big bulk into an armchair.

"Here's looking at you," she said.

Brady peered at the glass, sipped its contents, muttered: "What the dickens?"

"Dandelion wine."

"I heard of it, I didn't know anybody ever made the stuff nowadays."

"My brother sends it from Ohio, he has a farm south of Cleveland." Mrs. Drummond grinned. "I like it better'n gin or whiskey—to start the day off with, anyway."

"Yeah, it's okay."

48

She asked abruptly, "What's this about a job for Chuck?"

"Oh. Tell him to get in touch with Steve, is all."

"A garage job?"

"Kind of."

Mrs. Drummond lowered one eyelid, her left.

"Come on, Brady," she said, "you don't have to stall around with me. Spill the dope, mister. Exactly what Joppas wants, and what he's willing to pay, and then I'll see whether or not Chuck's interested."

"Well . . ."

"It's a hot car proposition, huh?"

Brady stared at her. He wouldn't have believed it; not when he first walked in here. Her white hair and bland face gave you the idea she didn't know what anything was all about. It began to look, though, like he had to deal with another Ma Barker.

"So what?" he said.

"Plenty. What happens if Chuck gets pinched?"

"Bail. We got a system."

"You'll stand back of him?"

"Sure. Same as we do all the guys. Steve's got this thing *organized.*"

Mrs. Drummond walked to the front window. Standing there, she asked:

"What's in it? How much?"

"Fifty a week."

"That's—that's pretty good for a nineteen-year-old kid."

"For anybody," said Brady, laughing.

"Uh-huh. I sh'd think you wouldn't have much trouble—paying that much—if it's safe as you claim."

"Sure. Steve's a good guy to be lined up with."

"I sh'd think he could get all the help he needs, without Chuck."

"Well, we like 'em to be a little experienced, too."

"But Chuck isn't the only one—with a little experience?"

"No," Brady said, "he ain't. There's others. He better look alive and let Steve know if he wants to go to work. Otherwise, like you say, we can line up some different guy."

"That's about what I thought."

Mrs. Drummond fingered the white lace window curtain. A smile grew on her lips.

"Well, Brady," she said, "I lied to you. Chuck didn't leave town."

"I figured."

"He's right here in the house. He was *going* to leave—I packed his suitcase this morning. I could tell he was in some kind of trouble and finally he admitted it to me," Mrs. Drummond said slowly. "I was going to send him to Ohio, to my brother's farm there."

Brady breathed shallowly. "Lucky I came when I did . . . He's right here in the house, huh?" He got up from his chair.

"Hold on," Mrs. Drummond said. "I've got something more to say to you."

Her voice froze Brady in his tracks.

"I thought it'd be all right if I helped him get away," she was saying. "I know Chuck, and I know my brother, and I believe a year on the farm would straighten him out . . . He's sick and ashamed of the mess he's in, and I guess what he mostly needs now is a fresh start in a new place. With plenty of good hard work."

Brady hesitated, puzzled and perplexed.

"But that's only Chuck," the white-haired woman said. "It doesn't apply to the others like him. The ones you and Steve Joppas want to make into professional automobile thieves, provided you can't hire my son to do your dirty work."

"Huh? Say, what's you getting at, anyway?"

Mrs. Drummond's face was as white as her hair. "I called the police when I went for the wine. I've just been talking like this to keep you here . . ."

Brady said hoarsely, "You're turning me in? And your own kid with me?"

"Both of you," Chuck's mother said. Her hand trembled on the lace curtain, but her voice now was steady and sure and defiant. "I'm going to tell this whole thing in court, Mr. Brady. I want the judge to hear about my boy's mistake, and what you and Joppas were going to do about it. Every word you've said to me here . . ."

"You're crazy!"

"No, I'm not. I've gone through enough in the last few hours to turn almost any mother's mind," Mrs. Drummond said, "but I'm not insane. It's just that I don't want any other woman to go through this, too, and I know plenty of them will unless some one has the courage to fight men like your Steve Joppas." Her eyes glittered. "The mothers of all those other boys . . ."

She broke off, smiled grimly as Brady swung and headed toward the door. "It won't do you any good to run. There's a squad car in front of the house."

Detective Brady hurried down the shabby steps. Teagle, the inspector in charge of the Hot-car Detail, was emerging from the official machine.

"Too late," Brady said.

Teagle said, "We got a tip one of Joppas' mob was here . . ."

"Sure, that's me. I faked it to see if she wouldn't tell me where the kid was," Brady said, "and she did."

"Well?"

"He's on a farm out in Ohio, working for his uncle there."

"Ohio?" Teagle looked nonplussed. "That's a hell of a break. I don't know whether we can extradite a guy on what evidence we've got."

"We can't, but don't let it worry you," said Detective Brady. "From what I found out, I'd say right now the kid's in better hands than ours, Inspector."

# The Bloodless Corpse

*by O. R. Dale*

Spying from behind carefully drawn curtains, Mrs. Leona Carlin, young, with all the curves in the best of places, watched her day maid pick her way gingerly along the slush-covered walk. Not until the maid's full, swaying hips disappeared around the corner did Mrs. Carlin turn from the window. Breathing a deep sigh of relief, she hurried upstairs, entered her bedroom—and locked the door. Nervousness suddenly overcame her and, copying the age-long habit of men when beset by worry, she began a slow but steady march back and forth across the carpeted floor.

There was no trace now on her face of that gayety that had so pleased the simple maid during the day. No song issued from Mrs. Carlin's tightly-pressed, sensuous lips. There was no hint of the warm friendliness that had animated her eyes but an hour earlier.

With frenzied hands she suddenly tore off her dress and stood forth clad only in the filmiest of lingerie. Then the pacing began again. Back and forth she strode with the grace and freedom of some jungle animal, pausing every now and then to throw anxious, furtive glances at the tiny ivory clock ticking away on a nearby dresser.

Suddenly a muffled jingle from the telephone brought her to a rigid stop. She stood there, poised for a moment as though for flight, head erect, delicate nostrils distended, eyes alert, expectant, breast forward, as though about to run. The bell jingled again, more insistently this time, and the woman approached it with a look of something akin to despair flashing across her beautiful, pale face. At the third ring, which she seemed to take as a challenge to her self-control, she smiled, whipped the receiver off the hook and placed it firmly to her ear.

"Hello-o," she breathed softly. A smile parted her soft, moist lips as she recognized the voice that whispered in her ear.

"Yes, this is Leona . . . not so loud, Joe," she cautioned. "Yes, darling," then, after a moment's pause, "everything's all right . . . no, he isn't home yet—not until six. Hurry over, dear."

Her face lighted up as she listened to the purring, mellow, deep-toned laughter that poured through the receiver.

"The maid and I brought down the chairs from the attic," she trilled, her voice taking on a note of nervousness. "I dismissed her early. Told her we—John and I—were going out to dinner. I phoned John you'd be here to buy them . . . what? No, no, darling. He'll leave the car at Smith's garage on 27th street and walk home from there . . . It's two blocks away."

The voice at the other end of the wire broke in hurriedly and the woman listened with lips compressed, eyes tightly closed, the phone crushed to her breast. A tremor ran through her.

"Sh-sh-sh!" She cautioned. "Not so loudly, Joe. Be here soon? Oh, that's fine, darling, I'll be waiting, so anxiously. Yes . . . yes . . . I guess . . . so. Goodbye, darling."

She placed the receiver carefully on the hook and then, as though exhausted by this single physical effort, threw herself on the bed with a frightened cry. Her breasts pressed into the coverlet were crushed but she didn't notice. Beads of perspiration stood out on her forehead. Her eyes burned and delicate shivers made her lithe body quiver.

The gray March dusk seeped into the room and enshrouded her in a ghostly blanket as she lay there hiding her face, biting her lips, trying with every atom of willpower to conquer a rising tide of terror that shook her. Finally, in a frantic movement, as though surrendering to a force greater than herself, she jumped up, rushed over to a wall switch and turned on all of the lights. Snatching up a flimsy dressing gown she sheathed her natural loveliness.

"It's madness!" she breathed fiercely to herself. "I shouldn't do this to John. I hope Joe doesn't come, I don't love him." She repeated this over and over again like one who tries in vain to memorize a little verse.

The tiny ivory clock struck the half hour.

52

*  *  *

Scarcely had the sweet echoes of its soft chime died away when the doorbell rang. And somehow, despite its sharp, imperative summons, the sound of it seemed to bring back her courage. The strange fears, doubts, uncertainties that had assailed her completely vanished. A grim, determined smile parted her lips as she unlocked her bedroom door. There was no hesitancy, no nervousness in her lithe walk as she went down the broad stairway.

The slim, calculating man who eagerly pushed his way through the half-opened door paused only long enough to feast his eyes in one sweeping glance at her beautiful form, revealed as her dressing gown fell open, before taking her in his arms and crushing her against him. After that first breathtaking contact his hands became active, and he rained kisses upon her face and neck. The ardor of his love, the warmth of his hands, met a response as warm as his own as they stood there, melted together, in the darkened hallway, swept by a storm of passion that knew no bounds.

Joe's seeking lips found their mark as he lifted her into his arms. The touch of her flesh thrilled him and drove all thoughts but one from his mind.

It was the woman who first came to her senses, who pushed away with a breathless little moan of protest.

"We mustn't . . . we mustn't now, dear. We'll have plenty of time after . . . after tonight." She stammered weakly.

And the man, this Joe, young and slim, hot-eyed, nodded his sleek head and whispered: "All right, Leona, have it your own way. There's plenty of time, but you're beautiful." He stroked the firm, living flesh of her as he spoke these words. "The most beautiful thing in the world. That's all your lips are for—to be kissed!"

She clung to him, the billowing mounds of her breasts crushed against him, raised her depthless eyes to his face.

"It's nice to hear you say that. I—I love you, Joe!"

Arm in arm, ecstatically brushing together they walked into the living room.

"He'll—John—my husband—will be here soon," she warned as she broke slowly away, fastening her negligee to cover her tempting bosom. As she drew down the curtains, Joe watched her through half-closed eyes, smiling hungrily, took an eager step toward her.

"Oh!" he breathed hoarsely, "there was never a woman like you!"

He reached her side, pulled her down beside him and rained kisses on her neck and lips, holding her so tight against him she could scarcely breathe. She struggled once, made a half-hearted effort to push him away, and the light in his bold eyes became suddenly cold and hard.

"You—needn't be afraid of me, Leona," he said in a throaty whisper of anger and surprise. "You needn't be afraid of me. I wouldn't hurt a hair of your pretty head! Only I can't stop myself. You're like wine in my blood."

"I know you wouldn't hurt me. How silly to think of such a thing. When I love you so. But we haven't much time. The—the kisses will come later, Joe." She bathed her lover with a provocative, tantalizing smile as she alluringly moved farther from him on the davenport.

"You're the boss," he replied, grinning his approval. "I understand."

As Mrs. Carlin got to her feet and turned on a light in the stand lamp, her eyes, hot and burning with a strange fire, darted swiftly about the room. Once she swayed, and when she grasped the table-edge for support, her knuckles showed blue-white under the light.

The man—the man she called Joe—keen, hard eyes, took it all in, and he smiled as if it amused him.

"Haven't lost your nerve, have you?" he questioned with a shrug. "Haven't decided to call off the—the sale, have you?" He stood there facing her, his cruel but handsome face devoid of all expression. "Listen to me," he shot at her suddenly, "if there's a catch in this, God help you!" He was all business now, bold, cruel, crafty and suspicious.

With a tremendous effort the woman regained her composure. She even managed to smile, to go to him and kiss him passionately.

"No," she said in a loud voice, "no, I haven't lost my nerve. See!"

The white arm she thrust out was as steady as so much marble.

"Not even a quiver," Joe smiled his compliment. "That's fine! I'll take it all back, but for a second I thought you were going to chuck it. Nerve! Why, Leona, you've got it to spare!"

Joe's praise was accepted with a warm caress.

"The day you came down to Jerry's place," he went on, "and gave me the money to pay that fine, I right away you weren't afraid of hell-or-high-water. You saved me a trip up the river, and I'll never forget that. And as I agreed last week, when—when we talked—business, I'm willing to do anything for you. I'm here. I'm crazy about you." He charmed her into his arms. "Now, cheer up, little lady."

The mere mention of the word "business" seemed to electrify Leona, to make her wary. Her inviting face suddenly became drawn and pinched as though the hand of fear was upon it.

"Did you get here unnoticed?" she questioned.

"Not a soul in sight," Joe responded genially. "Slipped in like a
54

shadow. Lonesome neighborhood you live in around here. And your walks! Like canals. Got my feet all wet sliding through the slush."

"He'll be here any minute now. Let's—let's get down to . . ."

"To business," Joe broke in with a hard laugh. "All right. Give me the lay."

"The what?"

"The lay—the next move. How are we going to surprise the old gent?" he asked with brutal frankness.

The woman pointed out three old-fashioned pieces of furniture.

"The maid and I brought them down from the attic this afternoon," she explained. "I phoned John that a collector named Barlintto wanted to buy them. That's you, Joe Barlintto. Remember the name. And be careful when you bargain. The pieces are worth more than you think."

"I'll take your word for that," came the disdainful answer. "I'm not up on antiques. Tell me some more. Maybe you *had* better tell me how much they're worth—real money. I don't want to appear too dumb."

"Well," Mrs. Carlin informed him, "they're worth at least two hundred dollars apiece. Offer him less than that, of course. Make an effort to buy them cheaper; that is—if you . . ."

"Oh, I understand." Joe smiled knowingly. "I understand. But I don't believe I'll have time to bargain much. We'll surprise him right off the bat, eh?"

He raised his right hand and brought it down in a significant gesture that wrung a sharp cry of protest from Mrs. Carlin's grey lips.

"That's the idea, isn't it?" Joe asked nonchalantly. "No use in being touchy, now, is there?"

The woman did not answer, but she looked into the man's cruel, hardened face, saw the slow grin, the hot, narrow eyes and succumbed to waves of terror.

"I—I—I can't, Joe," she began in a stammering, terrified voice.

Joe jumped toward her before she could finish. Anger blazed like a hot flame within him.

"Keep away from me," the woman warned, desperately. Then, in a sharp whisper, "Quick! He's at the door!"

Joe rushed to a wall switch, snapped on the lights and, with the silent swiftness of a cat glided back to the table.

"Now get busy!" he rasped out curtly. "I'm looking at that chair. And I've made you an offer. Tell him about it when you've introduced me. Come on! Come on!"

A tall, thin man, well past middle age, appeared at the living room door. He regarded Joe with mildly interrogative eyes, then he bent slowly and removed his rubbers. His wife rushed across the floor and greeted him with a lingering kiss.

"Not ill, are you?" he inquired solicitously. The pallor of her face disturbed him. "Who's that?" he asked quite suddenly, nodding in Joe's direction.

Mrs. Carlin's laughter, brittle with nervousness, rang out high-pitched, thin-edged, hysterical. "No," she said, "I'm not ill. Just excited and—happy. Don't take off your overcoat," she protested. "Mr. Barlintto, the collector of whom I phoned, is in a hurry. He's here to buy those chairs."

She led her husband close up to Joe.

"This is Mr. Barlintto, John," she said calmly.

Joe bowed gracefully.

"Very glad to meet you, Mr. Carlin."

"My wife tells me you want to buy these," Carlin began, indicating the antiques. "They'll come high," he warned.

Joe walked over to the chair nearest him. "I like this one," he announced quietly. "One hundred and fifty dollars, Mr. Carlin. That's my limit."

"You're like all of them," Carlin replied wearily. "Trying to get something for nothing. What's your price on the others?"

"Let's settle this one first," Joe insisted stubbornly. "How about adding another twenty-five." He tipped the chair back. "Say look here! There's a crack in one leg!" He bent over to examine the fault more carefully. "See for yourself, Mr. Carlin!"

Joe stood erect, face flushed, eyes gleaming.

"See it?" he questioned again, handing the chair to Carlin and moving so that he stood a little to one side and back of the owner. "It's right here." He placed a long, cigarette-stained finger on the crack.

Carlin stooped over. Peered intently to discover the flaw.

As he did so, Joe cast a quick, meaning glance at the woman. His hand slipped—with a stealthy movement toward his hip pocket.

"Yes," admitted Carlin, still squinting at the crack, "yes, I see it—but it's nothing much. It doesn't change my price any. You can have it for two hundred dollars, nothing less."

Joe's hand, raised above his head, held a club-like object. Carlin's wife, fingers digging into her luscious throat as though trying to get air, watched it with wide, staring eyes.

"Look again, mister," Joe insisted, giving the woman a wink. "It might be a fake."

"Oh, let's forget it!" Carlin snapped and made a move to straighten up.

56

"Sure," Joe roared, bringing down his arm, "let's forget it!"

They stood there, these two, Joe and the woman, tense and alert. They were breathing hard, like runners who have reached the tape completely exhausted.

The woman began to sob. Joe's lips curled in a sneer. Her mature beauty was cheapened in her weakness. He put his arms around her slim waist, drew her roughly to him.

"Well," he announced grimly—as though satisfied with a job well done—"that's that." And as an after-thought: "I'd bump off a regiment like him—for you. You won't be sorry." He placed one hand lightly on one of her surging breasts, sought out her face and kissed her. "Don't worry, baby," he murmured. "I'll take care of you."

He left her standing there staring down at the inert body of Carlin at her feet, went to the door and so out onto the porch.

"Not a soul in sight," he said upon his return. "But we've got to hurry."

Leona dumbly nodded assent.

"Turn out the lights," Joe commanded, suddenly all "business" again. "We must be careful, too."

When the room was dark, he stooped, picked up the limp form in his strong arms and carried it outside.

Back of him like a shadow came Mrs. Carlin.

Certain that the coast was clear, he hurried with his burden along the narrow path that led to the street. He cursed under his breath as he slipped through the slush and almost fell.

But he reached the sidewalk without mishap, placed the body on the walk so that the head rested against the cement step that connected with the path to the house. Satisfied with the arrangement of the body, he stepped close to the woman, thrilling with her nearness as he said:

"Keep your head up," and whispered, "not a chance for a slip-up. Let me know when you get the insurance money. I'll be at . . ." He placed his lips to a pert ear and gave an address.

Jim Crawley of the Vice Squad eased his long form into the most comfortable chair in the receiving room of the Emergency Hospital and complained in no uncertain terms of life in general and sleuthing in particular.

"I tell you, young fellow," he said, addressing the efficient-looking interne, "this business isn't what it's cracked up to be. Nothing much happens any more."

He was interrupted by a white-clad nurse who burst through the door and held it open for a man bearing a limp form in his arms. The interne rushed up a wheeled cot and helped the man deposit the body on it.

A luscious woman, tight-lipped with determination, idly dabbling at her face with a filmy lace handkerchief, attracted Crawley's attention, and he hastened to her, gently urging her to take the chair he had just vacated. He drank the full measure of her ripe beauty and asked her a question, glancing at the cot:

"Automobile?"

"No," she replied with a sob that was none too genuine, "he—he must have fallen on the slippery walk in front of our house. He—he must be hurt terribly."

"When did it happen?"

"The neighbor next door found him lying there. About six it was. He's usually home about five-thirty." The woman's sobs were becoming more convincing as she gave this information.

Crawley, somehow, could not keep his eyes away from the cot, glanced at it again and again as he became less satisfied with the woman's answers, sensed something haywire in the case. Finally he went over and stood by the interne.

"Hurt bad?" the detective whispered.

"Dead," the interne whispered back.

The detective stiffened. "Play with me," he whispered in the interne's ear. "I gotta hunch something's up. Keep working over him until I ask a few questions." He ran practised fingers over the dead man's clothing, touched the shoes, and then strode back to the sobbing woman.

The man who had carried the body in was talking.

"I'll have to go home, Mrs. Carlin," he said. "The children are all alone. I'll be back shortly." He gave her a smile of encouragement and departed.

"He—your husband was walking home?" The detective smiled as he put the question, unable to ignore the soft curves revealed by the V in her coat.

"Not far," the woman explained monotonously. "He put the car in the garage in 27th Street and walked in from there. It's about two blocks."

"Where is that, Mrs. Carlin?"

"1516 Keppert Street."

"Well," the detective went on in a matter-of-fact voice, "a man's taking an awful chance on these slippery streets. That's a fact. Almost fell myself coming down here. Slippery out your way, too, you said."

Leona nodded. A vague, undefined dread clutched at her heart. She wished with all her soul that this hard man would stop asking her questions, would leave her alone.

The house doctor arrived and Crawley watched him as he worked over the body.

"We'll take him upstairs," the doctor announced suddenly.

Crawley, in a mild voice, told Mrs. Carlin of the seriousness of the accident and suggested she wait there where she could rest until he sent down word.

"You may think I am the prize busybody—and maybe you're right," he declared smiling. "But I'm around here so much off and on that I sometimes get a bit officious. But I like to help folks when trouble comes. Everything is all right. Just be patient. If it's anything serious I'll come right down."

"He's dead," the house doctor announced gravely when Crawley entered the operating room. "Dead when he got here."

"Thought so," came the gruff reply. "Knew it when they brought him in." He suddenly became very determined, very officious.

"I want you to leave the body just as it is—don't touch it until I come back," he commanded from the door.

Mrs. Carlin was quiet in her chair, eyeing him invitingly as he entered the room.

"Tell me," she questioned softly, "how is he?"

"We'd better go up," he replied breathlessly, unable to resist placing his strong fingers about her shapely arm.

Leona gave a little cry, fell towards Crawley, melted in his embrace as he crushed—fiercely pressed—her to him. Passion beat through his veins as he smothered her carmine lips with fiery kisses.

Almost all self-control had left him, when Crawley hurled the woman to the floor in a heap, stood over her glowering.

"What the hell kind of a woman are you anyway? Doesn't your husband mean a thing to you? You gutter snipe!"

Mrs. Carlin struggled to her feet, put her hands on the detective's shoulders. "Is he—dead?" she asked humbly.

"He is." Crawley spoke quietly.

She stumbled back a step, her hands dropping to her sides.

"*Murdered!*" roared Crawley.

She slumped into the chair, nearly spent.

Crawley came closer, stood before her, a pointing finger almost in her face and pronounced distinctly, "Your husband's shoes were dry!"

In a split second he saw her erect, saw the flash of a short knife, heard her piercing scream as she plunged it to the hilt in her breast.

Crawley shook his head sadly as, hands still bloody, he started for the operating room to report Leona Carlin's suicide.

# Bread Ahead

*by C. J. Henderson*

I'd gone down to Caesar's Bay to get away from everything. It had been a foul, grey, humid day—one of disappointments—one I didn't want to remember. I'd solved another sad little case, brought another sniveling, cheating husband to ground like the big bad hero I am. I'd made the monthly office rent by ruining a family with pictures of Daddy grunting in the back seat of their station wagon with a woman who didn't look anything like Mommy at all. As a daily occupation, it was getting to me.

My name's Jack Hagee. I make my living, I put food on my table, buy my toothpaste and subway tokens, by rooting through people's lives and their garbage, by turning over rocks for lawyers and crying spouses and tired shopkeepers and more lawyers. I'm a private detective and that day I was hating my job as much as anyone else. That's why, when midnight had passed and I still couldn't get to sleep, tossing in my bed, dying in the clogging humidity steaming in off the ocean, that I'd gotten dressed and driven down to Caesar's.

Caesar's is a shopping mall at the end of Bay Parkway, the main drag through the neighborhood I live in. Most people stay away from it after closing—with good reason.

After dark, Caesar's parking lot, and the park adjacent, become one large dark criminal carnival land. Dopers sell their wares, johns pick up their ladies, kids strip cars, smoke dope, shoot craps and sometimes each other. And the worst thing about it all is, it isn't in some terribly seedy neighborhood. Not a home between my apartment building and the river would sell for under a hundred and fifty thousand. It's not a ghetto—just simply the same as the rest of New York City, bursting at the seams from too many people, all with painfully clear visions of the nowhere toward which they are headed.

For those who haven't tasted the city, haven't felt the cold, leaden knuckle it digs into the backs of those who flock to it, let me just say that it is a hell—a black, indifferent hell, one which beckons to all types, the stupid and the arrogant, the talented, the conning, the naive, the hopeful, and the self-destructive, to come from around the country to lick at the festering black syrup leaking from its million-and-counting wounds, begging them to call it honey.

Those who had begun to catch on to what the city had in store for them, however, sat in their cars, staring, or prowled the darkness of Caesar's. I parked my Skylark at the rail meant to keep people from driving into the ocean and got out to prowl with them. I walked down along the massive stone sea wall, looking out into the storm front crawling in toward me over the black, oily water. The Verrazano Bridge was lost in the fog, as was the parachute tower at Coney Island, both usually easily visible to my spot. Not then. That night the clouds were hanging thick—waiting.

Ignoring the clouds and whatever they were waiting for, I threw myself up and over the steel railing in front of me, settling down on the foot-and-a-half of ledge on the sea side of the barrier. My legs dangling over the dashing waves below, I stared out at the ocean, my eyes not focusing on anything, my brain relaxing for the first time in weeks. I was tired. Tired and alone, dying of despairing old age while still in my thirties.

Leaning back against the rail, I pulled a cigarette and managed to light it in the wet of the surrounding mist. I sucked the smoke in deep, holding it down as long as I could, maybe hoping to choke myself. No such luck. The nicotine did start to relax me, however, which at the moment was good enough.

I'd left my apartment in a foul mood. I don't own an umbrella— ridiculous, effeminate props—but in my anger I'd slammed my way out leaving hat and coat behind. The thickening mist was soaking into my hair and clothes, drenching me. By the time I was ready for a second smoke, the sky had started drizzling to the point where I could barely get it lit. I downed its fumes one breath at a time, watching the lightning splash along both the far shores before me. The coasts of Brooklyn and Staten Island were illuminated over and over, the random split seconds of light revealing the increasing press of the waves below and the rain above.

The truth of the image depressed me. Even nature worked for the city. It squeezed people, crushing them, forcing them to huddle and shiver, always prepared to wash them away forever for the slightest mistake. Part of me railed at the image, but a larger part spoke in calmer tones, implying that perhaps hopelessness was the only sensible feeling one could have living in New York.

I leaned back with eyes closed, the rain lashing, surf below pounding hard enough to almost reach my shoes. I thought of all the reasons people come to New York and wondered what mine had been. As a friend once said, "People don't pull up in covered wagons to the center of Times Square and say, 'Here it is, honey—a good land, a strong land, a decent land where our children can grow strong and free.'" They didn't say it when people actually rode around in covered wagons, and they sure as hell don't say it now. New York is not a good land or a strong land, and it certainly is not a place to bring children. Not by a long shot.

New York is an aching scum hole, a never-closing maw always willing to let anyone—no matter how corrupt, or illiterate, or evil—call it home and hang up their shingle. It is a giant con, a government-owned-and-operated money drain, constantly sucking the life and joy and wealth out of its inhabitants the way a dying man sucks oxygen—greedily, as if each breath were the last. It grabs everything in sight, using guilt and law and lies and finally thuggery, if nothing lesser will suffice, to strip those who can't fight it every single minute of every day, week in, decade out, of everything they have—their money, their needs, their dreams, and wretched, desperate hopes—until finally it either gets the last juice left within them, piling their useless bones with the rest, or drives them away in pitiful defeat, frustrated and humiliated and wondering how anyone, *anyone* as tough as them could have lost—everything—so easily, to an enemy so impartial.

And, I thought, still they come. Every day by the hundreds—*by the hundreds*, they arrive by plane and bus, in rented trucks, old cars, on bicycles, motorcycles, or they walk and hitch if they have to—all of them desperate to follow some simpleminded plan they've mapped out for themselves that is just foolproof. One that shows how easy it will be to make it on Broadway, or in television, or as a painter, a broker, writer, dancer, restaurateur, publisher, actor, reporter, agent, or whathaveyou, willing to work hard now for their bread ahead, not realizing how many waiters and convenience store attendants and busboys, cab drivers, keyboarders, bartenders, store clerks, menials, drug dealers, hookers, homeless starvlings, and corpses the city requires for every you-have-made-it golden meal ticket it passes out.

As the rain slacked off, I tried to get another cigarette going, ruefully asking myself what my excuse for being in New York was, knowing all along that I hadn't come to the city to find anything. I'd come to lose myself, to hide a person I didn't think anyone should see. I was tired when I did it, tired of corruption, tired of hate—of jealousy, pettiness, violence, and anger. I was tired of these things in myself and others.

So naturally, I came to New York, where all the above vices and sins were long ago renamed art forms, encouraged to grow with wild abandon like kudzu, or social welfare. It was the move of a desperate man—trying to hide in a sweltering sea of desperation—hoping the heightened insanity of those around him would make his own reflection look normal. It hadn't worked.

Not knowing what to do about any of it, though, I let the big problems rest and concentrated on lighting my cigarette. I had just gotten my first lungful when the city gave me something new to think about.

So skillfully I almost didn't notice, a pickpocket had reached through the railing my back was against, going for the wallet in my front pants pocket. His hand out with its prize, I managed to snag his wrist a split second before it could snake back behind the railing.

"Oh no you don't!" I growled.

The pickpocket pulled hard, pushing with his feet against the rail, tearing my fingers at the knuckles as he scraped them against the steel rails. I pulled back, determined to keep my wallet, fighting for balance on the foot and a half of slick rock which made up my side of the fence.

"Let go, damnit! Let go o'me!"

Sticking his free arm through the rails, the pickpocket slammed me in the side, knocking me over the sea wall. I held his wrist in a death grip, feeling his shoulder slam against the rails as my weight pulled him tight. He cursed nonstop, his free hand tearing at my fingers around his wrist. I punched him away as best I could, hitting him sometimes, sometimes myself, sometimes the rails. My mind raced over my options, not finding much.

I could release my grip and hope to be able to catch a rail or the sea wall's edge, but the rain made my chances slim at best. It was possible I might survive the fall to the water, but it was only a fifty-fifty possibility. The rocks hidden beneath the violently pounding waves, slamming against my legs and the sea wall, were jagged and slimy with sea growth. Walking along the wall back to shore was impossible. So was swimming. The tide was too low for that, but quite ample to mash a man to death. I had no choice—I hung on.

"C'mon, man—let go o'me! I mean it—I mean it!!"

He shook at me, pulling back and forth, jerking my armpit painfully across the edge of the rock wall. I bit at the rain, growling in agony, but didn't let go.

"Le'go, le'go, le'go—you bastard—le'go, le'go!!"

"Just pull me up—fer Christ's sake!" I told him. "let me grab the rail so I don't have to die over five goddamned bucks!"

"No—shut up!! Let go o'me—le'go, le'go! Shit. I makes you le'go. I makes you!"

The pickpocket reached inside his coat. Bracing myself, I thought, okay, you want it—you got it, and then dug my heels into the wall. The pickpocket's hand emerged with a straight razor. My left foot slipped back into the water. The pickpocket's free hand came through the rails at me. My foot almost caught, but slipped again. The razor took my distance, cutting open my sleeve and flaying a fine layer of hair and skin away. My foot caught. I hovered into balance, finding my center of gravity. The razor waved above my line of sight.

"Now. Now you let go."

"Not yet."

I threw my weight back, my legs pushing me out from the wall. The extra leverage broke the pickpocket's hold, bringing him slamming into the rails face first. The razor flipped out of his hand, arcing past my right ear. Blood splashed from the pickpocket's face, catching me in the eyes and mouth. Not slowing up, I leaned forward and punched, nailing the part of his face that the steel to either side of my fist had missed. Blood arced again, running over his shoulder, down his arm to mine. The blow caused me to slip, but I managed to get half my body back up on the ledge. Releasing the pickpocket, I caught rails in both hands, dragging myself into a secure position as fast as I could.

Once on the ledge I turned to face the pickpocket in case he was going to be any more trouble. He wasn't. He was unconscious or dead. I didn't care which. Then I spotted it—my wallet was still in his hand. Catching my breath, I reached over and pried it free. He didn't stir. I slid back over to the landward side of the railing. I sat down in relief a few feet from the pickpocket, exhausted from my ninety seconds of past-event reruns, glad for life and breath and safety. After a few minutes of being overjoyed with having remained alive, though, I noticed it was starting to rain harder. Tired of abuse for one night, I pushed myself to my feet and walked over to the pickpocket. Patting him on the back, I told him,

"Nice try."

Then I walked back to my car and drove home. When I got there, I had no trouble sleeping.

# Cache and Carry

*by Marcia Muller
and Bill Pronzini*

"Hello?"

" 'Wolf'? It's Sharon McCone."

"Well! Been a while, Sharon. How are you?"

"I've been better. Are you busy?"

"No, no, I just got home. What's up?"

"I've got a problem and I thought you might be able to help."

"If I can. Professional problem?"

"The kind you've run into before."

"Oh?"

"One of those things that *seem* impossible but that you know has to have a simple explanation."

"  . . . ."

" 'Wolf,' are you there?"

"I'm here. The poor man's Sir Henry Merrivale."

"Who's Sir Henry Merrivale?"

"Never mind. Tell me your tale of woe."

"Well, one of All Souls' clients is a small outfit in the Outer Mission called Neighborhood Check Cashing. You know, one of those places that cashes third-party or social-security checks for local residents who don't have bank accounts of their own or easy access to a bank. We did some legal work for them a year or so ago, when they first opened for business."

"Somebody rip them off?"

"Yes. For two thousand dollars."

"Uh-huh. When?"

"Sometime this morning."

"Why did you and All Souls get called in on a police matter?"

"The police were called first but they couldn't come up with any answers. So Jack Harvey, Neighborhood's owner and manager, contacted me. But I haven't come up with any answers either."

"Go ahead, I'm listening."

"There's no way anyone could have gotten the two thousand dollars out of Neighborhood's office. And yet, if the money is still hidden somewhere on the premises, the police couldn't find it and neither could I."

"Mmm."

"Only one of two people could have taken it—unless Jack Harvey himself is responsible, and I don't believe that. If I knew which one, I might have an idea of what happened to the money. Or vice versa. But I don't have a clue either way."

"Let's have the details."

"Well, cash is delivered twice a week—Mondays and Thursdays—by armored car at the start of the day's business. It's usually five thousand dollars, unless Jack requests more or less. Today it was exactly five thousand."

"Not a big operation, then."

"No. Jack's also an independent insurance broker; the employees help him out in that end of the business too."

"His employees are the two who could have stolen the money?"

"Yes. Art DeWitt, the bookkeeper, and Maria Chavez, the cashier. DeWitt's twenty-five, single, lives in Daly City. He's studying business administration nights at City College. Chavez is nineteen, lives with her family in the Mission. She's planning to get married next summer. They both seem to check out as solid citizens."

"But you say one of them has to be guilty. Why?"

"Opportunity. Let me tell you what happened this morning. The cash was delivered as usual, and Maria Chavez entered the amount in her daily journal, then put half the money in the till and half in the safe. Business for the first hour and a half was light; only one person came in to cash a small check: Jack Harvey's cousin, whom he vouches for."

"So Chavez couldn't have passed the money to him or another accomplice."

"No. At about ten-thirty a local realtor showed up wanting to cash a fairly large check: thirty-five hundred dollars. Harvey doesn't usually like to do that, because Neighborhood runs short before the next cash delivery. Besides, the fee for cashing a large check is the same as for a small one; he stands to lose on large transactions. But the realtor is a good friend, so he okayed it. When Chavez went to cash the check, there was only five hundred dollars in the till."

"Did DeWitt also have access to the till?"

"Yes."

"Any way either of them could have slipped out of the office for even a few seconds?"

"No. Harvey's desk is by the back door and he was sitting there the entire time."

"What about through the front?"

"The office is separated from the customer area by one of those double Plexiglas security partitions and a locked security door. The door operates by means of a buzzer at Harvey's desk. He didn't buzz anybody in or out."

"Could the two thousand have been removed between the time the police searched and you were called in?"

"No way. When the police couldn't find it in the office, they body-searched DeWitt and had a matron do the same with Chavez. The money wasn't on either of them. Then, after the cops left, Jack told his employees they couldn't take anything away from the office except Chavez's purse and DeWitt's briefcase, both of which he searched again, personally."

"Do either DeWitt or Chavez have a key to the office?"

"No."

"Which means the missing money is still there."

"Evidently. But *where*, 'Wolf'?"

"Describe the office to me."

"One room, with an attached lavatory that doubles as a supply closet. Table, with a desktop copier, postage scale, postage meter. A big Mosler safe; only Harvey has the combination. Three desks: Jack's, next to the back door; DeWitt's in the middle; Chavez's next to the counter behind the partition, where the till is. Desks have standard stuff on them—adding machines, a typewriter on Chavez's, family photos, stack trays, staplers, pen sets. Everything you'd expect to find."

"Anything you *wouldn't* expect to find?"

"Not unless you count some lurid romance novels that Chavez likes to read on her lunch break."

"Did anything unusual happen this morning, before the shortage was discovered?"

"Not really. The toilet backed up and ruined a bunch of supplies, but Jack says that's happened three or four times before. Old plumbing."

"Uh-huh."

"You see why I'm frustrated? There just doesn't seem to be any clever hidey-hole in that office. And Harvey's already starting to tear his hair. Chavez and DeWitt resent the atmosphere of suspicion;

they're nervous, too, and have both threatened to quit. Harvey doesn't want to lose the one that isn't guilty, anymore than he wants to lose his two thousand dollars."

"How extensive was the search you and the police made?"

"About as extensive as you can get."

"Desks gone over top to bottom, drawers taken out?"

"Yes."

"Underside of the legs checked?"

"Yes."

"Same thing with all the chairs?"

"To the point of removing cushions and seat backs."

"The toilet backing up—any chance that could be connected?"

"I don't see how. Harvey and I both looked it over pretty carefully. The sink and the rest of the plumbing, too."

"What about the toilet paper roll?"

"I checked it. Negative."

"The extra supplies?"

"Negative."

"Chavez's romance novels—between the pages?"

"I thought of that. Negative."

"Personal belongings?"

"All negative. Including Jack Harvey's. I went through his on the idea that DeWitt or Chavez might have thought to use him as a carrier."

"The office equipment?"

"Checked and rechecked. Copier, negative. Chavez's typewriter, negative. Postage meter and scale, negative. Four adding machines, negative. Stack trays—"

"Wait a minute, Sharon. *Four* adding machines?"

"That's right."

"Why four, with only three people?"

"DeWitt's office machine jammed and he had to bring his own from home."

"When did that happen?"

"It jammed two days ago. He brought his own yesterday."

"Suspicious coincidence, don't you think?"

"I did at first. But I checked both machines, inside and out. Negative."

"Did either DeWitt or Chavez bring anything else to the office in recent days that they haven't brought before?"

"Jack says no."

"Then we're back to DeWitt's home adding machine."

" 'Wolf,' I told you—"

"What kind is it? Computer type, or the old-fashioned kind that runs a tape?"

"The old-fashioned kind."

"Did you run a tape on it? Or on the office machine that's supposed to be jammed?"

". . . No. No, I didn't."

"Maybe you should. Both machines are still in the office, right?"

"Yes."

"Why don't you have another look at them? Run tapes on both, see if the office model really is jammed—or if maybe it's DeWitt's home model that doesn't work the way it should."

"And if it's the home model, have it taken apart piece by piece."

"Right."

"I'll call Harvey and have him meet me at Neighborhood right away."

"Let me know, huh? Either way?"

"You bet I will."


" 'Wolf,' hi. It's Sharon."

"You sound chipper. Good news?"

"Yes, thanks to you. You were right about the adding machines. I ran a tape on DeWitt's office model and it worked fine. But the one he brought from home didn't, for a damned good reason."

"Which is?"

"Its tape roll was a dummy. Hollow, made of metal and wound with just enough paper tape to make it look like the real thing. So real neither the police nor I thought to remove and examine it before. The missing money was inside."

"So DeWitt must have been planning the theft for some time."

"That's what he confessed to the police a few minutes ago. He made the dummy roll in his workshop at home; took him a couple of weeks. It was in his home machine when he brought that in yesterday. This morning he slipped the roll out and put it into his pocket. While Maria Chavez was in the lavatory and Jack Harvey was occupied on the phone, he lifted the money from the till and pocketed that too. He went into the john after Maria came out and hid the money in the dummy roll. Then, back at his desk, he put the fake roll into his own machine, which he intended to take home with him this evening. It was his bad luck—and Jack's good luck—that the realtor came in with such a large check to cash."

"I suppose he intended to doctor the books to cover the theft."

"So he said. You know, 'Wolf,' it's too bad DeWitt didn't apply his creative talents to some legitimate enterprise. His cache-and-carry scheme was really pretty clever."

"What kind of scheme?"

"Cache and carry. C-a-c-h-e."

" . . . "

"Was that a groan I heard?"

"McCone, if you're turning into a rogue detective, call somebody else next time you come up against an impossible problem. Call Sir Henry Merrivale."

"What do you mean, a rogue detective?"

"The worst kind there is. A punslinger."

# Calling Dr. Death

*by C. William Harrison*

The owl, swooping through the pines along the lake shore, sent its harsh cry whipping out through the darkness. The cry caved in the night silence and brought a backlash of echoes down from the black humps of the hills above the lake, and Dr. Paul Lanning shivered.

He stood motionless where he had parked his car well off of the narrow blacktop road, listening to that harsh sound bound off across the lake. It was only the nocturnal cry of an owl on the hunt—he knew that—but he couldn't stop the shiver that ran up his spine and into the short hairs on the back of his neck. He was a tall, slender man, city bred, and he couldn't rationalize the wildness of this resort lake high in the San Bernardino mountains. By day the lake offered beauty and sport and the comforts of a fashionable mountain resort. But by night unseen things moved among the pines and combed the air above the restless surface of the lake. He didn't like the utter darkness of night in the mountains; he hated it.

He stood there beside his car, almost crouching as he waited for the owl's cry to come back again. It didn't. But he shivered again, and it was like mice running up the bare skin of his back on icy feet. He reached into his coat pocket and gripped the handle of the butcher knife, and somehow that made him feel better.

"I've got to take it easy," he told himself. "There's nothing out here to be afraid of."

It was true. There was nothing in the wildness of this mountain resort to fear. The bears or mountain lions, if there were any in these peaks, would be on the Mojave Desert side of the range, away from this heavily populated resort section.

If Dr. Paul Lanning had anything at all to fear it was in the cabin showing its drapery-diffused lights through the pines a hundred paces back from the lake shore. In that small redwood cabin was Dr. Lanning's only danger—Steve Thorne. But that danger would not threaten much longer. Dr. Lanning smiled as he gripped the long-bladed knife. Thorne was going to die tonight.

He left the key in the ignition of the car, as he had planned. He had thought all this out with the precise care of a surgeon diagramming a delicate operation. There would be little likelihood of him having to make a quick flight after he murdered Steve Thorne, but he was not taking even that small chance. So he left the key in the ignition as he stepped away from his coupe.

He walked slowly, his footsteps silenced by the thick matting of pine needles under the trees. He came to the clearing, paused and turned, carefully laying out the direction of his return route to the car. He might be frightened after he drove the knife into Thorne, confused or panicked by the shock of the murder he had committed, and he didn't want to become lost in the darkness. He laid out his route carefully, past the grey outcropping of granite and the pine whose top had been lopped off by lightning—a direct line that would return him to his hidden coupe.

He nodded his satisfaction and went on across the clearing to the cabin. He wasn't afraid, now that the time had finally come. He had imagined he would be, but he wasn't. He went up the steps and rapped on the door. Someone moved audibly inside, like a chair being shifted, and a voice called out.

"Who is it?"

Dr. Lanning didn't answer. He knocked again.

Inside the cabin, a voice grunted impatiently, and footsteps tramped across the floor. The door swung back, and there was Steve Thorne, just waiting to be murdered.

Thorne frowned irritably, a short, loose-fleshed man with sour eyes and a red Cupid's bow of a mouth. "You knew I'd be settled down for some reading, Doc. Why didn't you sing out your name and come on in?"

And perhaps let someone at another cabin overhear his name? No, Lanning thought. He smiled pleasantly. "You needed the exercise, Steve."

"I get all the exercise I want with a knife and fork," Thorne snapped. "Or depositing checks in my bank." His red mouth curved into a mocking smile as he pushed the door shut. "You bring your monthly payment with you, Doc?"

Dr. Lanning didn't answer at once. He watched the fat man pad his way back across the room to his easy chair. Thorne sat down, sighing audibly. The draperies were opaque across the windows, Lanning saw, and except for himself and Thorne, the cabin was empty.

Thorne's smile was malicious. "How about your monthly payment, Doc? You bring it with you?"

Lanning crossed the room and stood beside the fat man's chair. He looked down, mildly surprised at his own calmness. But then he understood the reason for that. Plan a man's murder long enough and the actual act, when it is committed, is easy; you have conditioned your mind to the swift strike of your arm and the shocked agony of violent death.

He said, "This is going to be the last payment, Steve."

Thorne's smile shaped into a slow grin. "You've said that before, Doc, but you've never meant it. As long as I've got the evidence against you that you're selling dope to those female hop-heads in Beverly Hills, you'll never make your last payment to me. Too many movie and society gals pay you big money for morphine for me not to get a monthly cut. You get cute with me, and I might slip the police that dictagraph record I've got. Or maybe give them an idea who sold the sleeping pills to that actress who knocked herself off last year."

The fat man's voice flattened out. "Don't ever try to get cute with me, Doc. Don't even think about stopping your payments. Now get your business over with and clear out of here."

"All right," Lanning said, and smiled. It was easy. There was nothing to it. He reached into his pocket and gripped the knife. He looked at the third button down from the collar of Thorne's shirt, took the knife out of his pocket and drove it home.

There was no outcry, not even much blood. He saw the shocked agony that contorted the muscles of the fat man's face, but he had witnessed death in too many shapes and forms to be bothered by that. Thorne sagged in his chair, twisted around in a spasm of movement, as though trying to kneel, and slid to the floor.

The man was not yet dead. His eyes looked up from the floor, bright-glazed with pain, and his groping hand came away from his

72

chest with blood on it. He whispered, "Doc . . . my God . . . Doc!"

Lanning's smile was steady, without pity or remorse. "Last payment, Steve. I told you this was it."

He turned away, and he knew where to look. Steven Thorne, wherever he went when he left Los Angeles, always carried the camera case with him. He was too lazy a man to ever interest himself with a camera, and money was his only hobby. So the dictograph record, Lanning knew, would be in the camera case.

He smiled as he lifted the cylindrical black tube out of the camera case, guarding against leaving fingerprints on the leather. He turned back, looked down at the man on the floor.

"The human mind can take some funny quirks, Steve. Money and feeling of power over me was your main pleasure in life. You got money from me, and you liked to keep this record near you for the feeling of power it gave you. That was a mistake, Steve. You know that now, don't you? I could have stolen this record a long time ago, but that wouldn't have kept you from talking."

He bent to the man on the floor, rubbed his handkerchief over the handle of the knife. He kept looking down into Thorne's fading eyes. "This way I have the record, and you can't talk."

He straightened, pleased with his own calmness. No dread or uncertainty; no sickness at what he had done. Consciousness was a feeble flickering in Thorne's dying eyes, and when that was gone, Steve Thorne would be gone. The police could not connect him with the dead man, and the cheap knife he had stolen from the hardware store in Los Angeles could not be traced. The dying man's eyes closed, then fluttered slowly open again. His fingers, red with his own blood, were trying to move on the floor in front of him. Dr. Lanning stood there at the cabin door, watching the man and waiting for him to die. The eyes remained open, but the fever in them had become shallow, fading. The blood-reddened fingers stopped moving. . . .

The telephone in Paul Lanning's room rang once, stopped, then rang again, insistently. He sat up in his bed, still drugged by sleep, and picked up the handset.

"That you, Doctor?"

"Yes." His voice was thick from the heavy sleep of the bromide he had taken late the night before after getting back to his room. "Yes."

The man's voice came leaping through the receiver, quick and urgent. "This is the deputy sheriff talking—Jim Keene. I need your help,

Doctor. A man has been stabbed. Come over as fast as you can." The telephone clicked dead.

Paul Lanning's mind came awake. It jarred awake with fear slamming through it, with his heart pounding the walls of his chest and a cold wetness of sweat breaking on his face and hands.

So Steven Thorne had not died after all. He had remained alive—somehow—and was still alive. He had been found alive, with the knife driven into his chest, and now the sheriff was calling for medical assistance to keep life in him long enough for him to talk.

Panic went rushing through Paul Lanning. He leaped out of bed and grabbed for his clothes. He halted that movement, instantly realizing that trying to escape now would be proof of his guilt. It was an instinctive thought, rooted in guilt and desperation.

He stood there in his hotel room, rigid in his crouch, trying to settle the wild lunging of his mind. He thought, "They wouldn't have telephoned me if Thorne was conscious and able to talk."

The thought took some of the panic out of him. If Thorne was unconscious, then he offered no danger. The miracle was that he still lived. But he would die soon. A man couldn't live for long with a knife in his chest at the place where Lanning had driven that honed blade. Lanning thought with a sharp fingering of cunning, "All I have to do is stall getting there until after he dies."

But that thought wasn't so good. There was too much uncertainty in it, too much risk. The deputy sheriff would not have pinned all his hopes on one doctor. He had undoubtedly telephoned every hotel in the resort, asking for any doctor who might be vacationing at the lake, and giving the same request to each.

"If I don't answer his call," Lanning told himself, "they'll be suspicious. If I don't go out there, some other doctor will. I've got to be the first there. If I can be the first doctor there, I can give Thorne something that will keep him unconscious until he dies."

He tore off his pajamas and dressed, fumbling at the buttons with fear-stiffened fingers. He rammed his arms into the sleeves of his coat, ripping the lining without even knowing it. He grabbed up his black leather bag and went out of his room, running hard through the hotel corridor. Outside, the sun was already above the high spikes of the pines across the lake, and he was dimly surprised that he had slept so late. And that Steve Thorne could have lived so long with that knife in his chest.

The road followed the contours of the lake shore, pine-flanked and cool at this hour. He drove with desperate speed, topping the hills and plunging down into green-shaded valleys. The road forked, and the blacktop slanted in toward the north shore of the lake, along a white sand beach where small waves rolled in, flattened and retreated, leaving a thin lacy foam behind them.

Dr. Lanning braked his car in the driveway at the side of the Thorne cabin, and relief spilled through him as he saw only a sheriff's car ahead of him.

The sheriff's deputy opened the door for him. The man was tall and lank, with cool grey eyes and skin that was as dark as old leather. "Come on in, Doc. You made good time."

That was all he said. There was something behind his tone, though, a grimness and a satisfaction, and Lanning wondered about that. But the thought only scraped the surface of his mind, making no mark.

He was staring at Steve Thorne's body, at the dry brownness of blood on Thorne's hand and at the cryptic lines the man had managed to trace on the bare floor. D-o-c. Thorne had tried to leave a message behind him, naming his murderer, and he had managed to trace out only those three letters before consciousness had left him.

Lanning bent, jerking open his medical bag. He picked up Steve Thorne's hand, and instantly dropped it. There was no pulse in that hand. The flesh was cold to his touch, with rigor mortis already beginning to set in.

Lanning pushed to his feet, staring down at the body on the floor. "Why—" His voice was slow, hoarse. "Why, this man has been dead for hours."

"That's right," the deputy said. "That's right, Doc."

Paul Lanning was slow to absorb that. His mind was a sponge soaked through with fear and dread. It was slow to register what the deputy sheriff had said. And then understanding finally built its implacable pattern in his mind, and he shuddered. He turned and looked at the deputy dully.

The officer was smiling, but his hand was on his gun. "I guess you know how this is, don't you?"

Lanning only stared at the man, stupidly. Yes, he knew. He could look into the black hell he had created and see the horror of his own future staring back at him. He knew.

"I telephoned every doctor on the lake that I could locate," the deputy was saying. "I telephoned them all when I saw what Thorne had tried to write on the floor, and I told them the same thing I told you—to get over here as soon as they could. *But I didn't tell them where to come!* You're the only one who knew where to come, Lanning. So you can see how this is for you. It's not good, is it? And it'll be worse for you later."

Paul Lanning closed his eyes. It didn't help. He could still see his own fate on the screen of his mind, like something etched by acid, implacable in its black promise. Even with his eyes tightly closed, he could see it, and there was no escape.

# The Cap'n Sleeps

*by John Earl Davis*

There was no moon over the North River, which was fine; but there was a noise just beyond the end of the dock—throwing the hooks into sleep—which was not fine at all.

Cap'n John "Lefty" Curhew, supine, lifted one forearm at right angles to the dock floor, elevated his chin to the hollow support of a large but supple paw, and swore expressively in Armenian. He could swear quite well in any language that has ever been known among modern seafaring men.

It was very irritating. His stomach a bit off, because of a temporary imbalance of diet. This disturbing habit of waking up at any sound less familiar than a tug whistle. The growing uncleanliness of docks on both sides of town—distressing indeed to a fastidious man. And now an alien invasion of his private quarters—his summer Sailors' Rest.

He wished he knew what time it was. To a methodical man, it was of importance to know at what time he was awakened during the long night watches.

Continuing to weigh a third of his body on one elbow, Cap'n John automatically classified the commonplace warnings that had fetched him forth out of slumber. A car had driven up to the edge of the dock. The lights were out. There was a car door opening, an arch giggle, a scutter of light steps and a succession of heavier ones.

Cap'n John sighed and swore again (this time in Greek) and *wished* he knew what time it was. Too late for decent people to be out. And the Lonergans . . .

He swiveled his head toward the lighter riding drowsily to starboard of his position on the dock. The Lonergans had come home from the neighborhood movie in good time, were in bed long ago. Nothing could wake them.

Nice people, the Lonergans. Against their tiny cabin rested the mop with which Cap'n John had swabbed their foredeck late that afternoon. He sighed happily, remembering the meal which had rewarded him; and then, feeling a twinge of indigestion, halted his sigh, so to speak, in midair.

But it was not indigestion alone. Without deigning to turn, he knew that something most unpleasant was approaching; that sleep was over for the nonce. The footsteps clomped close on the dock planking. More arch giggles; soft, fatuous words. A toe rammed the Cap'n's hip. A voice said:

"*What* the Hades—Pardon me, Baby. Should never swear before you—let you swear first."

There was another giggle. A quick shuffle and, then, a sharp thin beam of light directly in Cap'n John's eyes. One of those phony fountain pen flashes. The Cap'n drew himself up, leaned back against straight arms, palms flat on the deck, and blinked indignantly.

"Really, sir, a man's bedchamber should be his castle. May I ask—"

"Scum!" The flashlight executed a wavering arc, and the ungentle toe again prodded the Cap'n's shortribs. The captain said, "Whoosh," and observed the course of the light beam. Its penumbra revealed a stockily built man in conservatively cut, well-tailored clothes, adorned in the coat lapel by a slightly wilted gardenia. His face showed a man well pleased with himself and with the world surrounding him—except, no doubt, for Cap'n John "Lefty" Curhew.

But the beam of light itself showed an object of considerably greater interest; a gold watch, very nicely made, studded around its edge with what appeared to be diamonds. An expensive and undoubtedly accurate timepiece.

Cap'n John said, "Pardon me, sir, but what time—"

"Time for you to be on your way," said the man. "Scat!" He emphasized the admonition with a final dig of his toe.

Final, because Cap'n John was in no fettle for argument. He could be pushed so far—and this was not So Far. He rose and bowed gracefully, giving one glance to the man's companion. The casual lights of the river were enough to indicate the nature of the lady. Dressed for a night out. Cute. And beyond that the less said the better.

Cap'n John moved back into the shadows, and quietly attained the deck of the Lonergans' barge. Brushing aside a few odd bits of coal, he lay down and conscientiously invited sleep.

In this endeavor he was less than successful. The well-tailored man and his lady moved toward the end of the dock, the lady evidently acting as pilot. She giggled. He guffawed.

Cap'n John contemplated murder, decided temporarily against it, and wondered what time it was. The voices went on:

"So nice meeting you, Daddy. . . . And the places we went— yumm! . . . Don't you love the water? I told you you'd like it if you came down here with little me."

And so on. Cap'n John peered over the deck edge. They faced the water, their backs to him and to the dead-end street. One little push, only; and unless they were good swimmers . . .

Cap'n John sighed and began to lower his head to the canvas bag which he kept always with him, as pillow and as storehouse for personal effects. . . . And then it started.

There were quick, furtive steps along the dock floor; a shape materialized out of the shadows, heading directly for the well-tailored man's back. The man heard not nor saw, his arm being around his companion's waist, her head on his shoulder. It was undoubtedly a very pretty scene, though to the ex-seafarin' Cap'n it looked kind of silly.

But there was nothing silly about the shape which crept up behind the well-tailored man. To speak plainly, this was a footpad: an uplifted blackjack, poised over the well-tailored man's head, attested to the authenticity of this fellow's profession.

The blackjack descended, and so did the well-tailored man, making quite a noise as he hit the dock. The lady screamed realistically and ran; yet the sound of her running ceased at the end of the dock, and did not continue up the street. The footpad himself bent over his victim, making the least noise of all.

Yet, to be perfectly just, it must be admitted that he had been a contributing cause to the entire disturbance; and Cap'n John was irked beyond reason. This was, indeed, being pushed. So Far. A man was entitled to some sleep.

Cap'n John therefore arose, albeit very quietly, and seized the mop reclining against the Lonergans' tiny cabin. It was, he noted happily, still wet.

With the quietness and forthrightness of a panther he crept over the lighter's side to the dock, and so to the rear of the industrious footpad. He raised the mop very high, gripping it with no uncertainty at the handle's end; and he then brought the business part of that mop down with great force upon the footpad's head. The force of the blow

78

resulted in some splattering, even upon the well-tailored man; but this could not be helped.

The footpad howled in rage and bewilderment; but his howl ended abruptly because he fell flat on his face. Cap'n John, deeming it both unwise and uneconomic to await developments, lifted the footpad bodily and dropped him over the side of the dock. Thus, with small difficulty, he disposed of the *source* of the noise.

But not of the noise itself. There was now a scream, and the sound of footsteps running rapidly up the street away from the dock. Odd, perhaps, that a lady should have been waiting there; yet Cap'n John felt no surprise whatever. He now turned his attention to the last remaining annoyance.

By the application of river water and patience he finally brought the well-tailored gentleman around, and assisted him to his feet. The gentleman swayed groggily, felt the lump on his head, and said, "Wh-what happened?"

He was not in the pink. His necktie was mussed, and so was his hair. His face and collar bore traces of coal dust and other things; for mops are no respecters of persons. His countenance, so far as it showed anything at all, indicated that he was bewildered, betrayed, and deeply hurt.

Taking his hand quickly away from the lump on his head, he fiddled nervously with the gold watchchain which stretched across his comfortable middle.

"You have been taken for a ride," said Cap'n John gravely. "You were fortunate to escape with your life. Stand still, sir, and I shall brush you off."

The well-tailored man looked at him with quickened interest. He gasped and gulped. He said, "My name is Eckles—Cyrus N. Eckles. Mittens, hosiery, and undergarments. I was walking here with a—uh —friend, when everything went black. Where is she? What happened?"

"Mr. Eckles"—Cap'n John paused to spit over the edge of the dock, casting pointblank at a spluttering sound that had just arisen from the water beneath—"Mr. Eckles, you have been victimized by an unscrupulous woman, the accomplice of an ordinary footpad. . . . Stand still!"

Cap'n John began to brush Mr. Eckles industriously. "This woman," he continued, "lured you to this lonely spot and distracted your attention so that you could be slugged and robbed: a technique which I myself have often—ahem—observed before.

79

"This woman was waiting to divide the spoils; but with the intrusion of a fourth party"—he spat over the dockside, whence came an occasional glubbering—"she quite naturally took to her heels."

Cyrus N. Eckles said, "Why the dirty—" and then thought better of it. He said, "But my good man, then you must be the one who saved me. How did you happen to see—"

"You kicked me," said Cap'n John modestly.

Mr. Eckles gasped and gulped once more, and looked more closely at the man before him. His eyes were focusing better now, and the light at this point was good enough for a closeup view. He observed a man of about fifty years, clad in grayish duck pants and turtle-neck sweater; the eyes mild and watery, the chin thrust upward and wavering a little, as if the man were about to cry.

"I'm sorry, my good man," said Mr. Eckles. "Terribly sorry. Here, let me—"

"Stand still, now!" Cap'n John stayed him in the act of reaching for his wallet, continued his brushing. "I do not wish any reward, sir, for doing my duty. I am a man of numerous professions, more or less connected with the sea; and I am able to earn my own living.

"Besides"—he spat a third time toward the glubbering just beneath the dock-edge—"I have a strong aversion toward all types of crime. I cannot bear to see a man robbed. And now, sir, you may go—and be careful of your companions in the future. New York is, unhappily, full of wicked men."

With a final fillip of his hand against a well-brushed lapel (with care not to disturb the gardenia), he sent Mr. Eckles rejoicing on his way. He waited for the sound of the car's starter, the further token of its retreat from the dock.

One thing still remained to be done.

Cap'n John went to the edge of the dock and grappled with a pile, lowering himself almost to the water's edge. Just far enough, in short, to put his foot firmly upon the head of the blubbering footpad who was clinging to that very pile. He pushed the foot downward, dunking the head. This he did three times, whistling a gay hornpipe as he did so. Finally he reached down an abnormally long arm, seized the footpad by his hair, and hauled him dripping to the dock. "I despise a thief," he said reprovingly.

For all his exhaustion, the footpad stayed not upon his going. Perhaps he was lent a kind of second wind by the sole of a size eleven shoe, unceremoniously applied to his stern. Whatever the circumstance he went quickly, and did not return.

Picking up the blackjack which the footpad had inadvertently left behind him, and stuffing it into his pocket, Cap'n John "Lefty" (in certain quarters known as the Dip) Curhew sighed and lay down in his favorite spot near the edge of the dock. It was very quiet now; the river was peaceful and kind and decent. He could sleep now.

But first . . .

Smiling happily, Cap'n John removed from his pocket a gold watch, very nicely made, studded around its edge with what appeared to be diamonds. An expensive and undoubtedly accurate timepiece.

It was one forty-two. Good, very good, for a methodical man to know what time he turned in.

Cap'n John slept.

# The Carnival Caper

*by R. L. Stevens*

It was only by chance that Detective Sergeant Nancy Trentino was the first to reach the Glenside Amusement Park that Saturday morning. She'd been driving back to headquarters after checking out a narcotics tip when she picked up the report on her police radio of a holdup in progress.

Her unmarked car skidded to a stop at the park entrance and she was out and running, reaching into her purse for her .38 service revolver. A uniformed security guard tried to block her path and she shouted, "Police! Report of a robbery in progress!"

"It's all over," the guard told her. "Mr. Blackthorn shot the guy while he was trying to escape."

Nancy Trentino slipped the revolver back into her shoulder bag but kept her hand on it as she followed the security guard into the park. Already a large crowd had gathered near the merry-go-round.

A stocky man wearing a striped shirt stood in the center of the circle. The body of a long-haired young man was sprawled at his feet. Nancy identified herself and knelt to examine the body. There was a single bloody hole in the center of the back where the bullet had hit him. "He was running away with my money," the stocky man told Nancy. "I warned him to stop and then I shot him."

"Keep back, everyone!" Nancy shouted as the circle of the crowd began to tighten. "Are you Blackthorn?" she asked the man.

"That's right," he said, "Sam Blackthorn. I'm one of the owners here."

She noticed the automatic pistol stuck casually in his belt. "Is that the weapon you used?"

"Yeah."

"Give it here." She wrapped it in a clean handkerchief and placed it in her purse.

Two uniformed patrolmen pushed their way through the circle of spectators. One of them knew her. "Hi, Nancy. Did you nail this guy?"

She shook her head. "This gentleman did the honors. See if you can break up the crowd, will you, Phil?"

The officer turned and held up his arms. "Okay, the show is over. Everyone back to the rides!"

Nancy led Blackthorn aside and took out her notebook. She needed a statement.

"I was counting the money from last night," he told her, "getting it ready for the bank. Friday is always a big date night here, and I had just under nine thousand dollars in the sack when this punk barged into the office waving a gun. I pushed the silent alarm button under my desk and gave him the sack. He ran out and I grabbed my gun from the desk drawer and went after him. Hell, no young punk gets the best of Sam Blackthorn!"

They were standing by the merry-go-round and Nancy became aware of a girl wearing paint-streaked jeans and a T-shirt with GLEN-SIDE PARK printed on it. She had straight blond hair and seemed to be of college age—one of many students the amusement park liked to hire during the vacation period. "Are you painting that zebra?" Nancy asked, distracted from her questioning.

The young girl grinned. "That's what I'm doing—touching up the stripes. Then I have to add some color to the horses' manes and re-paint the white on that unicorn's horn."

Nancy stared at the row of paint cans—black and white and orange and brown, large and small, some opened, some still closed. "It looks like fun," she admitted. Then, getting back to the business at hand, she said, "You must have seen the shooting if you were working here."

The blond girl nodded. "I saw the whole thing. This fellow came running along and then I saw Mr. Blackthorn yelling at him. All of a

82

sudden there was a shot and he went down. Mr. Blackthorn ran up to him with a gun. He looked like he was going to shoot again, but he didn't."

Nancy turned back to Blackthorn. "Is that what happened?"

He nodded agreement. "I yelled at him to stop, but he kept on going. When I brought him down, he fell right against the carousel here and then rolled over a couple of times. I was afraid he might shoot back, but then I could see he was a goner."

Nancy glanced around. "Where's his gun? And the sack with the money?"

"He didn't have any sack," the girl in the T-shirt said. "And I guess that must be the gun you're looking for." Half hidden by the wooden steps up to the carousel was a little snub-nosed automatic. Anyone could have dropped it there—including, of course, the dead man.

"He must have ditched the money somewhere when I started chasing him," Blackthorn grumbled. "Have a couple of your officers search the trash barrels."

"We'll do that," Nancy said. She turned back to the girl. "What's your name?"

"Linda Brice. I'm working here for the summer."

She made a note of it. "Go back to your painting. I'll talk to you later."

Nancy found one of the officers and suggested he check the barrels and other likely hiding places for the sack of money. "It should be on a line between Blackthorn's office and the merry-go-round."

The police photographer, the medical examiner and an ambulance had all arrived on the scene, along with a pair of detectives from the violent crimes squad. She told them what she knew and handed over Blackthorn's gun. The park had a strangely quiet air, with most of the rides stopped while the operators joined the gawkers.

Nancy found the security guard she'd first encountered at the gate. His name was Donovan and she said, "Tell me something, Mr. Donovan. When I got here, you told me Blackthorn had shot the robber. How'd you know, when it had just happened?"

"I saw it," he explained. "The alarm rang at my gate when he pushed the button in his office. I called the police and said there was a robbery in progress. Then I saw this guy running, only he didn't head toward the gate. He ran toward the carousel."

"Is there another exit that way?"

"No, no other."

"When you saw him, was he carrying anything—a sack or a gun?"

"I think he had something, but I was too far away to see for sure."

"Had you ever seen him before? Was he a regular here?"

He shook his head. "I was just looking at the body. Never saw the fellow before."

Nancy smiled. "Thanks, Donovan. See you later."

She went back to the carousel building, pausing to study the blacks and whites and browns and tans and grays of the wooden animals. The body had been removed and the crowd was finally breaking up. The officer, Phil, told her, "No luck in the trash barrels, but we found a driver's license on the dead man. Name's John Torres, 24 years old, with an address on Andrew Street. We're checking to see if he has a record."

"Good."

Phil looked at her. "This one bothers you, doesn't it? How come?"

"He was running the wrong way, not toward the exit. I want to know why."

She went back to Linda Brice, who was kneeling beside the wooden zebra as she applied the final touches of paint. "Back at work, I see."

The girl smiled. "Mr. Blackthorn wants this job finished so he can reopen the merry-go-round tomorrow. Did you find the money?"

Nancy Trentino shook her head. "Not a trace. Funny thing—the dead man wasn't running toward an exit at all."

"You noticed that, too?"

"What does it mean?"

Linda Brice wiped some paint from her hands and shrugged. "If he wasn't trying to escape, maybe he didn't commit the robbery. Maybe Mr. Blackthorn made up the whole story."

"Why would he fake a robbery to steal his own money?"

"It isn't his money. He's got a flock of partners, and I hear he's in debt."

"You think he killed an innocent person?"

The girl shrugged. "You're the detective."

Nancy saw the squad men leaving with Blackthorn and walked over to their car. "What's up?"

"We're taking him downtown for a full statement. It'll have to go to the grand jury."

Nancy nodded. "Looks funny to you, too?"

"We can't find the money. There's no evidence of a crime except his word.

84

She watched the car pull away. The park was getting back to normal and she could hear the screams of happy terror as the roller coaster plunged into one of its dips. She stared out at Donovan by the main gate and then made her decision.

Linda Brice had finished the zebra and was opening the can of brown paint to touch up a horse's mane. "Back again?" she asked Nancy with a smile.

"This is the last time, Linda. The man who was shot was a stranger here. And yet he knew where and when to rob Blackthorn of last night's receipts. He had to have inside knowledge, a tip from someone."

"That's if you believe the robbery story."

"I believe it, Linda. He ran this way so he could hide the sack of money with you. You scooped it up from the carousel steps just as he went down with his fatal wound."

"I don't—"

"There are lots of colors on these animals, Linda, but not one of them is orange. I think that big can of orange paint is empty, and if you'll take off the lid, I believe we'll find the missing sack inside."


# The Case of the Barking Beagle

*by R. L. Stevens*


The green shingled house with the fenced-in yard was strangely silent as Sergeant Nancy Trentino approached it. If it had not been for the two squad cars with their pulsating red lights parked on the street, she might have thought it was the wrong address.

Bennett, a patrolman she knew slightly from her days on the narcotics squad, opened the door as she reached the porch. "Hi, Nancy. Got a bad one here. Old guy shot through the head. Neighbors noticed he wasn't in the yard like he usually is, and they phoned."

Nancy Trentino stepped into the living room and stared at the crumpled body. "Robbery?" she asked, glancing around at the open drawers and scattered papers.

The officer shrugged. "Supposed to look like one, but I don't know. Here's a framed collection of old postage stamps on the wall. Don't you think a thief would take that?"

"Sometimes they just like cash," Nancy answered. "What's his name?"

"Conrad Peterson. He owned a chain of ice cream parlors around the state, but his nephew's been running the business."

Suddenly the stillness of the house was shattered by loud barking from a dog in the next room. Another police officer entered the house with a middle-aged man wearing jogging shorts and a T-shirt. "Damn dog," the officer grumbled. "Near tore us apart when we arrived."

"That's Shep," the man said. "Best watchdog in the neighborhood." He held out his hand to Nancy. "I'm Hank Isles from next door. Are you working with the police?"

"I am the police," Nancy said sweetly. "Detective Sergeant Trentino of the violent crimes squad. What do you know about this?"

"Well—nothing, really. Peterson is usually out in his yard when I do my morning jogging, but he wasn't today. When I phoned and nobody answered, I got worried. That's when I called the police."

"Didn't you try the door?" Nancy asked.

"What, and get my legs chewed up by Shep? No, thanks!"

"We locked the dog in the other room," Bennett told her.

"He wasn't much of a watchdog if he let his master get killed."

The dog was barking again as the police photographer and lab technician arrived. Nancy opened the door gingerly and peered into the adjoining room. Shep proved to be a brownish beagle with white markings who eyed her suspiciously and made a dash for the door. "No, you stay in there a while," she decided.

Nancy returned to the other room and found a slim, pale young man and a pretty brown-haired woman waiting with the police. "Sloan Peterson," he introduced himself, "and my wife Betty. Who's in charge here?"

"I am," Nancy said. "You're Conrad Peterson's nephew?"

"That's right."

"Your uncle's been murdered. I'm sorry."

"Was anything stolen?" Betty asked, glancing in at the disarray.

"We don't know yet. Robbery may not have been the motive."

"But what—?"

Nancy cut her short and gave instructions to the police photographer.

86

"Where's Riley today?" the man asked.

"Riley's busy. This is my case," said Nancy, trying not to bristle.

The man shrugged and focused his camera on the body. "You'd better wrap it up quickly, Nancy. They don't like murders in this part of town. You're supposed to keep 'em in the inner city."

"Just take your pictures," she said. Shep was barking again, peering out of the window at a gathering crowd of curious neighbors. Nancy turned to Hank Isles. "Doesn't he ever stop?"

"Barks all day, and half the night. Some of the neighbors complained but it didn't do any good."

"Did you hear him barking last night?"

"Not after dark. He'd only bark if someone came to the door."

"But someone did," she pointed out. "The person who killed Conrad Peterson."

"That's right," he agreed, as if realizing it for the first time.

The medical examiner arrived amidst more barking and announced that Peterson had probably died around eleven o'clock the previous night, which was the time indicated by his broken watch.

"Did you hear Shep barking around eleven?" Nancy asked Isles.

"Not a sound."

"Could he have had a visitor who arrived early and stayed that late?"

"No, he had no visitors. I could tell because he only had this little den light on. He always turned on more lights for visitors."

Officer Bennett came in from outside while the dog barked anew. "The neighbors all say there was no barking last night," he said. "So how do you think the killer got inside the house?"

"Was the door forced?" Nancy asked.

"Not a mark on it. He either had a key or Peterson let him in."

Nancy went over to where Sloan Peterson stood with his wife. "Do you have a key to this house, Mr. Peterson?"

"Certainly, but you can't suspect me of murdering my uncle! What motive would I have? He'd already given me control of the family business."

"Does anyone else have a key?"

"Not that I know of."

"Where were you last night, around eleven?"

"I was checking on the ice cream parlors. They close at that hour, and on weekends I drive around and pick up the cash."

"Alone?"

"I was alone last night."

"So you have no alibi?"

"Do I need one?" he countered. "I think I'd like to speak to your superior."

"You'd find him just as tenacious as I am. Maybe more so."

"Why are you questioning my husband?" Betty Peterson demanded. "You can see there was a robbery here!"

"The killer wanted it to look like a robbery. But the door wasn't forced, and those rare stamps weren't stolen. In fact, it appears that Mr. Peterson was dozing in his chair or watching television when the killer entered and shot him through the back of the head."

"But how could he do that without the dog barking?" Hank Isles asked. "I'll swear that dog never stirred last night."

"Maybe Shep was locked in a room somewhere," Nancy reasoned, but at once she remembered the police officers saying they'd put him in the other room when they arrived. He'd been in here all the time during the murder."

And he hadn't barked.

Nancy walked over to the window, then back to Betty Peterson. "Do you have a map of any sort out in the car? One that would show the route your husband traveled last night to visit the ice cream parlors?"

"I think there's a map out there," she replied. "Sloan, she wants the map of your route last night."

He started for the door, but Nancy called him back. "Your wife can get it. I want you in here."

Betty Peterson returned in a moment with the folded map. The house was silent, and she paused, realizing they were all watching her. "What is it?" she asked Nancy. "I brought the map like you asked."

"The dog didn't bark," Nancy said simply.

"What?"

"The dog didn't bark when you came back in just now. And he didn't bark last night when you used your husband's key, or a duplicate, to enter this house and shoot Conrad Peterson."

"That's crazy!"

"Not at all. Shep's obviously been trained only to bark at men. I realized it when I remembered that he didn't bark at me when I arrived this morning. He barked when you and your husband arrived together, but not when you came in alone."

Sloan Peterson was on his feet. "Betty, did you—?"

"You wanted Peterson out of the way so your husband could own the entire business, didn't you? I'm afraid, Mrs. Peterson, that since your husband has no alibi for late last night the chances are you have none either. While he was driving around, you came here and committed a somewhat inept murder. I should warn you that you have the right to call a lawyer, and—"

That was when Betty Peterson broke down.

Later, as the body was being removed, the medical examiner came out to where Nancy stood by her car. "I'm finished here," he said. "But I need a name for my report. Whose case is this, anyway?"

Nancy sighed and managed a smile. "Mine," she told him. "Sergeant Nancy Trentino."

# Checkmated!

*by Coretta Slavska*

The table where Delph Mayers had sat playing his last game of chess was covered with dust. There was a thin layer of dust on the ivory chessmen, and the stub of a cigarette in the ashtray was almost buried under a gray mound that looked curiously like a grave.

And Delph will soon be dust, thought Vera, and she covered her eyes with her hand. She could not go into the room where Delph had died, but from every corner where she stood in the adjoining living room she imagined she could see the chessmen standing guard.

Flynn, the detective from the local police station, had given her specific instructions about the room. "Don't go in there, Mrs. Mayers. Nothing must be touched. It's important to the inquest that everything remain as it is until the final examination is all finished."

Inquest, examination, strange words. But they could only mean the police were not entirely satisfied about Delph's sudden death.

Vera had been sure the doctor's certificate of death made it clear Delph had died of a heart attack. Now all this silly talk of an inquest. It was absurd! Nothing would come of it. It was just routine!

Vera turned her back to the game room where the chessmen stood. She was a tall, well-built woman in her early thirties. Her gray eyes which could look hard and cold when she was angry, usually appeared serene and soft. She had a slow, languid walk but now her steps quickened as she almost ran to a mirror.

With an effort, she looked at herself. No, she had not changed. She looked the same, a little pale perhaps, but not unduly nervous or frightened. She looked like a widow should look, weary and unhappy. After all, Delph had been buried only a few days ago.

Considering the circumstances, she and Karl had been bearing up very well. It was understandable that Karl had not returned since the day Delph died. After all, Karl had been playing chess with Delph. It would be natural if Karl looked nervous.

Vera hoped he would keep himself in check. Sometimes it seemed he needed only a slight shock to make him lose control. But nothing could go wrong now.

Soon their friends would come to visit. They would bring a cake, candy, perhaps some more flowers. They might play a game of cards. This was modern times. Distraction was good for a widow. It helped her to forget her sorrows.

Karl would come too. He had telephoned, saying he would be here tonight. Karl. Sleek-looking, gay, everything that Delph had never been! A good chess player too! Too good for Delph, who had been the acknowledged champ of Sparkhill until Karl moved to town.

Vera remembered the day she first met Karl. At the local gas station. Repairs were being made on her car.

Karl had smiled at her as he walked by, on his way to work. She smiled back, suddenly reckless.

"You live here?" he asked.

Vera nodded, almost afraid to speak. Something in his black eyes appraising her, warned her this would be no casual friendship, but something more exciting.

"I suppose we'll meet at the usual town festivals," Karl said slowly.

"We don't go out often," Vera told him. "But my husband likes to play chess." Suddenly she knew Karl played too! It had been that way between them. She always knew a few moments before when he would telephone her. When he first brought her a box of candy, his hand seemed to burn on her arm as he touched it softly, and then went into the gameroom to play chess with Delph.

He would come again tonight. For the first time, they would be together without Delph!

Vera's hands moved restlessly. She felt chilled suddenly, and ran back to the living room, hoping Karl would come soon so they could have a drink together.

The bell rang sharply. But it was not Karl. For the first time her instinct had failed her. Was it a sign, a warning that all was not going well!

Flynn, the detective, stood at the door. Flynn had come once before when the undertaker had phoned the police station. It seemed

90

when a man died so suddenly as Delph had, the police had to be called if a doctor was not immediately available.

Vera looked sharply at Flynn. She felt her smile freeze on her lips as she led him into the room. She could feel his eyes on her every movement.

"How are you feeling?" Flynn asked.

"Better! Much better. I try not to think about it, the suddenness of it. The confusion when I couldn't get the doctor at once, and the undertaker wouldn't touch the body until he called you! It's hard being here with that room staring at me, but the dust getting thicker every minute! When can I have it cleaned out?"

"Easy does it," Flynn said quietly. "Have a cigarette."

Vera regained control. Her hand was steady as it held the cigarette, and she smiled into the detective's eyes.

"I'm not satisfied about your husband's death," Flynn said slowly. "I need your help. Tell me again what happened during the last chess game."

"Delph was playing chess with our friend, Karl Sommers."

Flynn nodded. "Well, chess seems to me to me to be a quiet game. The players sit there calmly, hour after hour. Of course, I know nothing about it, but it seems a quiet hobby," Vera continued.

"Is it a quiet game?" Flynn asked softly. Then he added, "No, it isn't —not to the players of the game. Actually the players can become quite excited inwardly. When a player makes a move his heart beat quickens, his blood pressure rises!"

Vera looked at him intently.

"Yes, of course you are right! I guess that's what did happen, for the doctor who examined Delph did say it was heart failure. Delph's heart had never been strong."

Flynn nodded. "Yes, the death certificate said heart failure. Poor Delph! You said he made the last move and then fell back in his chair?"

Vera didn't like the way Flynn was looking at her.

"Yes, Delph made the last move. Why do you keep harping on that? You asked me that the night you came here. Don't you believe me?"

"Don't get excited," said Flynn. "You'll sign a statement to that effect, won't you?"

"Of course, and you can check with Karl Sommers! I think he's coming now."

It was Karl. He came in quickly, his movements light and cautious as a panther's step when he senses danger. His keen eyes focused on Vera.

Flynn watched him and turned away suddenly, quite sickened.

"Sit down, Mr. Sommers," he said to Karl. "Mrs. Mayers has told me again how her husband died. She said he had just finished a chess move, leaned back in his chair and slumped to the floor. You'll verify that, of course."

Karl nodded. "That's about it."

Flynn stood up. "Yes, I've heard about his reputation as a chess player. Would you mind coming into the game room with me?"

Karl nodded. Suddenly the door opened and there were people, two policemen, the local police sergeant. They were moving toward Karl.

Karl turned away, his eyes on the game room. His mouth twitched slightly. He moved automatically toward the room where Delph had died, and Flynn closed in after him.

Vera's hand moved toward her throat, her fingers dug into her cheek. Something was wrong. Was it something she had said? This was not going according to plan. But the doctor's certificate had said heart failure. It had all seemed so easy—there was nothing to worry about. She stood motionless in the middle of the room, the policemen watching her.

Then Karl came out of the gameroom, his face white.

"You touched those chessmen! You fool—you idiot! You've spoiled everything!"

"Stop it!" screamed Vera.

Flynn turned to Vera. "It's all over. Even Karl had to admit it couldn't have been Delph's last move! You see, we did an autopsy on your husband—there were traces of poison in his stomach. He probably died during the chess game, fell across the table. While Karl carried him into the living room, you fixed the chessmen to make it look as though he had just finished a move."

Vera looked puzzled. "But what does that prove? The doctor didn't say anything about that!"

Flynn grinned. "The good doctor doesn't play chess—but I do! When I saw the chessmen, I knew you had lied about it being Delph's last move. I ordered an autopsy on your husband. But we needed a confession from one of you. I figured if Karl saw the chessboard it would give him enough of a jolt to say something incriminating! Karl has already said enough to satisfy us. He, also, was quite stunned to see two black bishops on white squares!

92

# The Clarion Call

*by O. Henry*

Half of this story can be found in the records of the Police Department; the other half belongs behind the business counter of a newspaper office.

One afternoon two weeks after Millionaire Norcross was found in his apartment murdered by a burglar, the murderer, while strolling serenely down Broadway, ran plump against Detective Barney Woods.

"Is that you, Johnny Kernan?" asked Woods, who had been nearsighted in public for five years.

"No less," cried Kernan, heartily. "If it isn't Barney Woods, late and early of old Saint Jo! You'll have to show me! What are you doing East? Do the green-goods circulars get out that far?"

"I've been in New York for some years," said Woods. "I'm on the city detective force."

"Well, well!" said Kernan, breathing smiling joy and patting the detective's arm.

"Come into Muller's," said Woods, "and let's hunt a quiet table. I'd like to talk to you awhile."

It lacked a few minutes to the hour of four. The tides of trade were not yet loosed, and they found a quiet corner of the café. Kernan, well dressed, slightly swaggering, self-confident, seated himself opposite the little detective, with his pale, sandy moustache, squinting eyes, and ready-made cheviot suit.

"What business are you in now?" asked Woods. "You know you left Saint Jo a year before I did."

"I'm selling shares in a copper mine," said Kernan. "I may establish an office here. Well, well! and so old Barney is a New York detective. You always had a turn that way. You were on the police in Saint Jo after I left there, weren't you?"

"Six months," said Woods. "And now there's one more question, Johnny. I've followed your record pretty close ever since you did that hotel job in Saratoga, and I never knew you to use your gun before. Why did you kill Norcross?"

Kernan stared for a few moments with concentrated attention at the slice of lemon in his high-ball; and then he looked at the detective with a sudden crooked, brilliant smile.

"How did you guess it, Barney?" he asked, admiringly. "I swear I thought the job was as clean and as smooth as a peeled onion. Did I leave a string hanging out anywhere?"

Woods laid upon the table a small gold pencil intended for a watch charm.

"It's the one I gave you the last Christmas we were in Saint Jo. I've got your shaving mug yet. I found this under a corner of the rug in Norcross's room. I warn you to be careful what you say. I've got it put on to you, Johnny. We were old friends once, but I must do my duty. You'll have to go to the chair for Norcross."

Kernan laughed.

"My luck stays with me," said he. "Who'd have thought old Barney was on my trail!" He slipped one hand inside his coat. In an instant Woods had a revolver against his side.

"Put it away," said Kernan, wrinkling his nose. "I'm only investigating. Aha! It takes nine tailors to make a man, but one can do a man up. There's a hole in that vest pocket. I took that pencil off my chain and slipped it in there in case of a scrap. Put up your gun, Barney, and I'll tell you why I had to shoot Norcross. The old fool started down the hall after me, popping at the buttons on the back of my coat with a peevish little .22 and I had to stop him. The old lady was a darling. She just lay in bed and saw her $12,000 diamond necklace go without a chirp, while she begged like a panhandler to have back a little thin gold ring with a garnet worth about $3. I guess she married old Norcross for his money, all right. Don't they hang on to the little trinkets from the Man Who Lost Out, though? There were six rings, two brooches and a chatelaine watch. Fifteen thousand would cover the lot."

"I warned you not to talk," said Woods.

"Oh, that's all right," said Kernan. "The stuff is in my suitcase at the hotel. And now I'll tell you why I'm talking. Because it's safe. I'm talking to a man I know. You owe me a thousand dollars, Barney Woods, and even if you wanted to arrest me your hands wouldn't make the move."

"I haven't forgotten," said Woods. "You counted out twenty fifties without a word. I'll pay it back some day. That thousand saved me and—well, they were piling my furniture out on the sidewalk when I got back to the house."

"And so," continued Kernan, "you being Barney Woods, born as true as steel, and bound to play a white man's game, can't lift a finger to arrest the man you're indebted to. Oh, I have to study men as well as yale locks and window fastenings in my business. Now, keep quiet while I ring for the waiter. I've had a thirst for a year or two that worries me a little. If I'm ever caught the lucky sleuth will have to divide honours with the old boy Booze. But I never drink during business hours. After a job I can crook elbows with my old friend Barney with a clear conscience. What are you taking?"

The waiter came with the little decanters and the siphon and left them alone again.

"You've called the turn," said Woods, as he rolled the little gold pencil about with a thoughtful forefinger. "I've got to pass you up. I can't lay a hand on you. If I'd a-paid that money back—but I didn't, and that settles it. It's a bad break I'm making, Johnny, but I can't dodge it. You helped me once, and it calls for the same."

"I knew it," said Kernan, raising his glass, with a flushed smile of self-appreciation. "I can judge men. Here's to Barney, for—'he's a jolly good fellow.' "

"I don't believe," went on Woods quietly, as if he were thinking aloud, "that if accounts had been square between you and me, all the money in all the banks in New York could have bought you out of my hands tonight."

"I know it couldn't," said Kernan. "That's why I knew I was safe with you."

"Most people," continued the detective, "look sideways at my business. They don't class it among the fine arts and the professions. But I've always taken a kind of fool pride in it. And here is where I go 'busted.' I guess I'm a man first and a detective afterwards. I've got to let you go, and then I've got to resign from the force. I guess I can drive an express wagon. Your thousand dollars is farther off than ever, Johnny."

"Oh, you're welcome to it," said Kernan, with a lordly air. "I'd be willing to call the debt off, but I know you wouldn't have it. It was a lucky day for me when you borrowed it. And now, let's drop the subject. I'm off to the West on a morning train. I know a place out there where I can negotiate the Norcross sparks. Drink up, Barney, and forget your troubles. We'll have a jolly time while the police are knocking their heads together over the case. I've got one of my Sahara thirsts on tonight. But I'm in the hands—the unofficial hands—of my old friend Barney, and I won't even dream of a cop."

And then, as Kernan's ready finger kept the button and the waiter working, his weak point—a tremendous vanity and arrogant egotism,

95

began to show itself. He recounted story after story of his successful plunderings, ingenious plots and infamous transgressions until Woods with all his familiarity with evil-doers, felt growing within him a cold abhorrence towards the utterly vicious man who had once been his benefactor.

"I'm disposed of, of course," said Woods at length. "But I advise you to keep under cover for a spell. The newspapers may take up this Norcross affair. There has been an epidemic of burglaries and man-slaughter in town this summer."

The word sent Kernan into a high glow of sullen and vindictive rage.

"To h—l with the newspapers," he growled. "What do they spell but brag and blow and boodle in box-car letters? Suppose they do take up a case—what does it amount to? The police are easy enough to fool; but what do the newspapers do? They send a lot of pin-head reporters around to the scene; and they make for the nearest saloon and have beer while they take photos of the bartender's oldest daughter in evening dress to print as the fiancée of the young man in the tenth story, who thought he heard a noise below on the night of the murder. That's about as near as the newspapers ever come to running down Mr. Burglar."

"Well, I don't know," said Woods, reflecting. "Some of the papers have done good work in that line. There's the *Morning Mars*, for instance. It warmed up two or three trails, and got the man after the police had let 'em get cold."

"I'll show you," said Kernan, rising, and expanding his chest. "I'll show you what I think of newspapers in general, and your *Morning Mars* in particular."

Three feet from their table was the telephone booth. Kernan went inside and sat at the instrument, leaving the door open. He found a number in the book, took down the receiver and made his demand upon Central. Woods sat still, looking at the sneering, cold, vigilant face waiting close to the transmitter, and listened to the words that came from the thin, truculent lips curved into a contemptuous smile.

"That the *Morning Mars?* . . . I want to speak to the managing editor. . . . Why, tell him it's someone who wants to talk to him about the Norcross murder.

"You the editor? . . . All right . . . I am the man who killed old Norcross . . . Wait! Hold the wire; I'm not the usual crank . . . Oh, there isn't the slightest danger. I've just been discussing it with a detective friend of mine. I killed the old man at 2.30 A.M. two weeks

96

ago tomorrow . . . Have a drink with you? Now, hadn't you better leave that kind of talk to your funny man? Can't you tell whether a man's guying you or whether you're being offered the biggest scoop your dull dishrag of a paper ever had? . . . Well, that's so; it's a bob-tail scoop—but you can hardly expect me to 'phone in my name and address . . . Why! Oh, because I heard you make a specialty of solving mysterious crimes that stump the police . . . No, that's not all. I want to tell you that your rotten, lying penny sheet is of no more use in tracking an intelligent murderer or highway man than a blind poodle would be. . . . What? . . . Oh, no, this isn't a rival newspaper office; you're getting it straight. I did the Norcross job, and I've got the jewels in my suitcase at—'the name of the hotel could not be learned'—you recognise that phrase, don't you? I thought so. You've used it often enough. Kind of rattles you, doesn't it, to have the mysterious villain call up your great, big, all-powerful organ of right and justice and good government and tell you what a helpless old gas-bag you are? . . . Cut that out; you're not that big a fool—no, you don't think I'm a fraud. I can tell it by your voice. . . . Now, listen, and I'll give you a pointer that will prove it to you. Of course you've had this murder case worked over by your staff of bright young blockheads. Half of the second button on old Mrs. Norcross's nightgown is broken off. I saw it when I took the garnet ring off her finger. I thought it was a ruby. . . . Stop that! It won't work."

Kernan turned to Woods with a diabolic smile.

"I've got him going. He believes me now. He didn't quite cover the transmitter with his hand when he told somebody to call up Central on another phone and get our number. I'll give him just one more dig and then we'll make a 'get-away.'

"Hallo! . . . Yes. I'm here yet. You didn't think I'd run from such a little subsidised turncoat rag of a newspaper, did you? . . . Have me inside of forty-eight hours? Say, will you quit being funny? Now, you let grown men alone and attend to your business of hunting up divorce cases and street-car accidents and printing the filth and scandal that you make your living by. Good-bye, old boy—sorry I haven't time to call on you. I'd feel perfectly safe in your sanctum asinorum. Tra-la!"

"He's as mad as a cat that's lost a mouse," said Kernan, hanging up the receiver and coming out. "And now, Barney, my boy, we'll go to a show and enjoy ourselves until a reasonable bedtime. Four hours' sleep for me, and then the west-bound."

The two dined in a Broadway restaurant. Kernan was pleased with himself. He spent money like a prince of fiction. And then a weird and gorgeous musical comedy engaged their attention. Afterwards there was a late supper in a grill-room with champagne, and Kernan at the height of his complacency.

Half-past three in the morning found them in a corner of an all-night café, Kernan still boasting in a vapid and rambling way, Woods thinking moodily over the end that had come to his usefulness as an upholder of the law.

But, as he pondered, his eye brightened with a speculative light.

"I wonder if it's possible," he said to himself. "I won-der if it's pos-si-ble!"

And then outside the café the comparative stillness of the early morning was punctured by faint, uncertain cries that seemed mere fireflies of sound, some growing louder, some fainter, waxing and waning amid the rumble of milk wagons and infrequent cars. Shrill cries they were when near . . . well known cries that conveyed many meanings to the ears of those of the slumbering millions of the great city who waked to hear them. Cries that bore upon their significant, small volume the weight of a world's woe and laughter and delight and stress. To some, cowering beneath the protection of a night's ephemeral cover, they brought news of the hideous bright day; to others, wrapped in happy sleep, they announced a morning that would dawn blacker than sable night. To many of the rich they brought a besom to sweep away what had been theirs while the stars shone; to the poor they brought—another day.

All over the city the cries were starting up, keen and sonorous, heralding the chances that the slipping of one cogwheel in the machinery of time had made; apportioning to the sleepers while they lay at the mercy of fate, the vengeance, profit, grief, reward and doom that the new figure in the calendar had brought them. Shrill and yet plaintive were the cries, as if the young voices grieved that so much evil and so little good was in their irresponsible hands. Thus echoed in the streets of the helpless city the transmission of the latest decrees of the gods, the cries of the newsboys—the Clarion Call of the Press.

Woods flipped a dime to the waiter, and said:

"Get me a *Morning Mars.*"

When the paper came he glanced at its first page, and then tore a leaf out of his memorandum book and began to write on it with the little gold pencil.

"What's the news?" yawned Kernan.

Woods flipped over to him the piece of writing:

The New York *Morning Mars:*

Please pay to the order of John Kernan the one thousand dollars reward coming to me for his arrest and conviction.

BARNARD WOODS.

"I kind of thought they would do that," said Woods, "when you were jollying 'em so hard. Now, Johnny, you'll come to the police station with me."

# The Clincher

*by Jack Foxx*

They were forty-five minutes from the Oregon-California border when Cord noticed that the red needle on the fuel gauge hovered close to empty. He glanced over at Tyler. "Almost out of gas," he said.

Tyler grinned. "So am I. I could sure use some food."

In the backseat, Fallon and Brenner sat shackled close together with double cuffs. Fallon's eyes were cold and watchful—waiting.

"There you go," Tyler said suddenly, touching Cord's arm and pointing.

Cord squinted against the late afternoon sun. A couple of hundred yards to the right of the freeway was a small white building, across the front of which was a paved area and a single row of gasoline pumps. A sign lettered in faded red and mounted on a tall metal pole stood between the building and the highway. It read: ED'S SERVICE— OPEN 24 HOURS.

"Okay," Cord said. "Good as any."

A short distance ahead was an exit ramp. He turned there and doubled back along a blacktopped county road that paralleled the freeway, took the car in alongside the pumps. He shut off the engine and started to get out, but Tyler stopped him.

"This is Oregon, remember? No self-service here. It's a state law."

"Yeah, right," Cord said.

An old man with sparse white hair and a weather-eroded face came out of a cubbyhole office, around to the driver's window. "Help you?"

"Fill 'er up," Cord told him. "Unleaded."

99

"Yes, sir." Then the old man saw Fallon and Brenner. He moistened his lips, looking at them with bright blue eyes.

"Don't worry about them," Cord said. "They're not going any-where."

"You fellas peace officers?"

Tyler smiled, nodding.

Cord said, "I'm a U.S. marshal and this is my guard. We're trans-porting these two down to San Francisco for federal court appear-ances."

"They from McNeil Island, up in Washington?"

"That's right."

Fallon said from the back seat, "Say, pop—"

"Shut up, Fallon," Tyler said sharply.

"Where's the rest rooms?" Fallon asked the old man.

"Never mind that now," Cord said. "Just keep quiet back there, if you know what's good for you."

Fallon seemed about to say something else, changed his mind, and sat silent.

The old man went to the rear of the car and busied himself with the gas cap and the unleaded hose. Then he came back with a squeegie, began to clean the windshield. In the front seat, Tyler yawned and Cord sat watching Fallon in the rearview mirror. The old man's eyes shifted over the four men as he worked on the glass, as if he were fascinated by what he saw.

There was a sharp click as the pump shut off automatically. The old man went to replace the hose and to screw the cap back on the tank. A few seconds later he was leaning down at the driver's window again.

"Check your oil?" he asked Cord.

"No, the oil's okay."

"That'll be twelve even, then. Credit card?"

Cord shook his head. "Cash." He got the wallet from his pocket, poked inside, gave the old man a ten and a five.

"Be right back with your change and receipt."

"Never mind, pop. Keep it. We're in a hurry."

"Not that much of a hurry," Tyler said. Then, to the old man, "You got anything to eat here?"

"Sandwich machine in the garage."

"Where's the garage?"

"Around on the other side. I'll show you."

"Better than nothing, I guess." Tyler looked at Cord. "What kind you want?"

"I don't care. Anything."

"I'll take ham on rye," Fallon said from the back.

Tyler said, "I thought we told you to shut up."

"Don't Brenner and I get anything to eat?"

"No."

"Come on, come on," Cord said. "Get the sandwiches, will you, Johnny? We've got a long way to go yet."

Tyler stepped out of the car and followed the old man around the side of the building. When they were out of sight Cord swiveled on the seat to stare back at Fallon. "Why don't you wise up?"

"I could ask you the same thing."

"Easy, Art," Brenner warned him.

"The hell with that," Fallon said. "This—"

"You keep pushing and pushing, don't you, Fallon?" Cord asked him. "You can't keep that smart mouth of yours closed."

Fallon's black eyes bored into Cord's; neither man blinked. Before long Brenner began to fidget. "Art . . ."

"Listen to your pal here," Cord said to Fallon. "He knows what's good for him."

Fallon remained silent, but his big hands clenched and unclenched inside the steel handcuffs.

Cord slid around to face front again. Pretty soon the old man came ambling back across the paved area, alone, carrying a square of rough, grease-stained cloth over one hand. He moved around to the driver's window again, bent down.

"What's keeping my guard?" Cord asked him. "Like I said before, we're in kind of a hurry."

"I guess you are," the old man said, and flicked the cloth away with his left hand.

Cord froze. In the old man's right hand was a .44 Magnum, pointed at Cord's temple.

"You make a move, mister, I reckon you're dead."

Fallon sucked in his breath; he and Brenner both sat forward. Cord remained frozen, staring at the Magnum.

The old man said to Fallon, "Where's the key to those cuffs?"

"On the ignition ring. Watch out he doesn't make a play for the gun."

"If he does he'll be minus a head." The old man reached down with his free hand, never taking his eyes from Cord, and pulled open the door. "Step out here. Slow. Hands up where I can see 'em."

Cord did as he was told. He stood holding his hands up by his ears, still watching the Magnum. The old man told him to turn around, pressed the muzzle against his spine, then removed the .38 revolver from the holster at Cord's belt. "Walk ahead a few steps," he said then. "And don't look around."

Cord took three forward steps and stopped. Behind him, the old man took the keys out of the ignition and passed them back to Fallon, who unlocked his and Brenner's handcuffs. Then the two of them got out and the old man let Fallon have the .38.

"The other one's around back," the old man said. "I slipped into the office while he was at the sandwich machine and got my gun and tapped him with it, then disarmed him. Here's his piece."

Brenner took the .38. "Go see about Tyler," Fallon told him, and Brenner nodded and went around the side of the building.

Fallon said to Cord, "You can turn around now." And when Cord had obeyed, "Lean your chest against the car, legs spread, hands behind you. You know the position."

Silently, Cord assumed it. Fallon gave the handcuffs to the old man, who snapped them around Cord's wrists. Then Fallon slipped the wallet out of Cord's pocket, put it into his own.

Brenner came back, shoving a groggy Tyler ahead of him. There was a smear of blood on Tyler's head where the old man had clubbed him. His hands were also cuffed behind him now.

When Cord and Tyler were on the back seat of the car, Fallon gripped the old man's shoulder gratefully. "What can we say? You saved our lives."

"That's a fact," Brenner said. "All they talked about coming down from Washington was shooting us and leaving our bodies in the woods somewhere. They'd have done it sooner or later."

"What happened?" the old man asked.

"We got careless," Fallon admitted. "We stopped this morning for coffee and made the mistake of letting them have some. The next thing we knew, we had hot coffee in our faces and Cord there had my gun."

Brenner said, "How did you know, pop? They didn't give us the chance to say anything, to tip you off."

The old man had put the .44 Magnum into the pocket of his overalls; the heavy gun made them sag so much he looked lopsided. "Well," he said, "it was a number of things. By themselves, they didn't mean much, but when you put 'em all together they could only spell one thing. I was county sheriff here for twenty-five years, before I retired and opened up this station two summers ago. I seen a few federal marshals transporting prisoners to and from McNeil in my

102

time. Housed federal prisoners in my jail more'n once, too, when an overnight stop was necessary. I know a few things about both breeds.

"First off, things just didn't seem right to me. The way they was acting, the way you was acting—there was something wrong about it. The way they looked, too, compared to you two. Whiter skin, kind of pasty, the way some Caucasians get when they've been in prison a while. And then neither of you lads was wearing those plastic identity bands around your wrists. I never seen a federal prisoner yet had his off outside, no matter what."

Fallon nodded. "They broke the ones they were wearing, so there was no way to get them on us."

"Another thing," the old man said, "they didn't want to let you go to the can or have anything to eat. No marshal treats his prisoners that way, not nowadays. They'd go screaming to their lawyers and anybody else who'd listen about abusive treatment, and the marshal'd find himself in hot water.

"Then there was the gasoline. The fella behind the wheel . . . Cord, is it?"

"Cord."

"Well, he paid me in cash," the old man said. "I never seen a marshal in recent years paid for gasoline 'cept with a credit card. Like the one I noticed peeking out of the wallet Cord had when he give me the two bills. Am I right?"

"Absolutely."

"And you get reimbursed for mileage, don't you?"

"We sure do."

"Well, that was the clincher," the old man said. "When I offered to give Cord a receipt he told me to keep it *and* a three-buck tip. No man on the federal payroll is gonna hand a gas jockey a three-dollar tip; and he sure as hell ain't gonna turn down a receipt that entitles him to get his money back from the government."

The old man passed a hand through his sparse white hair. "I'm getting on in years, but I ain't senile yet. I used to be a pretty fair lawman in my day, too, if I do say it myself. Reckon I haven't lost the knack."

Fallon glanced in at Cord and Tyler, now both sullen and quiet. "As far as Brenner and I are concerned, sir," he said, "you're the best there ever was."

# The Cop
# and the Lady

*by Booton Herndon*

"Me, I'm just a dumb cop, an' I been admittin' it for thirty years," O'Toole said. "Those other birds with their psychology and scientific crime-detectin' try to make it sound like a detective book. Imagination don't pay in this racket."

"I don't get you," I said. O'Toole and I were sitting in the dingy detective office. O'Toole was there on the late shift to answer the phone if it rang. That's what you do with a flatfoot who won't retire. I was there because I'd be the guy who'd go out and do the work if the phone did ring.

"Yeah, you're just like the rest of them guys," O'Toole said. "Nothin' makes sense unless they got it in college or high school and it's a big word. Minute they get on a case they begin thinkin' about thinkin'. Psychology and stuff. Character an' behavior patterns. They begin to talk about manias an' them things an' can't tell when you're just plain nuts."

He squinted at me over his nose. It was a strain because his nose was shaped to match his belly. "Got a cigar?"

"No," I said. "And if I did, I'd keep it. If you think your theories on psychology are worth a cigar to me, you're suffering from dementia tremendous."

"Just like all the rest of the guys," O'Toole said grumpily. "Can't talk plain English. Well, I'll tell you what I mean about bein' nuts.

"This guy Folkes was found all slashed up in his bedroom. We walked in after Mrs. Folkes called us, an' there he was, lookin' like ten dollars' worth of chopped steak. Mrs. Folkes was cool as the bottle of beer I'd like to be drinkin' right now." He looked up quizzically, but I shook my head. No beer. "Well," he said, sighing, "all the brainy boys said she was so cool because she was so well bred. They said she was a lady of quality an' wouldn't show emotion. As for cuttin' a guy into hash, they never dreamed of such a thing. So they went out lookin' for the murderer.

104

"They looked up the street an' down the street, but they didn't see no murderer. They read all their books over again, an' they finger-printed everything in the house. They questioned the servants an' the gardener, an' spouted theories all over the place. But they couldn't find who done it."

"Let me get this straight," I butted in. "Not that I care, but if I have to listen to this stuff I'd better try to understand it. Why weren't there any fingerprints? What did the servants say?"

"Somebody wiped the knife off, and the servants were all asleep. That suit you? Mrs. Folkes said she didn't know anything about it; she slept in her own room, and she found him that way when she went in to say good-mornin'. She let out a yelp, refined an' lady-like, of course, an' told the maid to call the cops.

"That's all there was to it, except that the guy hated animals. That's why Mrs. Folkes slept in the other room—she had this little dog that looked like a rat, an' she always kept him in the room with her, 'cause Folkes didn't like the mutt.

"I told the Cap'n that she probably sliced him up herself an' he says for me not to act dumb. Any poor fool could see, he says, that no lady who loved animals as much as this dame could dump off a guy, espe-cially like that. He says that psychology shows that a lady of such refinement and love for dumb animals couldn't bear to harm any living thing, much less chop her hubby to pieces. He went on like that for a couple of weeks, an' finally he gave up an' they put me on the case 'cause I'm so dumb I was in their way everywhere else."

"Come on," I said. "I know how dumb you are. Let's get to the point."

O'Toole looked up and sighed.

"Since there wasn't nobody else around that night that I could find out about, I figured Mrs. Folkes killed him. That's the easiest thing to do, ain't it?"

I sneered, but O'Toole went right on.

"So I figured that maybe he slapped her dog or somethin'. Y'see, I'd been talkin' to one of the maids, an' I found out that she washes this shaggy pooch of hers in all kinds of fancy shampoos, an' powders the thing up, an' sprays it with perfume, an' buys clothes for the fool dog, an' treats it like a baby, an' Folkes hates it, so what else could I think?"

"I'm beginning to think you can't think."

"I've known that for years," he said. "Any rate, I decide that, since I can't get no proof on her, I'll have to get her to confess. So I pay a little call on her an' her dog, an' ask her does she kill this guy. She gives me a stuck-up look an' picks up her dog an' begins to stalk outa the room. So I grabs the dog outa her arms an' I landed a kick on that mutt that shook a quart of perfume off its hide."

"I don't much see the point in that," I said. "Just because you're a disgruntled old flatfoot is no excuse to kick a little dog around."

"Well, I kinda hated to do it myself," O'Toole said, "especially with my achin' feet, but it worked. This dame makes a dive for me and begins to claw my eyes out. Just about the time she tells me she's gonna kill me, too, the other cop waitin' outside the door comes in and we take her to the bughouse. Y'see, I'm dumb enough to call a dame what's nutty nutty. An' that's all there is to it. Psychology? Humph."

O'Toole took his feet down off the desk, groaning with every motion of his three hundred pounds, and reached down under his chair. He came up with some gruesome looking object, like a half-starved marmoset with a wig on.

"My God, O'Toole," I said. "Is that . . . ?"

"Yeah," O'Toole said sheepishly, chucking the mutt under the ear. "I'm just dumb enough to figure I oughta take care of it now."


# Cop Maker

*by Ronald Henderson*


Barney Conroy hunched behind the wheel of his cab, still smarting from his most recent encounter with Detective-Sergeant Sullivan. The fact that Sullivan was admittedly riding him for a purpose proved small comfort to the youthful hack driver. His thoughts were as gloomy as the cold drizzle that had settled on the city earlier in the evening.

"Jump a light once more," Sullivan had said, "and I'll see that your hack license is revoked, even if I have to get a radio car to pull you in." His gray mustache fairly bristled and his dark eyes reflected an anger entirely out of keeping with the situation.

Barney knew that it wasn't his habit of jumping lights that had infuriated the old detective. Every hack driver in the city of New York did that. It was the knowledge that Jean, his daughter, was in love with Barney and they were planning on getting married as soon as Barney received his appointment to the police force.

Everything else having failed to change Jean's mind, Sullivan had set about blocking Barney's appointment. He knew Barney would never ask Jean to share the uncertain future of a hackman's prospects.

Because of the unusually large number of young men who had passed the preliminary tests, the few chosen ones would have to be sifted by a process of elimination. And the revocation of a hack license would hardly be considered a recommendation.

Although there were times when Barney resented the old man bitterly, deep in his heart he felt sorry for him. He knew that it wasn't anything that Sullivan held against him, personally, that was the reason for his determined opposition. It was just that he couldn't reconcile the thoughts of his daughter being married to any man. In his mind there was no man living that was good enough for her. He had been father and mother to the girl ever since Jean's mother had died when she was a baby. In his hard-bitten way, he had lavished his affections on Jean until he was totally blinded to her own happiness.

But why couldn't the old man see that he also worshipped Jean? Had worshipped her ever since they were kids in school together.

Barney's musings were interrupted by a man who jumped into his cab.

"Drive around the corner to Jay's Bar and Grill."

Without turning to look at his fare, Barney shifted gears and eased away from the curb. He turned the corner, pulled up in front of the bar, and braked to a stop.

His passenger said: "Be back in a minute." He dashed out of the cab, leaving the door open and ran into the bar.

Barney lit a cigarette and was letting his thoughts drift back to Jean and their future when he heard a shot from the barroom. He looked up quickly and saw a man backing out of the place, holding a gun in his right hand. It was his passenger. Before Barney could do anything, the man wheeled and ran to the cab. He jumped inside, slammed the door and held the gun on Barney.

"Get going," he gritted through clenched teeth.

In the brief moment when Barney had looked his passenger full in the face he had recognized him. His picture was in all the evening papers. "Bugs" Mayhew, the notorious killer who had slipped his guard at Grand Central while being taken to Sing Sing to die in the electric chair. Every cop in town was on the lookout for him with orders to take no chances but to shoot on sight.

Barney had no choice but to obey. If he refused to drive he knew that Mayhew would have no compunction about shooting him. Here was a golden opportunity. To capture this much-wanted criminal would clinch his appointment and he was helpless to do anything about it. He shifted the gears and shot away.

"Take it easy buddy—don't try breaking the speed limit." Mayhew's voice was close to Barney's ear.

The fact that he was at the mercy of a blood-crazed killer didn't enter Barney's head. All he could think of for the moment was the definite end to his hopes of becoming a cop and all that it meant to him. If Mayhew got away, it would spell doom to his chances of ever wearing a policeman's shield. It wouldn't matter to the board that he was helpless to bring about Mayhew's capture. It was up to him to do something to stop this killer before he could add more victims to his list.

A number of wild ideas flitted through Barney's mind but he discarded them as impractical. He could run his cab into another car or up onto the sidewalk, but it would only result in more shooting. A desperate man like "Bugs" Mayhew wouldn't hesitate to kill anyone who stood in his way. And even though Mayhew was caught and Barney was praised for his assistance in the capture, he couldn't become a cop at the expense of innocent people.

Suddenly, he realized that the one-way street they were driving down, led right past the intersection where Detective-Sergeant Sullivan was generally on duty. He remembered Sullivan's threat.

He pulled up to the intersection and stopped for the red light. As he had hoped, Sullivan was standing on the sidewalk, not ten feet away, watching the stream of traffic flowing by. Barney saw him glance casually in his direction, then become suddenly alert. His gaze riveted on Barney's cab.

Barney looked up at the light. In the other direction it flashed red but had not yet flashed green on his side. Pedestrians were still crossing the street. Intersecting traffic had stopped. Barney shifted to first and shot across the street a brief second before the light changed. It was nothing unusual, but technically it was a traffic violation.

He looked in his rear vision mirror to see what Sullivan's reaction had been. He had expected to see the detective run into the corner cigar store to make good his threat to send a radio car after him. With a sinking sensation he saw Sullivan commandeer a passing car. He was standing on the running board, pointing to Barney's cab.

Barney cursed under his breath and stepped on the accelerator.

Instead of everything working out as he had hoped, he was in a worse predicament than ever. Sullivan, evidently anxious to have his hack license revoked, had decided to have the satisfaction of bringing Barney in himself.

Through Barney's dismayed mind raced a vivid picture of what would happen.

Not knowing that Barney had "Bugs" Mayhew for a passenger, he would be taken completely unawares. The minute Sullivan's commandeered cab pulled up alongside, Mayhew would shoot him down without a second's hesitation. Whatever happened to Barney, he knew he couldn't let the old man in for this.

Another quick glance in the mirror showed him that Mayhew had noticed nothing unusual.

The killer sat on the edge of the seat, his gun in his hand. But it would only be a matter of minutes before he realized they were being chased. If he looked back he couldn't miss seeing the pursuing cab with Sullivan hanging on to the side.

Mayhew rapped on the glass panel that separated the driver from his passengers. Barney slid it open.

"Turn west at the next corner," Mayhew ordered.

"Okay," said Barney. He slid the panel shut.

He knew what this order meant. As soon as they got to a deserted street, Mayhew would tell him to pull up to the curb, then probably club him with his gun, and make his getaway.

At the corner he turned west and headed for the river. The pursuing car was now only about a block behind them. Barney stepped on the gas and felt the cab leap forward under him. A glance upward in the mirror showed him Sullivan's car take the turn recklessly, speed after them down the block.

Barney squeezed the accelerator to the floor boards but he could see that his cab didn't have the speed to shake off the other car. Slowly the distance between them grew shorter. He knew it would only be a matter of minutes before the other car drew alongside. When that happened, Sullivan was as good as dead.

Mayhew was rapping on the panel again. Barney slid it open. His decision was made.

"What do you want?" he said, over his shoulder.

"Stop this cab, you lunatic."

Barney kept his eyes on the road, holding the handle of the panel with his right hand.

"I can't hear you."

Mayhew stuck his arm over the seat. Through the corner of his eyes, Barney could see the glint of steel.

Before he could finish, Barney slammed the panel shut, holding Mayhew's arm as effectively as if it had been held in a vise.

He let go the wheel, jammed his foot on the brake. Before Mayhew realized what had happened, Barney grasped his arm, forcing it downward. He heard Mayhew curse, then the gun clanked to the floor. The cab slowed down, swerved to the right, then stalled to a stop against the curb.

The other car pulled alongside and Barney saw Sullivan leap to the ground. He was surprised to see the detective holding a gun. Without bothering with Barney, Sullivan flung open the door of the cab. In a few seconds he had Mayhew handcuffed, then he turned to Barney.

"What's the idea of trying to give me the slip? Were you in cahoots with Mayhew?"

"In cahoots!" Barney sputtered indignantly. "I jumped the light while you were watching me, figuring that you'd send a radio car after me like you threatened. I didn't think you'd take after me yourself."

"That still doesn't explain why you tried to get away."

"I couldn't let you be shot in cold blood, could I? You didn't know I had Mayhew in my cab."

Sullivan looked at Barney curiously. "So that was it." He was silent for a moment. His flushed and angry face slowly softened. Then, he said: "You thought I was chasing you because you jumped a light?" For the first time in his life, Barney heard Detective-Sergeant Sullivan laugh. A warm, friendly laugh.

"I spotted Mayhew in the cab while you were waiting for the light."

# The Course of Justice

*by Hugh B. Cave*

It happened very much sooner than John Houghton expected, and he was glad he had written the two letters beforehand. At that, he might not have had a chance even to mail them had the Immigration Officer been certain.

Apparently the officer was not certain. Not quite. His routine glance at Houghton's face did freeze into a searching stare; he did look down again at the name "John Harper" on Houghton's tourist card; he was still staring when Houghton glanced back after leaving the desk; but he was not sure.

As soon as Houghton had picked up his suitcase in Customs and entered the main part of the St. Joseph airport, he dropped the two letters into a mailbox. They were already stamped. Norma, his wife, had bought several dollars' worth of stamps as souvenirs when they had honeymooned in the Caribbean three years before.

Houghton then took a taxi to the Pension Etoile, where he and his wife had stayed on their earlier visit.

Little Max Haun, the proprietor, shook his hand warmly. "You haven't changed a bit, John," Max said. "Not a bit. And how is Norma?"

"She doesn't know I'm here, Max."

"Doesn't know you're here? What do you mean?"

"I'll explain later over a drink. Let me get rid of this suitcase."

"You must have the room you had before," Max said. "Come." He took the suitcase himself—it was that kind of hotel, small and intimate—and led Houghton upstairs to the large front room which on that other occasion the proprietor had jokingly called the bridal suite. It was the best room in the house, with a little balcony that offered a fine view of the Parc de l'Indépendence and the glittering white Palais National across the square.

"It brings back fond memories, I hope," Max said, his eyes twinkling.

Houghton turned himself slowly to look around the room, then stepped onto the balcony to scowl at the President's palace. "It brings back memories. Not fond ones. Sit down, please, Max. We'll have the drink later."

Puzzled by his guest's strangeness, Max sat down.

"Haven't you wondered," Houghton said, pacing as he spoke, "why I kept asking you in my letters to keep me posted on the political progress of Emile Nerette?"

"You said you were interested in his career."

"And you didn't wonder why I was interested? No, I suppose not. You're not a man to question the motives of your friends." Houghton turned and stared. "You remember the night my wife was arrested by the Palace Guard and taken to headquarters?"

Max almost smiled, but not quite. "For failing to stop her car when the President's cavalcade was passing. Yes, of course."

"How we searched for her for hours and finally found her in this room, on this very bed, crying, when we returned?"

"I remember."

"She said then, Max, that everything was all right, that nothing had happened. She was only upset. You remember that? But the truth, which I didn't find out until weeks later—the truth, Max, is that she was raped."

"*Mon dieu!*" Max said.

"Yes, Max, and the man who did it was Nerette, then head of the Palace Guard, now your President."

Max Haun placed his hands on his knees to stop their trembling. "So that is why you have come back."

"I waited, Max. It was not enough just to kill him. Anyone can die. In this country of yours men die by violence all the time. You wrote in one of your letters that Nerette was ambitious to be President. Good, I thought. In another letter you said it was rumored he would soon marry one of the most desired women in St. Joseph. Again I thought: good. Let him marry her. Let him have a son or daughter, even. Then when my time comes, he will have that much more to lose."

"*Mon dieu!*" Max said again, whispering now as though a normal voice would be unsafe. "As you say, he has much more to lose at this time—a wife, an infant son, the presidency of the republic—but you must be mad, my friend. You would never get near him. In this country a President has enemies always, and is on guard every moment against them."

"I have taken precautions."

"Suppose it is remembered who you are. Suppose someone goes to him and says, 'M'sieu Président, the husband of that American girl whom you—you mistreated—is here again.' Think about it. Such an event is not only possible, it is likely. Very few Americans come to this country now. The political upheavals have ruined our tourist trade."

Houghton said, smiling coldly, "I will get to him, Max. Before leaving home I wrote two letters. At the airport here I mailed them. Not only will those letters protect me, they will get me into the palace and bring me face to face with Nerette himself."

"Impossible. How?"

"You will see. Remember, I've had three years to think about this. All I need is time enough for the letters to be delivered. Until tomorrow, say. Then it will be easy. I've used an assumed name on my tourist card." Houghton turned to the door. "Come on. Let's have that drink together for the sake of things remembered—the *good* things remembered. Then—where are you going?"

"You take too much for granted," Max muttered, stepping onto the balcony to gaze in a trance of terror at the Palais National across the square. "You think because you have used a name not your own—*Mon dieu*, look!"

Houghton, frowning, stepped to his side.

"Those three in uniform by the monument, coming this way across the grass!" Max whispered. "They are coming here!"

"How—"

"I tell you they are coming here! Where else?" Houghton was seized by an arm and pulled back into the room. "You were recognized at the airport!"

"Perhaps." Houghton felt his lips go dry. "An Immigration man looked at me closely. Tall, thin, not so dark—a man with beady eyes and bad teeth."

"God in heaven. Beliard! A former captain in the Palace Guard."

"Would he know me?"

"*Know* you? He was one of those we talked to that night when we searched for your wife—one of those who pretended to know nothing when all the time she was there at headquarters. Now he is the President's eyes and ears in the Immigration Service, planted there to keep Nerette informed of dangers!"

Houghton had turned pale. "Hide my suitcase, Max. I'll go out the back way, through the garden."

"Where will you go?" Max said, wringing his hands.

Houghton had no answer. Where *could* he go, he asked himself as he sped through the garden at the rear of the pension. With the rest of the day ahead of him, and the night to live through, where would he hide?

St. Joseph was a big city, to be sure. It was home to a hundred thousand people. But it was patrolled these days by hundreds of police and more hundreds of Nerette's private goons, and in every part of the city a foreign face would be conspicuous.

He climbed the wall at the garden's end and dropped into an alley on the other side. Ran down the alley. Stopped running and turned left, slowly, into a street of small shops. Could he hide in a hotel? They were practically empty these days, and watched. In a theater? Theaters did not open until evening and even then were almost never frequented by foreigners. Dear God, where?

He kept to the side streets and walked. Hands in pockets, slowly. Not a tourist enchanted by the sight of *marchandes* singing their wares,

113

peasants riding the rumps of clop-clopping donkeys, naked children playing noisily at games—not that but like a foreign resident on some routine errand, made listless by the noise and tropical heat. An old hand here. Only the eyes alert, reaching ahead like radar to glimpse danger in time . . .

So many policemen in this city! So many footsteps! So many swift changes of direction, crossings of streets, dartings into doorways. If he had any doubt that he was hunted, it was dispelled quickly. Less than a block away a khaki-colored car screeched to a stop beside a pair of uniformed men on a corner. The officer in the car briskly gave them orders. The two looked this way and that along the street, jerked their heads in understanding, and swiftly went their separate ways. Houghton fled.

He crept into an empty church and sat there watching the stained-glass windows break the sunlight into floating flecks of color.

"Dear God, I'm tired. And there's a whole night of this ahead."

An organ began to throb. People came ghosting in. He fled again.

Mustn't walk the same street twice . . . but it's a big city and there are many streets. And the sun is sliding behind the hills now. Darkness is moving in.

"Stop! You, there! Halt!"

He means you, Houghton. Don't stop. Don't run, either. Don't turn, don't hesitate, don't even walk faster. Here now, the corner! Get around it. Now! Run!

The street was empty, thank God, and the next corner close. There was an alley between high wooden buildings, and at the end of the alley he saw a district of peasant hovels, like a jigsaw puzzle dropped from a box. Hands in pockets, mumbling to himself, he trudged through it. The naked children backed out of his way, goggle-eyed. The peasant women squatting at their cookpots peered at him through fogs of charcoal smoke, and some of them laughed.

Now it was dark.

Now by avoiding the streets where there were lights he could walk slowly, stop when tired, then walk on again when the silence bred footfalls. The greatest danger was on wheels—cars that came lurching around a corner with glaring headlamps that made him a performer on a floodlit stage. Each time it happened, he turned to stone and the car sped by trailing a woman's laughter. *That could have been a chatter of gunfire, Houghton.*

Then he would move faster between hiding places and at the sound of approaching cars he'd press himself into cracks where the head-lights could not reach him.

114

At midnight, lost in a part of the city he had not seen before, he found an empty house. First a high stone wall. Then gateposts, but only half a gate. A yard knee-high in weeds. A wooden bungalow—the shell of one—with a collapsed veranda and only empty black holes for window and door.

He stood on the veranda listening, and there was no sound. There was only a car horn on a distant street and a rattle of *chacha* pods on a tree in the garden. With hands thrust in front of him for eyes, he staggered inside and sat down in the dark. Would they look here? They could not look everywhere in one night.

Dear God, I'm tired. I'm dirty. I stink.

I wish I were a nothing

So I could not be seen.

I wish to—get—where I must go

And not be—where I've—been—

Don't go to sleep, Houghton. Don't . . . go . . . to . . . sleep . . .

"Get up," a voice said, and the room was splashed with sunlight stabbing through gaps in the walls, and over him stood men in uniform.

"Get up!" and a hand seized him by an arm and jerked him savagely to his feet, but another man muttered in French and the hand became more gentle.

Houghton looked at his watch. It had stopped. He had forgotten to wind it.

"What time is it?"

"A little after ten o'clock, m'sieu. You are to come with us."

After ten. By now the letter . . .

"Where to? Where are you taking me?"

"To the Palace."

He let his breath out.

They led him through the overgrown garden to a khaki-colored car. They were gentle with him, he noticed. No pushing, no shoving. "Between us, if you please, m'sieu."

He was surprised at how short the journey was. In no time at all the car had left the grubby streets and was speeding through the business district. It swung into the Parc de l'Indépendence, past the Pension Etoile, past the monument and the statues, and into the Palace driveway. Last night he must have traveled in circles.

"For your audience with the President, perhaps you would like to freshen yourself, m'sieu?"

There was motive in their generosity, of course. When they took his clothes and shoes away to "make them more presentable," there was the opportunity to search for hidden weapons. As if he would be foolish enough to carry a weapon they might discover!

He dressed again slowly after his shave and shower. Even the lining of his jacket had been slit and resewn, he noticed. Had they ripped the soles and heels off his shoes and rebuilt those too?

"The President will see you, m'sieu."

They walked him down a shining white corridor, a man on each side of him, into a kind of reception room. An officer of the Palace Guard, a colonel, rose from a desk to open an inner door.

He stepped into the sanctum. The door clicked shut behind him.

Windowless. Air-conditioned. A gleaming mahogany desk with a top like a dance floor. Behind the desk a man rose to greet him, and the memory of that three-year-old night came back in a rush. Houghton clenched his hands and stepped forward.

The man behind the desk reached down and produced a pistol. "Be seated, m'sieu."

Houghton regained control of himself. He sat in a large red-leather chair and looked at the man he hated. Photographs in newspapers and magazines had prepared him for the fantastically ugly face, but he was stunned by Nerette's hugeness. The man was a bull.

Houghton shuddered. Norma, his wife, was so small and dainty . . .

"I have your letter, m'sieu." The letter lay on the desk and Nerette tapped it with the pistol. "Let me see if I understand it correctly." He sat as though lowered into place by a crane, and the mountain of flesh overflowed the chair.

"You understand it," Houghton said.

"I must be sure. You say you have written also to my wife, giving her Madame Houghton's account of what happened that night. In your letter to my wife you admit you have no proof other than madame's statement. You expect to obtain proof, but as yet you do not have it."

"Go on."

"You point out to my wife that if I am guilty as charged, I will undoubtedly take steps to eliminate you. So you will telephone her daily. If the calls cease, she will know that I have silenced you—and why."

"You have it right," Houghton said.

"You are ingenious, m'sieu. By writing so to my wife, and making me aware of what you have written, you have made sure you will stay alive—with freedom to use the telephone. What now?"

"I intend to kill you."

"Really? How?"

"There will be ways. You have to travel about the country a good deal, and I will be here. I'm an excellent shot with a high-powered rifle, Nerette. For more than a year now I've been practicing."

"It may take a long time, m'sieu," the bull said with a twisted smile.

"I have time."

"What about your wife? Your work?"

"Thanks to you, Nerette, my wife doesn't know she has a husband. She is in a mental hospital. My work is not important."

"So I am to be shot, eh?"

"Or blown up. Or poisoned. I am several kinds of expert."

"You have thought of everything."

"I hope so."

The huge man leaned over his pistol and looked at Houghton and laughed. His laughter boomed through the room like thunder. "What a fool you are, M'sieu Houghton. What a charming, childish fool!"

"Childish?" Houghton said, rising.

"Sit down. Yes, childish. Your plan, your whole ingenious plan, is based on the assumption that I cherish the woman I married, that I will do anything to keep her from knowing the truth about that night." The fat hands oiled themselves, fondling the pistol between them. "Let me tell you something. Now that I am President, I could not care less what my wife thinks of me. If she leaves me, there are a hundred other women eager to take her place. I married her for one reason only—because her brother was a dangerous political rival."

Houghton slowly sat down, speechless.

"As for you," the President went on with a gigantic shrug, "you came here under an assumed name. Mr. John Houghton is not in St. Joseph at all. Only Mr. Harper is here. But there is really no John Harper—is there?—so he will not be missed."

He turned the pistol and pointed it at Houghton's chest.

Houghton stared at it.

"But I dislike violence," Nerette said. "Personal violence, that is. It is well known how much I dislike violence. So, instead—"

He pressed a button.

The door opened and the colonel from the outer office stepped in. It seemed to Houghton—though perhaps he was not thinking too clearly now—that the door opened even before the button was pressed.

"You have your pistol, Colonel?" Nerette murmured. "Ah, yes. Good. Use it, please."

"Certainly, mon President," the colonel said.

He drew the weapon from its holster and without expression stepped forward. Before Houghton could rise, he halted and turned.

"Your wife's orders, M'sieu Nerette," the colonel said, and taking aim at the big man's heart, squeezed the trigger.

There was almost no sound except the President's gasp.

A slender, attractive woman came into the office, shut the door, and walked to the desk. After glancing at the dead man, she turned to the colonel and nodded. "You had better remove the microphone, Victor," she said calmly.

The colonel reached far into a drawer of the desk and took something out of it. He moved the desk a few inches and ripped some wires from a small hole in the floor. Only then did the woman turn to Houghton.

"In this country we find these things necessary," she said. "I, especially, have found them necessary. Go now, please. Forget that you came here."

She opened the door for him.

As Houghton passed her, an expression of sadness touched her face. "I am so sorry about your wife," she said. "I wish there were something more I could do."


# Curtains for Kelly

*by John Randolph Phillips*


Kelly's voice, buzzing over the wires into the chief's office, was saturated with a flat self-disgust. "Yeah, Chief, I been kidnapped. Ain't that a hell of a note? It's George Eddins and Bucky Marcum's brother, Wolfe, the last of the Bucky's gang. Ouch . . . Nothing, Chief, except Marcum just nudged me with his gun and told me to cut out the talk and get down to business.

"They got a fool proposition to make. They'll trade me for Bucky. I told 'em the law didn't do business that way, but they think different. If you turn Bucky Marcum loose by four o'clock, I go free. If you don't, the undertaker can pick me up sometime thereafter. I know it ain't any use, but they insist on me giving you the setup.

"You turn Bucky loose and call off the cops. He goes to some hideout they've got, and if he's sure he ain't been tailed he puts in a call and tells his pals you've played square. Shortly after that, they tell me, I'll be a free man again. Beautiful idea, ain't it? Me kidnapped!

"They want it plainly understood that Bucky must be turned loose by four. Otherwise, curtains for Kelly . . . Now, Chief, don't go sentimental on me. In this game you got to take it as it comes."

Kelly replaced the receiver and faced the two men. Short, heavy, dark, middle-aged Wolfe Marcum; slender, boyish George Eddins. Kelly regarded them sourly.

"Told you it wouldn't work. Tried to make you understand the law don't do business that way. Why, the chief couldn't do it even if he would. Bucky Marcum has got a date with the chair. Well, when does the party start?"

"Not till four o'clock," Marcum answered. "We'll wait."

"Wait! What for?" Eddins demanded shrilly. "I told you the thing was cock-eyed. I knew it when Bucky sent us that message."

"So it was Bucky's idea?" Kelly said.

"Yes, it was Bucky's idea," Eddins snapped, "and a bum idea, too. I told you that, Wolfe. Of all the—"

"Shut up," Marcum said. "We'll wait. Have some sense, George. The chief was only stalling. They'll come across. Think they're going to lose their best man? He's their star. The whole force would go to hell for Kelly. Don't worry, George."

The heavy man's quiet, confident tones seemed to relieve young Eddins. He seated himself on the bed. Kelly looked around. He had not had time to inspect the place when they ushered him in. He saw now a small room, furnished with a bureau, an iron double bed, three straight chairs, and a small table. It was on the second story. The one window, open from the bottom, faced another window in a house across a narrow alley.

"A movie guy," Kelly thought, "would throw himself out that window and not be killed when he hit the alley below."

Kelly glimpsed himself in the bureau mirror. So far, he reflected, his appearance didn't betray his agitation. Rather handsome, Kelly. Tall and well-proportioned, running a little to the lean side. Gray eyes. An unlined, clean-cut face. The face said he was twenty-five. But the contradictory gray already showing in his black hair claimed he was considerably more.

"Sit down if you want to," Marcum said, taking one of the chairs himself and sliding his automatic into a side pocket.

Kelly dropped into a chair across the table from Marcum. Eddins leaned back on the bed, puffing at a cigarette. Outside sounded the hum and clatter of the city's traffic. Kelly wondered if he'd ever be outside again to listen to it. Being an optimist, he figured that he would. Always before something had turned up in the nick of time.

"Smoke if you want to," Marcum told him.

"Thanks," said Kelly. "It's a favor." He lit his cigarette. "Not many furnished rooms are fitted up with telephones," he observed.

"We believe in conveniences," Marcum said. "Been renting this room for years. Me and George hid out here all the time you coppers were staging your big drive."

"It was a swell drive," Kelly told him. "We broke the Bucky Marcum outfit. Got every man but you and George, and we missed you awful close. Well, well. And to think I'm sitting here in the same room with you two."

"And can't do a thing about it," George sang out triumphantly.

"That's right, son," Kelly admitted.

Kelly looked at his watch. Twenty-five minutes past three. It seemed unbelievable that less than twenty minutes ago he had been a free man. He had been standing on Fifth, with his back to the street, gazing into a jeweler's window when he felt a tap on his shoulder. Turning, he came face to face with Wolfe Marcum.

"This thing making a bulge in my pocket is a gun," Marcum told him. "Hop in that car."

Kelly hopped in, on the back seat beside Marcum. George Eddins was at the wheel. The car slid into traffic, stopped a few minutes later before this house at the corner of Pine and Harrison. A traffic cop was standing at the intersection. Kelly started to yell to him, but, not quite ready to die yet, he chose to play for time. They marched him upstairs to the room, gave him his instructions, and made him telephone.

Now he sat there and, as Eddins had said, couldn't do a thing about it. A little of Kelly's habitual nonchalance fell from him, like a garment that no longer fitted. A bead of sweat rolled down his forehead. His cigarette was tasteless. Three-thirty now. Only thirty minutes to wait.

"A really game guy," Kelly thought, "would suggest a session of poker to pass the time, but I ain't that game."

In spite of their tastelessness, he smoked two more cigarettes in
120

rapid succession. His eye strayed to the window across the alley, strayed back. His mind turned this way and that in the coils of his dilemma. There had to be a way out. There always had been before. He concentrated on every detail of the situation. Sure, there had to be a way out, but what was it?

"Stop thinking so hard, kid," said the bulky Marcum. "Ain't nothing you can do. Buck up. You've always shot square, you've never been dirty, and you can rest assured we won't bump you unless we have too. And we won't. The chief'll trade. He won't let you—"

"I wish I thought that as strong as you," Eddins interrupted from the bed.

"Shut up," Marcum told him gently. "Nerves," he explained to Kelly. "Put George behind the wheel of a fast car and there ain't a nerve in his body. But—well, he's jittery in a case like this. Take a drink if you want, George. Just one, though."

"Can I make it as big as I want to?"

"No," laughed Marcum. "I'll pour, as they say in the society columns."

"No, thanks," said Eddins. "I don't want the thimbleful you'd pour me."

Kelly rose abruptly. Every muscle in his body grew tense, then relaxed.

"Can't you get it through your thick heads that the law doesn't play ball that way? You ain't that dumb. What'll you do when the chief don't turn Bucky loose? Where'll you be? In the doghouse, that's where!"

"You'll be there, too," Marcum said. "We've drawn our cards, Kelly, and we're standing pat."

"You fool," Kelly said, "don't you know that by now the chief has had that call traced? He knows where we are just as well as we know it ourselves. He'll have a squad down here that'll—"

"Sure," Marcum interrupted, "if he decides not to trade. I'm betting he'll trade. Anyway, that's the chance we got to take. It's my brother they're fixing to burn, Kelly, and this is the only way I know to get him out."

"But—" Kelly began again.

"There ain't no buts. If he don't trade, and if he sends a squad down here to shoot it out with us—why, we lose. But it's a gamble we got to take. I've already figured it from every angle. So you can't tell me anything. Just don't forget that in a shooting match you'll be the first casualty. Sit down, Kelly, before I knock you down."

121

"Who's jittery now?" Eddins demanded.

"You still are," Marcum responded calmly. "Do something to take your mind off this business. Anything. Play yourself a game of solitaire or write a letter to that girl in Louisville."

Kelly watched the slender man on the bed, watched his yellow fingers quiver as they brought a cigarette to his lips. Without Marcum there to steady him, to serve as ballast, the kid would go haywire. He wasn't built for this kind of strain. Kelly knew he could handle Eddins alone. But Marcum was another proposition.

"Ever been shot, kid?" he drawled.

"Let him alone," Marcum said, "if you know what's good for you."

"You're the worst jailer I ever saw," Kelly grumbled. "You won't even let me talk to the turnkey."

"Shut up."

"I reckon you've been shot lots of times," Eddins said sarcastically, in an attempt to throw off the jitters. "You're the big hero of the police force, ain't you?"

"Oh, I've been shot a few times," Kelly answered casually. "But once I saw a cop turn a machine gun loose on a guy down by the river. George, I'll swear that guy's insides—"

Marcum leaned across the table and hit Kelly hard on the jaw. "I told you to shut up, didn't I? Let the kid alone."

"You're the first guy, Wolfe," said Kelly, "that ever hit me and didn't get hit back. Maybe my turn will come."

Marcum offered no reply. Kelly rubbed the lump on his jaw. He could make a break here. He could leap to his feet and knock Marcum out with one punch and be on top of Eddins before the latter realized the situation. There was just one hitch. Only in the movies were men like Marcum knocked out with one punch.

And then the germ of an idea trickled into Kelly's suffering brain. He turned it over. He rehearsed it. He laughed suddenly.

"You boobs," he said. "Going through all this for a guy that's already sold you down the river!"

"Now what, sweetheart?" Marcum asked sourly.

"It might interest you to know that Bucky Marcum has confessed a lot of stuff about his brother and a fellow named Eddins." The slender man on the bed sat up instantly, his eyes popping. "It might interest you also," Kelly continued, "to know that your big hero is going to turn state's evidence so he can get life instead of the chair. How do you like them apples, Georgie?"

Eddins bounded to the floor. His wild eyes fastened accusingly on

122

Marcum. "The doublecrosser!" he yelled. His breath came in gasps. Kelly's heart leaped. "The dirty doublecrosser!"

"Gee, but you're dumb, George," Marcum said wearily. He pushed Eddins back to the bed, keeping at the same time an alert eye on Kelly. "That one is as old as the hills. Don't you see what the guy's trying to do, George? Try again, Kelly."

But Kelly couldn't try again. Always before he had been able to grin at defeat, at temporary setbacks. But he couldn't now. The answer probably lay in the very evident fact that this defeat was not temporary. It appeared to be about as permanent as anything under the sun. A drop of sweat fell to the bare top of the table and lay there as if mocking him.

Kelly slumped in his chair, with his spine cold and his forehead burning. He thought of many things: of sunlight on the river, of dawn stealing up city streets, of a girl with blue eyes who lived in the West End. She had watched the sunlight with him and the dawn after a glorious night of merrymaking.

His eyes strayed again to that window across the alley, that window which was merely a blank, unwinking eye in the house opposite. But suddenly it wasn't blank. Suddenly it seemed to wink back at him.

"Marcum," Kelly said, "I want to ask you a favor. You seem pretty sure of things, but just in case the chief doesn't trade— Well, Marcum, there's a girl I'd like to leave a last word for."

"Well?"

"Let me call the chief again and leave the word with him."

"Whyn't you call the girl and leave it with her?"

"I couldn't say it to her. Can't you see that? Besides, she's a visiting nurse and out on her rounds. I wouldn't know where to reach her. How about it, Marcum?"

"I guess not. In case things don't pan out right, the other cops can make up a story to tell her. She—"

"Aw, let him call," Eddins broke in. "The guy deserves a little consideration."

"You're a softy," Marcum growled. "You're thinking about that girl in Louisville. Oh, all right."

"Chief," said Kelly over the phone a minute later, "I want you to tell Nora not to feel too bad. In this game a man's got to take it. Tell her I did the best I could. And by the way, since I'm checking out, I might as well make my last report. When these fellows nabbed me, I was on my way to the eight hundred block on Webber Street to investigate a complaint about a kid with an air rifle. Seems he was in

123

one window shooting the panes out of another window across the street."

"Aw, cut it out," Marcum grumbled, and yanked him from the telephone. "Think we enjoy standing here listening to you being heroic?"

"I ain't feeling so heroic," Kelly said. He looked again at his watch, probably for the hundredth time. Seventeen minutes to go. No, sixteen. What a difference one minute made! He stole a glance at the window across the narrow alley. A good man with a rifle could pick off two men in the length of a heartbeat. There was a man named Kemp Ormsby on the force who was the second best rifle shot in the state.

At eleven minutes to four he sneaked another look at the window. Its very blankness seemed to gleam with promise. He was hot and cold by turns. Was that a shadow beyond the window? Had Ormsby had time to get down here from headquarters? Had the chief caught on? But it was foolish asking that, because even yet he could hear the chief saying, "Yeah, I get it."

"Go over there, Kelly, and pull that shade down."

He had been so engrossed that he hadn't noticed Marcum rise and move out of line with the window. Now Marcum pointed the automatic at him. Kelly rose, stumbled to the window, reached the cord, and pulled the shade down. He shook his head once, for beyond that other window he had glimpsed for one tantalizing moment Kemp Ormsby's white, strained face.

"Down good," Marcum said. "Clear to the sill." Kelly obeyed. Marcum threw a glance at Eddins. "Our detective got cute with us. Little boy with an air gun shooting from one window to another. I was dumb not to get it before."

Kelly gazed into the mirror and hardly recognized his own image. He wasn't nonchalant any more. His eyes seemed to have faded. The gray in his hair no longer gave him a distinguished touch; it merely made him look old. He felt weak all over, but weakest of all at the pit of his stomach. He guessed you always felt that way when your last forlorn hope was gone.

"Sit down," Marcum told him. "What time is it, George?"

"Eight minutes to four," Eddins said, in a voice that shook. "Wolfe! Wolfe, I'll take that drink now—no matter how small it is!"

Marcum took a half-pint bottle from his pocket and a glass from the bureau and measured the thimbleful Eddins had previously predicted. Eddins gulped it straight. "One more," he pleaded.

"No," said Marcum, and returned bottle and glass.

"Those damn cops," Eddins said. "Kelly was right. They ain't going to play ball. We'd heard by now. We—"

"You're forgetting," Marcum reminded him, "that the deadline is not till four. Seven minutes to go. Now get yourself—"

"But we said *by* four. If they were going to play ball, they'd of turned him loose right away. They wouldn't of waited. Bucky'd be out. He'd already of called us. We didn't say four on the dot."

"Ah, shut up," Marcum snapped. "I got enough on my hands with Kelly. Don't make it any harder for me, George."

There was a silence. Eddins lay back on the bed, shifted in a way reminiscent of a man unable to get to sleep, sat up, and lit another cigarette. Marcum, who had returned the automatic to his pocket, sat down and folded his hands across his considerable belly. Outside still sounded the hum of a city at work. Never had it seemed as sweet to Kelly. The clang of street cars, the growl of starting motors, the din of horns—they were all music; and he was hearing them for the last time.

He wasn't fooled any longer. Optimism was out. He'd played his string to the finish, had schemed and plotted, and had brought one scheme to the point of culmination only to see it explode in his face. He'd been lucky a long time. Now the breaks were running the other way. It was curtains for Kelly.

"Four minutes to four," came the thin, shrill voice of Eddins.

"Shut up, can't you?" Marcum said. "I can read time as well as you."

Marcum, too, was showing the strain. He took the bottle out again, looked at it, and after a moment of indecision returned it to his pocket. He glanced worriedly at young Eddins. All of a sudden he came to a decision.

"George, I was wrong to bring you into this. You're a lot younger'n me and life is sweeter to you. For me it don't make a hell of a lot of difference." He paused, then went on with difficulty: "If they burn Bucky—well, I'd just as soon be dead. That's why I was willing to take this gamble. But—in your case—hell, Bucky's not your brother. I was wrong. You can beat it if you want to, George."

"Let's both beat it!" Eddins cried. "Turn this guy loose and both of us beat it." Marcum shook his head savagely. He was one man, Kelly reflected, who didn't mind dying. "O.K., then," Eddins concluded. "I never run out on you before. I won't start now."

Marcum passed him the bottle. "Drink what you want," he said gratefully. "All of it if you like."

Kelly said: "You fooled me, George. I'd have thought a guy with the jitters wouldn't've jumped at the chance to—"

"Shut your mouth," Eddins said. "We came in this together, we'll go out together."

It was the whisky talking, Kelly knew, and he felt a fugitive sensation of pity for young Eddins. Doubtless Marcum had been smart enough to know what the whisky would do.

"Four on the dot," said Eddins.

Marcum's face slowly purpled with rage and disbelief and frustration. And in the silence that fell upon them, a silence like the weight of the world, Kelly heard a rustle, no louder than a whisper, in the hall outside. Tense, he waited and heard it again. Marcum caught it, too, and slewed round in his chair. Suddenly coming to his feet, he bounded half the distance to the door.

"You, out there!" he called. "If you start anything, Kelly goes out like a light."

"I want to hear Kelly's voice," came the answer. "I want to know you ain't already done him in."

"I'm here, Johnny," Kelly called.

"Marcum!" Johnny Mallon shouted through the door. "Marcum, you can't get by with it. I've got men enough—"

"But we got Kelly, see?" Marcum told him. "Listen, Johnny, we're coming out in just a minute. Make it a shooting match if you like. But my gun will be in Kelly's back and I gamble he'll go down first."

Kelly stood up. He had discovered that he could take it after all. It made little difference just what moment he died. His voice rang when he called: "Open up, Johnny. Break the door down. I'm going to die, anyway."

"We'll do this, Mallon," said Marcum quickly. "If you let us through, we'll take Kelly with us, but we won't hurt him. We'll turn him loose when we're safe. But if you try to follow us, we'll bump him and make a run for it. Want to trade with us, Mallon?"

"He's lying!" Kelly shouted. And, from the savage glow in Marcum's eyes, he knew that was the truth. He could see the killer light in Marcum's gleaming eyes. Marcum had played a desperate gamble and lost, but he would cash at least one chip before the game ended. "He's lying!" Kelly shouted again. "Break the door down, Johnny. I'm your superior. I say break that door down!"

From unseen Johnny Mallon came something that sounded like a sob. "The hell with you being my superior. I can't do it. I can't murder you, Kelly."

"It's a trade, then, Mallon? It's a trade?" Marcum called triumphantly.

"Yes," came Mallon's voice, "it's—a—trade."

"It ain't!" Kelly raged. "It ain't, because I don't agree to it. Get this, Johnny. You're so dumb— Hell, you're dumber than you were out on Dulaney Street. That's going some. Listen, Johnny, I'll give you ten minutes to get going on that door. Ten minutes, you hear?"

*"You'll* give him ten minutes?" Marcum marveled. "Say, who you think is running this show?"

"Shut your mouth!" Kelly was beside himself with rage. His voice rose in thunderous imprecations. The veins in his forehead threatened to burst. Sweat rolled off his brow. Again and again he ordered Mallon to break the door down. Finally he came to a weary, reluctant pause and glared at Marcum. "The coward," he whispered.

A new voice spoke beyond the door, the dry voice of Kemp Ormsby: "That was a swell description you gave of Johnny, but he didn't hear it. He's gone to get more reserves. We're going to hold this place till Marcum gives you up if it takes till Christmas."

Rage mottled Marcum's face. "So that's the game. Well, when you give him his orders, Kelly, with all that ranting and cussing, you signed your own death warrant."

Kelly, sparring desperately for time, said: "I thought you were the guy who didn't mind dying. Wolfe Marcum, the guy without fear!"

Marcum brought the automatic up slowly, an inch at a time. Eddins shifted, put his own gun back into his pocket, and used both shaking hands to steady the bottle as he drained the last drop. Marcum's eyes held Kelly's, and Kelly knew that the payoff had come. The relatively small aperture that was the muzzle of the automatic loomed larger and larger. Clammy hands seemed to fasten on Kelly's throat. He saw the second knuckle of Marcum's trigger finger grow white as the finger tightened.

The noise of the suddenly released shade whipping to the top of the window was like an explosion. Kelly flung himself out of line. Even then Marcum's shot plowed his side. One shot sounded from the window. But Kelly was too busy hurling himself on Eddins and subduing him to look around. Finally, after he had knocked Eddins half senseless with a punch to the jaw, he lurched to his feet and faced Johnny Mallon.

Very matter of fact, Mallon snapped handcuffs on the dazed Eddins. Ormsby and half a dozen other policemen came through the shattered door. Mallon indicated Marcum on the floor with a jerk of his thumb. "Ambulance for him. Damn it, I shot too high. He's out

127

now, but he'll live to join Brother Bucky in the chair." For the first time he appeared to notice Kelly. "Fancy meeting you here."

"You came damned near being too late," Kelly complained.

Ormsby crossed the room, leaned out, and regarded the ladder leaning against the outside wall. "Well, you had better luck with the window than I did," he observed with his customary dryness.

Mallon looked at Kelly. "I got good fast legs."

"They're dandies," Kelly gravely agreed.

"Took me less'n five minutes to sprint half a block down to the fire department, get a ladder, and sprint back." He paused. Then: "And ain't I got a good memory, son?"

"You got the best in the world."

"Memory?" Ormsby asked blankly.

"Sure," said Kelly. "That time on Dulaney Street I reminded him of —well, one time when Johnny and I were rookies, some old dame went batty out on Dulaney and locked herself in a room. Instead of breaking the door down, Johnny got cute and put a ladder to her window thinking to surprise her. She laid his head open with a flat-iron."

Kelly put his hand inside his shirt and it came away wet and sticky. But the wound amounted to little. Just a crease. Still, he was glad the blue-eyed girl in the West End was a nurse, because he planned to let that crease along his ribs make him sick for a week at least.

"No curtains for Kelly," he whispered. "Lord, Lord!"

# Cut Glass

*by Frederick Arnold Kummer, Jr.*

Lopez walked slowly; there was, he decided, no especial need for haste. Even if there had been, a hurrying pedestrian on Hilton Street would have seemed out of place, for the few people on that murky thoroughfare appeared to slip in and out of the shadows with silent ease.

A dim light in the next block attracted his attention. That would be Abelson's shop. Unconsciously he quickened his pace, and almost before he knew it, he was standing in front of the window. With great caution he bent down and glanced into the little basement store. Seated behind the counter was a man, the light from a green-shaded lamp giving his face a deathlike hue. Lopez opened the front door and descended the steps. As he entered, old Abelson looked up, his gnarled features twisting into crooked smile.

"So it's you," he croaked, rubbing his hands nervously. "I was beginning to think you would never get here!"

Lopez lit a cigarette.

"Ready?" he asked.

Abelson fumbled with his wallet, extracted a slip of paper.

"Here is the combination," he whispered, stepping from behind the counter.

Lopez glanced up at the street; it was deserted. From beneath his left arm he drew a heavy automatic, gripped it by the barrel. The jeweler bent his head; his face was tense.

"Gently now," he cautioned.

With an easy motion Lopez swung the weapon. Abelson silently crumpled to the floor, blood seeping from his forehead. At once his assailant knelt beside him, felt his pulse. The old man would have a headache tomorrow, he reflected. The blow had been a bit too hard.

Satisfied as to Abelson's injury, Lopez turned toward the safe. With the combination in his hand, it was a matter of seconds only until the iron door yielded to his touch. As he peered into the dark interior, fear and anger swept over him. The safe appeared to be empty.

Then, in one of its many compartments, he noticed a familiar object—a slender leather case with gold letters stamped upon it. Smiling, Lopez picked up the box and opened it. A row of diamonds gleamed dully in the pale green light. He slipped the case into his pocket and quickly turned toward the door.

Suddenly the sound of footsteps above froze him to the spot. A man's feet and legs appeared before the window.

A swinging night-stick caused sweat to ooze from Lopez's face. The policeman hesitated momentarily and Lopez's hand sought the butt of his gun.

Unconscious of his danger, the patrolman brushed a speck of dust from his sleeve and continued on his beat. Lopez stood still, for what seemed an age. Finally, the pounding of his heart and the officer's footsteps both died into silence. With the utmost caution, he ascended the stairs and stepped lightly to the sidewalk. Save for an occasional automobile, the street was empty.

When Lopez's feet touched the pavement, new life and assurance seemed to flow through his veins. Squaring his shoulders, he strolled along in his most jaunty manner.

It had been a good night's work, he decided, and delightfully simple. Possibly he and Abelson could try it again, with higher stakes. It had, of course, cost them each ten G's to buy the bracelet. Yet Abelson would get the fifteen grand theft insurance; while he, Lopez, would receive about the same amount for the diamonds.

Since they were now hot ice, Speer, the fence, would scarcely give more than that. At the same time, fifteen thousand for ten made a profitable investment, especially when it entailed so little risk. Lopez hummed to himself and patted the slight bulge in his pocket. The diamonds would not go to Speer until the end of the week. Abelson had made him promise that. The old man had been afraid to have them in circulation until the insurance money was paid. Well, he could afford to wait. Unlike most things, diamonds were constant in their value.

Lopez glanced at his watch. The hour was twelve-thirty. It would do him good to go to bed early, he decided. There had been too much fun of late, especially since he had been going around with Myra. He would take things easy tonight and celebrate with her tomorrow. They would make it a big evening. He waved to a passing taxi. The driver snapped out of his coma and ground to a stop.

"Guilford Apartments!" Lopez smiled pleasantly as he entered the cab.

The next morning Lopez slept late; it was after twelve o'clock when he arose. Donning a dressing gown, he unlocked the apartment door and picked up his newspaper. The robbery, he noticed with pride, had been given headlines. Automatically his eyes ran down the column: "Abelson described the man as being a large burly individual with a deep voice."

Lopez gazed in a mirror at his small sleek person. The jeweler, he reflected, was making the game doubly safe.

Like a child with a new toy, Lopez went over to his bed and drew the leather case from beneath his pillow. Returning to the window, he held the bracelet up to the sunlight, revelling in its sparkle, the very feel of the stones. Suddenly the bit of jewelry slipped from his grasp and fell, sliding across the glass top of his desk. Idly Lopez glanced at the smooth surface; it was not scratched.

For a moment his eyes dimmed, as though the black cloud of rage which rose within him had obscured his view. Seizing the bracelet, he rubbed it vigorously over the glass. No marks appeared upon the

130

desk-top. Shaking with fury, Lopez began to dress as fast as his trembling fingers would permit.

The rat! The dirty double-crossing rat! Not only would he get the insurance, but the diamonds as well! Lopez's mind was a maze of dark twisted thoughts.

Bitterly he reflected on his own stupidity. Abelson's little scheme was horribly clear to him now.

As a jeweler, Abelson had had no difficulty in making this imitation of the real bracelet—the one they had bought together at Brongier's. This, then, was why he had insisted that the stones were not to be taken to a fence until the insurance money had been paid.

As soon as he received the fifteen grand, he would have left town, left him, Lopez, with a bit of cut glass in exchange for his ten G's.

Murderously Lopez thought of the previous evening. How he wished he could swing his gun butt at Abelson's head once more! A thin cruel smile on his lips, he gazed a moment at the automatic before placing it in his shoulder holster. Then, tossing the bracelet carelessly in his pocket, he strode into the front hall. As though in a trance, he ran down the steps, through the front door. A single thought kept pounding through his brain. He, the wise guy, the con man, had been taken by a jeweler, an amateur! The blow to his pocketbook was severe—but that could be replaced. The blow to his pride was infinitely more serious. If this were to reach the ears of the "boys," he would be the joke of every bar, every "hot spot" along the main stem. Like many small men Lopez's ego was greatly out of proportion to his size.

Fifteen minutes of steady walking found him in front of a dingy little building; its faded sign read, "J. Speer, Importer." Lopez pushed open the creaky door and entered. A large man with the look of a moth-eaten vulture was gazing through a magnifying glass at an emerald ring. On seeing Lopez, he slipped the ring into his pocket and grinned cadaverously.

"Hiya, Tony!" he said.

"Okay," Lopez answered briefly. Taking the bracelet from his coat pocket, he laid it on the table. "I think this ice is phony. Let me know if I'm right."

Speer picked up the bracelet, disappeared into a back room. Five minutes later he returned, chuckling to himself.

"What've you been doing?" he demanded. "Heisting the five-and-dime? This isn't even a good imitation!"

Lopez snatched it from him.

"I just wanted to make sure!" he said, his voice dangerously soft. "So long, Joe!"

All that day Lopez remained in his room, drinking and thinking. From a tangle of ideas one thought resolved itself. Above everything else, he must get the bracelet—and in doing so "get" Abelson as well. Lopez had never killed a man before; his methods were usually more suave, more subtle, as becomes a con man and swindler. The gun had been bought for an emergency. This was it.

Nightfall found him once more walking through the mottled shadows of Hilton Street. As he strolled along the gloomy avenue, a vague foreboding of disaster stole over him. Laughing almost audibly at himself, he loosened the gun in its holster; the feel of its rough grip gave him new courage.

When Lopez descended the steps, old Abelson's wrinkled visage contracted into a frown; a suspicious light gleamed in his yellow eyes.

"What do *you* want?" he snarled at his visitor.

Lopez assumed a furtive, hunted look. "I'm in trouble," he muttered. "I gotta have help. Let's go back into your office. Someone might come in." To complete the illusion, he glanced over his shoulder.

Abelson's face bore a puzzled expression; for a moment he thought, then led the way to his private office. With a somewhat pompous manner, he seated himself behind his desk and looked up at Lopez.

"Well," he demanded, "what is it?"

Lopez kicked the door shut and, drawing his automatic, shot Abelson through the chest. The old man rose halfway from the chair; his clutching hands knocked to the floor several books and a green glass vase which broke into bits. Panic-stricken, Lopez fired again. This time the jeweler fell limply across his desk. For a moment Lopez stood still, listening.

Carefully, he wiped the automatic with his handkerchief and threw it on the floor. Bullets and guns were so easily identified with one another that it was folly to keep a gun after having used it in a murder. Long before he had filed the serial numbers off the weapon.

He stepped over to the desk; there was no sound except the crackle of glass beneath his feet and the dripping of Abelson's blood. The steady pit-pat of the latter did strange things to Lopez's nerves. It seemed to grow louder and louder until it filled the room with its booming; then it would fade away only to return louder than before.

With an effort Lopez regained control of himself. Wrapping his hand in the handkerchief, he went through the old man's pockets.

Since these smart coppers had learned how to get finger prints from cloth, you had to use the greatest care. This cautious search was, however, not a lengthy one. From Abelson's vest pocket he drew the real bracelet, a strip of glowing white fire. Its beauty dazzled Lopez, drove all fear from his brain. Placing it in his own pocket, his hand encountered the false piece of jewelry. With a contemptuous laugh he tossed the glass bracelet upon the desk beside the dead man and turned to go.

Carefully stepping to avoid those dark stains upon the floor, he walked into the front room. As he did so, two blue clad legs and a swinging night-stick passed by the window. Lopez cringed against the wall. Was he seeing things! The same cop up there! With twitching fingers he rubbed his eyes. When he looked again, the figure was gone, but the echoing footsteps proved that it had been no vision. Silently Lopez waited. He seemed to hear strange noises from the other room; a mad desire to drown them out seized him. If he could only sing or whistle! Fear gripped him. Rushing up the steps, he once more gained the street.

Lopez took a deep breath. Boy, the air felt good! It was so cool, so fresh. Why that crazy shop seemed to be miles away, years in the past. It had nothing to do with him; he was a free man. No one could connect him with the killing. If you were smart and left no clues, you could get away with almost anything. Some men made careless mistakes. Some boasted to women. Not Lopez—he was too careful for that.

A young couple were walking toward Lopez. They were too lost in one another to notice him. Pretty girl, Lopez thought. How frightened she would be if she knew that she had brushed against a murderer! For a moment he wished he could tell her, just to hear what she would say. Being a woman she would probably look at him skeptically and ask, "So what?" Lopez chuckled. Women were strange—even Myra. She was so assured, so indifferent, that he could not help loving her—as much as it was possible for him to love anyone.

He turned into Seventeenth Street. The rows of dancing, multicolored lights pleased him with their cheerful glow. He would go to Rossiter's, meet Myra, and drink wine. He would forget everything that had taken place—the dicks would never know. Why should they suspect him? Wasn't he a friend of Abelson's? He found it hard to realize himself. Had it not been for the bracelet in his pocket, he might have swept the whole affair into oblivion like a mad dream.

Tomorrow he would exchange the ice for cash and then go away. The West Indies would be a good trip—maybe Myra might go with him.

Lopez looked up. The big red sign of Rossiter's restaurant winked ahead. As he drew near, he could see the show window with its pyramids of bottles. Italian wine, German beer, Scotch whisky, all glistening in the soft, warm lights of the store. They whispered of travel, adventure, romance. Lopez smiled and opened the door. Inside it would be pleasant, devoid of shadows, mental or actual.

Myra was waiting for him, her cool young beauty as soothing to his raw nerves as April rain.

"I bought a bottle of Chianti," she smiled at him. "Your favorite brand."

Lopez tossed down a glassful, then another. There was a leaden weight in his brain—lead—like bullets. The caressing glow of the wine would melt that—burn it from his mind. Myra was talking, her rich, low voice giving some trivial incident the sound of music. What she was saying did not matter; the nearness of her, the melody of her voice, was all that he wanted.

Mentally he went over the murder, step by step. There had been no slip, no mistake. He had thought of everything. Lopez drank deeply and dismissed the whole affair from his thoughts. He must tell Myra how lovely she looked, ask her about the trip.

It was about one o'clock when the newsboy came in. Lopez, on his second bottle, was feeling very expansive.

"Here, son," he handed the boy a quarter. "Keep the change."

Lopez hurriedly read the report of Abelson's murder. "Jeweler Shot, Stolen Bracelet Returned. Police today are mystified by the murder of Solomon Abelson, Hilton Street jeweler. Last night Abelson was attacked and robbed of a twenty-thousand dollar bracelet. Early this evening his body was found by Patrolman Joseph Eberts, in the back room of his store. The bracelet was lying beside him and . . ."

"What's wrong?" Myra asked. "You look so funny."

"Friend of mine got bumped," Lopez answered casually.

At that instant a hand fell upon his shoulder. Lopez glanced up into the blue eyes of Detective-Sergeant Murphy. For a second there was a sick feeling in the pit of his stomach; the room seemed to whirl. This dick couldn't know! Couldn't!

"What's the trouble?" Murphy smiled. "Guilty conscience about one of those con games of yours?"

Lopez took a deep breath, forced a laugh. "Ever since they transferred you to the Homicide Squad," he said, "you don't worry me. Have a shot of ink!"

"Thanks." Murphy sat down and removed his hat, grinning bashfully at Myra. "Just finished the night's work on that Abelson job. He was a friend of yours, Tony—can you help us out on the case?"

Lopez bit his lip to keep from laughing. This was a riot! That dumb dick asking *him* for help! In a way he felt sorry for Murphy. He was a nice guy but so stupid! A plodder with no brilliance, no finesse. He, Lopez, was his absolute opposite.

"Sorry, Murph," he answered. "I'd give anything to find out who opened my old pal Abelson—but I haven't the slightest idea. There's plenty of smart guys in the prowl racket who might have done it. The same one who stuck him up last night, maybe. Abelson said he was a big, tough guy. But why he'd return the ice beats me."

The detective took a swallow of wine. "Just found out," he said, "that the bracelet we found is phony. A dizzy case! Doubt if we ever land the mug who shot him!"

Lopez leaned back, crossed his legs. "You shouldn't feel discouraged, Murph," he said genially. "Every one of these killers makes a mistake somewhere. You'll probably catch up with him sooner or later."

Murphy's gaze swept Lopez from his shiny black shoes to his shiny black hair. Suddenly he bent over and brushed at Lopez's lapel.

"Spider on your coat," he explained. "Well, I reckon I'll mosey along. After thinking over that case all evening, my brain needs rest. Thanks for the drink."

In his embarrassed, awkward manner he nodded to Myra and slipped out into the night. Chuckling, Lopez watched him go. The irony of the situation had delighted him, tickled his vanity. Maybe after he sold the stones he would anonymously send Murphy a little piece of change. Poor devil, he deserved it—losing sleep over a case he could never solve. Lopez turned once more to Myra.

"We've got a lot of fun ahead of us, baby," he whispered. "Life comes easy when you're smart."

After leaving Myra at her apartment, Lopez was troubled once more by shadows. One in particular seemed to be following him. He could see it out of the corner of his eyes, but when he turned around it was gone. With an exclamation, he hailed a cab.

Once inside the familiar lobby of the Guilford Apartments, he grinned to himself. Decidedly his nerves were in bad shape! A grown

135

man seeing things! It was ridiculous! Too many cigarettes, too little exercise. That trip now, would do him lots of good.

Glancing at his watch, he started up the stairs. Three o'clock! No wonder the place was quiet!

The steps creaked noisily. Kinda like the ones in Abelson's shop, he reflected. Must stop thinking of that—it was all over now. Think about Myra. It would be wonderful to marry her. No more being alone. That's what the trouble was—being alone.

He whistled loudly as he entered his room. Things seemed better with the lights on. He threw his coat over a chair, slipped off his shoes. The empty holster had been tossed in an ashcan on the way uptown. He was playing safe, making sure of everything. A wave of exultation rose within him. He was revenged upon Abelson. He had the bracelet. And he had fooled the coppers.

For a complete triumph one could ask nothing more.

Lopez was just loosening his tie when the knock came at the door. He stood still, a tight feeling in his throat. Hot blood pounded through his temples, roared in his ears.

Stiffly he walked to the door, pulled it open.

Murphy's shy grin broke the tension. He stepped hesitantly into the room.

"Sorry to bother you, Tony," he apologized. "Just wanted to see something. After I left you I bought a magnifying glass—regular Sherlock Holmes stuff. Look."

Lopez stared uncomprehendingly at him; his bewildered mind raced in circles. Murphy strolled over the bedside, picked up Lopez's smart, black shoes. While examining them through the glass, he kept on talking.

"Noticed something shiny in one of your rubber heels," he said. " 'Member you were sitting with your legs crossed? When you pulled that crack about every killer making a mistake, I got to thinking."

He paused a moment, chuckled. "Brushing that 'spider' off your lapel gave me a chance to see that your holster was empty—and people don't strap on empty ones just to go out and have a few drinks. Don't chuck them in ashcans, either, 'less there's a reason. . . ."

Instinctively, Lopez poised himself for a spring. His flat black eyes, however, telegraphed the message. Murphy drew his gun, twirled it carelessly on his finger.

Lopez took a step backwards, glaring. "An empty holster's no proof!" he muttered defiantly.

"Mebbe not," Murphy drawled, "but y'see when Abelson got

bumped, a green cut glass vase was smashed. Cut glass is your jinx, I guess—you got some pieces of it in the heel of your shoe!

"Funny," he went on reflectively, "this afternoon I was helping one of my kids with his homework—all about a Greek guy named Achilles. That's what gave me the idea. His weak spot was his heel, too . . ."

For an instant Lopez stared at the shoes. Suddenly, very bitterly, he laughed.

# Damsel with a Derringer

*by Stephen Dentinger*

Sergeant Connie Trent had been driving back to headquarters from an arson investigation when she heard the report of a woman with a gun on her police radio. Facing her now in the foyer of Byron Cheviet's waterfront apartment, she thought a more apt description might have been a damsel with a derringer. The girl was blond, blue-eyed and very young—the sort poets see in their dreams—and the tiny gold-plated derringer pistol looked not at all out of place in her small hand. It seemed perfect for the occasion.

"Sergeant Trent, police," Connie identified herself, holding up her ID case. "Give me the gun before someone gets hurt."

"I've come to kill Cheviet," the girl announced, "and you're not going to stop me!"

Connie's hand was resting on the shoulder bag with her own pistol inside, but she was reluctant to draw it. Derringers were notoriously inaccurate, yet at this range the girl could hardly miss. If shooting broke out, one or both of them could end up dead.

"Suppose you give me the gun and we talk about it," Connie suggested calmly, moving another careful step forward as she spoke. She knew another squad car would be arriving momentarily, and that might bring a delicate situation to a head. "Why are you so anxious to kill him?"

137

"Because he killed my father! He sent him a bottle of poisoned wine!"

"All the more reason for us to talk. If you can prove what you're saying I'll arrest this man here and now. But you won't make things any better by shooting him." Connie was within reach now and she slowly stretched out her hand till it was almost touching the weapon. "Or me, for that matter."

The girl jumped a little at the sudden sound of a siren in the street. Connie's hand grabbed the derringer, deflecting it to one side just as it went off. Then she twisted the weapon free and pinned the girl against the wall. A door opened behind them and a middle-aged man stood there looking terrified.

"Did you get her?" he asked. "My God—she tried to kill me!"

"Are you Byron Cheviet?" Connie asked.

"I am. I'm pleased to see the police have this matter under control."

"Next time you hear a gunshot, don't open your door right away. You might get yourself killed."

"I'll remember that," he replied.

The girl's name was Clare Grody and she cried all the way to police headquarters. Captain Leopold was taking one of his rare vacation days, and Lieutenant Fletcher suggested she use Leopold's office for the questioning rather than the drab interrogation room down the hall. "She's just a kid," he said, looking across the room at her tear-streaked face. "How old is she?"

"Nineteen. She's home from college this week."

"Go easy on her. Her father's death obviously shook her up."

Finally, relaxed a bit in the worn leather armchair in Leopold's office, Clare Grody agreed to make a statement. "My father, Sam Grody, died yesterday. He and Cheviet were partners with a man named Russell in a large real estate development scheme. Cheviet sent him a bottle of French wine for his birthday a few days ago. I fixed dinner for my father last night and he decided to open the wine. He poured some for me too, but before I could taste it he became violently ill. I called an ambulance and had him rushed to the hospital. By the time we got him there he was dead."

"You say the wine came from Cheviet? Are you certain?"

The girl nodded. "After it arrived by messenger father phoned Cheviet to thank him for it. The bottle was an especially good 1975 Bordeaux. And then it killed him!" Tears came to her eyes once more. "As soon as the doctors confirmed it was poison, I went home and got out a set of gold-plated derringers he kept in his study. I sat there and

138

thought about it all night, but this morning I loaded one and went to Cheviet's apartment."

"What did he say when you accused him?"

"He denied it, of course! He slammed the door in my face and phoned the police. But there'd been trouble among the three of them before."

"Your father and Cheviet and Russell?"

She nodded. "Father suspected someone was cheating him. They're partners in a venture to build a big shopping mall north of the city."

Connie picked up the phone and pressed the button for Fletcher's line. When he came on, she asked, "What have we got on this Grody poisoning?"

"Beckett's out at the hospital now, talking to the doctor. We don't have the autopsy report yet but it appears to have been some fairly fast-acting poison. We're analyzing the rest of the wine."

"Has anyone questioned Cheviet yet?"

"Beckett was going to head over there from the hospital. You want to take it instead?"

"I might as well."

Connie hung up and turned back to Clare Grody. "All right, your lawyer will probably have you out on bail in a few hours. Go home and behave yourself. I'll have a talk with Byron Cheviet."

Sam Grody's business partner remembered her from that morning. "You're the one who saved my life," Cheviet said, leading her into his spacious penthouse living room overlooking Long Island Sound. She noticed he had a monkish bald spot on the back of his head. "That crazy girl would have killed me!"

Connie Trent sat down. The apartment was furnished in a mod style, with several pop art paintings on the walls. Expensive, but not her taste. "Mr. Cheviet, Clare Grody says the bottle of wine that poisoned her father came from you. Is that true?"

"Of course not! I had no reason to want him dead!"

"She seems to think you did. Something about a real estate deal—a shopping mall—involving a third man named Russell."

"Ernest Russell. Yes, he's our partner. And you might as well know that the bottle of wine I sent to Grody originally came from Russell. He and his wife brought it when they came over for dinner last week. I needed something for Sam's birthday and I knew he'd like it."

"The very same bottle?"

Cheviet hesitated only an instant. "Yes. It wasn't a vintage I cared for too much."

"Grody's daughter said it was a very good Bordeaux."

The balding man was silent for a moment. Finally he said, "All right, I may as well tell you. I changed the label. Russell brought me a 1976 Bordeaux. I happened to know 1975 was a better year for that wine so I soaked off the label and replaced it with a '75 label I'd kept from an earlier bottle. It was the same vineyard, and I figured Grody would be impressed with the year without really noticing the inferior quality. It was a bit of a joke, you see."

"Only Brody didn't die laughing."

"I swear I didn't know the bottle was poisoned! Why would Russell and his wife want to poison me?"

Connie Trent got to her feet and closed her notebook. "That's what I intend to find out. Thanks for your help, Mr. Cheviet. I think I'd better call on Ernest Russell next."

"Miss Trent?"

"Yes?"

"Don't tell him I changed the label."

On her way to Russell's home Connie telephoned Fletcher and learned that Clare Grody had indeed been released on bail. She called the Grody apartment and told the girl, "Cheviet claims he got the poisoned wine from Ernest Russell last week. I'm on my way there now. What can you tell me about him? Would he have had a motive for killing Cheviet or your father?"

Clare Grody hesitated, then said, "He's the third partner in the shopping mall project, of course. He did have a violent argument with my father at Christmas time, when I was home, but I thought they'd patched it up. The terms of the corporation are such that if one of the three partners dies the other two can buy his share of the business back for just what he originally invested. That would be a low price now, with much of the work completed. Viewed in that light, Russell would have a motive for killing either Cheviet or my father."

"Thank you," Connie said. "I'll get back to you."

Ernest Russell met her at the front door of his expensive brick ranch home, with his wife right behind him. He was middle-aged and running to overweight. She was young and sleek, with brown hair and matching eyes. Connie suspected she was the second Mrs. Russell.

"Come in, Sergeant Trent," Russell said, leading her to a sunken living room with plush overstuffed couches. "This is Helen, my wife. Tell us how we can help you."

Connie sat down, crossed her legs and opened her notebook. "Naturally you've heard about Samuel Grody's death. We expect the autopsy to confirm that he died from drinking a bottle of poisoned

140

wine—a Bordeaux which was a birthday gift from Byron Cheviet. Now Cheviet says it was the same bottle you brought to his house when you came to dinner last week."

"That old fox! Passing our bottle on to Sam as a gift!"

"The point, Mr. Russell, is that the bottle was poisoned," Connie reminded him.

Russell and his wife exchanged glances. "You'd better tell her, Honey," Helen Russell suggested.

"All right," He nervously lit a cigar. "That bottle came to us as a gift. It was delivered by messenger service a few weeks ago, on New Year's Eve."

"Who sent it?"

"The card with it was simply signed *From an admirer.* It caused a bit of a stir around this house, I'll tell you." He looked ruefully at his wife. "Helen thought it came from another woman."

"Darn right I did! I even phoned the messenger service to find out who paid to have it delivered. They'd received a call to pick it up at a hotel checkroom and deliver it here. No one remembered much about the order, and payment for the delivery had been in an envelope attached to the bottle. The only name they had was one given over the telephone—Melody Sugar."

Connie frowned. "A woman?"

"Either a woman or a race horse," Helen Russell said dryly. "It sounds like the name of a showgirl."

"I swear I don't know any Melody Sugar," Russell insisted.

"So you said." His wife moved to a small bar at one end of the sunken living room and began fixing herself a drink.

"Anyway, with Helen so upset about the gift there was no chance of our drinking it," Russell told Connie. "We kept it in our wine rack a few weeks and then I took it over to Cheviet's place last Thursday."

Connie was doodling something in the margin of her pad. "Is it possible . . . ?" she began, but was interrupted by the door chimes. Helen Russell went to answer them.

"What was your question?" Russell asked, drawing on his cigar.

Before Connie could ask it again there was a screech from the front door. Helen Russell was shoved to one side and Connie saw Clare Grody run into the room. There was a tiny derringer pistol in her right hand.

Connie rose unsteadily to her feet, letting the notebook slide to the floor. She had the decided feeling she'd been through all this before, just a few hours earlier. Clare had mentioned a pair of derringers, of course, and Connie should have remembered that before Clare was released on bail.

"Don't be foolish all over again," she said sharply. "Put that down!"

"Not this time! I've got the right person now—the man who poisoned my father! When I got to remembering that fight they had, I realized I should have known it all along."

Connie Trent stepped toward her, moving into the line of fire. "Ernest Russell didn't poison your father, Clare, and neither did Byron Cheviet."

"Then who did?"

Connie let out her breath. This part would be difficult. "The poisoned bottle was sent here by someone who used the name Melody Sugar to have it delivered. The bottle went from here to Cheviet's apartment last week, where he soaked off the label and substituted one from a better vintage year. That was the bottle he sent to your father for his birthday."

"I'll be damned," Russell said softly.

"Don't you see, Clare?" The poisoned bottle arrived here only a week after your father and Russell had their fight at Christmas. It wasn't Russell trying to kill your father. It was your father trying to kill—"

"No!" she screamed. "That's a lie!"

"—to kill Ernest Russell. He tried to murder Russell, but the bottle was passed on to Cheviet instead. It was re-labelled and returned to your father. With a different label he never realized it was the same bottle. He waited for Russell's death all these weeks, and it must have been a terrible shock when he drank the wine and realized in his dying moment that it was the bottle he'd poisoned."

Clare Grody stood shaking her head. "I don't believe it."

"He poisoned himself, Clare. Nobody else did it."

The gun wavered in her hand. There were tears in her eyes. "I can't believe that about father."

"Believe it, Clare," Connie insisted. "The poisoner had to disguise his identity somehow. Your father pulled a name out of the air. Perhaps it was a name he'd used before, or discovered in playing with the letters of his own name. Perhaps subconsciously he really wanted to be discovered. Don't you see—Melody Sugar is an anagram for Samuel Grody. They're really the same person."

Then she reached out and took the gun from Clare's hand.

# The Dead Go Overboard

*by Fenton W. Earnshaw*

A few yards to starboard the bell buoy clanged in solemn, broken cadence. Gus Draper strained brooding eyes to catch a glimpse of it, but the fog was too thick.

The dank white mist shrouded the buoy as completely as it had hidden Balport's rock jetties astern. The boat lifted easily in the ground swells and slid with a hiss into the following troughs of leaden water. Gus waited until the unmeasured banging of the buoy's iron clappers was well astern. Then with a glance at his watch, he put the wheel over and set a course for Clemente Bank.

He turned finally to stare aft where Andy Hill was working on the trammel net. The young man's lank figure was barely visible in the fog which clung to the deck of the Monterey fisherman. A tall, blurred form moving about in heavy sea boots and thick wool jersey.

Gus felt his lips tremble involuntarily, and he steeled himself against a shudder that ran like a current through his massive frame. Turning quickly, he tried to concentrate on the impenetrable path ahead.

Seconds later he started as Andy's hand fell upon his shoulder.

"All set, Gus," Andy said. "I'll see if the coffee's hot."

"Yeah, you see," Gus answered. He didn't trust himself to say more.

Andy brushed past and stooped to enter the tiny cabin. In a minute he was back with two steaming cups. Gus took one with a grunt and swallowed deeply. It burned his throat, but he hardly noticed it.

Andy stood beside him, staring into the gray nothingness of sea and air. "It's thick, all right," he said. "But I'll bet it lifts by noon." He hesitated. "Say, Gus, I'll take her out. You get some sleep. You look tired."

Gus slid away from the wheel willingly. "I am," he said. "I am tired. Thanks, Andy. I'll get some sleep."

But when he'd curled atop the port bunk below, Gus couldn't sleep. And he'd known he couldn't, because he wasn't tired. His mind was wide awake—so wide awake that every faculty was ten times keener than ever before.

So he lay quietly as the *Irma H* rocked herself out toward Clemente Bank. Once, Andy cut the throttle of the engine and touched the horn button. Gus came upright on the bunk and cried out.

"It's okay," Andy called in a minute. "Thought I heard another boat. Go back to sleep."

The exhaust stack above the cabin top coughed as Andy set the throttle again and the two-cylinder Hicks thumped into action. Gus listened to the steady, patient strokes.

*Get ready, get ready, get ready . . .*

He listened to the tantalizing rhythm so long that suddenly, despite himself, he shouted: "I am ready, damn you! I am!"

"What?" Andy called from the cab. "What'd you say?"

So he climbed from the bunk, cursing himself and wondering what Andy would think. "I was dreaming, I guess," he mumbled, going on deck. "And talking—" He let it trail.

"Well, it's time you were up, anyway," Andy said pleasantly. "I figure we're over the Flat. The swell's heavier. Shall we sound?"

Gus turned so that Andy couldn't see his trembling hands as he drew out his pocket watch and gazed at it.

"Yeah, this is it," he agreed. "Go drop the lead. I'll take the wheel."

Gus noted that the fog had lifted some. Not much. Not too much, he told himself. He closed the throttle and kicked the gear into neutral. The *Irma H* coasted several yards and then began to swing broadside to the swells.

There was a splash forward. Gus watched Andy pay out the lead line. Finally he had bottom and was hauling in. Gus plastered the woolen stocking cap lower on his head and moved out on deck. His boots thumped heavily on the fog-slicked wood.

Andy joined him. "We're on top, Gus," he announced. "Let's hope the halibut are waiting for us."

He bent to lift the grapnel which would anchor one end of the net they were about to sink. Gus stiffened and walked behind to the high-board coaming on the port side. His hairy hand closed firmly on the shark billy which hung there. Two feet of rounded oak, shaped for the hand, drilled at the core and loaded with lead.

Andy was still busy with the grapnel line. His back was turned. He was whistling tunelessly.

Gus took one full step and regripped the club with both hands. He raised it high above his head, crashed it down upon Andy's skull. The

144

boy crumbled to his knees. Gus beat a second time in fury. Without a murmur Andy's tall form fell headlong upon the nets.

Gus moved swiftly then. His face reflected openly everything that had burned so fiercely within his heart. He talked aloud to himself.

"The stick's not bloody, but I'll wash it."

Lifting a bucket of sea water from over the side, he doused the stick and scrubbed it with a brush. Then he dragged the body of Andy Hill from the nets and onto the deck, face up. Thrusting a horny hand beneath the sweater, he felt for any heartbeat.

"No," he said quietly, "he's dead."

Dead! Panic iced his blood. The first sense of guilt and fear struck at him sharply. He sought escape in action.

Springing aft to the litter of lines and nets, he dragged out a twenty-pound anchor. He hacked away the line. It was too heavy for his purpose. Then with his knife he slashed a length of smaller rope which he fastened to the anchor. With shaking hands he wound the rope about the body of Andy Hill.

He cursed the fog, cursed the confusion which made him fumble lubber-like as he tightened the knot. And when he finished, he wasn't satisfied. He snatched blindly at another rope-end from the coils draped over the coaming, and made it fast around Andy's waist.

Gus had lifted many a two-hundred-pound shark inboard. And so he found it easy to hoist Andy's body and the anchor to the gunwale. The body splashed dully overside. The anchor disappeared swiftly. Then the corpse was jerked downward out of sight in the gray water.

Carefully Gus looked about the deck. There was no blood on it, nor upon the nets. But, like the shark billy, he washed everything just the same. Finally he went below to take a drink and stare once at the picture of Mollie, Andy's wife.

It was nine o'clock when he started the Hicks. The propeller kicked a white whirlpool astern in the sullen water. Gus set a course for the Balport buoy and took another drink of whiskey.

He didn't look back. Not once. Everything was perfect. What lay ahead mattered. But Gus had figured that all out, too.

The engine thumped monotonously.

*It's done, it's done, it's done . . .*

Mollie would never guess. Or if she did, she'd never speak about it after they were married.

Married! His blood pumped warm again. He pictured Mollie with her flaming red hair and full red lips. An eager creature with an unquenched thirst for love.

And she had never loved Andy Hill. The only complication—the one thing that had stood between Mollie and Gus—had been Andy. Well, that was finished, Gus thought grimly.

A few weeks, months maybe, and then Mollie would be his. How natural, Gus reflected, that his dear, dear partner's wife should turn to him in her grief.

The clanging of the bell buoy two hours later brought Gus back to reality. He tore his mind from contemplation of the money he and Andy had banked jointly. With an effort he erased the picture of Mollie.

The throttle of the *Irma H* had been set full since he'd left the graveyard on Clemente Bank. Now Gus was suddenly aware of the stifling engine heat. The old mill hissed a protest against the fierce speed at which he had driven it. But that had been on purpose.

When he ran the boat alongside the harbor master's dock, every sign must bear out the story he would tell.

Two other fishing boats passed him in the channel. They appeared swiftly and swept by like ghosts, swallowed again in the fog. He used his horn, moving up the bay. There'd be little traffic except fishermen, so he didn't slacken speed.

Then ahead he made out a schooner anchored near the City Wharf. A minute later shapes along the shore—the Pavilion, the small-boat anchorage and the board walk—appeared in a patch of clear air.

At the top of the ramp which led from the float stood Tom Grandon, the Captain of the Harbor Police. Grandon was watching the *Irma H* nose in to the float. Gus felt himself grow taut as he reached out and cut the throttle.

It was like some strange nightmare then. The fog rolled away and as if by magic the bay was clear. The *Irma H* slid up against the dock. Tom Grandon seized the bow line and made it fast.

Gus jumped from the gunwale and ran to him.

"Oh, God! Andy Hill's drowned! He went overside and I didn't even hear him. The fog—the damned fog! I went back to find him but he—he was gone. His boots must have pulled him down!"

Gus paused breathlessly, eyes wide, and clutched at the captain's sleeve. Tom Grandon stared at him and then at the *Irma H.*

"Andy's drowned!" Gus repeated with a moan. "What'll I do? Think of poor Mollie! You got to help me, Grandon."

It was good; Gus knew it. The words and the way he threw them off were natural. If only Grandon would say something quick or shake

146

his head sympathetically or offer to take him home. If only he'd speak . . .

But Tom Grandon's eyes were still fixed upon the water. He turned back to Gus and Gus felt cold.

"I said you got to help me," he mumbled uncertainly.

The captain pivoted and called up the gangway. Two men came running from the office and down the ramp.

"He says Andy Hill fell overboard," Grandon began carefully. "Just where was it, Gus?"

Gus answered eagerly. "Clemente Bank. Maybe just before we got to the bank. He made coffee and we drunk it and then he went aft to work on the nets. He must have slipped overboard and his boots dragged him down."

Grandon still did not speak. Gus went on hurriedly: "I looked all over for two hours! I did everything I could!"

"Everything you could," Grandon repeated softly. "Tell me, Gus, why did you murder Andy Hill?"

Gus turned like one hypnotized and his eyes followed Grandon's, which were riveted on the water.

Astern of the *Irma H*, floating face downward, was the battered corpse.

Gus Draper couldn't understand how the anchor had gone adrift. But instantly he realized that the second piece of rope he had wrapped round Andy's waist had been fastened to the boat!


# Death Racket

### by Frederick Arnold Kummer, Jr.

Across the street pneumatic riveters roared an angry staccato chorus. Pawley's nerves, tight as piano wires, quivered in accompaniment. He bent over his desk, tried to work, but the figures were driven from his mind by the long, shuddering bursts of sound that made all his attempts at normal routine seem unreal. Sometimes he felt that the riveters were inside his head, pounding to get out.

Pawley walked to the window, ran his fingertips over a crack in the ancient woodwork of the sill. Old—of course, it was old. Fifty-odd

147

years since his father had built the place. It had done well, the past half-century. *The* Eastport House, in fact as well as in name. Age, dignity, had come to it as the town grew. Pawley thought of his father, in cutaway coat and top hat. Dinners in the old gas-lit dining-room, with the tinkle of glassware, the *frou-frou* of silk, the clop-clop-clop of carriage horses in the street. And now. . . .

Pawley glanced through the window at the network of girders thrusting toward the sky. To stand there, day after day, watching the new hotel inch its way upward! To stand there, helpless! Anderson, its builder, planned a ballroom, recreation center, cocktail lounge, a swimming pool. Everyone knew that the old Eastport House would have no chance to compete, that it was doomed to failure. Numb with despair, Pawley shook his head. Outside, the pneumatic riveters roared in wild, cackling laughter.

Like splinters of steel the sharp sound tore at his brain, tortured it. A strange picture began to form before his eyes. Anderson dying, his face twisted in agony. Anderson dead! Anderson dead! The jarring racket of the riveters took up the chorus. *Deaaaaaaaaaad! Deaaaaaaaaaaad!*

With Anderson staying here at the Eastport House, the thing would be easy. All that he needed was to establish an alibi and then . . . But the people in the other rooms would hear the shot! As though in answer, the pneumatic riveters ground out their savage chant. Pawley straightened up. *They'd* cover it—Anderson's own riveters! The irony of it moved him to flat, colorless laughter. They'd cover it—if—if someone wanted to commit a murder. Not that he, Pawley, would ever . . .

A fierce stuttering blare from outside deafened him. Fingers twitching, he picked at a bit of lint on his sleeve. Easy . . . it would be so easy. . . .

All night the harsh monotonous rhythm crowded the darkness. Pawley could see the sound as a row of black dots, dancing before his eyes. Feel it, stabbing relentlessly at his nerves. Hear it, pounding in his ears, keeping pace with his racing heart. At times the thundering cacophony would increase until it threatened to crush him, then dwindle away into faint pinpricks of sound, only to return louder than before. He tore at the sheets, vainly imploring the riveters to stop. That devil Anderson! If he were only dead. . . .

The next morning he was quite calm. Seated in the rococo lobby, he read his newspaper with slow determination. The furious rasping of the riveters made the small smoking stand beside him tremble. Pawley

148

smiled, nodded. The chattering machines were with him now. Friendly. They were going to drown out the sound of the shot, when he killed Anderson, who was planning to ruin him.

Pawley drummed his fingers upon the arm of his chair in time to the shattering blast. Yes, they were friendly now. . . .

At eleven o'clock Anderson came in to look over his mail. He took a sheaf of letters from Morgan, the desk clerk, and went to the elevators. Pawley, watching him, smiled. Then he, too, sauntered toward the desk.

"Hot, isn't it?" The clerk mopped his shiny face.

"Yes. Hot." Pawley raised his voice harshly to make himself heard above a renewed outburst from the riveters. "I'm going downstairs to check the liquor supplies in the storeroom. I'll be there if you want me."

"Yes, sir." Morgan nodded.

Pawley crossed the lobby, made his way through the dining-room, the kitchens. A nod to the cooks, busy with luncheon, and he was descending to the basement.

The supply-room was small, dark, filled with barrels of flour, sacks of potatoes, crates of canned goods, with liquor in demijohns, bottles on the shelves above. Pawley thought of the rainy afternoons when as a boy he had explored the cellars of the old hotel, discovering nooks and crannies all his own. This place had been forbidden territory then, but he had found a way to enter it. He moved a flour barrel, felt the rough wooden wall behind. There it was—the loose board leading to the tool closet in the engine-room. Smart. He was plenty smart! The cooks would swear that he had spent at least an hour in the supply-room, since there was no way out other than through the kitchen. No legitimate way. He would have plenty of time to go upstairs, attend to Anderson, and return unsuspected. He could hear the riveters jabbering their approbation. *Saaaaaaaaaafe! Saaaaaaaaaafe!*

Pawley wriggled through the opening. Tougher going than when he had been a kid. Now he was in the little closet near the entrance to the engine-room. He opened the door a crack and, seeing no one, stepped out. Up the narrow brick stairway to the first floor, the second! Another moment and he'd be at Anderson's door. Pawley moved along the hallway, chuckling. The riveters were sweeping toward a triumphant crescendo, now. They seemed to shake the entire building. Pawley shook, also, his face twitching. Just nerves. That damned shattering sound inside his head—churning his brain to a pulp. But soon Anderson, whom the riveters obeyed, would be dead, and they

149

would be stilled. First though, they must drown out the sound of the shot! That was the beautiful, the sardonic part of it!

Pawley glanced at the room numbers. 217 . . . 218 . . . 219 . . . Here! He leaned forward unsteadily, commenced to hammer on the panels. Hard—he'd have to knock hard because the riveters were so loud this morning—so deafening.

The knob turned and Anderson appeared on the threshold, round, red-faced, sweaty. "Well?" Anderson snapped. "What is it?"

"Business. We'll talk business." Pawley smiled inanely. "Just for a moment." He almost shouted the words so that Anderson could hear.

"O.K." Anderson shut the door. "Suppose you want me to buy you out," he grumbled. "Well, I'm up to my neck in grief now. These damned labor unions—"

Pawley stood still, listening. How furiously the riveters were pounding! No one would ever hear the shot!

"Hurry up!" Anderson said impatiently. "What's the proposition?"

Pawley snatched the gun from his pocket, fired. Anderson coughed gently, slid to the floor. Pawley stared at him a moment, fired again. Best to make sure. Another shot did not matter with that noise going on outside! Anderson, he thought, looked rather silly lying there. Fascinated, he watched the trickle of blood writhe like a red snake toward him. What was he supposed to do next? Oh, yes. Pawley bent down, took Anderson's watch and wallet from his pocket. Robbery, the police would think. He'd get rid of the things, along with the gun, later. And the window leading to the fire-escape was already open. Now he had only to go back to the storeroom and continue to check stock for the next hour or two. He moved toward the door, smiling. The roar of the riveters seemed suddenly to become mocking laughter.

Pawley's hand was on the knob when he heard voices, the sound of running feet in the corridor outside. For a moment he frowned, then shook his head. Nerves. Just nerves, of course—

The door of the room burst open. Morgan, followed by Wentzel, the house detective, appeared in the entrance.

"Mr. Pawley!" the clerk gasped. "Two-nineteen just phoned down that he heard shots and . . . Good God!" Wide-eyed, he stared at Anderson's body.

"No!" Pawley's voice rose to a scream. "He couldn't have heard any shots! Nobody could have! Don't you understand! Nobody could have! How would you expect them to, with those riveters hammering out there like mad! Listen to them, Morgan! Hammering! Hammering! Hammering! Can't you hear . . . ?"

150

A ghastly silence filled the room. Wentzel took a deep breath.

"Screwy," he whispered to Morgan. "Plumb nuts. Anderson's men are on strike. Them rivet gangs stopped work an hour ago."

# The Deer that Ate a Diamond

*by Edward D. Hoch*

The odd tale that I am about to narrate reached my ears at a small gathering of poets and editors in London in September of 1937. It was one of those delightfully pleasant evenings in late summer when old friends had returned from their holidays in the country and good conversation abounded. The weather was still warm enough so the large second-storey windows had been left open, and a gentle breeze had sent the lace curtains billowing.

There were about fifteen people present, and when I grew tired of the endless debates about the Spanish Civil War I'd broken off from the main group to chat with a young poet named Julian Symons who'd recently launched a magazine called *Twentieth Century Verse*. It was he who introduced me to Gabriel Gale, a visiting poet who supported himself by painting inn signs.

"Is this your first time here?" Gale asked, taking a sip of the drink he'd been holding. He was in his early forties, a slender man of better than average height and a friendly smile. He wore a grey suit that seemed a bit rumpled, perhaps from the train journey into the city.

"I came once in the summer," I replied, "but there was a very poor turnout."

"Yes, so many are away in the summertime."

"Tell me, do you live in the London area, Mr. Gale?"

"No, no. I do quite a bit of traveling, actually. Painting inn signs is a traveler's occupation."

"More suited to a gipsy, I would think." The remark was hasty and meant nothing, but Gabriel Gale took it up at once.

"In my younger days I was quite the radical firebrand, always defending lunatics and gipsies in a variety of causes."

151

"You must have some stories to tell."

Gale nodded. "The late poet Mr. Chesterton recounted some of my tales. I wish he were alive today."

"Why is that?"

We'd moved into a quiet corner of the room, and the others were ignoring us as they carried on their own conversation. "Just this past summer I had a most amazing adventure in the Suffolk countryside not far from the village of Boulge. I'd gone there to seek out the grave of the poet Edward Fitzgerald."

I smiled at that. "Didn't he call it one of the dullest and ugliest places in England?"

Gale's face brightened. "He did indeed! I'm glad to find a really literate person who's familiar with Fitzgerald. You know, Boulge today is a serene, thickly wooded countryside—quite beautiful, really. I had to walk up a sandy path through a stand of beechwoods to reach the wrought iron gates of the small Norman churchyard where he's buried. St. Michael and All Angels, it's called."

"What adventure could you have in a place like that?"

Gabriel Gale smiled. "Why, a poetic one, of sorts. After visiting Fitzgerald's graveside I drove on to the village itself. I've learned there are always inn signs in need of painting, and *The Brave Hart* was no exception. It was located at the village crossroads in a building that had been painted white so it could be seen from either direction, but the sign itself, with a red deer leaping a stream, had become hopelessly weatherbeaten. I stared up at it and saw a job waiting to be done . . ."

Gabriel Gale sought out the owner of *The Brave Hart*, a man named Thomas Splend who'd lived in the area all his life. He was a lanky, middle-aged fellow who stared up at the creaking sign swaying in the wind and confessed, "You know, I never look at it. Now that you point it out, Mr. Gale, it certainly does need to be repainted. But that's a job for an artist."

"I am an artist," Gale responded. "My materials are in the car. I could undertake the job for a reasonable fee and I guarantee the result will be better than the original."

After a bit of dickering it was decided that he should do the job, beginning the following morning. He would be put up at the inn for the length of his stay, estimated at about three days, and receive an agreed-upon sum if the work was satisfactory.

"So you're a painter," Splend said as they shook hands on the deal.

"Actually I'm a poet," Gale replied, "but there is very little money in poetry these days. There is little money in painting, either, unless one has the talent and the temperament for painting inn signs."

In the morning, after a hearty breakfast, Gale took down the faded and weatherbeaten sign and carried it around to the inn's small courtyard, an area with a few tables and chairs surrounded by a white wall. He placed the sign on a table and started work on its restoration. He labored through the morning and had begun work on the painting of the great hart itself when the pangs of hunger seized him. It was after one o'clock and he decided to pause for lunch.

Another traveler had stopped by the inn for lunch, and he seated himself at one of the tables in the courtyard while Thomas Splend's buxom wife Gertrude saw to his needs. He was stouter than Gale, and slightly older, and since they were alone in the courtyard he called over to ask, "Tell me, sir, would you join me in an ale?"

"With pleasure," Gabriel Gale responded, walking over to the other's table.

He introduced himself and the man replied, "I'm Baxter Ward, traveling through here on my way down to Ipswich."

"It's good country," Gale said as Gertrude brought their pints.

Baxter Ward lifted his glass. *"Shoulder the sky, my lad, and drink your ale . . ."*

"Ah!" Gale said with a smile, "A poet—and an admirer of Housman, at that!"

"Indeed. The poor man died last year, you know."

Gale nodded. "It is a bad year for poets when we lose the likes of Housman and Chesterton."

"I fear I'm not in their league," Ward admitted, wiping the excess foam from his mouth as he set down the ale. "I quote much more than I write. But I do like good verse."

Gale had warmed to the man, who seemed to be in good physical shape despite a few grey hairs and some extra weight around his middle. "If you're interested in poets, you must know that Edward Fitzgerald is buried here in Boulge. He was born not far from here, of course, near Woodbridge. I visited his grave yesterday at St. Michael and All Angels."

"Interesting. I might stop by there if I have the time."

There was some commotion inside, and the voice of a young woman, obviously distressed, reached their ears. "What's all that?" Gale asked Gertrude Splend when she returned with their food.

The proprietor's wife gave a snort. "Young lady lost a valuable diamond ring. Claims she laid it down and a deer ate it! Ever hear anything so foolish in your entire life? Deer eating diamonds!"

153

Baxter Ward grinned. "That's one young woman I have to see! Coming, Gale?"

"Why not?" He picked up his glass and followed along inside.

The woman was both young and attractive, dressed in an elegant riding habit with a little cap covering her blonde hair. She carried a short riding crop, but Gale could see no sign of a horse out the window. Thomas Splend was attempting to calm her, as she seemed close to tears.

"I've been thrown by my horse and a deer has eaten my diamond engagement ring! I come here asking for help and I'm treated with ridicule!"

"Not by me, certainly," Baxter Ward said, stepping forward gallantly. "Exactly what happened, Miss?"

As if suddenly aware that a reasonably handsome older man was addressing her kindly, she brushed a tear from her eye and managed a tentative smile. "My name is Millicent Grady. I rode up from Little Bealings. Just south of here I was crossing a large estate—"

"Sir Albert Bush's place."

"—when my horse tripped in a rabbit hole and threw me. Before I could remount she galloped away without me. I started walking toward the spire of the church, the only landmark I could see among the trees. There's a little stream in the woods with berries growing alongside it. I stopped to pick some, and then I wanted to wash my hands before I ate them. I put the berries in a little heap and slipped off my engagement ring so it wouldn't come off in the water. I put it right by the berries and went downstream about ten feet to a place where I could kneel and reach into the water. I'd just finished washing when I looked up to see a large hart standing at my pile of berries, head down, eating them. It seemed completely unfazed by my presence, not ten feet away. I started toward it and it backed off, then bolted. That's when I realized my ring was missing."

"Perhaps the ring fell into the water," Ward suggested, cocking his head a bit as if to better hear her story.

"The water was not close at that point, which is why I'd moved downstream to wash. Believe me, I spent ten minutes searching the ground in all directions, and found nothing. That big deer had to have swallowed it!"

"Most unusual," the innkeeper Splend remarked, shaking his head. "Never heard anything like it."

"The diamond was no bigger than the berries, and the ring itself could easily have passed down the hart's throat. I think the beast was nibbling on the berries and accidentally swallowed the ring along with them."

Gale joined in the conversation. "Do deer eat berries?"

"They've been known to," Splend replied. "Usually they exist on a diet of leaves and grass and twigs, but sometimes berries are an extra treat."

"But not diamond rings."

"No," the innkeeper agreed. "If what she says is true, it's a wonder the poor creature didn't choke."

"I must get it back!" the young woman insisted. "Whatever would I tell my fiancé?"

"I'm afraid the possibility of that is quite remote," Baxter Ward told her. "Even if you could identify the specific deer, what would you do? Follow it around?"

"I'd kill it," she replied firmly.

He stared at her with open admiration. "I believe you would, at that." Turning to the innkeeper, he asked, "Whose land is it?"

"Sir Albert's. He has most of the open acreage in that area."

"And do you have a hunting rifle I could borrow, Mr. Splend?"

"Well, yes. But you can't go up there shooting deer—"

"I will of course seek the permission of Sir Albert first. Gale, would you like to accompany us?"

Gabriel Gale smiled. "It's not something I'd want to miss."

He set off with Baxter Ward and the young woman in Ward's lorry, a small van with the inscription Ward's Husbandry Services on its side. "Exactly what services do you offer?" Millicent Grady asked as she climbed in.

"I give advice on the production of profitable crops and animals," he explained. "There are some pamphlets in the back on thrift management for the small estate, if you'd care to pursue the subject."

"No, thank you. I just want my ring back."

Ward had borrowed a weapon and some ammunition from the innkeeper, who'd decided to follow along in his own car. Thus there were two vehicles that negotiated the winding drive up to the manor house to see Sir Albert Bush. The butler who admitted them eyed the group with some uncertainty, but finally Sir Albert himself was summoned. He was a fiftyish man with balding head and red cheeks, and all the time he listened to their story he kept eyeing Millicent Grady's form-fitting jacket and spotless riding breeches, full of open admiration for the young woman.

"Thrown by your horse on my property? My, my, this is dreadful! It's a wonder you suffered no injury."

"Only to my pride," she answered with a smile. "But somehow I must retrieve my diamond. We ask your permission to seek out the hart that ate it and dispatch him."

"But could you recognize the very animal?" Sir Albert asked. "We have more than a hundred head of deer living wild on our property."

"It was an older hart with a full rack," she explained. "That would eliminate most of your herd, wouldn't it?"

He hesitated. "I suppose so, but I can't have you shooting haphazardly at my deer. What will you do after you've killed one?"

"I've had some experience with dressing animals after a hunt," Baxter Ward told him. "I have a large hunting knife in my lorry. If the ring is in the animal's stomach, I'll find it."

"Please!" Millicent appealed. "You don't know how much this means to me."

Thomas Splend chuckled. "If they find that ring inside a hart's stomach I'll get your name in the papers. I'll guarantee that!"

"It would be a first," Sir Albert admitted. "I'll tell you what I'll do. Let me ride along with you and if we spot any likely suspects I'll make the decision about what to do."

That seemed to be the best way to proceed, since Sir Albert obviously was not about to give them a free hand in slaughtering his herd to recover the missing diamond. They departed from the manor house in Baxter Ward's lorry and the innkeeper's car, heading for a ridge that gave them a good view of the meadow and the adjoining woods.

"Late in the day is when they're usually on the move," Sir Albert said when they stopped to study the lay of the land.

"There's one!" Millicent cried softly, pointing toward a small doe that had just emerged from the shelter of the trees. A moment later it was followed by a male with a large rack. "That could be him," she said a bit uncertainly.

Baxter Ward alighted from the lorry and took out the rifle. He glanced in Sir Albert's direction. The balding man sighed and said, "All right."

Ward seemed to aim the weapon with a casual grace before he squeezed the trigger, and Gabriel Gale was surprised when the hart toppled over as if hit with a sledge hammer.

"A clean kill!" Splend exclaimed. "That's quite a shot at this distance."

They hurried down to the fallen animal, with Ward drawing the hunting knife from its sheath. He knelt by the hart and made one quick incision. After a moment's search he withdrew his hand. "I'm sorry. It's not here."

Millicent uttered a single heart-wrenching sob. "I was so certain."

Sir Albert tried to comfort her. "Perhaps you were mistaken, my dear young woman. I've never known a deer to eat a diamond."

Baxter Ward glanced over at Gale and the innkeeper. "We really must clean up the area. Could you two give me a hand with the carcass?" They lifted it with some effort, trying to keep the blood from their clothes, and placed it in the back of the lorry.

They continued along the ridge, uncertain of their next move, when suddenly another large hart, perhaps frightened by the whine of the lorry's motor, burst from cover not fifty feet ahead of them. Almost without thinking Baxter Ward's hands left the steering wheel and went for the rifle propped against the door beside him. He fired through the open window as Sir Albert gasped and tried to restrain him. The deer ran for several yards before it toppled over.

"I can't have you killing any more of my animals," Sir Albert said.

Ward was already out of the driver's seat with his knife, but the result was the same. "I'm sorry," he told Millicent, bowing his head. "There is no ring."

There were two dead animals in the lorry now, and Sir Albert insisted they return to the house. "What was the value of the diamond, dear lady? If I am even remotely responsible for its loss perhaps I can—"

"It belonged to my fiancé's mother. The monetary value is secondary compared with the sentimental value. You must understand that."

"Indeed I do, Miss Grady, and I wish there was something more I could do for you."

"Perhaps if we abandoned the lorry and went on foot we'd have better luck. The animal might still be near the stream."

After some discussion Sir Albert reluctantly agreed it was worth a try. Watching the drama unfold, it seemed obvious to Gabriel Gale that chivalry was not dead, at least not in this part of Suffolk. They set off toward the woods that bordered the stream, moving as quietly as possible so as not to frighten the deer.

At the water's edge, by a natural pool, they came upon several animals drinking. Baxter Ward managed to bring down the largest hart before the others fled. Again, his knife and searching fingers yielded nothing. They carried the animal out to the clearing, to be picked up later by the truck.

"This is all," Sir Albert decided reluctantly. "No more deer must be slaughtered like this."

"Please!" she begged. "One more! If my ring is not recovered, I will

157

have to live with my sorrow. There was another large hart in that group and I feel he might be the one."

But the animals had scattered now that the scent of blood was in the air, and they searched the woods for a full half-hour before Baxter Ward suggested he should go on alone. "The rest of you stay here," he said. "And be still!"

Gale and the others waited in silence for what seemed an eternity while Ward moved off into the woods, disappearing from view. Presently, from some distance away, came the crack of two shots, close together. They broke into a run with Millicent in the lead, tromping through the underbrush with no thought of silence now.

When they reached Baxter Ward they found him with his knife out, standing above the bodies of two fallen harts. "They were together," he explained. "I had to kill them both."

"My God, Ward!" Sir Albert started forward with fire in his eye. "This is the absolute end! All of you people must leave my property."

Ward's hand felt around inside the first deer and suddenly emerged holding a bloodied piece of metal. As he wiped it off, Millicent Grady gasped. "It's my diamond!"

Even Gabriel Gale was caught up in the excitement of the moment. A small cheer went up in the woods, with Sir Albert himself stepping forward to shake Baxter Ward's hand. "I'm just pleased that you found the ring before my entire herd was wiped out," he said.

"How can I ever repay you?" Millicent asked Ward.

"No payment is necessary," he insisted, "Though I would enjoy dining on venison if Sir Albert has no use for these carcasses."

"Take them as your reward," he agreed with a wave of his hand. "To see Miss Grady's smiling face is enough for me."

Baxter Ward returned the rifle to the innkeeper and the three men dragged and carried the dead animals back to the lorry. Sir Albert strolled a bit with Millicent and then invited them all up to the manor house for some wine.

"I really should be getting back," Millicent decided. "If my horse returned home on her own, the family will be worried."

"Did you say you came from Little Bealings? I'll be passing close to there on my way down to Ipswich," Ward told her. "I'll be honored to drive you home."

"Thank you very much." She finished wiping off the diamond ring and returned it to her finger. "I'll never take it off again," she promised.

Gabriel Gale shook hands with them both, and with Sir Albert, and watched Baxter Ward drive away with the young woman. He felt as if he had been watching a master at work. "Like St. George slaying the dragon," he said, half to himself.

"What was that?" the innkeeper Splend asked.

"Nothing. I was just talking to myself. Let's get back to the inn so I can finish your sign."

". . . and that's what we did," Gabriel Gale concluded, his eyes twinkling a bit as he finished the story. "I never saw Baxter Ward after that."

"An interesting tale," I agreed. "Though I don't know if I would have left her alone with him. Ward may have been a jewel thief after her ring. Why else should he have gone to such lengths to find it in the first place?"

"Oh, I can assure you that Millicent Grady was a charming young woman. She completely enchanted Sir Albert. And Baxter Ward was not a jewel thief. Quite the opposite, in fact."

The evening breeze was picking up in London, and someone had closed the window of the room. A few of the poets were taking their leave, going off for a late supper together. "What do you mean by that?" I asked Gale. "What is the opposite of a jewel thief?"

"I was watching Ward when he slit open that last deer. He had the ring palmed in his hand the whole time. It didn't come from the hart's stomach."

"What? But how is that possible? It was Millicent's ring."

"Ah, yes—Millicent. Charming Millicent! She'd fallen off her horse, knelt by the stream to wash her hands, and searched the grass for ten minutes, presumably on her hands and knees. Yet her riding breeches were spotless. There was not even a grass stain!"

"Do you mean she made up the story? The deer never ate her diamond?"

"Of course not! Baxter Ward had it the entire time, until he pretended to find it inside the fifth deer."

"But what did Ward and Millicent accomplish by their charade? What was the object of it all?"

Gabriel Gale smiled. "Even a minor crime can be a work of art, if performed with enough skill. Baxter Ward was not a jewel thief. He was a poacher."

# Detective for a Day

*by Walt Sheldon*

Just because I had Blowtorch Foley on the phone doesn't mean that I'm not a perfectly respectable citizen. I just happen to be desk clerk in the Billings Hotel, and the Billings Hotel happens to be a place where people like Blowtorch Foley abound. Of course, not everybody who comes to the Billings is ripe for rogue's gallery—we get everybody from science guys like Dr. Anathy Polt, to bright-eyed kids like J. Eugene Demwood, III.

This J. Eugene Demwood, III came in to register about the same time I was talking to Blowtorch. He stood in front of the desk and clutched two suitcases in his hands like he was afraid somebody was going to snatch them. I nodded to him and kept barking into the phone.

"Look, Blowtorch," I said, "these locksmiths always rip things apart as though they were cans of kippered snacks. I want a nice, neat job so we can use the safe again, see? . . . What's that? . . . No, I don't know what's in it. Nobody around here does. We just found the thing in the cellar—nobody even knows where it comes from. . . . You'll be right over, eh? . . . Okay. So long, Blowtorch."

I hung up and pushed the register in front of the youngster. He had a nice fresh skin like you don't often see around the Billings, and the way he smiled was like a big St. Bernard dog dying to make friends with somebody.

I said, "Single room, buck and a half. Double, two bucks."

"Thank you," said the young fellow. "Mighty reasonable. Yes sir. I'll take a double room."

He was dressed in a herringbone tweed and one of those light sweaters like those Harvard fellows. Only when he spoke his voice had a twang and I could hear the tall breeze blowing in the corn. He put his bags down reluctantly and signed the register, "J. Eugene Demwood, III."

"Bernie!" I yelled.

Our bell boy, a little, mussy-haired guy, trotted into the lobby. He
160

made a dive for J. Eugene's bags and then J. Eugene yelled, "Hey—hold on!"

Bernie looked up from under his brows. "Don't touch that one." J. Eugene said pointing to the larger of the two bags. It was a square, black case and looked pretty strong. Bernie shrugged, took the other one, and left the lobby.

Then J. Eugene Demwood, III, leaned over the desk confidentially and said to me, "That's my crime detecting kit."

It took me a full thirty seconds to squash the laugh that mushroomed up in my throat. I pretended I was blotting the register. Finally I was able to say, "Crime detecting kit? You—er—you don't look like a detective, Mr. Demwood."

"Well, no," he said, blushing with pleasure. "The modern detective doesn't."

"Hm," I said. I eyed him sideways. "What department you work for, Mr. Demwood?"

"Hinkelstown, Pennsylvania," he said without batting an eyelash. "I'm here on a special assignment."

"Special assignment?" This was getting hot. I knew Hinkelstown was a middle sized burg in Pennsylvania inhabited by a lot of pretty well-to-do families, such as this kid might come from.

"Yes," he said. He lowered his voice. "I'm here to find Justice Grooter."

I almost choked. Justice Grooter! He'd been missing for years. It was a joke, even. If you dropped a quarter through a grating and got down on your hands and knees looking for it, some wise guy would be sure to come along and say, "What you doin', bud—lookin' for Justice Grooter? Ha ha." I just stared blankly at J. Eugene Demwood, III and bared my chest for the next screwball.

"He was last seen here, you know," he whispered.

"Here?"

"Sure. Don't you remember? He'd taken a room here for a rendezvous with some of the underworld. That was the last ever seen of him."

"It's a little before my time," I said. "How come you're lookin' for him?"

"Well, when my father got me a job on the Hinklestown police force, I guess they sort of recognized my scientific ability. I studied criminology at school. Anyway, nothing really scientific ever happens in Hinkelstown, so they sent me on this case."

"Oh, I see," I said. I could see all right. I could see a bunch of coppers back in Hinkelstown thanking their lucky stars they got rid of J. Eugene, III so easily.

"Look, kid," I said, "Take it easy—don't speak to anybody about anything here. This is a funny place this Billings, and funny things happen here. You don't know who you're gonna run into. You read about that department store robbery yesterday where a watchman was killed? Well, for all you know the guy in the room next to you was the murderer. And I could say the same for practically any crime that's happened lately."

"Oh, yes—I read about that robbery," Demwood started to bubble. "The watchman had a club in his hand and there was blood and hair on it, and—"

I put out my hand. "Forget it, young fella. Take it easy."

He looked a little hurt. "All right," he said, "Thanks." Then he picked up his crime detecting kit, as he called it, and turned toward the door.

Just then Blowtorch Foley blew in. There was another man next to him, and I frowned. The other one was smaller than Blowtorch, he had a sallow skin, and greenish eyes that kept sliding from one side to the other. He was dressed in a sharply cut suit that tripled the width of his shoulders. This was Sharkskin Storn, and I wished that Blowtorch hadn't brought him along.

And all of a sudden I had something else to wish it wasn't. J. Eugene, lugging that crime detecting kit of his; trying to say so long to me at the same time, and trying to steer himself toward the door, bumped smack into Blowtorch Foley.

"Hey!" yelled Blowtorch.

His voice was big, like the rest of him; when he talked I could feel it in the floor. J. Eugene's nice pink skin got pinker and he stepped back and sort of grinned and sort of said, "huh!" and sort of fumbled at his tie.

Then Sharkskin Storn suddenly stepped in front of J. Eugene and stabbed him in the chest with his forefinger. "Look, punk," he said, "Why the hell don't you put out your hand?"

That was Sharkskin. Sometimes I thought being nasty was his hobby.

"Why," said J. Eugene, looking like a wounded deer, "I'm sorry, but you don't have to get nasty about it."

"Yeah," said Sharkskin. "On your way, mooch." He flipped J. Eugene's tie from his sweater.

There was a small red sunrise on the back of J. Eugene's neck and then there were two sound effects. One was a soft thud, the other a
162

hard *clop!* Before my eyes Sharkskin bent double from a blow to the midsection and went to sleep from a sweetly placed crack in the jaw. J. Eugene Demwood, III, rubbed the knuckles of his right hand a little, then pulled at his fingers. About that time Blowtorch Foley started one of his big fists traveling from his side.

J. Eugene rolled his head to the right, stepped inside of Blowtorch's punch and snapped one of those short ones straight into Blowtorch's mouth. Blowtorch's eyes got as shiny as ball bearings and he staggered backward into a corner.

I said, "Well, scratch my ear!" and watched J. Eugene Demwood pick up his bag and leave.

Blowtorch and Sharkskin started to get into focus again, and in a moment they were both standing in the middle of the lobby looking dumbly at each other. At that time a stranger came in the door.

First a little pointed Van Dyke beard came, and behind it a little, scrawny man in dark gray clothes. He stopped and looked Blowtorch and Sharkskin up and down.

The little beard quivered. "Had an accident, gentlemen? I'm a doctor."

Blowtorch blinked a little at the beard. "Naw. We're okay."

It suddenly occurred to me that if anything disabled Blowtorch for a while I wouldn't get my safe opened. I used my best foreign minister type tones. "Let the Doc take a look at you," I coaxed Blowtorch.

"Well—" he said grudgingly.

"Somebody sneaked up behind him and socked him on the chin," I told the Doc. I didn't want to embarrass Blowtorch.

The beard walked right up to Blowtorch, started to finger his face and peck away in a peppery voice: "Well, well, let's see now, just a bruise or two. Interesting phenomena, propensity of the inferior mentality to deny pain. Probably due to repressions in childhood caused by father forbidding normal urge to cry. Yes, yes. Closely allied to the Oedipus complex."

Blowtorch said, "Huh?" and he and Sharkskin stared at the Doc.

All of a sudden the beard stopped jiggling. The Doc's hand was on the back of Blowtorch's head, he frowned and said, "Where did you get this bump?"

"Aw, that?" said Blowtorch. "Aw, a screw in stir batted me wit' a billy onct."

The Doc went, "*Tch, tch, tch.*"

"Why? What's a matter?" asked Blowtorch.

"Are you sure you don't get pains in your forehead? Do you ever have hallucinations?"

"Naw! Whaddaye mean! Are you tryin' to tell me I'm nuts?"

"No," said the Doc gravely. He pulled at his beard. "Not yet."

Blowtorch jerked away from the Doc and stood at the door, snarling at him. Sharkskin took his arm and said, "Come on, let's go get some witch hazel. This joint is gettin' a screwier element in it every day." The two of them turned and walked out.

The Doc walked up to the desk, and as though nothing had happened, said to me, "How do you do. I'm Doctor Anathy Polt. I'll need accommodations for about two weeks. I came here to study criminal types. I'm writing a book, you see, on criminal psychology."

"Oh," I said. I handed him the register and looked in the drawer to see if I had any aspirins.

When Doctor Anathy Polt had left for his room I took two aspirins and buried myself in the ledger so I wouldn't start thinking too much about some of the guests at the Billings. Just when I was hot on the trail of a stray dollar and twelve cents. Blowtorch and Sharkskin came back.

Blowtorch asked. "Where's 'at safe you want busted, Wally?"

I pointed to the storeroom door. "In there."

"I'll try the dial first," said Blowtorch. "If I can't open it like that, I'll get some tools."

"All right, sure," I said. I opened the storeroom door for them and they went in. I was just about to follow them when I heard somebody come into the lobby. I turned. There was J. Eugene Demwood, III, with a little tin box in one hand and a pile of old clothes in the other.

I figured if Blowtorch and Sharkskin heard J. Eugene's voice they'd try to start things again, so I carefully closed the storeroom door on them. J. Eugene came up to the desk, and I faced him.

He had the look of Destiny in his face. "Hello," I said a little apprehensively.

"I'm going," said J. Eugene in a low voice, "to reconstruct the crime."

"Huh?" I asked.

"The scientist," he replied, unloading his junk on the desk top, "to learn an unknown fact, recreates the conditions surrounding that fact. Now, I'm going to be Justice Grooters. And I'm going to come up here and register. Then I'm going up to the room Grooters occupied. 207, I believe. I see by the key rack that it's empty."

164

"What's all this?" I waved my hand at the old clothes and the tin box.

"A make-up box, and an exact replica of Grooter's costume at the time of his disappearance," said the kid eagerly. He added: "All the great detectives of history were perfectionists."

"Now, wait a minute—" I said.

J. Eugene interrupted me. "Just think!" he said. "If I can find Grooters, I'll have surpassed every detective in the country! On top of that, there's a ten thousand dollar reward for him. I'll see that you're taken care of."

I didn't believe I'd ever see a pale green flash of that ten thousand, but I figured maybe I could keep the kid and the two gorillas in the storeroom from meeting. I said, "Okay. Go in that little office on the side there to put your costume on."

"I'll be right out!" whooped J. Eugene, III. He dashed into the office. I shook my head sadly, took another aspirin and went back after that dollar and twelve cents.

Just when I almost had it Blowtorch Foley and Sharkskin Storn came stumbling out of the storeroom. Sharkskin looked nastier than ever and Foley seemed to be a slight spearmint color around the gills.

"What's the trouble?" I asked.

"Nuttin'." replied Blowtorch. His voice was a ragged whisper. "Nuttin'. I can't open your safe." Sharkskin just sort of glared at me. They started to walk across the lobby, and I noticed Blowtorch was placing his feet carefully one in front of the other, like a drunk tries to walk a chalk line. And then, when they were only a few steps from the door, Dr. Polt suddenly popped in.

Dr. Polt's beard vibrated at Blowtorch.

He said, "I'd like to ask you a few questions, Foley."

I wondered where Polt had learned his name, and I had another misty idea that the Doc's voice had lost its Ph.D. peckiness.

"I ain't got time," Blowtorch said, "I got an appointment."

"Just a minute," Polt interrupted. "Where were you Thursday night?"

In a flash, then, Sharkskin had backed away and had a gun in his hand. "I get it," he said quietly. "Blowtorch, get your gat out. This guy ain't a nut doctor. He's a dick."

Polt nodded. "Right. An insurance detective. You got some valuable furs from that department store. If I were you I'd tell where they are and come along quietly. Save a lot of trouble in the end."

Sharkskin's eyes squinted under his dark brows. "Mr. Insurance," he said, "I'm gonna let you have a bullet right in the belly."

165

I could see Polt stiffen where he stood. I could see that he knew Sharkskin wasn't fooling. I could see where I'd better get ready to duck under the desk.

The door of the office rattled open. Sharkskin said from the side of his mouth, "See who that is, Foley."

Blowtorch Foley turned around. I saw him stiffen, then saw a rippling shiver grab him by the toes and travel all the way up his body to the top of his head. I saw every bit of color fade from his face and leave an oyster white mask. Then Blowtorch Foley screamed.

*"Arrrr!"* He yelled, *"I'm goin' nuts!"*

I swung my head around to what Foley was looking at, and jerked a sharp breath into me. J. Eugene Demwood, III was there. The kid was wearing a dark gray business suit, he had his paunch stuffed to make it fit; there were grease paint lines in his face and his hair was sprinkled with gray. Even his nose was molded with putty. I recalled pictures I'd seen of the missing Justice Grooters. . . .

*"Get outa here!"* wailed Blowtorch, "You ain't real! Scram!"

Sharkskin turned to see, no doubt, what the hell was making a blubbering idiot out of Blowtorch, and in that minute, Polt jumped him. Polt grabbed the gun and they began to waltz back and forth in the middle of the lobby.

Sharkskin grunted. "Foley! It's a gag! Come on, get this guy!"

"Yeah, yeah," said Blowtorch, staring at J. Eugene, "It's a gag. Sure, it's a gag."

He brought his gun up with a trembling hand, turned, and pointed it at Polt.

In that instant J. Eugene Demwood was bounding across the lobby. He crashed into Blowtorch and knocked his gun arm upward, just as the weapon went off. One of his big hands torpedoed into Blowtorch's face for the second time that day; caught him at perfect right angles on the front of his jaw. Blowtorch's knees forgot what they were for and Blowtorch fell flat on his face.

J. Eugene turned to Sharkskin and Polt. He turned just in time to see Sharkskin jerk his automatic loose and hatchet the butt down on the insurance detective's forehead. J. Eugene took two steps, flung his hand at Sharkskin as though he were throwing a ball and sent the automatic tumbling across the lobby.

Sharkskin crouched low and put every ounce in his body behind a hard jab into J. Eugene's solar plexus. Sharkskin's fist must have been surprised to find itself sink into a lot of padding.

There wasn't much more to it. J. Eugene lashed out with a rhyth-

166

mic one, two, three, and then Sharkskin was draped limply over the insurance detective.

J. Eugene turned to me. "Gee!" he said, "What—"

I motioned toward the storeroom. "Don't ask questions," I said, "I've got a sneakin' idea. Come with me."

J. Eugene picked up one of the fallen guns and followed me into the storeroom. The safe that had been found in the cellar was standing in the corner. It was about as high as my waist, as wide as the spread of my arms. I stepped over to it and pulled at the knob of the dial. The door swung open ponderously.

"Good God!" breathed J. Eugene.

"Not very pretty after all these years," I said. "Even with that airtight safe."

"But—but—what's it all about?" asked J. Eugene. He put his hand lightly to the side of his forehead.

"Come on," I said, "We'll call some cops, then I'll tell you."

After I had phoned the law I said to the kid:

"This guy Polt posing as a psychologist, or whatever he was supposed to be, was snooping around to find who robbed the department store and killed the watchman. The watchman's club had a little hair and blood on it, so there must have been a struggle and the thief must have been hit on the back of the head. Polt felt the bump on Foley's head, and went out again to check and make sure. Then Foley came in to open this safe which we found in the basement. He and Sharkskin saw the corpse of Justice Grooters. Sharkskin decided they'd say they couldn't open the safe, then swipe it later and collect the reward for themselves.

"Then when they came out, and Blowtorch saw you made up as Grooters, he thought that bump on the head had made him nuts. You know what happened after that."

"Gee!" said J. Eugene Demwood, III, "What's gonna happen now?"

"You're going to get a reputation as the greatest detective in the country." I said, "But heaven help you if they ever give you a case!"

# Die Before Bedtime

*by Walt Sheldon*

Detective Cubbs wasn't so sure how this Miss Skeeley was going to act when she saw the body. A frail little trick like her—coal-black, curly top, perky nose and small mouth—wasn't likely to go for the sight and smell of blood. And this one promised to be bloody.

"Sure you want to go?" he asked her. That was maybe the twelfth time. And each time he asked it he leaned his elbow on the desk, pressed a finger against the side of his nose and cocked his blond eyebrows; one up, one down.

Every cop on the force had fun with that gesture of Detective Bayer Cubbs. He didn't mind. He didn't mind much of anything. He had a nice, round face that would have looked good in a baby talcum ad.

Miss Pearletta Skeeley stood up and hugged her handbag under one arm. "Of course I want to go, Mr. Cubbs. I had a hard time getting permission for this interview and I don't want to miss one single thing!"

Cubbs took his finger away from his nose. "Okay. Only you won't see much."

Miss Skeeley drove him to where the murder was, and they started up three flights of stairs. The house was an old brownstone converted into studio apartments. Cubbs said, "To tell you the truth, Miss Skeeley, these things are all the same. Routine."

"Maybe you don't see the glamour, because—well, maybe you're too close to it." She had a sharp, capable way of speaking and a funny habit of waggling her head sideways with each word.

"It's a business," said Cubbs. "When you're in it long enough, you know exactly what's gonna happen."

"What's going to happen here?"

"Huh?"

"I said what's going to happen here?"

"Oh." Cubbs tapped his nose. "Well, let's see. Trana Thorne was a gorgeous dame. A model. The landlord found the body. Now, I'll bet she'll be in the bedroom, and there'll be lots of blood, her hair'll be sticky with it . . ."

Pearletta Skeeley's step wavered a little.

"I'm sorry," said Cubbs quickly. "I'm used to hard-boiled newspaper folk. This isn't exactly stuff for a columnist on a ladies' magazine. . . ."

Pearletta forged ahead grimly. "Please, Mr. Cubbs, forget that. This is an assignment for me, and I'm going to finish it."

She would, too, thought Cubbs. She had that determined zip to every move she made. Also, the backs of her legs were damned attractive. "Hm," said Cubbs.

A couple of bluecoats let them inside the apartment, and Doc Drickers, the medical examiner, brought them to the body. It was in the bedroom all right. Jardin, the fingerprint man, was blowing powder on things.

Pearletta Skeeley said softly, "Awrrgh," and got a little pale. She went to the corner of the room and sat down weakly on a slender green and gold chair.

Cubbs gazed at the body and muttered, half to himself, half to Doc Drickers, "Covers half over body, position slumped on one side—murdered while she slept. Big bruise and blood on forehead. She got smacked with something big and heavy. It oughta turn up soon."

Doc said, "She's been dead since early this morning. Frontal and part of parietal plates fractured . . ."

"Yeah. Sure. Okay," said Cubbs. He put his finger to the side of his nose and swung his eyes in a lazy circle around the room. He saw a blue lamp on the vanity table.

"Hey, Jardin."

The fingerprint man stopped blowing powder and looked up. Cubbs jerked his thumb at the lamp and Jardin nodded.

He turned to Pearletta who was sitting white and rigid. "After we question this landlord," he said, "we'll get a line on some of Trana Thorne's boy friends. And we'll question them and have the murderer by supper time. Strictly routine."

Pearletta's dark eyes got wide. "Oh, I think it's *too* fascinating," she said.

Cubbs turned his head and sniffed to himself. He wondered why women always sounded so phony when they were raving about something.

Jardin stepped back from the lamp and looked at Cubbs over his glasses. "That's it," he said. "Traces of blood and hair—though it's been wiped carefully. No prints, I'm afraid."

"Okay," said Cubbs. He pressed his nose. "Something damn awful familiar about this murder," he mumbled.

Pearletta was out of her chair. "The lamp, Mr. Cubbs!" she said, "Remember—a few years ago a chorus girl was murdered that way? And this gambler—what's his name—was tried for it, but acquitted?"

"Yeah, yeah," said Cubbs, looking steadily at Pearletta. "That's all right. O'Connan was his name—Kane O'Connan. . . ."

She grinned all over with pleasure. "See, I'm learning."

"Yup," said Cubbs.

"Aren't you going to look around, now?" she asked. "I mean for clues and things?"

"Oh, sure," said Cubbs lightly. "Routine checkup. Doesn't usually tell much. In rare instances maybe."

"Well, do you mind," asked Pearletta, "if I look around myself? I mean, just for fun?"

"Nope," said Cubbs.

He watched her go into the kitchen, shrugged, and went into the living room.

Mr. Joseph P. Morfit, the owner of the building, who lived in the first floor apartment, had found Trana Thorne's body. He was a skinny man and his bald head, with its few arid, gray hairs on the sides, made him look skinnier. He had one massive, gold tooth in front.

"Let's see, now," said Cubbs, "Miss Thorne didn't trust alarm clocks and you always called her at twelve noon."

Morfit nodded his head. His eyes were deep set and he looked at Cubbs around the corners of their sockets.

"She always got in late?" asked Cubbs.

"Mm."

"Who with?"

"Oh, several gentlemen. Mostly Mr. O'Connan. Or Spanky Smythe."

"Oh," said Cubbs. He rubbed his nose and stared at Morfit until the man started to fidget. Then he said, "That's all, thanks. Don't leave town or anything, though. May want you again."

"Mm," said Morfit. He went out.

Cubbs called Pearletta out of the kitchen. "You know all these society folks from your column," he said. "What dope have you got on Spanky Smythe?"

"Is he mixed up in this?"

170

"Maybe. What about him?"

Her head popped from side to side. "Oh, he photographs well in night clubs. He can afford to go to them, and he can afford to take girls like Trana Thorne with him. He's not thirty yet, and all the liquor he drinks hasn't started to work on his figure. . . ."

One of the bluecoats tapped Cubbs' arm. "Young fella just came to the door. Name's Spanky Smythe."

Pearletta looked surprised, then said, "I'll go in the other room so you can question him."

"Okay," said Cubbs.

Spanky Smythe was horrified to hear about Miss Thorne's death. He propped his slim figure on the edge of the davenport and kept shaking his head slowly at the carpet. "I can't understand why anyone would want to murder Trana. She was so lovely—so . . ."

"Yup," said Cubbs sympathetically. "I guess all of Miss Thorne's friends treated her pretty nice."

Spanky Smythe nodded absently. Then he looked up. "All except Kane O'Connan. How she could stand that guy, I don't know. . . ."

"Hm," said Cubbs thoughtfully. He fingered his nose. "Of course you can prove where you were this morning when the murder happened. . . ."

"Well—no—I don't think so," muttered Smythe. He blushed a bit. "I was out for a bender. Last thing I remembered was drinking at the bar in O'Connan's place."

"O'Connan was there with Miss Thorne, huh?"

Smythe looked sheepish and nodded.

"Okay," said Cubbs. "You can go. Don't leave town, though."

After Smythe had left he called up Kane O'Connan. O'Connan was deeply shocked—yes, he certainly would come to headquarters and answer questions. Anything to help the police.

Cubbs hung up and said to Pearletta, "Come on, we have an interview."

"Any clues yet?" she asked eagerly.

"Nope," said Cubbs. He was idly thumbing a copy of *Mesdames*. It had Trana Thorne's picture on the cover. "Guess that gorgeous pan sold a lot of magazines, huh?"

"She was a beautiful woman," said Pearletta.

On the way to headquarters Cubbs asked, "Isn't *Mesdames* the magazine you write for?"

"Yes."

"How you gonna do this thing? I mean do women want to read about all that blood and stuff?"

Pearletta waggled her head. "I think I can manage to treat it without sordidness."

"You mean you'll just skip over the actual murder lightly, huh?"

"Well—no—" said Pearletta. "I'll say something about this lovely creature entering her boudoir for the last time, like a flower folding for the night, little knowing that the end of that glamorous day meant the end of her glamorous life—not dreaming as she carefully folded her expensive silken gown, sipped her last glass of warm milk and stepped into her soft, warm bed . . . oh, you know how it goes."

"Sure," said Cubbs.

He was silent for a few minutes.

"You must get to know all these people you write about pretty well," he said, "I mean their private lives and all that."

She shrugged. "Oh yes, I suppose so."

They met Mr. Kane O'Connan at headquarters. He was sitting in the squad room chinning with the boys when Cubbs and Pearletta came in. He jumped up, crossed the floor and waved a big hand toward the detective. His cigar tilted at the ceiling.

"Well, well," he said. "Detective Cubbs. How's the smartest ol' dick on the force, huh?" He had big, black eyes in his paunchy face. They fastened themselves on Pearletta. "Well, well, who's the young lady?"

"Hello, O'Connan," said Cubbs. "This is Miss Skeeley. Writes a column for *Mesdames*. She's getting some firsthand dope on the detective business. It's a business, you know."

Cubbs noticed the long, coarse hairs on O'Connan's brow bristle away from his eyes. "Oh, so you're Miss Skeeley," he said. "Well, I'm pleased to meetcha. Yeah, I heard a lot about you, Miss Skeeley."

"How do you do," said Pearletta.

"Oh—you read ladies' magazines?" asked Cubbs.

O'Connan laughed. "Haw haw!" he waved his cigar. "Naw, I just heard about her aroun' town. You know."

"Oh," said Cubbs. He crossed the squad room and whispered something to one of the other detectives. The man left. Then Cubbs beckoned to O'Connan and Pearletta.

He spoke to the night club owner. "Of course you have an alibi?"

O'Connan put his cigar in his mouth and started to chew on it. "Well, Cubbs, to be frank, no. I guess maybe I'm in a pickle. I had a date with Trana Thorne last night. I was probably the last person to see her alive—outside of the killer. . . ."

172

Cubbs studied the ceiling. "O'Connan," he said finally, "That's the first time you ever admitted being near the scene and time of a crime. I'm inclined to believe you're telling the truth. But I gotta hold you. That other murder you were mixed up in . . . the girl was killed the same way. . . ."

"Sure, Cubbs. I understand. I got a lawyer."

"When'd you leave Miss Thorne?"

"Maybe four—half past. The milk was at the door when I left."

"She always took warm milk to make her sleep, huh?"

O'Connan wrinkled his nose. "Yeah. How'd you know?"

"Found out," said Cubbs. He stared dreamily at an invisible point somewhere in the middle of the room. Then: "Wonder if you'll excuse me a minute. Gotta make a phone call."

Cubbs used the phone in the Captain's office.

"Hello," he said when he had the number. "This Detective Cubbs, Twenty-first precinct. I'd like to speak to the driver that delivers around the Grand Street section. I want to find out if he left any milk this morning for Miss Trana Thorne, 436 Grand Street, third floor."

There was a long wait. Then Cubbs listened carefully and said, "None left, eh? Okay, thanks."

About the time he got back into the squad room, a bluecoat was coming in the other door escorting both Joseph P. Morfit and Spanky Smythe. Smythe looked sharply at Miss Skeeley, then at Cubbs. He was pouting and frowning. Morfit was looking at the floor.

"Sit down everybody," said Cubbs pleasantly. "I'm just going to run over the whole thing lightly. There's no reason to be scared."

A bluecoat with a large, enamel coffee pot in his hand came in the other door. "Here y'are, Cubbs. I got it at the Greek's next door. You owe me two bits."

"Okay," said Cubbs.

The officer set the coffee pot on the desk. Then he went back and got four cups and a pint bottle of milk and set that on the desk, too.

"Thought maybe some coffee'd make this more pleasant," grinned Cubbs blandly. He got up and poured the steaming liquid into the cups. Then he picked up the milk bottle and opened it. "I saved money on this though." He winked in the general direction of his guests. "We found this bottle on Trana Thorne's dumbwaiter. It's this morning's milk—so it shouldn't go to waste. And it's still more than half full."

Each of the four stared at Cubbs. Morfit wrinkled his nose acidly.

173

Then Cubbs handed the coffee around. He leaned back lazily in one of the chairs and smiled.

Pearletta Skeeley said, "I don't think I want any coffee."

"Nor I," frowned Spanky Smythe.

Kane O'Connan brought the cup to his lips. "I can always drink coffee," he said.

Pearletta was suddenly up, out of her chair. She snatched the cup from O'Connan, and put it down on the desk. "Oh, this is all very silly!" she said. "Why do we sit here and drink coffee, with a murderer going free somewhere?"

Cubbs grinned. "Thank you, Miss Skeeley," he said. "I think we should get down to business." He put his fingertip to his nose. "Pearletta Skeeley," he said, "I arrest you for the murder of Trana Thorne!"

For a floating second her eyes opened wide, and in the next instant she was dashing toward the door. Almost magically a policeman appeared in the doorway and grabbed her. He held her while she screamed and kicked and raved.

Afterward Cubbs told the newspaper men, "Well, it was like this. Pearletta had been blackmailing some folks she learned about while snooping for her column. Spanky Smythe was one. She had all her dope in a little book. Spanky, a dumb lovesick kid, told Trana Thorne all his troubles, including Pearletta. Trana told O'Connan, her sweetheart, about it. O'Connan decided that book would be a good thing to have and hold over people. So when Trana got into the offices of *Mesdames*, she swiped it. Pearletta learned about it and decided the only way to clear up things was to murder Trana Thorne and get O'Connan blamed for it."

Cubbs stretched and yawned. "Well, Pearletta knew O'Connan was mixed up in a killing where a chorus girl got brained with a lamp. She decided to make this one similar. First she got permission to interview me and made the appointment for this morning. O'Connan always dated Trana on Sunday nights. She poisoned a pint bottle of milk and delivered it to Trana, after first calling the company and telling them not to leave milk there as usual. She waited until Trana let O'Connan out and took the milk in.

"She gave Trana time to die, went in, hit her with the lamp, wiped the lamp and beat it quick.

"Today she comes out there with me, gets time to snoop and find the poison milk, then get rid of it. After I sent a man snoopin' for it, he found it in the dumbwaiter. I had him bring a duplicate in with the coffee, and Pearletta gave herself away."

Cubbs' digit dwelt for a moment on his nose. "I guess you fellas want to know how she slipped up, huh? Well, she was saying how she was gonna write this article and she mentioned Trana drinking her last glass of hot milk before she went to bed. Nobody knew about that—not even me. It was screwy enough to start me thinkin' and investigatin'."

Cubbs got off the desk and went to his locker. He'd had a good day's work.

# Dogs Know

*by Gary Lovisi*

Sometimes I think back on things. When Larry used to be alive. He was the best partner a cop ever had, the only friend I'd ever known. So damn real.

I was always the wild one. Larry was calm, logical, orderly, quiet. He had a good life, loving wife, great kids, he proved it could be done. It was incomprehensible to me, but Larry did it. He made the good things happen.

I wouldn't have stayed a cop if it hadn't been for Larry. I was always in trouble. He would always straighten me out, cool me down. We'd talk a lot, and he'd always give me the best damn advice. Free. Not like a lot of the shitheads that want to latch onto your life or get influence over you. Larry didn't care about that crap. Larry just wanted what was best for his friends and family. To Larry, his friends were family too.

I know what he used to do. Something no one ever does anymore. He used to go outside himself to help a friend. Help his family. I know he considered me family and the thought brought tears to my eyes when I saw him lowered into the ground. He went outside himself for me time and again. No one's ever done that for me before or since. Not friends, not family. Especially not family. All they ever wanted was to drain me dry and throw out what was left—or ignore me. Pretend I was dead. That I didn't exist. That I was nothing. I

175

wanted to go outside myself for Larry now. To show him. I would. Somehow.

I remember the last time I was over Larry's house. It was when he got the dogs. They were monstrous brutes. One was a big German Shepherd, the other two silk black Dobermans. They were all big as hell and ugly as sin. Larry's dogs meant business.

I don't know where he got them but I know he was training them. They'd make good pets for his boys and protect the house and family when he wasn't home. Being a cop, he wasn't home much. Now he wouldn't be home ever again. The dogs were still there though, to watch over Susan and the boys. Larry saw for the protection of his own.

On that day long ago, the dogs sat quietly watching me as I approached the high chain-link fence Larry had around the house. It was one of those cool spring days, bright sunny mornings. Even the air smelled good. He was doing some junk in the yard. He was always working on the house, worked like a damn dog himself, but never complained. He looked happy as shit when he was working. He waved me in.

I just laughed. "Shit man, I ain't coming in there. The dogs'll tear me apart."

"Don't worry about them", he said with a laugh.

I nodded, "Sure. As long as I'm on *this* side of the fence I won't worry at all."

He just laughed. He was hammering something, making something out of wood for his boys or the neighborhood kids. He always tinkered with stuff.

When he saw I wouldn't budge he got up and came over to the fence. "What's wrong, scared of a few puppies?"

"Yeah, puppies. Suppose they think I'm some slimebag coming to mug you? Rob the house? Steal your tinker toys?"

"Nah, don't worry, they won't hurt you. I'm telling you, Vic, they can pick up on things better than people. Things like feelings, friendship, belonging. You belong, Vic. Believe me, dogs know."

I said, "Fine, Larry, dogs know," but I didn't move until he came out of the gate to where I was standing nice and safe.

It was funny back then. We joked around. Talked a lot. We had dreams. He busted my chops because I was being a peckerhead by fooling with this fast girl that was no good for me but a lot of damn fun all the same. Larry always told me to be careful, keep it in my pants. Fun ain't all there is. I never could see what else there was

176

beside fun. The other side only seemed to be pain and hurt and I'd seen enough of that.

Self-control and clear thinking was Larry's thing. He had it. I never did. That could be why we partnered so well together. It's sure as hell why I lasted on the force for so long after all the crap we saw in the day-to-day.

I was real shook when the cop killer got Larry. It bothered me, even though it hadn't been my fault. I mean, I told him not to leave me, not to go after the guy alone—but Larry didn't listen. The *one* time I was right—he didn't listen to me!

I'd been hit. Leg wound and it was bleeding badly. Larry seemed so calm about it, like usual, so by-the-book. I thought, OK, we're cool, things will be OK. Larry quickly made an improvised tourniquet for my wound, ran back to the car and pulled the shotgun from the trunk.

I didn't know what was happening. I thought he was going to stand guard over me or something until backup arrived. Logical right? The way it should be done. Larry was always so calm, doing the smart thing. Only this time he acted more like me than I'd ever done. He saw me hit, bleeding, maybe dying, and he freaked for vengeance.

It all happened so fast. The cop killer had struck once before in this borough. We were in our usual prowl area and were on the look-out for him like everyone else. We never expected to find him. We didn't. He found us. He was hunting cops. The whole thing was a set-up and we'd walked right into it.

"No!" I shouted, "Don't do it!"

"Shut up and stay put," Larry whispered, calm, smiling now, "This won't take long. I'll be back in five minutes."

He slipped two cartridges into the shotgun, then blended into the darkness of the night so damn fast—like between heartbeats.

I tried like hell to get up and follow him. I knew the backups would be here soon, but they'd be too late. I remember crawling across the wet asphalt, moving forward, leaving a sticky smear of red behind me like I was a damn snail. I'd knotted the tourniquet, tied it as tight as I could. It wasn't working so great, too much leakage. So much blood now. I tried to get up on my good leg, stumble, hop, do anything to catch up to Larry. It wouldn't work. By then I was dizzy and much too weak. So I crawled. Crawled like a motherfucken bug. My revolver drawn, my eyes searching desperately for Larry in the darkness, searching for the killer, seeing nothing but the blackness of the night. The shadows, the black of the bricks, the asphalt and con-crete were all closing in on me.

Finally, I spotted Larry. I was about to yell out to him to get back to the car, when I heard the shots. They came out of the blackness around me, and they struck him down.

It was weeks before I recovered. At least physically. Mentally, I don't know. I'm Vic Powers, I got my own way of dealing with things. It's different from most people. Let's leave it at that for now.

It was weeks later when I was able to really move around. The first thing I did was extend my time off. Wounded cop. Line of duty. I got it, no sweat. Then I decided to perform my own investigation and get Larry's killer.

I had some good hunches. Better facts. Facts I had not put in my report. I'd seen the killer. Clear. After he'd shot Larry he came out from his hiding place. He came out to look at his handiwork. He stood there. Laughing. It was only for a minute. He didn't know I was there, but I saw his face as clear as daylight in the flash of a headlight from a passing car. That was all I needed. I could wait. I'd never forget that face.

Rounding up the creep was no problem. It didn't take me long to dig around and find him. I'm good at that stuff. Once I get the scent I run all the way with it. Hungry. Non-stop.

The piece-of-shit was my meat now. I had him tied and gagged in the trunk of my car. I was driving around the city thinking about what the hell I was going to do to him. There were a lot of possibilities. This was something I wanted to think through real good. It was for Larry.

It was a good feeling to have Larry's killer just where I wanted him. I kept thinking about that. I thought about what Larry would have done. Shit, he'd have done the right thing and brought the guy in.

"I can't do that, Larry," I said out loud. It went against the grain. What if the killer got off from some soft-bellied judge? What if some liberal idiots figure he didn't get as many "rights" as he was entitled to and he got a light, easy-tit sentence? I'd seen that shit too much.

Damn weasels!

That's the bullshit they call justice—but the only justice for a murderer is a quick bullet in the brain and six feet of dirt.

I hung a turn onto the parkway. Floored the gas pedal. The speed felt good and there was no traffic. Speedometer moving up to 60, past 65 now. I popped another upper. Been driving a long time. Thinking. Thinking so much it hurt.

When I finally became aware of the sounds I didn't know what the hell they were. Then I realized, banging from the trunk. The killer was awake, kicking around in the darkness, trying to get out.

"Shut up! You fucking murdering bastard!"

He kept kicking. The sound went right through my brain.

I took a sharp turn, I knew that would rattle his cage a bit.

"Now shut up and let me think!"

The banging wouldn't stop. It was driving me crazy.

"Larry, what should I do with this piece of garbage?"

Larry wouldn't answer me just then. Maybe it was the drugs. Or me being so tired. I mean, I knew Larry was dead and couldn't talk to me, but I really needed to hear his voice just then. I really needed to talk to him. The fact that we'd never talk again just burned me up. It couldn't be! It just couldn't be! Maybe Larry was dead, but I could still talk to him. I *needed* to talk to him just then.

"I'm alone, man, help me. I don't know what to do."

The banging began again. Into my brain.

"I need you, Larry. Why'd you leave me? Why'd you put yourself out there to save me? I wasn't worth it!"

The banging continued. Drowning out the sound of the car.

"I'm all alone now, Larry. I don't know what the fuck to do anymore!"

The banging grew louder. Intense.

"Shut up back there! You fucken killer! You killed the only friend I ever had! He was like a brother to me and you killed him for no damn reason!"

The killer tried to yell but the tape over his mouth made only tiny sounds. But I heard them. I heard them! I HEARD THEM!

"Shut up! I'll stop this car right now and rip your fucking face off with my damn hands if you don't shut up!"

The kicking stopped. The noise stopped.

OK, that was better. I tried to open another bottle of beer. Finally got it open and chugged it down between the tears. Threw the empty in the back seat. It shattered on another bottle. I didn't even notice.

The guy was quiet now. Now I could think. So I drove around the city. Thinking. Talking with Larry's ghost. Trying to figure out what we should do.

I thought about how lovely it was going to be to plug that murdering son-of-a-bitch. Plug him real good. Permanent customize job on that fucker. But it had to be good. It had to be special. Just killing him wasn't enough. It had to mean something, just as Larry's life had meant something. So much.

"What should I do, Larry?" the highway lights rushing over my tearful eyes, fogging my glassy vision, leaving me alone and confused. "Why'd you leave me! I'm so lost now. I don't know what the hell to do. Help me, Larry!"

I knew it had to be the drugs talking. I didn't care. Before I crashed I popped some more uppers, letting the car drive me. We drove all over. It eventually took me to the old neighborhood, the place where Larry and I had grown up. I don't know how I got there but it was significant. It was the place where Larry had chosen to live his life with Susan and raise their family. I knew then that Larry was guiding my hand.

I passed the house slowly. Everything looked the same, nothing seemed to have changed since the killing. Except for Larry. He was gone now forever. The feeling of loss was heavy in the air, like a thick fog swirling all around me, everything so sad, so lonely. I could feel what Susan and the boys were going through. Susan's quiet determination, her bravery, the sadness, that cold loneliness in bed at night as she slept alone. Without Larry for the rest of her life. That was an aching loss that would always be an open wound. Then there was the anger of the boys, all they'd miss growing up without a father. Just when they'd really need him—he couldn't be there for them. I knew what they felt. I felt it too.

My fist smashed the dashboard.

I stopped the damn car.

I knew what I had to do.

It was dark. Just right for what I'd decided. I parked the car. It was a quiet street. No one was around. I unlocked the truck and took out the garbage.

"If you make one move, one whisper, I'll blow your fucking brains out. Got it!"

He nodded, shivering, eyes ablaze.

He was cuffed, hands behind, duct tape over the mouth. I cut off another piece of tape. A long piece. Wrapped it around his head so it covered his eyes. Tight. He wasn't seeing nothing.

"We're going for a walk, don't give me no problems."

I pulled him out of the trunk and he fell to the asphalt. I pulled him to his feet by his hair. I took my right hand and dug it into the back of his neck leading him forward to the gate. I saw the dog house Larry had built for the three monsters. The three monsters weren't anywhere in sight. I knew Susan kept them in the house since the murder. It helped having them around, helped with the loneliness. They were Larry's dogs and he loved them, a small part of Larry left

180

alive in the world. The dogs were a part of the family, they were Larry's children too. They were the boys' brothers now.

I opened the gate to the backyard. It slid open silently. I pushed the killer forward.

There was a metal pole in the center of the yard. It was about twenty feet high, made of thick gauge piping Larry had cemented into the ground. It was real solid. Larry was going to make an oldtime swing or something for him and Susan someday. That day would never come now but I hoped to put it to good use. I pushed the killer to the ground, unlocked one of the cuffs, quickly putting it back on again with his arms behind the pole. I left the tape on his mouth and eyes.

He got nervous and tried to kick me, almost hitting my sore leg. I smacked him upside the head. He bled a bit, was stunned. I held myself back from finishing the job.

I left him there and went to the house, rang the bell.

Susan answered. Behind her were Larry's four teenage sons, the three dogs stood strangely quiet in the background. Waiting. Anticipating. Watching so damn interested.

Susan was surprised. "Vic? What are you doing here?"

I said, "Susan, I've got something for you, for the boys. Something for Larry too. He's chained in the back yard. It's the man who killed Larry. I saw him do it. He's yours. Do whatever you want to him. No one need ever know. I'll be back this time tomorrow night to take care of what's left."

Then I left. Their faces blank, stunned. None of them knew what to say. Neither did I. I'd said enough. I got in my car and drove away.

I drove around for hours. Thinking things through. Trying to figure it out in my own way. Why did this guy want to kill cops? Not one particular cop, just any cop. I couldn't figure it. Maybe he didn't even know why he did it. He just did it. I didn't care now. He'd murdered Larry and that was enough for me. It didn't have to make sense. Not everything makes sense. Damn little really does anymore. To me.

I didn't know what Susan and the boys would do to him. I figure they deserved the opportunity to make him pay, they were owed that much, at least. Hey, isn't that what America's all about? Opportunity. And Justice! Let the family decide what the killer deserved.

I know it was a stupid thing to do. Not only career-wise. Hell, my cop career was going right down the toilet since Larry's death. I knew that. I didn't care now. I'd never be able to handle it again. Not that I did so well before. And now, the more I thought about it, I realized I'd messed up again. Real bad. I'd put Susan and the boys in terrible jeopardy, made them have to make nasty choices they should have been spared. I'd also placed them in considerable danger. What if that bastard got loose? It would be on my head. If he didn't get away Larry's boys would just tear the bastard apart. They weren't so much like their dad, but they loved him fiercely. They'd destroy the guy who murdered him if they could. I'd made that possible now. And it might destroy *them* if they did it and word got out.

"Stupid shit! Why do I always fuck up the worst when I try to do good?"

I looked at my watch. It was already 5 A.M. I'd been driving most of the night. I hadn't slept in two days. I was running on coffee and uppers. And beer. Where the hell was I anyway? I had to hurry. I hit traffic on the way back. By the time I got into Brooklyn it was already rush hour.

I was nervous. Flying from the pills and lack of sleep. Worried about what I'd find in the back yard. Susan and the boys had been through so much, now I'd put this shit on them. I felt like crap.

I pulled up to the house with a screech, got out of the car, ran to the front porch. Susan opened the door. She was alone, the boys were probably on the way to school that time of morning. Or were they out in the back with the killer!

Susan saw me but didn't say a word.

"Susan . . . ?"

She shook her head. Stunned.

"Is he dead?" I asked.

She ignored my question. There was anger in her face.

"Vic, we had a very bad night last night because of you."

"Sue, I know. I'm so sorry, I wasn't thinking right . . ."

"The boys went wild. I lost control over them for the first time. I thought they were going to kill that bastard, tear him apart, but they didn't. It was so weird, Vic, it wasn't like they didn't want to do it, even I thought about it last night when I was alone in bed. Alone in the bed Larry and I used to share. But the boys stopped. They were really going to kill him—but they stopped."

"I'm glad, Sue. I'll go get him and bring him in."

"Vic, that was such a stupid thing to do," but she gave me a sad little smile as she said it, "but we all love you for it. Don't think we don't understand. I wish it could have brought Larry back, and if it would have, I would be the first one to pull the trigger on that piece of filth, but please, Vic, get that garbage out of our back yard. Take it

182

where it belongs. I don't want his presence fouling our house anymore."

I nodded. A bit subdued for once. She slowly closed the door, looking so tired. I went to the side of the house, through the gate, out to the back yard.

The killer, his name wasn't important, was where I'd left him the night before. Same position. Same condition. Untouched. His mouth and eyes were still covered with the duct tape. His hands still cuffed behind him to the pole. He lay stretched out, quiet, motionless.

I moved up close. He stiffened. I whispered into his ear.

"So no one touched you. You're a lucky piece-of-shit! These are good people, you don't deserve their mercy. I'm taking you in for the murder of policeman Larry Jenkins. I saw you do it. I'm his partner, the one you wounded in the leg. The one that didn't die."

I moved behind him and bent down low to put my key into the left cuff. It snapped open. He lashed out with his leg, his boot smashing into my bad leg. His wrist slid out of the cuff. I let out a gasp of pain. He let loose with a roundhouse swing, the metal cuff catching me square on the side of the head near the eye. I reeled, fell back stunned, seeing stars for a moment. By the time I could see images again the killer had ripped the duct tape off his eyes and mouth and was on me like a madman.

He knew I was the only thing between him and freedom. I was the only witness. Take me out and no one would ever know. He wasn't a big guy, normally I could have smashed him a dozen ways to Sunday, but he was wiry and frantic, and his attack had me off balance. I was having trouble fighting him off, seeing two of him, four hands at my throat pressing tighter and tighter. I tried to shake him off, but he was good, and I knew I was in a fight for my life with a killer who had everything to gain by my death and nothing to lose.

I tried to reach inside my jacket to get at my revolver, but it wasn't there. Then he hit me again. Hard. Two, three times. It was hard to think straight anymore, the hands at my throat were cutting off my breathing. Things started to get fuzzy all around me. I felt the killer's fingers digging deeper and deeper into my throat, my corded muscles slowly giving way as he pressed, cutting off my breathing.

I remember seeing his face up so close. Young, almost handsome, now all twisted with hatred and bloodlust. The son-of-a-bitch was smiling, he knew what was coming, soon he was going to add one more dead cop to his tally.

My head lolled over to the side, I tried to hit him, knock him off me, but my fists could only hit weak and glancing blows that hardly seemed to bother him.

I saw Susan at the screen door on the back porch. Her attention had finally been drawn by the noise of the fight. The alarm in her face said it all to me, she knew I was a goner too.

Then Susan opened the screen door.

My voice was able to let out one tiny gasp of terror as I saw Larry's pack of monstrous dogs charging down at me. They ran like bats out of hell. The giant Shephard with slavering jaws and long razor teeth, the two silk-black Dobermans, eyes ablaze with the killing lust. They were on us instantly. They were on the killer like white on rice. And they held onto him while he screamed. No matter what he did, he couldn't get away, he couldn't shake them off. It was wonderful.

They left me alone, coming real close but not touching me at all, they were after my attacker. They knew the difference. They took a chunk of him here, a bite there, drawing blood in a dozen places, moving in on his neck, chomping his hands as he tried vainly to defend himself. I was able to roll away, watching the dogs close in on the killer's throat, cutting it with bloody teeth, crushing it with jaws that could deliver over 500 pounds of smashing, killing, demolition pressure.

Susan came out of nowhere, muttered a command, the dogs quickly moved off to sit quietly behind her.

I prodded part of the bloody carcass of Larry's killer with my hand. There wasn't much left in one piece and it was obvious he was deader than hell. That pile of garbage never looked so good.

Susan helped me up. I was really shaky, covered in blood, but I didn't care because all of it was the killer's. That was OK by me, he wouldn't need it anymore. It would wash off real easy too.

I watched the dogs, growing a little nervous. They were watching me so closely. Guardedly. They looked like they were ready for some more action. That's not what I wanted to see.

Susan smiled at me, "What a mess."

"Just what he deserves," I said.

"Not him, Vic. You. And don't be scared of the puppies. It's OK now."

Puppies, I thought. When I found my voice I said, "They make me nervous."

"You make them nervous too, but don't let them bother you."

"I know, that's what Larry always used to tell me."

She smiled at the mention of Larry's name. So did I. We both missed him, both felt him with us just then. I swear, he was there. Smiling.

She said, "The dogs won't hurt you, Vic. They only hurt the enemy. You're not the enemy. Larry was right. Dogs know."

I didn't say a word. Larry was right. Dogs know.

So I tried to pet one of the ugly brutes. He took a snap at my hand, almost taking it off!

Susan laughed. "Larry always said dogs know, Vic. He didn't say they were fucking geniuses!"


# Duck Behind that Eight-Ball!

## *by Nick Spain*

You run a pool hall long enough, you get so you can tell these things. The minute the guy walked in, I knew he was a dick. He said, "Fellow named Giles hang around here?"

I said, "Seems I've heard the name. What do you want him for?"

"They tell me he's here all the time."

"He comes in now and then," I said.

"I'll be back."

"Any time," I said, and watched him walk away. It didn't surprise me none. This Giles, he is all right if you care for that sort of guy— completely worthless and working at it full time. In the first place, he's a braggart of that worst kind, the kind that can make his boasts stick or else weasel out of them some way.

Take the time in '39 this Tiger Cline, he come down to Lake Mellow to train. The lake was still there, but that was the only thing that hadn't burnt down except an outdoor stage the Tiger was using to spar on. He stayed at the Garden City Inn, in town, and run out to Lake Mellow every morning and back and then run out again and worked a few rounds with what local talent he could get cheap. The Tiger was kind of a beat-up looking guy and no kid, but from his clippings he was a fair fighter.

Giles saw him in my pool hall one night. Giles was sitting around waiting for a fish, as usual, and he saw this Cline come in and shoot a couple of games of pool and go out.

"So," he said, "that's the jerk that's gonna fight Armstrong. I can beat that guy myself."

"Playin' pool?" somebody asked.

"Boxin'," Giles said.

"Boxin' oranges?" somebody asked him. We ain't strong for wit in Garden City.

Giles turned to the guy that made the crack. "I'll tell you what I'll do, wise guy," he said. "I'll play you a game of rotation and let you shoot offa the big end for a fin."

Now that's a hell of a handicap. If you ever played pool, you know. One guy starts shooting at the one ball and the other guy at the fifteen ball. It's three to one odds.

"Okay," this chump says. I forgot who he was. He got his fin up and Giles let him break the balls and then Giles beat him. This Giles shoots a hell of a cue. He gets the two fins out of the side pocket where they stuck them and he says, "I'll bet you the ten I can beat that Tiger Cline boxin'."

There ain't any question this guy was sore by then and I guess he figured that he'd fix Giles up. He didn't say nothin' but he went out of the door and in about ten minutes he was back and he said to Giles, "I got it fixed for you. You get to work with the Tiger tomorrow afternoon."

"For five or ten?" Giles asks.

The guy gets kind of pale, he's that mad. He turns to me. "Al," he says, "will you cash me a check for a sawbuck?"

The guy probably didn't have no ten in the bank but with a check you can collect, generally. "Okay," I told him. I didn't like this Giles myself. I didn't like him good.

This kid scribbles me off a little lumber for ten and I give him the ten. "For ten," the guy says to Giles. "Get yours up."

Giles he started welching then. "Now what have I got to do?" he asks. "Go out there and knock a professional boxer kickin' that's trainin' to fight Lefty Armstrong in St. Louis next week?"

"You said for ten you could beat him," I said.

"Well," Giles said, "one round, how's that? I'll go out there and work one round with him and let the Tiger's manager figure who won." He gets the ten out and gets it up. Then he comes over to me and asks real respectful, "You don't mind if I walk Margie home, do you? It may be my last night on earth."

186

Margie, she's my step-daughter and she's twenty-one, only a couple

Margie, she's my step-daughter and she's twenty-one, only a couple of years younger than Giles, and of course what I say wouldn't change her mind a quarter's worth. That is, about Giles. She likes the guy or something and they kind of go together in spite of me. Margie runs the fountain and we close that down at ten though I run the poolhall till twelve. "She's twenty-one," I says, kind of surly.

"And I'm twenty-three," he said. "Ain't it hell to be fifty?"

I wasn't but forty-nine at the time but—well, what the hell!

I got home at twelve-ten and run him out of the porch swing. "You better get your beauty sleep," I told him. "You got a date with some leather tomorrow. Right in the puss."

Margie says, "Giles, what in the world . . . ?"

"I beat a chump out of five tonight," he says, "playin' rotation, and for a gag I told him I'd bet him the ten that I could beat a guy named Tiger Cline boxin'."

"Who's Tiger Cline?" Margie asked.

"Oh," Giles says, "he's a never-was that's trainin' out at Mellow Lake to be beat up by Lefty Armstrong down in St. Louis next week."

"Giles," Margie said, "you make me sick. Why don't you get a job? I hope Tiger Cline beats your brains out."

"Aw, honey . . ."

"I hope he does. I hope he beats you—"

"Till you can't recognize me, honey? If that happens and you see some bloody hulk come into the pool hall tomorrow night and if he meows like a cat that'll be me."

"Go home," Margie says.

Giles, he gets up and goes on down the street, gay as a lark. And of course he crosses us all up. He must have gone down and talked to Cline and give him a great song and dance, because the next day we go out to Mellow Lake and Giles he takes off his shirt and puts on some boxin' shoes and they lace the big gloves on him and him and the Tiger start sparrin' around on the old stage that they have roped off for a ring. The Tiger stabs him four, five times and roughs him around in close, but Giles gets in some good solid licks and keeps his left hand out pretty good and he actually shakes the Tiger up toward the end of the round. He turns to the Tiger's manager.

"Who win that one?" he asks.

"I'd give you a shade," Tiger's manager said.

"Okay," Giles says, "lemme out of these mittens."

"But," the Tiger says, "you said last night you'd work three rounds if I—"

Giles has got the gloves off. "Give me the twenty," he says to me, and what else can I do?

He come in the pool hall that night meowing like a cat and he took Margie home but the next day he drawed I-A in the draft and we got rid of him shortly. That was the draft before the war. The draft for one year.

I didn't run him offa the porch the last night, because Margie was cryin'.

"She ain't got anybody but herself to blame," Giles says. "If she'd have wed me, I'd be safe as a church."

"What if I married you now?" Margie asked. I felt pretty funny there for a minute.

"Why," Giles says, and his voice is even in the dark, "you'd be makin' a eighteen-carat mistake." He stops a minute. "Good-night, Al" he says to me. "I'll see you in the guardhouse." I go on in the house and Margie comes in pretty soon. We don't say nothing much to each other and she goes on to bed.

That all seems like a million years ago. Giles he gets back on leave a couple of times and he sees Margie when he's back and I keep on running the pool hall and Margie she keeps on running the soda fountain. I get one card from him. "Dear Al" he writes. "I have done so much K. P. that my fingers have got so stiff I probably couldn't make a froze combination in the corner pocket. However, I win fifty-five last night shooting dice. Did they let go on a blanket in the last war without no cup? Your, Giles."

That seems like five hundred thousand years ago, because Giles came in one day. Margie dashed around the counter and threw her arms around him and kissed him and I went up and shook him by the hand. To me he looked just the same but he had a limp in his walk and he carried a cane. He wasn't in uniform.

"How are you, Giles?" I said. "I'm glad to see you, kid."

"I'm glad to see you, Al," he said over Margie's shoulder. He hadn't let go of Margie.

"Giles, why didn't you write?" Margie said.

"I wrote every year," Giles said. "Anyway, you know me, solid as a rock."

I nodded toward his knee.

"I fought a short war," Giles said. "I got offa one of them landing boats and run up the beach and I kick a mine they had missed. Then they carried me down and put me on a boat and took me back to England."

188

"That the McCoy?" I ask him.

"Naw," he said. "Matter of fact, I was over there a coupla days and got me two medals for bein' brave and stuff, besides a Purple Heart."

I shrugged my shoulders. He'd be tellin' me something else if I asked him, I knew.

"I was in a hospital in England and a hospital in New York and in a hospital in Washington and then they give me the toss."

"Skip it," I said.

"How's the pigeon crop?" he asked.

"There's dough around," I said.

"Were you—did you get to be an officer?" Margie asks.

"I got to be a first class private a coupla times, only they busted me. But I was gainin' on 'em. I was a Corporal when I went over."

Well, he hung around and he was the first guy back in Garden City and he told 'em some wonderful lies, I guess. One day he'd got run over by a jeep, the next day he'd stormed a machine gun nest bare-handed, or something. He had a lot of fun, I guess, and really, believe it or not, he hadn't changed. I know that it changes guys, but Giles, he wasn't changed. It took him about a week to get to shootin' his stick again and he was making pretty good money shootin' pool in ten days.

He walked Margie home every night though he didn't walk very good and it took him longer to get from the pool hall out to the house. I didn't like the guy. He could have gone to work for good money, even with that bum knee. I said something to him one time about it. He was knocking the balls around and waiting for a sucker.

"Everybody you know, pretty near," he said, "has got a knee that will bend one way. But me . . . why I'll just make you a little bet that I can bend mine the wrong way out to here," and he held his hand down. It made me kind of sick.

"Of course," he said, "it ain't so good for prayin' or shootin' craps. I done a lot of both in the Army, but then I ain't in the Army any more."

"I don't see what Margie sees in you," I said, and I must have sounded real sincere because he answered me.

"She sees my soul, Al, shinin' out of my limpid blue eyes. She also knows I'll always be for her, do I write her or not, and she furthermore knows I won't do nothing wrong."

"Just nothing," I says. "You don't have to stick that *wrong* on there."

He laughs and cuts a ball back into the side pocket. He can make shots I never seen anybody else even try.

"If you don't do nothing wrong," I said, "what do you consider it is to lay around and hustle pool and play cards all day and all night?"

"The guy that runs the pool hall says it's wrong to play pool," he says.

I didn't say nothing more and pretty soon a foreman from one of the shops comes in and Giles beats him for sixteen bucks in a nice, smooth way. He don't wrench it out of him; he just beats him a little —just for all he's got with him and I'll swear he makes it look like he's just lucky.

It goes on that way until about a month ago he limps over to the counter and talks to Margie a while and then he comes on back to where I'm brushing the farthest back table.

"Al," he says, "what you got against me? Really?"

"You ain't got a job," I tell him. "The war's been over a long time, but you don't act like you want to get a job. You're—you're just a adult delinquent."

"You mean like some of these kids around the cities runnin' around in hot cars, knockin' off joints and such?"

A couple of kids I don't recognize walk in the front and I go up to see what they want. First they want some cigarettes and then they want some liquor. I ain't got any cigarettes and I don't handle nothing but beer, of which I am out.

One of them reaches under his coat and he fishes out a gun that the front end of looks like you can crawl in it and turn around. He points it right at me. "That your heap settin' in front?" he asks.

I admit it is. Giles, he limps out. "Just what we was talking about," he says. "I ain't like these kids, at all, at all. I wouldn't be carryin' no gun like that around for all the tea in China."

"Gimme the key to the heap," this kid says and his eyes look funny, dilated, and I know he's hopped up. The other kid, about eighteen, he just stands there. He looks like he's about half drunk.

I start fishing for the keys and toss them over. "Help yourself, son," I says, kind of shaky. "It's insured."

"Get their dough," the kid with the gun says. The dark complected one, the one that looks half crocked, he comes over and Giles and I, we hand them our money.

"You read about that daylight job down in St. Louis yesterday?" the kid with the gun asks. "We pulled that."

"He's tougher'n Dillinger," the dark complected one says. "Let's go."

"These guys will bleat soon as we get outta here," the one with the gun says. "Let's take the broad with us."

190

Giles goes pale and I see the sweat start on his brow and he moves up a little closer.

"Bud," he says, "I ain't got any folks an I'm kind of a tough guy myself, not like you all but kind of a underworld character and you don't want to take the girl with you. It'll just make you trouble. We'll let you go."

"You're some hero," Margie says from behind me, and I see one good thing coming from the setup. It shows Margie really what kind of a guy this Giles is, back from the wars or not.

"Honey, you want with one leg I should fight this guy and him with a gun in his hand that would blow a hole in me as big as your head?"

"Let's lam," the dark one says. "Come on, baby."

Giles, he gets closer to the guy. "I'm a real hero," he says and reaches in his pocket and he hauls out a medal and tosses it to the guy with the gun. "I win that in France, with ten million Jerries shootin' exclusively at me."

The kid looks at the medal, and Giles reaches out with his cane and jerks the kid to him with the crook of it around his neck and with his good foot he kicks the gun and the dad-blasted thing goes off.

Giles' bad leg folds up under him like a accordian, but he has got the hand that holds the gun in his two hands by then and he's got the kid down on top of him and the kid ain't got a chance. I grab up a cue ball and score on the dark complected one. I drop him cold and break out my plate glass window where I bank it off his head. Then I help Giles with the kid. Giles has like to bit his wrist off and the gun is layin' on the floor. I bust the kid over the head with it.

We get 'em tied up good before they come to and I go call the sheriff.

Giles gets up off the floor very shaky. "I hurt my knee," he says, but he is hobbling around on the floor looking for something and he finds it and drops it in his pocket. It's the medal.

"Lemme see the medal," I says.

"Al, don't be silly. I told you I was in France for three days and really was decorated before I was shot up."

"You've told me everything. Lemme see it."

But Giles, he is kind of white and moves over and leans against the counter. "As for you," he says to Margie, "I don't know whether I'll marry you or not. You seemed to prefer that I get a big chunk blowed out of me rather than taking a short motor ride with those two delinquents."

The sheriff comes up, wakin' everybody with his siren, and takes the kids away after much conversation and so on.

"There ain't much use lockin' up," I says, lookin' out at the crowd and my broken window, "but let's go home."

And Margie, my own step-daughter, she turns on me. "You come out with us, Giles," she says. "Al's been treatin' you like a dog for years, but I'm gonna tell him. We been married for four years and he's a hero, won those medals on the square. He was in France five days and—"

"Aw, honey," Giles says, "skip it." He turns to me. "You don't mind if I stay with you a few days, do you, Al? While I look around. I wasn't gonna tell you till I was settled and could support Margie in style."

Well, that was a month ago and he's still here livin' at my house. Not that I mind much. I kinda got used to him after all of these years, and he and Margie are sure happy. . . .

Up till now. And now Giles walks in and the detective is right behind him. The dick says, "Your name Giles?"

Giles grins and says, "You called it, friend. You like snooker?"

"Some other time. Right now I'm due back in St. Louis. There's a man whose son was killed. He sent me down for you."

Giles says, "Yeah? What for?" And I look at him. He's the coolest guy in town, but I'm thinking of Margie and what to tell her. Whatever I thought of Giles, I never pegged him for this.

The detective slaps down a paper, pulls out a pen and says, "Sign. It's a matter of five yards reward for those punks you grabbed. Before they got down here, they pulled a daylight job in St. Louis, shot up half the town."

Giles looks down at the paper and says, "Tell the old boy to drop down some time. I'll play him a thousand or nothing. Sure you ain't got time for a game?"

I gave Giles a dirty look, and I guess he saw I meant it. I picked up the check, and Giles owned a piece of the pool hall.

Which didn't matter at all to him. But the detective allowed he could play one game, and that made Giles pretty happy. They went to the back table, and two hours later the shamus gave me a marker, and I lent him five to get home.

# Dust

*by James W. Holden*

Patrolman Hammer wore a new gray pepper-and-salt topcoat and carried a new brown leather billfold. But the two-dollar bill he shoved under the ticket window had a corner missing. It was the sort of bill you might find in the pocket of a superstitious cop.

"Two," he rumbled.

Puckering her ruby lips, the blonde in the booth saw that one corner of the bill had been clipped off as if by a circular tool.

"Do you-all bite the corners of two-dollar bills?" she asked as she punched out the tickets.

Yanking his watch chain, Dave Hammer showed her a flat penknife with a round hole through it.

"No, sister—I clip off a corner with my little cigar cutter."

"You're a nut," said the blonde.

Dave rejoined a girl who was standing by the door. "She says I'm a nut because I clip off a corner of a two-dollar bill for good luck," he remarked to Lucy as they went into the theater.

"That's right," agreed Lucy cheerfully.

The feature throbbed to a finish. A newsreel banged through. The next picture was a Western. At one point, when the screen cowboy raised his gun, Dave squeezed Lucy's hand. He got a kick out of shooting on the screen.

"I nevah kills a man in cold blood," drawled the screen hero, letting the six-shooter fall to his side.

*Bang* went the gun. People snickered.

"He must be shooting at the ground," said Dave to Lucy.

"That wasn't on the screen—it was in the back of the theater!"

Dave put his topcoat down on the seat and walked back. Apparently every one else thought the shot was a bum sound effect, but he was glad he had a .32 revolver in his side pocket. He asked the ticket chopper, a tall and serious young man with black hair, if he had heard a shot.

"Only on the screen, mister." The chopper tore a brace of tickets in half. "Did you?"

"I don't know."

Blinking at the glare, Dave went into the lobby, which was papered with lurid posters. At the ticket booth he shoved up to the window where the ruby-mouth blonde was punching change and shouted through a hole in the glass.

"Hear any shooting, Scarlett?"

"Why don't you-all get in line and let—" But she was susceptible to a good-looking, tough, tanned face. "Oh, it's you-all. Did I hear any shooting? I did not."

"Did a car backfire?"

"I can't hear nothing in this booth. However, this is about the time" —she shot a glance at a flashing wristwatch—"nine-thirty, yeah, it's about the time Mr. Pearsall generally gets held up. Better try his office. It's at the head of a stairs opening on the inside foyer."

"He's been held up before?"

"Six–eight times. He's an old circus man—he *likes* it. Lemme know."

Patrolman Hammer looked up and down the street, choked with Saturday night cars and people, and saw a harness cop chinning with the man who ran a popcorn machine next door to the theater. He knew the cop, Slim Duggan.

"Hi, Slim, do me a favor? Keep an eye on this alley. All the exits open on it, don't they? Don't let anybody out and I'll give you a cheroot when I get married."

Slim nodded. "All the exits that don't open on the other side of the theater. I can cover both sides. Chase 'em out and gimme a shot at 'em —I'm getting rusty."

Patrolman Hammer blinked back through the glaring lobby. He was pretty sure nobody had just come out. To the black-haired ticket chopper, giving him an eyeful of a nickel-plated badge in his hand, he said:

"Is there any way you can lock these doors and not let anybody out for five minutes?"

"What for?" The chopper knew his job; he'd be manager some day. "We can't keep people in—that would amount to false arrest."

"Don't be so damn sure it's false," Dave snapped. "I can order the doors locked and I'm doing it."

"Can I let people in?"

"Sure."

The young man unlocked, closed and bolted two sets of double doors, stood by the third and continued to take tickets. Dave found a small door opening on a stairway as steep as a ship's companionway, but halfway up he saw glaring lights and heard a tinny voice: "Mary won't have no truck with your kind." He hastily backed down; it was the projection room. Farther along the foyer he found another door and a similar stairway.

He took the gun out of his pocket, unlocked it and oozed up the treads as quietly as an Indian snaking up on your great-great-grandmother. He sneezed.

"Damn!"

He was in a dusty little office painted a violent pink with poisonous green furniture. Sitting on a big gilt chair and sprawled over the desk, almost as if he'd gone to sleep, was the manager. Dead as a herring. His wavy, light-colored toupée had fallen to the desk, exposing a pink dome with a few hairs on it. The top of the desk was a pond of fresh blood, which was pattering to the floor.

On the floor was a small canvas bag such as people use to carry cash to a night depository. Dave kicked the bag. There was nothing in it.

There was dust on the desk edges. Dave walked around to the other side, but saw no wound from which the blood still oozed; Pearsall must have been shot in the chest. The manager's right hand hung down emptily, and on the floor under it was a quaint single-barreled derringer with a pearl handle.

Again Dave sneezed. "Another lousy cold," he muttered. "Poor guy—he got worse than a cold."

Pearsall must have been a character. His face, turned to one side, was florid and paunchy with bags under the eyes. He was dressed like a carnival man in a checked jacket such as hardly anybody wears any more, light-gray trousers, spats. There were gold rings on his fingers, and over in a corner was a gold-headed cane. On the desk was a fancy silver item which Dave picked up and puzzled over.

*Chew!* Again Patrolman Hammer sneezed. "Sure is draughty in here. Well, the guy that shot Pearsall didn't want gold, only cash. Guess he didn't expect to shoot the old boy. Wonder where he went?"

He opened a small locker, but this contained only a brown gabardine coat and a black Homburg hat. Nothing was under the desk except the manager's spatted feet. Dave pocketed his revolver and crept downstairs feeling rather baffled. At the main door three people were waiting to get out—a man, a woman and a little boy.

"Are you three together?" he asked.

"Yes, and we want to go home. My baby is sick," replied the woman sharply.

"Let 'em go," he said to the ticket chopper. "But don't let anybody else out."

Dave felt dubious by this time. It was probable that the man—he was sure that only one man could slip up there without being noticed—had hidden among the audience. Nothing to it, he thought grimly—there weren't more than three hundred people in the theater. For a minute he looked over the rows of heads, like bowling balls, before the blue-white screen. One of these people had just killed a man. But which one?

When he began to feel conspicuous, Dave walked down the aisle and Lucy took his topcoat in her lap.

"Was it a shot?" she asked in a low voice.

Dave nodded. "Hold on to my coat, honey—I'll be going out again." He was listening hard. Everybody in the theater seemed to be coughing. To his tense ears the audience and the screen voices were as noisy as a battle. Rangers were galloping over the Hollywood hills in the picture. *Cloppety-clop, cloppety-clop. Bang-bang!* This shooting was in the screen play as the hero, clutching his horse by the mane, twisted in his saddle and took aim at his quarry. But the picture had lost its thrill.

"Damn all this racket," Dave muttered. Then his fists knotted. He slipped out of his seat and marched to the back of the theater.

"Did you sneeze?" he demanded of a big gray man sitting on the aisle.

The man blinked and said: "What?"

"Did *you*?" he asked the man in the seat behind, less heavy but just as gray.

"Not me."

A girl in the next seat was staring. "He did too, mister—he nearly blew my hat off. Some sneeze!"

Patrolman Hammer was taking no chances. He shoved his six-shooter in the fellow's ribs.

"Put down your coat and come outside. Don't think I won't plug you just because this is a theater. Keep your hands at your sides and walk ahead of me."

People gaped as they went out.

"Down in the smoking room."

The man knew he didn't have a chance. He just stared ahead of him, his watery gray eyes as dull as bullets. There was nothing inter-

196

csting about him—he was all gray. Even his carefully brushed hair was gray around the edges. It would be a lot grayer, Dave thought, before he got out of stir, if he ever did. Only once did the man show signs of life. He sneezed.

"Quiet," growled Dave.

The man didn't even fight when Dave stuck his hand into a side coatpocket and fished out a huge roll of bills—ones, twos, fives, tens.

"I guess I got this coming to me . . . I didn't want to plug him." The man's voice was dull. "He shouldn't have tried to pull a fast one on me when I—"

"Yeah, he blew snuff in your face. Made you sneeze. Good thing he did."

"He shouldn't have tried—"

"Aw, snap out of it," said Dave Hammer.

He locked the man's wrists and took him out to Slim to be delivered to Sergeant Moses. Then he went into the candy store, called Moses and explained he would be in later with the roll of cash. On the way back he told the ticket chopper what had happened, and went to his seat. In snatches he told Lucy, and her hand bit his fingers, glad he was back safe.

"You took a big risk, honey. Suppose he hadn't talked. Anybody can carry a bale of money—He might have been a collector for a furniture company."

Dave chuckled as he thumbed through a large roll of money and took out a two-dollar bill with one corner neatly clipped off.

"No furniture man is getting two-dollar bills from me—not yet."

# Escape

*by Jack Foxx*

I had been on the road for more than two hours, pushing the sedan as fast as I dared, when I came down out of the mountains and saw the lights of Santa Alta spread across the valley below.

The twisting black ribbon of highway straightened here, and my foot crashed down harder on the accelerator. The cool night air sang through the open wind wing.

I glanced down quickly at the luminous dial of the dashboard clock. It was eleven-fifteen.

I had almost reached the outskirts of Santa Alta when they interrupted the recorded music on the radio for a news broadcast.

I kept my eyes riveted to the blurred white line beneath my headlights, and fumbled with my right hand to turn up the volume.

". . . *state-wide manhunt for escaped murderer Frank Vernon continues into the night*," the announcer was saying. "*Vernon, who was apprehended on suspicion of inter-state bank robbery this afternoon in Colman, shot and killed one of the Federal agents who was transporting him to the State Capitol and affected his escape in a stolen automobile. He is believed heading for Santa Alta, where his wife Marianne is a resident.*

"*Mrs. Vernon disappeared after drawing some four thousand dollars from her bank account shortly after her husband's flight, and it is theorized by police that Vernon contacted her by telephone and arranged a rendezvous. Vernon is armed and extremely dangerous. Citizens in the vicinity of Santa Alta are advised . . .*"

I didn't pay any attention to the rest of it. My hands were knuckle-white around the steering wheel. I could feel the hard outline of the gun against my side.

Grimly, I reduced my speed as I entered the city limits of Santa Alta. The streets were deserted. I drove through the industrial sector, near the river, until I came to the county highway that wound east up into the low foothills on the other side of town.

I followed the county highway for something over seven miles until I saw the entrance to the private road that angled off of it there. I made the turn, and drove over the graveled roadbed for another mile.

There was a sharp bend ahead, and I pulled the sedan off the road before I reached it, into a clump of scrub pine where it would be hidden from anyone approaching.

I switched off engine and lights, then stepped out. It was cold up here, the air thin and clear. There was a moon tonight, but it was hidden now behind a rolling bank of clouds.

I ran back to the road and crossed it. There was a short, rocky field on the other side. At the end of it was a densely-grown slope that rose at a sharp forty-five degree angle.

I paused at the edge of the field. The bend in the road brought it around on the other side of the slope.

That was where Marianne would be, hidden in a copse of trees.

I started off across the field, moving quickly, keeping my eyes on its rough surface. I reached the slope moments later and started up, my heart thumping in my chest.

Just before I crested the slope, I dropped prone. The ground was spongy and fertile here, and I inched my way over it on my belly to where I could look down through the heavy growth on its opposite side.

Marianne's car was there in the copse of trees. I could see the empty gray line of the roadway beyond.

I peered intently at the car. I could see a shadowy figure sitting behind the wheel, but at this distance and through the darkness I couldn't tell if it was Marianne or not.

My throat was dry as I made my way slowly and as silently as possible down the far slope. I kept my hand wrapped around the gun at my belt.

I was almost to the bottom, hidden by a thick growth of ferns, when I stopped moving. I was only about fifteen feet from the car. The figure behind the wheel was Marianne, all right.

I lay listening for a moment. There was only the night sounds of insects. I lifted my head and called her name in a soft voice. She didn't hear me. I called again. Her head jerked this time, swiveling around. She recognized my voice.

"Darling!" she breathed. "Oh, God, I thought you'd never come!"

"Are you alone?"

I saw her head bob, blonde hair dancing. "Yes. I've been so frightened, waiting here, just waiting."

"It's all right," I said. "Everything's all right, now."

"But suppose—"

I cocked my head, ears straining. "*Shh!*"

"What is it?"

"Listen!"

In the distance, barely audible at first but growing louder now, was the sound of a car engine. It was coming from the upper end of the private road, opposite the way I had come in. I knew that the road branched off a mile or two further on in that direction, and that one of those branches led to another county highway.

Marianne had heard the car engine, too. I could see her face, a pale cameo, her eyes huge and alive with fear. She was on the verge of losing control.

"Marianne!" I whispered. "Don't panic! Just sit still and be very quiet. Keep your eyes straight ahead. Do you understand?"

After a moment she said in a hushed voice, "Yes."

The sound of the car engine grew closer. I couldn't see any headlights, or even any sign of it. Abruptly, the sound ceased and the night was still again.

I lifted the gun from my belt and held it in my right hand. With my left, I made a part in the growth of ferns so that I could see Marianne and her car through it.

Time halted. I waited, my stomach knotted, my eyes probing the darkness for some sign of movement. There was nothing.

Suddenly I heard a gentle rustle of leaves from a point directly to the rear of Marianne's car, near a giant oak. I focused my eyes there. One of the shadows moved, detaching itself from the silent, blacker ones cast by the trees.

My finger tensed on the gun's trigger.

At that moment, the moon came out from behind the cloud bank and I could see the outline of a man. He stood absolutely motionless, one arm extended out in front of him. Then he stepped into the open and started toward Marianne's car, coming around the rear to the driver's side.

I could see his face clearly in the white lunar light. And I could see that in his extended hand he held a large, square automatic.

I stopped breathing. I let him get by the rear fender, on the side nearest me, before I raised up onto my knees, my own gun thrust out before me.

"Hold it!" I shouted. "Hold it right there!"

He spun toward the sound of my voice, the gun in his hand spitting flame. The bullet ploughed up earth inches to my right, spraying me with dirt.

I shot him twice.

Marianne screamed as the sound of the gun crashes reverberated through the trees. He went down, rolling onto his back by the rear tire, the automatic slipping from his fingers. He lay very still.

I scrambled to my feet and ran down there. I knelt beside him and put my hand on his chest. He wasn't breathing.

I stood up. Marianne threw open the car door and came running to me, flinging herself into my arms. I could feel her trembling. I held her tightly.

She whispered, "Is he—?"

"Yes."

Her arms tightened around me. She began to cry convulsively. "I—I don't know why I didn't call you sooner," she sobbed. "If I'd waited only a few minutes longer to get to a phone—"

"It's all right, Marianne," I said, stroking her hair. "I made it in time. That's all that matters."

"When he called I was terrified. I did what he told me as if I were in a trance. I drew the money out of the bank and I came up here to wait. He said he'd kill me if I didn't do exactly as he instructed. He said—"

"Easy, honey," I said. "It's over now. It's over."

"Oh, Paul. I don't know what I'd have done these past few months if I hadn't met you. Never knowing when he'd come back, when he'd—"

I kissed her tenderly. Then we walked back to where my car was hidden. We sat close together on the front seat while I lifted the microphone from the shortwave radio under the dash and put in a call to Colman Police Headquarters.

"This is Special Agent Barrows of the FBI," I said, when they answered. "You can call off the manhunt for Frank Vernon now. He's dead."

# Exhibit D

*by John Maclay*

Yes, Walter, you're a judge. And I've had a few drinks here at the country club, so perhaps that's why I'm telling you this story. But please don't give me that look which says it's beneath your dignity to listen. Because, appropriately, you *are* a judge. And, drinks or no, I'm worthy of your respect; I'm a doctor.

The late Harvey Newsome's doctor. And all of this is why you must believe me, Walter, when I contend that you should have put him away for . . . *murder.*

You'll remember Harvey, though I don't think you knew him as well as I did. A man in his sixties, as you and I are now. A member of this club, a professional; had a big accounting practice. Had gone to the right schools, made the right marriage. Was a good-looking fellow, even at his age, with his thatch of white hair, twinkly eyes, and infectious smile.

But now that you do remember Harvey, you'll also recall something else about him.

How—and I'll try not to be guilty of the same—he could *talk.*

So, to use your terms, let me present my case . . .

Exhibit A.

I was a guest at a garden party some years ago; a big affair, with one of those yellow-and-white tents. That was the first time I really noticed Harvey at work. Yes, we'd all been buttonholed often enough by him, yet being his peers, had been able to handle it. But this time, toward the end of the evening, it was a young woman he was talking to. A blond, willowy girl, who'd just gotten married. And Harvey Newsome, standing close to her—of course, with his personality, he'd been quite a ladies' man in his day—was talking on and on, about anything and everything . . . and even in *depth*.

You'll remember, I think, the little tricks he had? To *hold* you? Such as, just when he saw you were getting bored, his coming up with something so interesting that you just had to listen? Or when you thought you'd never again get a word in edgewise, his becoming for a moment the most sympathetic listener in the world? Or—the worst one—his meeting your polite excuses, your "just have to go's", with that hurt-puppy look of his?

Well, he was doing all of it with that girl. She'd already said good-night five or six times, and so had her new husband, who was standing beside her, but it hadn't made any impression at all. And now her poor mate was at his wit's end. He'd even noticed in her eyes, he appeared to be thinking, an *attraction* for Harvey—the man's personality, experience—which had made him jealous!

So finally, in desperation, the young fellow did the only thing left; I wished then I could have stopped him.

He went over to Harvey's wife—you'll remember her; stout, white-haired, outgoing too—and said:

"Will you *please* take your husband *home?*"

Of course, in a marriage as new as his, it was the fatal mistake.

"How *could* you be so cruel?" I overheard the young woman sobbing to her husband, as they all departed. "To a nice old man like that? I know we wanted to leave, but I will *not* be embarrassed, be told what to . . ."

In short, Walter, they divorced a few months later.

And Harvey Newsome. I contend, had murdered a marriage.

But I know, of course, that that really isn't murder. So I present to you:

Exhibit B.

It was at another party, several years later. Indoors, this time; I think it was even here at the club. Harvey was at it again, with a man about forty. A tall, polite fellow; and, I couldn't help noticing from my place across the room, one of those born listeners, the kind of person

202

everyone likes. At first, I smiled inwardly at the beauty of it: the talker and the listener, together at last.

Yet presently—as others moved around, joined different groups, and those two still stood there—I began to worry. Because the younger man's face . . . his whole body . . . slowly took on a stiffness, an unease, which told me that perhaps even he, the eternal listener, had limits. I decided to walk over . . .

But, before I could get there . . . it happened.

The man—who was in that tense, heart-attack season, which if you survive you live to be our age, but if you don't—went *down*.

I'm a doctor; I did everything I could for him, Walter, I truly did. C.P.R., injections—my wife ran to get my medical bag out of the car—everything.

But by the time the ambulance came, he was gone.

And—oh, yes—there's one thing more.

While the poor fellow was struggling there on the floor, he was able to gasp out something. Something . . . which I've never told anyone until now.

"*Air*," he panted. "Can't . . . *breathe*. Need . . . *air*."

Then he raised a rigid arm, pointed . . . *to Harvey Newsome*.

"*Away* . . . from *him*. Must get . . . *away*."

So, what about that, Walter? You're the judge. The evidence: that talk can *kill*; that someone can literally be *talked to death*.

But you're still not convinced?

Well, then, I'll open up a new dimension in these proceedings. I'll contend . . . that there are fates *worse* than death. That at least, if you want to be philosophical about it, that polite listener is in Heaven now, while another of Harvey's victims is still alive . . . but in *Hell* . . .

Exhibit C.

One more party. This time    therefore it hurts me most to tell it— it was a patient of mine. A brilliant young man, just out of Princeton. Had already had a book of stories published: a *writer*. The sky was the limit for him, it seemed, *until* . . .

And this time, I was close by; not just observing from across the room. In the group with the young genius . . . and Harvey. Listening to Harvey tell him *stories*: you'll recall how that old man remembered *everything*, and the way in which it would come out of him, *complete*, as if you were really there along with him? His experience . . . and how he could *talk* it?

In short again, Walter, a week later the young fellow came to my office.

"I have . . . nothing *left*," he mumbled to me, his face pale. "You'll understand that we writers . . . *live* in ourselves, our stories?"

Then he slapped my desk . . . in anger.

"I will *never* write as well . . . as that damned old fool—not even a writer—*talks*. My confidence . . . is *gone*. And even if I could, I'd have to wait *years* . . . to equal his *experience*."

. . . Of course, I referred my patient to a psychologist; even sat in. Heard my colleague tell him that he didn't have to be Harvey's age in order to understand the world. And that he shouldn't worry about others' creations—in whatever form—because his own, were *his*.

But it was in vain. Because at the end, after many sessions, all that that young "writer"—he's now an advertising executive—could say, was:

"That old man . . . *overwhelmed* me. He'd . . . *told* all the stories.

"He took away . . . my *soul*."

. . . Well, Walter, that's it. My case—against the late Harvey Newsome—is closed. Besides, I'm concerned, my having spent this time talking to you *about* the talker, that you'll be tempted to put me in his same category. So I'll let you go: as Harvey never did, I'll simply *walk away*. And leave you to decide whether or not you, as a judge, should have put him away as the *murderer* I firmly believe him to have been . . .

Yet there's one thing more, my friend.

Something that . . . you'll forgive me, I hope, for taking your arm now, but in truth, I'm so *afraid* . . .

Afraid of something perhaps I should call Exhibit D . . . for Death.

You see, when Harvey *himself* was dying, I attended him.

And at the end—in that moment in which, sometimes, patients seem miraculously to come *back*, with an indescribable look on their faces, and to *tell* something, presumably from the other side—

I feared for Heaven itself, Walter, with a horror I'd never known. When Harvey Newsome croaked, as the last of his trillion words:

"No, God.

"*You* listen . . . to *me*!"

# Extra Service

*by John Mallory*

Eddie's Diner stood like a sentry at the intersection of the new Super-Highway and the famous Shore Road. A brilliant neon sign above the door of the converted railway dining-car flashed redly, SERVICE DELUXE.

Lloyd Tober, wizened and leathery, sniffed as he looked up at the sign, his loose lips curling to reveal small yellowish teeth. In Lloyd's estimation, Eddie was a fool. After fifty-odd years, Eddie still believed that moss-covered hokum about giving service in order to succeed. Lloyd grunted. If Eddie had thought less about service and more about the changes going on around him, perhaps that letter from the People's Drug chain wouldn't be reposing on Lloyd's desk. Lloyd had sensed the strategic location of Eddie's corner long ago. So it appeared, had the drug people . . . now.

Lloyd scuttled across the road as the traffic signal halted an unending stream of cars. Two men were beginning belated suppers in the tiny spic-and-span eating place when he walked in. It was a little after eight-thirty—the dull hour.

As Lloyd seated himself, Eddie was in front of him instantly, wiping the already immaculate black linoleum counter, polishing each piece of silver with a clean napkin before setting it on the counter. Lloyd had seen Eddie go through this polishing routine a thousand times and it always irritated him.

Why didn't Eddie just slosh off the counter with a wet rag and let it go at that? And cloth napkins were a luxury. It cost money to launder them. Paper napkins would be good enough. Lloyd had mentioned this to Eddie a long time ago. But Eddie had only grinned and said: "People like 'em. Makes 'em feel things are nice and clean. Just a little extra service, Lloyd."

"Where's your helper tonight?" Lloyd asked, as he picked up the menu.

"The kid wanted to go to a dance," Eddie said, his faded blue eyes smiling. "I gave him the evening off."

"Makes double work for you."

"I don't mind. It doesn't hurt a fellow to do something for somebody else once in a while."

Lloyd ordered and watched Eddie as the proprietor of the diner moved swiftly among gleaming kettles and pans. Eddie's face was homely but good-natured. His hair was getting very gray, almost white, around the temples. The way Lloyd saw it, Eddie had arrived at a time of life when he should have been alive to the hard ways of a self-seeking world. He should have lived long enough by now to see the silliness of all this super-service stuff. But that he hadn't was Lloyd's good fortune. Lloyd was glad there was no foolish sentiment in his own make-up. He came immediately to business when Eddie brought his toast.

"That mortgage I hold on this property is due tomorrow," he reminded Eddie. "Twenty-five hundred."

Eddie leaned on the counter. His blue eyes were trusting. "I haven't forgotten, Lloyd. But I can't take it all up, right now. Guess you know why. Excuse me a moment."

He moved down the line of stools to the two men at the other end of the diner. "Is everything all right?" he inquired. There was a note of solicitude in his voice. "Is your steak cooked the way you like it? Would you like more butter?"

Just a sucker, thought Lloyd. Eddie would never see this customer again. The man was only a transient. Suppose the steak wasn't right? And butter cost money. Oleomargarine would be plenty good enough for the transient trade. Lloyd shook his head.

Eddie came back to his place in front of Lloyd. "I can give you half," he said in a low tone. "I know you won't mind extending the balance another six months. It shouldn't take me any longer than that with the business this new highway's bringing in."

Lloyd fastened his eyes on his coffee cup while he dropped his little bombshell. "Mighty sorry, Eddie. I'd like to accommodate you, but business is business. If you can't take up the whole mortgage, I'll have to exercise my option."

Eddie looked incredulous. He started to say something, but just then one of the other customers finished his meal and stood up. Eddie went in his direction and said: "Was everything satisfactory?" And when the man dropped his money into the shiny, nickel-plated automatic cashier by the door, Eddie called: "Thank you, sir. Come back and see me again, please."

All part and parcel of the same extra service idea of Eddie's, and

206

unmitigated tommy-rot, Lloyd thought. Except for the automatic cashier. That was smart. The thing was completely hold-up proof.

The other customer left and Eddie brought Lloyd's eggs. He said: "You wouldn't treat an old friend that way, Lloyd. You know I'm only short because I helped out my sister when her husband died. It's temporary. Your loan couldn't be safer. Why, I could sell today for four times the amount of the mortgage."

Lloyd shrugged. "No, Eddie. You couldn't. You know the terms of our agreement. If you don't take up the full amount of the loan at the moment it's due, I have the right to buy your property at the valuation we set at the time the mortgage was made."

Trouble sprang into Eddie's face finally. "That was before the new highway," he said. "Now it's worth—"

Lloyd held out his empty cup and, quite automatically, Eddie refilled it with hot coffee. "I'll go to the bank in the morning," he started.

Lloyd cut him short. "Sorry. The bank isn't interested in a loan." Lloyd knew, for he was a director and owned a sizable block of the bank's stock. Furthermore, he knew there wouldn't be time for Eddie to make arrangements with any city institution.

Eddie's face started to get red, but at that moment the door opened and in came a young man in a white sharkskin suit with a rosebud in his lapel. He flopped negligently onto a stool and said: "Cup o' 'java."

Eddie turned to the big chromium percolator. He was wiping a spoon carefully on a clean napkin when in came Dan Fowler, sheriff of the country. Dan smiled at Eddie, nodded rather curtly in Lloyd's direction.

The young man in the white suit was staring around the diner. Swiveling on his stool, he coolly appraised the whole place, frowning as he saw the automatic cashier. Then, as he swung back, he noticed the little mahogany frame on the wall next to the coffee percolator. There was a ten-dollar bill in the frame and under it Eddie had printed the words:

THIS IS THE FIRST TEN DOLLAR BILL EVER CASHED IN THIS DINER AND IT
WILL REMAIN HERE UNUSED AS LONG AS WE STAY IN BUSINESS.

The young man laughed and suddenly there was a gun in his hand as he announced: "This is a stickup! Reach for the sky, all of you." He pointed the gun in Eddie's direction, laughed again. "Gimme that bill on the wall."

207

Eddie didn't hesitate an instant. Calmly he reached for the frame, opened its back and took out the money. There was actually a smile on his face as he handed it to the gunman.

The man's face was black when he found less than three dollars in Lloyd's wallet. Sheriff Fowler's pockets yielded only a dime sandwiched between two nickels.

"You hicks are lousy with dough, ain't you?" he sneered.

He backed toward the door. "Don't try to follow," he ordered. "It wouldn't be healthy."

Eddie said: "Good night. Come back and see me again, please." He spoke in the same courteous tone he used with all his customers.

Lloyd swung on Sheriff Fowler. "Aren't you going after him, Dan? You're an officer of the law."

The sheriff held up his hand for silence. "I'll tend to it, Lloyd. Just keep your shirt on. I don't aim to do nothing headstrong, like rushing after a guy with a gun.

"Them listed serial numbers on them ten spots in that frame of yours are proving *a real service*, Eddie. I just got a wire that the guy who stuck you up two weeks ago was nabbed this morning. He's a real tough egg and there's a five-thousand-dollar reward for his capture. You're getting half of it, 'cause they caught him on account of the number of that bill of yours. Come see me in the morning and collect."

Lloyd sat stupefied. Eddie was just grinning.

He said: "Good night, Sheriff. Come back and see me again, please."

# Eye-Witness

*by Donald S. Aitken*

Judd eased open the screen door at the rear of the cottage and slipped from the warm afternoon sun into the cool kitchen. He closed the door noiselessly behind him. Then he stood perfectly still, listening. When he caught the faint *clack-clack* of a typewriter in another part of the house, his bearded lips spread and became an oily smile of satisfaction. He drew an automatic from his pocket.

208

In the front room of the cottage a man in a spotless linen suit was seated with his back to the door, bent over a typewriter. His fingers moved over the keys swiftly, without hesitation. He did not hear the door open. The first intimation that he was not alone came when a menacing voice behind him breathed softly:

"Hello, Patterson!"

The clatter of the typewriter ceased abruptly. The man in the linen suit froze in his hunched-up position. He did not look around.

Judd circled to the front of the desk. There was a wariness in his narrowed eyes.

"No fast moves!" he warned. "This gun's liable to go off!"

With the two men facing each other, the effect was startling. They were strangely alike. Each had a brown, pointed beard. Their noses were long and lean. They were not old men; both looked under forty.

"Who are you?" Patterson demanded in a deep, booming voice. His wide-open eyes did not blink.

A chuckle came from the man with the gun. "You don't recognize me with the beard, eh? What about my voice—isn't that familiar?"

The man in the linen suit caught his breath sharply. Shock registered on his face.

"Harry Judd!" he gasped.

"Yes. Harry Judd's back!" the intruder snarled.

Patterson's hands gripped the edge of the desk convulsively.

"My God!" he cried in an agonized voice. "Haven't you done enough to me? Don't you know I'm—"

"Yes, I know. You're a cripple. I watched you hobbling around in the garden just now. You've been like that, I suppose, since the day twelve years ago when I hit you over the head with a monkey wrench and pushed you off the cliff along High Point Road. I hated you then. I intended your death to look like an accident, but by some miracle you were still alive when the searching party found you. I had to leave Penfield in a hurry. And now—I've come back!"

Sweat beads had broken out on Patterson's white face.

"What do you want?" His deep voice sounded choked. This man had already injured him terribly.

Judd went on. "Six months ago I came across your picture in a newspaper. It was the first I'd heard of you since I left Penfield. You've risen in the world—become a successful playwright. You're wealthy." Grim determination came into his eyes. "I want money, Patterson. Understand? Money!"

Patterson gulped helplessly. "I don't keep money in the house— there isn't twenty dollars."

"I didn't expect there would be. I want to see your bank book."

"You can't—"

"Shut up!" Judd made a threatening motion with the gun. "Get your bank book, I said!"

Patterson sat breathing hard for a moment. Then he reached over and opened the right hand drawer of the desk. Without lowering his eyes he fumbled among some papers, finally producing a slim book secured by an elastic band. Several canceled checks were laid lengthwise in it.

Judd took the bank book eagerly, glanced into it. His buttonhole eyes glittered.

"You've done even better than I thought," he said finally. "Now listen! You're going to write a check for twenty-five thousand dollars, payable to yourself. Then you're going to call up the National Merchants Bank in Penfield and tell them you're coming down right away to cash it. Ask them to have the money ready. Understand?"

Patterson balked. "That's all the money I have!" he cried. "You can't force me to do this!"

Savagery swept over Judd's face.

"You see this gun, don't you? I can put a bullet through you if you refuse!" His expression softened a little. "Do as I tell you, and there's nothing to be afraid of. I don't want to kill you but—" his face hardened again—"I will if you drive me to it!"

Patterson deliberated only a moment. Then he took out his check book, felt for his fountain pen. He made out the check.

Judd compared the signature with those on the canceled checks.

"Good!" he said. "You're being sensible. Now phone the bank."

He held the gun close against Patterson's side while the call was put through. Then he moved the telephone out of Patterson's reach again.

"All right, that finishes your part," he announced. "I'm going to tie you up and leave you here now."

Patterson looked surprised. "But I thought—"

"You thought I was going to force you to come down to the bank with me and cash that check?" Judd laughed. "No, Patterson, I'm not fool enough to risk a stunt like that. I planned all this six months ago, the day I saw your picture in the paper. People always said you and I looked a lot alike, so I waited and grew a beard like you've done. With a suit of your clothes on and your Panama hat I can go into that bank and collect the money without anyone knowing the difference.

I'm good at imitating voices and I know the way you hobble around. I watched you in the garden."

Fifteen minutes later, Judd came out of the adjoining bedroom. He wore a freshly laundered linen suit. The drooping brim of a Panama hung over his eyes.

Patterson was lashed to his desk chair, bound hand and foot, unable to move. Strips of adhesive plaster sealed his lips.

Grinning, Judd picked up the blackthorn stick which was propped against the desk. Leaning on it heavily, he practiced limping back and forth across the room. When he felt he was proficient in this, he picked up the telephone. Imitating Patterson's deep, booming voice, he called the Penfield Taxicab Company and ordered a cab to be sent out to Elm Cottage.

Then he took a pair of scissors from the desktop and hacked through the telephone wires. He tossed the instrument into the fireplace.

Patterson sat with unblinking eyes, helpless.

When the bell rang, Judd opened the front door of the cottage. The taxi driver was outside, a plump little man with a double chin and red face.

"Good afternoon, Mr. Patterson. Cab's here."

Judd kept his head low.

"Thank you," he said.

As he commenced to shuffle across the wooden porch the fat driver caught his arm and assisted him down the steps, then piloted him along the garden path.

They negotiated the garden gate.

"How's the old leg today, Mr. Patterson?"

Judd put extra weight on his stick. "About the same," he said gruffly. "No better."

The red-faced driver helped Judd into the cab, then squeezed his fat form behind the wheel. He threw a glance over his shoulder.

"Where we bound for today?"

"The bank."

"Okay, Mr. Patterson."

As the cab commenced to roll, Judd leaned back against the cushions and eased out a deep sigh of relief. In spite of himself he'd been a bit shaky. Apparently this driver knew Patterson well. The first test had been a severe one but he'd come through all right. He felt his confidence returning.

By the time they reached the outskirts of the little town of Penfield, Judd's thoughts had drifted back to the cottage. As soon as the money was safe in his hands, he'd return there, dismiss the taxi, then put a bullet through Patterson. He had intended all along to murder him. He wanted first to gloat over this man he hated. Hold before him the wealth he had stolen. That was why he had not shot him as soon as Patterson signed the check.

The cab was bowling along Main Street now. In the center of the town it slid to the curb in front of the National Merchants Bank. A traffic policeman out in the center of the street was operating a Stop-and-Go stanchion.

The driver climbed down and opened the door of the cab. As Judd alighted, he caught his arm and steered him across the sidewalk.

The door of the bank was open. On each doorpost hung a printed sign: WET PAINT!

Judd halted at the doorstep. He disengaged his arm from the taxi driver's.

"Thank you," he said. "I can manage now."

But the driver caught his arm again. "Better let me take you in, Mr. Patterson: I know you can make it, but there's fresh paint everywhere."

"I'll be able to manage."

The fat driver persisted. "But you'll get your suit messed up!"

Judd was annoyed. He didn't want the man to witness the cashing of the check.

"Let go of me!" he snapped. "I'm not so helpless that I can't keep away from wet paint when I see a sign!" He shook his arm free and hobbled across the threshold into the bank. The taxi driver stood staring after him.

Inside, Judd limped slowly across to the teller's cage. There were no other customers in the bank. The man behind the grille greeted him.

"Good afternoon, Mr. Patterson. Thanks for calling us up. Sometimes a big withdrawal like this catches us short."

Blood was pounding to Judd's face as he extracted the check from the pocket of Patterson's suit. The teller glanced at it, stamped it, put it away in a drawer and took out a sheaf of large bills. He counted the money over twice, then pushed it carelessly under the grille.

"There you are, Mr. Patterson. Twenty-five thousand dollars."

Judd's heart gave a little bobble of joy. Only with a great effort was he able to keep his hands from shaking as he picked up the money and thrust it into his wallet. Then, leaning heavily on his stick, he turned.

His jaw dropped. Every vestige of color drained from his face.

The fat taxi driver was entering the bank. With him was the traffic policeman from the street. The driver extended a short, thick arm, pointed at Judd excitedly.

"There he is, officer—that man there. He's not Mr. Patterson!"

With an angry snarl, Judd took a step back. He dropped his stick. His right hand clawed desperately for his automatic. But the officer was quicker. Before Judd could clear his weapon, an explosion racketed from the policeman's gun. Flying lead tore into Judd's side, spun him half around. The whole bank started to revolve; the floor tilted up and hit him.

When Judd opened his eyes, he was in a hospital bed. Chief Butler of the local police was standing beside him, a sarcastic smile on his lips.

"Nice of you to come back, Judd!" he said. "You had a clever scheme. Too bad you had to tell the taxi driver you knew enough to keep away from wet paint when you saw a sign. That was the tip-off."

Judd stared up from the pillow with an expression of mingled pain and bewilderment.

"What do you mean?" he gasped.

The police chief grinned.

"That knock over the head with the monkey wrench you gave Patterson twelve years ago threw his optic nerves all out of gear. Since then he's been stone blind!"

# Eye Witness

*by David X. Manners*

A thin bluish vapor still writhed and curled from the muzzle of the automatic as Frankie Sardi shoved it back into the holster under his arm. With cold unconcern he turned and walked from the room, and as he slowly shut the door behind him, he took one last sneering, triumphal glance at the lifeless body of Vince Salica slouched in a straight-backed, wooden chair on the far side of a card table.

Five bullets remained in the magazine of Sardi's .38 automatic as he noiselessly slipped down the outside stairs out of the now-deserted roadhouse. Four slugs had buried themselves in quick succession in the head and body of Vince Salica.

Sardi was chuckling to himself as he climbed into the car that waited for him at the bottom of the flight. "Home, James," he sang out merrily to the driver who sat behind the wheel.

The tough-faced driver turned slowly. "Usin' four shots again, huh, Frankie? Don't you think that's gettin' like leavin' a calling card behind?"

Sardi eyed him disdainfully. "Aw, forget it," he said with a wave of his hand. "Anyway, do yuh think I'm scared? I believe in doing my work for keeps." His words rolled fast and smooth from his well-oiled tongue. "What do you want me to do? Just take two shots at a guy? Why, you can't even be sure with three. But there ain't no guy livin' who can take *four* slugs without trippin' down the primrose path."

Sardi settled down comfortably in his seat and puffed forcefully on a newly lighted cigar. He liked that little speech about his "four-shot" philosophy. In fact he liked everything about himself. He was a "plenty wise guy," and he knew it.

The moon-washed hills of the countryside slipped by, and soon they were back in town again. At Sixth and Eastlake, Sardi got out, and with a parting wink to the driver, he turned and walked into his place of business.

Behind the door inscribed "Private," Sardi spent the better part of an hour meticulously cleaning his gun. The glum, vacuous expression on the rotund blob of fat that was his face showed that he had something on his mind. It seemed that he still had one little detail to attend to.

When Manny Zwick dropped by around an hour or so later, Sardi made known to him that the "little detail" was Babyface Joey Fine.

"Joey?" Manny repeated in unbelievable surprise. "Why, he's just a kid. Why he—"

"Yeh, I know, I know," broke in Sardi. "I heard all that kind of stuff about him, but that don't mean nothin' to me. It's just a business proposition. He's getting a little too wise for his tender years, and he's gotta go."

Manny nervously bit his lower lip. "Listen, Frankie," he urged, "you got rid of Mauri Sneller, and wiped out that little rat Vince Salica without so much as a buzz from the cops. But those guys were bad eggs. This boy Joey Fine is well liked down at headquarters. Those dicks'll haul yuh in."

Sardi's nervous lips quivered in impatience. "Listen, Manny, you know dicks don't cut no ice with me. Anyway, when I get through,

214

those coppers won't have enough evidence to hang a necktie on." A smile broke on his face as he lowered his voice. "It's all gonna be innocent and sweet."

A short while later Sardi squeezed into the mahogany-stained phone booth in the rear corner of his drug store. There was the clink of a nickel in a slot, half a dozen winding zips of the phone dial, and Fine was on the other end of the wire.

"Frankie speakin'," Sardi grunted as he flicked the ashes off a stubby cigar in his right hand with his little finger. "I got something lined up for you in San Diego. Drop around and see me at my room tonight. Yeh, ten o'clock's all right."

At nine-thirty the beefy gangster walked between the white columns that stood on either side of the entrance to the Colonial Hotel. He got his mail at the desk, mumbled something about "catching a rattler for the East" to the clerk, and asked that he be called at five-thirty in the morning.

The elevator dropped him off on the nineteenth floor and he walked directly to his room. He undressed, and put his wallet under a half-dozen or so shirts in the top drawer of his dresser and quietly placed his reloaded automatic under his pillow.

He took a look out of each of the two windows in his room before he pulled down the shades and drew together the heavy, écru drapes. He crawled into bed, and it was no later than nine forty-five when the lights in his room went out.

At ten sharp there was a knock on the door. Sardi breathed a quiet, quick "Come in." The door opened part way and Joey Fine slipped through. For a moment the boy fumbled in the dark for the light switch near the door, but Sardi quickly rolled over and snapped on the switch near his bed.

Fine's slim, young face looked clean-cut, and his pearly white teeth showed as he half smiled in awkward self-consciousness

Sardi nodded. "I got a wire from Hy Williams down in San Diego today okayin' a little proposition that would be just the thing for you, Joey," he said in a confidential tone. He pointed a tobacco-stained finger toward his dresser. "The wire's in the top drawer. You can get it out."

Sardi's eyes glinted and a frown spread over his face as Fine unsuspectingly turned his back and walked toward the dresser.

The gangster's hand slid under his pillow. It came out clutching his automatic.

Sardi thrust it calmly under the blanket as Fine turned momentarily. There were two top drawers.

The gangster smiled wryly. "It's in the left-hand drawer," he explained patiently. "You'll find it in my billfold under those shirts. Just take it out."

Fine reached down into the bottom of the drawer, and pulled out the wallet. Instantly four shots rang out in quick succession. The impact of the bullets seemed to swing him half around. His eyes were glassy wide in incomprehension. With a throaty groan he pitched face forward to the floor. Sardi's upper lip curled in surly disgust. He tossed the gun on a low table near his bed, and from the same table, he lifted a phone receiver.

"Call the police—quick!" he jerked. "I've just shot a robber!"

Slowly he cradled the receiver, and still holding the instrument in his hands, he thoughtfully pondered over the situation. Confidently he slipped his tongue in his cheek. "It's the oldest game in the world," he whispered, "but I'll get away with it."

Sardi had no sooner slipped on a robe than the door of his room opened. In came the house detective. His face was flushed, nervous.

"I'm Detective Moorehead of the house," he began brokenly. "What is it you—" He sucked in his breath sharply as his eyes fell on the body.

Slowly he treaded over to the dresser and stood by the lifeless form. He seemed a little frightened. "Robbery, eh?" he asked gravely.

Sardi nodded with a feigned dejectedness. Inwardly he was pleased by the detective's timidity at the sight of death.

"We've got in touch with Lieutenant O'Rourke," the detective said, clearing his throat. "This is a matter for the police, of course."

His last words were almost lost in a confused scuffle of pounding feet as four men barged into the room. Two were patrolmen, the others plainclothesmen, all of the homicide squad.

The tallest of the group was apparently Lieutenant O'Rourke. With darting eyes he took in the layout.

"Well, Frankie, so at last we've got you red-handed," he growled, leveling a gun at Sardi. "And for out-and-out murder, too!"

Sardi sneered contemptuously. "Put down the rod, flatfoot," he jeered. "I'd be sprung in two minutes if you ever took me in for this, and I wouldn't need a crooked mouthpiece or a phoney writ, either. Believe it or not, it so happens that I was asleep in bed when this mug busts into my room and tries to lift some dough of mine. So I let him have it, and I don't mean the dough."

The police lieutenant took one look at the dead man. "Babyface Joey Fine! You know him, don'cha?"

216

"It so happens that I do. And I'm sorry for his folks that he was so dumb as to try a stunt like this." Sardi paused as he saw his story wasn't making the impression he wanted it to make. "If I'd had cat's eyes and could have seen in the dark that it was Joey, I'd have given him a break. But how in hell could you expect me to take a chance, not knowin' who it was?"

O'Rourke knelt down beside Fine's body and studied the manner in which the billfold was held. "It looks legitimate enough," he confessed, after a short study. "The wallet wasn't planted on him." Suddenly his face brightened a bit. "A dresser drawer's an awful funny place to keep five thousand in cash, ain't it, Frankie?"

Sardi regarded the lieutenant sourly. "Listen, gumshoe, I expect dough to be safe any place when I'm around. Anyway, a place like that should be about the last place a smart crook should think of looking."

O'Rourke was plainly puzzled. "I'm achin' to pull you in for this," he began with a resigned bitterness, "but I know how damn foolish it'd be. It'd be just like it's always been. We wouldn't have a thing on yuh, except your bum rep. I guess all we can do is to ask you to come down to headquarters and make a statement."

Sardi smiled appreciatively. "I only wish you knew how sorry I am that such a thing has happened."

O'Rourke nodded sullenly and walked over to the dead man for a last look. He grasped the boy's shoulders firmly and rolled him over on his back. Fine's jaw dropped. A dried, red thread of blood snaked down the side of his face from a head wound. His eyes were glassy, unseeing.

O'Rourke arose slowly and faced the porcine gangster. "You say the room was dark, and that you wouldn't have shot him if you could have seen who it was?" he asked casually.

A faint trace of worry spread over Sardi's face. "That's what I said," he admitted. "You might think I'm tough, but killing people ain't exactly my idea of an after-dinner sport."

O'Rourke turned as if to go, but just as he reached the door he stopped, and, pulling a three-celled flashlight from his hip pocket, he walked back toward Sardi and flashed the light full in his eyes.

Sardi started in surprise.

"Don't be afraid, it's just a gag of mine," O'Rourke explained quickly. "I like to watch how the pupils of the eyes contract when you shine a light in them."

Sardi scratched the back of his head. "Are you nuts?" he snapped. "What in hell are you talking about?"

O'Rourke disregarded the gangster's query. "Put the cuffs on him, boys!" he commanded. Then: "I'm arresting you for the murder of Joey Fine. And if you want to know why, just take a look at his eyes. Once a person dies, they never change, and his contracted pupils show this room was as light as day when you shot him!"

# A Friend of Davy Jones'

*by Dan Gordon*

The morning activity on the pier didn't bother Lew Guyon, but he awakened when someone stepped aboard the boat. His hand found the .45 beneath the pillow, released it as the legs came down the ladder. He said, "Enter, Angel. Stumble in, O Vision."

Sue Brandon said, "Go right on sleeping. Don't let *me* keep you awake."

Lew said, "It is as nothing, baby. I was just getting up. Come on in, fairest lady."

"Just getting up," the girl repeated. The sweetness went out of her voice. "Listen, did or did not my father hire you to protect people here in the cove?"

"He did. And I did. I visited each yacht, all but tucked each chubby millionaire into his downy bed."

She nodded. "And right after you left they held up the *West Wind.* The women lost their jewelry, and the men lost thousands of dollars."

Lew Guyon walked to the porthole, looked out at the water, at the flotilla of luxury craft riding easily on the placid surface of Millionaire's Cove. It wasn't absolutely necessary that he follow through on this job. Brandon had seemed like a nice guy, but this daughter of his was a menace. She had, he reflected, a pleasant voice when she used it pleasantly. But why wait around for that?

"Did I ever tell you," Lew said, "how I feel about millionaires?"

"No," Sue Brandon said, "but I'm dying to hear."

"Don't give a damn about 'em," said Lew. "Especially at this hour of the day." He found a roll of bills, kept two, shoved the balance toward her. "You owe me for a night's sleep. I tied up here an hour ago, after spending the night put-putting around this cove."

218

Sue Brandon ignored the money. "My father hired you. I didn't. Give it to him. And if you find it convenient to move your things ashore by this afternoon, I'd like to use my boat."

Lew touched his forehead and said, "Yes'm." The girl bit her lip, turned away and went up the ladder. Lew looked after her thoughtfully. He'd have to hang around for a day or two. Having sent the wire to Sammy Sultan, he'd have to wait for Sammy to tell him the job was off.

He had intended to feel quite well as he shaved and ate breakfast. He didn't. Maybe a stretch. Maybe a walk on the dock. . . .

The first thing he saw when he went topside was Sammy Sultan's schooner, *Sea Maid*, as she slid in beside the pier.

The olive-dark man standing aft by the wheel called aloud to Lew. "Hi, chum. They don't shoot you yet?"

"Not yet," Lew said. "How's Cuba?"

"Hot," said Sammy Sulton. "Cuba is very warm." He swung a leg over the schooner's rail, leaped and landed cat-like on the dock beside Lew Guyon. "Down there is too hot; up here is too cold."

"Hotter'n the gulf?"

"No," Sammy said. "No, not *that* hot."

"It was a good job."

"Yeah," said Sammy Sultan. "If the chump had lived to pay us it would have been an excellent job."

"Like the one we just lost."

"We?" said Sammy Sultan. "You work for Cipelli too? I wonder where he hears of me. Now I know. It is like old times. Here you are, and here I am. It is like that, eh?"

"No," Lew told him, chuckling. "It is not like that. Cipelli must have heard of your lily-white reputation. I was on the other side of this war—until this morning."

"So?" What happened?"

"Fired," Lew said shortly. "But let's not stand here. Get a bottle of your number one rum. There's not a barroom on the cove, but I know where to find a tea room."

The woman who ran the tea room wasn't too happy about the rum, but Sammy Sultan topped his brilliant smile with a crackling bill, and she went away and left them alone.

Lew poured an inch of rum in the bottom of Sammy's cup, took his own coffee straight. "This lad," Lew said, "this Cipelli. After he made his pile during prohibition, he settled down here to enjoy a life of exclusive ease with the other millionaires."

"It's nice," Sammy Sultan commented.

"If you like it, or can afford it. Apparently Cipelli can't. Or at least he can't any more. Coupla months ago, some gang began a series of sea-going stickups, knocking off the yachts at anchor. Brandon, the guy who hired me to stop it, wanted it done quietly. He felt that bringing in the law would give the place too much publicity."

"Reasonable," said Sammy Sultan. "Very reasonable. I never heard of Millionaire's Cove until Cipelli sent his man."

"They've kept it that way. Mostly old families who've had their moola for years. They can afford to pay to stop Cipelli without calling in the cops. Which is why I sent for you. The boys I have on the tug are tough enough for diving work, but they wouldn't stack with Cipelli's gang. Now, I dunno. I'd say Cipelli is going to make one big haul, shake down every yacht in the harbor, load everything aboard and ship it south with you."

Sammy Sultan said virtuously, "Me, I know nothing. I carry cargo for the man—as long as the price is right. Of course, I would rather work with you, but if you have no money . . ."

"I've got some," Lew Guyon said, "but I've got to give it back. Want to come along for the ride? We'll use Miss Brandon's boat."

"Young girl?" Sammy Sultan inquired, moving his eyes. "Pretty?"

"Yeah. But not your type. Strictly uptown."

"Good," said Sammy. "I been thinking of going into society."

"She talks," Lew said with some bitterness. "Has a yap like a tiger shark. Which is why I quit."

"So," said Sammy. "Well, it is regrettable. But no matter. You work with me for our friend Cipelli."

Lew grinned. "Cipelli wouldn't like that."

Sammy Sultan spread his hands expressively. "Who cares what he likes? Come on."

They walked back to the dock, and Lew looked out over the water at the fog bank rolling in from seaward, glancing sideways at Sammy Sultan. "Sammy, I ought to tell you. I've been legit since the war."

Sammy looked at him. "So? What's your racket?"

"Marine investigation. Anything that comes up. I'm a sea-going private dick."

Sammy Sultan seemed faintly embarrassed. "What the hell," he said. "You are my friend."

They dropped it there and began to discuss the old days, the rough days. Pearl fishing off Australia, the business in South America. They had taken their chances and mostly won and sometimes lost and tried again.

The fog was all around them by the time they reached the boat. Lew stepped into the cockpit and gunned the motor while Sammy threw off the lines. Sammy said, "You know where she lies?"

"I can find her." Lew eased the cabin cruiser away from the dock, and they went ghosting along through the fog in the general direction of Brandon's yacht. The mist, hurrying along close to the surface, enclosed the boat in a tiny pocket of visibility.

They were, Lew thought, about halfway out when Sammy Sultan touched his arm and said, "What—"

They both heard it, the sound of a shot, vague and directionless. Lew pulled the throttle back, allowing the engines to idle. Listening, they heard nothing but the slapping, hissing waves.

Then, with a roar of a high-powered engine, the other boat was upon them, flashing into view, skidding in a wild turn as the man at the crew spotted the cabin cruiser. Lew saw Cipelli at the wheel, and beside him a thin, spidery little man he didn't know. He saw the thin man's arm come up, and together he and Sammy Sultan flung themselves to the deck.

The bullet, splintering the cockpit glass, made a high tinkling sound. The exhaust of the flying speedboat growled derisively as the boat vanished in the fog.

Sammy Sultan sat up, slipped his gun back into its shoulder holster. "Where do you keep it?"

"What?"

"The gun. What you think I want? Your address book?"

"Below," Lew said, "Under the bunk."

Sammy ducked below, returned with a sub-machine gun. He said: "They come back, Louie, my boy?"

"Maybe." Lew booted the stern around and sent the boat ahead slowly, at right angles to her original course. "The fat guy at the wheel," he told Sammy, "was Cipelli."

Sammy, his brows rising, said, "Careless, isn't he?"

Lew didn't answer. Instead, he cut the engine and reached for the chopper. Sammy Sultan handed it over, patted his ribs, and came up with a gun in his hand.

The boat had loomed suddenly out of the fog. It wasn't the one that had passed them. This boat was small, a runabout. It lay in the trough and rolled with the sea. The cockpit seemed empty.

When they were closer, Lew saw the man on the floorboards. They lowered their guns and boarded. "Brandon," Lew Guyon said.

"From the back," Sammy Sultan commented. "Close up."

"No fight," said Lew.

"No fight," Sammy Sultan agreed.

Lew looked down at the lean grey face. He had liked Brandon pretty well. "Dirty," he said. "Damned dirty."

Sammy said, "Easy," as the sound of another boat's engines came through the mist. Lew and Sammy leaped aboard the cruiser.

Lew cut his own engine, hoping he'd been quick enough. The sound they'd heard diminished, came closer again.

"Patrol boat," Sammy whispered.

"There isn't one."

"Don't tell me! I can smell cops a mile away. Let's breeze, Louis."

"And leave this guy to bleed to death?"

"They'll find him. Hurry!"

Lew nodded and brought the engine to thundering life. Sammy cast off from the smaller boat and the sleek cruiser went heeling and careening into the fog.

Looking back, Lew saw the shadow of a bow emerge from the mist. It looked like Cipelli's boat, but he couldn't be sure. The dim shape changed, became small and symmetrical as the other boat altered her course to give chase. Lew crowded the throttle and looked at Sammy Sultan. "That guy'll bleed to death."

"Okay," Sammy said. "He'll bleed. If they catch us, we'll burn to death."

Lew said, "Hell, we didn't shoot Brandon."

"No? Suppose I'm the law. I hear you're running away in a pea-soup fog. You got a dead man behind, and Sammy Sultan for a passenger. Nice, baby?"

"Lovely," Lew said. Glancing back at the pursuing boat, he spun the wheel hard right, ran for a heavier fog bank broad on the starboard bow. "Just the same," he said, "we'll lose these tramps, go back and patch up Brandon. I'll feel better then."

The whine of bullets forced them down in the boat. Behind them, they heard the unhealthy chatter of a machine gun. Lew brought the rudder amidships and the firing ceased as they ploughed into the fog bank. They headed back in a slow circle, found Brandon's boat on the nose.

"Nice maneuver," said Sammy, "but foolish."

"Save it," Lew told him. "Let's get this guy aboard."

They lifted Brandon aboard the cruiser and Sammy examined his wounds while Lew kicked the boat ahead. "Bad?" Lew asked without looking back.

"Pretty bad. Maybe he makes it, maybe not. What now?"

"We take him in?"

"And he dies on the way?"

Lew shrugged and altered his course as the sound of the other engine came faintly across the water.

They made it into the pier. Lew and Sammy remained with Brandon, and sent a boy to phone for a doctor and Brandon's daughter.

Sue Brandon got there first. She knelt, silent and grief-stricken, beside her father. Lew, seeing the question in Sammy Sultan's eyes, nodded.

The doctor was coming aboard, but Sue Brandon ignored him. She looked at Lew Guyon and said very distinctly, "Why didn't you finish the job? I should have known when you quit that you'd sold out to the gang."

Vince Cipelli stood on the dock and said, "Who is it? Mr. Brandon? We thought we heard a shot."

Lew looked at the former gang boss, at the spidery man beside him. Cipelli moved his bulk to step down into the boat and Lew said sharply, "Stay off her."

"Is it your boat?" Cipelli asked gently.

"No. But I'm the guy don't want you aboard."

The spidery man crawled forward. "Now, buddy," he began.

"Here's the meat wagon," Sammy Sultan said hastily.

The ambulance stopped, its crew came with a stretcher and removed the still-unconscious Brandon. As the stretcher was handed up, Cipelli made another move to board the boat.

"Coming aboard," Cipelli said.

"Don't," Lew said quietly.

The spidery man moved his hand. Sammy Sultan's hand flickered briefly and a gun leaped into his fist. "You gentlemen," he murmured, "have more persistence than brains."

Lew said, "Thanks, Sammy." He glanced up at the ambulance. The men were closing the doors and Sue Brandon was watching the play on the boat. Lew called "I'd like that job back, Miss Brandon."

Wordlessly, she shook her head.

"I'll do it cheap. The service won't cost you at all."

She hesitated, then came to the edge of the dock, looked at him, and pressed the roll of bills into his hand. Then she ran for the ambulance, climbed in front with the driver.

Sammy Sultan leafed the few limp bills. "This isn't money," he said plaintively.

"No money," Lew agreed, "but a good job." He jerked a thumb at Cipelli. "You wouldn't work for Tubby, there—now, would you?"

"For a price," said Sammy Sultan, "I would work for Mr. Hoover. I mean Edgar, of course."

Lew smiled and said, "What about me? For a marker?"

"*Your* I.O.U.!" Sammy shook his head in sorrow. "Why I ever knew you is a mystery I cannot explain." Then, as Cipelli started forward again, "Shove off, my fat friend. And believe me, I hate to see you go. With you goes my last chance to make an honest dollar here in these putrid waters."

Lew watched Cipelli and the spidery man walk away. He kept his eyes on them absently, wondering if Brandon were to die, whether Cipelli would attempt to pin a murder rap on Sammy and himself to cover his own operations.

"Well?" Sammy Sultan said.

"What?" Lew answered vaguely.

"I would not interrupt your dreams, but I have a schooner tied up near here. I have just pulled a gun on the man I came to work for. I believe he will act like a substantial citizen and call the local cops. I also believe his boys will carry out his original plan and stick up these yachts tonight. If I am now not mistaken, I hear the sound of a siren. He has already phoned the constabulary. They are coming to take us in. Now. Can you do something?"

"I guess we'd better shove off," said Lew, cocking an ear at the siren.

"I guess," Sammy Sultan said.

The fog stayed with them as they left the pier. It was chilly and close to the surface. Sammy Sultan, below, brewed a pot of coffee, while Lew remained at the wheel. Staring intently ahead, he found the effect of the swirling vapor hypnotic. Then he made out the sailboat, the grey-white belly of the sail, the little curl of water at the bow. Lew rubbed his eyes, looked again, and flung the wheel hard right.

The cruiser heeled, and her stern, skidding, barely missed the sailing craft. Looking back, Lew made out two figures dimly outlined on her deck before the fog closed in again.

Sammy Sultan came up the ladder and said, "What the hell? I'm now wading in coffee."

"Couldn't help it, Sammy. Some fool out in a sailboat. We almost ran him down."

Grumbling, Sammy slid back down the ladder and returned with two cups of coffee. He handed one to Lew.

"Thanks, Sammy, I'm glad you came along."

"I'll mop it off the deck, then I wring the rag. Good, no? Where you headed?"

"All the way across. Our best move is to stay out of jail and clear of Cipelli until we can get your boys off the schooner. Next time we see Cipelli, he'll have more hired help. Not just one underfed hood."

Zinging in from the starboard side, the bullet passed through the cockpit. Lew hurled himself to the right, scooped up the sub-machine gun and turned to face the boat that was bearing down upon them.

Too late. The other boat opened fire before Lew could bring his gun to bear. They flattened themselves on the deck and heard the lead burn the air, watched it splinter the woodwork. Lew raised his head and saw the speedboat rocket away.

Recognizing the spidery man, Lew was bringing his gun up when the other man fired first and caught him high in the shoulder. Lew gritted his teeth and clapped one hand to the wound. With the other, he picked up the gun. Then, turning, he saw Sammy Sultan. Sammy's face was contorted, his hands clamped tight on his belly. Sammy said, "How do you—" His voice trailed off.

Lew shifted his eyes to the curtain of fog. The roar of the boat came then.

Slowly, Lew squeezed the trigger. The gun leaped and bucked against his hand.

He saw the surprised expression on the thin little face, watched while the stream of lead ate into the bow of the oncoming craft. The roar of its engine died abruptly. Somebody let out a scream. Lew Guyon leaned against the rail, dropped his gun.

When he looked again, the fragile hull of the speedboat was slipping under the waves. Behind Lew, Sammy Sultan sat in a pool of blood. His face was very pale.

From the other side of the boat, there came a scraping sound. Lew saw the hand on the rail. He dragged himself to it, grasped it and leaned back, feeling the tearing strain in his shoulder. He gave a final tug, and the spidery man slid aboard and flopped like a fish on the deck. . . .

Crouched in a blanket on the starboard bunk, the spidery man looked like an Indian chief.

Sammy Sultan lay in the other bunk. He said faintly, "We get Cipelli?"

Spider said, "I guess he couldn't swim."

Lew's shoulder was hurting. His shoulder was hurting like hell. The bunks were full, and somebody had to take the boat in. . . . He

225

grasped the edge of a bunk and hauled himself up off the deck. "Goin' topside," he announced. He fought his way up the ladder, poked his head through the hatch and gratefully gulped the air—and saw the sailboat not fifty yards away.

An ancient and bearded Negro sat cross-legged on the bow.

"Here's one of them," the old man said. "Come look at him, Miss Brandon."

She came aboard and said, "You're wounded."

Lew started an airy wave. The pain interfered with the gesture, stopped the wave in mid-air. He said, "You ought to see the other fellow."

"Cipelli?"

Lew let his eyes go blank. "Never heard of him," he said. "Couple of guys below got in a fight. We were drinking and—you know how it is. How's your father?"

"Grand. He's going to be all right."

Lew nodded and staggered below. With the girl close behind him, he steadied himself against the door frame and looked at the spidery man. Lew said, "You got any more interest in this racket, or were you in it strictly for Cipelli?"

"For Cipelli," the man said, "and the dough."

"You sure drew a blank," he said.

"Not me, I never draw a blank. Cipelli floated a while, see?"

"Well?" said Sammy Sultan.

"Well what?"

"Come up with half."

Reluctantly, Spider pulled out a soaking roll. "All twenties," he said. He split the bundle in two, tossed one half to Sammy.

"Fine," said Sammy Sultan. "Now I don't hurt so bad. If we dropped you on the other shore, you think you could pull a fade?"

"*Could I?*" he breathed. "If anybody'd told me I'd come out of this with nothin' more than a headache—" He eyed Sammy Sultan searchingly. "You're a funny guy," he said.

Lew Guyon, watching Sammy, realized that the wounded man wasn't paying much attention. Sammy was staring at the girl, and the girl was looking at Sammy. Lew said, "A funny guy is right. To me he looks like a guy who will soon be settling down."

Sammy Sultan said very thoughtfully, "I got a clean record here."

226

# Granny Gumption
# Solves a Murder

*by C. J. Henderson*
*and Charles Hoffman*

Granny Gumption sat quietly, composing her notes on the frontboard of the Townshend Goddard breakfront secretary. Gumption, of course, was not her real name, nor was she anyone's grandmother. But the name given her by a whimsical newsman so many years previous when she had solved her first murder had stuck and now, to everyone in the northern Worshire fishing village which she loved so dearly, she was Granny Gumption, the luncheon party woman who solved all those beastly crimes the police could not.

With a sigh, knowing she was right as usual, she consulted the hands of the handsomely polished Simon Willard grandfather's clock in the corner of the mansion's sitting room. Nine o'clock. The others would be gone. Now was the time. Pushing herself up with the dignity of her age, Granny crossed to the hall to confront young master Wayne alone in the burgundy drawing room. He was pouring a brandy for himself as she entered.

"Such a waste," she thought, and then proceeded forth to do her duty.

Seeing her enter, the young man quipped airily, "Can I offer you a drink, Granny?" indicating the Waterford crystal set at his elbow.

"No thank you," replied Granny coldly. She rested her weight on her cane, her owl-like eyes seeming to pierce young Wayne's soul.

"So, have you solved the murder yet?"

"As a matter of fact, I have, young Wayne," Granny answered accusingly, "*You* murdered Doctor Carstairs."

"You'll be expected to *prove* that."

"I imagine the missing diaries can be found under the flagstones in front of the groundskeeper's shed," snapped Granny succinctly.

A dark expression settled on young Wayne's brow. "Indeed. So, what was it that tipped you off?"

"Your hands. Those well-manicured hands. Hardly the hands of the prodigal son who supposedly spent ten years laboring in the Peruvian tin mines."

227

"And have you told anyone of this?"

"No. I wanted to offer you the chance to come forward on your own first, to preserve what's left of the honor of the Prescott family name," Granny retorted tartly.

"Thank you, Granny. I'm not sure you understand how much I appreciate that."

And, with that said young Wayne reached out in one quick, serpentine motion, snatching Granny's cane from her liver-spotted fingers. The old woman tottered forward, off-balance, then jerked awkwardly back, spinning her arms in circles to keep her balance. Young Wayne tapped the cane against his palm, testing its weight.

"My cane!" Granny squawked frantically, "Give me back my cane!"

"Oh—Sure."

Young Wayne held the cane loosely like a pool cue, then swung, shooting the hook end sharply into Granny's solar plexus. Granny folded broken and hurting, dropping to the floor coughing blood. Young Wayne snapped a kick that caught Granny on the jaw, breaking it in two places, stretching the old woman supine. Then, the young heir raised the cane above his head, only to bring it down hard on Granny's face.

The old sleuth's sharp, beak-like nose shattered into a bloody misshapen blob. Several more stout blows shattered her glasses, driving razor-sharp slivers slicing through her eyeballs until they broke apart like soft-boiled eggs, their greyish jellied mass oozing down the old woman's wrinkled cheeks.

Granny writhed helplessly on the floor, futilely flailing her withered arms to ward off further blows. Her keening cry of anguish and terror echoed through the empty mansion, a single, sustained, high-pitched squeal sounding like nothing but the devil's tea kettle.

Laughing at the old woman's bloody pain, the young millionaire launched his athletic body upward into the air and then came down hard, striking Granny squarely in the center of the chest with both feet, shattering her ribcage—crushing her like a bug. The keening cry ended abruptly then, but young Wayne, his face flushed red, contorted by his rage, jumped up-and-down, up-and-down on the old woman until long after she was dead.

And later, when his fury had finally expended itself, young Wayne downed another brandy, bathed, and then changed to a fresh suit of clothes. Going to the master safe, he removed all the family monies and jewelry, along with a sealed envelope containing a full set of false

I.D. complete with passport. He left the manor for the last time without regret. As for the crushed corpse in the drawing room, the servants would take care of that.

# A Hand of Pinochle
*by Theodore Tinsley*

"This goes for all of you," Captain Daley snapped. "Don't think that
because you've been assigned to duty in a rural precinct in Queens
that you have nothing to do but chuck old ladies under the chin. The
commissioner sent me out here to pep up this precinct, and I intend
to get results or there'll be men up on charges."

His eyes focussed meaningly on Patrolman Kirker. Kirker shuffled
his big feet nervously and wished old Captain O'Brien were still alive.
O'Brien had been easy-going, not like this new skipper with the
youthful frown and the crisp snap to his voice. "If only I could get
him to play pinochle!" Kirker thought sadly.

Eleven years on the force hadn't made much change in Patrolman
Adolph Kirker. His feet were a little flatter, his uniform a bit tighter
across the stomach, his sun-wrinkled smile deeper. He had served in
three boroughs and had made exactly three arrests. The first was an
under-sized Sicilian junk peddler whom Adolph had caught viciously
larruping a bloated white horse from a rental stable in lower Manhattan. The second was a Bronx janitor who had celebrated an alcoholic
birthday by blacking his wife's eye. The third, a taxi driver in Queens,
had tinkered unlawfully with his meter and had tried to collect the
surcharge with his fists.

Adolph Kirker had drifted to Queens on the border of the city
line, because there was no further spot to which a mild and inoffensive cop could be transferred to make room for the stronger-jawed,
more ambitious rookies who poured out of the police school every
year.

Each time a new commissioner stepped up, Kirker stepped down.
He was not at all bitter about it; quite the reverse. In Queens there
were shady trees, friendly folk in neat frame houses who called him
Mr. Kirker and were like as not to bring out a bottle of cold beer

when he passed and asked about the health of his wife. In Manhattan Kirker had lived in a dark, dismal flat. Here he owned his own grass-plot and home, or would as soon as he finished making the payments. And every Sunday afternoon, while his wife attended the Ladies' Auxiliary of the Lutheran church, Kirker and his friend Otto Muller played pinochle.

Pinochle! That was the one thing that gave meaning and pleasure to the easy-going existence of Kirker. Even in Queens the virus of bridge had bitten deeply, so that it was hard to find a good steady pinochle player. But Otto Muller, an ex-cop who had taken a lighter job after being wounded and partly crippled, knew the finer points of pinochle and was fond of beer and Liederkranz. Kirker walked his beat, not from block to block but from Sunday to Sunday. In two years he was two dollars ahead of Muller and hopeful of increasing his lead. He smiled dimly at the prospect, the irate face of young Captain Daley a meaningless blur. Daley's curt question cut ruthlessly through his daydream.

"Anything particularly exciting happen on *your* beat?"

"Some kids were playing baseball in a vacant lot on Division Avenue," Kirker mumbled. "One of 'em broke a window, so I—I—"

"Ahh. . . . A broken window. Did you make your annual arrest?"

Kirker's ears were bright red. "I walked the kid a coupla blocks and talked to him like a—a Dutch uncle. He was scared stiff, a big overgrown kid. So I gave him a half dollar and told him to get the window fixed."

"And reconstructed a potential criminal, eh?"

"Yes, sir," Kirker said quietly. "I've watched kids like him before. All they need is a tap on the pants and a bit of help sometimes. Treat 'em rough, sir, and they start robbing tills and buying a cheap gun in Jersey."

"I see," Captain Daley murmured. The red in his own face deepened. "A broken window and a bit of welfare work." His voice rose as he struck the typewritten report in his hand a resounding whack with his palm. "Seven Long Island banks knocked over by Rod Cantor and his pal—no arrest. Thieves made a haul yesterday not a mile from this squad room—no arrest. From now on that kind of police work is ended. You'll devote your attention to crooks and killers, or I'll have you wishing you had."

There was discreet silence. "That's all," Daley snapped and strode off to his sanctum with a brisk click of his heels.

"Try *that* on your pinochle deck, Adolph," a sardonic voice mut-
230

tered. Kirker grinned feebly. He was used to being kidded about his Sunday game with Muller.

Mrs. Kirker clucked indignantly when he told her about the new captain's ultimatum. "Why didn't you talk up to him, Adolph? Did you tell him what you did for young Charlie Franklin? Or how you put the fear of the Lord into Dave Martin and made him get busy and support that sweet little family of his?"

Kirker shrugged and didn't answer. What was the use? Those were things the skipper wouldn't understand.

"Anyone would think," his wife sniffed, "that cops were a lot of quarrelsome thugs, running around day and night to shove people into cells. I've a good mind to go around to the station house tomorrow and give that whippersnapper a talking to."

Kirker said mildly, "Now, Hattie!" He was sitting comfortably in a kitchen chair, his uniform coat off, the weight of his gun sagging his hip pocket. His wife bustled between cupboard and stove, preparing the coffee they always drank before they went to bed. She lifted the lid of the bread box and the irritation she felt toward Captain Daley transferred itself suddenly to household affairs.

"Oh, dear. I forgot the crumb cake. Tomorrow's Sunday and the bakery will be closed all morning. Here, take a quarter and get some. The coffee'll be ready by the time you get back."

Kirker sighed. Without crumb cake, dipped in soggy chunks, coffee lacked savor. He padded heavily across the front porch and walked bareheaded up the dark street to the corner. He grunted with disgust as he saw that the bakery was already closed. His tired glance wavered hopefully toward the adjoining bank. He'd stop awhile and say hello to the watchman. Suddenly his blurred smile faded. There was a sedan parked at the curb, its motor quietly purring; and the locked door of the bank wasn't locked—it was slowly opening.

As the door widened Kirker saw two strangers sneak cautiously out, carrying heavy suitcases. In a flash he darted toward the parked automobile to head off the thieves, his hand tugging at his gun. Pistols flared at him with a staccato roar, but the sedan shielded him. He fired and saw one of the crooks drop his suitcase and fall to the sidewalk. The other kept on and reached the car, and Kirker, puffing, sprang to the running-board as the sedan got under way.

A hot streak flicked across the flesh of his neck as he ducked. A quick clutch inward and his fingers jerked at the steering wheel. The sedan curved across the street and rammed head-on into a wooden telephone pole. The impact threw Kirker into the street on his face. A man who had peered out of a window down near the corner, began to blow shrilly on a police whistle and through the darkness came the *thud-thud* of running feet.

The crook, his escape cut off by a dead-end street, hesitated and then dashed straight for the open door of the bank. As the dazed Kirker staggered to his feet and clutched for his dropped gun, the bank door slammed and locked.

Kirker hesitated. He knew the inside of that bank better than the crook did! If he waited out front he could keep the killer bottled up until the precinct reserves arrived. He remembered the thin, taut-lipped sneer he had seen on a placard posted in the station house. He was facing Rod Cantor, the killer who had knocked over seven banks on Long Island. Cantor would fight a frontal attack to a finish, shielding himself behind the helpless body of the watchman.

Whitefaced, Kirker sprang to the tall telephone pole and climbed swiftly up the spiked footholds. It was a dangerous leap across to the roof of the bakery, but he made it. The bank roof was six feet higher. Kirker's bleeding hands hauled him up a rusted vent pipe; a bat of his gun smashed the pane out of the bank's skylight.

Down below Kirker could see Cantor's gun jerk upward, and the sight sent a wave of grim rage through Kirker's aching body. He dropped recklessly, feet first, through a crash of pistol fire. His body struck the crouched gunman and rebounded to the paved floor. Pinwheels of fire whirled through his brain. He lay for a moment, breathless and paralyzed; then, as he swayed to his knees, the glass of the front door crashed and policemen spilled into the bank. A hand clutched at Kirker and helped him to his feet. It was Captain Daley, wildly excited, shouting like a young fool. Kirker stared past him at Cantor and saw steel cuffs on the sprawled crook's wrists. He lay motionless on the tiled floor, his head twisted at a queer angle. The slugged watchman was stirring, groaning feebly.

In a daze Adolph Kirker found himself back in a crowded precinct house where every light was ablaze. The commissioner himself was there after a swift twenty minutes run from Manhattan. Flashlights popped, reporters jammed the tiny squad room. Kirker felt very tired.

"Why did you climb to the roof and pull that wild Tarzan jump?" a reporter asked. "Why didn't you plug Cantor from the back door?"

"When you have over four hundred dollars in a bank, you get to know it," Kirker said quietly. "There isn't any back door."

"Ummm. . . . You got fighting mad when you realized you'd trapped Cantor, huh?"

Another camera popped and Captain Daley beamed. "Kirker was

on his toes, that's all. There's been a shakeup in this precinct. You see, boys, the commissioner sent me here to—"

Kirker's weary eyes were staring at the bandaged head of his friend, the watchman.

"I guess I did get a little mad," he admitted. "The gall of that rat, Cantor! Damn him, he tried to kill Otto Muller—the only pinochle player in town."


# Harsh Light of Day

### by Wayne D. Dundee

Pimps, like vampires, are creatures of the night. They thrive on neon-fringed darkness, strutting peacockishly across the shadowed underbelly of a city, lording it over their whores and, through them, sucking their lifeblood from the endless parade of nameless, faceless johns who are desperate enough to pay money for a few seconds of tainted pleasure.

But in the harsh light of day, pimps are nothing but furtive-eyed little hustlers; maggots avoiding the brightness, soft and vulnerable, squirming anxiously as they await the return of their only friend, the night.

This was the harsh light of day. Six A.M., to be exact, on an already sweltering July morning. The pimp I was after called himself The Champion of Charm; Champ for short. The address I'd been given on him was the basement apartment of a converted Victorian just off North Main. The snitch who'd provided this information was reliable enough—and the picture he'd painted of Champ was slimey enough —for me to have no qualms about kicking open the front door and skidding in unannounced. I entered with .45 drawn and ready, just in case Champ wasn't aware how vulnerable he was supposed to be.

The apartment was a shrine to gaudy taste and materialistic whims. Goodies achieved via the exploitation of others, the muddy underside of the American dream. It was all there: from the giant-screen TV in the living room to the gleaming microwave in the kitchen to the home gym paraphernalia scattered across the purple shag carpeting to the empty ice cream cartons in the garbage. The price tag on each had been paid by more than just dollars and cents.

I took in all of this from the vantage point of the semi crouch I'd dropped into after making my entrance. The apartment was quiet. The only sound was the hum of the kicked-open door still vibrating on its hinges.

When I was satisfied there was going to be no violent reaction to my arrival on the scene—at least not for the time being—I straightened up, lowering the .45, turned and propped shut the door. Turning back, I began to move through the apartment. I kept the .45 drawn, carrying it down alongside my thigh.

The layout was simple, it didn't take a genius to figure out where the bedroom would be. I checked the bathroom and the hall closet on the way by, to be sure I was leaving my wake clear, then nudged open the bedroom door.

There were three of them lying naked on a huge, satin-sheeted waterbed—Champ flanked by two females. One was a dusky-skinned Chicana with floppy, oversized breasts, the other a pale, painfully thin blonde who couldn't have been more than fifteen. Champ lay on his back with the Chicana nestled against one shoulder. The blonde lay partially on her side, turned away from them, facing toward me as I entered the room.

Like the rest of the place, the bedroom was crammed with expensive gadgets and ostentatious furnishings. The scent of marijuana hung heavy in the air. That fact, combined with a scattering of brightly-colored pills and the matching mirror, razor, and straw coke-snorting set I spotted atop the nightstand, told me the slumber of the three wasn't likely to be easily disturbed.

I moved around to the foot of the bed, leaned over, put the .45 between Champ's legs. I pressed the snout hard into the black satin a half inch from his balls and squeezed off a round.

The rubbery casing of the mattress and sixteen inches of water absorbed most of the sound—enough, anyway, not to have to worry about the neighbors. But within the bedroom itself, the gunshot was a sudden, shocking boom. It jarred Champ awake and sent him scrabbling backward, crablike, until he slammed hard against the ornately carved headboard. The Chicana rolled away with a squeal while the blonde on the other side, stoned to the gills, stirred only slightly. Water arced up from the bullet hole and came back down with a dog-pissing-on-shoes sound.

I planted a foot in the middle of the bed, reached across the spouting water, and this time pressed the snout of the .45 against the shiny

234

blackness of Champ's forehead, nailing him to the carved mahogany like a fly on the end of a pin.

"One wrong twitch," I said, "your brains are part of the wallpaper."

Off to my left, the floppy-titted Chicana was scrambling to her feet, grunting loudly with the effort.

I flicked her a glance and said out of the corner of my mouth, "You understand English, puta?"

Her movement froze. "Si," she answered in a hoarse whisper.

"Then hear this: Put on some clothes and get out of here. Take the blonde girl with you. Go fast and go far. Your man here is in big trouble, you don't want any part of it. If you try to help him in any way, try to cause trouble for me in return, I will come after you and make you very sorry. Comprende?"

"Si," she said again.

"Then move it."

A flurry of activity, more grunts of effort, the snap of elastic as she pulled on some clothes. Then she was around on the other side of me, dragging the near-catotonic blonde from the bed and forcing clothes on her as well. When the blonde made mewling protests, the Chicana shushed her and cursed her in Spanish.

All the while I kept my eyes boring into those of Champ, following the progress of his two playmates only through peripheral vision. Beads of sweat were standing out on the face of the pimp like droplets of tar on a freshly-blacktopped street.

As the Chicana herded the blonde out of the room, he finally worked up enough courage to speak. "What the fuck this all about, man?"

I lifted the muzzle from his forehead and backhanded him across the right ear with the long barrel of the gun. When his head rolled back to center, I pinned it there once again with the business end of the .45.

"Rule one," I said. "I ask the questions."

He hated me with his eyes. The beads of sweat started to run down his neck, mixing with the worm of blood that crawled from his ear.

"The name's Hannibal," I told him. "You've heard of me because I've squashed your kind of cockroach before."

A rush of anger and humiliation overcame his good sense. "You nuthin' but a lousy private dick, man. You got no right bustin' in here. You just a pretend pig, not no real cop!"

I slapped him across the other ear with the gun barrel. Gorilla treatment for a gorilla pimp. The only language he'd understand.

"I'm looking for a girl," I said when his eyes were focused again.

"Her name is Alice Grant and you bailed her out of jail two months ago, after you set her up for the bust that put her there in the first place because she was freelancing in your territory. Then you turned her out as part of your stable. Her parents are in town and they've hired me to find her. They want to take Alice back and help her try to put her life together again. Trouble is, I can't find anybody who remembers seeing Alice in over a week. What I did find, though, was plenty of street talk that says you were having to slap her around pretty heavy in order to get her to turn the kinds of tricks you wanted. So what did you do to her, Champ? Where is Alice Grant?"

"I let that bitch go, man. Like you say, she nuthin' but trouble."

"You spent all that money and time bailing her out and turning her out, then you just let her go?"

"Yeah. Yeah, man. I didn't need the aggravation."

I slid my foot forward across the slick satin, lifted it suddenly and brought it down on his shriveled penis and balls, shoving them into the rapidly deflating mattress. I didn't apply much pressure but the pimp's eyes bulged and his body tensed and became as rigid as a steel bar.

"Rule two," I said, just before giving a single toe tap that made him cry out more in apprehension than in pain. "Don't lie to me."

I withdrew the foot, gave him time to catch his breath, then said again, "Where's Alice Grant?"

Whatever answer he might have given was cut off by a commotion from behind me. It came from the Chicana and the blonde, who I'd figured were long gone by now.

"No," I heard the Chicana say loudly. "You cannot go in there—he is a very bad man and he will kill us all."

"But he's hurting our Champ," protested the high-pitched whine of the blonde.

"No! Give me that—"

There came the sound then of a gunshot, unmuffled this time, shatteringly loud.

I whirled in time to see the Chicana pitch into the room, mouth working guppylike, blood spraying high and far from a grapefruit-sized hole in her stomach that she was trying unsuccessfully to cover with both hands. Behind her, emerging through a haze of gunsmoke, stepped the blonde. She moved with a stiff, zombie-like jerkiness and her eyes were wild, unfocused, frightening things. She held a huge, nickel-plated Magnum revolver in front of her.

Those wild eyes swept the room, found me. "Leave Champ alone,"
236

she said in a faraway voice, spacing the words very carefully. As she spoke, she began to raise the Magnum.

There was no other way. No place to hide, no chance to talk her out of it, no time to think or to aim. I swung the .45 around and snapped off a shot. The bullet tore away half her throat and the hinge of her jaw. She slammed back against the wall, instantly loose and lifeless, and collapsed like a pile of rags. The Magnum discharged once, harmlessly.

While the .45 was still throbbing in my fist, Champ launched himself from the headboard and slammed a vicious punch into my kidney. I dropped to my knees, a groan of agony escaping from between my lips. I twisted instinctively and lashed out with my gun hand. I caught him as he was aiming another punch, driving the butt of the .45 into his cheekbone. I heard the bone splinter and he fell away with a howl, tumbling off the bed. Ignoring the pain that boiled through my midsection, I lunged after him. I wrestled him onto his back, then knelt on his chest with a shinbone pressed across his throat and once more brought the muzzle of the big automatic to rest in the center of his forehead.

"Where's Alice Grant?" I demanded for the third time.

"Fuck you," he sneered.

"One way or another, you bastard, you're going to tell me."

"You ain't got time enough to *make* me tell you. Not now, motherfucker. You think all them shots ain't gonna bring the cops? You in a world of shit, man. You offed that girl."

"It was self-defense, maggot."

"You bust in a man's home an' members of that man's household try to make you leave an' you blow them away—that ain't self defense, motherfucker. Even a black man—even a black *pimp*—got more rights than that."

"Then I may as well blow you away, too. What have I got to lose?"

"Off me, I never be able to tell you what you want to know."

"There are other ways. If Alice Grant rubbed up against you, she'll leave a trail of slime."

"Then best you go find that trail of slime to stick your nose in, bloodhound man, cause I ain't tellin' you shit."

I looked around the room at all the trashy luxury and thought about what it stood for. Then I looked at the blood and the bodies. Champ hadn't put the bullets in either girl, but he was every bit as responsible for their deaths as the fingers that pulled the triggers. More so, in a sense. And I could only wonder how many other young

237

girls' lives he had ruined—ended either directly or indirectly. And how many more to come.

I considered my own predicament. A simple missing person case gone sour in an unexpected and terrible way. A world of shit, Champ had called it. And I knew I could count on him to do everything in his power—embellish every point, put on every kind of act—to see me suffocate in it. I looked back down at him. After years of operating on the edge of the law, was *this* what I would end up taking a fall over?

Even with his face smashed and my .45 jammed against his skull, the cocky bastard was smirking at my dilemma.

"Rule three," I said. "Don't ever back me into a corner."

And I pulled the trigger.


By the time the cops got there, I had things rearranged as best I could and I had my story ready for them. They didn't buy it for a minute, but they couldn't break my testimony and none of it made sense any other way they tried to figure it.

I'd taken the Magnum from under the blonde's body, smearing any fingerprints she might have left on it, then pressed the weapon into Champ's hand and fired one more shot into the soggy waterbed, doing my best to make sure he left at least one good lift. The way I told it, I'd gone there to ask about Alice Grant. When I arrived at the front door I could hear shouting and arguing from inside. Then I heard gunshots. I'd kicked down the door and gone in. The Chicana was already dead and I saw Champ chasing the blonde into the bedroom. I wasn't fast enough to save the blonde and I'd had to shoot the drug-crazed pimp in self defense when he turned on me. The bullet trajectories and various other ballistic aspects as well as the accounts of neighbors regarding the spacing of the shots and so forth didn't match most of this worth a damn, of course. But they still couldn't get me to change my story and the whole thing refused to fit together more convincingly any other way.

Two days into the investigation, Alice Grant's body turned up in a drainage ditch over near the county line. She'd been tortured and savagely beaten to death. The discovery of her remains probably helped save my butt. Nobody put it into words, but once it was generally accepted that her death most likely came at the hands of Champ, then all enthusiasm for nailing the guy who'd burned the pimp suddenly seemed to dissipate.

I returned the retainer fee Alice's parents had paid me and told them I was sorry. The old man called me a dirty name and slammed

238

the hotel room door in my face. I never heard from them again and I hardly ever think about them anymore, or about Alice or Champ.

But sometimes late at night, when sleep won't come and there's no one lying beside me to occupy my mind with other thoughts and not even a few belts of bourbon will work its magic, I think about the blonde girl I had to shoot. My mind's eye replays and replays the way she bounced off that wall so immediately limp and dead, until I want to scream for the repeating image to stop.

No one ever came forward to claim her body—or the Chicana's. No one even knew where they came from or what their real names were; only their street handles, their whore names. The county buried them in unmarked plots and to this day they remain listed in the files only as Jane Doe #546 (aka Priscila) and Jane Doe #547 (aka Conchita).

Once in a while, usually on those same nights when the booze won't work and I'm all alone, I'll drive out to where their graves are and maybe shed a tear over them. It doesn't change anything, doesn't bring them back, doesn't buy them markers or names to put on them.

But it gets me through to the next day.

# Heir-in-a-Hurry

*by Morris Cooper*

The only time Sylvester Hanson came to see him, Tony Brun still had three years to go. Tony didn't especially care about having his recreation period broken up, but he followed the guard across the walled yard. After all, it would be a novelty having a visitor for the first time in the two years he'd been in prison.

Tony Brun sat on the other side of the screen and waited for his visitor to speak. He saw a little dried-up old man, with an old-country mustache that looked as if it was almost too heavy for the face that carried it. The visitor placed a hand on the screen, then jerked it away. He looked at the guard who sat at the end of the table and smiled apologetically. Then he turned to Tony.

"I am Sylvester Hanson." He peered at Tony as if he hoped the name might mean something to him. "Your papa and me, we were

239

friends in the old country." The accent, smoothly guttural, reminded Tony of the lectures his old man had given him when he was a kid.

"That's nice," said Tony. He wondered what the old fool wanted, and almost regretted the fact that he'd consented to see him.

"For a long time, now, I look for your papa. But when I find him, it is already too late." He smiled at Tony. "The grave, it is very nice, but it has no headstone. So I have one put up." He peered at Tony. "You do not mind?"

"No, I guess not," he mumbled. "I was kind of short at the time—" He broke off. What the heck was he apologizing for? This old duffer sure had his nerve coming around to tell him about a headstone.

"It is not until later that I find out you are here," said Hanson. "For me it is difficult to travel much. The doctor, today, did not wish for me to go, but I said yes. I wanted once to look at the son of my old friend."

Tony fidgeted. "I got a bad break. . . ."

Hanson held up a hand. "A mistake we all make. It is later what we do that counts." Tony felt like grinning. It looked like the old boy had gotten himself all primed up to give him a lecture.

"When you are released, you will please come to see me?" asked Hanson. "It is possible that I may be able to give you some help."

"Sure thing," said Tony. He got up. "I gotta go now, but I'll keep you in mind." Tony turned at the door and waved. "See you around." Every time he thought of the old man, the rest of the afternoon, he couldn't help laughing. They were all the same, always preaching to a guy when he was in no position to talk back.

Tony got the first letter a week later. It was a rambling affair, full of good advice and a couple of long words that sent him to the prison library looking for a dictionary. They came regularly after that, once a month, and always with some money enclosed, that was credited to his account at the prison store.

From the letters he found out that old Sylvester Hanson was alone in the world with only a housekeeper to look after his needs. And, from an occasional word or phrase, he gathered that the old man had a sizeable chunk of cash in the bank. He'd retired from business ten years ago.

The idea hit Tony three months before his time was up. He showed one of the letters to Del Saugus. "Do you think you could copy this?"

Saugus laughed. "Sure I could. But what's the percentage? The only way I'll ever leave this joint will be feet first."

240

"A guy in stir can always use an extra luck," said Tony. "And maybe I might be able to make a connection that'll get you over the wall."

Saugus fingered the letter. "If I thought there was half a chance . . ."

Tony said, "If this goes through, I'll have a wad. And if it doesn't pan out, what the hell have you got to lose?"

Saugus made up his mind. "I'll do it."

"Swell," said Tony. "What I want is a will—one of those holographic things. Hand-written, you know. This guy knows he's gonna pop off any minute and hasn't got time to get a lawyer."

"You got a crystal ball?" asked Saugus.

"Leave the date blank. And do a good job."

Saugus snorted. "Don't tell me my business. Just tell me what you want Hanson to write."

"That he's leaving everything he owns to Anthony Brun, son of his old friend Otto Brun."

The day before he was released, Tony got the will from Saugus. "You put today's date on it, like I asked you last night?"

Saugus grinned. "Makes a good alibi, doesn't it, being in stir the day it was written?"

"Insurance," said Tony, patting the envelope. "In more ways than one."

The wreath hung over the old-fashioned knocker and Tony had to push it aside to rap on the door. He heard a tired voice call out, "Come."

Tony opened the door and saw Hanson sitting in an easy chair in the living room to the right of the hallway. Ahead was a banistered stairway.

"Tony." Hanson held out a hand, and Tony walked over. The old man's flesh felt dry and tired. "Sit down." He waved to a chair next to him.

"I promised you I'd come to see you when I got out," said Tony. He pressed his hands together.

"It is good you come," said Hanson. "I would offer you some refreshments, but I am alone."

"That's all right," said Tony. That's a break, he thought.

"You have come for help, no?" The old man caressed the ends of his mustache.

Tony nodded his head. "I figured with a new start, maybe a little business—" He waited. There was the off-chance that the old man would give him a sizeable chunk now, and he wouldn't have to use the will.

"I have found out a lot of things about you, Tony. You have been very bad. Your papa died early because he worried for you." Hanson held up a silencing hand when Tony started to speak. "I am not trying to preach. All of us, sometimes, we do wrong, and then maybe we are sorry." He looked at Tony.

"I guess maybe I am," he said. "But if I had another chance . . ."

"That is what I think," said Hanson. "So I have for you a job. It is on a farm, and the pay, it is not much. But plenty to eat you will get, and a lot of hard work. It is good for a man that he work hard."

Tony nodded. There was no point in arguing with the old man. He'd have to do what he'd started out to, and get it over as quickly as possible.

"It sounds good," agreed Tony. "Do you think I could stay here tonight? I haven't had a chance to get settled yet."

"But yes. The bedrooms, they are upstairs."

That was all Tony wanted to know; it fitted in nicely with his plan. He stood up. "I'll go down to the station after my bag." Tony walked over to Hanson and put out his hand. When the old man lifted his, Tony cracked his left fist against Hanson's jaw.

It wasn't much of a punch, but it was enough to knock the old man out. Tony hadn't wanted to hit him too hard—he didn't want to leave a bruise that might be difficult to explain.

Tony carried the frail body of the old man into the hallway. He laid Hanson on the floor, held his head in his hands like a basketball, and brought it crashing down on the bottom step. The crunch reminded Tony of a watermelon dropping on a concrete floor.

It didn't need an expert to know that old Sylvester Hanson was dead. Tony lifted the body, carried it halfway up the stairs and let it drop. He watched it roll slowly down, come to a rest on the bottom step.

The story would be obvious when they found the old man. He'd started to go up to bed and he'd slipped, or maybe even had a dizzy spell. If they noticed a mark on his jaw, they'd just figure he'd hit it on a step on the way down.

Tony shook the will out of the envelope and held it with his handkerchief while he reached down and tucked it into the pocket of Hanson's smoking jacket. He left by the front door, hands in his pocket and whistling jauntily. The future looked bright for Tony Brun.

\* \* \*

Tony waited until the next afternoon before he went calling. When he reached for the knocker he noticed that the wreath was no longer there. The man who opened the door wore civilian clothes, but Tony could see copper written all over him.

"Yes?"

"I'm looking for Mr. Sylvester Hanson." The cop motioned Tony in, and he followed him into the same room the old man had been sitting in the evening before.

"What do you want to see Mr. Hanson about?"

"It's kind of personal."

The man took a badge from his pocket. "I'm Sergeant Whitt, Homicide."

"Oh," said Tony. "Mr. Hanson asked me to call when I—ah—got a chance. I'm Tony Brun." He tried to put a tone of casual surprise in his voice. "Anything wrong?"

Sergeant Whitt stood with his back to the fireplace. "Mr. Hanson is dead."

"Dead!" Tony reached for a chair, remembered it was the one Hanson had been sitting in, but it was too late to change.

"Know Hanson long?" Whitt asked casually.

"I only met him once," Tony said, "but I got a lot of letters from him." He sat down. "I got out of State Prison yesterday."

"Parole?" asked Whitt.

"I did my full time." Tony formed his hands into a pyramid, supported his chin on twin thumbs. "Mr. Hanson came up to see me once —he used to be a friend of my father's in the old country."

"You thought Mr. Hanson might do something for you if you came around?" Whitt asked.

"I did," Tony answered. "What happened to the old man, anyway?"

"Looks like he started up the stairs and fell down."

"Tough," murmured Tony.

"We found a will." Sergeant Whitt studied his fingernails. "The old man left everything to you."

"Say!" Tony stood up. "That's something."

"Funny about that," the sergeant said. "His lawyer told me he drew up a will just a week ago leaving everything to an orphanage."

"Tough on the orphans," said Tony, "but lucky for me."

"You say you received letters from the old man while you were doing time?"

"Yeah." Tony reached into his inside breast pocket. "Here's the last one I got, about three weeks ago."

The sergeant looked at the letter, turned it over and put it in his pocket. Tony started to protest, changed his mind. "I guess Mr. Hanson's lawyer will get in touch with me," he said, moving toward the hallway.

"That was a nice pen job on the will," the sergeant said. "Even the date to give you an alibi."

Tony looked at the sergeant. "What are you talking about?"

"Did you do the writing job yourself, Tony, or get one of the boys in stir to help you?"

"Listen, copper, if you got anything to say, spill it," snarled Tony. "I did all my time and there's nothing you can pin on me."

"You didn't know the old man had been sick and bedded down in the library, did you Tony? His doctor told me he couldn't have climbed those stairs if his life depended on it."

"You're still talking through your mouth, copper. What has all this got to do with me?"

Sergeant Whitt moved next to Tony. "Bet you didn't even know that all the English the old man could write was his name."

Tony laughed. "I suppose those letters came out of my head? Besides, what difference does it make if he could write English or not?"

"The will, Tony, the will. Or have you forgotten that it's handwritten."

"Nuts," Tony said.

"Mr. Hanson's housekeeper did all his writing for him."

Tony sighed. "So maybe she wrote the will."

"He still would have signed it himself."

Tony shrugged his shoulders. "So I guess that means the orphans get the break after all. Hanson should have thought about that."

"It's no good, Tony. The housekeeper never wrote that will."

"But you just said—"

Whitt shook his head sadly. "Didn't you notice that wreath on the door when you were here yesterday?"

"I wasn't here—" Tony's voice trailed off.

"The wreath was for the housekeeper, Tony. She died two days before the date on the will."

Tony thought of Saugus. It looked like he'd been right in his prediction that he'd go out feet first—only from the way it stood now, Tony would beat him to it.

# Higher Education

*by Sidney Waldo*

I'm a police detective, and I've had my education. Only it's been local—New York, Chicago, Boston, U.S.A. While this dame . . .

But I'll tell you.

We get a call from the Second National Bank, and I hop over there. A man had been shot—down in the safe deposit vault.

They let me in through an iron-grilled door and I see three well-dressed guys and a dame sitting around a big oblong table. None of them is looking at any other one. These four, and the bank clerk on duty, had been there when the shots were fired. The clerk had telephoned up for one of the vice-presidents, and he was now in charge of things.

He shows me the dead guy, lying face down in one of the bond clipping rooms. The man's name is Newhall. He was a big stock market gambler. The dame was his secretary. They were just stepping into the little room, when two shots exploded somewhere, and Newhall pitches in on his face. I bent over him. I could see where the big bullets had punched through his clothes, low in the back.

"The coroner'll be along any time," I said. "But, now, where in hell is the gun?"

They hadn't found any gun. And, of course, that was the nuts. The one place on earth you couldn't hide a gun would be a bank vault. The three guys and the dame had been searched, and the four open safe deposit boxes, and there wasn't any gun.

"That's what *you* say," I told the vice-president. I stepped over to him and ran my hands down his sides. "Somebody could have slipped it to you," I grinned. But he had no gun. "Now stand still where I can watch you," I said as I frisked the clerk.

No gun on him either. I let him stand beside his boss, while I called the dame over. She was a slim, blue-blooded looking doll, a lot of class, and a gun would have showed on her. But just to be sure, I felt for the weight of one down round the bottom of her skirt.

The next guy was short and plump. He wore a gray suit with a

245

white edge to his vest. He acted nervous, but he had no gun on him. Nor did the next one.

The last man, when he stood up, was tall—over six feet—and thin. He looked sick and touchy. He picked up a heavy curved-handled cane from the table, and as he came over toward me, I saw that he needed it. He walked with a bad limp. He had no gun either.

There was something about this guy, though, that I didn't like. "Where was you," I asked, "when the shots went off?"

He pointed to the half-open door of the bond room exactly opposite Newhall's. He could have plugged Newhall from there, easy.

But I had to find the gun.

It had to be there, some place. The long table had a glass top and no drawers. I looked underneath. I also looked underneath some other, smaller tables; and under all the chairs. I made them all go and sit down at the big table again, while I went through all the bond-clipping rooms. I even frisked the dead man. I don't pass up one bet.

And there isn't any gun.

I can't go back and report a thing like that. It don't make sense. And these birds around the table are getting impatient. Just to keep their minds occupied, while I fish for another hunch, I sit down and begin taking their names. The dame is right opposite me and when the lame man says his name is Flint—Richard Flint—I see her give a start.

I turned on her quick. "That name give you any ideas?"

She thought for a minute. "It reminded me of a letter Mr. Newhall got from Paris. It was partly in French. I helped translate it. It was signed 'Dick.'"

"What did it say?" I asked.

She seemed excited. "It sounded very friendly. But Mr. Newhall seemed to take it as a warning. I couldn't see it that way. If this man intended any harm to him, why would he advertise it beforehand?"

"Sometimes they can't resist it, sister," I explained. "It's how they get their fun."

But she was hurrying on. "The letter spoke of increasing lameness. A lameness that shut him out of all the activities that meant life. That was the part that worried Mr. Newhall. This man, he said, held him responsible for that lameness."

"So there we have the motive," I thought. A big, six-foot athlete could brood plenty over a thing like that. But I still didn't have the gun. "Anything else?" I asked.

She nodded. "There was something about Mr. Newhall's great busi-

246

ness success; some joke about cutting coupons. Then the man used a French idiom. '*Ça-y-est!*' It has a number of meanings. 'So much for that,' or 'Let it ride,' or 'You see?' There was more in French. I remember this part clearly, because we couldn't make any real sense out of it: '*The French are not only clever, but also discreet. I have bought from them a new cane and a new foot.*' And the final word was in Italian, '*Arrivederci,*' which means:

" 'Until we meet again,' or 'I'll be seeing you.' "

But, already, I thought I had it. Sure! A cane. The cane from Paris. One of those foreign pistol canes. I made a grab for it, as it lay on the glass-topped table.

Then I caught the dame's smile. "I thought of that, too," she said. "I've seen them, in the Paris gun shops. But they fire only a single shot."

Still, I hated to let go the idea. While I was looking for some gadget that would open up that cane, the dame spoke again.

"But that word, 'discreet.' Why did he use *that* word? 'The French are not only clever, but also discreet. I have bought from them a new cane *and a new foot.*' "

Lord! It dawned on me as if I'd been hit with a brick. What a sweet revenge! A new foot! A new foot that was hollow.

"I'll just have a look at that new foot," I told him.

He pushed back from the table and drew himself up, straight and tall. He was game, I'll say that much for him.

"If it's the same to you," he said, "I'll spare myself that indignity. I admit it. There *is* a gun—"

But I had to make him go through with it. There might still be some catch in this.

"Sorry," I told him. "I've got to actually have my hands on that gun before anybody goes out of here."

His face darkened, but he saw the point. With that limping step, he walked over to another table and sat down with his back to the rest of them. I kept right there beside him. Bending down, he unbuckled some straps and handed the foot up to me. And maybe that didn't give me a squirm! It had the sock and the shoe still on it.

Then I saw the gun. A smart workman had fixed it up, all right. Fitting into its slot, as close as a hand in a glove, was the prettiest little double-barreled derringer you ever set your eyes on.

I lifted it out, and handed the foot back to him. He buckled it on and stood up. I almost felt sorry for him. He'd sure had a tough break. Once he had got outside the vault and disposed of the foot, the whole

247

secret would have died with Newhall. If it hadn't been for that blond dame. Who'd expect a stock gambler's secretary to be tops on languages?

I looked over at her. Yeah, that was his bad luck. That dame had been around. She was educated.

# Hip and Thigh

*by H. H. Matteson*

This Hoh-hoh Stevens he comes in the back way furtive and mysterious. He sets down. I never did see him look so miserable and dejected. Usually Hoh-hoh comes in grinning and smart talking. He don't this time. He looks plumb downcast and wretched.

"Dode," he says to me, "I got the toughest problem of my career to solve. I require counsel and advice. I dassent tell Joe Albright, the U.S. Commissioner about it, so I come to you. At that, though, I aim to shoot square with Joe even if I have to turn in my badge and resign a lot."

"Whatever is the run-in, Hoh-hoh?" I says serious, seeing how he hain't in no jocular mood.

"Well," he says, "I been over to Nagichak Island. I never was to that island before. It's account of no one there knowing me or that I'm a deputy marshal, that I gets betrayed into this dilemma. I'm going past the trading post store there on Nagichak, and a passel of beachcombing outcasts is setting on the steps talking plenty ribald and obscene. Them beach bums, they was five–six of 'em, was exulting very offensive that they had broke up the meeting in the gospel ship the night before. Yes, the Reverend John Benner, and his sister that plays the organ and sings, is at Nagichak with their gospel boat.

"Them sculpins setting there in front of the store are laughing hearty as they review how they caterwauled, and bellered, and took on when this Benner woman began her singing. Then they just about bust with delight when they recount how this Bottlenose Needham dragged the preacher, John Benner, right out of his pulpit, and near beat him to death.

"Seeing how this breaking up of gospel meetings is agin the law—

248

or at least is agin decency—I'm about to step up to them beach rats and demand explanations. Yes, this identical Bottlenose is setting there amongst 'em, the hero of the occasion, and he grins very complacent when they tell how complete he licked the preacher.

"This here Bottlenose speaks up important and he boasts how he aims to break up all gospel meetings whatever from then on.

" 'But you won't have to break up no meetings soon again, Bottlenose,' says one, 'account of you busted this pastor so severe they've had to pack him off to the hospital.'

"Then again them rats all laugh hearty at the jest.

"I restrains myself with difficulty. Constant Joe warns me, and you do too, Dode, not to act impulsive. I figure I better go first to the preacher boat, and if them swabs hain't lied, and the pastor wants to make complaints, I'll make earnest endeavors to induce this Bottlenose to accompany me back here to jail.

"So I walks on down the shore to where the gospel ship is moored, with a long plank running from the deck to shore-side.

"This here is a sizeable ship, with a long cabin, with seats into it so that fifty–sixty people can set down at once. At one end there's a platform where the little organ is, and where the preacher does his discoursing and leads the hymn singing.

"I walks up onto the deck, and they hain't a soul on board. So I sets down in a little cubby where a desk is, and I see at once from books and so forth it must be the pastor's study. I figure I'll just wait till someone does come, and I can get the straight of the busting up of this meeting.

"I'm setting there, and I glances through a port, and I seen a girl paddling frantic acrost the bay in a skin boat. She comes alongside, and up onto the deck, and into this study office where I'm setting.

"She hain't but about thumb-size, but she's got nice brown eyes, and she comes in timorous, and I indicates polite for her to set down, and she done it, and busts out bawling.

" 'Whatever can the matter be?' I asks sympathetic.

" 'Oh, I'm so worried,' she says. 'I just got to tell you. My brother, Eddie won't tell, and he'd kill me if he knowed that I told. But I got to tell. I just can't stand it no longer.'

" 'But still I don't know what this trouble you're into is,' I says.

" 'It was my brother, Eddie, that pirated the Thunderbird trap last week and stole five thousand dollars' worth of fish,' she blurts out. 'Yes, my brother, Eddie, done it. Him and another. Bottlenose Needham, into the job with Eddie, he says how he's got a way figured to

249

lay the whole job onto Eddie, and he aims to make Eddie blow the big safe in the cannery office now some night soon.

" 'Oh, what will I do?' she sobs. 'What will I do? I just know, soon or late, Eddie will get ketched. I hear how they now got a terrible brute of a deputy marshal in the islands, and when he goes out after a criminal, he always gets him, and they call him Hoh-hoh Stevens.'

"This here left handed compliment gives me a terrible jolt, Dode. I seen right away this little thumb-size girl, confessing her brother's crime, thinks she's telling her troubles to John Benner, the boat preacher.

"And that's my problem. Though I and you have been plenty chagrined we hain't solved that Thunderbird pirate job as yet, I just can't caper out now and arrest this Eddie. No, though under false pretenses, what this girl tells me is a privileged communication. Why, it's almost sacredly so! Whatever can I do, Dode?"

I sets and ponders. "I just don't know exact, Hoh-hoh," I says. "A man that is a man can't take advantages of breaks like this girl's confession."

"I know well that I can't," says Hoh-hoh. "If I was to prance out now and arrest this Eddie, I'd never dast look in the mirror again for fear I'd spit."

"Well, leave us consider," I says. "Later, if we decide we got to, we'll tell Joe. Meantime, Hoh-hoh, I'll string along with you. If and when Joe does find out about it and lays back in the britchin and starts to paw, I'll share the blame with you for holding out the information on him."

"Good!" explodes out this Hoh-hoh, terrible relieved. "Now I got to encroach further onto you, Dode. You explain to Joe why I hain't going to be home tonight, or possible several nights."

"For why?" I asks.

"I got duties emphatic laid out for me tonight that I promises to perform."

"What duties, Hoh-hoh?" I asks. "And further, Hoh-hoh, what did you say final to this thumb-size girl?"

"Oh, I gets reckless, Dode, I'm that sorry for her. I guarantees her that she dassent worry, that a way will be found to keep Eddie out of further misdemeanors, and for her not to fret none.

"Then she stands up terrible relieved, and she lays that little paw of hern in mine, and thanks me ardent, and then she says, 'Pastor, will you just say a word of prayer for Eddie?'

"That there was a facer, Dode. I swallers hard. I can feel my eyes

250

beginning to bulge. But I says, 'Yes, I will.' So I says, 'Oh, Lord, learn this Eddie boy some sense, or I will. Amen.' "

"What is them emphatic duties you got to perform, Hoh-hoh," I asks, "that may keep you absent from our midst, and concerning which I got to fabricate lies to Joe Albright, who, you must remember, is the United States Commissioner here, and our boss?"

"Why," says Hoh-hoh, "after the little thumb-size departs, I still sets there aiming to remain till someone comes that can tell me about the busting up of the meeting and the belting of the pastor.

"Final a timid little woman comes on in, and she reminds me all ways of a sparrer wren. She looks surprised when she seen me in the study. She sets down and says how she is the sister of Preacher John Benner, and she plays the organ and sings in them meetings.

"Not to get ketched in no further jams, I tell her prompt that I am Hoh-hoh Stevens, Deputy United States Marshal, and honing to know details of the busting up of their meeting and the assault on her brother.

"At that she begins to bawl, too. It's a day for me with bawling women. She sobs and takes on, and tells me at intervals how this Bottlenose and his gang did break up the meeting in disorder, and how Bottlenose drug her brother right out of the pulpit, and beat him so severe she'd just come from putting him on the boat for the hospital at Dutch Harbor.

" 'I take it your brother must be a little man, and feeble?' I says.

" 'Little! Feeble!' she says.

"She gets up and goes on into a adjoining cabin, and she comes back with one of them long-tail, black preacher coats.

" 'Take off your coat, and put on this, Mr. Stevens,' she says. 'Little! My brother is big as you. He's plenty *skookum.*'

"I shucks my coat, and put on the long-tail pastoral garb, and it fits me exact.

" 'What I can't understand,' I says to Sister Benner, 'is how any gent capable of filling this here coat would take a belting off this Bottlenose, or any one.'

" 'It's my brother's principles,' she says, 'to turn the other cheek. He just stood there, my brother did, his arms hanging down, while Bottlenose struck him brutally, again and again in the face.'

" 'Them's practices and doctrines plumb foreign to me,' I says, 'but I got to respect a gent that will stand up to the rack and take punishment for his principles.'

"Well, I and Sister Benner set for a while, and talk and a idea begins to glimmer. I puts on the long-tail preacher coat again and kind of

251

parades around, aiming to soak up some piety and sanctity out of the garment if possible.

" 'Sister Benner,' I says, 'you play the organ, and sing at them meetings, do you not?'

" 'Yes,' she says proud. 'I can play. And I can sing.'

" 'Then why hain't it a good idea for I and you to rehearse?'

"She looks kind of wild for a minute. Then she begins to smile. She gets up and I and her go into the long meeting cabin, and she pulls some stops on this organ and steps on the bellows, and I and her bust into song.

"Dode," Hoh-hoh says, "sin-hardened old buzzard that you be, if you could hear Sister Benner and I render 'Oh, Beulah Land,' you'd stagger sobbing to the mourners' bench, and repent your manifold sins.

"I and Sister Benner we render two–three tunes more, all very sweet, and we go back into the pastor's study, and I instructs her as follows:

" 'Sister Benner,' I says, 'I aim to be absent for a little while. In the meantime, you circulate around industrious, and you tell the folks of Nagichak, how that account of John Benner is indisposed, a new preacher has came in to take his place. Special you try to get the word to Bottlenose and his gang of beach rats, that services will be held this evening, as usual, in this gospel ship.'

"So there now, Dode, you know why I'll be absent tonight from here," Hoh-hoh says. "I aim to preach tonight and I got my text all selected out. It's from Isaiah, and it says, 'Smite 'em hip and thigh!' That there text, I'll admit, Dode is some obscure to me. Whacking a gent on the thigh I don't figure is good fighting tactics. I generally always aim to connect with his jaw or belly. But it's Bible, and it's my text."

## II

I then tells Hoh-hoh how simple it is to square his absence with Joe, just by revealing out the preacher attack, and how Hoh-hoh aims to rebuke this Bottlenose, I'll just forget to mention this here confession made by the little thumb-size girl. Hoh-hoh he goes sliding out then, climbs into his skin boat, and away he goes.

Seems like Sister Benner had spread it on thick. She figures if Preacher Hoh-hoh can expound good as he sings—which of course he can't—why he deserves a abundant congregation.

252

When the meeting opens that night they is a crowd that fills every seat, and folks standing along the wall besides. Hoh-hoh, him wearing John Benner's long-tail preacher coat, he gets up very grave, and announces how they'll open the services with song, and invites all hands to join in hearty.

In the very front row, grinning up imbecile and insulting, is this Bottlenose, and he's got four–five of his beachcombers with him. Hoh-hoh he walks back and forth slow on the platform, and he pauses a minute to fix this Bottlenose with his eye.

"It was most unfortunate," says Hoh-hoh solemn, "that the services last night were disturbed by unseemly conduct. Let us hope, brothers and sisters, that there will be no repetition of such rude and impious demeanour."

Hoh-hoh he walks over to the organ then, and Sister Benner and he leads off with "Beulah Land." They sing it very sweet. Fact is, this here brand new music on the program even stopped Bottlenose for a spell. He sets there staring up wopper-jawed at Hoh-hoh.

They sing two–three songs more, Hoh-hoh urging the flock to join in, and him singing personal so loud you could a-heard him clean to Puffin Bird.

After this singing Hoh-hoh steps to the edge of the platform, and says how he'll announce his text, and expound it later.

"I aim to preach emphatic to you all," he says, "from a text out of Isaiah, or somewhere, and it's entitled, 'Smite 'em hip and thigh.'"

Just then Bottlenose nudges on his gang. "Which this is the most stupidest meeting I ever did attend," says Bottlenose, loud and offensive, and yawning and stretching. "I aim to take over these services personal, and conduct 'em more animated."

"Sure, Bottlenose," says one of the beachcombers. "Fine idea! You got it all ways over this new preacher, who I esteems to be a false alarm."

Bottlenose he stands up then, though many of the congregation is saying, "Shame! Set down, Bottlenose! Keep still!"

Bottlenose he looks around defiant at the congregation, and then he looks up at Hoh-hoh, who's standing on the edge of the platform, his hands folded together pious.

"Brothers and sisters," says Hoh-hoh calm and cold—too calm if them beachcombers had had wits to understand—"until this rude interruption, this here was a gospel ship. But the wicked have invaded the sanctuary. So now this peaceful meeting place is going to get transformed sudden into a arena of action."

With that, Hoh-hoh shucks off this long-tail preacher coat, and in

253

one jump offen the platform he's down amongst them beach rats. The first two *chukkins* he leaves go, he knocks two of them sculpins colder than storage fish.

But he takes a mean one from Bottlenose. Bottlenose had his reputation as a preacher-buster at stake, so he tears into Hoh-hoh fierce. He belts Hoh-hoh on the side of the head, and it kind of knocks Hoh-hoh off balance, and before he can come back to a even keel, Bottlenose gives him another, and one of the gang hits Hoh-hoh on the other side of the head.

Folks in the congregation is milling around, and the women is running out screeching and down the plank to the shore.

This here beachcomber that had swung in the lick, just as Bottlenose had hit Hoh-hoh, too, he runs in jubilant. He is all organized to give Hoh-hoh another one, when Hoh-hoh he just lifts up his leg, and he plants a foot in this party's belly, and he kicks him clean acrost the bench.

Now this leaves the fight to Bottlenose and Hoh-hoh exclusive. Bottlenose he runs in, and he swings wild and misses, and the force of his own lick kind of spins him around. And Hoh-hoh snatches out and gets him by the scruff of the neck and Hoh-hoh held him there and give him some slaps alongside the head that would rock a walrus.

This Bottlenose just bellers, and rears and pitches, and he twists loose, and Hoh-hoh leaves him have one right on the jaw, and it knocks this Bottlenose quivering, and he sets on the floor, gasping like a beached bull cod.

Hoh-hoh he leans and he picks this Bottlenose up bodily and sets him on his feet, again clinging to the scruff of Bottlenose's neck.

"Brethren and sisters," says Hoh-hoh as solemn as squinch owls, "my text is, 'Smite 'em hip and thigh.' "

With that Hoh-hoh just drug this Bottlenose acrost the bench, face down, and he spanked him till he smoked, this Bottlenose squirming and kicking and howling for mercy.

Final, Hoh-hoh, still maintaining that scruff holt, he lets him up. "Brothers and sisters," says Hoh-hoh, "you are about to listen to a confession. Bottlenose, you tell the assemblage how you planned and helped to pull the Thunderbird pirate job. And how you got poor, weak Eddie Bower in to help you. You tell further how you aimed to use this Eddie as a tool to blow the Thunderbird safe."

This Bottlenose, through them puffed lips of hissen, he begins to splutter how he won't confess to nothing.

"Oh, yes, you will," says Hoh-hoh, and he doubles that pile-driver fist of hissen and he goes to menacing at Bottlenose with it. "You tell," says Hoh-hoh, "or I aim to knock you loose from your keel."

Hoh-hoh he puts that ship-clamp grip of hissen onto the back of this sculpin's neck, and he kind of weighed his own big fist, and balanced it, like he was selecting out a place to land it forceful.

This Bottlenose begins to blubber, and he owned up he done the pirate job with Eddie, and did kind of have a notion, seeing times was hard, to blow the Thunderbird safe.

Hoh-hoh he then drug Bottlenose up onto the platform, and he makes him set down, and then Hoh-hoh and Sister Benner sings "Abide With Me," and Hoh-hoh he dismisses the congregation, saying how he's got hopes the regular pastor, the Reverend John Benner, will be with them soon again.

The congregation files out, and Hoh-hoh similar, clinging ardent to the arm of this Bottlenose.

We never did ketch Eddie Bower. Seems like his sister, after telling about the pirate job, she kind weakened, and she tells Eddie, and he took it on the *klatawa*, and we hain't none of us seen him since.

Bottlenose, we give him plenty.


# If the Body Fits—

*by Larry Holden*


"For three days now . . ." Joe was saying thoughtfully. "He ain't showed for three days on that old wagon of his, and it got me to thinking. He's dead."

"And it hasn't been reported?" I asked. Joe was chief of police, and he'd know.

He shook his head. "No. That's what got me to thinking. Between you and me, there's more funny business going on out at that farm than we know about, them two hating one another's gizzards the way they do. Let's get Doc and take a run out."

I stammered. "You—you think he was murdered, Joe? Is that what you think?"

He shrugged. "What's *your* guess?"

Old Jake Stence was a miser.

He wasn't merely economical, thrifty, parsimonious or even just stingy. He was a fanatical, money-crazed miser.

Let me give you an example of the kind of thing he did. Eighteen years ago, just after young Johnny was born, his wife dropped dead with the baby in her arms. She rolled down the stairs from the second floor, and the baby wasn't expected to live. Jake hitched the horse to his wagon and disappeared for twelve hours. When he came back, he had two battered, paintless coffins in the back of the wagon—a large one for his wife and a little, four-foot one for the baby. How or where he had gotten them was anybody's guess, but from the looks of those old relics, you knew darned well he had gotten them for a song.

But there was a joke in it—if you can imagine a joke in a pair of coffins. The baby didn't die, and Jake was stuck with that second four-foot coffin on his hands. He went out one morning with it in the back of the wagon again, but when he returned that evening his face was as dark as midnight in a wolf's throat—and the coffin was still in the wagon.

From that day on he hated young Johnny. There are charitable folks around who said he hated the baby because he blamed his wife's death on it. Me, I know better. He hated the baby because it didn't die and use that coffin. Jake never forgot a wasted penny, and he never forgave it, either.

The kid got through as much school as he had to, and every extra minute he spent working on old Jake's poultry farm. And not learning the poultry business, as you might think. No. Learning the business of being a miser. Jake drilled it into him from morning till night, sixteen hours a day, until in the end Johnny was just as miserly as old Jake himself.

And don't think for a minute that Jake ever let the kid forget that useless little four-foot coffin. He kept it in the parlor so he could brood over it, so he could beat his breast every time he looked at it— so it would be a continual reproach to the kid for being alive.

You don't have to be a psychiatrist to know that that's no life for a kid. Young Johnny was saving string and making one nail do the work of four when most kids are still playing with dolls, and at the age when he should have been teasing the young girls and offering them sodas in exchange for a furtive kiss later, he was working sixteen and sometimes twenty hours a day, piling penny on top of penny, and nickel on top of nickel, watching them turn into precious dollars. As I said, it was no life for a kid. It was no life for anybody.

They were a familiar sight around town, young Johnny and old Jake, perched side by side on the hard seat of that old wagon. Every day they came through to sell their eggs from door to door because they could squeeze out a few extra pennies that way. And they were as alike as brothers, both six feet tall, as skinny and bony as a piece of scaffolding, dressed in rag-ends and tatters, their hair home-cropped to the skull to save barber bills. The horse was spraddle-legged and tottering, and the wagon moaned as if haunted by all the weary years it had spent past its prime.

In the evening they returned, sagging with fatigue, the wagon empty, old Jake driving and young Johnny sitting beside him, carefully counting a handful of loose change and dropping it piece by piece into a small leather sack under the old man's steely eye.

They lived on the refuse of the garden they kept, eating the chickens that died of old age, or any other way except chopping their heads off. I sometimes wondered if Jake made the kid eat dinner on the lid of the coffin just to remind him what a dirty trick he had played by insisting on staying alive; and sometimes I was darned near to being convinced that if the kid had had his choice, that little four-foot coffin would have been under the turf of the cemetery these eighteen years.

Those were idle thoughts, though, and I had no proof. So I kept my mouth shut.

But Joe had a fact that day when he came through my front gate, fanning himself with his hat. Joe was chief of police. He and I hunted duck and deer in season, and whenever he had a job in which he had to depend on a steady hand with a gun, he usually called on me to go along.

"Harry," he said, "have you noticed anything funny about old Stence's wagon these past few days?"

I laughed. "Don't tell me he's gone and got a new one."

"Not much chance of that. But I been watching it for three–four days and he ain't been on it."

"Maybe he's sick."

"Jake's never too sick to ride that wagon, never too sick to let young Johnny make the collections without his being there to keep one eye on the accounting."

We looked at each other.

"For three days now . . ." he said thoughtfully. "He ain't showed for three days on that old wagon of his, and it got me to thinking. He's dead."

A half-hour later the three of us—Joe, the Doc and I—were riding in silence out toward the Stence farm on the Pike. We stopped at the rickety fence, and Joe got out of the car soft and easy, went up the path, not making a sound. There was a feeble, flickering light in the kitchen, and when we peered through the window we saw young Johnny sitting there, listlessly turning over the pages of an old magazine someone had given him. On the table, stuck in its own grease, stood about an inch of candle. It threw an eerie light, fitful and shallow, and it filled young Johnny's gaunt face with darkness. He looked as if the bones of his skull were impatiently thrusting against his skin.

But there was no sign of old Jake. It was too early for bed, and old Jake would certainly not have been in another part of the house when one candle would have done for two.

Joe opened the door without knocking and walked in.

He said casually, "Hello, Johnny."

Johnny looked up. "Hello, Joe." His voice was creaky and rusty, as if he were just as miserly about using it as he was about everything else.

Joe went on, "I notice Jake ain't been to town these past few days, and I dropped in to see if anything was the matter."

Keeping his finger in the magazine to mark his place, young Johnny said emotionlessly. "He drapped daid three–four days ago. Bury him t'morra—if I can spare time from the egg route."

Six feet tall, harsh-boned and scrawny, the image of the old man, you'd never have taken him for eighteen. He looked a hard-used forty. And his words, as calmly as they were spoken, were callous enough to have curdled lead. But what else could you expect, when everything had been squeezed out of him except the bleak desire for money?

"Mind if I take a look at him?" Joe's voice hardened.

Johnny shrugged. "Go right ahead," he said disinterestedly. "He's in there." He tossed his thumb limply toward the parlor.

Joe gave him a sharp glance and he and Doc went into the other room, while I stayed in the kitchen to keep an eye on young Johnny. I had a gun stuck in my waistband, under my coat.

From the tail of my eye, I saw the beam of Joe's flashlight flick around the parlor; then I heard both of them gasp. I sharpened my ears. Johnny hunched over his magazine.

Having difficulty with his tongue, Doc mumbled something about a stroke. Joe stumbled through the doorway with a small hatchet in his hand, his face the color of spoiled veal.

He said hoarsely, "You chopped him off at the knees!"

Johnny didn't even look up from his magazine. "What of it? He

258

was dead, wasn't he?" Then, with sudden, blazing hatred. "That was the only way I could get him in that little coffin. Now he should feel better, damn him! Now that he knows that little coffin didn't go to waste after all!"

# Ignorance of Art

*by Vincent Hall*

They speak enviously of Pop Townsend in the art circles; an artist who won recognition painting the portrait of a murderer from a photograph in the Rogues' Gallery. "For copying old masters in the Museum, he hardly made enough to pay his rent," they say. "But for a killer's picture, they gave him five thousand dollars."

Paradoxically, it was ignorance of art that started Pop on to success; ignorance of a trio of killers not up to the elementals. Pop's masterpiece hangs in the Art Museum. And three killers were hanged for murder.

It all started when Mr. Swinburne of the Ninth National Bank criticized Pop Townsend's paintings of six veteran employees standing outside the bank entrance.

"You've caught the speaking likeness of each man," Swinburne graciously admitted. "But our depositors will never recognize their building unless you paint in our sign, NINTH NATIONAL BANK."

Pop stroked his trim Van Dyke, took a long pull at his pipe. "And would it be more of a building if I painted unimportant details?"

"To us, details are important," Mr. Swinburne replied. "I suggest that you go up to the elevated station platform outside and copy our sign from there."

Pop did as he was told. Early that morning before the rush hour crowds would jam the station, he set up his easel and canvas; and scowled at the faded, carved letters on the Ninth National Bank's two-story building. "Always I get kicks about details," he muttered. "It isn't a building unless I put a label on it."

His attention was suddenly attracted to the man standing on the bank's roof opposite the elevated station platform. Pop studied the profile of the man, who was dressed in a natty tweed suit and gray felt hat. There was no exit to the roof. Pop guessed that the stranger must have stepped from the tenement roof adjoining.

"A regular cutthroat," he mused. "Might make a good sketch to show at the Academy exhibition." He reached for his sketchbook.

"Hold it!" the man called. "And act natural."

Shifty black eyes murderously regarded the old man; the .38 caliber pistol threatened instant death. It never wavered from Pop.

Pop's heart pounded, and his spine chilled. Chancing a glance downward, he observed what was taking place on the street below. A gray limousine had swept to the curb. Two men, one carrying a black bag, emerged and started for the bank entrance.

Quick staccato barks of guns suddenly broke the early morning stillness. The man with the black bag toppled to the sidewalk; his companion sagged to his knees.

Pop shouted. The man on the roof instantly fired. Pop crashed to the floor, easel and canvas draping his still figure. For a moment he lay there rigid, amazed that his heart was beating; that his temples throbbed. The distance from the bank's roof to the elevated station was a scant twenty paces. How could the killer miss?

The station agent dashed out of his cubby-hole, leaned over the old man.

"Are you hurt?"

Pop staggered to his feet. "I saw them. Telephone the police."

"Easy," the man said. "They're on the way." He pulled at Pop's vest. "Why, your clothes are soaking blood."

"Never mind me," Pop answered. "I must phone the police a description of the man I saw on the roof."

"Here they are now," the station agent said. "A regiment of cops."

Detective Sergeant Mike Glennon took one look at Pop, and snapped an order to a patrolman. "Get hold of that ambulance doctor before he goes back to the hospital."

He jotted down Pop's detailed description of the killer, tore a sheet of flimsy from the pad and handed it to a detective. "Broadcast that."

The doctor probed the old man's chest. "Nothing but a flesh wound. Two men below killed instantly."

"They were making an early morning deposit of fifty grand. The killers got it," Glennon said.

The pungent liquid the doctor put on Pop's wound hurt, but he bore it stoically. He was lucky to be alive. He straightened the frames around his eyeglasses, put them on and took out his sketchbook. There was a charred hole squarely in the middle of the cardboard
260

cover and right through the pages to the cardboard on the other side. Pop smiled wanly. "For once this sketchbook was worth something."

They took Pop to the Rogues' Gallery at Police Headquarters. He studied predatory faces, sullen faces; hard expressions that frighten children into hysterics. For well over two hours Pop studied one photograph after another. Suddenly he singled out a full face and a profile alongside.

"There's your man," he declared.

"Trigger Madden!"

Glennon dashed out, followed by his men. Three detectives remained to guard the old man. O'Brien read from the late morning newspaper. "We've got you down as a dead man unidentified," he said. "That's to make the killers think they're in the clear."

At noon, Glennon came back. "Madden surrendered on his own hook," he announced. "He has an alibi supported by five responsible persons who swear Madden was with them in a bungalow sixty miles out of the city at the time of the double murder."

"Liars!" Pop exclaimed.

Glennon looked dubious. "We didn't find the bullet that went through your sketchbook. And with five alibi witnesses against us, we'll have a tough time making your identification stick."

Pop shrugged. "They're still liars," he insisted.

"I see you wear eyeglasses," Glennon observed. "Can you see good with them on?"

"Of course."

Glennon stepped out of earshot, exchanged worried glances with his men. "A smart shyster will challenge the old man's vision," he said. "He'll make cracks about the glare of sunlight, harangue the jury about reasonable doubt—" He stopped as Pop came over.

"Take me to a room that has strong sunlight from the north," Pop suggested.

"What for?" Glennon wanted to know.

"I'm going to paint what I saw this morning."

"Go ahead, Sarge, humor him," Detective O'Brien said.

They took him to the top floor, let him in a small room. Pop set his canvas on the easel, tacked Madden's photograph alongside. He smiled as he soaked a brush into turpentine and erased the six figures of the bank employees he had painted for Swinburne, the president. "I wonder what my associates would say if they caught me painting in a rogues' gallery."

The detectives tapped their heads significantly and went out. "We'll kid him along and then spring him," Glennon said.

Pop put all his life and energy into his composition. The thought that Madden might be freed because of false alibi witnesses made him angry and spurred him on. "Maybe those liars will sing a different tune when they get a look at this painting," he told himself.

Late that afternoon, Glennon poked his head into the room. "We've decided that you can go home, Mr. Townsend," he said.

"Look at my painting," Pop invited.

Glennon gasped. "The very spit of Madden."

"Any criticism?"

Something about the painting jarred on Glennon. "You told us Madden was dressed in a tweed suit when you saw him on that roof. Why do you paint him in a blue suit?" Glennon objected.

Pop looked sour. "It never fails. Always somebody points out unimportant details when they're asked to criticize a painting."

Glennon frowned. "If you were painting my picture would you do me in a tweed suit if I had a blue one on?"

"You recognized Madden's likeness, didn't you?" Pop came back.

"Sure, but you're cockeyed on the details."

Pop put down his palette and brushes. Patiently he explained the meaning of a likeness; of light and shade; perspective and background.

"A professional critic overlooks absence of details that have nothing to do with the likeness of a portrait. Whether you're painted in a green suit, or a black, it is still the man, if the artist has caught the likeness."

"Sounds reasonable," Glennon admitted.

"Of course it's reasonable. Take this man, Swinburne, for example. He admitted I had made a likeness of those bank employees. But what does he see? He sees that I didn't paint in his damn sign . . . wants me to put in a label so you'll know it's a bank and not a jail."

Glennon ran his fingers through his hair. "Anybody who knows Madden will say your painting is the spit of him. But painting him in a blue suit when he had a tweed on is going to give us static."

Pop smiled. "Let's confront Madden," he said.

Headquarters men escorted Pop into a large room in the basement. There was a stage in the front. Glaring lights were played on the man seated in the chair. It was Madden.

Glennon walked up the steps to a raised platform that looked like a preacher's pulpit.

"Madden," he began, "you said you were with your alibi witnesses in that bungalow at the time of the double murder?"

"I told you that before."

"And you still stick to it?"

"Sure."

Detective O'Brien caught his cue. He took Pop's arm, escorted him to the stage. A bright light was shifted on the old man's face.

Madden's olive skin became a greenish hue; his breath caught in a sob.

Glennon said, "Bring up that Exhibit B."

O'Brien handed up a forty-two-by-twenty-inch canvas. Pop set it against the wall.

Madden sucked his breath.

The Ninth National's building was in the background. The painting showed two figures getting out of a gray limousine at the curb, two men with flaming pistols shooting them down. On the bank's roof, painted in a fourteen-inch length, was the figure of Madden in a nice blue suit. His .38 caliber pistol was aimed in the direction of the elevated station platform.

"It's a dirty frame!" Madden shrieked.

"Isn't that a likeness of you standing on the roof?"

Madden regarded the painting sullenly.

"Go on, please criticize it, Mr. Madden," Pop suggested affably. "See anything wrong?"

"Yeah. I wasn't wearing no blue suit; it was a tweed—"

Madden gasped, overwhelmed by the slip of his tongue that convicted him. He cracked under the grilling that followed. He named the two who had committed the murders; he confessed where the money was cached.

Pop never gets tired repeating the story. "I couldn't have painted that picture in the three minutes it took those men to rob their victims and kill them—

"And always my customers kick about details. They force me to paint their lapels plainly; put buttons on their coats. I had a hunch Madden would criticize me for painting him in a blue suit instead of the tweed he wore that morning."

# Incident in a Neighborhood Tavern

*Bill Pronzini*

When the holdup went down I was sitting at the near end of the Foghorn Tavern's scarred mahogany bar, talking to the owner, Matt Candiotti.

It was a little before seven of a mid-week evening, lull time in working-class neighborhood saloons like this one. Blue-collar locals would jam the place from four until about six-thirty, when the last of them headed home for dinner; the hard-core drinkers wouldn't begin filtering back in until about seven-thirty or eight. Right now I was the only customer.

But the draft beer in front of me wasn't the reason I was there. I'd come to ask Candiotti, as I had asked two dozen other merchants here in the Outer Mission, if he could offer any leads on the rash of burglaries that were plaguing small businesses in the neighborhood. The police hadn't come up with anything positive after six weeks, so a couple of the victims had gotten up a fund and hired me to see what I could find out. They'd picked me because I had been born and raised in the Outer Mission, which to them meant I understood the neighborhood better than any other private detective in San Francisco.

So far, though, I wasn't having any more luck than the SFPD. None of the merchants I'd spoken with today had given me any new ideas, and Candiotti was proving no exception. He stood slicing limes into wedges as we talked; they might have been onions the way his long, mournful face was screwed up, like a man trying to hold back tears. He reminded me of a tired old hound.

"Wish I could help," he said. "But hell, I don't hear nothing. Must be pros from Hunters Point or the Fillmore, hah?"

Hunters Point and the Fillmore were black sections of the city, which was a pretty good indicator of where his head was at. I said, "Some of the others figure it for local talent."

"Out of this neighborhood, you mean?"

I nodded, drank some of my draft.

264

"Nah, I doubt it," he said. "Guys that organized, they don't crap where they eat. Too smart, you know?"

"Maybe. Any break-ins or attempted break-ins here?"

"Not so far. I got bars on all the windows, double locks on the storeroom door off the alley. Besides, what's for them to steal except a few cases of whisky?"

"You don't keep cash on the premises overnight?"

"Fifty bucks in the till, that's all." He scraped the lime wedges off his board, into a plastic container. "One thing I did hear," he said. "I heard some of the loot turned up down in San José. You know about that?"

"Not much of a lead there. Secondhand dealer named Pitman had a few pieces of stereo equipment stolen from the factory-outlet store on Geneva. Said he bought it from a guy at the San José flea market, somebody he didn't know, never saw before."

"Yeah, sure," Candiotti said wryly. "What do the cops think?"

"That Pitman bought it off a fence."

"Makes sense. So maybe the boosters are from San José, hah?"

"Could be," I said, and that was when the kid walked in.

He brought bad air in with him; I sensed it right away and so did Candiotti. We both glanced at the door when it opened, the way you do, but we didn't look away again once we saw him. He was in his early twenties, dark-skinned, dressed in chinos and a cotton windbreaker. But it was his eyes that put the chill on my neck, the sudden clutch of tension down low in my belly. They were bright, jumpy, on the wild side. He had one hand in his jacket pocket and I knew it was clamped around a gun even before he took it out and showed it to us.

He came up to the bar a few feet on my left, the gun jabbing the air in front of him. He couldn't hold it steady; it kept jerking up and down, from side to side, as if it had a kind of spasmodic life of its own. I eased back a little on the stool, watching the gun and the kid's eyes flick between Candiotti and me. Candiotti didn't move at all, just stood staring with his hound's face screwed up tight.

"All right all right," the kid said. His voice was high-pitched, excited. You couldn't get much more stoned than he was and still function. Coke, crack, speed—maybe a combination of drugs. The gun that kept flicking this way and that was a goddamn Saturday Night Special. "Listen good, man, I don't want to kill anybody but I will if I got to, you believe it?"

Neither of us said anything. Neither of us moved.

The kid had a folded-up paper sack in one pocket; he dragged it out with his free hand, dropped it, broke quickly at the middle to pick

265

it up without lowering his gaze. When he straightened again there was sweat on his face. He threw the sack on the bar.

"Put the money in there, Mister Cyclone Man," he said to Candiotti. "All the money in the register, no coins, you hear me, man?"

Candiotti nodded; reached out slowly for the sack and then turned toward the backbar with his shoulders hunched up against his neck. When he punched No Sale on the register, the ringing thump of the cash drawer sliding open seemed overloud in the electric hush. For a few seconds the kid watched him scoop bills into the sack; then his eyes and the gun skittered my way again. I had looked into the muzzle of a handgun before and it was the same feeling each time: dull fear, helplessness, a kind of naked vulnerability.

"Your wallet on the bar, man, all your cash."

I did as I was told. But while I was getting my wallet out I managed to slide my right foot off the stool, onto the brass rail, and to get my right hand pressed tight against the edge of the bar. If I had to make any sudden moves I would need the leverage.

Candiotti finished loading the sack. There was a grayish cast to his face now—the wet gray color of fear. The kid said to him, "Pick up this dude's money, put it in the sack with the rest. Come on come on *come on!*"

Candiotti added my wallet to the contents of the paper sack, put the sack down carefully in front of the kid.

"Okay," the kid said, "okay, all right." He glanced over his shoulder at the street door, as if he'd heard something there; but it stayed closed. In his sweaty agitation the Saturday Night Special almost slipped free of his fingers. I watched him fumble a tighter grip on it, reach out and drag the sack in against his body. But he made no move to leave with it. Instead he said, "Now we go get the big pile, man."

Candiotti opened his mouth, closed it again. His eyes were almost as big and starey as the kid's.

"Come on Mister Cyclone Man, the safe, the safe in your office."

"No money in that safe," Candiotti said in a thin, scratchy voice. "Nothing valuable."

"Oh man I ain't playin' no games here, I want that money!"

He took two steps forward, jabbing with the gun up close to Candiotti's gray face. Candiotti backed off a step, took a tremulous breath. "All right," he said, "but I got to get the key to the office. It's in the register."

"Hurry up!"

Candiotti turned back to the register, rang it open, rummaged inside with his left hand. But with his right hand, shielded from the kid

266

by his body, he eased up the top of a large wood cigar box nearby. The hand disappeared inside; came out again with metal in it, glinting in the backbar lights. I saw it, and I wanted to yell at him, but it wouldn't have done any good, would only have warned the kid—and Candiotti was already turning with it, bringing up that damn gun of his own in both hands. There was no time for me to do anything but shove away from the bar and sideways off the stool just as Candiotti opened fire.

The state he was in, the kid didn't realize what was happening until it was too late; he never even got a shot off. Candiotti's first slug knocked him halfway around, and one of the three others that followed took him in the face. He was dead before his body, driven backward, slammed into the cigarette machine near the door, slid down it to the floor.

When I came up out of my crouch, Candiotti was standing with his arms down at his sides, the gun out of sight below the bar. Staring at the bloody remains of the kid as if he couldn't believe what he was seeing, couldn't believe what he'd done.

Some of the tension in me eased as I went to the door, found the lock on its security gate and fastened it before anybody could come in off the street. The Saturday Night Special was still clutched in the kid's hand; I bent, pulled it free, broke the cylinder. Five live cartridges. I dropped the gun into my jacket pocket, thought about checking the kid's clothing for ID, didn't do it. It wasn't any of my business, now, who he'd been. And I did not want to touch him. There was a queasiness in my stomach, a fluttery weakness behind my knees—the same delayed reaction I always had to violence and death.

Candiotti hadn't moved. I walked over to him, pushed hard words at him in an undertone. "That was a damn fool thing to do. You could have got us both killed."

"I know," he said. "I know."

"Why'd you do it?"

"I thought . . . hell, you saw the way he was waving that piece . . ."

"Yeah," I said. "Call the police. Nine-eleven."

"Nine-eleven. Okay."

"Put that gun of yours down first. On the bar."

He did that. There was a phone on the backbar; he went away to it. While he was talking to the emergency operator I picked up his weapon, saw that it was a .32 Charter Arms revolver. I put it down again when he finished the call.

"They'll have somebody here in five minutes," he said.

I said, "You know that kid?"

"Christ, no."

"Ever see him before, here or anywhere else?"

"No."

"So how did he know about your safe?"

Candiotti blinked at me. "What?"

"The safe in your office. How'd he know about it?"

"How should I know. What difference does it make?"

"He seemed to think you keep big money in that safe."

"Well I don't. There's nothing in it."

"That's right, you told me you don't keep more than fifty bucks in the till overnight."

"Yeah."

"Then why have you got a safe, if it's empty?"

Candiotti's eyes narrowed. "I used to keep my cash receipts in it, all right? Before all these burglaries started. Then I figured I'd be smarter to take the money to the bank every night."

"Sure, that explains it. Still, a kid like that, looking for a big score to feed his habit, he wasn't just after what was in the till. No, it was as if he'd gotten wind of a heavy stash—a grand or more."

Nothing from Candiotti.

"Big risk you took, using that .32 of yours," I said. "How come you didn't make your play the first time you went to the register? How come you waited until the kid mentioned your safe?"

"Listen, what're you getting at, hah?"

"Another funny thing," I said, "is the way he called you Mister Cyclone Man. Now why would a hopped-up kid use a term like that to a bar owner he didn't know?"

"How the hell should I know?"

"Cyclone," I said. "What's a cyclone but a big destructive wind? Only one other thing I can think of."

"Yeah? What's that?"

"A fence. A cyclone fence."

Candiotti made a fidgety movement. Some of the wet gray pallor was beginning to spread across his cheeks again, like a fungus.

I said, "And a fence is somebody who receives and distributes stolen goods. A Mister Fence Man. But then you know that, don't you, Candiotti? We were talking about that kind of fence before the kid came in—how Pitman, down in San José, bought some hot stereo equipment off one. But that fence could just as easily be operating here in San Francisco. Right here in this neighborhood, in fact. Hell, suppose the stuff taken in all those burglaries never left the neighbor-

268

hood. Suppose it was brought to a local place and stored until it could be trucked out to other cities—a tavern storeroom, for instance. Might even be some of it is *still* in that storeroom. And the money he got for the rest he'd keep locked up in his safe. Who'd figure it? Except maybe a poor junkie who picked up a whisper on the street somewhere—"

Candiotti made a sudden grab for the .32, backed up a step with it leveled at my chest. "You smart son of a bitch. I ought to kill you too."

"With the police due any second?"

"There's still enough time for me to get clear." He was talking to himself, not to me.

"I don't think so," I said.

"Goddamn you, you think I won't use this gun again?"

"I *know* you won't use it. I emptied out the last two cartridges while you were on the phone."

I held up the two shells I'd palmed, so he could see them. At the same time I got the kid's Saturday Night Special out of my jacket pocket and showed him that too. "You want to put your piece down now, Candiotti? You're not going anywhere, not for a long time."

He put it down—dropped it clattering onto the bar. And as he did, his sad hound's face screwed up again and wetness began to leak out of his eyes. He was leaning against the bar, crying like a woman, submerged in his own outpouring of self-pity, when the cops showed up a little while later.

# In the Library

*by W. W. Jacobs*

The fire had burnt low in the library, for the night was wet and warm. It was now little more than a grey shell, and looked desolate. Trayton Burleigh, still hot, rose from his armchair, and turning out one of the gas-jets, took a cigar from a box on a side-table and resumed his seat again.

The apartment, which was on the third floor at the back of the house, was a combination of library, study, and smoke-room, and was the daily despair of the old housekeeper who, with the assistance of one servant, managed the house. It was a bachelor establishment, and had been left to Trayton Burleigh and James Fletcher by a distant connection of both men some ten years before.

Trayton Burleigh sat back in his chair watching the smoke of his cigar through half-closed eyes. Occasionally he opened them a little wider and glanced round the comfortable, well-furnished room, or stared with a cold gleam of hatred at Fletcher as he sat sucking stolidly at his brier pipe. It was a comfortable room and a valuable house, half of which belonged to Trayton Burleigh; and yet he was to leave it in the morning and become a rogue and a wanderer over the face of the earth. James Fletcher had said so. James Fletcher, with the pipe still between his teeth and speaking from one corner of his mouth only, had pronounced his sentence.

"It hasn't occurred to you, I suppose," said Burleigh, speaking suddenly, "that I might refuse your terms."

"No," said Fletcher, simply.

Burleigh took a great mouthful of smoke and let it roll slowly out.

"I am to go out and leave you in possession?" he continued. "You will stay here sole proprietor of the house; you will stay at the office sole owner and representative of the firm? You are a good hand at a deal, James Fletcher."

"I am an honest man," said Fletcher, "and to raise sufficient money to make your defalcations good will not by any means leave me the gainer, as you very well know."

"There is no necessity to borrow," began Burleigh, eagerly. "We can pay the interest easily, and in course of time make the principal good without a soul being the wiser."

"That you suggested before," said Fletcher, "and my answer is the same. I will be no man's confederate in dishonesty; I will raise every penny at all costs, and save the name of the firm—and yours with it— but I will never have you darken the office again, or sit in this house after tonight."

"*You* won't," cried Burleigh, starting up in a frenzy of rage.

"*I* won't," said Fletcher. "You can choose the alternative: disgrace and penal servitude. Don't stand over me; you won't frighten me, I can assure you. Sit down."

"You have arranged so many things in your kindness," said Burleigh, slowly, resuming his seat again, "have you arranged how I am to live?"

"You have two strong hands, and health," replied Fletcher. "I will give you the two hundred pounds I mentioned, and after that you must look out for yourself. You can take it now."

He took a leather case from his breast pocket, and drew out a roll of notes. Burleigh, watching him calmly, stretched out his hand and took them from the table. Then he gave way to a sudden access of rage, and crumpling them in his hand, threw them into a corner of the room. Fletcher smoked on.

"Mrs. Marl is out?" said Burleigh, suddenly.

Fletcher nodded.

"She will be away the night," he said, slowly; "and Jane too; they have gone together somewhere, but they will be back at half-past eight in the morning."

"You are going to let me have one more breakfast in the old place, then," said Burleigh. "Half-past eight, half-past—"

He rose from his chair again. This time Fletcher took his pipe from his mouth and watched him closely. Burleigh stooped, and picking up the notes, placed them in his pocket.

"If I am to be turned adrift, it shall not be to leave you here," he said, in a thick voice.

He crossed over and shut the door; as he turned back Fletcher rose from his chair and stood confronting him. Burleigh put his hand to the wall, and drawing a small Japanese sword from its sheath of carved ivory, stepped slowly toward him.

"I give you one chance, Fletcher," he said, grimly. "You are a man of your word. Hush this up and let things be as they were before, and you are safe."

"Put that down," said Fletcher, sharply.

"By ——, I mean what I say!" cried the other.

"I mean what I said!" answered Fletcher.

He looked round at the last moment for a weapon, then he turned suddenly at a sharp sudden pain, and saw Burleigh's clenched fist nearly touching his breast-bone. The hand came away from his breast again, and something with it. It went a long way off. Trayton Burleigh suddenly went to a great distance and the room darkened. It got quite dark, and Fletcher, with an attempt to raise his hands, let them fall to his side instead, and fell in a heap to the floor.

He was so still that Burleigh could hardly realize that it was all over, and stood stupidly waiting for him to rise again. Then he took out his handkerchief as though to wipe the sword, and thinking better of it, put it back into his pocket again, and threw the weapon on to the floor.

The body of Fletcher lay where it had fallen, the white face turned up to the gas. In life he had been a commonplace-looking man, not to say vulgar; now—

Burleigh, with a feeling of nausea, drew back toward the door, until the body was hidden by the table, and relieved from the sight, he could think more clearly. He looked down carefully and examined his clothes and his boots. Then he crossed the room again, and with his face averted, turned out the gas. Something seemed to stir in the darkness, and with a faint cry he blundered toward the door before he had realized that it was the clock. It struck twelve.

He stood at the head of the stairs trying to recover himself; trying to think. The gas on the landing below, the stairs and the furniture, all looked so prosaic and familiar that he could not realize what had occurred. He walked slowly down and turned the light out. The darkness of the upper part of the house was now almost appalling, and in a sudden panic he ran down stairs into the lighted hall, and snatching a hat from the stand, went to the door and walked down to the gate.

Except for one window the neighbouring houses were in darkness, and the lamps shone up a silent street. There was a little rain in the air, and the muddy road was full of pebbles. He stood at the gate trying to screw up his courage to enter the house again. Then he noticed a figure coming slowly up the road and keeping close to the palings.

The full realization of what he had done broke in upon him when he found himself turning to fly from the approach of the constable. The wet cape glistening in the lamplight, the slow, heavy step, made him tremble. Suppose the thing upstairs was not quite dead and should cry out? Suppose the constable should think it strange for him to be standing there and follow him in? He assumed a careless attitude, which did not feel careless, and as the man passed bade him good-night, and made a remark as to the weather.

Ere the sound of the other's footsteps had gone quite out of hearing, he turned and entered the house again before the sense of companionship should have quite departed. The first flight of stairs was lighted by the gas in the hall, and he went up slowly. Then he struck a match and went up steadily, past the library door, and with firm fingers turned on the gas in his bedroom and lit it. He opened the window a little way, and sitting down on his bed, tried to think.

He had got eight hours. Eight hours and two hundred pounds in small notes. He opened his safe and took out all the loose cash it contained, and walking about the room, gathered up and placed in his pockets such articles of jewelry as he possessed.

The first horror had now to some extent passed, and was succeeded by the fear of death. With this fear on him he sat down again and tried to think out the first moves in that game of skill of which his life was the stake. He had often read of —— people of hasty temper,

272

evading the police for a time, and eventually falling into their hands for lack of the most elementary common sense. He had heard it said that they always made some stupid blunder, left behind them some damning clue. He took his revolver from a drawer and saw that it was loaded. If the worst came to the worst, he would die quickly.

Eight hours' start; two hundred odd pounds. He would take lodgings at first in some populous district, and let the hair on his face grow. When the hue-and-cry had ceased, he would go abroad and start life again. He would go out of a night and post letters to himself, or better still, postcards, which his landlady would read. Postcards from cheery friends, from a sister, from a brother. During the day he would stay in and write, as became a man who described himself as a journalist.

Or suppose he went to the sea? Who would look for him in flannels, bathing and boating with ordinary happy mortals? He sat and pondered. One might mean life, and the other death. Which?

His face burned as he thought of the responsibility of the choice. So many people went to the sea at that time of year that he would surely pass unnoticed. But at the sea one might meet acquaintances. He got up and nervously paced the room again. It was not so simple, now that it meant so much, as he had thought.

The sharp little clock on the mantel-piece rang out "one," followed immediately by the deeper note of that in the library. He thought of the clock, it seemed the only live thing in that room, and shuddered. He wondered whether the thing lying by the far side of the table heard it. He wondered—

He started and held his breath with fear. Somewhere down stairs a board creaked loudly, then another. He went to the door, and opening it a little way, but without looking out, listened. The house was so still that he could hear the ticking of the old clock in the kitchen below. He opened the door a little wider and peeped out. As he did so there was a sudden sharp outcry on the stairs, and he drew back into the room and stood trembling before he had quite realized that the noise had been made by the cat. The cry was unmistakable; but what had disturbed it?

There was silence again, and he drew near the door once more. He became certain that something was moving stealthily on the stairs. He heard the boards creak again, and once the rails of the balustrade rattled. The silence and suspense were frightful. Suppose that the something which had been Fletcher waited for him in the darkness outside?

He fought his fears down, and opening the door, determined to see what was beyond. The light from his room streamed out on to the landing, and he peered about fearfully. Was it fancy, or did the door of Fletcher's room opposite close as he looked? Was it fancy, or did the handle of the door really turn?

In perfect silence, and watching the door as he moved, to see that nothing came out and followed him, he proceeded slowly down the dark stairs. Then his jaw fell, and he turned sick and faint again. The library door, which he distinctly remembered closing, and which, moreover, he had seen was closed when he went up stairs to his room, now stood open some four or five inches. He fancied that there was a rustling inside, but his brain refused to be certain. Then plainly and unmistakably he heard a chair pushed against the wall.

He crept to the door, hoping to pass it before the thing inside became aware of his presence. Something crept stealthily about the room. With a sudden impulse he caught the handle of the door, and, closing it violently, turned the key in the lock, and ran madly down the stairs.

A fearful cry sounded from the room, and a heavy hand beat upon the panels of the door. The house rang with the blows, but above them sounded the loud hoarse cries of human fear. Burleigh, half-way down to the hall, stopped with his hand on the balustrade and listened. The beating ceased, and a man's voice cried out loudly for God's sake to let him out.

At once Burleigh saw what had happened and what it might mean for him. He had left the hall door open after his visit to the front, and some wandering bird of the night had entered the house. No need for him to go now. No need to hide either from the hangman's rope or the felon's cell. The fool above had saved him. He turned and ran up stairs again just as the prisoner in his furious efforts to escape wrenched the handle from the door.

"Who's there?" he cried, loudly.

"Let me out!" cried a frantic voice. "For God's sake, open the door! There's something here."

"Stay where you are!" shouted Burleigh, sternly. "Stay where you are! If you come out, I'll shoot you like a dog!"

The only response was a smashing blow on the lock of the door. Burleigh raised his pistol, and aiming at the height of a man's chest, fired through the panel.

The report and the crashing of the wood made one noise, succeeded by an unearthly stillness, then the noise of a window hastily opened. Burleigh fled hastily down the stairs, and flinging wide the hall door, shouted loudly for assistance.

274

It happened that a sergeant and the constable on the beat had just met in the road. They came toward the house at a run. Burleigh, with incoherent explanations, ran up stairs before them, and halted outside the library door. The prisoner was still inside, still trying to demolish the lock of the sturdy oaken door. Burleigh tried to turn the key, but the lock was too damaged to admit of its moving. The sergeant drew back, and, shoulder foremost, hurled himself at the door and burst it open.

He stumbled into the room, followed by the constable, and two shafts of light from the lanterns at their belts danced round the room. A man lurking behind the door made a dash for it, and the next instant the three men were locked together.

Burleigh, standing in the doorway, looked on coldly, reserving himself for the scene which was to follow. Except for the stumbling of the men and the sharp catch of the prisoner's breath, there was no noise. A helmet fell off and bounced and rolled along the floor. The men fell; there was a sobbing snarl and a sharp click. A tall figure rose from the floor; the other, on his knees, still held the man down. The standing figure felt in his pocket, and, striking a match, lit the gas.

The light fell on the flushed face and fair beard of the sergeant. He was bare-headed, and his hair dishevelled. Burleigh entered the room and gazed eagerly at the half-insensible man on the floor—a short, thick-set fellow with a white, dirty face and a black moustache. His lip was cut and bled down his neck. Burleigh glanced furtively at the table. The cloth had come off in the struggle, and was now in the place where he had left Fletcher.

"Hot work, sir," said the sergeant, with a smile. "It's fortunate we were handy."

The prisoner raised a heavy head and looked up with unmistakable terror in his eyes.

"All right, sir," he said, trembling, as the constable increased the pressure of his knee. "I 'ain't been in the house ten minutes altogether. By ——, I've not."

The sergeant regarded him curiously.

"It don't signify," he said, slowly; "ten minutes or ten seconds won't make any difference."

The man shook and began to whimper.

"It was 'ere when I come," he said, eagerly; "take that down, sir. I've only just come, and it was 'ere when I come. I tried to get away then, but I was locked in."

"What was?" demanded the sergeant.

"*That*," he said, desperately.

The sergeant, following the direction of the terror-stricken black eyes, stooped by the table. Then, with a sharp exclamation, he dragged away the cloth. Burleigh, with a sharp cry of horror, reeled back against the wall.

"All right, sir," said the sergeant, catching him; "all right. Turn your head away."

He pushed him into a chair, and crossing the room, poured out a glass of whiskey and brought it to him. The glass rattled against his teeth, but he drank it greedily, and then groaned faintly. The sergeant waited patiently. There was no hurry.

"Who is it, sir?" he asked at length.

"My friend—Fletcher," said Burleigh, with an effort. "We lived together." He turned to the prisoner.

"You damned villain!"

"He was dead when I come in the room, gentlemen," said the prisoner, strenuously. "He was on the floor dead, and when I see 'im, I tried to get out. S' 'elp me he was. You heard me call out, sir. I shouldn't ha' called out if I'd killed him."

"All right," said the sergeant, gruffly; "you'd better hold your tongue, you know."

"You keep quiet," urged the constable.

The sergeant knelt down and raised the dead man's head.

"I 'ad nothing to do with it," repeated the man on the floor. "I 'ad nothing to do with it. I never thought of such a thing. I've only been in the place ten minutes; put that down, sir."

The sergeant groped with his left hand, and picking up the Japanese sword, held it at him.

"I've never seen it before," said the prisoner, struggling.

"It used to hang on the wall," said Burleigh. "He must have snatched it down. It was on the wall when I left Fletcher a little while ago."

"How long?" inquired the sergeant.

"Perhaps an hour, perhaps half an hour," was the reply. "I went to my bedroom."

The man on the floor twisted his head and regarded him narrowly.

"You done it!" he cried, fiercely. "You done it, and you want me to swing for it."

"That'll do," said the indignant constable.

The sergeant let his burden gently to the floor again.

"You hold your tongue, you devil!" he said, menacingly.

He crossed to the table and poured a little spirit into a glass and took it in his hand. Then he put it down again and crossed to Burleigh.

"Feeling better, sir?" he asked.

The other nodded faintly.

"You won't want this thing any more," said the sergeant.

He pointed to the pistol which the other still held, and taking it from him gently, put it into his pocket.

"You've hurt your wrist, sir," he said, anxiously.

Burleigh raised one hand sharply, and then the other.

"This one, I think," said the sergeant. "I saw it just now."

He took the other's wrists in his hand, and suddenly holding them in the grip of a vice, whipped out something from his pocket—something hard and cold, which snapped suddenly on Burleigh's wrists, and held them fast.

"That's right," said the sergeant; "keep quiet."

The constable turned round in amazement; Burleigh sprang toward him furiously.

"Take these things off!" he choked. "Have you gone mad? Take them off!"

"All in good time," said the sergeant.

"Take them off!" cried Burleigh again.

For answer the sergeant took him in a powerful grip, and staring steadily at his white face and gleaming eyes, forced him to the other end of the room and pushed him into a chair.

"Collins," he said, sharply.

"Sir?" said the astonished subordinate.

"Run to the doctor at the corner hard as you can run!" said the other. *This man is not dead!*"

As the man left the room the sergeant took up the glass of spirits he had poured out, and kneeling down by Fletcher again, raised his head and tried to pour a little down his throat Burleigh, sitting in his corner, watched like one in a trance. He saw the constable return with the breathless surgeon, saw the three men bending over Fletcher, and then saw the eyes of the dying man open and the lips of the dying man move. He was conscious that the sergeant made some notes in a pocket-book, and that all three men eyed him closely. The sergeant stepped toward him and placed his hand on his shoulder, and obedient to the touch, he arose and went with him out into the night.

# Ink's Jinx

*by Anthony Clemens*

After considering every angle of it, Kemmerer finally decided upon strangling as the best means of doing away with his employer, Jake Banff. In the first place, it would be a noiseless affair; in the second place, Kemmerer was a husky sort of fellow and kept himself in trim despite his clerical job by doing setting-up exercises every morning, while Banff was only a half-pint man and would strangle easy.

So Kemmerer got up as usual at six-thirty on Monday morning and turned on the radio in his room. The Freling family, with whom he lodged in the squalid tenement on the lower east side, was used to that, and never disturbed him. The station that broadcast the setting up exercises wasn't on the air yet; it would come on at six forty-five.

He had not removed his clothes on going to bed, and now stepped fully dressed through the window onto the fire escape. He was on the top floor and it was a short climb to the roof. He crossed two roof tops, opened a skylight, walked down four flights of stairs, and was in the street. Not a soul was about.

As he hurried along, he cast a glance at the row of old-law flats and made a wry face. What a sleazy place to live in—unwashed stoops, dirty "to let" signs, bedding being aired from dozens of windows. Well, he'd soon have money enough to get away from all this.

The Banff Metal Works occupied a two-story building two blocks away. Jake Banff always got there at six-thirty sharp, went over the memos that Kemmerer had left for him the night before, and departed in his truck to make the rounds in Long Island, Connecticut or Jersey, as the case might be, buying old metal. He had built up a nice business in thirty years, and being sixty-four now, and alone in the world, had made a will leaving the business to Kemmerer and two other employees.

The only thing that made Kemmerer glum on this vital morning was the fact that the other two employees wouldn't even know enough to thank him when they inherited their share of the business.

He put on a pair of gloves, entered the old building, and walked up

278

the flight of squeaking wooden stairs to the second floor where the office was located.

Jake Banff had heard the steps and was looking up from the desk at which he'd been working. When he saw Kemmerer, he put down his fountain pen and said, "Hello, there. What brings you around so early? You getting ambitious, maybe?" This with a friendly grin, for he always treated his employees as equals.

Kemmerer didn't allow himself to hesitate. He had planned too well, and time was important. He first went over to a radio in the corner and tuned it into the same station as the one in his room. He told Banff, "I couldn't sleep, Mr. Banff, so I came over. I got something to see you about."

Banff laughed. "Always nuts about radio. Why did you ever buy a radio for the office?"

Over the air came the voice of the announcer. "All right, get ready everybody. Setting-up—"

Kemmerer nodded. He had put the radio in the office just for this purpose—to make sure there was no accidental change in the program.

He crossed over to Banff.

The little old man must have seen something peculiar in his eyes, for he said, "Kem—what's the matter?"

Kemmerer's face was hard. "Nothing," he muttered, and bent, put his two hands around Banff's throat. . . .

Banff was weak, and old, and his resistance was negligible. But his body thrashed spasmodically; he tried to shout, but the sound resembled a croak more than anything else. In his eyes there was astounded unbelief. His arms flailed wildly, and his fingers caught in Kemmerer's vest pocket, and the red Parkinson pen the murderer carried was flipped out. It sailed in a short arc, and just as Banff gasped his life out, it struck the floor and shattered to pieces.

Kemmerer sat the limp, purple-faced body back in the chair and swore to himself. He stooped quickly to recover the pieces. Then panic assailed him. Suppose some of the pieces should be overlooked by him? Suppose they had fallen under the desk? A clever detective might find them.

He stood up, surveyed the room, started to tremble.

Then his eye lighted on the desk, and he grinned. Banff's pen was lying there, and it was exactly the same as his. The boss had bought them both at the same time.

Kemmerer picked up Banff's pen, capped it, wiped it off with his gloves, and put it in his pocket. There was one thing he'd have to remember, though—Banff always used green ink in his pen—an old habit. He'd have to change the ink; but not now, time was short. The voice of the instructor was coming over the radio, "One-two-three, one-two-three—" The exercises were drawing to a close.

He bent to the floor again. There was only one piece of the broken pen large enough to retain prints. He wiped it off carefully. The sack had burst, splattering black ink on the floor. He shrugged. That couldn't be remedied. They'd know it was some one else's pen. They'd surely check on the three employees. But he'd have the red pen—and he'd be sure to have *black* ink in it when he was questioned.

He turned off the radio, switched the dial away from the station, took a last look at the body of Banff, and stole downstairs.

Four minutes to get to his street. Two minutes to get to the roof of the house he had come through. So far so good. Three more minutes and he was across the roof tops, down the fire escape, and in his room.

His own radio was just saying, *"These exercises come to you through the—"*

He'd have to work fast now. Stoner, the cop on the beat over at the Banff Metal Works, always said hello to the old man as he left with the truck in the morning. When Stoner failed to see him today, he'd be sure to go up and investigate. He knew where Kemmerer and the other employees lived, and would surely give the addresses to the detectives, and Kemmerer knew he could expect a visit from the police in a very short time. He counted on that.

First he took out the fountain pen, opened it, and squirted the green ink it contained out of the window. Then he filled it from a bottle of black ink in his dresser.

He was careful to see that there were no stains anywhere, that the pen was dry on the outside and showed no signs of having been recently filled. He tried it on his memo book and nodded. It wrote good and black.

He replaced it in his pocket, then proceeded to strip off coat, vest, tie and shirt. He turned off the radio, picked up a towel, and unlocked his door.

Mrs. Freling was in the kitchen preparing breakfast. She called out a cheery "Good morning, Mr. Kemmerer. You have good exercises, no?"

He said, "Good morning, Mrs. Freling. I smell bacon. Turn my eggs over this morning, will you?" Then he went on into the bathroom and shaved. He was very cool. This didn't surprise him; he had planned long and well. The incident of the pen had been annoying, but he'd covered every angle of that.

He finished, taking his time. He slicked his hair back and left the bathroom.

A man was waiting for him in the kitchen. Mr. Freling was eating his breakfast undisturbed, but Mrs. Freling was fluttering about, excited.

"Mr. Kemmerer!" she exclaimed. "This man iss from the police. He wants—"

The detective motioned to her. "All right, lady, I'll talk for myself." He turned to Kemmerer. "You been here all morning?"

Kemmerer said angrily, "What do you mean—have I been here all morning? What's it to you? What you doing here anyhow?"

The detective held up a placating hand. "Don't get excited. I'm just checking up. Your boss, Jake Banff, was choked to death at a quarter to seven this morning!"

Kemmerer acted well. He had rehearsed. He clutched the detective's coat. "Good God, no!"

Mrs. Freling let out a little bleat. Mr. Freling, with a mouth full of egg, said, "Too bad. But Kemmerer had nothing to do with it. He was in his room doing setting-up exercises, like he does every day. We heard the radio."

The detective looked at Freling. "But you didn't hear him—did you?"

Kemmerer said, "Well, of all the—"

The detective stopped him. "Wait a minute—we can settle this quick, if you'll cooperate. If you had nothing to do with it, you'll show me what I want to see, and then I can go."

"What's that?" Kemmerer asked.

"Your fountain pen!" The detective rapped it out, watching him keenly.

"My fountain pen!" Kemmerer looked blank, then shrugged. "Okay. If you want to act crazy—"

He went to his room, the officer following. The officer stood in the doorway while he got out the pen, then snatched it from him, removed the cap, and wrote with it in his note book.

He looked up disappointed. It had written black. "I guess you're all right," he said. "If this was Banff's pen it'd be filled with green ink. You see, the guy who bumped Banff, took the old man's pen, as near as I can figure out, because his own got smashed in the—"

He was interrupted by a loud rapping at the outer door.

Mrs. Freling, who had come after them and had been watching with open mouth, went to answer it.

When she opened the door, an immense woman in a house dress came in, carrying a pillow. She said in a loud, angry voice, "I'm Mrs. Reilly, from the flat below. An' I wanna know what you people mean by throwing green ink down on my bedding what I was airing!" The pillow case had a large green stain, hardly dry yet, across the top.

# An Irreducible Detective Story

*by Stephen Leacock*

The mystery had now reached its climax. First, the man had been undoubtedly murdered. Second, it was absolutely certain that no conceivable person had done it.

It was therefore time to call in the great detective.

He gave one searching glance at the corpse. In a moment he whipped out a microscope.

"Ha! Ha!" he said, as he picked a hair off the lapel of the dead man's coat. "The mystery is now solved."

He held up the hair.

"Listen," he said, "we have only to find the man who lost this hair and the criminal is in our hands."

The inexorable chain of logic was complete.

The detective set himself to the search.

For four days and nights he moved, unobserved, through the streets of New York scanning closely every face he passed, looking for a man who had lost a hair.

On the fifth day he discovered a man, disguised as a tourist, his head enveloped in a steamer cap that reached below his ears.

The man was about to go on board the *Gloritania*.

The detective followed him on board.

"Arrest him!" he said, and then drawing himself to his full height, he brandished aloft the hair.

"This is his," said the great detective. "It proves his guilt."

"Remove his hat," said the ship's captain sternly.

They did so.

The man was entirely bald.

"Ha!" said the great detective, without a moment of hesitation. "He has committed not *one* murder but about a million."

# Kansas City Connection

*Wayne McMillan*

Francine Ware sat up with a start. Her little black eyes darted about the car. As long as the train was moving, her thoughts carried her swiftly into the future. But when the fluid motion stopped, time stopped, too. The hours just passed raced up again and she was back in Chicago in the big stone house on the North Shore. Warren lay sprawled on the floor. Once more her fascinated eyes watched the red stain widen on his stiff, white dress shirt. Again she forced his nerveless fingers around the cold metal of his revolver. Warren's fingers had been still warm, slightly moist. . . .

Francine jumped up and walked quickly to the platform. "What's this place?" she asked the conductor. "What are we stopping for?"

"We pick up mail here. Cayote Junction it's called." She stepped off the train and he called warningly: "It's just a two-minute stop, lady."

The damp night air was sweet in Francine's lungs, but it didn't quiet the nerve that twitched at her temple, or put strength into her water-weak knees and elbows. Gravel crunched under her restless feet.

The raw arc light gleamed on the sleek sides of the crack Transcontinental, on the silver ribbons of track that ran off over the plains to Kansas City. It glistened on the gossamer film of a spider web spun across a small, black box near the huge engine wheel. Francine unconsciously stretched out a brown suede toe to tear the web down. Then she checked the impulse. She felt a curious kinship for the spider. Hung precariously near the powerful wheel, it worked quietly, weaving its web.

Thread by thread, Francine had woven her own web. Somewhere ahead another train puffed its slower way to Kansas City. It had left Chicago nearly three hours before the Transcontinental, but they would be in Kansas City together for fifteen minutes. From there, the Transcontinental sped north, and the other train trudged south across the desert to El Paso. And on the slow El Paso train, in a drawing room of Car N-64, Francine's traveling bags were stowed. Her dressing case was open, her powder and creams on the shelf before the mirror. The bed was turned down and a sign was on the door, PLEASE DO NOT DISTURB.

She had chosen this day because Warren was with his board of directors until seven o'clock. She said good-by to him on the phone and made certain he would come home to dress before going to the Crowley's dinner. James put her on the slow train at six-fifteen. "That will be all," she said sharply. Was he going to fuss with the bags until the train pulled out? "Send the porter in and you can go."

She had her bed made immediately. The porter grinned at the size of her tip. "I'm going to bed now," Francine told him. "I don't feel well and don't want to be disturbed. Give this to the conductor for me." And she handed him her ticket to El Paso.

The porter would remember her. He and James both would testify that she had left Chicago on the six-fifteen train. But just before it left the station, while the porter was settling his last-minute passengers, Francine had slipped off the train, into the hurrying crowds.

That gave her nearly three hours before she boarded the swift Transcontinental. Three short hours. But long enough to free herself forever from a man who had grown repulsive. Whose lightest touch made her flesh shrink.

Standing alone in the night beside the throbbing engine, Francine felt no remorse. Only the exhilaration of freedom. And this clammy, twitching nervousness that would soon be over. In those uncertain days before Warren asked her to marry him, she thought money was all she wanted. Now she would have money and freedom.

One more strand and her web would be complete. She would leave the Transcontinental at Kansas City. Somehow she would dispose of her single, nondescript bag. Then she would slip back into her own compartment on the other train. If the porter or conductor saw her, they would think she had stepped off for a breath of air.

The spider started another cross-piece; its body dangling at the end of the delicate filament. Francine held her breath. Her own fate hung by a thread as fragile. The thread of those fifteen precious minutes in Kansas City.

The train gave two sharp whistles and Francine hurried back to her car. The train started, then jerked to a stop. Five priceless minutes slipped away. She craned her neck to peer out the window. The dark was broken by bobbing lanterns of the trainmen hurrying up the track. Six minutes . . . seven . . .

She rang for the porter. "What's the trouble?" Her voice sounded hoarse above the roaring in her ears.

"Just a little engine trouble. They'll find it soon."

Ten minutes . . . This motionlessness was maddening. The slower train was puffing steadily across the plains, widening the distance between them.

The minutes raced away. Fifteen . . . twenty . . .

Francine knew what would happen. Back in Chicago, James would bring Warren his morning coffee. He would knock discreetly, then push the door open. He would find Warren just as she had left him, except now his fingers would be stiff and cold. She shook her head to clear the picture from her mind. That was over. She was free. Or would be after Kansas City . . .

But when the wheels started turning again, fifty-three minutes had passed. Frantically, Francine sought out the conductor. "No, lady," he said in answer to her question. "The El Paso train won't wait for us in Kansas City. It's not a regular connection."

Cold fear seeped into Francine's brain. James would call the police. They'd try to reach her on the El Paso train and they would find her empty compartment. The porter would remember he hadn't seen her since they left Chicago. If only she had stayed boldly at home! The police might have called it suicide—dismissed her with a routine questioning. But she had needed so desperately to be completely safe —safe with an alibi that she was miles away when her husband was shot.

Now, sooner or later, they would question her. Those men with the steel-trap jaws and cold eyes. "Why had she left the El Paso train before it pulled out of Chicago?" "Where had she spent those three hours?" "Why had she made reservations on both trains?" They would go over and over the same ground until she was hopelessly enmeshed in her web of lies.

She ran to the end of the car. For a long minute she stared at the shining rails as they slipped from under the train. Then she shuddered and shrank back in the car. No, she couldn't jump. Her body would be hurled onto the sharp, tearing rocks of the roadbed, or caught under grinding wheels. But maybe—maybe she could disappear in Kansas City.

The conductor came down the aisle droning: "Kansas City. All out for Kansas City."

It was like a nightmare—this sensation Francine had of being physically bound, caught in the web of her own clever alibi. To her panic-
stricken eyes the window seemed to be crossed by steel prison bars.
Abruptly she jerked down the shade, and saw the conductor glance at
her.

Her plan had been so perfect. Why had it failed? She *had* to know.
She clutched the conductor's sleeve with taut fingers. "What—what
was it held us up?"

The conductor's uniformed crispness vanished for a moment. He
pushed his cap on the back of his head. "Believe it or not, lady," he
said. "It was a spider web. Yes sir, a spider web spun across the electric
control box near one of the engine wheels."

*A spider web!* Francine remembered the spider web she had seen—
her impulse to tear it down, her sudden sympathy for the spider weaving a web as perfect as her own had seemed then. But it was ridiculous. Her mouth twisted with contempt. "Don't tell me a spider web
could stop a locomotive—"

"Sure," answered the conductor cheerfully. "Happens every so
often. It tripped the automatic air brakes and shut off the power."

The train slowed to a stop. Two keen-eyed men entered, pushing
in past the line of outgoing passengers. Francine turned quickly to the
other end of the car. But the exit was blocked by the huge bulk of a
man whose swift eyes seemed to be measuring her height and weight,
noting her coloring. He was headed straight for her.

Francine felt the blood drain from her face, felt her body tremble
with the cold fear that gripped her, and she heard the conductor's
voice.

"Don't be upset about it, lady," he was saying soothingly. "It was
just a spider web. It didn't do any harm."

# Knit One—Kill Two

*by Fergus Truslow*

Miss Van Arsdale's beautiful hands with the red-lacquered nails kept right on knitting when the clocks in Max Kunkel's jewelry shop next door began to bong and cuckoo for eight o'clock and his lights winked out.

Her hands didn't tremble. She watched them, to make sure.

*"Max,"* she would say, *"Max, I'd like to see those unset diamonds again, if you don't mind."*

Of course it would mean police and questions. She wondered if John Martin, the absurd, freckle-faced boy next door who had grown up to be a detective, might come.

He used to try to scare her on Halloween. He hadn't moved her from her calm then, and he wouldn't now.

Outward calm came easy for Miss Van Arsdale. Her dark eyes, her heavy, pale features, seemed as dully placid as landlocked waters.

Inside her, things were different. Her heart felt hard and hot, like a bit of carbon under terrible pressure.

She stood up, smoothed back a wisp of graying hair and checked carefully to make sure she had everything in her knitting bag.

Her fingers touched the hammer wrapped in newspapers. The big shoes. The box already wrapped, stamped and addressed to her sixteen-year-old nephew in Colorado, but with one end left open. The damp cloth.

Two steps took her across her own sill to the other half of the building she shared with Max Kunkel. She tapped on the glass. "Max," she called softly.

"Ah, it's you, Miss Van Arsdale!" Max Kunkel chuckled.

The bald little jeweler let her into the darkened shop, rubbing his hands.

She came directly to the point. "I'd like to see those unset diamonds again, Max, if you don't mind."

"Not at all, not at all, not at all!" he trilled at her. He led the way to his tiny back room workshop, which smelled of metals and acids.

287

One quick glance told her the dust barrel, the safe and the door were placed as she'd remembered them.

"I do a big business back here," Max Kunkel was saying, "making up settings for the big downtown jewelers. I don't care if many people don't come to the front of my shop."

"Yes, I suppose you're very busy," Miss Van Arsdale agreed calmly, as he cocked his bald pink head over the safe.

"Was you thinking of having a stone or two set for yourself some day?" he asked, intent on the combination.

"Yes, I was," she answered truthfully.

She stowed her knitting in one corner of the bag, took a firm grip on the hammer.

The bald little jeweler tugged open the door of the safe, reached in and brought out a leather wallet.

"Here I got some choice dia—"

He didn't finish. She struck—once, twice. It was enough. Miss Van Arsdale was a strong woman.

The sound of the blows sickened her a little. *But then*, she thought, *you couldn't make an omelet without breaking eggs. The worst was over now.*

She stooped, picked up the leather wallet, slid it into her knitting bag. The hammer she dropped, after taking off the newspaper wrapped around its handle.

Max Kunkel's body had slumped over against his dust barrel. With one easy pull Miss Van Arsdale overturned the barrel, sending a cascade of dirt across the floor.

The dirt didn't spread as far as the sill of the back door that opened on the alley. She'd thought of that. Without hesitation, she thrust her hand into the barrel and brought out more dust, scattered it carefully across the floor.

With the big shoes she made two heavy footprints in the dirt, as if an excited man had taken long strides and flung through the door to make his getaway.

Then she quickly put the shoes into the box addressed to her nephew in Colorado, closed it, tied the twine tight.

Her right hand, the one she'd thrust into the dust barrel, she wiped clean with the damp cloth. All was done. Hardly twenty seconds had elapsed since Max Kunkel had slumped over under the two terrible hammer blows.

Going back through the darkened shop to the front door, she paused by a showcase. A trayful of rings caught her eye.

She hadn't planned on what happened then. Before she knew it she had reached into the showcase and speared a whole row of the glittering rings with one of her long knitting needles.

Miss Van Arsdale gasped a little at her own recklessness. What if somebody had looked in the window and seen her stealing!

But the sidewalk was empty when she went out. She mailed the shoes to her nephew in Colorado in the mailbox on the curb.

Once back in the Yarn Shop she hid the rings and the wallet of unset diamonds in the heart of a ball of bouclé wool in a box on her shelves of stock and sat down again in her chair to knit.

Her needles had been clicking busily for more than half an hour when light, hurried footsteps passed her door. Presently a long, moaning scream rang out from Max Kunkel's jewelry shop. "Max! Max!" a woman wailed. *"Ah, Maxen!"*

Miss Van Arsdale calmly put down her knitting and called the police . . .

The late Max Kunkel's shop lights were blazing and his clocks were bonging and cuckooing ten o'clock at a throng of uniformed lawmen, when a young man in a neat gray suit tapped at the door of the Yarn Shop. He walked in.

"Remember me, Miss Van Arsdale?" he queried, smiling.

She glanced at his blue eyes, freckles, and mop of dark hair. "John Martin," she said. "You're a detective. You used to be the boy next door who—"

"Who tried to scare you by ringing your doorbell and jumping at you with a mask on," he finished for her. "Only you never would scream like the other women."

"If you've come to talk about the murder," she said, "I've already told the police I didn't see anybody."

*Better stick to the truth,* she reminded herself calmly.

"Do you know how it looks to me?" he said confidingly. "On the face of it, the killer scuffled with old Kunkel, upsetting the dust barrel, slugged him to death with the hammer, and made off through the back door. But I don't think so."

*He'll never prove anything,* she told herself. Aloud she asked: "Why don't you think, so?"

"One thing doesn't fit in," John Martin said thoughtfully. "The killer snapped up some rings from a full tray in the showcase. It looks like an afterthought to me—a last-minute decision on his way out."

"Yes?" she said. Her pale, heavy features were calm.

"Mmm," John Martin mused. "He carried a wire or a knitting needle

289

or something, and hooked the rings right out of the tray without touching anything else. It's the only way . . ."

Miss Van Arsdale sniffed. "Murderers don't carry knitting needles about with them."

The detective shrugged. "When I figured the front door had been the real exit and the killer had snatched the rings in leaving, I went back and took a close look at that dust barrel. You can see where he dipped the dust out with his hands. So the tracks in it were a plant."

Miss Van Arsdale permitted herself a bleak little smile. "You're still the little boy next door, aren't you? With a head full of wild notions."

She began to cast off stitches for the armhole of the suit she was knitting.

John Martin drew his chair close to hers. "You know one of the notions I had when I was a kid? That you hated life for passing you by."

Miss Van Arsdale's lips smiled coldly, but the hot, hard lump in her heart seemed to turn over.

"Other women had love, and husbands, and children, but you didn't. I used to think it wasn't fair. I still do."

She felt him touching her fingers. "You have beautiful hands," he said softly. "I'm sorry I have to do this."

His voice was kind. For the first time in her life she felt feminine and helpless and very close to tears.

He took out a clean white envelope and a nailfile.

*He can't prove a thing!* she told herself. *Even if I have got dust under my fingernails. Dust is only dust!*

"You cased the job O.K. except for one point," John Martin explained as he worked. "Where you dropped a stitch was in thinking sweepings from a jeweler's floor are just plain dirt."

He put away the envelope and nailfile. Miss Van Arsdale hardly felt the chill kiss of steel as handcuffs closed on her wrists. She was listening to John Martin's next words: "All jewelers save their floor sweepings for the gold dust mixed with the stuff. When you put your fingers into that dust barrel you struck it rich."

# The Leopard Man's Story

*by Jack London*

He had a dreamy, far-away look in his eyes, and his sad, insistent voice, gentle-spoken as a maid's, seemed the placid embodiment of some deep-seated melancholy. He was the Leopard Man, but he did not look it. His business in life, whereby he lived, was to appear in a cage of performing leopards before vast audiences, and to thrill those audiences by certain exhibitions of nerve for which his employers rewarded him on a scale commensurate with the thrills he produced.

As I say, he did not look it. He was narrow-hipped, narrow-shouldered, and anaemic, while he seemed not so much oppressed by gloom as by a sweet and gentle sadness, the weight of which was as sweetly and gently borne. For an hour I had been trying to get a story out of him, but he appeared to lack imagination. To him there was no romance in his gorgeous career, no deeds of daring, no thrills—nothing but a gray sameness and infinite boredom.

Lions? Oh, yes! he had fought with them. It was nothing. All you had to do was to stay sober. Anybody could whip a lion to a standstill with an ordinary stick. He had fought one for half an hour once. Just hit him on the nose every time he rushed, and when he got artful and rushed with his head down, why, the thing to do was to stick out your leg. When he grabbed at the leg you drew it back and hit him on the nose again. That was all.

With the far-away look in his eyes and his soft flow of words he showed me his scars. There were many of them, and one recent one where a tigress had reached for his shoulder and gone down to the bone. I could see the neatly mended rents in the coat he had on. His right arm, from the elbow down, looked as though it had gone through a threshing machine, what of the ravage wrought by claws and fangs. But it was nothing, he said, only the old wounds bothered him somewhat when rainy weather came on.

Suddenly his face brightened with a recollection, for he was really as anxious to give me a story as I was to get it.

291

"I suppose you've heard of the lion-tamer who was hated by another man?" he asked.

He paused and looked pensively at a sick lion in the cage opposite.

"Got the toothache," he explained. "Well, the lion-tamer's big play to the audience was putting his head in a lion's mouth. The man who hated him attended every performance in the hope sometime of seeing that lion crunch down. He followed the show about all over the country. The years went by and he grew old, and the lion-tamer grew old, and the lion grew old. And at last one day, sitting in a front seat, he saw what he had waited for. The lion crunched down, and there wasn't any need to call a doctor."

The Leopard Man glanced casually over his finger nails in a manner which would have been critical had it not been so sad.

"Now, that's what I call patience," he continued, "and it's my style. But it was not the style of a fellow I knew. He was a little, thin, sawed-off, sword-swallowing and juggling Frenchman. De Ville, he called himself, and he had a nice wife. She did trapeze work and used to dive from under the roof into a net, turning over once on the way as nice as you please.

"De Ville had a quick temper, as quick as his hand, and his hand was as quick as the paw of a tiger. One day, because the ring-master called him a frog-eater, or something like that and maybe a little worse, he shoved him against the soft pine background he used in his knife-throwing act, so quick the ringmaster didn't have time to think, and there, before the audience, De Ville kept the air on fire with his knives, sinking them into the wood all round the ring-master so close that they passed through his clothes and most of them bit into his skin.

"The clowns had to pull the knives out to get him loose, for he was pinned fast. So the word went around to watch out for DeVille, and no one dared be more than barely civil to his wife. And she was a sly bit of baggage, too, only all hands were afraid of De Ville.

"But there was one man, Wallace, who was afraid of nothing. He was the lion-tamer, and he had the self-same trick of putting his head into the lion's mouth. He'd put it into the mouths of any of them, though he preferred Augustus, a big, good-natured beast who could always be depended upon.

"As I was saying, Wallace—'King' Wallace we called him—was afraid of nothing alive or dead. He was a king and no mistake. I've seen him drunk, and on a wager go into the cage of a lion that'd turned nasty, and without a stick beat him to a finish. Just did it with his fist on the nose.

"Madame de Ville—"

At an uproar behind us the Leopard Man turned quietly around. It was a divided cage, and a monkey, poking through the bars and around the partition, had had its paw seized by a big gray wolf who was trying to pull it off by main strength. The arm seemed stretching out longer and longer like a thick elastic, and the unfortunate monkey's mates were raising a terrible din. No keeper was at hand, so the Leopard Man stepped over a couple of paces, dealt the wolf a sharp blow on the nose with the light cane he carried, and returned with a sadly apologetic smile to take up his unfinished sentence as though there had been no interruption.

"—looked at King Wallace and King Wallace looked at her, while De Ville looked black. We warned Wallace, but it was no use. He laughed at us, as he laughed at De Ville one day when he shoved De Ville's head into a bucket of paste because he wanted to fight.

"De Ville was in a pretty mess—I helped to scrape him off; but he was cool as a cucumber and made no threats at all. But I saw a glitter in his eyes which I had seen often in the eyes of wild beasts, and I went out of my way to give Wallace a final warning. He laughed, but he did not look so much in Madame de Ville's direction after that.

"Several months passed by. Nothing had happened and I was beginning to think it all a scare over nothing. We were West by that time, showing in 'Frisco. It was during the afternoon performance, and the big tent was filled with woman and children, when I went looking for Red Denny, the head canvas-man, who had walked off with my pocket-knife.

"Passing by one of the dressing tents I glanced in through a hole in the canvas to see if I could locate him. He wasn't there, but directly in front of me was King Wallace, in tights, waiting for his turn to go on with his cage of performing lions. He was watching with much amusement a quarrel between a couple of trapeze artists. All the rest of the people in the dressing tent were watching the same thing, with the exception of De Ville, whom I noticed staring at Wallace with undisguised hatred. Wallace and the rest were all too busy following the quarrel to notice this or what followed.

"But I saw it through the hole in the canvas. De Ville drew his handkerchief from his pocket, made as though to mop the sweat from his face with it (it was a hot day), and at the same time walked past Wallace's back. He never stopped, but with a flirt of the handkerchief kept right on to the doorway, where he turned his head, while passing out, and shot a swift look back. The look troubled me at the time, for not only did I see hatred in it, but I saw triumph as well.

"'De Ville will bear watching,' I said to myself, and I really breathed easier when I saw him go out the entrance to the circus grounds and board an electric car for down town. A few minutes later I was in the big tent, where I had overhauled Red Denny. King Wallace was doing his turn and holding the audience spellbound. He was in a particularly vicious mood, and he kept the lions stirred up till they were all snarling, that is, all of them except old Augustus, and he was just too fat and lazy and old to get stirred up over anything.

"Finally Wallace cracked the old lion's knees with his whip and got him into position. Old Augustus, blinking good-naturedly, opened his mouth and in popped Wallace's head. Then the jaws came together, *crunch*, just like that."

The Leopard Man smiled in a sweetly wistful fashion, and the far-away look came into his eyes.

"And that was the end of King Wallace," he went on in his sad, low voice. "After the excitement cooled down I watched my chance and bent over and smelled Wallace's head. Then I sneezed."

"It . . . it was . . . ?" I queried with halting eagerness.

"Snuff—that De Ville dropped on his hair in the dressing tent. Old Augustus never meant to do it. He only sneezed."


# The Man Who Collected "The Shadow"

*by J. V. Drexel*


Mr. Theodore Conway was a nostalgiac, a collector of memorabilia, a dweller in the uncomplicated days of his adolescence when radio, movie serials, and pulp magazines were the ruling forms of entertainment and super-heroes were the idols of American youth.

At forty-three, he resided alone in a modest apartment on Manhattan's Lower East Side, where he commuted daily by subway to his position of file clerk in the archives of Baylor, Baylor, Leeds and Wadsworth, a respected probate law firm. He was short and balding and very plump and very nondescript; he did not indulge in any of the vices, major or minor; he had no friends to speak of, and neither a
294

wife nor, euphemistically or otherwise, a girlfriend. (In point of fact, Mr. Conway was that rarest of individuals, an adult male virgin.) He did not own a television set, did not attend the theater or movies. His one and only hobby, his single source of pleasure, his sole purpose in life, was the accumulation of nostalgia in general—and nostalgia pertaining to that most inimitable of all super-heroes, The Shadow, in particular.

Ah, The Shadow! Mr. Conway idolized Lamont Cranston, loved Margo Lane as he could never love any living woman. Nothing set his blood to racing quite so quickly as The Shadow on the scent of an evildoer, utilizing the Power that, as Cranston, he had learned in the Orient—the Power to cloud men's minds so that they could not see him. Nothing gave Mr. Conway more pleasure than listening to the haunting voice of Orson Welles, capturing The Shadow as no other had over the air; or reading Maxwell Grant's daring accounts in *The Shadow Magazine*; or paging through one of the starkly drawn Shadow comic books. Nothing filled him with as much delicious anticipation as the words spoken by his hero at the beginning of each radio adventure: *Who knows what evil lurks in the hearts of men? The Shadow knows . . .* and the eerie, bloodcurdling laugh that followed it. Nothing filled him with as much security as, when each case was closed, this ace among aces saying words of warning to criminals everywhere: *The weed of crime bears bitter fruit. Crime does not pay. The Shadow knows!*

Mr. Conway had begun collecting nostalgia in 1944, starting with a wide range of pulp magazines. (He now had well over ten thousand issues of *Wu Fang, G-8 and his Battle Aces, Black Mask, Weird Tales, Doc Savage,* and two hundred others.) Then he had gone on to comic books and comic strips, to premiums of every kind and description—decoders and secret-compartment belts and message flashlights and spy rings and secret pens that wrote in invisible ink. In the 1950s he had begun to accumulate tapes of such radio shows as *Jack Armstrong, the All-American Boy* and *Buck Rogers in the 25th Century.* But while he amassed all of these eagerly, he pursued the mystique of The Shadow with a fervor that bordered on the fanatical.

He haunted secondhand bookshops and junk shops, pored over advertisements in newspapers and magazines and collectors' sheets, wrote letters, made telephone calls, spent every penny of his salary that did not go for bare essentials. And at long last he succeeded where no other nostalgiac had even come close to succeeding. He accomplished a remarkable, an almost superhuman feat.

He collected the complete Shadow.

There was absolutely nothing produced about his hero—not a

written word, not a spoken sentence, not a drawing or gadget—that Mr. Conway did not own.

The final item, the one that had eluded him for so many years, came into his possession on a Saturday evening in late June. He had gone into a tenement area of Manhattan, near the East River, to purchase from a private individual a rare cartoon strip of *Terry and the Pirates*. With the strip carefully tucked into his coat pocket, he was on his way back to the subway when he chanced upon a small neighborhood bookshop in the basement of a crumbling brownstone. It was still open, and unfamiliar to him, and so he entered and began to browse. And on one of the cluttered tables at the rear—there it was.

The October 1931 issue of *The Shadow Magazine.*

Mr. Conway emitted a small, ecstatic cry. Caught up the magazine in trembling hands, stared at it with disbelieving eyes, opened it tenderly, read the contents page and the date, ran sweat-slick fingers over the rough, grainy pulp paper. Near-mint condition. Spine undamaged. Colors unfaded. And the price—

Fifty cents.

Fifty cents!

Tears of joy rolled unabashedly down Mr. Conway's cheeks as he carried this treasure to the elderly proprietor. The bookseller gave him a strange look, shrugged, and accepted two quarters from Mr. Conway without a word. Two quarters, fifty cents. And Mr. Conway had been prepared to pay *hundreds* . . .

As he went out into the gathering darkness—it was almost nine by this time—he could scarcely believe that he had finally done it, that he now possessed the total word, picture, and voice exploits of the most awesome master crime fighter of them all. His brain reeled. The Shadow was *his* now; Lamont Cranston and Margo Lane (beautiful Margo!)—his, all his, his alone.

Instead of proceeding to the subway, Mr. Conway impulsively entered a small diner not far from the bookshop and ordered a cup of coffee. Then, once again, he opened the magazine. He had previously read a reprint of the novel by Maxwell Grant—*The Shadow Laughs!*— but that was not the same as reading the original, no indeed. He plunged into the story again, savoring each line, each page, the mounting suspense, the seemingly inescapable traps laid to eliminate The Shadow by archvillains Isaac Coffran and Birdie Crull, the smashing of their insidious counterfeiting plot: justice triumphant. *The weed of crime bears bitter fruit, crime does not pay* . . .

So engrossed was Mr. Conway that he lost all track of time. When at last he closed the magazine he was startled to note that except for the counterman, the diner was deserted. It had been nearly full when he entered. He looked at his wristwatch, and his mouth dropped open in amazement. Good heavens! It was past midnight!

Mr. Conway scrambled out of the booth and hurriedly left the diner. Outside, apprehension seized him. The streets were dark and deserted—ominous, forbidding.

He looked up and down without seeing any sign of life. It was four blocks to the nearest subway entrance—a short walk in daylight but now it was almost the dead of night. Mr. Conway shivered in the cool night breeze. He had never liked the night, its sounds and smells, its hidden dangers. There were stories in the papers every morning of muggers and thieves on the prowl . . .

He took a deep breath, summoning courage. Four blocks. Well, that really wasn't very far, only a matter of minutes if he walked swiftly. And swift was his pace as he started along the darkened side-walk.

No cars passed; no one appeared on foot. The hollow echo of his footfalls were the only sounds. And yet Mr. Conway's heart was pounding wildly by the time he had gone two blocks.

He was halfway through the third block when he heard the muf-fled explosions.

He stopped, the hairs on his neck prickling, a tremor of fear cours-ing through him. There was an alley on his left; the reports had come from that direction. Gunshots? He was certain that was what they'd been—and even more certain that they meant danger, sudden death. *Run!* he thought. And yet, though he was poised for flight, he did not run. He peered into the alley, saw a thin light at its far end.

*Run, run!* But instead he entered the alley, moving slowly, feeling his way along. *What am I doing? I shouldn't be here!* But still he continued forward, approaching the narrow funnel of light. It came from inside a partly open door to the building on his right. Mr. Conway put out a hand and eased the door open wider, peered into what looked to be a warehouse. The thudding of his heart seemed as loud as a drum roll as he stepped over the threshold.

The source of the light was a glassed-in cubicle toward the middle of the warehouse. Shadowy shapes—crates of some kind—loomed toward the ceiling on either side. He advanced in hesitant, wary steps, seeing no sign of movement in the gloom around him. At last he reached the cubicle, stood in the light. A watchman's office. He stepped up close to look through the glass.

A cry rose in his throat when he saw the man lying motionless on the floor inside; he managed to stifle it. Blood stained the front of the man's khaki uniform jacket. He had been shot twice.

*Dead, murdered! Get out of here, call the police!*

Mr. Conway turned—and froze.

A hulking figure stood not three feet away, looking straight at him.

Mr. Conway's knees buckled; he had to put a hand against the glass to keep from collapsing. The murderer! His mind once again compelled him to run, *run*, but his legs would not obey. He could only stare back in horror at the hulking figure—at the pinched white face beneath a low-brimmed cloth cap, at rodentlike eyes and a cruel mouth, at the yawning muzzle of a revolver in one fist.

"No!" Mr. Conway cried then. "No, please, don't shoot!"

The man dropped into a furtive crouch, extending the pistol in front of him.

"Don't shoot!" Mr. Conway said again, putting up his hands.

Surprise, bewilderment, and a sudden trapped fear made a twisted mask of the man's face. "Who's that? Who's there?"

Mr. Conway opened his mouth, then closed it again. He could scarcely believe his ears. The man was standing not three feet away, looking right at him!

"I don't understand," Mr. Conway said before he could stop the words.

The murderer fired. The sudden report caused Mr. Conway to jump convulsively aside; the bullet came nowhere near him. He saw the gunman looking desperately from side to side, everywhere but at him—and in that instant he did understand, he knew.

"You can't *see* me," he said.

The gun discharged a second bullet, but Mr. Conway had already moved again. Far to one side of him a spiderwebbed hole appeared in the glass wall of the cubicle. "Damn you!" the murderer screamed. "Where are you? *Where are you?*"

Mr. Conway remained standing there, clearly outlined in the light, for a moment longer; then he stepped to where a board lay on the floor nearby, picked it up. Without hesitation, he advanced on the terrified man and then struck him on the side of the head; watched dispassionately as the other dropped unconscious to the floor.

Mr. Conway kicked the revolver away and stood over him. The police would have to be summoned, of course, but there was plenty of time for that now. A slow, grim smile stretched the corners of his mouth. Could it be that the remarkable collecting feat he had performed, his devotion and his passion, had stirred some supernatural force into granting him the Power that he now possessed? Well, no matter. His was not to question why; so endowed, his was but to heed the plaintive cries of a world ridden with lawlessness.

A deep, chilling laugh suddenly swept through the warehouse. "The weed of crime bears bitter fruit!" a haunting, Wellesian voice shouted. "Crime does not pay!"

And The Shadow wrapped the cloak of night around himself and went out into the mean streets of the great metropolis . . .

# The Man Who Died Too Often

*David Crewe*

Doc Plummer bade adieu to the Big House, a free man after eighteen years, and at once set up practice at the old stand. Talk about your nerve!

Not that anyone had particularly mourned the discovery of Jem Tripp's charred remains in the smouldering skeleton of Plummer's summer house that day so long ago. Or that a certain measure of sympathy had not veered paradoxically to the young surgeon, when he was found dead drunk in his room, his revolver on the floor with his fingerprints on it—and the two bullets missing, which were later found embedded in the corpse.

The town had been fully aware, town fashion, of the young M.D.'s blind infatuation for Tripp's wife, of Plummer's crazy drunken rages— but damn it, the Doc had been regular in a lot of ways, and Tripp was a stinker, if there ever was one.

But it was one thing to sympathize with a man who had paid his debt to society, and another quite distinct thing to trust your life and those of your kids to his hands. So had the town reasoned.

And Plummer, no longer young, showing in every deeply etched line of his face the wreck of his unlived youth, read the verdict in his neat little expense book, and stared dully out into the night, drumming softly on the desk. So, it was no go, after all. He had been crazy to have tried it. Lucky that the income from his mother's estate would keep him going, with what little business he could eke out on the side. Well, a man couldn't think about it eternally without cracking, so—

He rose and paced restlessly about the office. Six months of it. Six months of hell!

The harsh *br-r-r-r* of the telephone broke into his reverie. He groped absently for the receiver.

"Hello."

"Doc!" The metallic, wire-distorted voice held a subdued undercurrent of excitement or fear. "Doc—I want you to come out to Melville's shooting lodge on Elk's Pond—at once. Case of ptomaine, I'm afraid. Hurry!"

"Right." Plummer mechanically jotted the directions on his memo pad. "What's the name?"

"Oh—" the voice stopped for an imperceptible pause—"someone who remembers you—from the old days. Hurry." The instrument clicked with an air of finality.

Doc swore softly as he picked up his kit. All of sixty miles through the worst roads in the state. Then his face softened. Someone of the old guard had called to him for help. The voice *had* stirred a vague chord of memory. Well—he'd know soon enough.

Nearly three hours later his old roadster jolted to a stop before a building nestled deep in the pine forest. Doc emerged, chilled and stiff, and stretched his cramped shoulder muscles luxuriously. Quite a layout. Man must have money. A tough place though, to be stuck alone with a bellyache or worse, miles from human contact.

The transition from purple blackness to the white brilliance within was too sudden for his tired old eyes, so that at first the man who huddled behind the large table was a blurred nonentity. Then as his retinas adjusted to permit clearer vision, he started violently, his groping fingers clutching the door knob for support.

"God!" he gasped incredulously, while the pink of his cheeks went slowly grey. "You!"

The supposed patient laughed, and the laugh held no vestige of mirth.

"Right the first time—Herman Jacobs to the wide open spaces— Jem Tripp to you, you two-timing heel. When I heard that my old friend was free, I couldn't resist this opportunity to see you once more. My," he sneered, "you sure are glad to see me."

"But," Doc murmured weakly, "I don't—understand—"

"Of course you don't, Plummer." Tripp laughed. "That's why I arranged this little rendezvous. Frenchy, take the gentleman's coat." A
300

servant glided noiselessly to his side and as silently departed with the apparel which Plummer mechanically gave him.

"Now, Doc—pal of my childish and wildish days—sit down." The resurrected Tripp gestured to a chair, and the Doc noticed for the first time the gun which lay on the table.

He obeyed, still dazed by the man who had sprung from the limbo of the past to haunt him. For a moment the spell of ghostly unreality claimed him. Then reason returned, and with it a blind surge of fury. He half rose, choking with emotion.

"You rotten—dog," came tensely from between clenched jaws, but even as his legs tensed for a leap he realized that it would be suicide to attempt it. The man before him was mad—mad with an accumulated jealousy and hate of two decades. And he had a gun. Doc sank back into his chair again, shrugging helplessly.

"Very wise of you, Doc." Tripp patted the revolver significantly. "And now"—he continued, "You're going to drink—drink until you're as drunk as you were in the old days—only *this* time you won't leave me under the table and make love to Elsie. Remember Elsie, Doc?" With a shrill cackle of satisfaction he noted the white knuckles strain impotently against the arms of the chair.

"Ah, Elsie"—he mused in mock reminiscence. "She was a rare piece, yet I find I like 'em younger, now, and with more looks. Y'know, Elsie died the week you were convicted. She never got over the thing. You knew it? Sorry. I wanted you to squirm under it before my face." He seemed almost childishly petulant that the doctor had not stirred at the news.

"Well," he resumed impatiently, "to business! Doc, you're a calm old quack when you're sober, but when the old firewater hits you—it never used to take long—you're as haywire as they come. I want to see you that way just once more. Want you to run amuck for me just once more—remember how the District Attorney brought out that at your trial? You even hit me once when you were that way—damn you." He rubbed his jaw reminiscently.

He pressed the servant's bell. "Two tall ones, Frenchy, and have 'em well chilled.

"Yeah," Tripp continued, picking up the gun and waving it baton-like before Doc, "I want to see that old pulse throb in your forehead, and you so blasted mad you really *would* kill me—if you could. Only, you won't. Just a few drinks together, you and me—and then I'll answer all those wild questions you've been asking yourself. Guess you'll get a reaction, all right. Only, so help me God, if you jump from that chair once, I'll shoot you apart like a dog! Now," he screamed, pushing a glass across the table, "Drink, my friend."

Plummer stared, gulped, and drank deeply, while the other shook in silent merriment. . . .

The clock astride the white mantel had ticked away a full hour. The two figures still sat as before. Tripp was slowly mellowing from the effects of the potent Scotch. Plummer—well, eighteen years of abstinence followed by eight stiff highballs—his lank figure wavered ever so slightly in his seat.

Tripp was tormenting him slowly, dragging it out to every subtle finesse of cruelty of which his mind was capable. Already he had explained how he had discovered the body of a tramp in the hedge that night long ago, how he had borne it under cover of the darkness to Plummer's estate.

His beady, rat-like eyes glowed with malicious satisfaction as he noted the Doc's face get hard and set as the points were driven home to his consciousness. He was, he reflected in half tipsy glee, a powerful cat toying with his prey. A sleek omnipotent tiger waiting for his game to move, so that he could have the peculiar ecstacy of crushing it to earth with one contemptuous gesture.

"Now Doc, strain your imagination. I want you to get a clear picture of this. There we were—you an' me, tipping our elbows in your study. You never knew, did you, that my drinks that night were spilled into the vase beside my chair. Nary a swallow did I take—I had business to do. Finally, you passed out, like you're almost doing now. I put the hobo in the summer house, poured gasoline over his body. Then I fired a coupl'a shots into him. Back in your room again I squeezed the gun butt in your hand so the prints would show clear.

"You can probably guess the rest of it. I set fire to the body, saw that the summer house itself was going good—and skipped town forever. Next day I read I was dead. Hah! I followed your trial thoroughly—it was swell. Ah! now you're getting hot."

He gazed expectantly at his visitor.

Doc stared at him dully, only the thin ribbons of scarlet in his high cheekbones betraying the emotions which were consuming him.

"And—so"—he enunciated the words slowly, thickly—"you framed me, Jem. Sent me to a lifetime of regret and remorse for a crime I never committed."

Tripp clapped his palms together in mock applause. "Always right, Doc!" he exclaimed. "At first I wanted to kill you. Maybe I could have. But this was safer—safer for me—and more gratifying. I didn't want

302

you to die—I wanted you to live, and never know what happened. Then somehow, it seemed to me that with Elsie dead and your youth gone—the best of your life unlived—it might edify you to know the truth. Well, there it is—I see you appreciate my efforts."

He tensed; his fingers tightened half fearfully on the gun as Doc's fury burst into full consummation.

"Tripp," the other stammered, "Here's one thing you may have overlooked. D'you realize that I have paid my debt to the state for the killing of you, that if I *should* kill you now, tomorrow, at any time, no jury on earth could convict me? The law says 'No man's life may be placed in jeopardy twice for the same crime.'"

"Ah-h-h-" Tripp for no apparent reason had slumped back into his chair, groaning. He held his right side in a queer cupped gesture, like a man with a toothache shields his jaw from the air. In spite of his fury, Plummer's professional training came to the fore. He noted the sudden pallor, the spasmodic diaphramic reflexes, the right leg doubled up almost to the abdomen.

"Say—let me look at you," he demanded, forgetting for the moment everything but the symptoms. Lurching slightly, he walked towards Tripp. The latter stiffened as he approached, and fear crept into his narrowed eyes.

"Wait!" he yelled. "Hey, Frenchy!"

The impassive servant again appeared. Tripp waved to him to take the gun. "Keep this bird covered, blast you. Now, Doctor—if you want to make a diagnosis—I'll allow you that pleasure. But no funny tricks, or . . ." His voice trailed off into a smothered cry of pain.

The examination required but a moment. Plummer arose again, a queer glint in his eye, and as he did so his drunken lurch was even more pronounced than before, due perhaps to the kneeling posture. He regarded the man he had murdered according to twelve good and true men, and a flicker which might have been pity twisted his features.

"Jem," he said slowly, "You *did* have a bellyache when you called me out here."

"Why—yes, had some lamb this noon—never did agree with me. What of it?" Despite his words, Tripp could not quite conceal the fear of the layman for the mysteries of medical science. The vague stirring of a half formed terror crept into his eyes and made his sneer theatrical.

"Pity you didn't tell me about it when I arrived," murmured Doc, lighting a cigarette with the clumsy, dogged ineffectiveness of the inebriate. "Well, I'm speaking as a physician now, not as a—friend.

303

My diagnosis is acute appendicitis. You'll have to let me operate right now—here. You'll never survive sixty miles of these roads to town."

He smiled, and to the panic-ridden Jem the smile seemed to combine Machiavellian cunning with the cruelty of the Borgias. Doc continued. "Get your little playmate here to carry out my directions, and place yourself in my care. You were right, you see, in summoning me —it *was* a hurry call, only it's a pity you forced me to disregard the first tenets of a surgeon about—firewater." His sardonic glance swept the other, and even as he started to unclasp his black kit, his knees buckled and he would have fallen had he not grasped Frenchy's shoulder for support.

Tripp was crying now, as much from fear as pain. Something in the quiet drunken logic of Doc's words carried conviction. Doc *was* blind, teetering on unsteady legs before him, and grinning a Cheshire mask of triumph, which belied the unctuous solicitude of his speech. Doc's voice had said he'd never live to get back to town, but his manner had said as plainly that the operation would be a homicidal travesty.

He rose unsteadily, pressing his side, and staggered to the threshold.

"Wait!"

He turned. Doc looked at him, still smiling. "I said, Tripp, you'll never reach the hospital. In about twenty minutes your pain will disappear suddenly. You'll think the attack is over, but it will only be the release of pressure caused by the bursting of your appendix. By the time you get on the table, you'll have a raging fever, peritonitis will have a head start, and in your present alcoholic state—curtains."

"For the love of God, man, save me!" In spite of himself, the words rushed unbidden to his lips, and he watched eagerly for a hairbreadth's deviation in Doc's set smile. None was forthcoming.

"Yes, Jem," Doc mused, with a faint trace of boredom, "let me operate—here—now. Your only chance. If it will take away any of the yellow from your spine, I'll promise to—operate—to the best of my present ability." As if in mute satire, the alert Frenchy was supporting him upright by sheer force as he uttered the reassuring words. Tripp's panic rose to a crescendo.

"I'm not drunk, y'know," Doc insisted, still smiling in that sly manner.

"No, blast you," sobbed Tripp, throwing on his ulster, "not drunk. That's what you used to say in the old days, when you couldn't even walk. Frenchy, keep him away from me. I don't believe you, damn your soul; slight—indigestion, that's all. But I'm going to the hospital to be sure. Frenchy, keep him here till I go, then follow in his car." He

304

lurched out, and a moment later the roar of a powerful eight cut the silence.

Doc watched the car bump crazily along the rough corduroy road and into the blackness around the first bend. Something inscrutable smoldered in his grey eyes.

He spoke over his shoulder. "Old boy, sure you won't let me go after him? Maybe I can save him, you know."

"Not a chance," snarled the servant. "I'm off now in your bus, like he said. S'long." Presently the lights of Plummer's car sought the distant bend, also.

With the second departure, Doc lit another cigarette. The blue flame of the match wavered not a trifle as it just sought the tip of the white cylinder. He snapped the flame out adroitly, and tossed the charred match into a receptacle some feet distant. Then he absently reached for his coat. Just at the doorway he paused, as he nestled the collar around his neck and part of his face, in preparation for the long hike to a state road and a lift. The same sardonic smile crept for a moment across his lips as he regarded a large vase beside the seat he had occupied for most of the evening. In it were innumerable cigarette stubs and match ends, floating idly on what had been eight perfectly good glasses of Scotch.

# The Mann Act

*by Michael A. Black*

"You think they're the ones?" Wally asked.

"Gotta be," said Frank. "They're supposed to be a sister act, and they sure ain't regulars. Dressed in leather, too."

"Ahhh, I don't know, Frank. Remember we're working with the Feds on this. We'd better be sure."

"Yeah, yeah," Frank said. But he was thinking, fuck the Feds. They'd come to him for help on this thing because they didn't know shit about working vice. Christ, they were all either fucking lawyers or accountants. Like that fucker Partial. He'd show them how a real cop worked. He just wished that he didn't have to wear this fucking wire. It cramped his style.

Wally scowled and took another sip of his beer. At least it was a good one. Some imported stuff. The Feds were sparing no expense on this one. Must be the key to something big. Bigger than he and Frank were used to, anyway. He remembered when the Lieutenant had called them into the office earlier that day.

"The Feds are requesting our assistance on a case," the LT had said. "Tonight at Henry's Bar. They want us to bust a couple of hookers for them."

"The Feds?" Frank said. "Since when are their high and mighty highnesses interested in hookers?"

"It involves a madam who sets things up over a 900 number," the lieutenant replied. "The broads travel over state lines and that's a violation of the Mann Act."

"Leave it to them to make a federal case outta a little free enterprise," Frank had said. He didn't like the FBI. Ever since they investigated him on that brutality rap five years ago. The one that had gotten him transferred from Homicide to Vice. From the top of the heap to the asshole patrol.

"Hey, Frank," Wally said. "Lighten up, will ya? It beats the hell outta bustin' fruits downtown, don't it?"

Frank grumbled a reply, hoping it would be indistinct for the federal agents who were recording their conversation in the surveillance van outside.

"Better get on with it," Frank said, getting up.

Just then Wally felt the vibrating signal of his beeper going off. He checked the number, then grabbed Frank's sleeve.

"Gotta check in first," he said.

Frank snorted in disgust and ordered another beer. If the "G" was picking up the tab he might as well make the most of it.

Wally went to the men's room where there was a pay phone on the wall. A drunk was futilely trying to dial a number. Wally took the receiver from him and said, "This phone's out of order."

The drunk lowered his chin and tried to focus his eyes, but seeing that Wally was younger than he was, decided not to push it. He nodded and stumbled out the door. Wally watched him go and then quickly removed the drunk's quarter from the coin return slot and redeposited it. He read the number on his beeper and dialed it.

"Detective Myers?" the voice answered.

"Yeah," said Wally. Jesus, didn't these federal guys know anything about working undercover? Answering the phone like that.

"This is Special Agent Partial," the voice said.

No shit, thought Wally. This was the van's car-phone number, wasn't it?

"Have you made contact with the suspects yet?" Partial asked. "It sounded as if you had."

"Yeah," Wally answered. "I think so. A couple of babes in their late twenties, blond hair, big boobs, black leather clothes. That was their description, wasn't it?"

"Yes," Partial said. "But it's imperative that we're sure."

Imperative? Where the hell did these federal guys get these words?

"Let me put it this way," Wally said, a hint of irritation creeping into his voice. "We're sure we got them. My partner can smell a hooker a mile away."

"All right," Partial said. "Proceed as directed."

"Roger willco," Wally said as he hung up. He kicked open the door of the toilet to see if there was anybody hiding in there listening. Jesus, he thought, this cloak and dagger stuff was making him paranoid.

Wally returned to the bar and ordered another beer. Frank looked across the bar and winked at the two blondes, who immediately perked up.

"What'd they say?" asked Frank, leaning close to Wally.

"They said, and I quote, 'Proceed as directed.' "

"Christ," muttered Frank. He got up and picked up his drink. "Time to make the donuts."

He walked around the horse-shaped bar and stopped next to the two blondes. Putting on his best middle-class businessman smile, he asked, "Anybody sitting here?"

As he approached he saw the one closest to him run her tongue over her lips as she shook her head. Frank smiled benignly and started to seat himself, then stopped abruptly.

"Bartender," he called sharply. "How can this be? This beautiful young thing has an empty glass. Correct this immediately."

Both of the blondes giggled. Frank asked them if they minded if his shy friend joined them. They giggled again and said that would be all right. Frank motioned to Wally as he set the empty glass onto the inner edge of the bar.

Al, the big baldheaded bartender, took the glass and put it in the sink. Who the hell did that asshole think he was ordering me about? he thought. Didn't he know who he was dealing with? Al decided to let them find out on their own. He replaced all the drinks and then

307

moved down the counter to check on the drunk who was nearly passed out with the twenty-dollar bill still sitting on the counter.

Frank introduced himself and Wally.

"I'm Sherry," the one with the big breasts said. "And this is my friend Bambi."

"So you girls from around here?" asked Frank.

"Actually," Sherry said. "I am. Bambi's not."

"I'm from New York," Bambi said.

"Ohh, you got a voice like Lauren Bacall," said Frank. "I love Lauren Bacall's voice. They call it a whiskey tenor."

Bambi smiled, then looked at Sherry.

"So you guys want to party?" asked Bambi. "We just love to party with big strong guys."

Frank looked at Wally and smirked. These girls didn't want to waste any time. Before he could answer Wally grabbed his sleeve.

"I gotta go drain the monster," he said. His beeper was going off again.

"Yeah," said Frank. "That ain't such a bad idea. Would you ladies excuse us a moment?"

Sherry and Bambi looked at each other and laughed.

"Drain the monster?" Sherry said. "You're really making me curious."

"Hurry back, boys," Bambi said.

Frank and Wally got up and went to the men's room. After checking the stall again, Wally started fumbling through his pockets.

"Frank, gimme a quarter"

"What for?" asked Frank who was standing at the urinal.

"I gotta call Partial," Wally said. "He beeped me again."

"Well, I gotta piss," Frank said. "My fuckin' bladder beeped me."

After he finished Frank reached in his pocket and gave Wally a quarter. Wally dialed the number.

"Whadda ya want?" he asked when Special Agent Partial answered.

"First of all, I want to caution you two about entrapment," Partial said.

"Yeah, yeah," Wally answered. "We know all about it. It's not a defense if the suspect's predisposed to commit the crime."

"Secondly," Partial continued. "You're both using excessive profanity. Remember, this is all being recorded. A federal grand jury will be listening to it."

"All right," Wally said. "Anything else?"

"Not at this time."

"Good," Wally said and hung up.

He walked to the urinal.

308

"Frank, hold up. I've got to urinate."

"Urinate?" Frank said sarcastically. "Ya got your tweezers?"

"Knock it off. We're gonna be listened to by a federal grand jury."

Frank rubbed his fingers over his temples. When Wally was finished, they returned to the bar.

"You girls miss us?" Frank asked.

"Yeah," Sherry said. He felt the huge, cantalope-sized breasts rubbing over his arm. "Didn't we, Bambi?"

Bambi's arms encircled Wally's neck and drew him close.

"We sure did."

Wally grinned and started to say something, but the next thing he knew Bambi's tongue was working its way into his mouth. Jesus, she was strong.

"Hey, you girls don't mess around, do you?" he said, purposefully grabbing his beer and swishing some around in his mouth, hoping that would kill any germs.

"Well," said Sherry. "We'd really like to party with you guys, but there's a catch."

"Oh?" Frank said. Here comes the sales pitch, he thought. Just then Wally felt the vibration of the beeper again. Dammit, he thought.

"I gotta go drain the monster again," he said, getting up and ambling toward the john.

"He got kidney trouble or something?" Bambi asked.

"Naw," Frank said. "Just a small dick. He wants to stroke it."

"Hmm, I'll do that for him," Bambi said demurely.

Inside the washroom Wally made dialed the now familiar number.

"What now?" he said into the phone.

"I've been checking with my supervisor," Partial said. "He states that it's imperative that I witness the arrest, in case I have to testify."

"Well, come on in and join the fucking party then"

"Detective Myers, remember what I said about excessive profanity."

Wally hung up. Frank pushed the door open and asked him what was going on.

"The Fed's are sending in a man to witness the arrest," Wally said.

"Who?"

"Special Agent Partial."

Oh great, Frank thought. Don Knotts in a three-piece suit to scrutinize their arrest. They went back to the bar. When Wally sat on his stool, Bambi French kissed him again. As he reached for his drink to sanitize his mouth, he felt a hand grope his crotch.

"You don't feel like you got a small dick," Bambi said.

"Huh?" Wally said, almost choking on his beer.

"Why don't we all go out to our car and I'll give you head like you never had before," Bambi said.

"Sounds good," Wally said.

"Come on, big guy," Sherry said. reaching down to Frank's groin.

"What's the catch?" Frank said. "You said something about a catch."

Sherry and Bambi both looked at each other and giggled. They didn't notice the slightly built, bespectacled man in a three-piece suit who came in and sat a few stools down. But Frank noticed. It was that Fucker Partial. Good. Let him see the bullshit they had to go through to get a vice arrest. Just then Sherry's tongue invaded his mouth.

"Let's go out to the car, Frank," Sherry said.

"But what about the catch?" he said.

"We'll discuss that later," Sherry said.

"You two are married or something?" Wally asked, playing dumb.

"No," Sherry said slowly.

"Oh, I get it," Frank said. "You two are working girls, is that it?"

Sherry and Bambi looked at each other.

Wally leaned close to Bambi's ear and whispered, "If that's it, we don't mind."

"Right," Frank added. "We got plenty of money. We're up here from Peoria for an insurance convention. He handed them each a phoney card with his name and an insurance company logo on it. A vice cop's best tool.

"You don't mind paying us?" Bambi asked.

"Lemme put it this way, babe," Frank said, lapsing into his routine of the suave drunk. "We're businessmen ourselves."

"And we got plenty of friends at the hotel too," Wally added.

"So you'll introduce us to some of your friends?" Sherry asked.

"Sure," Frank said.

"If the price is right," added Wally.

"You guys are so sweet, I'd feel bad charging you," Bambi said.

"I wouldn't want you to feel bad, sweet cakes," Wally said. "But I can understand that business is business."

"We don't mind paying for top of the line stuff," Frank said. He took out a fifty dollar bill and laid it on the counter. "There's plenty more where that came from."

"Well, we are trying to raise money for a good cause. Got some candy for my friend?" Sherry asked, palming the bill.

"Sure," Frank said. He took out his wallet. Sherry leaned forward and Frenched him again, while placing his hand on the huge silicone breasts. Suddenly, leaning back, Sherry's expression changed. Frank felt a hand on the transmitter he was wearing.

310

"Bam bam, this motherfucker's wearing a wire," Sherry said.

Bambi's mouth dropped open and she pulled back and spit in Wally's face.

"Too late, ladies," Frank said, pulling out his badge and slipping off the stool. "The money's already changed hands. You're both going down."

Sherry suddenly brought a foot up and snapped a kick into Frank's groin. His balls felt like they were going to explode. He sagged downward. Wally reached over but was snared by Bambi, who deftly twisted him to the floor.

"Hey, Partial," he called. "How 'bout some help?"

Special Agent Partial was fumbling for his identification as he stepped in front of the scrambling bodies. Frank had recovered enough to grab Sherry's tight black leather skirt, which twisted off.

"Halt, I'm Special Agent Par—" he started to say, but couldn't finish. Sherry's skirt had twisted completely off and under the translucent panty hose, no underpants could be seen. What could be seen was that Sherry was not a natural blonde. Sherry was not a natural anything, because bulging from beneath the nylon fabric was a full set of male genitalia.

"You . . . You're androgynous," Partial said incredulously.

Wally had Bambi on the floor now, locking the handcuffs over the slim wrists. Upon seeing "all" of Sherry, he reached under Bambi's skirt and felt the remnants of a fading erection. He ran his tongue over his lips, then thought about whose tongue had just been there. Leaning, he grabbed Special Agent Partial's pant-leg and puked all over the FBI man's shoes.

Partial did a little dance trying to get away, but Wally held fast, continuing to vomit. Sherry attempted to run, but tripped on the leather skirt. Two more Feds came running in. After a few more seconds, the squirming bodies were untangled and Sherry and Bambi were marched out in cuffs.

Al the bartender swore as he mopped the vomit off the floor.

"Perverts and cops," he muttered. "One as bad as the other."

Suddenly he felt a tap on his shoulder. He looked up to see two blonde identical twins, dressed to kill, in matching leather outfits.

"Excuse me," the one closest to him said. "Has there been anybody here looking for us? My sister and I just flew in from New York and were supposed to meet a couple of guys here for a . . . business meeting." She smiled demurely.

# Memento Mori

*Alex Saxon*

There are murder weapons and there are murder weapons, but the thing used to bludgeon Philip Asher to death was the grisliest I'd seen in more than two decades on the police force.

It was a skull—a human skull.

Ed Crane and I stood staring down at what was left of it, lying splintered and gore-streaked to one side of the dead man. It had apparently cracked like an eggshell on the first or second blow, but that had been enough to shatter Asher's skull as well. Judging from the concavity of the wound, he had been struck with considerable force.

I pulled my gaze away and let it move over the room, a large masculine study. Well-used, leather-bound books covered two walls, and a third was adorned with what appeared to be primitive Mexican or Central American art and craftwork: pottery, statuary, wood carvings, weaponry. There were two teakwood desks arranged so that they faced each other—one large and ostentatious, the other small and functional—and several pieces of teak-and-leather furniture. It should have been a comfortable room, but for me it wasn't; there seemed to be a kind of cold, impersonal quality to it, despite the books and art.

Crane said, "If I wasn't seeing it for myself, I don't think I'd believe it."

"Yeah."

He rubbed at the bald spot on the crown of his head. "Well, I've had enough in here if you have."

"More than enough," I agreed.

We crossed to the double entrance doors and went into the hallway beyond. At its far end was a large living room containing more teakwood furniture and primitive art. One of the two patrolmen who had preceded us on the scene stood stoically beside a long sofa; the other officer was waiting outside for the arrival of the lab crew and the coroner. Sitting stiff-backed in middle of the sofa was Douglas Falconer—hands flat on his knees, eyes blinking myopically behind thick-lensed glasses. He was about forty, with a thin, chinless face and sparse sand-colored hair, dressed in slacks and a navy-blue shirt. He looked timid and harmless, but when he'd called headquarters a half-hour earlier, he had confessed to the murder of Philip Asher. The dried stains on his right shirt sleeve and on the back of his right hand confirmed his guilt well enough.

All we knew about Falconer and Asher was that the deceased owned this house, an expensive Spanish-style villa in one of the city's finer residential areas; that Falconer had been his secretary; that no one else had been present at the time of the slaying; and that the crime had been committed, in Falconer's words, "during a moment of blind fury." We had no idea as to motive, and we hadn't been prepared at all for the nature of the murder weapon.

Falconer kept on blinking as Crane and I approached and stopped on either side of him, but his eyes did not seem to be seeing anything in the room. I thought maybe he'd gone into delayed shock, but when I said his name, his head jerked up and the eyes focused on me.

I said, "You want to tell us about it, Falconer?" We'd already apprised him of his rights, and he had waived his privilege of presence of counsel during questioning.

"I murdered Asher," he said. "I already told you that. At first I thought of trying to cover it up, make it look as though a burglar had done it. But I'm not a very good liar, even though I've had a lot of practice. Besides, I . . . I don't much care what happens to me from now on."

"Why did you kill him?" Crane asked.

Falconer shook his head—not so much a refusal to answer as a reluctance or inability to put voice to the reason. We would get it out of him sooner or later, so there was no point in trying to force it.

I said, "Why the skull, Mr. Falconer? Where did you get a thing like that?"

He closed his eyes, popped them open again. "Asher kept it on the shelf behind his desk. He was sitting at the desk when I . . . when I did it."

"He kept a human skull in full view in his study?" Crane's tone was incredulous. "What the hell for?"

"He had a macabre sense of humor. He claimed to enjoy the reactions of visitors when they saw it. It was his *memento mori*, he said."

"His what?"

"Reminder of death," Falconer said.

"That sounds pretty morbid to me."

"Philip Asher was a fearless, cold-blooded man. Death never both-

313

ered him in the least. In one sense, it was his life; he devoted his life to the dead."

Crane and I exchanged glances. "You'd better explain that," I said.

"He was an anthropologist, quite a renowned one," Falconer said. "He published several books on the Mayan and Aztec races, and was in great demand as a lecturer and as a consultant to various university anthropological departments specializing in pre-Columbian studies."

"You were his full-time secretary, is that right?"

"Yes. I helped him with research, accompanied him on his expeditions to the Yucatán and other parts of Mexico and Central America, correlated his notes, typed his book manuscripts and business correspondence."

"How long did you work for him?"

"Eight years."

"Do you live here?"

"Yes. I have a room in the south wing."

"Does anyone else live in this house?"

"No. Asher never remarried after his wife left him several years ago. He had no close relatives."

Crane said, "Did you premeditate his death?"

"I didn't plan to kill him today, if that's what you mean."

"The two of you had an argument, then?"

"No, there wasn't any argument."

"Then what triggered this murderous rage of yours?" I asked.

He started to shake his head again, and then slumped backward bonelessly. His eyes seemed to be looking again at something not in the room.

At length he said, "It was a . . . revelation."

"Revelation?"

A heavy sigh. "I received a letter yesterday from another anthropologist I'd met through Asher," he said, "asking me to become his personal secretary at a substantial increase in salary. I considered the offer, and this morning decided that I couldn't afford to turn it down. But when I talked to Asher about it, he refused to accept my resignation. He said he couldn't be certain of my continued silence if I were no longer in his employ or in his house. He ordered me to remain. He said he would take steps against me if I didn't . . ."

"Wait a minute," I said. "Your continued silence about what?"

"Something that happened six years ago."

"*What* something?"

He didn't speak again for several seconds. Then he swallowed and said, "The death of his wife and her lover at Asher's summer lodge on Lake Pontrain."

We stared at him. Crane said, "You told us a couple of minutes ago that his wife had left him, not that she was dead."

"Did I? Yes, I suppose I did. I've told the same lie, in exactly the same way, so many times that it's an automatic response. Mildred and her lover died at Lake Pontrain; that is the truth."

"All right—how did they die?"

"By asphyxiation," he said. "It happened on a Saturday in September, six years ago. Early that morning Asher decided on the spur of the moment to spend a few days at the lodge; the book he was writing at the time was going badly and he thought a change of scenery might help. He drove up alone at eight; I had an errand to do and then followed in my own car about an hour later. When I reached the lodge I found Asher inside with the bodies. They were in bed—Mildred, who was supposed to have been visiting a friend in Los Angeles, and the man. I'd never seen him before; I found out later he was an itinerant musician." Pause. "They were both naked," he said.

"What did Asher say when you walked in?"

"That he'd found them just as they were. The lodge had been full of gas when he arrived, he said, and he'd aired it out. A tragic accident caused by a faulty gas heater in the bedroom."

"Did you believe that?" I asked.

"Yes. I was stunned. I'd always thought Mildred above such a thing as infidelity. She was beautiful, yes—but always so quiet, so dignified . . ."

"Was Asher also stunned?"

"He seemed to be," Falconer said. "But he was quite calm. When I suggested we contact the authorities he wouldn't hear of it. Think of the scandal, he said—the possible damage to his reputation and his career. I asked what else we could do. I wasn't prepared for his answer."

"Which was?"

"He suggested in that cold, calculating way of his that we dispose of the bodies, bury them somewhere at the lake. Then we could concoct a story to explain Mildred's disappearance, say that she had moved out and gone back to Boston, where she was born. He insisted no one would question this explanation, because he and Mildred had few close friends and because of his reputation. As it happened, he was right."

"So you went along with this cover-up?"

"What choice did I have? I'm not a forceful man, and at the time I

315

respected Asher and his judgment. And as I told you, I was stunned. Yes, I went along with it. I helped Asher transfer the bodies to a promontory a mile away, where we buried them beneath piles of rocks."

Crane said, "So for six years you kept this secret—until today, until something happened this morning."

"Yes."

"These 'steps' Asher told you he'd take if you tried to leave his employ—were they threats of bodily harm?"

Falconer nodded. "He said he would kill me."

"Pretty drastic just to insure your silence about two accidental deaths six years ago."

"Yes. I said the same thing to him."

"And?"

"He told me the truth," Falconer said.

"That his wife and her lover *didn't* die by accident? That he'd murdered them?"

"That's right. He found them in bed together, very much alive; his massive ego had been wounded, the sin was unforgivable and had to be punished—that was how Philip Asher was. He knocked them both out with his fists. I suppose I would have seen evidence of that if I'd looked closely at the bodies, but in my distraught state I noticed nothing. Then he suffocated them with a pillow. I arrived before he could remove the bodies by himself, and so he made up the story about the faulty gas heater. If I hadn't believed it, if I hadn't helped him, he would have killed me too, then and there."

"Did he tell you that too?"

"Yes."

"So when you found out you'd been working for a murderer the past six years, that you'd helped cover up a cold-blooded double homicide, you lost control and picked up the skull and bashed his head in with it."

"No," Falconer said. "No, not exactly. I was sickened by his confession and by my part in the whole ugly affair; I loathed him and I wanted to strike back at him. But I'm not a violent man. It was his *second* revelation that made me do what I did."

"What was it, this second revelation?"

"Something else he'd done, a year after the murders. I don't know why he told me about it, except that he was quite mad. A mad ghoul." Falconer laughed mirthlessly. "Mad ghoul. It sounds funny, doesn't it? Like an old Bela Lugosi film. But that's just what Asher was, always poking around among the dead."

316

"Mr. Falconer—"

He let out a shuddering breath. "Asher's *memento mori* didn't come from Mexico, as I always believed; it came from that promontory at Lake Pontrain. I killed him, using the one fitting weapon for his destruction, when he told me I'd been working in that study of his all these years, *all these years*, with the skull of the only woman I ever loved grinning at me over his shoulder . . ."

# Mrs. Belcourt Draws a Bier

*by Alan Ritner Anderson*

Ching, the Chinese houseboy, found Mrs. Belcourt out on the moonlit terrace necking with a phony French count who grandly called himself Louis Henri Jean Pierre D'Valois.

Bowing, Ching said, "Dr. Orst, he call and say you phone sanitarium quick right away."

Wanda Belcourt languidly disengaged herself from D'Valois' ardent embrace. She was dreamy drunk. It showed in the glassiness of her pale blue eyes and the feverish redness of her cheeks. Voice savage, she said, "You stinking little rat! How many times do I have to tell you—"

"Excuse, please!" interrupted Ching impassively. "You say, Dr. Orst call, me tell you quick right away."

The name registered. Wanda Belcourt ran slim fingers through the glittering yellow curls of her upswept hair-do. The ruddiness faded from her cheeks and greyness spread out from the corners of her thin-lipped mouth.

"That's all!" she said jerkily.

Bowing, Ching backstepped into the house.

Pierre D'Valois' handsome face darkened with frustration and chagrin. He'd warmed Wanda Belcourt to the point where it would have been safe to ask for another hundred-dollar loan. Ching's announcement had destroyed the magic moment.

"What time is it?" she asked.

"Three," he replied sulkily after a glance at his wrist watch, added needlessly, "A.M."

In the faint moonglow, Mrs. Belcourt's eyes blazed with an unholy brightness. Her rapt, savage expression reminded D'Valois of a predatory animal after the kill. Shivering, he turned and glanced out across the formal gardens that sloped down to a young peach orchard.

"He's dead!" she cried, voice shrill with triumph.

"Who?"

"My husband. Why should Orst call at this hour if Larry hasn't died?" She hugged herself fiercely, said, "It's mine. All mine. The money, I mean."

D'Valois went cold with desperation. "If your husband is dead," he said, "you killed him."

There was a long, tense silence and far away they heard the hoot and rumble of a train. Wanda Belcourt stood ramrod-stiff and straight, and her eyes shaded from blue to indigo. Voice edged, she declared, "Larry was pronounced insane by a court of law. A judge committed him to the sanitarium on the advice of experts. However can that possibly make me at all responsible for his death?"

D'Valois decided that it was the opportune time to deliver his Sunday punch. He said, "Your so-called cousin, Frank Heath, talks too much when he's drunk. I understand that temporary insanity can be induced by secretly feeding the victim certain drugs."

"How droll!" said Mrs. Belcourt. "Frank has such a vivid imagination."

Pierre D'Valois went damp with nervous sweat. He took a stab in the dark. "Your husband has only been in the sanitarium two weeks. Perhaps if someone demands an autopsy . . ." He left the unfinished statement hang in mid-air.

Little flecks of blackness appeared in the pale blue of Wanda Belcourt's eyes, and her lips compressed into a thin, red line. In the moonlight the drops of sweat on her forehead looked like glass beads.

Seeing that the blow had scored, D'Valois, bored in, said, "Look, I'm twenty-six. You're thirty-three. We can get married and establish a residence in California where property is split fifty-fifty when a couple gets a divorce."

Mrs. Belcourt moistened her cold lips with the tip of her tongue. The stiffness went out of her shoulders. "You may have something," she confessed.

"Think it over," D'Valois urged. "As your husband, I would see that Frank Heath didn't make too much of a nuisance of himself."

Wanda Belcourt gave him a frosty smile, turned and walked stiff-leggedly into the spacious hallway where her spiked heels sank noiselessly into the thick nap of the wine-colored carpet. Sound and fury rolled out of the music room. The party was getting rowdy. Her guests were in a pattern—writers who never wrote, artists who couldn't paint, actors and actresses who'd done no better than a high school play. As she passed the archway, she saw Frank Heath sitting in an easy chair sipping champagne. He was a dumpy little man, pale and flabby, but his bald skull glittered with a pink sheen. He was morosely drunk, and tears beaded his eyelashes.

She entered the library and sat down behind the black gloss of the ebony desk. She said dramatically to the room at large,

"Oh, no, Dr. Orst!" She repeated it until she was sure her voice held just the right note of shocked tragedy and anguished grief. She dialed the sanitarium. One of the male attendants answered. She dropped her voice down to nervous apprehension. "This is Mrs. Lawrence Belcourt. Let me speak to Dr. Orst!"

There was a click, then Dr. Orst's thick voice came on the line. "I have bad news," he said. "Very bad news."

She fought down her fierce exaltation. "So I surmised. I am prepared."

Dr. Orst took a deep, gusty breath. "Your husband escaped an hour ago."

There was a sudden surflike roaring in Wanda Belcourt's ears, and chills marched up her spine on spidery feet. She gripped the handset until her knuckles whitened. "No! No!" She heard herself say. "No! It's not possible. You told me—"

"It couldn't happen in a hundred years," interrupted Dr. Orst, speaking fast. "The gardener piled hay for a mulch against the outside wall of the main building. Your husband leaped from a third-floor window. The hay broke his fall. I'm in touch with the state police. Your husband was seen entering the woods that adjoin your estate. The police have posted a trooper at the gate. Your husband can't climb the wall that surrounds your place. So you are perfectly safe."

Mrs. Belcourt's panic abated, and her eyes slitted with sly cunning. "Keep me informed!" she ordered crisply and replaced the phone with a steady hand. She lit a cigarette, took a reflective inhale, then plumed the smoke ceilingward.

The sanitarium was less than a mile away. She had selected it to give the impression that she was a devoted wife who wanted her mentally sick husband as near to her as possible. Her restive eyes surveyed the room. She got up and went to the French doors that opened on a flagstone walk. They were locked. She unlatched a door and opened it out an inch. Then she pulled the blue drapes closed.

Back at the desk, she opened the center drawer and took out the .22 target pistol that was her husband's pride and joy. Small arms were his hobby. There was a target range in the basement, one outdoors beside the miniature golf course. Wanda Belcourt had taken up pistol marksmanship with a ghoulish zest, seeing in it the opportunity to stage an accident that would make her a widow. Unfortunately, servants had always been present to care for weapons and targets.

The plan had blossomed in her brain so crystal clear, with details dovetailing so perfectly, that she had the illusion that she was about to enact a role in a well-rehearsed play. There was an oak door in the wall that surrounded the estate. The little-used entry was a quarter-mile from the main gate, just beyond a curve in the highway and opposite a gasoline service station that closed at midnight.

There was a tooled leather cigar box on the desk top. She emptied the cigars into the drawer, placed the pistol in the box, closed the lid and tucked the container under her left arm. She went out into the hallway just as Ching came out of the music room with an empty tray.

"Go to bed!" she ordered him, shouting to be heard above the tumult of the party.

Ching bowed and hurried back toward the kitchen. Pierre D'Valois came in from the terrace, smirking with triumph. He walked up to Mrs. Belcourt, gripped her bare shoulders and laid his cheek next to hers.

"Is he . . . ?"

"Signed, sealed and delivered," she said. "I'm going to the sanitarium. You stay here. Keep the party rolling hot and heavy. Don't tell a soul!"

D'Valois frowned, suggested, "Don't you think it better . . ."

"Shut up!" she snapped. "If you want a ride on the gravy train, do as you're told!"

He shrugged doubtfully, glanced at the leather box under her arm, then smiled broadly. "The will, I presume," he said. She didn't reply, so he turned and walked airily into the music room.

In her gay blue and ivory bedroom, Wanda Belcourt changed to a black suit and covered the white of her throat with a deep blue scarf. She transferred the pistol to her biggest handbag, added a well-filled wallet, then got the key to the oak door from the pin tray on her vanity. Since the cigar container would be out of place in her bedroom, she filled it with handkerchiefs and put it on top of the dresser.

Ready to leave, she picked up the ivory phone on the bedside table and dialed the state police barracks.

320

"State police, Corporal Swale speaking," said a firm voice.

"This is Mrs. Lawrence Belcourt," she said. "I understand that my husband is hiding in Jessop's woods."

"He was seen going in there," Swale hedged. "We'll search the woods in the morning. In the meantime, I've posted a trooper at your gate. Your husband can't climb the wall, so you'll be perfectly safe."

"Are you sure he went into the woods?"

"Yes. A motorcycle patrolman spotted him."

"Thank you," she said, and hung up feeling warm and excited.

The kitchen was deserted. She left by the back porch and walked to the garage. Ghostly moonlight flooded the scene with a silvery radiance and towering shrubs cast elongated shadows. Heart hammering, she slipped behind the wheel of her black convertible. Even at that distance she could hear sounds of revelry from the music room.

The trooper at the gate was a robust young man very much on the alert. Eyes wary, he stopped six feet from the driver's side of the convertible.

"I'm Mrs. Belcourt," she explained with a red smile. "I'm going in town and stay at a hotel."

"You'd be all right," said the trooper. "Your husband can't climb the wall and I have this gate covered."

"I'll rest easier in a hotel room," she said, then asked idly, "What time is it?"

The trooper consulted his watch. "Five to four."

She gave him a tight nod of thanks and drove out on the highway. There wasn't a car in sight. She drove at a sedate 25 miles per hour and switched off the lights as soon as she rounded the curve. She eased the convertible across the concrete apron of the gas station and let it roll to a stop behind the main service building. The concealment was better than she had hoped.

She wormed off her high-heeled slippers, then frowned. She should have remembered to bring along an extra pair of nylons. The soles of her stockings would be worn away by the time she got back. She sneaked to the south end of the building. The road was deserted. The pavement was hot beneath her feet.

The heavy oak door was partly concealed by vines. The lock turned easily with the pressure of the key, but the hinges grated chatteringly, and her heart started trip-hammering. She sneaked into the ground and left the door ajar. Then she tossed the key into a pool of water some ten feet from the gravel path. It struck with a soft splash and a tiny geyser.

"The faithful Ching," she whispered to herself. "As soon as he

321

heard of his master's escape, he sneaked down and unlocked the door."

She made a complete circle around the house. The light in Ching's room above the kitchen was burning and she imagined that she saw his shadow on the wall. Indianlike, she approached the music room by rushing from shrub to shrub and keeping where the shadows were deepest. Both windows of the music room were open and a profusion of bushes along the outer wall offered excellent concealment. She crouched beneath a window. The ceiling fixture was off and floor lamps diffused a soft orange glow throughout the room. The radio was waging a losing battle with a group of brassy males voices trying to harmonize on *How Dry I Am*.

She had to lock her jaws to keep her teeth from chattering as she lifted her head and peeked over the sill. She was in luck. Pierre D'Valois was slumped in a chair near the window studying the glowing end of his cigar with the rapt, dreamy expression his face acquired when he sank into a pleasant speculation of money matters. Frank Heath sat on an end of a davenport with his feet cocked up on the coffee table. The red-headed girl next to him sat leaning over the coffee table trying unsuccessfully to build some sort of a structure out of safety matches.

Wanda Belcourt got out the pistol and pumped a shell into the firing chamber. She steadied her hand and selected Pierre D'Valois as the first target. Her slim fingers took up the trigger slack.

The voices of the male chorus climbed up on a high note and hung there.

She fired. Magically, it seemed, Pierre D'Valois' forehead blossomed a red rose. The sharp thunder of the report had cut through the other noises in the room and some of the guests were staring around in bleary-eyed wonder. Frank Heath's pale face stood out like a beacon. The second shot caught him between the eyes, whipping his head back and jerking his arms. D'Valois was an inert heap on the floor.

Mrs. Belcourt faded back into the shadows. A woman's strident scream shattered the comparative silence of the night air. The singing ceased. Someone turned the radio off. The hushed calm was like the sudden silence after the fury of a thunder storm.

Frightened by the leather-lunged shrieks of the hysterical woman which could be heard by the trooper at the gate, Mrs. Belcourt lifted her skirt to her thighs and ran a zig-zag course between the shrubs and bushes of the garden. She reached the oak door panting for breath and tingling with apprehension. There were no soles left in her nylons and her feet were swollen and sore from rocks and gravel. She felt each foot anxiously, fearing a cut that would have left a blood spoor. But she'd suffered no cut, just bruises.

She reached the convertible without incident and slipped behind the wheel. Her swollen feet made her slippers painfully tight. Driving from the station, she waited until she saw an oncoming car in the distance before she turned on the lights. Halfway across the three-mile straightaway that crossed a swamp, she braked to an abrupt stop and hurled the pistol off to her right. It struck with a soft *plop* and in the glare from the headlights, she saw the weapon sink from sight in the muck.

She parked the car outside the main entrance of the hotel and grandly told the doorman to have it stored in the garage.

Safe within the privacy of the suite, Mrs. Belcourt undressed and sat on the edge of the bathtub soaking her aching feet. The hastily conceived plan had worked to perfection. In due time she would become either a widow or the wife of a man put away for life. Either way, she would come into possession of immense wealth, and with Pierre D'Valois and Frank Heath rotting in their graves, there would be no staggering blackmail payments to make.

She switched off the lights and climbed into bed. Faced with physical inactivity, her nerves tightened and worrying thoughts clouded her brain. The soleless stockings distressed her. Had the trooper at the gate run to the house after the double kill? Could Ching establish an air-tight alibi? She rallied, mentally rehearsed her story until she had it letter perfect.

The police came at five. They phoned from the lobby and gave her plenty of time to dress. She needed it. Even so, the soleless stockings refused to drape her ankles neatly. She lighted a smoke because she handled a cigarette with graceful flourishes that captivated men and which would draw attention away from her ankles.

There were two detectives. One was tall and lean, had a sad grey face dominated by a jutting jaw. His companion was short and stocky. Contrary to expectations, both removed their hats.

The tall one said, "Your husband was captured an hour ago."

"Where?" she asked warily.

The tall man sighed, said, "I'm not going to drag this out and play cat and mouse. You can add. Your husband escaped from the sanitarium wearing a strait-jacket. He was captured wearing a strait-jacket. A

323

man in a strait-jacket is on a par with a person with both arms cut off at the shoulders. Let's go, Mrs. Belcourt."

The words of Dr. Orst, Corporal Swale and the trooper at the gate marched through her memory on leaden feet. "Your husband can't climb the wall," they had all asserted with conviction. She should have asked why.

# Murder at Rose Cottage

*by Edward D. Hoch*

The threatening letters started arriving a month before the murder, and it was those that first brought Inspector Greene to the little English village of Merryside, nestled upon the Avon not far from Stratford. The autumn had been warm, and it was almost like a summer's day when he first visited Rose Cottage where Major Wen lived with his sister Grace.

"You came all the way from London!" Major Wentworth greeted him. "Didn't think my problems were that important."

"Death threats are always important, Major. The village constable requested our assistance." Inspector Greene settled into a comfortable chair by the window. "I believe this letter of October 5th is the first you received: *Major Wentworth—you must pay for the sins of your youth! Prepare to die in one month's time!* And it's unsigned, of course."

"But mailed right here in Merryside," Grace Wentworth pointed out. "That's what especially disturbed my brother. He has no enemies here." She was a slim woman, somewhat shorter than her brother and lacking his obvious charm. Inspector Greene imagined she spent much of her time tending the garden he'd glimpsed at the rear of the house.

"Were you indeed living in Merryside during your sinful youth?" he asked lightly. "The second and third letters also mention it."

"I grew up here," the major confirmed, "but of course I went away to school. I came back in the summers."

"Girl friends?" Inspector Greene asked.

The major hesitated and his sister answered for him. "Elizabeth Jennings. She still lives here and she's a bit touched at times since her husband died. Do you think she could be—?"

324

"I'll talk to her," Greene said with a smile. "Thank you for your time, and try not to worry about this. We'll get to the bottom of it."

The local constable was named Cedric Sloane, and he'd rung up Scotland Yard for help when the major's sister first told him of the threatening letters. "I'm only good at handling weekend drunks and stray dogs," he told Greene. "I knew I needed help on this one. Got any ideas?"

"I want to see a woman named Jennings—Elizabeth Jennings."

"Sure—I should have thought of her. I remember she was a beautiful girl. The major used to come down from Cambridge in his fancy car and take her to country dances. That was forty years ago and I was eighteen. I've married and raised a family since then."

"I'll have a talk with her," Greene said.

"Her mind's a bit wobbly since her husband died of a heart attack last year. You'd best be gentle with her."

"I'm gentle with everyone, except murderers."

Elizabeth Jennings still retained some of her youthful beauty, and she greeted Inspector Greene at the door with a winning smile. "You're investigating what?" she asked, still smiling. "Anonymous letters? Heaven help us—I thought Scotland Yard was busy with terrorists and murderers!"

"This could be murder. Major Wentworth's life has been threatened."

"Wentworth—yes. That would be Charlie Wentworth. I knew him in my youth, you see. A good man, even if he did bad things at times." Her expression was just a bit vague.

"What sort of bad things?" Greene asked.

"Oh, you know. He was at the university then. It was just after the war and everyone was so relaxed. He talked of marriage and I was foolish enough to believe him. I wasn't alone. His own sister had romantic troubles too. But when Charlie left me it was quite a blow. He told me after a party on Guy Fawkes Day."

Greene glanced at the wall calendar. "That's coming up next week. It will be the 40th anniversary of your parting."

"Not something to celebrate, is it?"

"That depends. Have you been threatening Major Wentworth?"

"Of course not! I wouldn't harm the dear man."

On the way out of town Greene paused to talk with Major Wentworth's neighbor, a middle-aged farmer named Paul McCrae. "Ever notice anyone prowling around the Wentworth place?"

McCrae scratched his head. "Haven't seen anybody. Grace does all the gardening, so I see her, but the major stays indoors. They keep to themselves since he retired from the army. She goes out on Wednesday afternoons, but he sticks close to home."

"Thanks for your help," Greene said, and drove off toward London.

It was the following Tuesday when Constable Sloane phoned from Merryside. Greene had all but forgotten it was Guy Fawkes Day. "We need you, sir," the excited voice told him. "There's been a murder at Rose Cottage."

"Major Wentworth?"

"No, sir. It's his sister Grace who's been killed."

The body had been removed by the time Inspector Greene reached Rose Cottage hours later, but Constable Sloane's car was still parked out front. The neighbor, Paul McCrae, was just leaving the house. "A terrible thing," he said, shaking his head. "The woman hadn't an enemy in the world."

"Where did it happen?" Greene asked.

"Out in her garden. Someone shot her from behind while she was picking the last of her vegetables. I heard the shot myself, but thought it was a hunter."

Inside, Greene found Constable Sloane with the major, trying to comfort him. "Tell me what happened," he said. "Had there been more threatening letters?"

The major shook his head. "Not since your visit. We were hoping that was over with. Grace went out in the garden just after breakfast to pick her vegetables. It was a damp morning and she slipped on one of my hunting jackets that was hanging by the back door. Could the killer have mistaken her for me?" His voice broke as he said it.

"It's likely," Constable Sloane replied. "She was much smaller than you, but it was misty out earlier. A frightened killer might have fired without thinking, seeing only a bent-over figure."

"Major Wentworth, do you remember anything that happened forty years ago today?" Greene asked.

"What? Forty years is a long time. It would have been my last year at Cambridge. I don't remember anything else."

"Elizabeth Jennings says you jilted her that night, after a Guy Fawkes party. Do you remember now?"

"Elizabeth—My God, do you think she wrote those letters?"

"It's a possibility. Tell me something else—did you or your sister discuss those letters with anyone? Your neighbor Paul McCrae, for example?"

"No one. It wasn't the sort of thing one bragged about."

"So only the two of you and the writer of the letters knew about them?"

"I suppose that's so."

Inspector Greene nodded. "I'll want to call on Elizabeth Jennings again," he told the constable. "Then I believe I'll have a solution to our mystery."

Elizabeth opened the door as he got out of the car. "I knew you'd be coming again," she said. "I heard someone killed Grace Wentworth."

Greene nodded and stepped inside. "You wrote those letters, didn't you. Mrs. Jennings?"

"I—"

"After your husband died you began to brood about the time when Charlie left you, forty years ago."

"I wrote them, yes," she admitted suddenly. "I must have been crazy. But I stopped after your visit last week. I didn't kill Grace."

"I believe you," he said after a moment's thought. "It was a known fact that Grace did all the gardening and the major stayed inside. Their neighbor told me that. No one could have mistaken her, even in the mist. Major Wentworth wasn't the intended victim. The killer was after Grace Wentworth and he got her. He used your letters to cover his real motive. That's why he struck on Guy Fawkes Day, hoping you'd be blamed."

He asked her one more question and then departed. Constable Sloane's car had pulled up behind his on the road outside. "Thought you might need help in making the arrest," Sloane said.

Inspector Greene shook his head. "The major wasn't the intended victim."

"You think he wrote the letters to himself and then killed his own sister?"

Greene shook his head. "Elizabeth Jennings wrote the letters, and that gave the killer the whole idea. But it wasn't Major Wentworth. He wouldn't have shot Grace in the garden where it was known he never ventured, not if he wanted to keep alive the idea of a mistaken victim. And I don't really think he remembered the significance of Guy Fawkes Day until I reminded him."

"Then who—?"

"The killer had to be someone who was here at the time Wentworth jilted Elizabeth Jennings, who saw that date on the first letter—October 5th—and realized the threat was for Guy Fawkes Day, one month later. He remembered what happened that day because he was

327

dating young Grace Wentworth at the time. I think they remained lovers, off and on, to the present time, though he had a wife and family. I suspect they met secretly when she went off alone on Wednesday afternoons. Maybe she decided it was time he left his wife. For whatever reason, he wanted to be rid of her for good. When he realized the meaning of those letters, he killed her on Guy Fawkes Day, hoping to blame Elizabeth Jennings."

"I don't—"

"The killer had to know about those letters, yet Wentworth said they told no one. Of course they did tell one person, Constable Sloane. They told you."

Cedric Sloane slumped forward. "You know."

"I know," Inspector Greene agreed. "Elizabeth Jennings just confirmed that you were Grace's suitor when they were young. You tried to remove suspicion from yourself by asking Scotland Yard for help, but you got more of it than you bargained for. I'm arresting you for murder."

# Murderer's Handicap

*by Alex Barber*

Gerald Beauchamp crumpled the letter savagely into a ball, and flung it with violence into the fire.

"Fifty pounds in three days!" he bit out venomously. "Well, he won't get it! The swine will have to wait!"

But even as he said it, he knew the truth. Hackett would not wait for the money. He would get it in three days, as he demanded—or he would strike, as a snake strikes.

Beauchamp stood there, rigid, staring down into the fire, an elegant man of perhaps thirty-five, with pale yellow hair brushed sleekly back, and rather protuberant blue eyes.

Gradually his pose slackened. A curious gleam came into his eyes. He lit a cigarette, and puffed out a cloud of smoke.

After all, it wasn't as if he was unprepared for this crisis, was it? It simply meant that a certain plan, which might not have proved necessary, would have to be adopted.

He took a deep breath.

"Murder!" he murmured, gazing at his cigarette with narrowed eyes.

He glanced at the gold watch on his wrist.

"Just time to get a note off to Hackett. And then—"

He dropped into a chair at the oval oak table near the fire. Writing materials were ready to his hand, for it was here that he wrote his murder-mystery novels and short stories. The deep leather chair at the end of the hearthrug was ideal for pondering plots, but too luxurious for the actual writing.

When he had finished his brief reply to the blackmailer's message, he slipped the envelope into his pocket, and rose, smiling confidently. But on his way to the door, a sharp sound brought him to a halt. Frowning, he crossed quickly to the window. Looking out through the leaded panes, he bit out an oath.

A homely woman of generous dimensions, with a figure like a loaf of bread, was waddling up the red-brick path between the lawns. Her round, happy face beamed with good-nature. Even her hat, a remarkable creation in what appeared to be antique green plush, with a jaunty feather wobbling precariously at the rear, had a happy sort of look.

Beauchamp strode angrily to the front door, and pulled it open just as the caller reached it.

"Ooh! 'Ow you did make me jump, Mr. Beauchamp! I didn't know you'd seen me coming!"

Mrs. Plucknett beamed at him with the motherly affection which she bestowed impartially, out of the infinite resources of her heart, on all human beings and most dogs, cats and canaries.

"You'll excuse me taking the liberty, I'm sure," she went on, fortified by a few gasping breaths, "but I always think a nome isn't a nome without you 'as a few flowers about, like. I know gentlemen like yourself can't be bothered seeing after flowers, but I thought, when old Wally Burchell come round today, I thought, 'There now,' I thought, 'if some o' them roses of his wouldn't be just all right for Mr. Beauchamp—and 'im all on 'is own, miles from nowhere, with nobody or nothink to cheer 'im up!' So I got these few."

She began plucking at the top of the newspaper cone which she was carrying.

"Beggin' your pardon for the liberty, sir," she added. "I 'ope you don't mind."

Gerald Beauchamp returned her motherly smile with a cold stare.

"I thought I engaged you, Mrs. Plucknett," he said frigidly, "for duties that finished immediately after lunch. If you want to know, I am

329

extremely annoyed at being disturbed like this at this hour. Good night!" And he stepped back, preparatory to closing the door.

"Oh, dear!" Mrs. Plucknett's face fell. "Oh, I'm sorry, sir, I'm sure." But she was not to be defeated without a struggle. Her good-hearted impulse to brighten the place up a bit for him was still strong in her, despite her reception. "Anyway," she pleaded, "you'll let me put them on your table for you now I've come, won't you, sir? It won't take me a tick. And they're lovely roses. You see, Wally Burchell, he used to be gardener to—"

"Mrs. Plucknett," broke in Beauchamp angrily, "I have already told you I dislike being interrupted." A sudden thought struck him, and he added, with marked emphasis: "I am writing. I shall be writing *all the evening*. If you must leave the flowers, come in and put them on my table—but for God's sake don't keep on babbling about them!"

And turning on his heel, he ran upstairs to the bathroom, and jerked savagely at the taps over the wash basin. Mrs. Plucknett or no Mrs. Plucknett, he had to get his face ready for the grease-paint.

Half an hour later, he had changed into a commonplace suit of cheap cloth and atrocious cut, and put on a pair of heavy boots. His face became grimmer when at length he drew on a pair of cheap woolen gloves.

"No finger-prints," he said slowly.

He went downstairs. Mrs. Plucknett, he knew, had gone. In the room that served as his study, he drew the heavy curtains across the window, lighted the hanging lamp, and stood the wire guard in front of the fire.

"That's everything, I think."

As he paused in the doorway for a final glance, his gaze flickered to the splash of deep red on his writing-table. Grudgingly he admitted that the old girl was right. They were certainly a lovely color, those roses.

He let himself out of the house by the backdoor, which he locked softly behind him. The back garden ended on the edge of a hazel copse. Soon he was slipping cautiously between the slender stems, to emerge presently on a path. His face looked rather strained, but he had himself well in hand for the grim task that lay before him.

As he strode along, his thoughts reverted to Mrs. Plucknett. Really, not half a bad thing that she had come over this evening! He knew she "charred" at Superintendent Jordan's place, in Keynesford Heath. And being incurably talkative, what could be more likely than that she should mention this evening's visit to Mrs. Jordan, who was well known for her habit of encouraging gossip from her "helps"? At any rate, there was more than a chance that the superintendent would hear of the visit. And if he did, and questioned Mrs. Plucknett, what would he learn?

"She'll tell him what I said," mused Beauchamp, grinning. "She'll explain that I was short with her for interrupting me at my work. And ten to one she'll remember what I said about intending to go on writing all the evening. Of course, it will be no proof that I did so—but every little helps, in the way of corroborative evidence!"

For an hour and a half he followed the winding path through the woods. Finally he reached a clearing, crossed it, and rapped on the back door of an old half-timbered cottage not unlike his own. It was opened, after a little delay, by a scholarly old man who peered at him over large, gold-rimmed spectacles.

"Who is it?" he demanded sharply. "What do you want?"

"It's only me, sir," said Beauchamp reassuringly; and he pulled off the cap which had shadowed his face.

"Good gracious, so it is!" exclaimed the old man, blinking in astonishment. "Come in, Gerald, my boy, come in! What in the name of goodness are you got up like that for, hey?"

"Just a sort of tryout for a murder story of mine, sir. I've come to see what you think of the plot."

Seated in a comfortable chair in the old man's cosy study, Beauchamp continued his explanation. Whilst he spoke, he was studying Sir Ephriam—the spare figure, the wizened, pear-shaped face narrowing down from the shining dome of his bald head to a tiny chin, the bright eyes, with their rather fanatical gleam—and the thin, stringy neck. It was going to be easy. As easy as puffing out a candle!

"A murderer," said Beauchamp thoughtfully, "suffers from the handicap of having to do his work perfectly—there must be nothing unprovided for. But to my way of thinking the way to achieve perfection is not by working out a multitude of details. What sort of job does one do best? A simple one. And that's the line I'm going on in this—this story."

"Simplicity is safety, hey?"

"Exactly, sir. And it occurred to me that if I used characters like ourselves, I could test my plot by, well"—Beauchamp laughed lightly—"shall I say a rehearsal? So I made myself the murderer, and you, sir, the victim!"

He laughed again, rather harshly. How hot this grease-paint made one's face feel!

Still, the brown complexion of a countryman had been a necessary adjunct to his rough clothes.

"The devil you did!" said Sir Ephriam. "So I'm to be the corpse, hey?" And he went off into a thin cackle of laughter that jarred on Beauchamp's strained nerves.

To cover his momentary agitation, Beauchamp hurried on:

"You see, it's all quite simple. There is a wealthy but rather eccentric knight, of about your own age. After the death of his wife, to whom he was intensely devoted, he chose to lead a life of scholarly retirement. He settled down, as you have done, in a simple country cottage, without ostentation, without even servants—alone with his beloved books."

"Was he," inquired Sir Ephriam, rather wistfully, "like me, looking forward to being with his wife again? Did he feel sure—as I do—that she would be there to meet him, when he went through that gate called Death? Or was he one of these stupid people who think it rather clever not to believe in God and the after-life?"

"I—I don't know," said Beauchamp hurriedly. "I hadn't thought about that point." He stirred uneasily in his chair before proceeding. "Anyway, like you, he struck up a friendship with a man half his age, an author. And in the course of a couple of years, his affections, which would normally have found expression in love for his wife— had she lived—and in a number of friendships if he had stayed in society—these affections came to a focus on this author-friend of his. So much so, in fact, that the old man altered his will. Instead of leaving his considerable fortune entirely to certain charities, he divided it equally between those charities and his young friend. And, having no reason to be secretive about it, he told the fortunate legatee what he had done."

"So far," remarked Sir Ephriam, "you seem to have kept strictly to the facts concerning ourselves. Where does the fiction part come in, hey? Must do your job, you know!" Again that thin chuckle which Beauchamp found almost intolerably jarring tonight.

## II

"I'm coming to that now," replied the author, forcing a smile and hoping that it looked less strained than it felt. "You see, this writer chap was a bad hat. Went in for gambling, belonged to one or two dubious so-called clubs in town, and lived—well, an immoral life.

"The old boy knew nothing of all this. How should he? He was buried down in the Sussex countryside. Besides, the author had a way of being discreet about his—er—pleasures. He knew that the old man had a strong religious streak, and would disapprove pretty thoroughly of his goings-on.

"In fact," said Beauchamp slowly, "there was no doubt whatever in his mind that if once the truth got to the old man's ears, he would be cut out of the will. That nice little half-share in a fortune would be gone—like that!" And he snapped his fingers.

Sir Ephriam was peering at him in a puzzled way beneath lowered eyebrows. To avoid questions, Beauchamp hurried on:

"The rest you can imagine without much trouble. A certain unsavory little man up in town gets to know too much, and puts the screw on this author laddie—threatens to expose him to the old boy, you understand. A rather nasty position. For a while it works all right, but there comes a time when the author can't pay.

"His pleasures are apt to be expensive, and perhaps he isn't turning out so much literary work, as a result of them. The blackmailer finds he doesn't receive a particular payment he was expecting. He turns ugly, issues an ultimatum. Fifty pounds in three days! And"—Beauchamp licked his lips, which felt hot and dry—"the author knows he can't possibly pay!"

He paused, breathing rather noisily.

"An extremely interesting situation," nodded Sir Ephriam. "I think I can see what comes next. The author murders the old man. He would be in a favorable position to do so—because he, too, lives alone, if he's like you. And, of course, he is known to be the old fellow's one friend—the one man who should be least likely to have committed the crime. As for the blackmailer, let me see—"

"The blackmailer," said Beauchamp softly, with a queer smile, "will have no hold left. His information has no market value when the old man is dead. The most he could do would be to reveal the author's immoral life to the police. But why should he? It won't convict the author of murder, and it means running the risk of being landed himself as a blackmailer. Even anonymous letters have been known to be traced. What is more, this particular blackmailer happens to have good reasons for not getting mixed up with the police. No, he'll see that his goose has given up laying golden eggs, and he'll get busy in safer and more profitable ways than writing spiteful letters to Scotland Yard.

"And so, as you have said, sir, the author is in a good position. He will be questioned, naturally. But suppose he says, 'I was at home all the evening. I was busy writing.' Well, why should anyone doubt it?

There is a faint chance, though it's most unlikely, because he hasn't encouraged callers, that someone might come to his house while he is out.

"They will see the light, but will get no answer when they knock. Why? 'I was writing a passage at white-heat—positively inspired,' says the author. 'Someone knocked at the door, you say? I shouldn't have noticed if they'd smashed it down!' The same applies to any telephone call. Everyone knows what authors are. So there you are! What do you think of it?"

"Very good," said Sir Ephriam, frowning. "Yes, undoubtedly a clever story. But I don't see why you should bother to come over here, dressed up like that, for what you call a rehearsal. It doesn't seem to me necessary, or even useful."

Beauchamp laughed.

"Perhaps it wasn't," he said gaily, rising. "But it helps my imagination. And there was just one thing I couldn't be sure of unless I actually tried it."

He crossed the hearthrug, and stood behind Sir Ephriam's chair.

"You see," he pursued, "the murderer has a talk with his victim. That enables him to make quite sure that there is no one else in the house—a most improbable thing, but just as well to be sure.

"Well, when he knows that everything is safe, he gets behind his victim's chair—like this. So far, so good. But what I want to know," said Beauchamp, in a curious whisper, "is whether the victim can be prevented from uttering any cry. That's what I want to know."

"Oh, I shouldn't think there would be much danger of that," said Sir Ephriam.

There wasn't. Beauchamp's gloved hands saw to that . . .

# III

Gerald Beauchamp rose late, as usual, next morning. He had fried two rashers of bacon and an egg for his breakfast, and was halfway through the process of consuming them, in the sunny little dining room, when Superintendent Jordan arrived with the news that Sir Ephriam Yardley had been found murdered in his study.

"Sir Ephriam? Good heavens, Super, what are you saying? Why—why, he was my best friend! You can't mean—"

That break in his voice—admirable!

"Brutally and foully murdered," said the big superintendent sav-

334

agely. "An old man that wouldn't have hurt a fly. The slug that did it deserves to swing, all right!"

Beauchamp sank into a chair. His emotion was not all acting. His legs felt suddenly weak. His heart was pounding madly.

"It's upsetting," he blurted out. "My best friend—"

"Quite so," said the superintendent, stroking his square chin thoughtfully.

Later, when Beauchamp was calmer, he faced the anticipated questions. The superintendent cross-examined him.

"We have to check up on people, you know, sir. Matter of routine."

"I quite understand, Super. Well, as a matter of fact I was in all last evening. I was busy writing in the room next to this."

"You didn't leave the house at all?"

"No."

"How long would you have been writing?"

"Several hours. I do, you know, when I feel just right for it. To be exact," added Beauchamp, caressing his plump cheek reflectively, "I was writing from the time Mrs. Plucknett came over—she happened to come with some flowers—until I went to bed at about half past eleven."

"I heard about Mrs. Plucknett coming over," nodded the superintendent. "She cleans up for us before she comes to you in the morning, and—well, there, women will talk! Brought you some flowers for your writing-table, didn't she?"

Beauchamp drew a long breath. This was better! The super was actually getting chatty! Evidently no suspicion.

"Why, yes," he smiled. "Some remarkably fine roses."

"Been in to give them any water this morning?" inquired Superintendent Jordan casually.

Beauchamp shook his head, with a faint smile.

"I never think of things like that. No doubt Mrs. Plucknett will give them water, as and when they require it. As a matter of fact, I haven't been in my study yet, this morning."

"Ah!" said the superintendent. "I wondered. I rather hoped you hadn't—in case I was right."

He stepped smartly forward. Beauchamp stared stupidly, as a heavy hand came down on his shoulder.

"Gerald Beauchamp," said the superintendent grimly, "I arrest you for the willful murder of Sir Ephriam Yardley, and I warn you that anything you say may be taken down and used as evidence at your trial!"

At the police station in Keynesford Heath, they got what they wanted. Beauchamp broke down, as he had known he would if it reached this stage. For one thing, arrest meant a search which would reveal the grease paint and clothes hidden in his wardrobe, things for which there was no innocent explanation. But then—it was a crime which never ought to have come to this!

When he had dictated and signed his confession, he turned savagely on the superintendent.

"You clever devil!" he bit out. "You couldn't have known I was lying about last evening!"

Superintendent Jordan returned the savage glare with a look of stern satisfaction. He was not afflicted with sentimentality where deliberate, brutal murderers were concerned.

"I should have believed you, I daresay, but for one thing. Those flowers. Of course, you might have known—but there was a chance you wouldn't, I realized. That's why I asked you if you'd given them water. Your answer told me you *didn't* know!"

Beauchamp was trembling now.

"Flowers? I don't know what you mean!" Suddenly his voice rose. "You devil," he screamed, "what d'you mean, flowers?"

"Hold him," said Superintendent Jordan calmly. "What I mean, Beauchamp, is just this! You didn't give Mrs. Plucknett a chance to explain. She tried to, but you wouldn't let her. And my question told me you still hadn't found out, this morning—what was the matter with those flowers.

"Well, I know those roses of Wally Burchell's are pretty good—he was a gardener before he got past it. Yes, they're very good, those roses—but you didn't sit at the same table with them for a whole evening. If you had you would have found out they were *artificial roses* —*made of paper.* . . . Splash some water over his face, Hobson; that'll soon bring him round."

# Murder Offstage

*by R. L. Stevens*

There's no other way," Garrison Smith said, putting it into words for the first time. "One of us will have to kill him."

Paul Drayer let his eyes shift to the others, seeking their reaction to the words. As he'd expected, Cliff Contrell was already nodding agreement; but most surprising, Aster Martin was offering no objection. She sat at the end of the table in a sort of imperious indifference, as if their decision had no bearing at all on her, as if they were not about to commit murder to protect their good name.

"What do you think, Aster?" Paul asked, fixing her with his deep-set eyes. He wanted her to say it, to take a stand for once in her life.

"I suppose there's nothing else to be done," she answered with studied effect. "You're all in those pictures with me. It's not just my reputation we're talking about."

"Then it's decided," Garrison Smith intoned. Always the director, even when it came to directing a murder. "Which one of us shall it be?"

Cliff Contrell cleared his throat. "What are the appointment times?"

Smith consulted the handwritten notes on the table before him. "Contrell at two o'clock, Drayer at two thirty, and myself at three thirty. He wants $12,500 cash from each of us, in return for the negatives."

"I'm first," Contrell said, "so I guess it's up to me." He was always the leading man in every production, and he wasn't about to yield his position now.

But Paul interjected a word of caution. "How do you know he'll even have the negatives in his office? You might kill him for nothing and then where will we be? Where will Aster be?"

"On the front pages of every paper in the country," Aster answered, but she wasn't joking. "Personally, I don't think any one of you has the guts to kill him, but it's got to be done. You three can't go on paying blackmail forever."

"All right, all right!" Garrison Smith was directing again. "How's this? Contrell shows up at his office at two o'clock this afternoon and pays the $12,500. Then Paul meets him outside and finds out if the negatives are really in the office. If they are, Paul goes upstairs at two thirty, kills our blackmailing friend, and collects both the negatives and Cliff's money."

After a few minutes of discussion it was agreed. "What about me?" Aster Martin asked.

"You stay here and wait," Smith told her. "You've caused us enough trouble already."

Leonardo Flood was many things to many people. An aging matinee idol, darling of the gossip columnists, king of yesterday's jet set— and clever blackmailer. It was in this last role that Paul Drayer and the others knew him best. When *Morning Five* opened on Broadway and catapulted Aster Martin into overnight stardom, they had all been too busy to give a thought to the pictures, a harmless indiscretion that had been quickly forgotten. Forgotten, that is, by everyone except Leonardo Flood.

He had obtained the negatives—stolen them, really—and telephoned the three men involved: Garrison Smith, the director of *Morning Five*; Cliff Contrell, the male lead; and Paul Drayer, its author. His terms were quite simple—each of them would pay him $12,500 and the negatives would be returned. Otherwise, Broadway's newest darling would be revealed to the columnists as something considerably less than that.

Whatever else they might be, Paul and the other two were loyal to Aster Martin—and to the play, of course. Now, carrying a little .22 automatic in his pocket, Paul Drayer rode the elevator to Flood's dingy office and the 2:30 appointment. It was easily the hottest day of a muggy Manhattan summer, and already the moisture on Paul's brow was evidence that the old building lacked air conditioning.

He walked in on Leonardo Flood without knocking and found the gray-haired man seated in a wooden chair behind a plain wooden desk. There was a filing cabinet in one corner of the room, next to a single closed window, and an electric fan oscillated slowly on top of the cabinet. Otherwise, the room was as bare and dingy as the building itself.

"Ah!" the aging actor greeted him. "The second member of the Aster Martin Fan Club! I'm pleased to see you're punctual. I like my visitors in their proper order."

"I came for the other negatives, Flood," Paul told him.

338

"Of course! The price is $12,500 from each of you." The actor smiled and adjusted his soiled necktie. "Some girls would almost pay that much to have a nude photo published, I suppose—but then of course our Aster doesn't need that kind of publicity now that she's a star."

Paul showed him the gun. "The negatives, Flood. All the rest of them—no tricks—or you're a dead man. And I'll take Contrell's money while I'm at it."

Leonardo Flood kept smiling. "You mean the Fan Club would kill me for dear, dear Aster? Even that?"

"The negatives!"

"Suppose I tell you they aren't here?"

"I saw Contrell downstairs. He said you had him wait in the hall and you brought one out to him. I know they're in this room and I want them."

"It'll do you no good to kill me. You'll never find them."

"We'll see," Paul said, and he swung the little gun at Flood's temple, catching the actor with a blow that knocked him unconscious to the grimy floor.

Now he had to work fast. The negatives were on strips of 35mm. film—easy to hide, and not too hard to find. First the body, every inch of it, and the clothes, which yielded Contrell's money but nothing else. Paul checked Flood's necktie, and the soles of his shoes, and everywhere else. He went over every stitch twice, without success.

He tore into the desk next, upending drawers, poking at the legs and sides and back for hidden compartments. He checked the chair legs, and its bottom and back. He searched the meager contents of the filing cabinet, even carefully lifted the whirling black fan to look beneath its base. He opened the window to feel along the ledge and sides. What else? There was no telephone, no closet, not even a coat rack. Flood obviously used the office infrequently.

After twenty minutes Paul gave up. Flood was beginning to regain consciousness, and there was nothing further to be gained—not unless Paul was willing to go the limit and really kill the man. And he wasn't willing to go that far, not even for Aster Martin.

He went out and closed the door behind him.

The street was hot, muggy, and unbearable. He walked a block, then stopped at a corner drug store and drank something cool. At 3:10 by his watch he decided he should call Smith and report failure. But in the phone booth he could get no dial tone.

"What's the matter here?" he asked the counterman.

"The phones are jammed up. We just had a power failure and the whole area's knocked out. All those damned air conditioners!"

Paul sighed and sat down to wait. Fifteen minutes later, the drug store's fluorescent lights flickered back on and the afternoon's minor power crisis was ended. The telephone traffic dropped to normal and he made his call to Smith's office. No one answered. Obviously Smith had gone to keep his 3:30 appointment with Flood.

Paul drove back across town and parked his car in the lot next to the theater. Aster and Cliff were up in the director's office waiting for him, but there was no sign yet of Garrison Smith. "Did you find the negatives?" Aster asked him.

"No. I tore the damned office apart and didn't find a thing." He sank into the familiar chair and took out his cigarettes.

"But I know he had them!" Contrell insisted.

"Here's your money. At least I found that." He tossed the thick wad of bills on the table just as Garrison Smith walked in.

Smith was smiling slightly. "You did a nice job, Paul. I didn't think you had it in you."

"What do you mean?" Panic started deep in his stomach.

"Flood's dead, of course. You got him right between the eyes."

Paul Drayer stared at Smith with unbelieving eyes. "I didn't kill him," he said finally. "I knocked him out and searched the place, but didn't find anything. He was still alive when I left."

"Well, he's dead now," Smith said, and nobody doubted him.

"Someone else killed him, then. One of us."

Garrison Smith shrugged. "Does it matter? We're all in this together anyway."

"Maybe it does matter," Paul said. "Maybe it matters a lot. One of us killed Flood and that means one of us has the negatives. As long as that person keeps his secret, he could continue the blackmailing, posing as one of the victims."

"If you think I killed him—" Smith began.

And Cliff Contrell coughed nervously. "It certainly was not me, Paul. You know he was alive when I left him."

"It doesn't make sense," Aster Martin joined in, brushing the hair from her eyes. "How did the killer find the negatives if you couldn't find them, Paul?"

"I don't know," he admitted, speaking slowly. There was something in the back of his mind, something turning . . . "I left Flood, still alive, just before three. Smith's appointment wasn't till three thirty. That leaves a full half hour unaccounted for. If—"

340

Paul Drayer stopped speaking. The pieces had fallen into place.

"Well?" Smith prodded.

"Look—would a man with as orderly a mind as Leonardo Flood have blackmailed three people for $12,500 each, a total of $37,500? Odd amount for blackmail. Isn't it far more likely there was a fourth victim, and therefore a $50,000 jackpot? A nice round figure . . . That fourth victim could only have been you, Aster."

She gave a little gasp. "Me!"

Paul nodded. He was sure of himself now. "You didn't want us to know, first because of your pride, and second because maybe we'd have wanted you to pay the whole fifty grand. You wanted to seem completely innocent of the thing, especially if it led to murder. But you had an appointment with Leonardo Flood this afternoon too.

"At three o'clock," Contrell breathed.

"That's right," Paul said. "I got to thinking—why should Flood skip a half hour in his schedule? There were four half hours, and four of us involved. In fact, Flood actually told me he liked his visitors in their proper order. What order? Alphabetical, of course—Contrell at two, Drayer at two thirty, Aster Martin at three, and Smith at three thirty. You were supposed to be waiting here, Aster, but when I phoned at three twenty-five, nobody answered. You were on your way to Flood's office with your blackmail payment."

She smiled at him across the table, still the leading lady. "All right, suppose I did go there? I knew you wouldn't have the guts to kill him, so I went to pay him off. That doesn't prove I killed him."

"I think it does, Aster," he said softly. "Flood always spoke of us as your Fan Club, and I should have caught the hint long ago. The negatives were taped to the blades of his electric fan—in plain view but moving too fast to be seen. You were in the office at three, and there was a power failure in the area about that time. The fan stopped spinning, and you saw the negatives there before your eyes. You shot Flood and took them. Naturally you didn't tell us about it, since we were already set up to take the rap."

"All right," she said finally, wetting her lips with a darting tongue. "Are you going to tell the police?"

Paul Drayer glanced at the other two men and then back at Aster. He was smiling slightly. "If we keep quiet, Aster, what's it worth to you?"

# Murder on the Limited

*by Howard Finney*

A long wail from the engine's whistle rose above the vibrations of the pullmans as the Mississippi Limited peeled away the miles of western Ohio. It was the only reminder Stanley, the pullman conductor, had that there was anyone else awake on the Limited other than himself.

He glanced through the window of the men's smoking compartment and saw the lights of Bellefontaine rush up on their left and then drop behind. He set his watch back an hour to Central Standard time. Bellefontaine was the last point on Eastern time. What a break if he could do that with his own life—set it back and gain a handicap, as the Limited did.

Above the hum of steel on steel and the song of the wheels he heard the ring of the porter's buzzer at the other end of the car. Queer that—at this hour in the morning.

A moment later steps sounded in the vestibule and Jeb, the porter, pushed his head through the curtain. His black face, extra dark against the spotless white of his jacket, was set in a frown halfway between worry and fear.

"Boss, lady wants to see you. Lower Three—"

A woman pushed by him hastily, pulling a thin kimono about her nightgown. She was middle-aged and plump. Stanley recognized her. She and her husband had made the run from New York. Her white face and haggard eyes brought him to his feet.

"My husband's vanished—disappeared right before my eyes," she blurted huskily.

"Vanished?"

"Yes. He went to get me a drink of water and he hasn't come back."

The frown left Stanley's face for a moment.

"But my dear madam, why alarm yourself so quickly? Maybe he stepped out on a platform for a smoke. Take a look, Jeb."

As the porter went out, she pulled back a loose strand of hair from her gray face, and shook her head.

"No, no. You're wasting precious time," she half-whispered in a low, urgent tone. "He doesn't smoke. And the only place he would stop would be here. Something's happened to him, something strange. He vanished before my very eyes."

She shivered and clutched her kimono more tightly about her. It was chilly in the car this time of night. But Stanley saw in her face that it was more than the temperature that made her shiver and turn her stricken eyes toward the slightly swaying curtain to the corridor. He nodded for her to go on.

"He was coming down the aisle with a cup of water when he disappeared. It was so strange and sudden I thought I was dreaming at first.

"A few minutes after he had gone for the water, I looked through the curtain and saw him coming down the aisle with the cup in his hand. I pulled myself up in bed to take the water. A moment later, when I thought it strange he hadn't reached the berth, I looked out again. The aisle was empty. He'd vanished. It was just as though I'd never seen him there a minute before.

"The paper cup was lying in the middle of the car. I waited a few moments, thinking perhaps he'd spilled the water and gone back for more. But he didn't come and when I looked out again, the paper cup was gone too."

She glanced around the room and for an instant at the curtain, her features drawn and haunted.

The sinister import of her words stirred Stanley uneasily. Thirty years on the railroad had taught him to evaluate the excited demands of passengers for their true worth. But this woman's story was a new one, fantastic, and yet touched with truth.

The door of the vestibule slammed and he heard the voices of Kelley, the railroad conductor, and Hunt, the brakeman.

"Stay here and keep calm, Mrs. Saunders," he said evenly. "We'll look for him."

As he pushed through the curtains, he saw her fingers wandering instinctively over the tightly constricted cords of her neck, trying to shake back her steadily rising hysteria.

"This fellow Saunders has pulled a Houdini," he muttered to the two trainmen. "Vanished like a puff of smoke. It's a queer story."

Kelley nodded at the porter.

"He told us."

Stanley glanced toward the room.

"She's scared stiff. Got something on her mind she hasn't spilled yet. See what you can find out."

"O.K.", Kelley assented and slipped through the door.

Hunt peered into Stanley's face. "I don't like it," he ground out tensely.

Stanley turned away.

"We'll take a look in this car."

The light from the end of the Pullman shone dimly down the aisle, revealing the neat series of polished shoes. The snores of several of the sleeping passengers droned from behind the heavy green curtains and mingled with the steady clacking of the wheels on the rail joints.

Stanley walked down the aisle slowly, pausing before each berth, listening intently. He reached Number Three, the Saunders' berth and his knee rubbed against something.

The inert, bare foot of a man was protruding into the aisle.

A low whine of terror escaped the porter. Stanley gripped his arm in a warning for silence and pushed the curtains aside.

A man in pajamas was lying diagonally across the bed, face down. The small light above the pillow illuminated the shock of iron-gray hair lying against the white sheet and his tightly clenched hands. His body was inert, lifeless as a wax figure.

The section of his white pajamas from just below the shoulder blades to the small of the back was a dark, moist red that glistened like jelly in the yellow ray of the light. His head was half turned toward them, revealing the wild agony in his eye and the lips drawn back for the scream that had never passed them.

Stanley's unsteady fingers pulled at the pajamas. The shirt came away from the skin with a slight, sucking sound and revealed the wound.

"Stabbed," Hunt gasped.

Stanley pushed the door of the vacant drawing room closed and stared at Hunt's gray, shocked face. Murder on the Limited! Momentarily stunned as he was, he composed himself and answered the question on the brakeman's mute lips.

"Go forward and tell Schwartz to open up the throttle right into Muncie so no one can jump off. Drop a wire for the operator at Schyler Junction to the police at Muncie. Tell them to have men on both sides of the track when we run in."

Hunt stumbled out of the door.

"On your way," Stanley added, "send Kelley back. Don't let on to the woman."

A moment later Kelley's big frame pushed through the door. His rough-hewn features were like chalk as he wiped his brow on his blue sleeve.

"Well?" he breathed.

344

Stanley spoke mechanically.

"Saunders was stabbed from behind and throttled as he came down the aisle with the water. That's the way he vanished."

He opened the door and peered down the dark pullman.

"And the murderer is lying behind those curtains. Probably watching us now," he added softly. "Waiting for the next move." He thought of a deadly snake, coiled in the darkness, ready to strike if stumbled upon.

Kelley licked his lips. "Dumped Saunders back in his own berth while the woman was out giving the alarm. Playing safe."

"What did you get out of the woman?" Stanley asked out of the corner of his mouth, his eyes still searching the aisle speculatively, trying to penetrate the secret behind those gently swaying curtains.

"Saunder's life had been threatened before they left New York. It seems he was an eye-witness to a gang shooting in St. Louis a few months ago. There were some other witnesses but they won't talk, scared to death. Saunders was a pretty high-class man—refused to be intimidated. He was the state's star witness and on his way back for the trial.

"Before they left New York yesterday he got a couple of telephone calls, warnings to lay off. He laughed 'em off. He got a telegram on the train at Rochester. Just two words—*Coffin Car*—"

Stanley's thin, resolute face hardened and his lips set in a grim line. It would have been better for Saunders if he had listened to the warning. It would be better for himself if he heeded the threat embodied in Saunders' lifeless, staring face. He felt that warning now as his eyes roved down the aisle, felt himself being watched, and the menace of invisible eyes.

"We'll take a look in these berths," he rasped.

Kelley's glance shifted uneasily. "Suppose this guy is wise. If he lays low in his berth and doesn't get cold feet we haven't got a clue. Might be any one of the passengers in the car."

"Maybe," Stanley said softly. "But it's ten to one he's dressed. You can't make a getaway all of a sudden-like in your pajamas."

Kelley's eyes flickered and then steadied before the level gaze of the older man.

"O.K.", he muttered.

Stanley opened the curtains of the berths with deft, cautious fingers and played the light over the interiors. He was wary, alert. Some stirred and muttered vaguely but he quickly flashed off the light and passed on. He eliminated the women from consideration.

Lower Ten was a man, sunk deep in the covers, snoring fitfully. Only the top of his black hair showed. They were all like that, asleep, apparently innocent.

At the other end of the car Kelley cursed softly.

"How can a dirty killer lie there and look so peaceful?"

"Of course one of them might have clothes on beneath those covers," Stanley frowned. "But I can't go down the line and yank everything off them to find out."

Jeb moved closer and nudged him.

"They's a funny thing about one of them passengers."

"Yes."

"Well, now, you know all them passengers always leave their shoes beneath the berths so's I can shine 'em. Well, I done finished shinin' all the shoes tonight and I don't find none beneath Lower Ten. Dey ain't no one in the upper but that don' explain what the gentleman in the lower done with his'n less they's right on his feet."

Stanley gave Jeb one long silent look—but there were unspoken words in that look. He turned and his eyes fell on the shadowed curtains of Lower Ten, bored through it, and seemed to meet the sinister, watching eyes that he had been steadily conscious of.

He and Kelley and Jeb moved silently down the aisle and closed in on the berth. His sharp ears detected a rustle and then silence.

He spread the curtains and turned on the flashlight. The passenger was in the same position as when they had first gone through the car. Stanley watched him, could hardly detect his breathing. He got the impression of a coiled spring, held by a hair trigger. His free hand stole down, grasped the rim of the bedclothes, pulled them down gently.

He had a flash of the dark blue suit the man was wearing, saw an arm swing back. The flashlight was dashed from his hand, the berth plunged in darkness. As he tried to draw away, a stunning blow crashed down on his head and he stumbled back against Kelley.

The muzzle of a black, snub-nosed automatic thrust through the split in the curtains and fanned them menacingly.

The other two froze and raised their hands. He sucked in his breath from pain and pushed his up slowly.

"Turn around."

The voice behind the curtain was muffled but peremptory, and they obeyed, facing the opposite berths.

"The first one of you that makes a break gets what Saunders got," the voice whispered.

346

They heard him getting out of the berth.

"If you know what's good for you, you'll lay low until I get off this train."

There was the shuffle of a foot on the carpet—then silence. A moment later the vestibule door clicked.

Stanley swung around and ran for the vestibule. Kelley called to him.

"Stop. He'll drill you."

Stanley kept running—saw no one on the platform—and ran into the next car. The aisle was empty. Kelley caught up with him, seized his arm.

"We're almost into Muncie," pleaded Kelley. "If he doesn't make a break for it, the cops can help us take him."

Stanley cursed harshly. "Did you see his face?"

Kelley shook his head in the negative.

They went back and searched the berth. There was nothing, no clues—only blood-stained sheets where Saunders' body had lain.

"We're running into Muncie in a few minutes," Kelley blurted. "We'll get him there. At least we uncovered him."

Stanley's lips curled grimly.

They sped into the outskirts of Muncie, flashed by streets and factories. The long *whaaa, whaaa* of Schwartz's whistle screamed twice, flinging a warning ahead.

Stanley saw policemen and plainclothes dicks every few car lengths as they rushed down the platform. A great shudder ran through the train, a grinding, tearing jar, and the scream of protesting wheels under the squeeze of the brakes. The Limited came to a stop.

He swung off and in his momentum almost bowled over a tall, stout figure in blue and two plainclothes men.

"You the pullman conductor?" the stout officer shouted. "I'm Braden, chief of police here. We've got your train covered. What's the story?"

Stanley gave it to him tersely.

"Any passengers getting off here?" Braden barked.

"No. Only three or four pickups for St. Louis."

The station was deserted except for the police and men loading mail. The last of the pickups for St. Louis was climbing the steps of the car reserved for Muncie space, a plump traveling salesman with a loud, green suit.

Stanley felt tense, strained.

He said slowly. "We'll have to go in and take him. Give us the two plainclothes men."

Braden nodded silently and the two dicks walked down and got on the observation car with him and Kelley. Stanley explained to them tersely with set jaw.

"We'll work right through from here forward. I'm checking every passenger's ticket. He can't show the stub for Lower Ten without giving himself away. And if he can't show a ticket that puts the finger on him."

The two dicks kept their hands in their pockets, ready for trouble. Most of the passengers were still asleep. Stanley woke them and made them show their stubs. Some wanted to start an argument but he moved on, left them spluttering.

There was only one car further ahead when he took the ticket of the last Muncie passenger, a heavily built, ill-tempered fellow.

"What's the big delay?" he growled, drawing his watch and waving it before Stanley's eyes. "We've been sitting in this station almost a half hour now. Am I on the Mississippi Limited or a milk train?"

"Sorry," Stanley apologized.

"Sorry, sorry," the passenger exclaimed. "That won't get me into St. Louis on time."

The pullman conductor's eyes flashed but he handed back the stub in silence.

He glanced in the lavatory on the way out. It was empty, as he had expected. He was getting into that frame of mind. There was only one more car ahead. He wondered how the killer had tricked him. He had vanished into thin air more completely than the hazy, blue pall of cigarette smoke that hung in the stuffy lavatory.

Everything was in order in the last car.

"Come back to that drawing room in the next car," he said, still frowning.

Stanley knocked on the door again and pushed it open immediately. The man from Muncie was standing in the middle of the floor.

"Now what?"

Stanley smiled apologetically.

"Sorry to disturb you again. Was there anyone in this drawing room when you came on board?"

The man raised dark, heavy eyebrows curiously.

"Why, no. I don't get you."

Stanley opened the lavatory door again. The air inside was still thick with cigarette smoke and stale. Four or five butts were mashed on the floor. The drawing room was supposed to have been unoccupied until the man from Muncie boarded the train.

348

Stanley regarded the passenger with shrewd, appraising eyes. They rested on his smooth black hair. His glance turned toward the upper berth.

"Open that up," he said to the porter standing in the doorway.

The passenger started and leaned forward.

"What's this all about?" he rasped.

The porter's key rattled in the lock. As the shelf swung down, a hoarse cry burst from the negro and he sprang back. A man's head and shoulders rolled over the side, and dragged by their weight, the whole body crashed to the floor. The fellow was bound and gagged with strips torn from the sheets. His plump figure and loud green suit betrayed him as one of the passengers Stanley had seen getting on at Muncie.

The black eyes of the other passenger flamed and his hand stole toward his coat.

"Hold that pose," cried one of the dicks, flashing his service pistol.

Stanley knelt and examined the man on the floor.

"He's alive. Got a good crack in the head, though." He glanced up at the crouched, tense figure in front of him.

"A clever trick," he said harshly. "You almost got away with it."

"What's it all about?" the other spat.

"After you murdered Saunders and got away from us you hid in here in the lavatory. When this man got on at Muncie and the porter left, you cracked him down, took his tickets and hid him up there. Passed yourself off as getting on at Muncie. Very clever—except for one thing you forgot."

The fellow's dark face worked with fury.

"You meddling old fool," he hissed.

He struck with his foot—quicker than Stanley could dodge.

When he came to he was lying on the side cushion of the drawing room. Jeb and Kelley were the only ones in the room. Jeb was leaning over him, dabbling his head with a wet towel, muttering unintelligibly, while Kelley looked on. Beneath him came the hum of the wheels.

"We're moving," he exclaimed, sitting up.

"Sure," grinned Kelley.

"Where are the others?"

"Done take the one to jail and t'other to the hospital," Jeb drawled.

Stanley lay back with a great sigh of relief.

"There's one thing those dicks couldn't understand," Kelley grinned. "How'd you spot that guy?"

"Remember when we came through the first time and I took his Muncie ticket? He was so damned ornery and kept waving his watch in front of my face?"

"Yeah."

"And complainin' about the delay?"

"Yeah?"

"His watch was on Eastern Standard time. Muncie's on Central Standard time. I thought it was phony his watch should be on Eastern time, him supposed to be getting on at Muncie."

Stanley shook his finger at Jeb with a quizzical smile.

"Can't fool a couple of old railroad men, eh, Jeb?"

# The Mystery
# of the Rue de Peychaud

*by O. Henry*

'Tis midnight in Paris.

A myriad of lamps that line the Champs Élysées and the Rouge et Noir, cast their reflection in the dark waters of the Seine as it flows gloomily past the Place Vendôme and the black walls of the Convent Notadam.

The great French capital is astir.

It is the hour when crime and vice and wickedness reign.

Hundreds of fiacres drive madly through the streets conveying women, flashing with jewels and as beautiful as dreams, from opera and concert, and the little bijou supper rooms of the Café Tout le Temps are filled with laughing groups, while bon mots, persiflage, and repartee fly upon the air—the jewels of thought and conversation.

Luxury and poverty brush each other in the streets. The homeless gamin, begging a sou with which to purchase a bed, and the spend-thrift roué, scattering golden louis d'or, tread the same pavement.

When other cities sleep, Paris has just begun her wild revelry.

The first scene of our story is a cellar beneath the Rue de Peychaud.

The room is filled with smoke of pipes, and is stifling with the

350

reeking breath of its inmates. A single flaring gas jet dimly lights the scene, which is one Rembrandt or Moreland and Keisel would have loved to paint.

A garçon is selling absinthe to such of the motley crowd as have a few sous, dealing it out in niggardly portions in broken teacups.

Leaning against the bar is Carnaignole Cusheau—generally known as the Gray Wolf.

He is the worst man in Paris.

He is more than four feet ten in height, and his sharp, ferocious-looking face and the mass of long, tangled gray hair that covers his face and head, have earned for him the name he bears.

His striped blouse is wide open at the neck and falls outside of his dingy leather trousers. The handle of a deadly looking knife protrudes from his belt. One stroke of its blade would open a box of the finest French sardines.

"Voilà, Gray Wolf," cries Couteau, the bartender. "How many victims today? There is no blood upon your hands. Has the Gray Wolf forgotten how to bite?"

"Sacré Bleu, Mille Tonnerre, by George," hisses the Gray Wolf. "Monsieur Couteau, you are bold indeed to speak to me thus.

"By Ventre St. Gris! I have not even dined today. Spoils indeed. There is no living in Paris now. But one rich American have I garroted in a fortnight.

"Bah! those Democrats. They have ruined the country. With their income tax and their free trade, they have destroyed the millionaire business. Carrambo! Diable! D—n it!"

"Hist!" suddenly says Chamounix the rag-picker, who is worth 20,000,000 francs, "some one comes!"

The cellar door opened and a man crept softly down the rickety steps. The crowd watches him with silent awe.

He went to the bar, laid his card on the counter, bought a drink of absinthe, and then drawing from his pocket a little mirror, set it up on the counter and proceeded to don a false beard and hair and paint his face into wrinkles, until he closely resembled an old man seventy-one years of age.

He then went into a dark corner and watched the crowd of people with sharp, ferret-like eyes.

Gray Wolf slipped cautiously to the bar and examined the card left by the newcomer.

"Holy Saint Bridget!" he exclaims. "It is Tictocq, the detective."

Ten minutes later a beautiful woman enters the cellar.

Tenderly nurtured, and accustomed to every luxury that money

351

could procure, she had, when a young vivandière at the Convent of Saint Susan de la Moutarde, run away with the Gray Wolf, fascinated by his many crimes and the knowledge that his business never allowed him to scrape his feet in the hall or snore.

"Parbleau, Marie," snarls the Gray Wolf. "Que voulez vous? Avez-vous le beau cheval de mon frère, ou le joli chien de votre père?"

"No, no, Gray Wolf," shouts the motley group of assassins, rogues, and pickpockets, even their hardened hearts appalled at his fearful words. "Mon Dieu! You cannot be so cruel!"

"Tiens!" shouts the Gray Wolf, now maddened to desperation, and drawing his gleaming knife. "Voilà! Canaille! Tout le monde, carte blanche embonpoint sauve que peut entre nous revenez nous a nous moutons!"

The horrified sans-culottes shrink back in terror as the Gray Wolf seizes Marie by the hair and cuts her into twenty-nine pieces, each exactly the same size.

As he stands with reeking hands above the corpse, amid a deep silence, the old, gray-bearded man who has been watching the scene springs forward, tears off his false beard and locks, and Tictocq, the famous French detective, stands before them.

Spellbound and immovable, the denizens of the cellar gaze at the greatest modern detective as he goes about the customary duties of his office.

He first measures the distance from the murdered woman to a point on the wall, then he takes down the name of the bartender and the day of the month and the year. Then drawing from his pocket a powerful microscope, he examines a little of the blood that stands upon the floor in little pools.

"Mon Dieu!" he mutters, "it is as I feared—human blood."

He then enters rapidly in a memorandum book the result of his investigations, and leaves the cellar.

Tictocq bends his rapid steps in the direction of the headquarters of the Paris gendarmerie, but suddenly pausing, he strikes his hand upon his brow with a gesture of impatience.

"Mille tonnerre," he mutters. "I should have asked the name of that man with the knife in his hand."

It is reception night at the palace of the Duchess Valerie du Bel-lairs.

The apartments are flooded with a mellow light from paraffine candles in solid silver candelabra.

The company is the most aristocratic and wealthy in Paris.

Three or four brass bands are playing behind a portière between the coal shed, and also behind time. Footmen in gay-laced livery bring in beer noiselessly and carry out apple-peelings dropped by the guests.

Valerie, seventh Duchess du Bellairs, leans back on a solid gold ottoman on eiderdown cushions, surrounded by the wittiest, the bravest, and the handsomest courtiers in the capital.

"Ah, madame," said the Prince Champvilliers, of Palais Royale, corner of Seventy-third Street, "as Montesquiaux says, 'Rien de plus bon tutti frutti'—Youth seems your inheritance. You are tonight the most beautiful, the wittiest in your own salon. I can scarce believe my own senses, when I remember that thirty-one years ago you—"

"Saw it off!" says the Duchess, peremptorily.

The Prince bows low, and drawing a jewelled dagger, stabs himself to the heart.

"The displeasure of your grace is worse than death," he says, as he takes his overcoat and hat from a corner of the mantelpiece and leaves the room.

"Voilà," says Bèebè Françillon, fanning herself languidly. "That is the way with men. Flatter them, and they kiss your hand. Loose but a moment the silken leash that holds them captive through their vanity and self-opinionativeness, and the son-of-a-gun gets on his ear at once. The devil go with him, I say."

"Ah, mon Princesse," sighs the Count Pumpernickel, stooping and whispering with eloquent eyes into her ear. "You are too hard upon us. Balzac says, 'All women are not to themselves what no one else is to another.' Do you not agree with him?"

"Cheese it!" says the Princess. "Philosophy palls upon me. I'll shake you."

"Hosses?" says the Count.

Arm and arm they go out to the salon au Beurre.

Armande de Fleury, the young pianissimo danseuse from the Folies Bergère, is about to sing.

She slightly clears her throat and lays a voluptuous cud of chewing gum upon the piano as the first notes of the accompaniment ring through the salon.

As she prepares to sing, the Duchess du Bellairs grasps the arm of her ottoman in a vicelike grip, and she watches with an expression of almost anguished suspense.

She scarcely breathes.

Then, as Armande de Fleury, before uttering a note, reels, wavers,

353

turns white as snow and falls dead upon the floor, the Duchess breathes a sigh of relief.

The Duchess had poisoned her.

Then the guests crowd about the piano, gazing with bated breath, and shuddering as they look upon the music rack and observe that the song that Armande came so near singing is "Sweet Marie."

Twenty minutes later a dark and muffled figure was seen to emerge from a recess in the mullioned wall of the Arc de Triomphe and pass rapidly northward.

It was no other than Tictocq, the detective.

The network of evidence was fast being drawn about the murderer of Marie Cusheau.

It is midnight on the steeple of the Cathedral of Notadam.

It is also the same time at other given points in the vicinity.

The spire of the Cathedral is 20,000 feet above the pavement, and a casual observer, by making a rapid mathematical calculation, would have readily perceived that this Cathedral is, at least, double the height of others that measure only 10,000 feet.

At the summit of the spire there is a little wooden platform on which there is room for but one man to stand.

Crouching on this precarious footing, which swayed dizzily with every breeze that blew, was a man closely muffled, and disguised as a wholesale grocer.

Old François Beongfallong, the great astronomer, who is studying the ethereal spheres from his attic window in the Rue de Bologny, shudders as he turns his telescope upon the solitary figure upon the spire.

"Sacré Bleu!" he hisses between his new celluloid teeth. "It is Tictocq, the detective. I wonder whom he is following now?"

While Tictocq is watching with lynx-like eyes the hill of Montmartre, he suddenly hears a heavy breathing beside him, and turning gazes into the ferocious eyes of the Gray Wolf.

Carnaignole Cusheau had put on his W. U. Tel. Co. climbers and climbed the steeple.

"Parbleu, monsieur," says Tictocq. "To whom am I indebted for the honor of this visit?"

The Gray Wolf smiled softly and depreciatingly.

"You are Tictocq, the detective?" he said.

"I am."

"Then listen. I am the murderer of Marie Cusheau. She was my wife and she had cold feet and ate onions. What was I to do? Yet life

354

is sweet to me. I do not wish to be guillotined. I have heard that you are on my track. It is true that the case is in your hands?"

"It is."

"Thank le bon Dieu, then, I am saved."

The Gray Wolf carefully adjusts the climbers on his feet and descends the spire.

Tictocq takes out his notebook and writes in it.

"At last," he says, "I have a clue."


Monsieur le Compte Carnaignole Cusheau, once known as the Gray Wolf, stands in the magnificent drawing-room of his palace on East 47th Street.

Three days after his confession to Tictocq, he happened to look in the pockets of a discarded pair of pants and found twenty million francs in gold.

Suddenly the door opens and Tictocq, the detective, with a dozen gens d'arme, enters the room.

"You are my prisoner," says the detective.

"On what charge?"

"The murder of Marie Cusheau on the night of August 17th."

"Your proofs?"

"I saw you do it, and your own confession on the spire of Notadam."

The Count laughed and took a paper from his pocket.

"Read this," he said, "here is proof that Marie Cusheau died of heart failure."

Tictocq looked at the paper.

It was a check for 100,000 francs.

Tictocq dismissed the gens d'arme with a wave of his hand.

"We have made a mistake, monsieurs," he said, but as he turns to leave the room, Count Carnaignole stops him.

"One moment, monsieur."

The Count Carnaignole tears from his own face a false beard and reveals the flashing eyes and well-known features of Tictocq, the detective.

Then, springing forward, he snatches a wig and false eyebrows from his visitor, and the Gray Wolf, grinding his teeth in rage, stands before him.

The murderer of Marie Cusheau was never discovered.

# Naked in Darkness

*by Hugh B. Cave*

They were near the entrance now. Sheppard could see the slit of daylight ahead and hear the rain pounding the mountain. Had Hurricane Flora been drowning the island all the time he was in the cave?

She probably had. Just before his departure from Moore Town the weather office at Palisadoes had issued a warning. Flora was slowing down over Cuba. The island of Jamaica could expect torrential rains until she picked up speed again.

Sheppard frowned. The return trip down the mountain would be a nightmare, and he had already gone 36 hours without sleep.

Ahead of him, his prisoner stumbled on the rough stone floor and began cursing again. Sheppard only raised the barrel of his shotgun an inch. The man looked back, his small eyes blazing in the gleam of his captor's flashlight.

"You could at least take these handcuffs off before I break my neck!" he snarled.

"Keep moving."

"Why don't you shoot me and get it over with?"

"Try jumping me again," Sheppard said, "and I will."

Last time he hadn't. McCoy, taken by surprise in the depths of the cave, had come at him like a madman, but Sheppard had simply spun the little single-bore Beretta in his hands and slapped its stock against the man's jaw. He was fond of that little Beretta. It gave you only one shot, true, but it was feather-light for quick action.

McCoy looked into the muzzle of it now and stumbled on toward the entrance.

Then Sheppard heard the muttering.

It began high above their heads and swelled to a thunder. It became a spectral train careening down the mountain at top speed. Suddenly it exploded into a monstrous, earthshaking convulsion.

Sheppard braced himself and watched the slit of daylight at the mouth of the cave. He had lived in Jamaica's mountains as a boy, and had seen landslides before. The slit was vulnerable. It opened on a

356

scrap of ledge about the size of his yard in Kingston. The mountain above the ledge was all but vertical.

A boulder crashed on the ledge, rolled, and dropped over the edge. A rain of debris followed, piling up with fantastic quickness. Then came the slide itself, earth and trees and rocks, with a roar so loud that the shockwave staggered him.

He watched the earth fill the opening and block out the light. By the gleam of his flash he watched it flow toward McCoy and himself, filling the tunnel from floor to ceiling.

They backed away and it followed for twenty, thirty feet, like a giant worm, before it slowed and finally stopped. The awful thunder had stopped, too. The only sound now was a soft slithering as the face of the earth wall settled.

For a long moment neither man moved. Then McCoy turned his head. "Well, mister, what you suppose now, huh?" McCoy was Kingston-born, with a good schooling, but he looked like a peasant and thought it amusing to talk like one.

Sheppard said slowly, "Is there another way out of here?"

"No way 'ceptin' this one, mister."

Sheppard was silent. He did not know the cave well, himself. He had only known there *was* one in this almost inaccessible region, and it was a logical place to look for his quarry. He did know it was a big cave, with dozens of chambers and a maze of tunnels. To explore it would take more days than he could hope to stay alive.

He walked forward to examine the great worm of earth. Behind him McCoy said dryly, "Us can't dig through it, mister. It want a bulldozer, and them couldn't get any 'dozer up here even if them knew we was trapped. Anyhow, them would never know where to begin. That slide cover the cave mouth."

"Talk English," Sheppard said.

"Certainly, pal. Any other orders while we sit here and wait to die?"

Sheppard gave it a moment's thought. "Yes," he said then. "Walk back to that last chamber we came through, and sit down. I don't like the smell of you in a tight place like this."

McCoy grinned. "You hide in a cave for two weeks, pal, and you mightn't smell so sweet yourself. It's these clothes."

"Walk," Sheppard ordered.

The chamber was not a large one. In it they sat twenty feet apart, their backs against opposite walls. McCoy laid his manacled hands on drawn-up knees and gazed calmly at his captor.

"What are you, mister? What kind of work you do?"

"I'm in coffee."

357

"So you a planter, huh?"

"Something like that," Sheppard said quietly.

"Then why you so down on me? What me ever do you?"

Sheppard fixed him with a cold stare. "In the past two months you've assaulted four women, McCoy."

"So?"

"One was my sister."

McCoy shaped his slack mouth into an O of astonishment. "Now what a thing you say. That too bad, mister. If me know she you sister, me never do that."

"And you've murdered two policemen."

"Them get too close to catching me."

"You're an animal, McCoy."

The handcuffed man lifted his massive shoulders and let them fall. "Me told you is not me you smell. Is me clothes." He frowned at his rags. "You change clothes with me, you be the one that stinks." His laugh was half grunt. "You got any cigarettes, mister?"

"I don't smoke."

"A flash of white rum in you pocket, maybe?"

"I don't drink."

"Shoo!" McCoy said. "You not very good company. Me goin' get some sleep."

Sheppard's eyelids were heavy with fatigue, too, but he willed them to remain open. He sat with the Beretta across his knees, the flashlight glowing on the floor beside him. He had brought extra batteries for the light but they were in it now, burning themselves up. When they were finished, he and McCoy would be in darkness.

"Naked in darkness," Sheppard murmured, gazing at his prisoner.

McCoy opened one eye. "What that you say?"

"You wouldn't understand."

" 'Naked in darkness.' Me hear you say it. What that suppose to mean?"

"I said you wouldn't understand. It's a line from a poem. 'Naked in darkness we sit and wait.' "

"Very good," McCoy said, dropping the patois. "I like that." He closed his open eye and seemed to doze for a moment, then opened both eyes and looked at Sheppard and grinned. "Yes, man. 'Naked in darkness'—that's good. I'll remember that." After a while he said, "How did you find me, mister? You must be smarter than the police. They couldn't do it."

"I studied you."

"Studied me? How?"

"When that last girl identified you, I went to people who knew you. I talked to your teachers, and people you grew up with and worked with. I could write your life story, McCoy. I found out you're a man given to wild rages when things go wrong for you. I learned about your hunting pigeons in this region, and how when you shot those two fingers off your left hand you began calling yourself Three-finger Jack because you admired the original Three-finger Jack so much. He was a killer too."

"So?" McCoy said.

"The original Jack hid in caves when he was hunted, McCoy. I knew there was a big cave here where you did your pigeon shooting. So I tracked you down."

McCoy chuckled. "You're smart. You should be almost smart enough to figure a way out of here." He waited, and when Sheppard remained silent he chuckled again. "Are you married?"

Sheppard nodded.

"Kids?"

Again Sheppard nodded.

McCoy shook his head. "You poor slob. For me it was only the hangman—sooner or later, the hangman—but look what you've got yourself into. Well, it's your own damned fault. I'm going to sleep."

He closed his eyes again. This time he slept.

Half an hour later Sheppard, too, allowed his eyes to close. He was very tired. . . . He awoke with a grime-encrusted foot nudging his neck and McCoy triumphantly standing over him with the shotgun. The muzzle of the Beretta was an inch from Sheppard's head.

"Just give me the key to these handcuffs, mister," McCoy said.

Sheppard did not move.

"The key! You think I won't shoot you for it?" The Beretta's barrel was a long black tunnel in front of Sheppard's right eye. "This gun is loaded, mister. I thought maybe you'd emptied it while I was sleeping, so I looked. It's loaded, mister—so hand over that key!"

Sheppard took the key from his pocket and watched the handcuffs fall to the floor. He said slowly, "So there is a way out of here. You were lying."

McCoy laughed. "You're dumb, mister. You said yourself I turn crazy-wild when things go wrong. When you first found me I jumped you, didn't I?—even with this gun aimed at my gut. Did I go crazy when that slide blocked the entrance?"

"I see," Sheppard said.

"But only one of us is leaving here, mister. Take off your shoes and those clothes—all of them. They'll be a big help to me outside."

Sheppard looked away from McCoy's face at last and slowly made himself naked. McCoy reached for the handcuffs. "You can wear these."

The cuffs clicked shut on Sheppard's wrists. McCoy took off his rags, dressed himself in Sheppard's clothing, and laced on Sheppard's shoes. Then with his rags wadded under one arm, he gathered up the shotgun and flashlight.

"So long, mister."

Sheppard said slowly, "You're leaving me like this?"

" 'Naked in darkness,' " McCoy chuckled. "You put the idea right into my head—I was only going to swap clothes with you and take the gun. Anyway, you wouldn't feel clean in these rags of mine, not even crawling under them to keep warm. You said yourself they stink." He looked down at the naked man and laughed. "Now just try finding your way out of here," he said, "in the dark and without using your hands."

He slid along the wall to one of the chamber's openings. Just before disappearing he turned his head. " 'Naked in darkness.' Man, that's good. I'll just have to tell that to a little girl I got picked out in Spanish Town." He was gone.

Sheppard lay still as the sound of footfalls died away in the dark. He shivered. Then he squirmed along the floor until his manacled hands touched a flat stone.

He turned the stone over. His fingers found the spare key he had hidden beneath it while McCoy slept. The handcuffs fell from him and he stood up. He walked slowly toward the tunnel into which McCoy had vanished, and slowly along it, testing the shape of the floor before each step. His hands kept up a continual weaving in front of him.

In time he reached a place where the tunnel branched, and he hesitated. But not for long. On he went again, groping.

*Naked in darkness*, he thought. Naked he was, naked he felt. Still, bare feet were better than shoes for feeling out the irregularities of the floor or the edge of an unseen pit around which he must make his way.

The strain on his senses began to tell. He stopped to rest. But after he had rested he went on again through the maze, step by step by step.

Near the end of the second hour he found McCoy's discarded rags. He did not touch them. Twenty minutes later he saw daylight. It was only a shining pinpoint far ahead, but it grew in size as he approached it. It became an opening large enough for a man to crawl through.

The floor of the tunnel, slanting up to it, was littered with stones. He studied them. He stooped. A moment later he wriggled through the opening and found himself on a yard-wide ledge thick with stunted tropical growth. The mountainside fell steeply to a lush valley where wisps of kitchen smoke rose from a cluster of peasant houses. Rain was falling.

Twenty feet distant on the same ledge, McCoy snatched up the Beretta and lurched to his feet from a study of the houses. His expression of astonishment changed slowly to one of amusement as the naked figure of Sheppard emerged from the mouth of the cave, straightened, and then faced him.

"Well, I'll be damned," McCoy said. "You found it."

Sheppard's hands were at his sides. He was very tired. Still, he was relaxed.

"You left your trail, McCoy."

"Don't move, mister. This gun is still loaded," McCoy warned. "What trail did I leave?"

"The smell, McCoy. The smell of your clothes. Even after you dropped them, the smell stayed with you." With his gaze fixed on the gun, Sheppard shifted his bare feet ever so slightly, to grip the ledge better. "I told you I was in coffee. I didn't say I was a planter, McCoy. You said that. I'm a coffee taster. I can smell you from here."

McCoy, after a moment of silence, said with a sneer, "Can you smell the powder in this shell, mister?"

"There isn't any to smell."

McCoy laughed. "I looked, mister. You forgot."

The naked man at the cave mouth shook his head. "You looked to see if the gun had a shell in it. You should have taken the shell out and looked at that. I emptied it, McCoy, while you were sleeping. Pull the trigger. Find out."

McCoy fired. True to form, when there was no explosion he flung the gun down the mountainside and hurled himself, cursing, at his adversary.

Sheppard's right hand flashed up. As a boy, he too had hunted pigeons in Jamaica's mountains. Not with a gun, of course. With stones.

He was still good at it. He didn't miss.

# Night Watch

*by Scott O'Hara*

At five minutes of five the disc jockey topped off his program with a recording by the All Stars. Barney Bigard's clarinet was sweet and strong, to the counterpoint noodling of Fatha' Hines. He kept the car radio tuned so low that the rhythm was a whisper, the tune like a memory in the mind. As the piece ended he turned off the radio, cupped his hands around the lighter from the dashboard as he lit another cigarette.

When it was finished he eased the car door open and stood out in the crisp, predawn air, the wet spring-smell of the woods. Four months of waiting and watching. The tiredness was deep in him, and the boredom. A leaden-muscled, sag-nerved tiredness.

Behind the house, three hundred feet away, the roosters screamed brassy defiance at distant hen runs, and, lonesome through the dregs of night, came the far-off sigh and pant of a train.

Barry Raymes leaned against the side of the government sedan, sensing, for the hundredth time, his own unreality—neatly dressed, as the Bureau demanded, the regulation special making its familiar bulge, the regulation hammer on the regulation empty chamber, the entire picture anachronistic in the threat of dawn, in the sleepy peace of the Georgia countryside. In the war there had been the long time on the ship, so long that things that happened before faded away, and the future was immeasurably distant. This was not unlike that time on the ship. At eight Sturdevant would relieve him, to be relieved in turn at four in the afternoon by French, who would carry on until midnight, when once again Barry Raymes, with the thermos of coffee, the bundle of sandwiches from the hotel, would begin the vigil that had begun to seem pointless. But no agent of two years seniority can hope to point out to the Special Agent in Charge that the assignment, in his measured opinion, is of no value. Patience is a quality more precious than gold to the Bureau. A man without patience does not last long.

And so there has to be reconciliation to the night after night, the

362

hundred and twenty-six nights thus spent, and the possible hundred and twenty-six yet to come. Even though each night added another cumulative factor to the deathly weariness. Weariness came from recurrent alertness, the adrenalin that came hard and fast into the blood whenever a car seemed to slow on the highway. Or there would be an unidentifiable sound that made necessary a cautious patrol of the grounds with the Bureau variation of the wartime, infra-red snooperscope.

All because the Bureau was gambling that Craik Lopat would return to see the girl he had intended to marry. . . .

As dawn paled the eastern sky, the kitchen lights went on, slanting yellow-orange oblongs out onto the packed dirt of the dooryard, and he could see her, tall, as she moved about in the kitchen, putting the coffee on before going back to her bedroom to exchange the robe for the cotton dress and sweater that she usually wore. The sweater was a heavy maroon cardigan, too large for her, and he suspected that it had belonged to Lopat. Somehow, this past month, when he thought of Marra Allen wearing Lopat's sweater, an ugly anger thickened within him. He recognized the potential danger of his attitude and sought to recover his original indifference, but without any particular success.

In the night watch you could think of taking this Marra Allen, with her ignorance and her superstitions and her unlettered tongue, and becoming Pygmalion, because there was no denying that her slim loveliness was more than just an attribute of youth. The bone structure was good and she would take beauty to her grave. And French told of the innate fastidiousness, the kitchen shades drawn, the water heated each night in the big tub in a countryside where Saturday baths were a mark of eccentricity.

And also, in the long night, you could think of her breathing softly in sleep on her bed and think of how her warm breath would come from lips parted just a bit, probably, and the golden hair spread over the pillow. She was three hundred feet away, and one night you quite calmly stepped over to the birch which was white in the starlight and clubbed it hard with your clenched fist, later sucking the swollen knuckles, but cured for the moment.

Barry Raymes had always been a quick and competent, though somewhat shy young man—with a wide, dark line in his mind separating right from wrong. The frequency with which his thoughts and his dreams turned to Marra Allen disturbed him because he sensed wrongness in a Bureau agent involving himself personally with any female in any case, no matter what intrinsic worth said female seemed to possess.

Sturdevant and French both made the usual, the expected, jokes about the midnight-to-eight trick, and the obvious advantages pertaining to the hour, and in the beginning he had laughed in the expected way and hinted broadly of the mythical delights of such an assignment, but of late he had felt the flush on the back of his neck and laughter had not been as easy.

When she returned to the kitchen the dawn light was brighter, paling the artificial light from the kitchen. She opened the kitchen door and looked over toward the small side road where his car was hidden in the heavy brush. The light behind her outlined her and the morning wind caught at the hem of the cotton dress.

He had long since decided that there was no compromise of Bureau directives involved. The SAC—Special Agent in Charge—had made it quite clear that it would be impossible to carry out the assignment without tipping off the girl. And so his conscience had been made easy. And it had become a morning custom.

He came across the dooryard, taking out the Special when he was forty feet from her. She stepped aside, as usual, saying, " 'Morning, mister," that look of amusement on her face as though he were a small boy playing some absurd variation of cops-and-robbers.

He went through the house as he had been taught in the School. It did not take long. Four rooms, like small boxes, on one floor. Bedroom, sitting room, storeroom and kitchen.

When he came back into the kitchen she had put the coffee cups on the table, taking, as usual, as the one without the handle.

Without turning she said, "Find any crooks in my house?" She stood at the wood stove, turning the eggs.

"Not today."

"Gives me a funny feeling, kinda, mister. You don't trust me much, do you?"

"Of course I trust you, Marra. I just have to follow orders."

"Sure," she said, her tone weary. He sat down in his usual place, his back to the wall. She brought over the two plates of eggs, the thick-cut bacon, taking, as usual, the chipped plate for herself.

They ate in silence, and, as on every morning, she lowered her face almost to the plate for each forkful. In another woman it would have amused and partially revolted him. In Marra it seemed oddly pathetic. It seemed as though a girl of breeding sat there, intent, for some strange reason, on playing this part that had been given her. And in

364

the depths of her grey-blue eyes he saw the deadness, a nothingness, as though a part of her had been dead—for four months.

They finished breakfast and he found the fifty-cent piece in his pocket. He slipped it under the edge of the plate, without her seeing him do it. They had never spoken of the fee he had arbitrarily selected as proper for the morning breakfast, and he knew that she would not take the plate away until he left.

"When you people goin' ta give up?" she asked.

"When we get Lopat."

"He hid good, eh?"

"He hid very good. Maybe we'll find him. Maybe he'll come back to be found."

She took one of his cigarettes. She sighed. "For me, mister, it might just as well be jail. When Craik was around I got to go jukin' once in a while. Now none of the boys'll ask me. Solly, or Tad or Jesse or any of 'em. They know there'll be you G's taggin' along."

"Are you in love with Craik Lopat?"

"Love is a big word, mister. Craik's always good for laughs. Big husky guy with a mean eye on him. Like a—well, like one of them mountain cats. Mean. Big white teeth. See him work out once on one of them Turner boys from Patton Ridge. Gouged an eye out of him in about three seconds."

"Did he get into trouble just out of meanness, do you think, Marra?"

She frowned, took her time answering. "I can't say. He always wanted a big shiny car and money in his pocket. He got fired off the gas station and they wouldn't take him back in the mill again because of the trouble last time. I guess he was sore at the mill and that's why he done it."

Barry Raymes, thinking aloud, said, "And he had beginner's luck, all right. If they'd gotten the safe closed . . . if it hadn't been payday . . . if that guard hadn't lost his nerve . . . Lots of ifs. He got thirty-five thousand, in small bills and change, and drove off in the plant manager's car to boot and took that payroll clerk with him. That's how we come into the picture."

"Because of the state line?"

"He rolled the clerk out into the brush in Alabama, remember, and shot him through the stomach. The clerk didn't die easy, Marra."

"He was always wild-like," she said softly. "Even when he was just a kid."

"You were going to marry him," he said accusingly.

"Oh, I know what you mean. He'd have given me a bad time, that's for sure. Other women and getting likkered up and maybe slamming me around. He done that once, you know." She laughed, almost fondly. "Gee, did I have a fat eye on me!"

"After what's happened," he asked, "if you had a chance to go with him, would you?"

She regarded him steadily. "Mister, I couldn't rightly say."

"You would, wouldn't you?"

"I might."

He wanted to hurt her. He pushed his chair back and stood up. He said, "You'll find the half-buck under the plate."

She flushed. "That's all right."

Anger didn't fade entirely until he was back at the car. And then he was ashamed for speaking of the money, knowing that it would make a difference between them.

Sturdevant showed up a little before eight and Barry Raymes drove back to the small city eight miles away and went to bed.

He was up at five, had another breakfast and went to a movie. At eleven he finished his lunch, picked up the sandwiches and coffee and went out and relieved a bored and sleepy Paul French.

The long night hours went by without incident. She did not come to the kitchen door. He waited longer than usual and then went over.

"I want to search the house," he said harshly.

She stepped aside without a word. As before the house was empty.

He went back into the kitchen and said, "I could use some breakfast, Marra."

"I can sell you coffee, eggs and bacon for half a buck, if you want it."

"I—I'm sorry I acted like I did yesterday, Marra."

She looked directly at him. "You was ugly."

"I had a reason."

"What reason?"

"You said you might go away with—with him. Marra, I don't know what's happened to me, but . . ."

She moved a half step closer to him and, with dignity, lifted her face to look directly up into his eyes. He felt the warmth of her breath against his chin. As he bent to kiss her, her hands fastened with hard force around his arms above the elbows. His reactions were delayed. He twisted away, reaching for the revolver.

"I wouldn't try that," a man said softly. The Army Colt in his hand was aimed at Barry's belt buckle. "You did right well, Marra, and I thank you for it. Back real slow against the wall next to the stove

366

there, mister. Hands way up. That's right. Go git me some cloth, Marra, a wad of it."

Craik Lopat wore an expensive-looking suit, but the knees were stained with dirt and one button was missing from the suit coat. He wore no tie and his white shirt was open at the collar. He was thick in the shoulder, slim and flat in the belly and hips. Black eyebrows met over the bridge of his nose and the mouth was heavy with cruelty and sensuousness.

"A cop," he said, "tryin' to love up my woman! They musta got you outa the bottom of the barrel, sonny. I been here for two days, layin' up in the hills until I figured out your hours. When you looked around, I was outside the bedroom window. And it'll be nearly two hours before the next one shows up. You couldn't find me before, and you won't find the two of us, either. I got a good car stashed over beyond the grove."

Marra came back into the kitchen with a wad of sheeting.

"You want me to tear it into strips, Craik?" she asked.

"No. Give it here. I got to wad it around the end of this here .45 because it makes too damn much noise. You want to see me shoot him, you kin stand over there, f'you want. Sonny gets it low down in the gut. He woulda got it in the head except for what I see him trying to do to you."

Barry Raymes felt the sweat run down his ribs. His mouth was dry and he was dizzy. Some of it was genuine fear. More of it was anger and frustration that he should have been taken in so easily. He looked at Marra. Her face was pale and she moistened her lips.

"Right—right here in the kitchen?" she asked weakly.

"You got no more use for this little old shack, honey. You don't like it, go on in the next room."

"They'll never give up if you kill me, Lopat. Never," Barry said. He despised the tremble that came into his voice.

"They got no pictures of me, sonny, and no prints. I got a nice new name and a lot of good neighbors in a place you'll never find. I told 'em all I was going back to pick up my wife." He wrapped the barrel in the sheeting. "Brace yourself, sonny."

"Craik," she said. "Wait a minute. Let me get my stuff together afore you kill him. It'll make some noise and I don't want to have to run for it without my things."

"I'm going to buy you new stuff, honey."

"After we get married?"

367

Craik Lopat frowned. "If we get time to make out the papers, honey. You'll get the new stuff anyway."

"I'll hurry. Don't shoot him yet. I want to see it, Craik. I never did see a man get hisself killed yet."

She smiled, quite merrily.

"Make it fast, baby," Craik growled.

She hurried out of the room. Craik stood, whistling tonelessly, the muzzle, shrouded in sheeting, steady as a boulder. Barry made his plans. They hadn't taken the revolver. That was an oversight. He'd watch Craik's eyes. They might flick over to the girl when she came back into the kitchen. At that moment he'd throw himself to the left, snatching the revolver as he fell, hoping to get in at least one shot.

He heard Marra's quick footsteps. She appeared in the bedroom door. She lifted the shotgun and the full blast at short range caught Craik Lopat in the back of his thick, tanned neck. The big man stumbled one step forward, his head nearly severed from his body, and fell heavily, full length, the .45 spinning out of his dead hand, his face smashing against the worn floor boards.

Barry Raymes bent stupidly and picked up the .45. Marra Allen knelt beside the body, picked up the dead hand, sat back on her heels and crooned—a low, sad tone that was without tears.

"You were going to go with him."

"He was changed, mister. Changed. He was like a dog I see once in town, with suds on his mouth and his eyes crazy."

"Was it because he was going to kill me?" he asked softly.

She turned her head slowly and looked at the wall against which Barry had been standing. Her voice sounded far away. "You see that blue color, don't you? Last year I wanted to fix the place up. He bought the paint and painted it. I got those little red things. Funny little things. You wet the paper and then they slide right off onto the wall. He thought they were pretty. And we were going to live here, you know."

She still held the lifeless hand. He saw the expensive band of the watch, the black hair curling harshly on the back of the hand, between the knuckles of the fingers.

"That's where he was going to kill me, against that wall."

"It didn't mean anything to him, mister. It didn't mean a damn thing to him."

He shifted his weight uneasily and said, with mock joviality, "Well, no matter why you felt you had to do it, I want you to know that I really feel . . ."

368

She wasn't listening. She had started that toneless crooning again, and he suddenly realized that it was the sound many women make when they wish to soothe infants, wish to send them off to sleep.

He walked out the open kitchen door, then turned, saying, "Did you say something?"

"I just said, mister, that it'll scrub off the floorboards. It sure would have messed up that wall."

He walked through the door yard and across the vegetable patch, careful not to step in the freshly planted rows. The night mist was drying on the hood and top of the black government sedan. When the sending set warmed up he lifted the hand mike off the prongs and said, knowing as he did so, that not only had Craik Lopat died, but also a girl who had existed almost entirely in his mind, "Raymes reporting, Raymes reporting in."

"Go ahead, Raymes."

He licked his lips and planned how he would phrase it.


# Night Work

*by Gerald Tollesfrud*

Hogan's Roadhouse.

I'd never been there before. Damn sure wouldn't go there again.

Harry Doyle Investigations had been stiffed again, for the third time in two years. Chicago suburbs, usually out of my territory, what had looked like an easy fee. A strange twist with the fat, gray-haired old guy in expensive Burbridge coat and raw silk suit wanting me to find out what his shorts refused to believe in spite of what his head told him. Was his ripe, young plaything suckering him with her occasional steamy romps for the expensive gifts and paid ocean cruises he bestowed on her? With pledges of undying love? Was she at the same time hanging on to the young, yuppie stockbroker she had married and had sworn to have left for him?

Easy surveillance. Some thousand-speed film, a few red-eyed nights in the middle-aged Buick Century I still hadn't paid off. Five hundred in the coin of the realm to start, two large when I delivered. Package of glossies and audio cassettes exchanged for the fee.

Screwed without being kissed. Guy had disappeared in his Mercedes that turned out to be rented under a phony name leaving me with six hundred in expenses to cover with the front five hundred and a week of my life down the sewer.

Got madder as each mile of Interstate slipped away in the rain-splattered rearview mirror through the smoky haze my porous muffler spewed in my wake. Speed needle hit eight-five, faster than five minutes ago. My pocket contributed about twelve bucks to my fist, enough to buy a tonic of Scotch at the next exit.

Hogan's Roadhouse.

Just what I needed. Not a fancy, upscale oasis where I'd have to belly up with the rosy-cheeked affluent. That would depress me even more. Just a dump with booze and a lonely waitress with an empty mind and a full body.

The place was more neon than bricks, more noise than therapy, more bad than good. But what the hell. On the way across the dark, puddled parking lot I wondered if there was a camper-club meeting inside. The back lot was bordered with a string of truck campers, pop-ups, and one rusty-looking Winnebago. Inside, while my eyes accommodated the dimness, my ears fought against the heavy-metal shrieking that passed for music and the sour smell of old beer and new toilet chemicals.

Perfect!

I hung my wrinkled London Fog raincoat at the far end of a dark alcove ringed with wall-hooks and crowded by empty beer cases. With a buck stuffed into one of its pockets for the remaining highway tolls, just in case, I took the balance of my wealth to the bar.

At the far end a large room was filled with electronic dartboards, more noise, enough smoke to cure half the ham in Kentucky, and occupied by most of the population of northern Illinois. A long, scarred bar stretched along one wall of the nearest section of the dump where one man sat huddled in a trench-coat like mine. Newer and cleaner. All the stools beyond him were covered by young women, mostly white, one black girl about six-three, and a Hispanic spilling out of her blouse.

As I approached the bar, blinking away the smoke and tasting the drink in my mind, trench-coat heaved to his feet. The girl next to him walked ahead of him, hips pistoning under tight, denim cut-offs as she tugged her red halter top up with her left hand and reached the other for a transparent plastic poncho hanging on an oak hall-tree at the bar's end. The man shoved his full beer mug and small pile of bills onto the narrow border at the bar's edge, nodded to the woman behind the bar, and followed. His shoes and the bulge under his coat and the way his quick eyes scoped out the joint before fading into the haze spelled cop.

That was all right.

I came in for a mood-altering snort, not to knock over the joint.

Now I knew why the campers were out back. The place was a hot-bed, the rigs providing havens for whatever games the clientele wanted to play.

Nice choice of watering holes, Doyle.

I ordered a beer and a shot instead of my usual J and B. It seemed more fitting for my mood and for the joint. The old war-horse behind the bar served me silently, her pancake-makeup face impassive. She looked like every woman's worst nightmare whenever a birthday came along, like the proverbial twenty miles of muddy gravel road. She slapped my change next to my drinks, pendulous breasts swinging freely under a sweatshirt that had never become acquainted with a Maytag, and went down to chat with the members of the ecstasy corps.

I would soon become acquainted with the stocky, flat-nosed man who slipped through the entry door, at the edge of my vision. But at the moment my attention was drawn to the red-nailed fingers squeez-ing my left knee.

"Buy a girl a drink, pal?"

Her eyes locked on mine, but they couldn't see anything. The pupils were the wrong size. I checked her out as she pressed one hard, siliconed breast into my arm, wondering a long list of wonderings; needle or nose candy? how young? how had she fallen into this crap-shoot? how soon would she die, and how? I thought of the daughter I hadn't seen in nine years, who would be eighteen, starting at Arizona State in two months with her step-father's money, her mother in and out of booze wards. Eighteen and probably pretty and probably still certain that life is and always would be wonderful.

"Not tonight, honey," I answered. "It'd have to be a freebie. I never pay for it." Male macho pride bullshit. And six bucks left.

"Freebie?" she whispered, then reached with her other hand to feel under my left arm and across my back where it stopped on the gun, hard under my sport coat. "Aw, shit!" she spat. "You must be the other guy Eddie said would stop by for the grease. My lucky night. First I get a whip-freak, now it's Support Your Local Sheriff. Jeez! Could you at least buy me a beer? We hafta wait for Eddie and Bambi to get back anyway." She must have thought my eyebrows were raised as a ques-tion instead of confusion and explained, "Same pad."

Nice. The guy in the other raincoat—kinda looked like me, the only glimpse I'd had—was cop, maybe even Vice. Perks of the job. Occasional cream in his coffee for letting the girls' mineshafts produce the gold. Suddenly, I wasn't thirsty any more. I didn't know Eddie and didn't care and I sure as hell didn't need my ashes hauled by the Sweet Thing by my side.

"Later," I mumbled, and slid some bills in front of her. Then I headed for my coat, to be followed by my car, then forty minutes on the high road to the relatively chaste sanctuary of my own place and hopes that I didn't dream tonight.

I glanced at the swarthy guy near the door and saw him puff smoke around his face from a stumpy cigar and saw the cold, dead eyes that followed me. Must be the guy Eddie said was coming. Enjoy the buffet, butt-head.

At the far end of the narrow, closet-like space where my coat hung I was just pulling it off the hook when the guy's stocky body blocked some of the light. He was coming fast, leaning toward me, his right arm held stiffly straight at his side. At the end of it a long knife began an upward arc.

Instinct. Survival. Before my brain reacted I tossed my coat over his face and launched a knee into his groin. I was high, and it caught the soft belly between the spread sides of his black coat. Air exploded from his mouth under the tangle of trenchcoat covering it. I glanced at the death in his hand, pushed his heavy, doubled-up body against the wall and dug for my gun. His left arm clawed the fabric off his head just before the barrel of my Beretta sank into his skull above and behind his ear. Soundlessly, he crumbled and lay motionless, almost blocking my path between the wall and the stacked boxes.

I snugged my piece back into its holster, gathered up my coat, and bent over the guy, hearing his hoarse breathing, smelling sweat and wet wool and bad breath. I kneed him to the side, picked up the knife and button-retracted the blade, and put it inside my shirt. In his hip pocket a thin wallet, mine now. A thick envelope went from his breast pocket to mine. Then I walked unsteadily back to the bar. This time, Scotch. Neat. I needed it.

The ladies glanced at me appraisingly until my earlier friend leaned their way and whispered, then they turned their backs and some very nice bottoms to me and washed me from their minds.

The Scotch had hit my gut and was burning fiercely. I turned away, shrugged into my coat, and used it to shield my movements. The wallet ID'd my attacker as Vito Inglese, Chicago, a meaningless

372

address. Couple hundred in bills. Charge cards, same name. All bull-shit. No clues why he'd picked me.

The envelope was a shocker.

Six thousand, all in crisp hundreds.

Hit money? A mechanic?

I put it back in my pocket. My hands were shaking a little. I wondered if it was the six big ones or the fact some gorilla had tried to provide me with the big sleep.

Also wondered why. Was he really after me? This wasn't my turf and the guy was a stranger to me. He'd tried to ventilate me as if he had a mission.

I stood up to leave. Forever would do it.

As I headed for the door I saw the girl who had led the way for the cop fifteen minutes earlier. Her shoulders slumped under the plastic coat as she took her place silently among her business associates. He wore a self-satisfied smile and the same tan, all-weather coat as mine. Then it hit me. Same build, same coat, in the same grungy roadside ginmill. I was looking at the right target.

Maybe I'm a closet moralist. Maybe I saw the chance to lay out an I.O.U. I could collect another time.

Or maybe I'm stupid.

I fingered the envelope carefully in my pocket, sorting, dividing. Then I walked past him to the bimbo who'd just serviced him and held out a hundred dollar bill. "For your sick mother, sweetie," I muttered, watching her confused frown melt into a smile on her glossed lips. "And your bosom buddy's last name," I added, jerking my head at the guy. She hesitated, then whispered it to me and stuck the bill somewhere out of sight.

Then I turned back to the man.

"To the end of the bar, Sarge." I led him to the curved corner of the dark oak where a waitress's station interrupted its contours. When I turned around he was about five feet away, operating distance, one hand at his side, the other with thumb hooked in his belt. Near the leather strap that ran across his chest to his holster.

"So?" he said. "Who th' fuck put you in charge? Da hell you want?"

"You don't know me, pal. Out of town cop. Private. Used to carry tin out of the Four Two station in the city."

He raised his eyebrows, jerked his head to tell me to keep going, his time was valuable. Say your piece. I slowly moved my hand into the pocket of my slacks. He watched my eyes, but he could see my hand, too. It came out with five bills. I handed them to him, but he didn't reach out. I dropped them on the bar.

"That's just to get your attention." I added, "This could be your lucky day. Know a hired hit named Vito Inglese?"

A flicker of recognition in the eyes. He knew I'd seen it. "Who're you?" I could feel him measuring me, looking at the scar that ran into my sideburn, the nose that wasn't straight any more, the bulk in the shoulders.

"Doesn't matter. I need a favor from you down the pike I'll let you know, Sutton." I reached, slowly again, into my hip pocket while he watched, and put Inglese's wallet on the bar. "Same size, same tan coat, guy got mixed up. Tried to put a knife in me. While you were out back massaging Bambi's tonsils. Thought I was you. I used to be a cop, figured you'd appreciate knowing somebody had your number." I waited while he thought about it. While he tried to decide where this was going. Then, "The five hundred is for you to stay at the bar until I'm gone. After that you can send it to your favorite charity. Vito is in the nearest closet sleeping with a headache. If he's wanted you'll be a hero. Sound fair?"

He shook his head slowly from side to side, his eyes still boring into me. "You're goddamned crazy."

"Nah!" I said. "Even a cop gets some take now'n then's still a cop. Needs to know who's at his back. Name is Harry so you'll know who might be calling you for that favor. You give me five minutes. Deal?"

He nodded, collected the bills and the wallet next to him, and moved away. I went through the door. The rain was still falling, the parking lot was muddier, the night seemed darker than I remembered. I went to the edge of the mass of cars and waited while the sound of eighteen-wheelers carried through the wet air from the Interstate. Behind Hogan's the lights went out in one of the campers and two people dashed back into the bar, the pale legs of the girl flashing in the darkness. Inside, the sound of music and people pulsed. He didn't come out behind me so I walked to my old Buick and drove back to the highway.

Stiffed by the gray-haired guy in the fading light of early evening on a rainy day. Made a lady of the night smile. Dodged a shank meant for someone else but aimed at my gut. Got five thousand dollars richer.

I patted the bulge of the envelope in my pocket lovingly.

Not a bad night's work for momma Doyle's little boy Harry.

# A Novel Forgery

*by Rodrigues Ottolengui*

Mr. Barnes was wondering whether he would soon have a case which would require special mental effort in its solution. "Something that will make me think," was the way he phrased it to himself. The same idea had occupied him for some time. Not that he had been idle, but his "cases" had all been of such a nature that with a little supervision it had been safe to intrust them entirely to his subordinates. Nothing had occurred to compel his personal investigation. On this morning, however, fate had something peculiarly attractive for him. His office-boy announced a visitor, who, when shown into the detective's sanctum, introduced himself thus:

"I am Stephen West, cashier of the Fulton National Bank. Is this Mr. Barnes?"

"Yes, sir," replied the detective. "Is your business important?"

"It is very important to me," said Mr. West. "I am interested to the extent of forty thousand dollars."

"Forty thousand dollars! Forgery?" Receiving an assenting nod, Mr. Barnes arose and closed the door of the office after instructing the boy to prevent his being disturbed. Returning to his seat, he said: "Now then, Mr. West, tell me the story. All of it, as far as you know it. Omit no detail, however unimportant it may seem to you."

"Very good. My bank has been swindled out of forty thousand dollars in the most mysterious manner. We have received four checks, each for ten thousand dollars. These were signed with the name John Wood, one of our best customers. In making up his monthly balance these checks were sent to his house in the usual order of business. To-day Mr. Wood came to the bank, and declared them to be forgeries."

"Were these checks paid by you personally?"

"Oh, no. We received them through the Clearing-House. They had been deposited at the Harlem National Bank, and reached us in the routine way. They were taken on four different days."

"Who was the depositor at the Harlem Bank?"

"There is a mystery there. His name is Carl Grasse. Inquiry at the

375

Harlem Bank shows that he has been a depositor for about a year. He had a seemingly flourishing business, a beer-garden and concert place. Recently he sold out and returned to his home in Germany. Before doing so he drew out his deposits and closed his account."

"How is it that you did not yourself detect the forgeries? I supposed you bank people were so expert nowadays that the cashing of a worthless check would be impossible."

"Here are the forged checks, and here is one cashed by us since the accounting, which is genuine. Compare them, and perhaps you will admit that anyone might have been deceived."

Mr. Barnes examined the checks very closely, using a lens to assist his eyes. Presently he laid them down without comment, and said:

"What do you wish me to do, Mr. West?"

"To me it seems like a hopeless task, but at least I should like to have the forger arrested. I will gladly pay five hundred dollars as a reward."

Mr. Barnes took up the checks again, examined them most carefully with the lens, and once more laid them down. He strummed on his desk a moment and then said suddenly:

"Mr. West, suppose that I not only arrest the guilty man, but recover the forty thousand dollars?"

"You don't mean to say—" began Mr. West, rather astonished.

"I said, 'suppose,' interrupted Mr. Barnes.

"Why, in that case," said Mr. West, "I would gladly give a thousand more."

"The terms suit me," said the detective. "I'll do my best. Leave these checks with me, and I'll report to you as promptly as possible. One moment," as Mr. West was about to depart; "I will make a memorandum of something you must do yourself." He wrote a few lines on a sheet of paper and handed it to Mr. West, saying, "Let me have those today, if possible."

One week later Mr. West received the following note:

STEPHEN WEST, Esq.:

Dear Sir—I have completed my investigation of your case. Please call at my office at four o'clock. If convenient, you may as well bring with you a check for fifteen hundred dollars, made payable to

JOHN BARNES

"Great heavens!" ejaculated the cashier upon reading the above, "he tells me to bring fifteen hundred dollars. That means he has recovered the money. Thank God!" He dropped into his chair, overcome at the

376

sudden release from the suspense of the previous week, and a few tears trickled down his cheek as he thought of his wife and little one who would not now be obliged to give up their pretty little home to make good his loss.

Promptly at four he was ushered into the presence of Mr. Barnes. Impatient to have his hopes confirmed, he exclaimed at once:

"Am I right? You have succeeded?"

"Most thoroughly," said the detective. "I have discovered the thief, and have him in prison. I also have his written confession."

"But, the forty thousand dollars?"

"All safe and sound. Your bank does not lose a dollar—except the reward." Mr. Barnes added the last after a pause and with a twinkle of his eye.

"Oh, Mr. Barnes, that is a trifle compared to what I expected. But tell me, how was this trick played on us? Who did it?"

"Suppose I give you a detailed account of my work in solving the riddle? I am just in the humor for telling it, and besides you will be more appreciative."

"That is just what I should most desire."

"Very well," began Mr. Barnes. "We will go back to the moment when, after scrutinizing the checks, I asked what you would give for the recovery of the money. I asked that because a suspicion had entered my mind, and I knew that if it should prove to be correct, the arrest of the criminal and the recovery of the money would be simultaneous. I will not explain now why that should be a necessary sequence, as you will see that I was right. But I will tell you what made me entertain the suspicion. In the first place, as you know, of course, John Wood uses a private special check. The forgeries were upon blanks which had been stolen from his check-book. Thus the thief seemingly had access to it. Next, as is commonly done nowadays, the amount of the check was not only written, but also punched out, with the additional precaution of punching a dollar mark before and after the figures. It would seem therefore almost impossible that any alterations had been made after the check was originally drawn. Such things have been done, the holes being filled up with paper pulp, and new ones punched afterwards. But in this case nothing of the sort had been attempted, nor indeed was any such procedure necessary, for the checks were not raised from genuine ones, but had been declared by Wood to be forgeries outright. That is, he denied the signatures."

"Certainly. They were declared to be spurious."

"Exactly. Now that was all that I knew when you were here last except that the signatures seemed to be very similar. It was possible

377

that they were tracings. The plain deduction from this was that the forger was some one in John Wood's establishment; some one who could have access to the checkbook, to the punch, and also have a chance to copy the signature, if it was copied."

"All that is quite clear, but how to proceed?"

"I instructed you to send me a list of all the checks which had been paid out on John Wood's account, giving their dates, numbers, and amounts. I also asked you to procure for me from the Harlem National Bank a similar list of checks paid on order of Carl Grasse. These two lists you sent to me, and they have been very useful. As soon as you left me, and whilst awaiting your lists, I tried some experiments with the forged checks. First I argued that if the signatures were traced, having been made, as it were, from a model, it would follow necessarily that they would exactly coincide if superimposed the one upon the other. Now whilst a man from habit will write his name very similarly a thousand times, I doubt if in a million times he would, or could, exactly reproduce his signature. The test of placing one over the other and examining with transmitted light satisfied me that they were not tracings. I compared each check with each of the others, and with the genuine one which you also left with me. No two were exact counterparts of one another. Still this did not completely prove that they were not tracings, for an artistic criminal might have gone so far as to trace each check from a different model, thus avoiding identity whilst preserving similarity."

"Mr. Barnes," said Mr. West, admiringly, "you delight me with your care in reasoning out your point."

"Mr. West, in speculating upon circumstantial evidence the most thorough care must be used, if one would avoid arresting the innocent. Nothing, to my mind, is stronger proof against a criminal than a complete chain of circumstantial evidence, but again, nothing is so misleading if at any stage a mistake, an omission, or a misconstruction be allowed to occur. In this case, then, as I was starting out to prove what was merely a suspicion, I determined to be most careful, for indeed I dislike following up suspicion at any time. A suspicion is a prejudgment, and may prove a hindrance to correct reasoning. Not entirely satisfied, therefore, I took the next step. A tracing can be made in either of two ways: with a lead-pencil, or with a stylus of glass or agate. The former leaves a deposit of the lead, whilst the latter makes an indentation upon the paper. In the first case the forger will attempt to remove the lead with an erasing rubber, but will not succeed thoroughly, because some of it will be covered by the ink, and because of the danger of injuring the surface of the paper. In the
378

latter instance, if he be a very thoughtful man, he might undertake to remove the indentation by rubbing the opposite side with the end of his knife or with an ivory papercutter. In either case a careful scrutiny with a strong glass would show the burnishing upon the reverse side. I could find nothing of the sort. Taking one of the checks I applied a solution to remove the ink. A thorough examination disclosed that there was no sign either of the graphite, or of the indentation from the stylus. In fact, I became satisfied that the signatures had not been traced."

"But what did that prove? They might have been imitations made by a clever penman."

"They might have been, but I doubted it; and since you ask, I will give my reasons. In the first place, the signatures were accepted at your bank not once, but four times. It would be a remarkably clever man to deceive experts so well. However, I did not abandon this possibility until further developments showed conclusively to my mind that it would be a waste of time to follow up that line of research. Had it been necessary to do so, I should have discovered who in the place had the opportunity to do the work, and by examining their past I should have received a hint as to which of these was most likely to be my man. For any man who could have the ability to commit such a clever forgery must have acquired it as a sequence of special skill and aptitude with his pen of which his friends would be cognizant. Once I looked up such a man, and found that as a boy he had forged his parents' names to excuses for absences from school. Later he turned to higher things. In this instance I was satisfied that the only person having the access to materials, the knowledge of the financial condition of the concern, and the ability to write the checks, was Mr. John Wood himself."

"John Wood!" exclaimed the cashier. "Impossible! Why, that would mean that ——"

"Nothing is impossible, Mr. West. I know what you would say. That it involved his having an accomplice in this Carl Grasse? Well, that is what I suspected, and that is why I asked for an additional reward for the recovery of the funds. If I could prove that John Wood made the checks himself, they ceased to be forgeries in one sense, and the bank could rightfully charge the amounts against his account. But let me tell you why I abandoned your theory that an expert penman was at work. Observe that though you would have honored a check for forty thousand dollars drawn by John Wood, yet the forgeries were four in number. That showed that the man was not afraid of arousing your suspicion. The only man who could feel absolutely sure

379

upon that point was John Wood. But there is another pretty point. These checks being spurious, and yet being numbered, could arouse your suspicion in two ways. If the numbers upon them greatly varied from those upon genuine checks coming in at the same time, the fraud would have been detected quickly. On the other hand, he could not give you correct numbers without being either in collusion with his bookkeeper or else duplicating the numbering of other checks. That the latter course was pursued, exempted the bookkeeper. All the numbers on the forged checks were duplicates of those on genuine ones."

"But, Mr. Barnes, that did not arouse our suspicion, because———"

"Just so," interrupted Mr. Barnes, "but let me tell you why, as the *why* is a very significant link in our chain. Your list of this man's checks helped me there. About a year ago Carl Grasse appeared upon the scene in Harlem, buying out a beer-garden, and starting an account in the Harlem National Bank. Now observe that prior to that time, from the first check sent to you by Wood, the strictest regularity as to numbering obtained. There is not a break or a skip anywhere. But in February, the month after Carl Grasse moved to Harlem, there is a duplication in Wood's checks. Two have the same numbering, but both are for trifling amounts, sixteen dollars in one instance and forty in the other. You possibly passed it over. Next month, I find two duplications, and from then on this apparent mistake happens no less than ten times."

"Mr. Barnes, the bookkeepers did notice this, and we spoke to Mr. Wood, but he said it was simply a clerical error of his own due to haste in business hours."

"Exactly, but he was paving the way for his big coup. He was disarming you of suspicion. This one fact satisfied me that I was on the right track, but your list gave me even better corroboration. On February 1st I find that Wood cashed a check payable to himself for ten thousand and fifty-nine dollars. On February 2d, Carl Grasse opened an account with the Harlem Bank, depositing ten thousand dollars, paying in the amount, in cash. This might seem but a coincidence, but by looking over the books of the beer-garden, which is still in existence, Grasse having sold it out, I find that on February 2d, Grasse paid his employees just fifty-nine dollars. The difference, you see, between Wood's draft and Grasse's deposit."

"It certainly seems to connect the two, when we remember that the final forgeries were checks signed by Wood in favor of Grasse."

"Precisely, but follow this a little further. For several months there is nothing to connect the two so far as their banking goes, but note that during this lapse Grasse does not draw a single check in favor of himself, nor does he deposit any checks from others. His transactions with his customers are strictly cash, and his checks are all to dealers, who supply him with his stock. None of these are for large amounts, and his balance does not exceed twelve thousand dollars at any time. On October 1st he deposited five thousand dollars in cash. On the day before that, Wood drew that amount out of your bank. On the 12th, this is repeated by both, and on the 14th, Grasse cashes a check for twelve thousand dollars, taking cash. This goes through successfully, and the Harlem Bank is made to see that Grasse commands large amounts and uses large amounts. This is repeated in varying amounts in November, and again in December, the bank by this time being quite ready to pay out money to Grasse. On January 2d, Wood has his check account balanced. On the 3d, Grasse deposits Wood's check for ten thousand dollars. This goes through the Clearing-House, and is accepted by your bank. The Harlem Bank is therefore satisfied of its authenticity. On the 5th, Grasse deposits check number two, and at the same time cashes a check for ten thousand dollars. The second spurious check goes through all right, and on the 10th and 15th, the transactions are repeated. On the 20th, Grasse explains to the Harlem Bank that he has sold his business, and is going home to Germany. He closes his account, taking out his money, and disappears from the scene. You are forty thousand dollars out by a clever swindle, with nothing to prove your suspicions save a few coincidences in the banking records of the two men."

"But assuredly, Mr. Barnes, enough evidence upon which to arrest Mr. Wood?"

"To arrest him, yes. But to convict him? That is another affair. Without conviction you do not recover your money. No, my work was by no means finished. I first sought to follow Grasse. I did not have far to go. At the Hamburg-American line I found him booked, but investigation showed that he never sailed. The ticket which he bought has never been taken up."

"Then the accomplice is still in this country?"

"No; the accomplice is not in this country," said Mr. Barnes, dryly. "Don't get ahead of the story. At this stage of the game I made some singular discoveries. I found, for example, that Carl Grasse slept over his saloon, but that he frequently would be absent all night. I also learned that when he did sleep there, he would leave about nine o'clock in the morning for that mysterious realm, 'down-town.' When he slept elsewhere, he usually reached the saloon at eight, and still went 'down-town' at nine. It was his general custom to get back about five in the afternoon. Extending my researches in the direction of

381

John Wood, I learned that he was customarily at his office at ten o'clock, seldom leaving before four. Moreover, at his apartment the janitor told me that he frequently slept elsewhere, and that when he passed the night at that place, he would leave about seven in the morning. Do you follow me?"

"Do you mean that John Wood and Carl Grasse are one and the same person?"

"That idea entered my mind about this time. Up at the saloon I found some other small evidences that this was a probability. You see, a man may disguise his personal appearance, but it is difficult for him to change his habits with his clothing. For example, I found that Mr. Wood always uses Carter's writing fluid, and Mr. Grasse had the same predilection, as the empty bottles attest. Moreover, the bottles are of the same size in both places. Next I observe that both men used the same make of stub pens. Again note that though Carl Grasse is a German name and the man was keeping a beer saloon, he was never seen to drink beer himself. John Wood has the same antipathy to malt. But most singular is the fact that this man, who so carefully laid his plans, should have actually bought a check-punching stamp of the same make and style of figures as that used in the Wood establishment."

"Perhaps he did that so that he could make the spurious checks up-town instead of down-town, where he might be discovered."

"More than likely, but he should have taken it away with him. There is always some little detail of this kind that even the most skillful overlooks. He probably thought that the similarity of the instruments would never be detected, or made to count against him. It is nothing in itself, but as a link in a chain it mends a break. There was one fact, however, at wide variance with the theory of the identity of the two men. Wood is of ordinary build, with black hair and smooth-shaven face. Grasse is described as very stout, with red hair and whiskers. Of course, following the theory of impersonation, if Wood transformed himself into a stout man, totally different clothing would be needed for the two parts which he played. I found that Wood always dressed in the finest broadcloth, whilst Grasse wore conspicuous plaids. Supposing that he wore a red wig and false whiskers, I determined to find the man from whom he had procured them. I guessed that he would avoid any well-known place, and I began my hunt in the costumers' shops on Third Avenue. I went to several without obtaining any clue, when at last fortune favored me. I found a place where, upon their books, in last January was a record of 'red wig and whiskers' for the same costumer. Moreover, they had furnished
382

this person with a 'make-up' for a fat German, giving him the necessary 'pads,' as they are called, a suit of underwear wadded so as to increase the proportion of the body. Can you guess what I did next?"

"I think not."

"It was an inspiration. I ordered a similar outfit for myself, including the plaid suit. This morning they were delivered to me, and, dressed in them, I induced the costumer to go with me to Wood's place. As soon as I was shown into his presence, I began to talk in a most excited, angry tone. I said, 'Mr. Wood, I come for satisfaction. I am Carl Grasse, the man you have been personating up-town. I am the man whose name you forged to the back of your own checks. And this is the costumer who sold you the disguise. Am I not right?' This last speech I addressed to the costumer, who, to my intense satisfaction, said, 'Yes, that is the gentleman; but I did not know he was going to impersonate anybody.' "

"What happened then?" asked the cashier.

"Well," said Mr. Barnes, "I had better luck than I had expected, though, in line with my hopes. You see, my sudden appearance before him, my words, and my rapid speech, all tended to confuse him. He suddenly heard himself accused of forging the name of 'Carl Grasse,' and for the moment thought only of defending himself from that charge. He was utterly taken back, and stammered out, 'I did not forge anybody's name. The checks had my own signature, and the endorsement—that was "Carl Grasse." There is no such person.' Then suddenly seeing that he was making a mistake and incriminating himself, he exclaimed, 'Who the devil are you?'

" 'I am a detective,' I answered, quickly seizing his arms and putting on a pair of manacles, 'and I arrest you for swindling the Fulton Bank, whether your offense be forgery or not.' That settled him. He wilted and began to cry for mercy. He even offered me money to let him escape. I delivered him to the Central Office officials, and since then the Inspector has obtained a voluntary confession from him. Are you satisfied, Mr. West?"

"I am more than satisfied. I am amazed. Mr. Barnes, you are a genius."

"Not at all, Mr. West, I am a detective."

# Old Calamity's Stick-up

*by Joseph Fulling Fishman*

"The new warden's here, sir."

Deputy Warden Fletcher looked up from his desk at his inmate clerk's announcement, betraying on his placid face or in his keen gray eyes none of the interest which he felt. For weeks the prison had seethed under the surface. Warden Anderson had been forced out by politics. For weeks the place had been vacant while rumors flew around concerning this and that politician who was to get this political plum. Nor was this interest impersonal on the part of the prisoners. If the new man was easy or soft there might be more recommendations for parole. If he was hard-boiled, it might be too bad.

Old Calamity, as Fletcher was known to the three thousand prisoners in the institution, left his office and went to the warden's office in the administration to meet his new boss. "Probably never been in a stir in his life," he told himself. "Have to educate him like the rest of them."

He was right. The new official, who introduced himself as James J. Beckwith, greeted the deputy cordially and immediately announced that he was entirely new to the game, with the usual witticism which Old Calamity had heard so many times that he guessed it was easy enough to get into a prison but hard to get out.

"Have to rely on you to help me," he said genially. "Governor told me a lot about you. Praised you a lot. Could you show me around a bit, so that I can sort of get acquainted?"

"Certainly, sir," Fletcher replied with his usual courtesy. "You have a certificate of appointment, I assume?"

"Yes, indeed. Here it is." Beckwith handed Old Calamity a piece of parchment informing the world in general that the Governor did, by virtue of the powers invested in him by law, hereby appoint James J. Beckwith Warden of the State Prison at Cosmopolis, and so on.

"By the way," the warden went on, "could you have one of the prisoners make a little frame for it? I'd like to hang it up in my office."

"Yes, indeed, I'll be glad to. Shall we start now?"

384

"Might as well, I guess."

The next three or four hours were spent in making a tour of the huge prison, with its twenty-three buildings and its thirty-foot wall which was nearly a mile around. The deputy went patiently over various details of administration which he had explained so many times during the past thirty years to so many politicians who had come and gone as wardens. The warden, like all those unfamiliar with prisons, was particularly interested in inmates about whom he had read in the papers, the notorious swindlers, members of gangs, and highly placed bank and business officials who had come to grief.

"You've got the Darnley mob here, haven't you?"

"Yes, seven of them."

"Pretty bad bunch, aren't they?"

Old Calamity smiled to himself. The usual questions. "Well, they're not exactly Sunday school boys," he said.

"How're they behaving?"

"All right. They don't give any trouble. Men of that kind scarcely ever break any of the minor rules. They don't have to earn a reputation for toughness; they already have it. You never have to put them in the hole." He paused for a moment, and then went on. "It's only when they make a break that you have to look out for them."

"Well, thank you very much, Mr. Fletcher," said the warden, at the end of the tour. "I'm tired walking. Suppose we leave the rest of it until tomorrow. I'll probably familiarize myself with some of the book stuff tonight. I guess the boys who work in my office understand it, don't they?"

"Perfectly," replied Old Calamity. He was deep in thought as he walked back to his own office. For a few moments he sat intent in thought. Suddenly, his mind was made up, he reached for the telephone and called the *Daily Dispatch*.

"That you, Fred?" he inquired when he finally got the managing editor. "This is Fletcher, up at the Pen. I want you to do something for me, will you?"

"Sure," the editor replied, "anything you want."

An hour and a half later, Old Calamity, in the office of the *Dispatch*, received from the managing editor a small flat package. The deputy walked across the street to the telegraph office and had the chief clerk there pick out one of his brightest boys.

"Son," said Old Calamity, with his winning smile, "there's a train leaves for Springfield in about twenty minutes. I want you to take this to Governor Husted. Don't give it to anyone else. I'll telephone him,

385

so he'll be expecting you. Here's five dollars. The fare will cost you about three dollars and fifty cents. Make it snappy, now, and keep the change."

After the call to the Governor's office was completed, Old Calamity hurried back to the prison.

"Mr. Enslow," he telephoned the record clerk, "come down to my office right away, will you, please, and bring your fingerprint powder?"

In the course of a few moments Mr. Enslow appeared. He stared at the oblong piece of heavy paper which the deputy handed him and then glanced inquiringly at Fletcher. In twenty-three years at the institution Mr. Enslow had received some strange requests from Old Calamity. But this was a little *too* much. His eyes widened and his mouth opened slightly.

"You mean—on—this—this—"

"Yes," said Old Calamity. "That's what I mean."

Mr. Enslow sprinkled the fine black powder as directed. Ten or twelve fingerprints became plainly visible.

"See if you can classify them."

Mr. Enslow took out of his pocket a small pointer and a powerful magnifying glass which were as much a part of him as his arms and legs. There was a long silence as he went patiently over one print after the other, counting and checking the ridges, and then re-counting and re-checking. Old Calamity stood patiently by. At last Enslow straightened up. "I can classify five of them," he said, "five of them which are on one hand. Probably where someone held it."

"All right, give me the classification right now. Then search our records and see what we have."

The record clerk departed and a few moments later reappeared. "Nothing in our files, sir," he reported.

"All right, thank you."

Old Calamity again picked up the telephone. "Get the Fingerprint Bureau of the Department of Justice in Washington," he directed the operator. He sat drumming on his desk, waved Mr. Enslow out.

"Hello, Fletcher," came the voice of the Bureau's director. "What's on your mind?"

"Want to give you a classification. Got a pencil? All right: M L-10 WO L-6 L-9. Have you got it?"

He waited a few moments. Then, "Yes, we have it," came the reply. "Only one rap, September 3, 1921, Chicago, Robbery in the Second, Five Years, Joliet."

"Nothing else?"

"No, that's all."

"Thank you." Old Calamity hung up the receiver and once again walked slowly back to the warden's office.

"You going to be here tonight?" he inquired.

The warden glanced at the clock.

"Why, yes," he replied, "I might as well. My family won't be down for two or three days yet."

"Well, I had planned to go to the theater. But if you want me to stay I'll be glad to."

"No, indeed," said the warden, "not at all. You go right ahead. If I want anything explained I'll see you about it in the morning."

# II

It was a cold December night and darkness had already set in. Old Calamity started toward his home at the far corner of the grounds, then changed his mind and walked rapidly along the wall which started on the side of the administration building to the corner where the wall turned east. He rounded the corner and started down along the side of the thirty-foot-high piece of masonry until he reached the south sallyport, which constituted the entrance to the prison yard for trucks and freight cars. He was sunk so deeply in thought that he was startled when he heard a sharp, "Where you going?" and whirled around to find himself facing a gun in the hand of the outside patrol. "Oh, I'm sorry, Deputy," the guard said as he saw who it was.

"All right, Madison; don't say anything about seeing me here. Who's on the sallyport tower?"

"Fredericks, sir."

"Tell him to open the gate, will you, please?"

Madison yelled to the tower guard, who could be seen peering down from the balcony surrounding the tower. In a few seconds the solid steel gate operated by electricity slowly rose and Old Calamity entered.

He hurried across the empty and dimly lit yard and let himself into the end of the main corridor, through which the prisoners entered to go into the mess hall from the shops. Guard Delafield was on duty in the lower corridor.

"I—I thought you went out the cage a few moments ago, sir," he said.

"I did," Old Calamity replied. He whispered, "Get Henry, Martine, Shea, Crispen, Endicott and Rogers and you come with them to the chief clerk's office."

The deputy walked rapidly down the hall to the front cage. O'Brien, the guard on duty there, exhibited the same surprise as Delafield had.

"Anything wrong, sir?"

"I'm not sure. Got a couple of pieces of chewing gum with you?"

"Yes, sir," the guard said, and handed two pieces to the deputy, who, instead of putting the gum in his mouth, put it in his pocket. "Save it till later," he explained. "Warden's car still here, isn't it?"

"Yes, sir. Right out there."

"All right; don't tell anybody I came back."

Old Calamity returned to the chief clerk's office to find Delafield and the six guards he had sent for awaiting him. "All right, boys," he said, "go out the south sallyport one or two at a time and meet me at the southeast corner of the wall. I'll go first." As he hurried out Delafield ran after him. "Just a second, Deputy," he said, "I forgot to tell you that someone in Springfield called up and said to tell you 'No.'"

The Warden had his dinner sent to him in his office. Immediately he finished it he sent for Captain Kearney, in charge of the first night watch. He introduced himself and then handed Kearney a list of about twenty-five names of prisoners. "Bring these men down here," he directed. "I want to talk to them."

Captain Kearney glanced over the list, eyes widening in surprise. He turned to go, hesitated, and then faced around. "Excuse me, sir," he said courteously, "but I assume you know these men are members of the worst mobs we have in the place. Four of them belong to the Spider McGiven mob, seven to the Darnley mob, six to the—"

"Yes, I know," said the warden. "That's the reason I want to talk to them. If they think they're going to start anything while I'm here I'll show them that they're mistaken."

"Very well, sir."

Fifteen minutes later all the men on the warden's list were sitting on benches outside his office. The warden interviewed the members of each mob at a time. Captain Kearney was vigilant and nervous while the inmates were all together in the small side corridor in which they were placed while waiting to be called, but as one gang and then another was interviewed and sent back to their cells, until only the Darnley gang remained, he began to breathe more freely. One or two guards had been sent to accompany each gang back to the cell house, so that by the time the Darnley gang was summoned, only three remained. From the muttered conversations of the members of the gang who had been interviewed, Captain Kearney gathered that the warden, as he had announced, was "laying down the law" to them concerning their future behavior in a decidedly impressive manner.

"Stick 'em up!" Kearney whirled around. Before his startled gaze stood the seven members of the Darnley gang. And in front of them stood the warden, agitated and perspiring, his hands held high above him, beside him Ed Darnley, gun in hand, shifting the weapon from the warden to the guards and then back again.

"One squeak out of you screws and you're dead men. All right, boys, tighten 'em up."

The men in back of him stepped forward. Four of them held ropes. Within three minutes Captain Kearney and the guards were gagged and bound and lying on the floor of the warden's office. In thirty seconds more the gang was at the end of the side hall where it entered the main corridor.

With a bound they sprang into the main corridor and ran up the fifty feet of hall to the front cage. O'Brien had his back turned and was looking out the front door. He heard a soft rustle back of him and whirled sharply. It was too late. "Open up, you," said Darnley, "or we'll croak this bird and then you, too. C'mon, snap into it."

"All right," said O'Brien sullenly, "you've got the drop on me." He opened the door, and then—as they crowded in—the second door forming the cage. At the outer door McCabe, Darnley's chief lieutenant, turned. He raised his hand, there was a soft "plop," then a sighing exhaled breath as O'Brien sank unconscious to the stone floor.

Darnley slammed the steel grille door with a resounding clang and, followed by his gang, raced like mad down the steps and over the brick path to the warden's automobile. They piled in. The warden, evidently hurried by Darnley's prodding gun, fumbled in his pocket and inserted the key in the ignition lock. "Why—there's something wrong—it's choked—"

"Give it to me, you damn fool," hissed Darnley. He grabbed the key from the warden and jammed it into the lock! Something there!

"It's chewing gum, Ed," came from the other side of the car.

# III

Darnley straightened up. There stood Old Calamity and his guards.

"I'll never go back alive!" Darnley screamed.

But Old Calamity was too quick for him. He jerked the car door open, grabbed Darnley's arm as he turned the gun on himself, gave a powerful wrench which pulled the gangster sprawling out on the road.

Within five minutes the prisoners and the frightened warden were back in the latter's office. The warden finally found his voice, and told his story.

"And I finally came to the Darnley mob," he concluded. "No sooner had they come into the office than Darnley stuck this gun in my ribs and told me he'd kill me if I didn't come along."

"You're a liar," said Old Calamity. His voice was soft, almost caressing.

"What was that?"

"I said you're a liar," repeated Old Calamity. "Where have you got him?"

"Who? Are you talking to me?"

"Yes, I'm talking to you. I'm asking you what you did with the warden and where you've got him. And I'm not going to ask you again." As if by magic a gun appeared in his hand. "I'm going to count three. I'm going to shoot. One—two—"

"My God, don't do that. I'll tell you, I'll tell you! He's all right. We didn't hurt him any. We've got him tied up in a house out on the Morgan Road. About ten miles away. I'll take you there, I swear I will!"

"But what made you suspicious in the first place?" the Governor demanded. Old Calamity had just related to him the details of the attempted break the night before.

"Why, several things, Governor. The first was when he used the word mob, referring to the Darnley crowd. Only gangsters, cops and prison men refer to them as mobs. Other people call them gangs."

"Yes, but he might have picked that up from somewhere."

"No," admitted Old Calamity, "it wasn't. But after he did that I purposely used the word 'hole' when referring to the solitary. I waited for him to ask me what it was before I went on talking. But he didn't. This practically convinced me that he was prison-wise. Then there was something else which made me sure that he was a fake."

"What was that?"

"He told me," said Old Calamity, "that you had lavishly praised me to him. I know you are not the kind of man who does that, no matter what you may think of him."

The Governor looked searchingly at the man in front of him. Then he smiled. "Well," he said, "you're right, but if ever I felt like praising any man, it's you, particularly after the events of yesterday."

Old Calamity raised his hand. "So," he went on, "after all these things had aroused my suspicions I had the *Dispatch* take a photograph of him which they told him wouldn't appear until the next afternoon,
390

and I sent this photograph up to you. And then I got his fingerprints off the certificate of appointment, which he had, of course, taken from the real warden when they waylaid him. And I found that 'Mr. Beckwith,' as I suspected, *had* been in prison, and that he wasn't Mr. Beckwith at all, but someone entirely different."

"And his interest in the Darnley gang led you to believe—"

"When these other facts were coupled with his interest in the Darnley mob, it made me suspicious. I found out he wasn't Beckwith at all, but someone else. I searched his car and found the six revolvers and the machine gun. I simply planted the men out near the car. The rest you know."

"Was he actually a member of their gang?"

"Yes. He knew in a general way how to go about it because of the time he'd spent in prison."

For a moment the Governor sat silent. Finally he spoke: "You know, Fletcher. You're really the one I should appoint warden, but of course there's politics—you know how it is—"

"Oh, sure," said Old Calamity.




# Old Guy

### by Maitland LeRoy Osborne

"This is a stick-up old guy," announced the hard-eyed youth, showing the storekeeper a revolver and then replacing it in a side coat pocket. "Don't get funny with me now, old guy, and you won't get hurt. Just hand over that money you got this afternoon and I'll be on my way."

The hard-eyed youth might have been a broker's clerk, or perhaps a college undergraduate—if you noticed only his expensive-looking well-fitting clothes, his slicked-back hair, his rather elaborately bored expression. Only his movements were a little too jerky and abrupt for entire normality and his voice was tonelessly flat.

Smoke spiraled slowly up from a cigarette which drooped from a corner of his mouth as he leaned against the counter of the little store. He tilted his head slightly to keep the smoke out of his expressionless unwinking eyes.

The storekeeper himself was a spare, ramrod-straight man with once black hair that was mostly gray. The well worn, carelessly baggy suit that draped his form somehow failed to entirely disguise a faintly military bearing. His eyes were a frosty blue. Once they must have been piercing. He looked somewhat incongruous behind the counter of a store, as if he never really belonged there. He had big hands. Hands that looked as though they could batter the pasty white face of the youth on the other side of the counter into bloody pulp.

But there was a revolver in the young thug's pocket. He was potentially as dangerous as the most hardened killer. More so, perhaps—because he was unpredictable. The amateur gangster still intent on building up an underworld reputation.

"Why—" the storekeeper said slowly with studied deliberation, "there's only a little small change in the till—maybe a couple of dollars or so—and a few small bills. Hardly enough for you to bother with." There was no discernible trace of excitement in the storekeeper's voice. He was taking the hold-up, it appeared, pretty calmly —almost, you might have thought, as a matter of course.

"We don't have much trade here now since that other store around the corner on the main street opened up. This place used to take in sometimes fifty, or sixty, dollars on a good day—but it don't take in that much money in a week now. We're lucky if we sell ten dollars worth of goods in any one day. As a matter of fact it hardly pays to keep the place open. If it wasn't that—"

His emotionless voice flowed smoothly on. With his calmly considering gaze fixed on the face of the young bandit, the storekeeper seemed, for some doubtless sufficient reason, to be deliberately talking against time.

"Aw! Can the chatter, old guy," the hard-eyed youth impatiently broke in. His flat nostrils flared suddenly. Anger dangerously tinged the edges of his cold, flat voice. "I didn't ask you to tell me the story of your life—and never mind the chicken feed in the till. What I want is that rent money you collected this afternoon. I know you've got it right here in the store, so you'll only be wasting my time if you try to lie out of it—and I don't like to have old guys waste my time. Come on—hand it over!"

He stuck his hand in the pocket of his coat where the revolver was concealed and motioned suggestively.

The big green Brazilian parrot that had been shuffling sideways back and forth on his perch eyed the intruder malevolently. "Hell's bells!" the parrot suddenly squawked stridently. "Splice the main brace. Lively, lads—lively now!" He cocked his head and preened the sleekly irridescent feathers on his breast importantly.

The hard-eyed youth whirled suddenly and swore with vicious emphasis. "Smart bird, ain't you? Maybe you won't be so smart, if I take a notion to wring your neck." He turned again and motioned once more with the hand that was in his side coat pocket.

"The rent money?" The storekeeper's face—in some fashion curiously like the face of an old eagle—held no expression. "Why, I always—"

"Don't tell me you put it in the bank," the hard-eyed youth snarled, impatiently. "It ain't going to do you any good to lie. I was watching you through the window when that woman paid you this afternoon. You go around the first of the month to those four houses, collecting the rent. I know all about it, old guy. Like I know all about a lot of things. And last month you *did* put it in the bank—but this afternoon you were late in getting around, and came back here with the money. And you haven't been out of the store since. So you've got it right here, hid in a crack maybe. You see, I know all about you, old guy. I don't mind letting you know that I'm smart—that's why I never get— why I've only been nabbed a couple of times—and both times I beat the rap.

"I've been keeping an eye on you, old guy, for quite a while. I knew sometime you'd slip—and then I could walk in and collect a little rent money myself. This is the time. Come—hand it over. I've got a date with a classy dame who'll help me spend some of it, and I don't want to keep her waiting. She ain't the kind of dame that likes to be kept waiting."

The parrot cocked his head inquiringly sideways. "Who's a fool now?" he inquired raspingly. "Who's a fool—who's a fool—who's a fool—" he seemed to run down suddenly, discordantly, like a clock the mainspring of which has been abruptly released.

"It's in the safe here, under the counter," the storekeeper told him evenly, "and the safe is locked. It has a combination lock. You see, I have been afraid—"

"Never mind all that." The hard-eyed youth shifted his feet impatiently. "Open it up, and hand me over the money. And no funny business, mind you. Don't keep me waiting any longer, old guy. It ain't exactly healthy for old guys to keep me waiting."

The parrot, sliding along his perch, hiccupped realistically. "Drunk again, you old soak!" he moaned in a shrill falsetto, then relapsed into inarticulate mutterings.

The storekeeper thoughtfully rubbed the ball of his right thumb along his stubborn jaw. He seemed to be considering. His gaze was

393

still fixed speculatively on the face of the intruder. "I guess you'll have to open the safe yourself," he confessed after a slight hesitation. "It's pretty dark here under the counter, and I can't make out the figures on the dial very well. My eyes are not quite as good as they used to be. I suppose I ought to be getting some new glasses—"

"All right—all right! Can the chatter. I'll open the safe. What's the combination?"

The hard-eyed youth came around the end of the counter and looked at the small cheap safe contemptuously. "Do you call that sardine can a safe?" he asked with a sneer. "What's the combination?"

The storekeeper squinted his eyes in an effort to recall the figures. He shook his head helplessly. "Funny—it's because I so seldom lock it, I guess. I never seem to be able to remember what the combination is. I have to keep it written down on a card. I get the figures all mixed up. Sometimes I have to—"

"For cripes sake—quit your stalling, old guy. Old guys that try to stall with me are apt to get hurt. Where's the card?"

"It's right here in the till—I'll get it for you. I'm not trying to stall. I wouldn't want to get hurt, you know. Here's the card, tucked away in a corner. I'd forgotten just where I put it, to tell the truth. Anyway, I think this is it. When I'm a trifle nervous, things sort of dance before my eyes. If you'll wait till I get my glasses—"

The hard-eyed youth snatched the card from his hand. "I'm getting kind of nervous myself, old guy," he snarled. "Old guys that make me nervous sometimes get something to quiet their own nerves. I guess this is the combination, all right. There's nothing but some figures on the card, anyway. You stand right there, where I can keep one eye on you—and don't try to get funny, old guy. You might get hurt if you try to get funny—and that wouldn't be so funny, would it, old guy?"

He crouched on his heels before the safe and began to twirl the dial with nervously supple fingers.

The storekeeper, leaning at ease with one elbow on a showcase, watched the proceedings with interested eyes. There was the faintest suspicion of a smile on his thin lips, but otherwise his face was expressionless.

"Nine—four—eight—seven—three—" The hard-eyed youth was speaking the figures aloud as he worked the combination. "Hear 'em click, old guy," he exulted. "But you wouldn't be able to hear 'em, of course. You ain't smart like me. Well—here it is."

The storekeeper straightened up suddenly in an attitude of strained attention as the bandit swung back the door. There was a loud report —a blinding flash—a strangled cry, as the hard-eyed youth slumped
394

backward to the floor. He lay there quite still, huddled in an inert mass.

The storekeeper permitted his thin-lipped smile to measurably broaden.

"Well—it worked perfectly," he remarked conversationally to the parrot that had emitted a startled squawk of amazement and was now agitatedly shuffling back and forth on its perch with head drawn in and feathers ruffled.

He stooped down and took a small metal case somewhat resembling an old-style hand camera from the interior of the safe and set it carefully on the counter. He regarded it with a sort of restrained pride.

*I'll get the thing patented now—there ought to be a lot of money in it. Williams' safe-breaker's trap—that ought to be a good name for it. And then for a catch-line—Catches 'em alive. Takes their picture and calls the police. And I might never have thought again of working out that old idea of mine, if that other tough young thug hadn't held up this store six months ago. Funny how that sort of thing is sure to be repeated.*

The loud, penetrating, banshee-like wail of a police siren stridently rose and fell in the distance, filling the whole street with horrid sound, and presently a prowl car stopped with a squeal of brakes before the door. Two blue uniformed men burst into the store with automatics in their hands.

"They got the alarm at Headquarters and notified us over the two-way radio," the older of the two policemen told him. "There'll be a couple more cars here inside of a minute. That's sure a swell invention that you worked out, Inspector. Where's the bird that set it off? Oh there he is. He's a pretty guy, isn't he? I guess they didn't have quite so many of these slick looking young thugs in the days while you were still on the force, old timer. He isn't dead, is he?"

The pseudo-storekeeper shook his head.

"Just a touch of gas, supposed to render a safe-breaker insensible and allow plenty of time for the police to show up and gather him in. He'll be all right in an hour, or so. By that time I'll have the film developed and a couple of prints made. It ought to be rather interesting—the expression on his face at the very instant when he swung back the door and sprung the trap."

The two policemen had dragged the unconscious form of the bandit from behind the counter.

"He's so young—and correspondingly foolish," he explained, "that I hesitated just a little at the last minute about using him as a subject for trying out my invention. Even after I'd spent so much time in the last

395

couple of months playing at being a storekeeper while the owner of this place took a vacation at my expense—besides carefully baiting him along to stick me up. If he hadn't rubbed in the 'old guy' stuff quite so much, I might have just slapped him down, taken his gat away from him, and thrown him out."

The policeman who was stooping over to lift the unconscious bandit by the shoulders looked up and grinned.

"Well—I guess you could have done that, all right, Inspector. I happened to overhear the Skipper bragging about you only the other day. He was telling the Commissioner that you're the best instructor in jiu jitsu that the Department has ever had."

The parrot sidled along his perch. He cocked his head knowingly. "Lively," he squawked. "Lively now, lads!"


# The Outside Ledge

*by L. T. Meade
and Robert Eustace*

I had not heard from my old friend Miss Cusack for some time, and was beginning to wonder whether anything was the matter with her, when on a certain Tuesday in the November of the year 1892 she called to see me.

"Dr. Lonsdale," she said, "I cannot stand defeat, and I am defeated now."

"Indeed," I replied, "this is interesting. You so seldom are defeated. What is it all about?"

"I have come here to tell you. You have heard, of course, of Oscar Hamilton, the great financier? He is the victim of a series of frauds that have been going on during the last two months and are still being perpetrated. So persistent and so unaccountable are they that the cleverest agents in London have been employed to detect them, but without result. His chief dealings are, as you know, in South African Gold Mines, and his income is, I believe, nearer fifty than thirty thousand a year. From time to time he receives private advices as to the gold crushings, and operates accordingly. You will say, of course, that he gambles, and that such gambling is not very scrupulous, but I assure you the matter is not at all looked at in that light on the Stock Exchange.

"Now, there is a dealer in the same market, a Mr. Gildford, who, by some means absolutely unknown, obtains the same advice in detail, and of course either forestalls Mr. Hamilton, or, on the other hand, discounts the profits he would make, by buying or selling exactly the same shares. The information, I am given to understand, is usually cabled to Oscar Hamilton in cipher by his confidential agent in South Africa, whose *bona fides* is unquestionable, since it is he who profits by Mr. Hamilton's gains.

"This important information arrives as a rule in the early morning about nine o'clock, and is put straight into my friend's hands in his office in Lennox Court. The details are discussed by him and his partner, Mr. Le Marchant, and he immediately afterwards goes to his broker to do whatever business is decided on. Now, this special broker's name is Edward Gregory, and time after time, not invariably, but very often, Mr. Gregory has gone into the house and found Mr. Gildford doing the identical deals that he was about to do."

"That is strange," I answered.

"It is; but you must listen further. To give you an idea of how every channel possible has been watched, I will tell you what has been done. In the first place it is practically certain that the information found its way from Mr. Hamilton's office to Mr. Gildford's, because no one knows the cipher except Mr. Hamilton and his partner, Mr. Le Marchant."

"Wireless telegraphy," I suggested.

Miss Cusack smiled, but shook her head.

"Listen," she said. "Mr. Gildford, the dealer, is a man who also has an office in Lennox Court, four doors from the office of Mr. Hamilton, also close to the Stock Exchange. He has one small room on the third floor back, and has no clerks. Now Mr. Gregory, Mr. Hamilton's broker, has his office in Draper's Gardens. Yesterday morning an important cable was expected, and extraordinary precautions were adopted. Two detectives were placed in the house of Mr. Gildford, of course unknown to him—one actually took up his position on the landing outside his door, so that no one could enter by the door without being seen. Another was at the telephone exchange to watch if any message went through that way. Thus you will see that telegrams and telephones were equally cut off.

"A detective was also in Mr. Hamilton's office when the cable arrived, the object of his presence being known to the clerks, who were not allowed to use the telephone or to leave the office. The cable was opened in the presence of the younger partner, Mr. Le Marchant, and also in the presence of the detective, by Mr. Hamilton himself. No one left the office, and no communication with the outside world took place. Thus, both at Mr. Gildford's office and at Mr. Hamilton's, had the information passed by any visible channel it must have been detected either leaving the former office or arriving at the latter."

"And what happened?" I inquired, beginning to be much interested in this strange story.

"You will soon know what happened. I call it witchery. In about ten minutes' time Mr. Hamilton left his office to visit his broker, Mr. Gregory, at the Stock Exchange, everyone else, including his partner, Mr. Le Marchant, remaining in the office. On his arrival at the Stock Exchange he told Mr. Gregory what he wanted done. The latter went to carry out his wishes, but came back after a few moments to say that the market was spoiled, Mr. Gildford having just arrived and dealt heavily in the very same shares and in the same manner. What do you make of it, Dr. Lonsdale?"

"There is only one conclusion for me to arrive at," I answered; "the information does not pass between the offices, but by some previously arranged channel."

"I should have agreed with you but for one circumstance, which I am now going to confide to you. Do you remember a pretty girl, a certain Evelyn Dudley, whom you once met at my house? She is the only daughter of Colonel Dudley of the Coldstream Guards, and at her father's death will be worth about seven thousand a year."

"Well, and what has she to do with the present state of things?"

"Only this: she is engaged to Mr. Le Marchant, and the wedding will take place next week. They are both going to dine with me tonight. I want you to join the party in order that you may meet them and let me know frankly afterwards what you think of him."

"But what has that to do with the frauds?" I asked.

"Everything, and this is why," She lowered her voice, and said in an emphatic whisper, "I have strong reasons for suspecting Mr. Le Marchant, Mr. Hamilton's young partner, of being in the plot."

"Good heavens!" I cried, "you cannot mean that. The frauds are to his own loss."

"Not at all. He has only at present a small share in the business. Yesterday from a very private source I learned that he was in great financial difficulties, and in the hands of some money-lenders; in short, I imagine—mind, I don't accuse him yet—that he is staving off his crash until he can marry Evelyn Dudley, when he hopes to right himself. If the crash came first, Colonel Dudley would not allow the marriage. But when it is a *fait accompli* he will be, as it were, forced to do something to prevent his son-in-law going under. Now I think you know about as much of the situation as I do myself. Evelyn is a dear friend of mine, and if I can prevent it I don't want her to marry a scoundrel. We dine at eight—it is now past seven, so if you will dress quickly I can drive you back in my brougham. Evelyn is to spend the night with me, and is already at my house. She will entertain you till I am ready. If nothing happens to prevent it, the wedding is to take place next Monday. You see, therefore, there is no time to lose in clearing up the mystery."

"There certainly is not," I replied, rising. "Well, if you will kindly wait here I will not keep you many minutes."

I went up to my room, dressed quickly, and returned in a very short time. We entered the brougham which was standing at the door, and at once drove off to Miss Cusack's house. She ushered me into the drawing-room, where a tall, dark-eyed girl was standing by the fire.

"Evelyn," said Miss Cusack, "you have often heard me talk of my great friend Dr. Lonsdale. I have just persuaded him to dine with us tonight. Dr. Lonsdale, may I introduce you to Miss Evelyn Dudley?"

I took the hand which Evelyn Dudley stretched out to me. She had an attractive, bright face, and during Miss Cusack's absence we each engaged the other in brisk conversation. I spoke about Miss Cusack, and the girl was warm in her admiration.

"She is my best friend," she said. "I lost my mother two years ago, and at that time I do not know what I should have done but for Florence Cusack. She took me to her house and kept me with her for some time, and taught me what the sin of rebellion meant. I loved my mother so passionately. I did not think when she was taken from me that I should ever know a happy hour again."

"And now, if report tells true, you are going to be very happy," I continued, "for Miss Cusack has confided some of your story to me. You are soon to be married?"

"Yes," she answered, and she looked thoughtful. After a moment she spoke again.

"You are right: I hope to be very happy in the future—happier than I have ever been before. I love Henry Le Marchant better than anyone else on earth."

I felt a certain pity for her as she spoke. After all, Miss Cusack's intuitions were wonderful, and she did not like Henry Le Marchant— nay, more, she suspected him of underhand dealings. Surely she must be wrong. I hoped when I saw this young man that I should be able to divert my friend's suspicions into another channel.

"I hope you will be happy," I said; "you have my best wishes."

"Thank you," she replied. She sat down near the fire as she spoke, and unfurled her fan.

"Ah! there is a ring," she said, the next moment. "He is coming. You know perhaps that he is dining here tonight. I shall be so pleased to introduce you."

At the same instant Miss Cusack entered the room.

"Our guest has arrived," she said, looking from Miss Dudley to me, and she had scarcely uttered the words before Henry Le Marchant was announced.

He was a tall, young-looking man, with a black, short moustache and very dark eyes. His manner was easy and self-possessed, and he looked with frank interest at me when his hostess introduced him.

The next moment dinner was announced. As the meal proceeded and I was considering in what words I could convey to Miss Cusack my impression that she was altogether on a wrong tack, something occurred which I thought very little of at the time, but yet was destined to lead to most important results presently.

The servant had just left the room when a slight whiff of some peculiar and rather disagreeable odor caught my nostrils. I was glancing across the table to see if it was due to any particular fruit, when I noticed that Miss Cusack had also caught the smell.

"What a curious sort of perfume!" she said, frowning slightly. "Evelyn, have you been buying any special new scent today?"

"Certainly not," replied Miss Dudley; "I hate scent, and never use it."

At the same moment Le Marchant, who had taken his handkerchief from his pocket, quickly replaced it, and a wave of blood suffused his swarthy cheeks, leaving them the next instant ashy pale. His embarrassment was so obvious that none of us could help noticing it.

"Surely that is the smell of valerian," I said, as the memory of what it was came to me.

"Yes, it is," he replied, recovering his composure and forcing a smile. "I must apologise to you all. I have been rather nervous lately, and have been ordered a few drops of valerian in water. I cannot think how it got on my handkerchief. My doctor prescribed it for me yesterday."

Miss Cusack made a common-place reply, and the conversation went on as before.

Perhaps my attitude of mind was preternaturally suspicious, but it occurred to me that Le Marchant's explanation was a very lame one. Valerian is not often ordered for a man of his evidently robust health, and I wondered if he were speaking the truth.

Having a case of some importance to attend, I took my departure shortly afterward.

During the three following days I heard nothing further from Miss Cusack, and made up my mind that her conjectures were all wrong and that the wedding would of course take place.

But on Saturday these hopes were destined to be rudely dispersed. I was awakened at an early hour by my servant, who entered with a note. I saw at once that it was in Miss Cusack's handwriting, and tore it open with some apprehension. The contents were certainly startling. It ran as follows—

*"I want your help. Serious developments. Meet me on Royal Exchange steps at nine this morning. Do not fail."*

After breakfast I sent for a cab, and drove at once to the city, alighting close to the Bank of England. The streets were thronged with the usual incoming flux of clerks hurrying to their different offices. I made my way across to the Royal Exchange, and the first person I saw was Miss Cusack standing just at the entrance. She turned to me eagerly.

"This is good of you, doctor; I shall not forget this kindness in a hurry. Come quickly, will you?"

We entered the throng, and moved rapidly down Bartholomew Lane into Throgmorton Street; then, turning round sharp to the left, found ourselves in Lennox Court.

I followed my guide with the greatest curiosity, wondering what could be her plans. The next moment we entered a house, and, threading our way up some bare, uncarpeted stairs, reached the top landing. Here Miss Cusack opened a door with a key which she had with her, pushed me into a small room, entered herself, and locked the door behind us both. I glanced around in some alarm.

The little room was quite bare, and here and there round the walls were the marks of where office furniture had once stood. The window looked out on to the backs of the houses in Lennox Court.

"Now we must act quickly," she said. "At 9.30 an important cable will reach Mr. Hamilton's office. This room in which we now find ourselves is next door to Mr. Gildford's office in the next house, and is between that and Mr. Hamilton's office two doors further down. I have rented this room—a quarter's rent for one morning's work. Well, if I am successful, the price will be cheap. It was great luck to get it at all."

"But what are you going to do?" I queried, as she proceeded to open the window and peep cautiously out.

"You will see directly," she answered; "keep back, and don't make a noise."

She leant out and drew the ends of her boa along the little ledge that ran outside just below the window. She then drew it in rapidly.

"Ah, ha! do you remember that, Dr. Lonsdale?" she cried softly, raising the boa to my face.

I started back and regarded her in amazement.

"Valerian!" I exclaimed. "Miss Cusack, what is this strange mystery?"

"Hush! not another word yet," she said. Her eyes sparkled with excitement. She rapidly produced a pair of very thick doeskin gloves, put them on, and stood by the window in an attitude of the utmost alertness. I stood still in the middle of the room, wondering whether I was in a dream, or whether Miss Cusack had taken leave of her senses.

The moments passed by, and still she stood rigid and tense as if expecting something. I watched her in wonderment, not attempting to say a word.

We must have remained in this extraordinary situation fully a quarter of an hour, when I saw her bend forward, her hand shot out of the window, and with an inconceivably rapid thrust she drew it back. She was now grasping by the back of the neck a large tabby cat; its four legs were drawn up with claws extended, and it was wriggling in evident dislike at being captured.

"A cat!" I cried, in the most utter and absolute bewilderment.

"Yes, a cat; a sweet pretty cat, too; aren't you, pussy?" She knelt down and began to stroke the creature, who changed its mind and rubbed itself against her in evident pleasure. The next moment it darted towards her fur boa and began sniffing at it greedily. As it did so Miss Cusack deftly stripped off a leather collar round its neck. A cry of delight broke from her lips as, unfastening a clasp that held an inner flap to the outer leather covering, she drew out a slip of paper.

"In Henry Le Marchant's handwriting," she cried. "What a scoundrel! We have him now."

"Henry Le Marchant's handwriting!" I exclaimed, bending over the slip as she held it in her hand.

"Yes," she answered; "see!"

I read with bated breath the brief communication which the tiny piece of paper contained. It was beyond doubt a replica of the telegram which must have arrived at Hamilton's office a few moments

402

ago. Miss Cusack also read the words. She flung the piece of paper to the ground. I picked it up.

"We must keep this, it is evidence," I said.

"Yes," she answered, "but this has upset me. I have heard of some curious methods of communication, but never such a one as this before. It was the wildest chance, but thank God it has succeeded. We shall save Evelyn from marrying a man with whom her life would have been intolerable."

"But what could have led you to this extraordinary result?" I said.

"A chain of reasoning starting on the evening we dined together," she replied. "What puzzled me was this. What had Henry Le Marchant to do with valerian on his handkerchief? It was that fact which set me thinking. His explanation of using it as a nerve sedative was so obviously a lie on the face of it, and his embarrassment was so evident, that I did not trouble myself with this way out of the mystery for a single moment. I went through every conceivable hypothesis with regard to valerian, but it was not till I looked up its properties in a medical book that the first clue came to me. Valerian is, as you of course know, doctor, a plant which has a sort of intoxicating, almost maddening effect on cats, so much so that they will search out and follow the smell to the exclusion of any other desire. They are an independent race of creatures, and not easily trained like a dog. Then the amazing possibility suggested itself to me that the method employed by Mr. Le Marchant to communicate with Mr. Gildford, which has nonplussed every detective in London, was the very simple one of employing a cat.

"Come to the window and I will explain. You see that narrow ledge along which our friend pussy strolled so leisurely a moment ago. It runs, as you perceive, straight from Mr. Hamilton's office to that of Mr. Gildford. All Mr. Gildford had to do was to sprinkle some valerian along the ledge close to his own window. The peculiar smell would be detected by a cat quite as far off as the house where Mr. Hamilton's office is. I thought this all out, and, being pretty sure that my surmises were correct, I called yesterday on Henry Le Marchant at the office with the express purpose of seeing if there was a cat there.

"I went with a message from Evelyn. Nestling on his knee as he sat at his table writing in his private room was this very animal. Even then, of course, there was no certainty about my suspicions, but in view of the event which hung upon them—namely, his marriage to Evelyn—I was determined to spare no pains or trouble to put them to the test. I have done so, and, thank God, in time. But come, my course now is clear. I have a painful duty before me, and there is not a moment to lose."

As Miss Cusack spoke she took up her fur boa, flicked it slowly backwards and forwards to remove the taint of the valerian, and put it round her neck.

Five minutes later we were both communicating her extraordinary story to the ears of one of the sharpest detectives in London. Before that night Henry Le Marchant and James Gildford were both condemned to suffer the severest punishment that the law prescribes in such cases.

But why follow their careers any further? Evelyn's heart very nearly broke, but did not quite, and I am glad to be able to add that she has married a man in every respect worthy of her.

# Packed House

*by Robert Zacks*

I stared at Mr. Stanhope, the office manager. I was burning but didn't dare show it. As he knew damn well.

"I can't come," I said. "My wife and I have an appointment. With friends."

I promptly felt sick at the last remark. I hadn't intended any implications; my subconscious had intercepted my tongue and run it for a touchdown.

Mr. Stanhope lifted his eyebrows. "Ah," he said politely. "I see."

He nodded thoughtfully and went back to his desk. I began to sweat as I thought it over. After five minutes my legs got me up and reluctantly took me over to Mr. Stanhope.

"I might be able to make it," I said, each word coming as hard as a pulled tooth. "If I can I will."

Mr. Stanhope nodded, didn't look at me, and kept writing.

The rest of the afternoon was an exhausted blur. At five o'clock I went home. Mary had a hot supper waiting. She was brushing her hair before the mirror.

"Listen, honey," I said sourly, "Stanhope invited us to attend an office get-together Wednesday night at some joint called the Pink

404

Palace Bar. It seems that Mr. Markham the big boss is going to be there and—"

Mary stopped combing her hair. She said indignantly, "But our date—"

"I tried to say no. You know how it is. You don't *have* to go, but if you're smart you show up. If Mr. Markham is coming. . . ."

"What's the occasion?" demanded Mary. Her face was flushed.

"No occasion," I muttered. "Just a get-together. I suppose Stanhope wants to show Markham how he keeps morale up."

"Was he insistent?" asked Mary hopefully.

I shook my head. "I'd better go," I said. Mary understood. She made a face.

It wasn't pleasant, phoning Mac and Ellen, our best friends, and telling them. Mac was nice about it, but I could tell he was as annoyed as the devil. We always had such wonderful times when we got together.

Over the phone Mac said, "Well, it's a pity. I just got that record player and two hundred dollars worth of records. From Beethoven to Josh White."

I groaned. That hurt. We both loved music.

I felt pretty savage myself Wednesday night when Mary and I went down to the Pink Palace Bar. I'd never heard of the place, but then Brooklyn has thousands like it: ornate, brassy, dim with indirect lighting, a noisy jazz band blaring until you get a headache, and a dance floor so small it helped utter strangers get extremely acquainted. It was also out of the way, which didn't help my mood any.

Mr. Stanhope waved casually to us when we came in. I forced a smile back at him.

When we were seated at a regular table for two, Mary said doubtfully, "This doesn't look like a get-together. Everybody's at separate tables."

"Stanhope probably wants the boss to himself," I growled.

The crowd was terrific, the heat oppressive, the ventilation poor and the service terrible. After a few moments of jazzy blaring by the band I took my hand away from my ear and saw Joe Halliday, the fellow who works next desk to me in the office. He waved gloomily, came over and pulled up a chair.

"You get roped in too?" he asked.

"Yes," said Mary. Joe grunted and looked around.

"It sure doesn't look like the kind of place Mr. Markham would like," growled Joe, I looked at Mary and she was staring at me queerly.

405

Mr. Markham was a nice, old, quiet guy. He had the tact and delicacy of the well-bred, educated man, and his tastes ran to literary and artistic things. He wasn't the night club type, and this joint was far from a night club.

I looked at my watch. It was well into the evening. No Mr. Markham yet and I was beginning to burn. So was Mary.

"I'll bet he doesn't come," said Mary.

She had crystallized the feelings we all had. Joe said, slowly, "Well, I don't get it. Unless Stanhope—"

He didn't get a chance to finish because Stanhope's bland face suddenly appeared above him smiling down at us.

"Having a good time, folks?" he asked. He was a little high, but under control yet.

"Just dandy," said Mary brightly. I said, politely, it was terrific.

"Where's Mr. Markham?" Joe asked bluntly.

Stanhope shrugged. "Well," he murmured, "I told him we'd be here. He wished us a good time. It would certainly be nice if he dropped in tonight."

There was a moment of stunned silence. Then Stanhope said smoothly, "By the way, this party tonight is on me. It won't cost you a dime. Just initial the check with my initials."

He smiled at us and nodded, then walked over to another table. We stared after him in stunned amazement. Joe recovered first.

"Well, what do you know about that?" he breathed. "I'll bet he's got a piece of this place. He's a pretty nice guy after all."

I got up slowly.

"Where are you going?" asked Mary. She was really mad, but controlling herself.

"To look for a man," I said.

As I walked away the pieces of the puzzle fell neatly into place. Intently my eyes went over the joint looking for the fellow I knew would be there.

It wasn't hard to find him. He looked like I thought he'd look, anxious yet pleased, with a worried, calculating look as he watched the crowd. He wasn't drinking and he wasn't having fun, just watching. That's how I knew. He was middle-aged, pudgy, and I waited until I could get him alone because I didn't want anybody to see this.

Then, just to be sure, I said, "Why don't you join the fun?"

He smiled anxiously. "No, thanks," he said.

"Nice crowd," I said, feeling my way.

"Isn't it?" he said. He offered his hand. "My name is Raphaels. Jack Raphaels. You know—" he grinned sheepishly—"I'm thinking of buying this place. Been saving all my life to get a chance to be my own boss. This," he said, looking with satisfaction over the crowd, "looks like what I want."

"Is that so?" I said, giving it to him fast because a couple of men were anxiously coming toward us. "I was wondering why I got roped into coming here."

Raphaels stiffened. "You what?" he said sharply.

I told him straight and quick, with no holds barred. I finished just before the man came within hearing distance, with, "They're packing the house on you, mister, filling it with friends for a week or two to make business look good."

Then, with a polite smile, like I'd told a dirty joke, I drifted back to my table. I noticed Mr. Raphaels was smart enough to turn to the men with an agreeable look on his face.

"Who's that man?" asked Mary.

I didn't get a chance to answer because Stanhope was making the rounds of the tables again and had come to ours. He was now really high, giggly and getting silly.

"Having fun?" he asked gayly, wagging a reproving finger. "Aren't you glad you came?"

"I never had so much fun in all my life," I said happily, and I meant every word of it.


# The Pattern

*by Alex Saxon*


At 11:23 P.M. on Saturday, the twenty-sixth of April, a small man wearing rimless glasses and a dark gray business suit walked into the detective squad room in San Francisco's Hall of Justice and confessed to the murders of three Bay Area housewives whose bodies had been found that afternoon and evening.

Inspector Glenn Rauxton, who first spoke to the small man, thought he might be a crank. Every major homicide in any large city draws its share of oddballs and mental cases, individuals who confess to crimes in order to attain public recognition in otherwise unsubstantial lives; or because of some secret desire for punishment; or for any

407

number of reasons that can be found in the casebooks of police psychiatrists. But it wasn't up to Rauxton to make a decision either way. He left the small man in the company of his partner, Dan Tobias, and went in to talk to his immediate superior, Lieutenant Jack Sheffield.

"We've got a guy outside who says he's the killer of those three women today, Jack," Rauxton said. "Maybe a crank, maybe not."

Sheffield turned away from the portable typewriter at the side of his desk; he had been making out a report for the chief's office. "He come in his own volition?"

Rauxton nodded. "Not three minutes ago."

"What's his name?"

"He says it's Andrew Franzen."

"And his story?"

"So far, just that he killed them," Rauxton said. "I didn't press him. He seems pretty calm about the whole thing."

"Well, run his name through the weirdo file, and then put him in one of the interrogation cubicles," Sheffield said. "I'll look through the reports again before we question him."

"You want me to get a stenographer?"

"It would probably be a good idea."

"Right," Rauxton said, and went out.

Sheffield rubbed his face wearily. He was a lean, sinewy man in his late forties, with thick graying hair and a falconic nose. He had dark-brown eyes that had seen most everything there was to see, and been appalled by a good deal of it; they were tired, sad eyes. He wore a plain blue suit, and his shirt was open at the throat. The tie he had worn to work when his tour started at 4:00 P.M., which had been given to him by his wife and consisted of interlocking, psychedelic-colored concentric circles, was out of sight in the bottom drawer of his desk.

He picked up the folder with the preliminary information on the three slayings and opened it. Most of it was sketchy telephone communications from the involved police forces in the Bay Area, a precursory report from the local lab, a copy of the police Telex that he had sent out statewide as a matter of course following the discovery of the first body, and that had later alerted the other authorities in whose areas the two subsequent corpses had been found. There was also an Inspector's Report on that first and only death in San Francisco, filled out and signed by Rauxton. The last piece of information had come in less than a half-hour earlier, and he knew the facts of the case by memory; but Sheffield was a meticulous cop and he liked to have all the details fixed in his mind.

The first body was of a woman named Janet Flanders, who had

been discovered by a neighbor at 4:15 that afternoon in her small duplex on 39th Avenue, near Golden Gate Park. She had been killed by several blows about the head with an as yet unidentified blunt instrument.

The second body, one Viola Gordon, had also been found by a neighbor—shortly before 5:00 P.M.—in her neat, white frame cottage in South San Francisco. Cause of death: several blows about the head with an unidentified blunt instrument.

The third body, Elaine Dunhill, had been discovered at 6:37 P.M. by a casual acquaintance who had stopped by to return a borrowed book. Mrs. Dunhill lived in a modest cabin-style home clinging to the wooded hillside above Sausalito Harbor, just north of San Francisco. She, too, had died as a result of several blows about the head with an unidentified blunt instrument.

There were no witnesses, or apparent clues, in any of the killings. They would have, on the surface, appeared to be unrelated if it had not been for the facts that each of the three women had died on the same day, and in the same manner. But there were other cohesive factors as well—factors, that, taken in conjunction with the surface similarities, undeniably linked the murders.

Item: each of the three women had been between the ages of thirty and thirty-five, on the plump side, and blonde.

Item: each of them had been orphaned non-natives of California, having come to the San Francisco Bay Area from different parts of the Midwest within the past six years.

Item: each of them had been married to traveling salesmen who were home only short periods each month, and who were all—according to the information garnered by investigating officers from neighbors and friends—currently somewhere on the road.

*Patterns*, Sheffield thought as he studied the folder's contents. Most cases had one, and this case was no exception All you had to do was fit the scattered pieces of its particular pattern together, and you would have your answer. Yet the pieces here did not seem to join logically, unless you concluded that the killer of the women was a psychopath who murdered blonde, thirtyish, orphaned wives of traveling salesmen for some perverted reason of his own.

That was the way the news media would see it, Sheffield knew, because that kind of slant always sold copies, and attracted viewers and listeners. They would try to make the case into another Zodiac thing. The radio newscast he had heard at the cafeteria across Bryant Street, when he had gone out for supper around nine, had presaged the discovery of still more bodies of Bay Area housewives and had advised all women whose husbands were away to remain behind locked doors. The announcer had repeatedly referred to the deaths as "the bludgeon slayings."

Sheffield had kept a strictly open mind. It was, for all practical purposes, his case—the first body had been found in San Francisco, during his tour, and that gave him jurisdiction in handling the investigation. The cops in the two other involved cities would be in constant touch with him, as they already had been. He would have been foolish to have made any premature speculations not based solely on fact, and Sheffield was anything but foolish. Anyway, psychopath or not, the case still promised a hell of a lot of not very pleasant work.

Now, however, there was Andrew Franzen.

Crank? Or multiple murderer? Was this going to be one of those blessed events—a simple case? Or was Franzen only the beginning of a long series of very large headaches?

*Well,* Sheffield thought, *we'll find out soon enough.* He closed the folder and got to his feet and crossed to the door of his office.

In the squad room, Rauxton was just finishing a computer check. He came over to Sheffield and said, "Nothing on Franzen in the weirdo file, Jack."

Sheffield inclined his head and looked off toward the row of glass-walled interrogation cubicles at the rear of the squad room. In the second one, he could see Dan Tobias propped on a corner of the bare metal desk inside; the man who had confessed, Andrew Franzen, was sitting with his back to the squad room, stiffly erect in his chair. Also waiting inside, stoically seated in the near corner, was one of the police stenographers.

Sheffield said, "Okay, Glenn, let's hear what he has to say."

He and Rauxton went over to the interrogation cubicle and stepped inside. Tobias stood, shook his head almost imperceptibly to let Sheffield and Rauxton know that Franzen hadn't said anything to him. Tobias was tall and muscular, with a slow smile and big hands and—like Rauxton—a strong dedication to the life's work he had chosen.

He moved to the right corner of the metal desk, and Rauxton to the left corner, assuming set positions like football halfbacks running a bread-and-butter play. Sheffield, the quarterback, walked behind the desk, cocked one hip against the edge and leaned forward slightly, so that he was looking down at the small man sitting with his hands flat on his thighs.

Franzen had a round, inoffensive pink face with tiny-shelled ears and a Cupid's-bow mouth. His hair was brown and wavy, immacu-

410

lately cut and shaped, and it saved him from being nondescript; it gave him a certain boyish character, even though Sheffield placed his age at around forty. His eyes were brown and liquid, like those of a spaniel, behind his rimless glasses.

Sheffield got a ball-point pen out of his coat pocket and tapped it lightly against his front teeth; he liked to have something in his hands when he was conducting an interrogation. He broke the silence, finally, by saying, "My name is Sheffield. I'm the lieutenant in charge here. Now before you say anything, it's my duty to advise you of your rights."

He did so, quickly and tersely, concluding with "You understand all of your rights as I've outlined them, Mr. Franzen?"

The small man sighed softly and nodded.

"Are you willing, then, to answer questions without the presence of counsel?"

"Yes, yes."

Sheffield continued to tap the ball-point pen against his front teeth. "All right," he said at length. "Let's have your full name."

"Andrew Leonard Franzen."

"Where do you live?"

"Here in San Francisco."

"At what address?"

"Nine-oh-six Greenwich."

"Is that a private residence?"

"No, it's an apartment building."

"Are you employed?"

"Yes."

"Where?"

"I'm an independent consultant."

"What sort of consultant?"

"I design languages between computers."

Rauxton said, "You want to explain that?"

"It's very simple, really," Franzen said tonelessly. "If two business firms have different types of computers, and would like to set up a communication between them so that the information stored in the memory banks of each computer can be utilized by the other, they call me. I design the linking electronic connections between the two computers, so that each can understand the other; in effect, so that they can converse."

"That sounds like a very specialized job," Sheffield said.

"Yes."

"What kind of salary do you make?"

411

"Around eighty thousand a year."

Two thin, horizontal lines appeared in Sheffield's forehead. Franzen had the kind of vocation that bespoke of intelligence and upper-class respectability; why would a man like that want to confess to the brutal murders of three simple-living housewives? Or an even more puzzling question: If his confession was genuine, what was his reason for the killings?

Sheffield said, "Why did you come here tonight, Mr. Franzen?"

"To confess." Franzen looked at Rauxton. "I told this man that when I walked in a few minutes ago."

"To confess to what?"

"The murders."

"What murders, specifically?"

Franzen sighed. "The three women in the Bay Area today."

"Just the three?"

"Yes."

"No others whose bodies maybe have not been discovered as yet?"

"No, no."

"Suppose you tell me why you decided to turn yourself in?"

"Why? Because I'm guilty. Because I killed them."

"And that's the only reason?"

Franzen was silent for a moment. Then slowly, he said, "No, I suppose not. I went walking in Aquatic Park when I came back to San Francisco this afternoon, just walking and thinking. The more I thought, the more I knew that it was hopeless. It was only a matter of time before you found out I was the one, a matter of a day or two. I guess I could have run, but I wouldn't know how to begin to do that. I've always done things on impulse, things I would never do if I stopped to think about them. That's how I killed them, on some insane impulse; if I had thought about it I never would have done it. It was so useless . . ."

Sheffield exchanged glances with the two inspectors. Then he said, "You want to tell us how you did it, Mr. Franzen?"

"What?"

"How did you kill them?" Sheffield asked. "What kind of weapon did you use?"

"A tenderizing mallet. One of those big wooden things with serrated ends that women keep in the kitchen to tenderize a piece of steak."

It was silent in the cubicle now. Sheffield looked at Rauxton, and then at Tobias; they were all thinking the same thing: the police had released no details to the news media as to the kind of weapon in-

412

volved in the slayings, other than the general information that it was a blunt instrument. But the initial lab report on the first victim—and the preliminary observations on the other two—stated the wounds of each had been made by a roughly square-shaped instrument, which had sharp "teeth" capable of making a series of deep indentations as it bit into the flesh. A mallet such as Franzen had just described fitted those characteristics exactly.

Sheffield asked, "What did you do with the mallet, Mr. Franzen?"

"I threw it away."

"Where?"

"In Sausalito, into some bushes along the road."

"Do you remember the location?"

"I think so."

"Then you can lead us there later on?"

"I suppose so, yes."

"Was Elaine Dunhill the last woman you killed?"

"Yes."

"What room did you kill her in?"

"The bedroom."

"Where in the bedroom?"

"Beside her vanity."

"Who was your first victim?" Rauxton asked.

"Janet Flanders."

"You killed her in the bathroom, is that right?"

"No, no, in the kitchen . . ."

"What was she wearing?"

"A flowered housecoat."

"Why did you strip her body?"

"I didn't. Why would I—"

"Mrs. Gordon was the middle victim, right?" Tobias asked.

"Yes."

"Where did you kill *her?*"

"The kitchen."

"She was sewing, wasn't she?"

"No, she was canning," Franzen said. "She was canning plum preserves. She had mason jars and boxes of plums and three big pressure cookers all over the table and stove . . ."

There was wetness in Franzen's eyes now. He stopped talking and took his rimless glasses off and wiped at the tears with the back of his left hand. He seemed to be swaying slightly on the chair.

Sheffield, watching him, felt a curious mixture of relief and sadness. The relief was due to the fact that there was no doubt in his mind—

nor in the minds of Rauxton and Tobias; he could read their eyes—
that Andrew Franzen was the slayer of the three women. They had
thrown detail and "trip-up" questions at him, one right after another,
and he had had all the right answers; he knew particulars that had also
not been given to the news media, that no crank could possibly have
known, that only the murderer could have been aware of. The case
had turned out to be one of the simple ones, after all, and it was all
but wrapped up now; there would be no more "bludgeon slayings," no
public hue and cry, no attacks on police inefficiency in the press, no
pressure from the commissioners or the mayor. The sadness was the
result of twenty-six years of police work, of living with death and
crime every day, of looking at a man who seemed to be the essence of
normalcy and yet who was a cold-blooded multiple murderer.

*Why?* Sheffield thought. That was the big question. *Why did he do it?*

He said, "You want to tell us the reason, Mr. Franzen? Why you
killed them?"

The small man moistened his lips. "I was very happy, you see. My
life had some meaning, some challenge. I was fulfilled—but they were
going to destroy everything." He stared at his hands. "One of them
had found out the truth—I don't know how—and tracked down the
other two. I had come to Janet this morning, and she told me that
they were going to expose me, and I just lost my head and picked up
the mallet and killed her. Then I went to the others and killed them. I
couldn't stop myself; it was as if I were moving in a nightmare."

"What are you trying to say?" Sheffield asked softly. "What was
your relationship with those three women?"

The tears in Andrew Franzen's eyes shone like tiny diamonds in the
light from the overhead fluorescents.

"They were my wives," he said.

414

# A Point of Honor

*by Larry Segriff*

I was directing, not fencing, when it happened. We were in the finals of women's epee. My own event, men's sabre, wasn't scheduled until the afternoon, and I'd agreed to call these last few bouts.

Janet Aubrey, the top seed in the tournament, was on my right. She was an atypical epeeist, a small blonde, slender but packed with power. Her opponent, Laurie Thompson from Kansas City, was a taller, thicker brunette.

I gave the command to fence and Janet launched a strong, fast, and wicked attack. She brought her blade around Laurie's, binding it with a quick, tight spiral, and pressed her attack home.

Laurie's point, which had been high all through the bout, snagged somewhere in Janet's sleeve. As they both drove forward, Laurie's blade snapped, and the short, jagged end leaped free of Janet's bind.

I had just enough time to feel a moment's relief that Laurie kept her point high. Personally, I'd rather take a broken blade in the mask than anywhere else. Steel is a lot stronger than either nylon or duck, and Kevlar's too uncomfortable to fence in for long.

At least, that's what I'd always thought.

The two women came together, either unaware of the broken blade or unable to stop. The end of Laurie's blade thunked solidly into Janet's mask, but it didn't stop there. It penetrated, finding a weak spot somehow, and passed on through.

Janet never screamed. She simply dropped, moving forward a little ways with the momentum of her attack. We found out later that the point had punctured her left eye and went directly into her brain. She never had a chance.

I had the command, "Halt," on my lips, but it died along with Janet. The whole thing, from the breaking of the blade to the moment that the broken end entered Janet's brain, had taken somewhat less than a second.

\* \* \*

I think I had my suspicions even then, with the scoring box still buzzing in the background, and the first horrified murmurs just starting to rise among the spectators, but there was nothing I could do about them. My detective's badge was strictly private, and not valid in this state.

Laurie had gone into shock when, at the end, she'd automatically tugged on her epee. It resisted briefly before pulling free, and we all got to see the blood on the end. She collapsed then, falling into a heap right next to Janet.

I felt like doing that myself.

"And you are?"

"Carl Jackson. My friends call me Jax."

His name tag read, "Malone, Jeffrey," and his badge said he was with campus security. "And you saw it all?"

"I was directing the bout."

He gave me a pained look. "What does that mean?"

"The director calls the action, kind of like the referee in a boxing match."

Officer Malone gave me a long, searching look. I knew what he was going to say before he said it. "So you were responsible, eh?"

I gave him a level stare in return. "I was officiating, yes, which makes me about as responsible as the ref at a football game where some kid gets his leg broken."

"This is a lot worse than a broken leg," he replied.

I nodded. "Yes, but much more rare." I thought he might take that opportunity to dig a little, but he didn't. I mean, the last recorded fencing-related death occurred in an Olympics thirteen years earlier, and had been almost exactly the same thing as we'd seen here today. The only other death I knew about happened some twenty years before that, when a fencer in Hungary, sweaty from a series of hard bouts, leaned up against an outlet and electrocuted himself.

No, these kinds of things didn't happen often. One like this was certainly suspicious.

Officer Malone simply nodded. "All right, Jackson," he said. "You staying at the same hotel as all the other fencers?"

"Yes. Room 317."

"We'll be in touch if we need any more information." He started to turn away.

"Um, Officer Malone? When will the police be contacting me?"

He turned back, glaring. "They won't be. This happened on University property. It's our baby."

416

*Jesus,* I thought. *Janet's dead, and he's worried about prerogatives.*

He turned away again, and I let him go, but I knew the investigation wasn't over. Not for me, it wasn't.

A couple of hours later, most of us ended up in a nearby bar. I'd ordered a hamburger and fries, but I found I could only stomach the beer.

We had a table toward the back, as far from the blaring TV as we could get. The local football team was on, playing a conference rival, and the bar was filled with yelling fans. Our group was out of place, to say the least, somber and subdued as we were.

I ended up next to Chuck, and it wasn't totally by accident. He was the armorer for the meet, the man responsible for maintaining all the equipment, and also for checking it out before the fencing, and I had some questions for him.

He was drinking whiskey, and he was drinking it fast. A dumpy little guy, no more than five-seven or five-eight, his dark hair was already receding, and he looked at least ten years older than the twenty-six I thought he was. He wasn't much of an athlete; the couple of times I'd seen him on the strip he'd been almost comical, but he knew his way around equipment.

"Chuck," I said, keeping my voice as soft as I could and still be heard over the raucous fans. "Chuck, I need to ask you something."

He turned startled, haunted eyes in my direction, and I recoiled from the pain I saw in them. "Yeah?" He took another deep drink of whiskey.

I sipped at my own beer. "Janet's mask. Did you check it in?" Standard tournament rules required that every piece of every fencer's gear be checked by a qualified person and stamped prior to any fencing. This had been a smaller meet, though, and things tended to be a lot looser. My own mask, for example, had not been checked.

"Yeah," he said. "We had weapons check at eight this morning. I went over all her stuff then."

I had another sip. "You didn't check mine."

"Hell, Jax," he slammed his glass down on the table and glared at me. "You were fencing sabre. For one thing, that wasn't even scheduled to start till this afternoon. For another, you know damn well that about the worst thing that ever happens in sabre is a few welts and bruises. Epee's different. The blades are a lot stiffer, and the attacks are all thrusts. There's more chance of injury with the epee, or even with the foil, and I'm more careful about those weapons." He picked up his drink and took another long pull. I noticed his hands were trembling. "Dammit, Jax," he added. "You know all that. Christ, it's not like this is the first tournament we've been at, you and me. Of course I checked her mask, and it passed. I stamped her bib myself."

I nodded and finished my beer. "Thanks, Chuck." I dropped a couple of dollars on the table. "The next one's on me." And I took myself back to the motel.

Laurie was in her motel room, alone. Her eyes had the glazed look of Valium; even so, they were red with crying. She gave me a hug as she let me in, and clung to me for a long time.

"Oh, Jax," she said. "It was so horrible."

"I know, Laurie. I know."

After a moment, she pulled away, heading toward a table near the window. There was a Kleenex box there, and lots of them wadded up on the floor around one of the chairs. I followed her and took the seat across from her.

"That campus policeman called a little while ago," she said, staring out at the parking lot. "They've agreed it was an accident. There won't be any charges."

I reached out and covered her hand. "That's great," I said.

I couldn't remember ever being in a situation like this one, and I felt awkward as hell. I'd questioned a lot of people about a lot of things, including several who I'd thought guilty of some pretty awful crimes, but I'd never had to ask difficult questions of a friend before.

Laurie had turned to look out the window. I studied her profile for a moment, trying to marshall my thoughts.

She was not pretty. Even taking her condition into account—the red-rimmed eyes, the lack of make-up, the sweat from her earlier fencing—she was not pretty. I wondered, could she have been jealous of Janet?

"You've fenced Janet a lot, haven't you, Laurie?"

She kept her gaze directed at the parking lot. "Yes." Her voice had gone flat, as though the Valium was kicking in again. "We went to a couple of tournaments in Omaha every year, and they came to Kansas City to fence maybe three or four times."

I nodded, still holding her hand. "I've probably seen most of those bouts."

"Hell, Jax," she said, a hint of life returning to her voice, "you directed most of them."

I nodded again. "Don't you usually try for wrist shots on her?"

I was glad that she had faded again. If she ever understood the implications of my question, our friendship would be over.

418

She nodded, though, without turning her head toward me. "Sure. I don't know if you knew it or not, but Janet started out as a foil fencer. She tends—tended—to make her moves a little wider than necessary, and opened up her wrist on her attacks."

I squeezed her hand and said, as softly as I could, "But today you were going high line, Laurie. Why?"

She shrugged. "The wrist shots weren't working. You asked how many times I've fenced her; you didn't ask how many times I won."

She was right. I didn't ask. I didn't need to.

"I never beat her."

I patted her hand, a patronizing gesture I've always hated, but at the moment it was all I had. "I know," I said softly.

"Besides," she continued. "I've been working with Chuckie a bit, these past couple of months. He's pointed out to me that I should use my height more, keep my point out there and let my shorter opponents run onto my blade."

I nodded a third time. It was a standard tactic, and Janet was certainly one of the shorter fencers. Maybe the campus cop was right. Maybe it really was just an accident.

I didn't know any more. The only certainty I had left was the pain I could see on Laurie's face.

I'd run out of questions. Or, at least, I'd run out of the strength to ask them. It's a hard line we walk: too little compassion and you're not a person; too much and you're not a private eye.

"Thanks, Laurie." I gave her hand a final squeeze, the rose and headed for the door.

"Jax." Her voice stopped me as I reached the door.

"Yes?" I said, turning to face her once more.

"I killed her, Jax. I mean, it was an accident and all, but I killed her, didn't I?"

I looked at her, silhouetted against the bright window, and could find no words to answer her with. I felt my lips tighten in silent sympathy for her, and I left without replying.

The armorer's table was still set up at the field house. I didn't see anybody guarding it, but so far none of the basketball players had appeared to touch anything. I was looking at some fencing gear—a mask, several blades, and such—that had been left unattended when Chuck showed up.

"What are you doing, Jax?"

I stiffened. "She was a pretty girl, wasn't she, Chuck?"

"Who?"

"Janet, of course. Petite, but cute, and her smile could light up a room. Friendly, too. She had a way of making everyone feel special." I picked up the punch test from the table. It looked something like a pistol. There was a metal bar that, after cocking, was designed to strike a mask with a very specific amount of force. Grabbing the mask, I started almost idly punching it with the test, snapping it against the same spot, over and over again.

"Is that what happened, Chuck?" I pressed. "Did you mistake her friendship for something more? Did you ask her back to your place last night, and did she turn you down?"

"I don't know what you're talking about."

We'd known each other for a lot of years, he and I, and been good friends for most of them, but none of that showed on his face or in his voice now. Mine either, for that matter.

I'd snapped the mask about a dozen times, more or less. Setting the punch test down, I wedged the mask up against some other stuff on the table and picked up one of the epees lying there.

"I talked to Laurie," I said. "You've been coaching her. You knew she'd be keeping her point up against Janet. What I don't know is why, Chuck? Why?"

"I don't—" he started, but I didn't let him finish. Lunging forward, I drove the point of the epee into the very spot I'd been snapping on the mask, one of the holes in the mesh on the right front side. The epee tore through the metal and struck the object behind the mask.

I turned to Chuck and presented him with the impaled mask. "Three years ago that hotshot Canadian showed up at one of our meets. As I recall, he'd beaten you pretty badly a few months earlier. That was, in fact, the last time you ever fenced in competition. You were still mad about that, and I didn't blame you, but I thought you took it a bit too far when you doctored the punch test. It passed right through his mask on the first try, and he wasn't allowed to fence. I've never forgotten that, Chuck."

He took the mask I was holding out to him, slipping it off the epee and putting it back on the table. He turned, then, toward the basketball players and away from me.

"She was pretty," he said eventually. "And I thought she was nice. And I did ask her out last night; not to my room, but just out on a date. She laughed. Oh, she apologized, like it was an accident or something, but she laughed, Jax."

He fell silent again for a time. I looked at the mask I'd punctured and waited for him to continue. "Yeah, I set up a weak spot in her mask, but I swear to God, Jax, I didn't mean for her to die. I just
420

wanted Laurie to cut her a little, maybe leave a scar so that next time somebody asked her out, it might not seem so funny."

He turned, now, and I could see the same haunting pain in his eyes that had been in Laurie's. "My God, Jax, I didn't want her dead."

I didn't say anything to that.

His eyes flicked to the mask and then back to me. "What are you going to do?"

I sighed. What could I do? That campus cop had already made up his mind: it was an accident, and not even the doctored punch test was likely to convince him otherwise. I wouldn't be able to prove that Chuck had actually used it on Janet's mask. Besides, I believed him when he said it was an accident. If Laurie's blade hadn't broken, Janet would probably still be alive.

So, "I'm not going to do anything," I said, the words a bitter weight upon my tongue, "except to make sure that you never touch another piece of fencing gear. Ever."

He nodded, but I could see resentment shining out beneath his relief.

"And one more thing," I added.

"Yeah?"

I thought about Janet, and the way she'd collapsed on the strip. I thought about Laurie, and how long it would be before she recovered, if she ever did. Mostly, though, I thought about myself, and the pain I would carry with me for the rest of my life. Everyone had liked Janet, myself included.

And then I hit him, as hard as I could. He cried out and went down, but I was already walking away, heading back to my room to pack.

# The Rosary

*Michael A. Black*

It crunched under the sole of Doyle's shoe. He stopped to pick it up. A bead. Dark colored. Almost black, with a hole through the center, as if it had been strung on some kind of necklace. But it was wood. As he rolled it in his hand it seemed out of place, but at the same time

421

strangely familiar. Like something out of his past. Doyle's eyes scanned the floor. There was another bead. And another, leading like a trail to the buffet near the front hall. Doyle knelt and saw the tangled heap of the remaining beads, the string, and the crucifix.

"Hand me an evidence bag," he said. "I think I've found something."

Doyle used a pen to extricate the rosary from under the furniture. Then he bagged it and scribbled the crime report number on the seal.

"Find something, Jim?" asked his partner, Roger McKay, coming into the room.

"Yeah," Doyle said, holding up the bag.

"A rosary?" said McKay, his brows furrowing. "What do you make of it?"

Doyle shook his head. "Don't know."

"They're ready to take out the body," said McKay, holding his nose and grinning. "You got anything else?"

"Huh-un." He put the bag in his pocket.

It had been an exceptionally brutal crime, made more heinous by the obvious defenselessness of the victim. Margaret S. Page had been in her mid-seventies. A semi-invalid, partially crippled by a stroke. Now she lay half folded around the base of the stairway in a fetal position. The crime scene photographer snapped another picture, then looked at McKay, who nodded. Two men moved forward with the stretcher.

"Let me get one more facial shot before you cover her," the photographer said. He was breathing through his mouth because of the smell. The dress that Margaret Page had put on now barely contained her swollen body.

"The person that did this was a real sociopath," said Doyle.

"Nuts too," said McKay, trying to break the grim pressure. But from the intensity in his partner's eyes, he knew his attempt at levity had fallen flat. He placed a hand on Doyle's shoulder and said, "Let's go back and start writing this one up."

"I want to talk to some of the neighbors first," said Doyle.

The canvass proved negative. No one had seen or heard anything suspicious or out of the ordinary. They all described Mrs. Page as a quiet woman who seldom ventured out since her husband died a few years ago. Her only regular visitors were her devoted nephew and his wife, and the priest who came weekly to bring her communion. Most of the neighbors expressed shock that she'd been dead for over a week without them knowing it, but she was not frequently seen around the neighborhood.

422

"I can't believe that Aunt Peggy is dead." Ed Roberts covered his eyes briefly. His wife inhaled on her cigarette, then patted his shoulder.

"Mr. Roberts," said McKay. "Was your aunt in the habit of talking to strangers?"

Roberts raised his eyebrows quizzically, then accepted a cigarette from his wife. He lit it before answering.

"I don't know," he said, fingering his nose. Then added, "I don't think so."

"You know how old people are," said Paula Roberts. "Sometimes they're too trusting."

Ed scratched his head. "Is that what you think? That she let in some stranger?"

"It appears that she let the offender in," said Doyle. "There were no signs of forced entry." He moved uncomfortably in the chintz-covered armchair as he spoke. The furniture fit the house—upscale suburban—but looked as though it had been bought wholesale from a decorator, without any eye for taste or comfort.

"Dead is bad enough," said Ed, shaking his head. "But murdered . . ."

"It wasn't a very pleasant note to return from our vacation to all this," said Paula, blowing a cloud of smoke at Doyle. Her mouth was bracketed by hard lines.

Ed put his hands over his face and Paula snubbed out his cigarette in the ashtray.

"Is any more of this necessary?" she asked. Her voice was nasal and somewhat bellicose. "Can't you see how upsetting this is to my husband? He was very close to his aunt."

Doyle caught the stare of her green eyes. They looked protective. Almost feral.

"We realize how difficult this is," said McKay. "But we're trying to get some leads on the investigation."

"Then find out who did it and quit badgering us," she said.

"It's all right," said Ed. "I'd rather talk to them now and get it over with. I know how it is. I'm a special deputy myself." He pulled out a part-time baliff's identification and showed it to the detectives. "You will find out who did this, won't you? You see," he started to break down again. "We were all she had."

They devoted the next day to the case, completing reports and interviews. The only one lacking was Mrs. Page's priest, Father Sullivan. He was in Ireland on his annual vacation.

The Medical Examiner discovered that Margaret Page had been killed by a 9mm bullet that had entered at the base of her skull. Quick and neat. However, there was also evidence that the victim had been tortured before she died. Numerous bruises were found on her face and body. The fingers on her left hand had been bent backwards, fracturing the bones. The body had lain in the house for approximately a week. The more brutal aspects of the crime were not released to the press.

When the Robertses returned from their vacation and were unable to reach the victim by phone, the police were called. The responding officer forced the front door and found the old woman's body in the hallway. The house had been ransacked. An apparent burglary/home invasion. Only small items, jewelry, and cash appeared to have been taken. But without any solid leads the investigation slowed to a standstill. Other urgent work crowded Doyle and McKay's schedule—two rapes, a drunk who might have been murdered, a drive-by shooting in which a young teenager had been shot. But the Page case seemed to gnaw at them because of its brutality and senselessness.

The first real break came almost by accident. Doyle sat in the office mulling over the file. McKay was going through his messages. He found one from Frank Morrison, a retired copper who now worked in security as an investigator for a large metropolitan bank.

"Hey, Frank," McKay said, glad to reach him on the first ring. "How's it going?"

"Roger, I'm glad you called. You're working on that homicide of that old lady on the south side, right?"

"Right."

"Well, I got something that might interest you," Morrison said. "I got notified about a week ago that they'd pinched a junkie for shoplifting and he had one of our cards on him. It wasn't reported stolen so I didn't think much about it. Wasn't able to contact the owner. Then this morning I read about the murder in the papers. Guess whose card this fucker had?"

"Margaret Page?" McKay asked, the excitement creeping into his voice.

Doyle looked up. He stared at McKay, who nodded.

"Frank, where is this guy now?" McKay said.

\* \* \*

He looked like a sick monkey on a string: fidgeting, shivering, runny nose. McKay gave him a cigarette and held the lighter.

"So tell us, Jesus," McKay said. "How'd you get the card?"

Jesus Garcia looked up at him through the haze, his head cocked, his voice a hoarse whisper.

"What's in it for me?"

The detectives looked at each other.

"I gotta know," Jesus said. "What's in it for me?"

"Listen, asshole," Doyle said, leaning forward. "You've been in the County Lockup for a week. You were arrested with a murdered woman's charge card in your possession. You're gonna tell us how you got it."

"Then we talk deals," said McKay.

"Maybe that ain't good enough," Jesus said. He took a long drag on the cigarette.

"If it ain't," said McKay, "we can up the charge from retail theft to suspicion of murder."

The banter went back and forth, finally, Garcia leaned forward and cupped his hands around his face. He had no more cigarettes. Sensing that they had worn him down, Doyle leaned forward.

"You want to tell us your side of it?"

"Okay, okay," Jesus said. "It was Herman."

McKay and Doyle glanced at each other, then quickly looked back to Garcia.

"Herman Brinx. I met him in the joint. Cellmates. Both from Chicago. We exchanged numbers, you know. Then, a couple of weeks ago he calls me up. Says he got something going. An easy job." Jesus looked up at both of them and accepted a new cigarette from McKay. "I don't do no heavy stuff. Just shoplifting, auto theft, a couple of burglaries . . . that's what I thought this was gonna be. You can check my record."

McKay nodded reassuringly.

"Then when we get in there's this old lady. I thought we'd just put her in a closet or something, but Herman . . . he goes off on her. Really bad. Breaking her fingers, one by one, asking her where her stash is." He lowered his eyes and shook his head. "I ain't never been in on something like that before. I keep telling him to hurry up. Let's get outta here, I say, but he just laughs and says to be cool. I mean, he's like an iceberg, he's so cool about it. Then he *offs* the old bitch right there. Tells me to go mess the place up. To take small stuff like cash and jewelry. Nothing big. Nothing that can be traced. But I took the card, figuring I could maybe score something with it before it got reported stolen." He shrugged his narrow shoulders. "But then I get busted on this two-bit shit and got the fucking card in my pocket."

McKay offered him another cigarette. He took one and put it above his ear, then quickly grabbed another one and grinned. He had very bad teeth.

"How'd you get in?" Doyle asked.

Jesus inhaled deeply on his square. "That's the weird thing." Residual smoke lingered around his mouth as he spoke. "She let us right in. Herman made me dress up like a priest."

The address that Brinx's parole officer gave them was Herman's mother's house. An old, dilapidated, wooden structure on the south side. No, Herman wasn't there, she told them. Nor did she care where he was. They left the bitter old woman and went to the second address that they'd gotten from running the phone number that Jesus had given them. It came back to a pay phone in a transient hotel in Uptown.

They radioed for two uniforms to meet them at the hotel. Doyle showed them Herman's mug shot. It was easy to picture him as the shooter. The smug expression, the blank eyes. Killer's eyes.

"He's served time for offenses ranging from auto theft to armed robbery," Doyle said. "He's probably armed."

"Just recently arrested for attempted break-in," added McKay. "Got out of County Jail on an I-Bond."

"They give those fucking things out to anybody nowadays, don't they?" one of the uniformed patrolmen said with a grin.

His partner, an older veteran smirked. "The jail's so fucking overcrowded they got to. They got that fucking federal judge telling them he don't want no poor inmates sleeping on the floor."

They paired off and McKay and the older uniform went into the hotel. Once it had been a well-kept building. But after several years on the downslide, it had slipped into a state of disrepair and neglect. Dollops of paint hung from the ceiling in the lobby. McKay showed the mugshot to an ancient, bleary-eyed deskclerk. He gave them the pass-key to room 304.

They headed upstairs. The halls reeked of vomit, booze, and urine. Standing on either side of the door, McKay slipped the key into the lock and turned it slowly. The knob turned, but the door held fast. Double locked.

"Who is it?" a voice called from inside the room.

"Police," said McKay. "Open up." He signaled the uniform that he was going to kick the door. Suddenly two shots pierced the antiquated wood. McKay flattened against the wall, hoping it was sturdier than the door. He waited, looked at the other copper, then slammed his foot home, just below the doorknob. The door flew open, bouncing against the wall. Surveying the room, one aiming high, one low. No movement, except for curtains that drifted inward from an open window. They heard a clattering sound.

"Jim," McKay said into his radio. "He's armed and coming down the fire escape." Then to the uniformed copper, "Stay here and seal the room. McKay dashed down the hall to the stairs.

Doyle and the other uniform had been waiting at the mouth of the alley. They heard the sound of shoes striking the metal stairs. Doyle saw that Brinx was already jumping from the metallic scaffold to the ground. The big automatic in Herman's hand exploded twice, and Doyle hit the alley floor, calling out a warning to his uniformed partner. Herman turned to run and the two officers rose, starting on a cautious foot chase. Another shot. Doyle threw himself behind a dumpster, leveled his .38 Chief's Special, and squeezed off a round. The young uniformed copper ran past him. Doyle followed.

Brinx ran across the street. Doyle had a chance to get a clear shot, but there were too many pedestrians to risk it. They headed down the block, Brinx pausing to fire off two more rounds. People screamed and ran for cover. The uniformed cop crouched behind a parked car and returned fire.

"Watch out for civilians," yelled Doyle.

Herman rounded the corner. Doyle got there seconds later to see Brinx at mid-block, disappearing into a perpendicular alley. Jogging behind, Doyle got to the mouth of the alley. Particles of brick exploded over his head, inches from his face. Doyle fired twice at the muzzle flash, then quickly dived to a big metal dumpster. Lying flat, arms extended, Doyle suddenly had Herman framed in his sights. The detective squeezed off three more rounds, seeing Herman jerk with each one. Then, after a stutter-step, Brix curled forward, dropping to the ground.

The uniformed copper was at his shoulder. With guns outstretched, they moved forward to check the body. When Doyle swept the 9mm away from Herman's limp fingers he realized that his Chief's Special was empty. When they flipped Brinx over, they saw that Doyle's bullet had entered just under the killer's left eye.

"Well," the young copper said. "At least we won't have to worry about the fucker getting another I-Bond."

\* \* \*

Doyle fingered the priest's collar they had recovered from Brinx's room as he sat at his desk.

"Jim," said McKay, entering the room carrying a paper cup of coffee and a donut. "What the fuck you doing here? You're supposed to be off for three days because of the shooting."

Doyle's lips compressed into a thin line.

"You slept at all?" asked McKay. He sat down at his desk and leaned forward.

Doyle shook his head.

"Go home and get some rest. I'll finish up the paperwork."

"There's something missing, Rog," Doyle said, handing him a copy of Brinx's I-Bond release form from the County Jail and holding up the clerical collar.

"I already seen it," McKay said. "So?"

Doyle turned and looked up a number. "I'm going to see if Father Sullivan got back yet."

"Yes, detective, I was in the practice of going there every week." There was an almost triple-tonguing effect to his Irish accent. "But for the past few weeks I've been out of the country."

"Yes, Father, I know. But what I need to know is if another priest could have visited her?"

"Well, as devout as poor old Mrs. Page was, I knew she surely wouldn't want to miss her communion. I told her nephew that I'd arranged for Father Lopez to substitute for me. He was supposed to bring the parish handyman with him to see about some chores for her."

"Did Father Lopez see her?"

"When I asked him, he said he got a call cancelling the visit."

"A call?" said Doyle. "Could you explain that Father?"

They sat in the interview room at District Headquarters. Doyle stood at the far wall. McKay sat across from her, his arms rested on the top of his chair.

"So you see, Mrs. Roberts, the killers came to the door masquerading as a priest and a handyman," said Doyle.

"A priest?" she said. McKay slid his chair closer.

"Father Sullivan went there every week to bring her communion."

"Since she wasn't able to get to church," added Doyle.

"So what does that have to do with anything?" she asked.

"Father Sullivan's been in Ireland recently," said Doyle.

428

"To visit a relative," said McKay. "But he made arrangements for another priest to substitute for him."

"In deference to Margret," Doyle said. "Because she was such a special lady."

Her head twisted back and forth as the two partners continued their consecutive statements.

"But Father Lopez received a call cancelling the visit the day before Mrs. Page was killed," said Doyle.

"A call from a woman," added McKay. Then, lighting up a cigarette, he pulled his chair closer and said, "You might as well tell us, Paula."

"You see," said Doyle from across the room. "We've already picked up Ed. From work. He admitted arranging the Individual Recognizance Bond for Brinx when he was working at the jail."

McKay waited for a second, gauging her reaction, then said, "He's already spilled his guts." Staring directly into her eyes, he added, "Told us that it was all your idea."

"You badgered him into it," said Doyle. She glared at him with the same feral look that he'd noticed before.

"That asshole never could keep his fucking mouth shut," she spat. "So I forced him into it, huh? Gimme a cigarette and I'll tell you how much I forced that son of a bitch to do anything."

The corner of McKay's mouth twisted into a slight, almost imperceptible grin as he glanced at his partner.

Doyle stood before the mirror and rinsed his face. He wished he could cleanse himself of the sins he'd witnessed as easily as he could wash the city grime from his face. Lately even the grim seemed harder to remove. And the memories, too. The memories of this case bothered him. More than he felt they should. But why? The actual trigger man was dead. And those that had hired him, the poor victim's family, had been charged. They'd probably plead to a lesser charge, but at least they'd be brought before the court. There was some justice in that, wasn't there?

Justice. It had seemed so clear and exact to him when he'd graduated from the Academy. Right and wrong, indelible in black and white. He wondered if the law had ever seemed so exalted to Ed Roberts . . . before he'd used his part-time deputy status to recruit a killer to collect an early inheritance.

Maybe nothing existed in black and white anymore. Everything, even the most sacred of values, eventually was compromised into varying shades of gray. The dripping face in the mirror stared back at him. He'd glimpsed so many times into the primordial essence that lurks beneath the thin veneer of society. Was there no mercy for the Margaret Pages of this world? No solace?

Slowly he dried off, then went into his bedroom. He found it in the top drawer along with a discarded watch from his long ago graduation, his forgotten military medals, and his old patrolman's shield. Doyle grasped it and sat down on the bed. He felt for the large bead in the semi-darkness. Then he began:

"Our father . . ."

# Safety Deposit

*by B. B. Fowler*

Ace Davis, the detective, stopped under the street lamp on the corner and stared at the screaming headlines of the paper the newsboy thrust before him. They were scare headlines, big and black across the head of the page.

BIG TOM ARNOLD MURDERED

Mechanically he handed the boy a coin and read the type that trailed down the page to give the details. Not much beyond the headlines. Big Tom Arnold found shot in his office. Just that.

The hard lips of the headquarters dick puckered into a soundless whistle and little lights danced in his black eyes. Then he looked up as if he had suddenly thought of something. He had been alone, a second ago under the street lamp. Now there were three men with him, one on each side, another one behind him.

One of them was in a big polo coat with wide pockets. He looked at Davis and his eyes were blandly speculative. His fat face was a lustrous white. He had one hand pushed down into a pocket that bulged. The other hand was bandaged, and stuck in the front of the coat, which had one button unfastened to act as a sling.

The fellow on the other side wore a Harris tweed ulster. He had a peaked face with shiny eyes and a hooked nose. He was very cool,
430

just as if he had stopped casually to look at the paper over Ace's shoulder. He stared unsmilingly at the headlines.

"Funny how many guys get it that way," he said in a conversational tone.

Ace didn't show by a muscle of his face that it meant anything to him. "Yeah, damn funny. But it does happen."

The man in the polo coat said:

"You'd be surprised. We'd like to go up to your apartment with you, Ace."

Ace felt the hard pressure in his side. "That would be nice," he agreed. "I was just going up anyway."

The four of them started walking down the street, not too fast— just walking along, three of them abreast, the other man coming along behind. Ace hadn't seen his face, and made no attempt to see it. It didn't matter what the gunman looked like, anyway.

The elevator boy glanced at them as they rode up. Polo Coat made conversation. "Funny, us running into you right on the corner that way. We'd been looking all over for you. Haven't seen you since I hurt my hand, Ace. What have you been doing with yourself lately?"

Ace grinned. "You'd laugh if you knew." He winked at the elevator boy. No use making a holler. That would only get the kid a busted head.

Outside the apartment they stopped while Ace unlocked the door. Polo Coat went in first. He halted in the doorway and said to the man whose face Ace hadn't seen:

"Stay outside. We wouldn't want to be disturbed."

Then Polo Coat jerked his head for Ace to go in.

Ace brushed against him as he went by. The man swore thickly. "Jeeze, look out for that arm!"

There were little beads of sweat on his forehead and the white face was more lustrous than ever. Ace grinned crookedly. He walked into the apartment and dropped into a chair and stared up at Polo Coat.

"So what?" he asked.

The peak-faced man in the Harris tweed walked over and struck Ace left and right—hard.

Ace looked at him impassively, his dark face darker; especially at the corner of his mouth where a trickle of blood ran down. Polo Coat sat down on the divan, nursing the bum arm. He looked at Ace with eyes that were coldly blank.

"Come clean, dick. We know you were working to get the dope on the big-shot. We know that Big Tom had it all today. We know now that he got jittery before he got bopped and gave it to you to hand

431

on to the D.A. That envelope will burn the big-shot. Nice of us to come up for it this way, wasn't it?"

"Nice," Ace said tonelessly. He hardly seemed to notice when Peaked-Face was taking his gun away from him.

"Not so nice if you get nasty," Peaked-Face said flatly.

Ace shook his head. "Sorry, boys. You're on a bum steer. I haven't got it. I got rid of it quite awhile ago. Think I'm sap enough to carry that dynamite around with me?"

"I think you were," Polo Coat said. "I think you're a hell of a sap. Go on—give it to him!"

Peaked-Face hit Ace twice more, a little harder. Peaked-Face put one hand in his pocket, and then when it came out he had a blackjack that *thunked* on Ace's ribs. The dark face twisted and was turning a muddy color.

Polo Coat stopped the battering. "Hell, we didn't come here just to enjoy ourselves. Frisk him and get that envelope."

They laid Ace out on the floor and went through every pocket. Peaked-Face yanked off the coat and vest and went over them carefully. He felt along Ace's legs. He pulled off his shoes. He rolled up his pant legs to see if anything were snapped underneath the garters.

"He ain't got it!" said Peaked-Face. "And he ain't been home since he picked it up from Big Tom. And he ain't had a chance to get rid of it. What the hell do we do now?" he swore.

Polo Coat got up. "Stay with him. Work him over some more when he comes to. I'm going to see Lantz. We've got to have that envelope. They've got the big-shot down at headquarters now. That envelope will burn him—and us." He walked out, closing the door softly.

Peaked-Face rolled Ace over on his face. He rolled heavily as if he were far out. Peaked-Face got to his feet and stared down at him. He kicked him in the ribs with a detached viciousness. Then something happened that Peaked-Face hadn't figured on.

Ace caught the foot and jerked. Peaked-Face came down on top of him with one hand diving into his pocket for a gun. The hand stayed there. Ace's fist crashed on the narrow chin and Peaked-Face rolled over and out. Ace yanked the hand out of the pocket and took the gun. He reached in the other pocket and got the blackjack.

He walked over to the door shaking his head. He opened the door and whispered hoarsely:

"Here it is!"

A head came around the corner and Ace slapped down with the blackjack. He carried the lookout in and threw him on the bed, snapped a cuff around his wrist. He stuck the other cuff through the bars at the foot of the bed and snapped it on Peaked-Face.

"Try and get out of that," he said.

He shook his head vigorously as he stuck his feet into his shoes and shrugged into his coat. He raced down the stairs and went through the lobby on the run. He went out and stared up the street.

Polo Coat stood out in the light a block away. He was looking for a cab, but there was none in sight. That was a break for Ace.

Polo Coat got to the corner and glanced at two cops coming his way. Something jammed into his back and Ace's voice said:

"I'd freeze if I were you, rat."

He looked around as he felt something twitch the pocket underneath his bum arm. He saw an envelope in Ace's hand.

"Where in hell was that envelope?" he asked.

Ace's battered face was impassive. But the little lights were dancing in his eyes once more. "In your pocket, sap. I slipped it there when I pushed past you into the apartment. Nice of me, wasn't it?"

"Nice," Polo Coat grunted. He looked at the cops, who were hurrying toward Ace. He looked at the taxicab he had summoned, got in, and sunk into a corner, nursing his arm. In the light from the street lamps the lustrous white face was wet and glistening.

# The Seventieth Number

*Stephen Dentinger*

Gordan Kahn did not set out to kill someone every day, and so this particular Wednesday was special in his life. He dressed carefully, making certain that the conservative striped tie was positioned just right, taking an extra few moments to polish his shoes.

He was meeting Dennis Marret for a drink in a private room at the College Club, supposedly to discuss the possibility of a settlement. But he already knew there was no chance of a fair settlement. Dennis Marret had robbed too many men like Gordon Kahn, taken their life's work away for a few thousand dollars. The time for talking had ended. Now Dennis Marret must die.

Gordon Kahn took a subway to 42nd Street and then walked the

433

two blocks to the College Club. The woman at the front desk didn't even glance up as he entered. She was used to luncheon guests and business appointments held in the club's private dining rooms. He had only the waiter to contend with, and that wouldn't be difficult.

Dennis Marret rose from his padded armchair and greeted Kahn with a broad smile. "Well, well! Good to see you again! Glad we could meet here like this. Gets me away from the office for a few hours. I have a room reserved. Do you want lunch?"

Gordon cleared his throat. "No, just a drink, I think. I don't have much time."

He followed Marret into an elegantly furnished private room which could easily have held twelve people for dinner. The walls were decorated with elaborately spacious campus scenes, and the two men seemed lost along the sides of the big table, facing each other like opponents in some ritualized chess match.

Marret touched the service bell and almost immediately an elderly waiter appeared to take their order. Kahn managed to blow his nose and turn his head at that moment, so the waiter could not see his face. He mumbled an order for a Scotch and water through the folds of his handkerchief, and held it in place until the waiter had left.

"Well," Marret said again. Gordon Kahn remembered that word from the first time he'd ever met him, in the plush presidential offices of Marret Enterprises, Inc. "You asked for this meeting. Just what did you have in mind, Gordon?"

Kahn cleared his throat. It was a nervous habit that dated from his youth; and he'd never quite got over it. "About the transducer. I thought we might come to terms." He produced a little notebook and a ballpoint pen from his pocket, and carefully placed them on the table in front of him. The notebook was blank except for a single number he'd written on the first page months earlier.

"Terms, terms! Gordon, you don't seem to understand. That's all settled and done with. The transducer is now the property of Marret Enterprises. You were paid for it—a perfectly fair and aboveboard transaction."

"I received a payment of three thousand dollars with a promise of royalties for as long as I remained an employee of Marret Enterprises. I also received one thousand shares of stock in the corporation, again with the proviso that it reverted to the corporation when I left your employ. Six months later you fired me. I ended up with nothing for my invention but the original three thousand."

"Gordon," Marret said with an exasperated sigh, "these are the ways of the business world. I had to let you go because we're cutting back all along the line. You were our employee, so the transducer belongs to us. That's standard practice among corporations everywhere, and the courts have upheld it."

"The transducer was developed on my own time, before I joined Marret Enterprises."

"You would have a difficult time proving that in court. Besides, we took certain risks in its development. We invested a good deal of money."

The waiter returned with their drinks, and again Kahn covered his face with his handkerchief. "I seem to have a bit of a cold," he mumbled. As the waiter shut the door behind him, Kahn returned the handkerchief to his pocket. "You were saying?"

"I was saying you were damned lucky to have gotten what you did," Marret told him, his patience obviously wearing thin.

"Three thousand for an invention worth millions?"

Marret shrugged. "Or worth nothing. You had no money to develop and produce it. I did."

"How many others have you cheated like this?" Kahn asked.

"Others?"

"We should really start a club. People cheated by Dennis Marret out of their life's work."

Marret sipped his drink and then waved a hand in dismissal. "We have nothing more to talk about, Kahn. There's no point in my even being civil to you any longer."

Gordon Kahn slipped the pen back into his pocket. When his hand reappeared it held a .22 caliber automatic.

"What in hell—put that gun down, you fool!"

"Do I get a fair payment for my invention, Mr. Marret?"

Marret's hand reached for the service bell. Kahn's hand went quickly across the table until the gun was only inches from Marret's head. When Marret kept reaching, Kahn shot him once through the left temple. Kahn coughed loudly to help cover the sound, and kept on coughing for a few seconds afterward.

Dennis Marret slumped in death across the table, a thin trickle of blood widening into a stain on the white cloth. Kahn held his breath to see if anyone would come running, but the sound of the little .22 had not passed through the massive oak door. He glanced around the room, seeking anything he might have touched, but his fingers had carefully avoided the glass of Scotch and water, and the gun was now safely back in his pocket.

For a moment he considered cutting the cord of the service bell, but then decided against it. Marret wouldn't be ringing for help any more. He started to pick up his open notebook next to the glass when there was a tapping on the door. He froze.

"Yes?" he managed to say, quite loudly. He stepped quickly to the door to prevent its opening.

"Telephone call for Mr. Marret," a voice announced.

"He can't be disturbed now. Take a message."

"Yes, sir."

Kahn cursed silently and opened the door a crack, watching the receding back of the old waiter. He couldn't stay there any longer. The hallway was clear and he stepped into it, closing the door behind him.

Marret had told his office where he was, and that was one thing Kahn hadn't figured on. He'd purposely phoned Marret's New York apartment last evening to arrange the meeting, rather than contacting him at the office where an efficient secretary might have recorded Kahn's name in an appointment book. He knew Marret's wife was in Florida, and there was no one else he would be likely to tell of the meeting.

But of course Marret had called his office and told them where he'd be. Had he mentioned Kahn's name? That was something Kahn had to find out—at once. He paused in the downstairs lobby of the club and sought out a pay telephone. Then he quickly dialed Marret's office and asked for his secretary.

"Ah . . . this is Mr. Rogers. I was supposed to meet Dennis Marret at the College Club, but he hasn't shown up yet. Do you know if he's on his way?"

The girl's voice was puzzled as she replied. "He's there now, Mr. Rogers. I just tried to phone him and they said he couldn't be disturbed. Perhaps he had another appointment first at the same club. He didn't tell me who he was meeting."

"Well, I'll wait a bit longer, then," Kahn said, relief flooding over him. He hung up and left the booth, feeling good. No name, no clue —not a single thing to link him with the killing. His revenge had been carried out as skillfully as one of his inventions.

And then he remembered his notebook on the table.

That damned waiter had interrupted him as he was about to pick it up. He'd left so quickly he'd forgotten it till now. There was no danger of fingerprints on the notebook's pebbled cover, and he hadn't touched the pages at all—but there was that damned number he'd scrawled on the first page months before. That number could send him to prison for the rest of his life.

He headed back upstairs toward the private dining room. There

436

was no choice but to retrieve the notebook before someone else found it.

But as he turned down the hallway he saw the elderly waiter just opening the door. The waiter was holding a slip of paper in his hand —the phone message from Marret's secretary. No one had answered his knock and now he was going in.

Kahn hit him from behind, slamming his head against the oak door, but he was an instant too late. A scream sprang from the waiter's lips as he saw Marret's body.

Kahn tried to push him aside, but the man's frail body remained jammed in the doorway. His forehead was bleeding but he still kept screaming. Finally, hearing the sound of running footsteps, Kahn scrambled across the hallway and out through a fire door.

The fire stairs led directly to the street, and he hurried until he was outside mingling with the afternoon crowd. He'd gotten away, but just barely.

He knew the waiter hadn't seen his face, and no one in the lobby had noticed him. The secretary back at Marret Enterprises didn't know his real name, and he'd left no fingerprints. He'd gotten away with it—except for that notebook with its damned number written on the first page.

He could only hope now that the police would fail to discover its significance.

The case came to Lieutenant Burns of Homicide East, and it was the sort of case he could easily have done without. The murder of some bum or pusher was one thing, but the murder of Dennis Marret in a private dining room at the swank College Club was something else again. The story hit the front page of *The Times*, and for the first time in his life Burns had a personal call from City Hall inquiring as to his progress.

That progress, 24 hours after the murder, was just about nil. Only the waiter's prints were found on the Scotch glass, and there were no prints at all on the notebook. The waiter's meager description could fit half the men in New York, and Marret's secretary dissolved into tears when she told of only one phone call—from a mysterious Mr. Rogers who had never called before.

"Nothing," Burns said, speaking mostly to himself, but including the other detectives in the squadroom. "Frost, have you found any enemies who had a motive?"

"Hundreds, Lieutenant." Sergeant Frost flipped open his notebook. "Marret might have been a hero on the financial pages, but in business dealings he was a villain. His favorite trick seems to have been finding scientists with promising inventions and persuading them to join the firm. Marret got them to assign their patents to his company in exchange for a cash payment, some stock, and a lot of promises. After a few months he'd fire them and get back the stock. The inventors were left out in the cold, with maybe a few grand if they were lucky."

"A good enough motive for murder," Burns agreed. "Let's take a closer look at these guys."

"That's the trouble, Lieutenant. There are too many of them! Marret pulled the same stunt on thirty, forty people over the years. There are a dozen lawsuits pending against him right now. Marret Enterprises was big business, and bad business."

Burns began tapping his pencil against the edge of the desk. "What else?"

"The usual business enemies, and a couple of disgruntled husbands who claim he was fooling around with their wives."

"How'd he have time?" Burns asked. Then, to another of the detectives, "You've checked all the employees of the College Club, Riggs?"

"Every one. Nobody saw a thing except the old waiter."

Burns stared down at the murderer's notebook on the desk before him. "That brings us back to the number. 5560894. What in hell does it mean?"

"Does it have to mean anything, Lieutenant?"

Burns went on tapping his pencil. "According to the waiter's testimony, the killer returned and hit him from behind, trying to get back in the room. Why? It could only have been to retrieve this notebook, since he'd left nothing else in the room. The notebook itself is unexceptional—you can buy them for a dollar in any stationery store. So that leaves us with the number. The number was important enough to bring the killer back after it."

"But what does it mean?"

Burns walked to a blackboard they kept at one end of the squadroom for diagraming the scene of a crime. He brushed away some chalk dust and wrote the number, very large, in the center of the board.

5560894.

"Seven digits. It's some sort of identification number with seven digits. Let's list the obvious possibilities."

He continued writing, and after a moment stepped back to look at the board:

438

1. Social Security number
2. Telephone number
3. Army serial number
4. Credit card number
5. Membership number

"Let's start with these," he suggested. "Any comments?"

Frost shifted his weight in the chair, reaching for his wallet. "Social security numbers have nine digits," he said after a moment of checking. "So that's out."

"And Army serial numbers have eight," Riggs said.

Burns nodded and crossed out those two. "But it could be a phone number. 556-0894. Most cities use only numbers now, and even New York is gradually doing away with the old exchange letters."

Frost still had his wallet out, checking credit cards. "Most cards use eight or nine digits, but I suppose a smaller store could use seven. We can check some of the more likely ones."

"And check all the clubs in town for membership numbers, starting with the College Club itself."

For the next few hours four detectives were on the phone, checking out various possibilities. Burns himself took a break only long enough to phone his wife and tell her he'd be late. Then he was back at it.

By dinnertime they had nothing to show for their efforts. The College Club numbers never exceeded five digits, and a random sampling of a dozen department stores had turned up only one Fifth Avenue men's shop that used a seven-digit charge number. They informed Burns that 5560894 was unassigned at present.

Burns sipped some water from a paper cup and called across the squadroom to Frost. "How about the phone numbers?"

"Nothing yet, Lieutenant. None of the old exchanges started off with a double number like 55. Some of the newer ones do—we've got 777 and 889 now, but no 556."

"Put somebody on checking out-of-town phone companies. Especially the suburbs and large cities across the country. Our killer wanted that number back because he thought we could trace him through it. Let's show him he was right."

They came back to it in the morning, knowing that the phone number theory hadn't worked out. In the 20 largest cities they'd found only one 556-0894, and it was the number of a West Coast car wash.

"All right," Burns decided. "It's back to the blackboard." He erased what he'd written the previous day and started on a new list:

439

1. Auto license number
2. Auto registration number
3. Laundry or dry cleaning mark
4. Prison serial number
5. Gun registration number

"Auto license numbers usually have a letter in them," Frost pointed out.

"All right." Burns rewrote the number on the blackboard. 556-0-894. "Suppose the 0 is a letter rather than a digit. That would do it. Somebody check the Motor Vehicle Bureau, and send out teletype messages to other states."

They worked all day, and into the night, and by midnight Burns was ready to give it up. There was no such license number as 556-0-894 issued in New York or in any of the surrounding states. The New York State Motor Vehicle Bureau used seven-digit numbers for auto registration, driver's license, and other forms, but the number in question failed to check out. Seven-digit numbers also appeared on auto inspection stickers in the state, but here again they drew a blank. The number in question hadn't yet been used that year.

Riggs reported on the laundry marks. "It's like the private clubs yesterday, Lieutenant. Membership numbers and laundry marks just aren't that long."

By midnight they had received teletyped replies from every major prison in the country. Only the largest used seven-digit numbers for their prisoners, and 5560894 meant nothing to them. Likewise, the gun registration number failed to check out. Burns went home.

In the morning over breakfast he sleepily wrote the number in the margin of the newspaper. 5560894. He showed it to his wife.

"Betty, what would this number mean to you?"

She eyed it indifferently as she poured his coffee. "Zip code? My sister in Minnesota is 55614."

"What about the other two digits?"

She frowned at the number. "Couldn't you just cross those out?"

He went back to the squadroom and stared at the blackboard. The feeling had grown in him that the number was the key to the entire case—if they could only decipher it.

"All right," he said to Frost and Riggs and the others. "I want to hear the wildest ideas you can come up with. Anything that this number could possibly be. Start talking."

After fifteen numbing minutes he stepped back to look at the board. The list was truly amazing:

1. A code of some sort
2. Lottery number
3. Horse race winners
4. Football signals
5. Latitude and longitude
6. A date or time
7. Serial number on currency
8. Baseball lineup
9. Magazine circulation
10. Radio station call numbers

"We could go on like this all night," he decided. "Things like codes are out because our killer wouldn't have been so anxious to get the number back if it was in code. It's too long for the usual lottery number, but we can check the New York State lottery."

"They keep no record of who buys what number," Frost pointed out.

"Horse-race winners wouldn't include a zero," someone else said. "And how would football signals point to a killer?"

"Ham radio stations use letters along with their numbers."

"Baseball lineups, magazine circulation—all nothing, a big nothing," Burns said, crossing them out. "Currency serial number—what would that tell us? This has to be something the killer had a reason for writing down. Latitude and longitude would be . . . let's see . . . 55 degrees, 60 minutes latitude, and 89 degrees, 4 minutes longitude." He consulted the atlas in his desk. "Without north and south or east and west indicated, it could be in four spots on the earth—all of them near the north or south poles."

"A date or time doesn't make sense, either," Frost grumbled.

Burbank, a cop on robbery detail, came in and rummaged around on his desk at the other end of the room. "Can I borrow your stapler, Lieutenant?" he asked finally, coming forward to get it.

"Sure." Burns leaned over and passed it to him.

"Any break in your murder case yet?"

"None." He pointed to the number. "What does it mean to you, Burbank?"

"This is the Marret thing?" He went on stapling his papers. "How about an employee payroll number or something like that? Marret Enterprises is a big outfit."

"Nothing in seven digits," Burns mumbled. "We checked it the first day."

"How about the numbers of golf clubs?"

Burns sighed with growing irritation. "It has to be something that connects the killer with Marret. The number in the notebook meant something, or the killer wouldn't have tried to get it back."

Burbank finished attaching the papers and returned the stapler to Burns. "Thanks. Say, maybe it's a safe combination, or—no, I guess not."

"Not a safe combination," Burns said. "And no dog license number." He glanced at a pad scribbled with notes. "Actually, we've checked out sixty-nine types of numbers—sixty-nine dead ends. We've just about hit rock bottom—" He stopped talking and stared at the bottom of the stapler in his hand. He could feel his heart beating faster as he reached across the desk for the telephone. "Get me Washington," he told the operator. "I don't know the number, but I want to speak to—"

Gordon Kahn was humming a little tune as he opened his apartment door and stepped into the hallway. He stopped humming when he saw the three men waiting there.

"Gordon Kahn?" the oldest of them asked. He was a ruddy-faced man with graying hair who looked as if he hadn't slept in days.

"That's me. Can I help you?"

The man flipped open his wallet and showed a badge. "I'm Lieutenant Burns, Homicide East. We'd like to question you about the murder of Dennis Marret."

Kahn glanced around, looking for a way out. One of the younger men placed a hand on his shoulder. "Well," Kahn said with a sigh, "it took you three days to find me."

"You need not make a statement until a lawyer—"

"I know, I know," Kahn said with a wave of his hand. "How'd you get me? It was the number in the notebook, wasn't it?"

The man named Burns nodded. "That, and a seven-digit number I finally noticed on the bottom of a stapler on my desk. I phoned the Patent Office in Washington, and they told me 5560894 was the patent number on the invention you assigned to Marret Enterprises."

# A Shroud
# with a Silver Lining

*by Marion Lineaweaver*

Daisy Baldwin was a typical chorus girl, only more so. Her hair was blonder, her skin whiter, her mouth riper, her curves curvier. Underneath she was as tough as nails and, true to the romantic notion about her profession, pure as the driven snow.

"Be good," her father had told her when she decided to make use of her looks, "but don't broadcast it."

"Men are suckers for flattery," added her mother. "You can bank on that."

Such parental advice had brought her far—on this particular evening to the snow-banked entrance of a very secret little chalet in the Adirondacks. Daisy had just skied four miles, and she was tired.

"Where have you been?" The door was flung open by the chalet's owner, whose unwinking black eyes, and the mustache inadequately hiding a long razor scar made him look more like a gangster than a sportsman.

"Oh, I've just been trying to ski on a hill back there," Daisy gestured vaguely. "Gee! I could hardly stand up. I'll disgrace you at White Peak Lodge tomorrow, Louis—that is, if you get the car fixed."

"Stop kidding. There's nothing wrong with the car and you know it. You're not so dumb!"

Daisy pouted as they entered the firelit, pine-paneled room. "A girl shouldn't be alone with a man overnight. Her reputation—"

"We won't be alone. The gang's coming at seven. Put on something fancy, baby. I like to show you off."

Daisy's room was mirrored and chintzy, designed to please any female who might inhabit it, but Daisy was not concerned with interior decoration. While she insinuated herself into a black velvet skirt and a pink satin excuse for a blouse, she could hear Louis playing darts in the next room. Louis was good at darts; he could throw them almost as well as knives. Thoughtfully, Daisy completed her dressing

443

by placing in her pink satin bag a tiny mother-of-pearl-handled revolver.

"Your twenty-first birthday present, my dear," her father had said. "You're a big girl now."

But her mother had admonished her, "Use your brains instead. They'll keep you out of trouble."

Daisy was trying to use her brains. With the graceful walk that was second nature to her, and a feature of her job in the Palace Hotel floor show, she sauntered to the closet and took from her coat pocket a newspaper photograph.

It showed an assortment of diamonds: rings, bracelets, earrings, and a necklace of startling magnificence. The caption read: *Wealthy socialite robbed at her Palace Hotel apartment. Police baffled*—Daisy felt that pricking of the scalp that told her she was not alone, and turned. Louis had come into the room as quietly as a snake, and was watching her as a snake watches its prey. She was petrified for just a second, then she asked coolly, "Do you like my dress?" She paraded before him with one hand on her hip, the other swishing the clipping through the air.

"I like it fine," Louis said, not moving.

Daisy sank languidly down at the dressing table and began to comb her golden hair. She stuck the clipping in the mirror and studied it. "Diamonds would go fine with this dress, Louis."

He strode over to her and clasped his flexible hands tentatively around her neck. "Pretty baby. It would be a shame if anything happened to you."

She leaned back against him and gazed up at his expressionless face in the mirror with her beautiful violet eyes. "You're wonderful, Louis. How did you get away with it?"

"It was simple."

"You're a brain, Louis. You can get anything you want."

"If you meant that, you'd let me off the string." His eyelids flickered. "I want you, baby." He leaned down and rubbed his cheek against hers. It was hard and dry, rather like snakeskin, Daisy reflected, but she didn't draw away.

"You're handsome, Louis."

"Think so?"

"I know so." Her rosy lips parted in a dreamy smile. "We'd go well together."

"You can say that again."

Gently she pushed back the sleeve of his coat. "Your watch says ten of seven, Louis, or I would say it again, and then some."

"Kiss me, baby."

444

She fluttered her long lashes demurely. "A girl likes to wear a piece of jewelry from her boy friend, especially in front of his gang."

Louis laughed outright. "I said you weren't so dumb! Here." He pulled a handful of rings and bracelets out of his inside pocket and arranged them in front of her. "Try one for size—one of the bracelets."

He leaned over her again, but she whispered, "Listen! Don't you hear something?"

"It's them." Louis thrust the jewels back, all except one, the most spectacular of the bracelets. "I'll take my cut now," he said. "For you."

Daisy had met the gang before, two nights ago at the Palace Hotel, when three of them had walked out on the party for a whole hour. Now they sat before the fire at a round table laden with sandwiches and the mixings for a large supply of drinks.

"Relax, everybody," said their host. "Have a drink. We're miles from nowhere."

"Let's get down to business first," muttered somebody.

"Yeah," agreed another, "excluding the ice on baby-doll's arm."

"My cut," said Louis shortly. "Any reason I can't give it to my girl?"

"No, but let's get the business over, then worry about the babe."

They looked strangely alike to Daisy, hard, evil, nervous. Louis put the jewelry in the center of the table, then his gun, and the others followed suit. Daisy helped herself to a chicken sandwich with one hand; with the other she opened her pink satin bag and withdrew the revolver.

"Mine too?" she asked seriously.

A burst of astonished laughter and various comments resulted. "You got her trained, Louis!" "Can she use it?"

"But natch." Daisy tossed her golden curls. "Want to see?"

"Why not?" Louis leaned back in his chair, proud of her. "Show us, baby. Shoot at the darts target." They all laughed at the idea.

Daisy wiped her red mouth daintily and rose, swinging her skirt like a velvet bell. Then she pushed up the diamond bracelet so it wouldn't dangle, took aim, and hit the bull's eye three times. In the silence that followed she heard what she wanted to hear—men running in answer to her shots, and she said quickly, "My Dad gave me that and he taught me how to shoot it. It helps me in vaudeville. I do an act. My Dad says a girl should be ready for anything—"

Louis interrupted. "Your old man must be in some tough racket."

"Oh, he is," Daisy assured him, as the door burst open to admit a

445

large detachment of the constabulary, "Chief of Police James Baldwin
—sometimes I help him and the boys out."

Five minutes later, Louis, sullen and handcuffed, addressed himself
to Daisy as she lounged before the fire in her velvet and satin, the
picture of feminine helplessness.

"Just one thing I want to know: the nearest phone is two miles
away and you can't ski."

"Oh, but I can. I learned on that borax slide at Macy's."

Louis' voice rasped with irritation. "But why? Why does a dame like
you want to ski for?"

"Because," Daisy explained, widening her limpid eyes, "my mother
told me if a girl wants to get around, she ought to learn sports."

# The Sign

## by Tom Curry

The warning sign was missing at Green Spring and Arizona State
Trooper Ben Hale, on the trail of two lost greenhorns, improvised one
by scrawling, POISON, ARSENIC, on a report sheet which he fastened to
a sharpened stake driven into the ground.

"They stopped here," he told Whitey, his sleepy-eyed horse, "but
had brains enough not to drink."

Men did, but occasionally some thirst-crazed animal drank the poison water, as attested by sun-whitened bones near at hand. Another
sign proclaimed, 17 MI. TO NEXT WATER.

Trooper Hale permitted himself a swallow of tepid liquid from a
canteen; Whitey would have to hold out.

Mounting, he went on, sun wrinkles thick at the corners of his
slitted eyes.

"Three days since they passed here, Whitey."

Hale was twenty-four hours out of Gila Bend, the point from which
the two easterners, a nephew and his uncle, had ridden into the
painted desert.

When their horses, carrying canteens and food, had come home
with empty saddles the storekeeper, who also rented rooms and
mounts, had notified Trooper Hale.

446

The pilgrims had been staggering around, up to their ankles in shifting sand, baked by the brassy sun. The beauty of flowering yucca and giant cactus, and other colorful blooms, would not appeal to them; they would crave water.

Trooper Hale, rangy and smoothly browned, was experienced in the desert; he felt optimistic about their chances, figuring he would reach them before they perished. From the storekeeper he had learned that George Vernon, the nephew, had been around Gila Bend for a month and knew a little about the country, although the uncle, whose name was Stone, had arrived only a couple of days before.

By the running off of their horses, the two were bereft of supplies and water; but they could hold out, for the next spring was good to drink.

Yet when Hale reached this tank three hours later and Whitey began sucking in mouthfuls of the brownish stuff, he did not find them. They had, from the sign they left, been here and rested, but gone on.

"Now what's that?" he wondered aloud, as he noted a hole an inch in diameter and several inches deep in the earth close to the point where the steps led down to the spring.

He shrugged, for he found no explanation and, forging on after filling his canteens and letting Whitey replenish himself, passed a sign reading, NEXT WATER 22 MI.

On horseback he made it by dark; afoot it would mean long, weary hours, staggering through sandy stretches and across sharp rock.

He came to the waterhole, cursing his men because they hadn't the sense to remain in one spot by good water until found.

Unable to trail in the dark he slept till gray dawn. Spruced up, he set his wide hat on his bullet-shaped head; as he saddled up and put a boot in the stirrup to mount Whitey, he saw another small hole in the ground, similar to the one at the other spring.

Pushing on he read the weakening of the two, it showed in the trail; they stopped more often to rest and their foot indentations were dragging. Sometimes their prints overlapped and at others both sets ran close together.

"Nephew helpin' his uncle along, I reckon," decided Hale.

He began the long run between waterholes, forty-two miles, and it was not until the following day that he came up with the lost greenhorns.

They were lying near the edge of a shrunken waterhole, muddy but drinkable.

447

A tall fellow around thirty-five pushed weakly to his knees.

Trooper Hale had never seen him before but concluded this was George Vernon, the nephew; he had sparse black hair and his face was burnt lobster-red; his dark eyes were sunken and wild, lips dry. The elder, stouter man, Robert Stone, the uncle, lay on his stomach, face turned aside.

"Howdy," sang out Hale.

"Thank God you've come! My uncle's dead, and I nearly am!"

"Dead!" exclaimed Hale.

He dismounted, turned over the body. It was as Vernon said; Stone was gone, lips bluish.

"He drank the water," babbled Vernon, "and keeled over!"

Hale stared at him, for the water was good. Whitey was calmly partaking of it.

The trooper found no marks of violence on Robert Stone. "This water's okay," he informed Vernon.

"It killed Uncle Bob. He'd hardly taken it when he died. Give me a drink, will you?"

Hale handed the thirsty man a canteen and Vernon put back his head, greedily filling up.

The trooper was puzzled. Looking Vernon over, he decided he didn't like the nephew: Vernon seemed uneasy. As his trained eyes went on, searching the ground, he saw one of those unexplained holes.

"How come you let your horses get away, Vernon?"

"They—they pulled their stakes and ran."

"Huh! No stakes on the ropes they brought in." His eyes hardened as he watched Vernon. "I understand your uncle was a very rich man. You his heir?"

"Yes." Vernon's voice grew defiant. "What do you mean by that?"

Hale was suspicious, yet there was nothing on which to base this, no evidence of struggle, no weapon in sight. He pushed back his Stetson, scratched his close-cropped head: Vernon watched him, plainly worried.

"How about getting me back to town, officer?" he demanded. "I'm exhausted. There's nothing to be done for Uncle Bob now."

"Why did you bring your uncle way out into the desert, Vernon? You've been around long enough to understand what it's like. They told me he wasn't very well."

"That was the reason," replied Vernon sullenly. "He came to Arizona for his health. We got lost and our horses ran away. Anything wrong in that?"

448

Hale walked around the spring; beside the hole he found a bare spot, indented in the dirt. "A stone lay there," he thought.

A sudden hunch sent him to his knees, peering closely at the earth, Vernon watching every move he made.

Hale said, "Reckon I'll wash up, I'm mighty dusty." He unbuckled his gunbelt, holding his .45 caliber Colt revolver, and put it on a flat rock.

Lying on his belly, he began splashing water over his face; then he reached in his arms to the shoulder and fished around the bottom. It wasn't long till he pulled out the sign, the missing sign from Green Spring. It was of wood, and under a skull-and-bones were carved the words

POISON, ARSENIC, DO NOT DRINK!

It had been weighted by that stone, to hold it under.

"Now I savvy," said Hale, voice hardening. "You toted that sign along with you from waterhole to waterhole, hid in your shirt, Vernon, so's your uncle wouldn't dare take a drink! You lagged behind to pull it up, and ran on ahead to stick it up at each new spring. You didn't suffer much yourself, you could grab a mouthful of water when you had to. All those springs save the first were good but your uncle read the warnin' sign you put up and wouldn't drink!"

"You lie!" snarled Vernon. "I didn't touch that sign!"

"Nobody else has been through here for a month! You figured on him dyin' of thirst, if his heart didn't kill him; he couldn't hold out and finally drank here; thinkin' it poison, the fright finished him."

George Vernon's eyes blazed.

"No one'll believe that crazy yarn," he shouted.

"I'll have to arrest you," declared Hale solemnly. "What with your being his heir and havin' the motive, you should get you at least twenty years."

Vernon crouched close to the flat rock on which rested Hale's gun; Hale stood further away, firmly accusing him.

Suddenly Vernon jumped, got his hand on the belt, dragging the big revolver from its pleated holster.

"All right, it's true," he screamed. "Damn him, he wouldn't die, he wouldn't give me any more than enough money to skimp along on. The old coot was wrecking my life, wasn't he, staying alive? He scared himself to death, thinking he'd drunk poison water, but that's not my fault and you'll never get a chance to accuse me. Stand back—"

Hale was starting for him and Vernon pulled the trigger of the Colt but the hammer only clicked harmlessly. Before he could try again, Hale was on him, wrested the pistol from his hand, knocked him down with a hard brown fist.

"Maybe I couldn't have proved the story of the sign, Vernon, but attempted murder'll put you in prison! I thought gettin' hold of the gun would stampede you. We always keep an empty cylinder under the hammer to prevent accidents!"

# The Sign of the "400"

### by R. K. Munkittrick

For the nonce, Holmes was slighting his cocaine and was joyously jabbing himself with morphine—his favorite 70 per cent solution—when a knock came at the door; it was our landlady with a telegram. Holmes opened it and read it carelessly.

"H'm!" he said. "What do you think of this, Watson?"

I picked it up. "COME AT ONCE. WE NEED YOU. SEVENTY-TWO CHINCHBUGGE PLACE, S.W.," I read.

"Why, it's from Athelney Jones," I remarked.

"Just so," said Holmes; "call a cab."

We were soon at the address given, 72 Chinchbugge Place being the town house of the Dowager Countess of Coldslaw. It was an old-fashioned mansion, somewhat weather-beaten. The old hat stuffed in the broken pane in the drawing room gave the place an air of unstudied artistic negligence, which we both remarked at the time.

Athelney Jones met us at the door. He wore a troubled expression. "Here's a pretty go, gentlemen!" was his greeting. "A forcible entrance has been made to Lady Coldslaw's boudoir, and the famous Coldslaw diamonds are stolen."

Without a word Holmes drew out his pocket lens and examined the atmosphere. "The whole thing wears an air of mystery," he said, quietly.

We then entered the house. Lady Coldslaw was completely prostrated and could not be seen. We went at once to the scene of the robbery. There was no sign of anything unusual in the boudoir, ex-

450

cept that the windows and furniture had been smashed and the pictures had been removed from the walls. An attempt had been made by the thief to steal the wallpaper, also. However, he had not succeeded. It had rained the night before and muddy footprints led up to the escritoire from which the jewels had been taken. A heavy smell of stale cigar smoke hung over the room. Aside from these hardly noticeable details, the despoiler had left no trace of his presence.

In an instant Sherlock Holmes was down on his knees examining the footprints with a stethoscope. "H'm!" he said; "so you can make nothing out of this, Jones?"

"No, sir," answered the detective; "but I hope to; there's a big reward."

"It's all very simple, my good fellow," said Holmes. "The robbery was committed at three o'clock this morning by a short, stout, middle-aged, hen-pecked man with a cast in his eye. His name is Smythe, and he lives at 239 Toff Terrace."

Jones fairly gasped. "What! Major Smythe, one of the highest thought-of and richest men in the city?" he said.

"The same."

In half an hour we were at Smythe's bedside. Despite his protestations, he was pinioned and driven to prison.

"For heaven's sake, Holmes," said I, when we returned to our rooms, "how did you solve that problem so quickly?"

"Oh, it was easy, dead easy!" said he. "As soon as we entered the room, I noticed the cigar smoke. It was cigar smoke from a cigar that had been given a husband by his wife. I could tell that, for I have made a study of cigar smoke. Any other but a hen-pecked man throws such cigars away. Then I could tell by the footprints that the man had had appendicitis. Now, no one but members of the '400' have that. Who then was hen-pecked in the '400,' and had had appendicitis recently? Why, Major Smythe, of course! He is middle-aged, stout, and has a cast in his eye."

I could not help but admire my companion's reasoning, and told him so. "Well," he said, "it is very simple if you know how."

Thus ended the Coldslaw robbery, so far as we were concerned.

It may be as well to add, however, that Jones's arrant jealousy caused him to resort to the lowest trickery to throw discredit upon the discovery of my gifted friend. He allowed Major Smythe to prove a most conclusive alibi, and then meanly arrested a notorious burglar as the thief, on the flimsiest proof, and convicted him. This burglar had been caught while trying to pawn some diamonds that *seemed* to be a portion of the plunder taken from 72 Chinchbugge Place.

Of course, Jones got all the credit. I showed the newspaper accounts to Holmes. He only laughed, and said: "You see how it is, Watson; Scotland Yard, as usual, gets the glory." As I perceived he was going to play "Sweet Marie" on his violin, I reached for the morphine, myself.

# Smoke Sign

*by Dale Clark*

Tourists were queer people. Some weeks as many as a dozen parties drove up the steeply winding dirt grade to Jim Riley's station on Round Mountain; and they all seemed to think they were the first, that no one and nothing else ever broke the monotony of Riley's solitary vigil.

"Don't see how you stand it, young fella," the big, blue-suited man said—typically. "All by yourself. I'd go crazy."

It must have been an idea they got out of a book. Certainly it didn't square with the facts spread in front of—or under—their eyes. Round Mountain, elevation eighteen hundred feet and only two miles from the state highway, was the unlonesomest Fire Patrol lookout in the county. The valleys below were parallelogrammed into citrus groves. The smaller, sunstruck blue rectangle was the swimming pool on Dolores Deanne's ranch. A man isn't exactly wilderness-bound when he can look from his kitchen window across a movie star's backyard, is he?

There was the Patrol truck crew housed at the foot of the two-mile grade. Daily, Chuck and Lew or Ed Sturgis came up with water and rations and small-talk. When he unhooked the phone, he could gossip with lookout men at Wheeler, Big Bow, and the Pass; he had his one day a week off-duty. Tourists included, Jim Riley led an existence less solitary than the average farmer in his fields.

He did not tell the blue-suited man so. Knowing he wouldn't be believed, anyway, Riley had evolved a stock rejoinder.

"Civilization's close enough to satisfy me." He pointed, chuckling. "Gray dot over behind Sawtooth is Tepaki State Penitentiary. I figure I'm better off right here."

452

This one always rated a laugh. It made the big, blue-suited man laugh heartily as he scrawled his name in the guest register. *T. Smith, El Paso.* "I bet plenty of 'em would be mighty glad to change cells with you."

His glance went around the small, single-roomed, glass-walled station. Riley's kerosene stove filled one corner. His chair and table filled another. In the third stood the cot. The fourth corner held a desk, with the phone and radio.

"The radio must help you kill a lot of time," T. Smith said.

"It's a battery set," Riley told him dryly, "and the battery's low, so I haven't been using it much."

The most prominent article in the room stood on a tall steel table in the middle of the floor.

"You probably never saw one of these before," Riley said. He showed T. Smith how the Osborne fire-finder worked. By swinging the turntable, you could peer through the rear aperture and draw a bead on a smoke signal anywhere around the horizon. The turntable was marked in degrees. "When headquarters get readings phoned in from two stations, they plot the lines on a chart. Your fire is where those lines meet."

Little brush fires couldn't always been seen from two stations, of course. Riley pointed out how the front lens of the finder was crossed by upper and lower hairlines. A calibrated gauge sight could be moved up and down the rear aperture. "So we take an elevation reading along with the direction finding. Headquarters and the different crew houses all have panoramic photographs taken at each lookout. The photographs are marked off in these same degrees, up and down and across, so they can put a pencil right on the trouble."

T. Smith didn't seem interested. He peered speculatively toward the eon-old, wrinkled flang of Sawtooth. "I'm just wondering how you get to a fire after you spot one?"

"We use fire trails."

Riley spread the Patrol map on the desk. It showed trails threading back-country where not even horseback trails ran. The big, blue-suited man looked at this more intelligently than tourists generally did. His plump finger came down: "Looks like a short-cut through to Cresida. Not open to the public?"

"No, it's privately owned land. They keep the gates padlocked, so we have to carry keys. You couldn't get an ordinary car through anyway. Plenty of places we can't take a truck in," Riley said. "You notice

453

that rebuilt jalopy of mine outside, special high wheels and low ratio gears. Well, I've just about had to carry that on my back sometimes."

"You help fight the fires, too?"

"You bet. Brother, no Patrol guy sits on his tail while twenty, thirty thousand acres of watershed go up in flames."

T. Smith presently went away, saying: "I'll be seeing you." Jim Riley did not think it very probable.

Four days later, at high noon, Jim didn't even look up from his task of recording the twelve o'clock humidity score when footfalls came up the steps. "You're early, Chuck."

"Riley!"

He jerked around then. It wasn't Chuck with the pork chops, it was T. Smith with a gun in his hand.

Jim Riley hadn't heard about any prison break. He knew, though, as soon as he saw the second man's face. It was a harshly sunburnt face, unshaved, with a lot of quarry dust bedded into the stubble. And Tepaki's was the only active quarry within a hundred miles.

Riley felt a cold, tightening knot in the pit of his stomach. He admitted to himself that he was as scared as hell.

"You're going to drive us over that Cresida short-cut," announced T. Smith. "Where we won't run into any posses."

Riley's noon meal warmed on the stove. The percolator bubbled busily. His heart thudded about as loud, and much more rapidly.

"I can't." It didn't sound like his own voice at all. "I can't leave my station."

T. Smith laughed—a brittle and dangerous sound.

"I mean it," Jim Riley insisted. He passed his tongue between dry lips. "Look, I'm not supposed to. If I headed my jalopy down the grade, the whole truck gang would be out to see why."

"We'll take care of them," the man with the quarry dust on his face said.

"That's what I'm afraid of. They aren't cops, and they're friends of mine. I don't want to get them mixed in this, shot up or killed."

T. Smith asked: "You don't want to get yourself killed, either, do you?"

Riley had thought of this. Supposing he drove the pair to Cresida, would they turn him loose alive to set the police on their fresh trail? The chance looked slight.

"Wait." The first sweat drop started on his forehead. "Maybe I can fix it for you. So the coast is clear." There was little strength or sureness in his voice. "Let me call up and send the gang out on a false alarm. They won't know about me leaving here, see?"

The quarry dusted man cried: "Let you talk on the phone! You think we're nuts?"

"Listen, you got to. Suppose some other station might call me, and noon's the likeliest time they would. If they can't raise me," Jim Riley said, "somebody's going to get busy and find out why. If I turn in a fire, though, they'd think I went to help put it out."

T. Smith said: "Dutch, he's got something there." He pressed his gun against Jim Riley's ribs. "Just so you keep your fire away from Cresida." He closed his hand on the phone receiver. "Tell them it's west of here, and remember I'm the guy that hears what they say back."

Riley's mouth was almost too dry for speech. He gasped his name into the phone. T. Smith's gun gave him a warning prod. Riley said: "There's quite a smoke sign on Little Bow. One hundred seventy, elevation plus nine. It looks like plenty of trouble from here."

The receiver sounded thinly through the big man's fingers. It was Ed Sturgis, talking from the foot of the grade. "Which side of the ridge, Jim?"

"This side. Coming this way."

The receiver issued fresh sound, Ed Sturgis saying they'd get right busy on it.

"All right, Riley. Where's your keys?"

Jim Riley drove his jalopy down the grade, always painfully aware of the revolver Dutch gripped in his hairy, quarry-dusted fist. T. Smith, behind them, pored over the fire-trail map and fired questions at Riley. Since Riley hadn't been over the Cresida short-cut in two years, his memory frequently failed to tally with the map. The pair were becoming darkly suspicious of his hesitant replies. Then their attention shifted grimly to the buildings beyond the bridge at the foot of the grade.

At the last minute, Riley braked hard. Four planks torn out left a hole big enough to drop the front wheels of the jalopy through the bridge. Six paces away, the barrel of a deer rifle pointed through the roadside bushes. The voice belonged to Ed Sturgis:

"Get out. You're covered."

Two shotguns pushed into sight along the bank of the dry watercourse. Jim Riley saw with enormous relief that both of his companions held their hands high and empty.

He exhaled: "Gosh, Ed. I didn't know if you could figure anything out of it."

"It figured itself. There was a radio broadcast right after you told us where trouble was coming from."

T. Smith spoke dazedly. "You told—?"

Riley's laugh sounded neither Homeric nor heroic; it was more like a nervous giggle.

"Sure. One hundred seventy, elevation plus nine. I know that one by heart because darned near every tourist has me draw a bead on Tepaki prison."

# Smothered Mate

*by Stephen Dentinger*

When Sara Blake played chess with her husband after an especially busy day at the agency, it was often the only relaxation she got.

She enjoyed the games even though he usually won, enjoyed them perhaps because it was almost the only time he reminded her of the sweet, simple man she had married. Hunched over the chessboard, pondering his next move, there was no time for the money-making schemes that seemed to fill his waking hours.

"Check!" he announced in triumph. "It's a smothered mate. My knight has you in check and all your moves are blocked by your own pieces!"

"Oh, all right, Ken." She started to clear the pieces from the board.

"Another game?"

"No! You always win!"

"I thought you liked to play," he said, searching his pockets for a cigarette.

"I do! I just don't like to lose."

He picked up a magazine that was open on the floor, intent on pursuing a conversation that had started at dinner. "This contest your agency is running—"

"We're only judging it, Ken. That's what our division does—judges promotional contests for clients."

"The first prize is fifty pounds of gold!"

"It's their fiftieth anniversary. They wanted something to—"

"Sara, at today's closing price fifty pounds of gold is worth over three hundred thousand dollars!"

"It didn't cost them that much. They bought it when the market was lower, when they first had the idea for the contest."

"But that's what it's worth. And *you* draw the winning postcard."

It was the same old conversation all over again. "Ken, sometimes I do it and sometimes Marian does it. There'll be probably fifty thousand cards in that drum, and twenty people in the room watching us. Everyone comes in for a drawing. You think I could cheat and draw your card? You couldn't win anyway, you're my husband."

"I've got it all figured out."

She put the chessboard and pieces away. "I don't want to hear it. I'm going to bed."

But that night, her subconscious remembering the chess game's final move, she dreamed Ken was smothering her with a pillow. She woke up choking, gasping for breath. Beside her, he was snoring.

Over breakfast he resumed the conversation. "Look, all I have to do is count the number of Lazylark trademarks in this picture and write it on the back of a postcard with name and address. It's simple! Anyone can see there are thirty-four of them. I've counted three times and I always get thirty-four."

"Thirty four is the right number," she conceded. "They make it easy so a lot of people will enter. But the winning postcard is chosen in the drawing. It's strictly luck. And you'd be surprised at the number of wrong guesses we get. Some people just can't count, I suppose, or else they think we're trying to trick them."

He nodded. "I'm going to win that gold, Sara. *We're* going to win it!"

"Don't talk crazy. Everything is money with you these days."

"I don't like living on your salary. Is that a crime?"

"No, but what you're thinking about is. And it wouldn't work anyhow."

"We'll see."

He didn't mention it again for several weeks, and for a time Sara hoped it had gone out of his mind. She buried herself in her job, lunching occasionally with Marian Lendel, watching the daily mail arrive and the postcards get dumped into the big revolving drum in the conference room.

"This is going to be the biggest one yet," Marian decided two days before the contest deadline. "We've passed sixty thousand entries already."

457

"Will they all fit in the drum?"

"Oh, sure!" No one ever took the time to separate the correct entries from the incorrect ones. On the day of the drawing, either Sara or Marian would simply keep drawing postcards until they chose one with the correct number 34 on it.

On the evening before the drawing, Sara walked home along Third Avenue, enjoying the first warm day of spring. When she reached their apartment she was surprised that Ken wasn't home, and when he came in an hour later he seemed nervous and agitated.

"What's wrong with you?" she asked.

"Nothing's wrong. I just want to tell you about tomorrow, about the drawing." He took something from his pocket—a signet ring with a flat surface where one might have expected a seal or initial.

"What's that?"

"It's a gift—for you."

"It's awfully large, more like a man's ring."

"You can wear it. I want you to wear it tomorrow."

"What is all this, Ken?"

He took some cards from his pocket. They were the size of postcards, but light gray in color, with postage affixed by hand. "See these? It cost me plenty to have five hundred of them made up. There are tiny iron filings embedded in these cards, and this ring is a magnet. Look—the card clings to it! I want you to wear this ring tomorrow, and turn the flat surface in toward your palm when you reach into the drum of cards. I mailed in five hundred, and that's about one percent of the total. You dig through those cards a few times and you're sure to attract one."

"That's crazy," she argued. "Maybe I won't do it a few times. Maybe the first card out will be the winner."

"No, it won't. If it isn't one of these gray cards, you just say it has the wrong winning number and toss it back. You told me that happens a lot."

"It won't be me anyway," she insisted. "It's Marian's turn to draw the winner."

"It'll be you," he said quietly.

After dinner the telephone rang. It was Mr. Foxe from the office calling to tell her that Marian Lendel was dead. She'd fallen in front of a subway train on the way home from work.

Sara hung up the phone and turned to face her husband. "My God, what have you done?"

"It was an accident," he murmured. "I only wanted to hurt her so

458

she'd miss work tomorrow. But you're part of it, Sara. We've got to go through with it now."

That night she dreamed again that she was being smothered.

The detective's name was Sergeant Gresson, and he arrived at the office shortly after nine o'clock. He spoke with Sara and the others who worked with Marian, asking about boyfriends or possible enemies. He was still there when they went into the conference room at eleven o'clock to draw the winning card in the Lazylark contest.

While one of the others turned the drum, thoroughly mixing the entries, Gresson said to Sara, "I understand this would have been Miss Lendel's job today."

She shrugged, nervously fidgeting with the ring on her finger. "We take turns," she answered simply. "It's no big deal who does it."

The others had crowded into the room and she waited for Sergeant Gresson to leave but he didn't. He was watching as she opened the drum and stuck her hand inside without looking. The first card out had the number 33 on it. "A loser," she announced. "A thirty-three!" She tossed it back in and dug for another. Her vision was clouded so that she could barely see, but she knew it was a government printed postcard and not one of Ken's special ones. "Thirty-five," she announced without looking. "Another loser."

On the third try she saw one of the gray cards clinging to her ring finger as she withdrew it. She felt a sudden surge of relief as she closed her fingers around the card and blinked her eyes to clear her vision. "It's a winner! A thirty-four! Mrs. Erica Manning of Philadelphia." She passed the card over to Mr. Foxe, wondering vaguely who Erica Manning was, wondering about Ken's occasional trips to Philadelphia.

"All right," Mr. Foxe confirmed. "That's the winner." He turned to a Lazylark vice president who'd flown in for the drawing. "Should we call her with the good news?"

"Maybe you'd better wait just a few minutes," Sergeant Gresson suggested.

"Look here," Foxe bristled, "I know you're investigating a violent death, but our business has to continue."

"Just a few minutes," Gresson repeated. "Mrs. Blake, could we go into your office?"

He sat down across the desk from her, and she tried not to stare at the empty desk that had belonged to Marian Lendel. "How can I be of help?" Sara asked.

The detective took some folded reports from his inside pocket and glanced at them. "She was murdered, you know. Someone pushed her in front of that subway train. It wasn't any accident. It may have been someone who knew her, even someone from this office."

"No," Sara insisted. "Marian hadn't an enemy in the world. Everyone liked her."

"Was she in debt? Watching you draw that winning postcard it occurred to me how easily one of these contests could be rigged."

"Oh no! We're all standing there watching. Marian couldn't have done anything like that." Staring across the desk at her, he seemed for an instant like Ken on the other side of the chessboard.

"I suppose not," he said with a sigh. He started to return the reports to his pocket. "Could I have a paper clip for these?"

"Sure." She reached out and picked one from the little plastic container on her desk. It was only as she handed it over to him that she saw the other clips clinging to the face of her ring. "I—"

Sergeant Gresson seemed saddened. "Don't bother, Mrs. Blake. You forgot to turn the ring back after you drew the card. A magnet, isn't it? And the card was attracted by it? I thought it was something like that, so I figured I'd give it a test. I knew you'd reach for the paper clip with the same hand you reached for those cards."

She shook her head. "I don't understand."

"When you announced that second card was a loser, you were looking at the address side, at the printed government stamp. How did you know it said thirty-five when the number was on the back?"

Then she knew it was like the chess games, and her king was in check again. "But was it so necessary to kill Marian Lendel," he asked quietly, "just so you'd get to draw the card today?"

Somehow she wasn't being smothered any more. She could breathe, and she knew what she had to do. "Let me tell you about my husband," she began. "His name is Ken. . . ."

# Snapping Out of It

*by Bruce Holland Rogers*

He felt emptied out as he walked along the dark beach. Did he always feel this way after he killed someone? He couldn't remember.

He stopped walking for a moment to think about it, to try to remember. The sea was grey and the shore was a long curving line of black. Orange light tinted the farthest clouds, and the wind tousled his hair. It felt good.

The Sea Breeze terrace was up ahead. He could stop there to watch the sun rise. Of course, they'd look for him there. They always did. *Blake* always did.

Thinking of Blake made it easier to remember.

Dr. Weber was the first. They had argued about his medication. He didn't want to take it any more, but Dr. Weber insisted.

There were pillows on the couch and Dr. Weber wasn't a strong man. It wasn't all that hard to hold one of those pillows against his face until he stopped struggling.

After he killed Dr. Weber, he had walked to the beach. He liked the salt smell and the sound of the waves rolling in. The beach relaxed him. He walked all the way to the big hotels.

But they found him. When he stopped to rest at the Sea Breeze terrace, Blake came with the van and took him back to the Center. On the way, he told Blake all about the murder.

After Dr. Weber was Nurse Fitzgerald. She wanted him to get out of his room and visit with the others in the lounge. "Craig," she told him, "it doesn't do you any good to be alone so much. Now come on."

But he didn't come on. Instead he strangled her, hid her body under the bed, and then slipped out the window. He walked off the grounds and down to the beach.

Blake found him at the Sea Breeze terrace. Again, he told Blake all about it.

"You don't fool me, Craig," Blake told him. "You don't fool me for a minute. You could snap out of it if you wanted to. So snap out al-

461

ready. I've got better things to do than chase after you and haul you back, okay?"

But Nurse Fitzgerald wasn't the last. There was the fat guy in the dining room who wanted to talk when Craig didn't want to talk. Craig blew him up with dynamite. And then there was Dr. Weber again. He was still being pushy about Craig's medication, so Craig drowned him in the fountain out front.

"Craig, just stop it!" Blake said as they drove back. "I have a lot of things to do. What if everybody at the Center just decided to walk away?"

"I killed Dr. Weber," Craig said.

"You didn't kill anybody," said Blake.

"Oh yes I did. I pushed him into the fountain and held him under. You'll see. When we get back, the police will come for me."

"Uh-huh. Just like the last time you killed Dr. Weber? When you suffocated him? But he was there at the Center, waiting for us when I drove you back, wasn't he? And Nurse Fitzgerald was fine after you killed her, right?"

"That was different. I *really* killed him this time."

"Craig," Blake said, "you wouldn't kill anybody. You're harmless. You're not even very crazy. You just don't want to be responsible. I've worked at the Center a long time, and I can tell. You're the kind who chooses to be crazy."

"*I really killed Dr. Weber.* He's floating in the fountain. You'll see."

"Craig, who do you think told me to find you and drive you back?"

Craig looked at Blake, uncertainty in his gaze.

"It was Dr. Weber," Blake said. " 'Looks like Craig's gone for a stroll on the beach, Blake. Would you mind driving him home?' " Blake shook his head. "The thing is, I do mind. I mind because I shouldn't have to do this."

Craig was looking at his hands, twisting his fingers nervously.

"Life at the Center is just too easy for you," Blake went on. "You're not willing to face things. Being crazy is an excuse to be irresponsible."

"You shouldn't talk to me this way," Craig said.

"Why not?"

"Dr. Weber wouldn't like it."

"Aha! He has to be alive to not like it, doesn't he?"

Craig frowned and twisted his fingers some more. "He wouldn't like it. You're just an orderly, and you shouldn't talk to me this way."

"Listen," Blake went on, "I know how you feel. Life is hard. Look at me, for instance. I'm married, but it's no good any more. My wife and

462

I, we might as well live on different planets. We stay together for the kids. I've got five, and it's expensive keeping them in clothes and braces and stuff. So I work two jobs. You'd think I'd get some appreciation for that at home—"

Blake's knuckles were white on the steering wheel.

"Well, anyway," he said, relaxing his grip, "the point is that we all have something to run away from, don't we? I mean, don't you think I'd like to be crazy and have people take care of me?"

"I don't like you," said Craig.

"You can hate me," said Blake, "so long as you make my life a little easier, okay? If you can't snap out of it, then at least quit running away from the Center! Don't make me drive up to get you any more!"

"I don't like you at all," Craig said.

Neither of them spoke during the rest of the drive.

He used a tire iron. They were back on the grounds of the Center, and he picked up the tire iron and thought about Blake's five kids and the braces and the clothes and the wife from another planet. It all made him furious somehow. He brought the tire iron down hard.

He knew they'd look for him on the beach. He hid in a culvert until dark.

This time he'd done it. He'd really done it.

After dark, the pull of the beach was irresistible. He had walked slowly along the strip of wet sand, thinking about it. It was real this time. He had killed Blake.

Or had he? Now, as he walked up the steps to the Sea Breeze terrace, he thought about what Blake had said, the stuff about choosing to be crazy. Or not.

Maybe he hadn't killed Blake. Maybe, when the sun rose, Blake would come with the van. He sat down on the terrace to consider not being crazy any more.

But as the sun climbed into the sky, it wasn't Blake who came. It was Dr. Weber.

The psychiatrist came and sat down beside him and said, "I had a feeling you might come here."

"I expected Blake, Dr. Weber. It's always Blake who comes."

Dr. Weber hesitated like he was about to say something and changed his mind. "This time, it's me," he said simply.

For a moment, he was afraid. "Blake's alive, isn't he?"

"Yes," said Dr. Weber. "Blake's alive."

On the drive back, he told Dr. Weber about what Blake had said. Maybe it was true. Maybe he could snap out of it.

Dr. Weber looked at him thoughtfully.

"Blake's right, isn't he, Doc? People can decide to stop being crazy, can't they?"

"Not necessarily," said Dr. Weber as he drove onto the grounds of the Center. "But in your case, perhaps."

"Then I'm going to do it," he said. "I'm going to snap out of it. I'm going to take responsibility."

There were two police cars in the circular drive. Dr. Weber got out and talked to the officers. When the psychiatrist came back to his car, the policemen came with him.

Again, he was afraid. "You said Blake was alive!"

The policemen looked at each other.

"Yes, he is," said Dr. Weber. "Blake's alive."

"I didn't hit him with the tire iron?"

"No," said Dr. Weber. "But you have to go away with Officer Garner, here. You have to answer some questions. All right?"

Detective Kelly frowned as the squad car drove away. "Doc, are you sure he isn't faking?"

Weber shook his head. "I doubt very much that he is."

"But I don't get it. You said he was perfectly sane."

"No, I didn't," Weber said. "Sanity's a legal concept, not a medical one. I said he had a well integrated, healthy personality when he came to work for the Center. All of our employees are tested."

"Well, what happened to him?"

"It's a hazard of working with the mentally disturbed, Detective. One can begin to identify with their symptoms. It's not that psychosis is catching, exactly. But with an existing predisposition—"

"So Blake really thinks he's Craig Brown, the man he killed?"

"Apparently so."

Kelly shook his head. "Well, I'm no expert. I guess the DA's psychiatrists will judge if he's responsible for his actions. They'll know if he's really crazy."

"Mmm." Weber nodded thoughtfully. "If Blake hasn't talked himself out of it by then."

# Something Green

*Edward D. Hoch*

It was Sid Frazier's radio series on Washington's working women that led to his first meeting with Ginny Pratt late in 1942. The nation's capital swarmed with young men in uniform and young women who'd taken their places in every conceivable job. Frazier had been interviewing them all over Washington, in congressional offices and crowded apartments, on rooftops, and in the gray office buildings the Navy had erected for temporary use east of the Lincoln Memorial.

Late one Thursday afternoon in October, Frazier stood across the street from the main post office, waiting for the car pool from the Agricultural Research Center in Beltsville, Maryland. Like many other office workers, Agriculture Department employees had been squeezed out of the city into Maryland and Virginia. An elaborate system of car pools had resulted to ease the 12-mile journey. Women commuting to work was another change brought on by the war, one unusual enough to rate an interview for Frazier's radio series.

The car-pool vehicle was late that day, and he passed the time watching two helmeted soldiers drilling with antiaircraft guns on the roof of the post office. One could see soldiers all over the city these days, though the rumor was that at least a few of them were wooden replicas, like the wooden rifles the Army had trained with a few years earlier. Frazier gazed at them wistfully. One good war story would get him back on the hard-news beat.

Presently a gray sedanbus, an odd, stretched-out automobile with room for a dozen people, pulled up to the curb. He watched the young women and older men getting out. A slender woman in her late twenties with clear, pale skin and bright blue eyes caught his attention. He found himself wishing he weren't on the job. He'd prefer a flirtation, not a professional encounter.

She listened politely as he introduced himself. When he asked her for an interview, she smiled. "I'll miss my trolley."

"Could I come along? We can talk during the trip."

She glanced around uneasily and then looked at him again, taking

465

in his neat haircut and ready smile. He was at least 10 years older than she was, but his voice had a youthful quality. "If you insist," she said after a pause, "but I'm sure some of the other women have far more interesting jobs than I do. I'm a nutritionist with the Agriculture Department."

"That's great!" He followed her onto the trolley and they found a seat together. Taking out his notebook, he began writing rapidly. "What's your name?"

"Ginny Pratt. P-r-a-t-t. I'm 28 years old and I've been with the department for nearly a year. We plan menus for the Armed Forces. Is that what you want to know?" Her smile was mischievous this time. He smiled back.

"That's fine, but I was hoping for some funny little details. Human interest stuff, ways in which the war effort has complicated your work."

"Well, I have no secretary," Ginny said, brushing a wisp of brown hair from her forehead, "and there's no extra typewriter for me to type my reports. So I dictate the reports onto wax cylinders and ship them to New York for transcribing. Is that a funny little detail?"

"Well, it's not exactly . . ."

"My roommate, Nancy, could give you a few more. She's a secretary for the FBI." She paused. "Oh, here's one. The FBI won't hire women to work in their fingerprint files. The women would have to climb up on ladders to check the file drawers, and men could look up their skirts." She smiled at his embarrassment. "You see, Mr. Hoover won't allow women to wear slacks, even for the war effort."

"Those are interesting stories," Frazier admitted, "but not exactly what I had in mind." He tried to think of questions that would loosen her up, making quick notes of her replies as the trolley jostled them past gray government buildings.

"Here's where I get off," she said suddenly as the trolley slowed to a stop in a residential neighborhood. "It's been a pleasure talking with you, Mr. Frazier. If you want to walk a bit . . ."

"Everyone calls me Sid," he said, following her onto the street.

"All right, Sid." She walked briskly toward a row of big old houses converted to apartments.

"Tell me about your personal life. Your apartment, your boyfriends." He hoped he wasn't being too obvious in his interest.

"Nancy and I share one tiny room. Most mornings we have to stand in line for the bathroom. My boyfriend is in the Navy somewhere in the Pacific. I haven't had a letter in two months. Anything else?" She stopped walking and turned to face him. "Forgive me for

466

snapping at you. I'm a little on edge. Do you see that man across the street? The one in the black raincoat?"

Frazier turned to look in the direction she indicated. He saw a squat, middle-aged man with a fedora pulled down to shade his face.

"He's followed me home every night this week," she told Frazier. "That's why I suggested you walk with me."

"Who is he?"

"I don't know. He's beginning to frighten me."

"I'll find out," Frazier said. He left her and casually crossed the street. The man she'd indicated had a pale look that Frazier associated with ex-convicts. He stood at the trolley stop, smoking a cigarette. When Frazier reached the curb, he started walking away, tossing the half-smoked cigarette into the gutter.

"Wait a minute!" Frazier called out.

The man turned. "What is it?"

"That young lady says you've been following her."

"She's crazy!" He winked at Frazier. "You know how they get, with so few guys around."

Frazier met the man's sly smile with a grim stare. "Stay away from her," he warned.

The squat man shrugged his shoulders and walked away. Frazier watched for a moment and then followed at a distance. In the next block, the man got into a dark green Hudson and drove away. Frazier jotted down the license number and hurried back to where he'd left Ginny.

"Thanks," she said with relief. "Maybe that'll scare him off."

"Let's hope so. And if you really want to thank me, come into the studio this weekend and let me interview you on my show."

Ginny hesitated. "Why don't you talk with my roommate? Nancy is much more of a talker than I am. She tells me she bores her boyfriends with stories about work all the time."

"Well . . ."

"She's working late tonight, but I know she'll be home tomorrow. Why don't you come by around six? We can eat at the corner restaurant, and you can interview Nancy."

"Sounds good," he agreed, "but only if you let the network pick up the check."

"Fair enough!" She gave him a parting smile. "Tomorrow at six."

He left her at the door of the house, then went back to the station and asked his secretary to check on the license plate number he'd jotted down.

As Frazier left the station the following afternoon, his secretary handed him a note. The green Hudson was registered to a Joseph Taylor at 3387 O Street in Washington. He shoved the paper into his pocket. Since gasoline rationing, he hadn't been driving his car to work, but the station's Nash was available. He made it to Ginny's apartment in 10 minutes.

She met him at the door in a panic. "Sid, that man who was following me is inside. He's been murdered!"

He followed her to the second floor, past a tiny bathroom under construction, and down a hallway to a half-open apartment door. The wood around the lock had been splintered. In the center of the small room, between two beds, lay the squat man Frazier had accosted the previous day. He'd been stabbed in the back; the knife was still buried deep in the wound. If Frazier had been worried about Ginny before, his worry doubled now.

He bent to examine the body. "Have you called the police?"

"They should be here any minute."

Working quickly, Frazier used his handkerchief to remove the dead man's wallet. He found some small bills and a Washington driver's license in the name of Rosco Keen.

"Keen," he muttered. He looked at Ginny. "That car he was driving yesterday was registered to somebody else. And I think Keen's recently back from Hawaii."

"Why's that?" In the distance they heard an approaching siren.

"Look at these dollar bills." They had orange-and-brown seals on the front and the word *Hawaii* overprinted across the back.

"I've heard about those from Nancy," said Ginny. "They're used in Hawaii so currency can be devalued quickly if the Japanese invade."

"I didn't know that."

"There are a lot of things about Hawaii the government doesn't publicize."

Suddenly there was a gasp from the doorway. "What's happened?" A blond woman stood there, horrified, holding a bag of groceries.

"Nancy!" Ginny hurried to her, taking the groceries. "This is my roommate, Nancy Lambert," she told Frazier.

"What's going on?" Nancy demanded. "Who's that dead man?"

"The one I told you was following me. This is Sid Frazier, the radio commentator I mentioned last night."

Nancy was tall and attractive, a bit younger than Ginny. She stood shivering in her raincoat, trying not to look at the body. "My God, Ginny! What's happening to us?"

The siren stopped in front of the house, and they heard heavy footsteps on the stairs. Frazier stuffed the license and money back into the wallet and returned it to the dead man's pocket just before two uniformed officers and a dour-looking detective named Schwartz entered the room. Frazier knew him from Headquarters. He had a jowly look and a short cigar hanging from the corner of his mouth.

"You know the dead man, Frazier?" he asked without any greeting.

"He's been following Miss Pratt here. That's about all I know." Frazier fingered the paper in his pocket, deciding against revealing Taylor's name. He wanted to understand Ginny's involvement before he gave away any clues.

"You really get around town, don't you?" Schwartz commented with a sardonic smile. "The Army could use you for reconnaissance work."

"The Army doesn't want 40-year-olds," Frazier answered.

As an officer took flash photographs of the murder scene, Schwartz turned to the young women. "Anyone ever see the knife before?"

"He probably brought it with him to use on the door," Frazier suggested, remembering the splintered wood.

"Looks like a kitchen knife," the detective observed. "Where's your kitchen?"

"Downstairs," Nancy answered. "Each tenant gets part of the refrigerator."

"The landlord live on the premises?"

"In the house next door." Ginny gestured to her right. "His name is Norman Dengler."

Schwartz turned to one of the officers. "Bring him over here."

Dengler was a balding man wearing work pants and an old shirt. He had a bandaged left hand, and the whiteness of the gauze made Frazier guess it was a recent injury. Dengler nodded to the young women and viewed the body with distaste.

"Do you know the dead man?" Schwartz asked, shifting the cigar to the opposite corner of his mouth.

"Nope."

"How about the knife? Is it from your kitchen?"

"No, sir! That's not one of ours."

"How'd you hurt your hand?"

The landlord covered the bandage with his good hand. "Sawing a length of pipe this afternoon. It's just a cut. I've been putting in a new bathroom at the end of the hall."

"Could one of you show me the downstairs kitchen?" Schwartz asked.

"I'll go," Nancy volunteered. "I have milk and oranges to put in the refrigerator."

After Schwartz had completed his questioning and the body was removed, Dengler stared at the bloodstained carpet. "I thought you two were nice girls," he told Ginny. He shook his head as he disappeared down the stairs.

Frazier turned to face the two women. "Dinner would get us away from here, if you're up to it. You can't sit around this room all evening." Now that the body and the police were gone, Frazier realized just how small the room was. Besides two narrow beds, it held two dressers, a radiator, and a bookcase. A half-open closet door revealed hatboxes and suitcases.

He's right," Ginny decided. "Come on, Nancy. Let's have the Blue Network buy us dinner."

Nancy led them to her favorite booth and hung up her raincoat. Wearing a light blue sweater with a string of pearls and neatly tailored navy slacks, she looked like anyone's girl next door.

"I know you're upset," Frazier said after they'd ordered, "but I think we should try to figure out why that man was following Ginny."

"Maybe he was watching to see what time she got home," suggested Nancy.

"Or when we both got home," Ginny added.

"But why?" asked Frazier. "And hadn't Dengler been there all day?"

"Yes," Ginny agreed, "but apparently he left early when he cut his hand."

"So Keen saw his chance to get upstairs unnoticed."

"What was he after, though?" Nancy asked.

"I don't have a clue," Ginny sighed.

"Do either of you ever bring work home from the office?"

"Oh, no," Nancy answered quickly. "In my job that's forbidden."

"Is there any way that Keen could know both of you? How'd you two get together anyway?"

"Mr. Dengler ran an ad for the furnished room and we were the first two arrivals," Ginny explained. "With the city so crowded we decided to take it together."

"The rent is outrageous," Nancy chimed in. "We're supposed to be fighting this war for the red, white, and blue, but Washington landlords are only after something green, like money."

After dinner he walked them back to their apartment. Both women were nervous about spending the night there, but they felt a little better when they saw a patrol car parked across the street.

"Don't worry," Frazier said, trying to reassure them. "Murderers don't really return to the scene of the crime."

Frazier phoned Ginny and Nancy Saturday morning to see if they were all right, then he decided to drive out to O Street to Joseph Taylor's Georgetown address. When he reached Taylor's house, a green Hudson was parked in the driveway, the same car he'd seen Rosco Keen drive away in last Thursday afternoon.

He left his car and started up the driveway just as a young man with a deep tan came out the side door and headed toward the back of the house. Frazier followed, confronting him at the trash cans.

"Joseph Taylor?" he asked.

"That's me."

"I'm Sid Frazier, from the Blue Network. A man named Rosco Keen was murdered last night. You know him?"

"Never heard of him."

"That's odd. He was driving your car on Thursday."

Taylor started to turn away, then swung around, pulling an Army .45 automatic from beneath his jacket. Frazier dodged behind a trash can as the gun went off.

Suddenly two men appeared from the driveway. One of them made a flying leap at Taylor's back, bringing him down before he could fire again. The other knelt quickly to handcuff him.

"Who are you?" the man with the handcuffs asked Frazier.

"Sid Frazier from the Blue Network. I came to interview Taylor."

"Mr. Taylor is under arrest," the man answered, showing his FBI credentials.

"May I ask what the charge is against him?"

"Theft of currency from a Federal Reserve shipment."

"Hawaiian bank notes," Frazier said, as if he'd always known it.

The men exchanged glances. "You'd better come with us."

When Frazier reached Ginny Pratt's apartment later that day, he found Ginny and Nancy in slacks, scrubbing the floor. "Hard work," he sympathized.

"We're almost finished," Nancy said with a sigh.

"That's good. I thought you'd want to know the mystery is just about wrapped up. Rosco Keen's partner, Joseph Taylor, was arrested by the FBI this morning."

"I'm glad to hear that," Ginny told him. "Nancy and I were awake all night, terrified the killer might come back."

"Tell us what happened," Nancy urged, putting down her scrub

471

brush and going to the closet. She started to lift one of the hatboxes from the shelf.

"Taylor and the dead man, Keen, learned about a special Federal Reserve shipment of currency to Hawaii. They stole two packages containing $100,000 each, but one of the packages got away from them. Keen was trying to recover it when he was stabbed."

"Why was he trying to recover it in our apartment?" Ginny asked.

Nancy was walking toward the door with the hatbox when Frazier reached for it. "Because this is where it is. That's right, isn't it, Nancy?"

She tried to pull the hatbox away from him, and it fell to the floor. Two summer hats spilled out and a package that split open as it landed.

"Nancy!" Ginny gasped. "Where did that money come from?"

Nancy struggled in Frazier's grasp, fighting like a cornered cat. "Sit down," he ordered, dumping her onto the nearest bed. He turned to Ginny. "Taylor was one of her boyfriends. When she heard about the special Federal Reserve shipment, she misplaced the request for additional guards and sent Taylor and Keen instead."

"That's crazy!" Nancy insisted, struggling to her feet.

"The theft was a success," Frazier continued, ignoring Nancy's outburst, "until she made off with half the loot. But Keen spoiled her plans."

The color drained from Nancy's face. "Did you kill him, Nancy?" Ginny asked softly.

"I . . . it was self-defense! He had a knife. He would have killed me!"

Frazier looked at Ginny, who was still frozen with disbelief. "Remember the story you told me about Hoover not allowing women to wear slacks? Nancy was wearing them last night when she came in, supposedly right from work and grocery shopping. She covered them with her raincoat."

"I was too upset to notice," Ginny admitted.

"Nancy had been home earlier and changed her clothes. Why try to hide the fact unless she was the killer? After stabbing Keen she needed an alibi so she went out for groceries." He turned to Nancy. "That was something else that gave you away. You carried the groceries upstairs rather than putting them away in the kitchen. You wanted Ginny to see them."

Nancy stood there, shaking her head. "It was self-defense," she insisted. "That money belonged to me!"

She broke away and ran into the hallway. Two FBI men were waiting for her at the top of the stairs.

472

Ginny sank back into her chair. "I still can't believe it! She was awake with me all last night, as worried as I was!"

"But for a different reason. With Keen dead she feared Taylor would come after the money," Frazier explained.

Ginny looked at Nancy's rumpled bed and shook her head. "But why did she do it?"

"Like she said last night—for something green."


# Something Wrong

*by Bill Pronzini*


The instant I walked into my flat, I knew something was wrong.

I stopped a couple of paces through the door, with the hairs pulling at the nape of my neck. Kerry had entered ahead of me and she was halfway across the room before she realized I wasn't following. She turned, saw me standing rigid, and said immediately, "What's the matter?"

I didn't answer. I kept searching the room with my eyes: the old mismatched furniture, the shelves containing my collection of more than six thousand pulp magazines, the bay window beyond which a thick San Francisco fog crawled sinuously across the night. There were no signs of disturbance. Nor was there anything unusual to hear. And yet the feeling of wrongness remained sharp and urgent. When you've been a detective as long as I have, you develop a kind of protective sixth sense and you learn to trust it.

Somebody had gotten in here while Kerry and I were out to dinner and a North Beach movie.

Somebody who was still here now?

Kerry came back toward me, saying again, "What's the matter?"

"Go out into the hall," I said.

"What for?"

"Just do it."

We had been together long enough and she knew me well enough not to argue. Frowning now, worry-eyed, she moved past me and out into the hall.

I shut the door after her and turned back to face the room. Nothing out of place in here . . . or was there? Something didn't seem quite right, but I couldn't identify it—couldn't focus on anything right now except the possibility of the intruder still being on the premises.

This was one of the few times I regretted my fundamental distaste for guns; unlike some licensed PIs, I do not carry or even own one. I picked up a heavy alabaster bookend, not much of a weapon but the only one handy, and went across to the half-closed bedroom door.

Nobody in there; I opened the closet and looked under the bed to make sure. No evidence of invasion or forced entry, either—not that anybody could get in through the bedroom window, or any of the other windows, without using a tall ladder. The bathroom was also empty and undisturbed. So were the kitchen and the rear porch. The back door, accessible by a set of outside stairs from an alley off Laguna Street, was still secured by its spring lock and chain lock.

I returned to the bedroom, opened the middle dresser drawer. The leather case in which I keep my few items of jewelry and a small amount of spare cash was still in place under my clean shirts. The jewelry and money were likewise untouched.

But all of that reassured me only a little. The feeling of wrongness, of a violation of my private space, would not go away. As unlikely as it seemed, somebody *had* gotten in during our absence. I was as sure of it as you can be of something unproven.

In the front room again, I opened the door and motioned for Kerry to come back inside. Just in time, too. She is not the sort of woman to stand by passively for very long, danger or no danger.

She said as she entered, "What is it? Burglars?"

"Something like that."

I got down on one knee and examined the two dead-bolt locks on the front door. A professional burglar can get past the best dead-bolt made, but he can't do it without leaving marks; there were none on either of these locks. Nobody could have come in this way, then, without a key . . .

I asked Kerry if she had lost or misplaced her key recently; she said she hadn't. Mine hadn't been out of my possession either. And ours were the only two keys to the flat. Not even the landlord had one: I had lived here for more than twenty years and had had the locks changed more than once at my own expense.

Kerry asked, "Is anything missing?"

"Doesn't seem to be. Nothing disturbed, no sign of forced entry. But I can't shake the feeling someone was in here."

"For what reason, if not to steal something?"

"I don't know yet."

"How could somebody get in, with everything locked up tight?"

"I don't know that either."

We prowled the flat together, room to room and back again. There was absolutely nothing missing. I checked the locks on the windows and on the back door; all were secure and had not been tampered with as far as I could tell. I did find a half-inch sliver of metal on the floor of the utility porch, the same sort of brass as the chain lock. But it hadn't come from the lock because I checked to make sure. It could have been splintered off just about anything made of brass, then; could have lain there for days.

We were in the front room again when Kerry said, with an edge of exasperation in her voice, "You must be wrong. There *couldn't* have been an intruder."

"I'm not wrong," I said.

"Even great detectives have hot flashes sometimes."

"This isn't funny, Kerry."

"Did I say it was?" She sighed elaborately, the way she does when her patience is being tried. "I'm going to make some coffee," she said. "You want a cup?"

"Yes. All right."

She went out into the kitchen. I stayed in the middle of the room and kept looking around—turning my eyes and my body both in slow quadrants. Couch, end tables, coffee table, leather recliner Kerry had given me on my last birthday, shelves full of gaudy-spined pulps, old secretary desk. All just as we'd left it. Yet *something* wasn't as it should be. I made another slow circuit: couch, end tables, coffee table, recliner, bookshelves, desk. And a third circuit: couch, tables, recliner—

The recliner.

The chair's footrest was pushed in, out of sight.

It was a small thing, but that didn't make it any less wrong. The chair is a good one, comfortable, but the footrest has never worked quite right. To get it folded all the way back under on its metal hinges, you have to give it a kick; and when you sit down again later, you have to struggle to work it free so you can recline. So I don't bother anymore to boot it all the way under. I *always* leave the footrest part way out, with its metal hinges showing.

Why would an intruder bother to kick it out of sight? Only one conceivable reason: he thought it was supposed to be that way and wanted the chair to look completely natural. But why would he be messing around my chair in the first place . . . ?

"Jesus," I said aloud, and the hair pulled again along my neck. I moved over to the recliner, gingerly eased the seat cushion out so I could see under it.

What I was looking at then was a bomb.

Two sticks of dynamite wired together with some kind of detonator plate on top, set into a slit in the fabric so that it was resting on the chair's inner springs. The weight of a person settling onto the cushion would depress the plate and explode the dynamite—

"My God!"

Kerry was standing behind me, staring open-mouthed at the thing in the chair. I hadn't even heard her come in.

"Not a burglar after all," I said grimly. "Somebody who came in to *leave* something. This."

"I . . . don't hear any ticking," she said.

"It's a pressure-activated bomb, not a time bomb. Nothing to worry about as long as we stay away from it."

"But who . . . why . . . ?"

I caught her arm and steered her into the bedroom, where I keep my phone. I rang up the Hall of Justice, got through to a cop I knew named Jordan, and explained the situation. He said he'd be right over with the bomb squad.

When I hung up, Kerry said in a shaky voice, "I just don't understand. All the doors and windows were locked—they're *still* locked. How did whoever it was get in and back out again?"

I had no answer for her then. But by the time the police arrived, I had done some hard thinking and I did have an answer—the only possible answer. And along with it, I had the who and the why.

"His name is Howard Lynch," I said to Jordan. He and Kerry and I were in the hallway, waiting for the bomb squad to finish up inside. "Owns a hardware store out on Clement. He hired me about a month ago to find his wife; said she'd run off with another man. She had, too, but nobody could blame her. I found out later Lynch had been abusing her for years."

"So why would he want to kill you?"

"He blames me for his wife's death," I said. "I found her, all right, but when I told her Lynch was my employer she panicked and took off in her boyfriend's car. She didn't get far—a tree stopped her three blocks away."

"Pretty story."

"That's the kind of business we're in, Mack."

"Don't I know it. Did Lynch threaten you?"

"No. He's the kind who nurses his hatred in silence."

"Then what makes you so sure he's the one who planted the bomb?"

"He showed up here one night a week after the accident. Said it was to give me a check for my services and to tell me there were no hard feelings. I knew about the wife abuse by then, but I still felt sorry for him—sorry enough not to be suspicious and to let him in. He wasn't here long, just long enough to sneak a look around."

Kerry said, "I don't see why the bomber has to be somebody who was here before tonight."

"That's the only way it makes sense. To begin with, he *had* to have gotten in tonight through one of the doors, front or back. The windows are all secure and there's nothing but empty space below them. There are no marks of any kind on the front-door locks, no way he could have gotten a key, and he would have had a hard time even getting into the building because of the security lock on the main entrance downstairs. That leaves the alley staircase and the back door."

"But that one was—*is*—double-locked too."

"Right. But one of the locks is a spring type, the kind anybody can pick with a small tool or a credit card."

"You can't pick a chain lock with a tool or a credit card," Jordan said.

"No, but once the spring lock is free, the door will open a few inches—wide enough to reach through with a pair of bolt cutters and snip the chain. That explains the brass sliver I found on the porch floor. Easy work for a man who owns a hardware store, and so is the rest of it: When he was here the first time he noted the type of chain lock on the rear door; among the other things he brought with him tonight was *an exact duplicate* of that lock. After he was inside, he unscrewed the old chain-lock plates from the door and jamb and installed the new ones using the same holes—a job that wouldn't have taken more than a few minutes. Then he reset the spring lock, put the new chain on, and took the pieces of the old lock away with him when he was done planting the bomb."

"If he relocked the door," Jordan said, "how did he get out of the flat?"

"Walked out through the *front* door. The locks there are dead bolts, but you can open them from inside by hand, without a key; and you can reset them the same way to lock automatically when you leave. Simple as that."

There were a few seconds of ruminative silence. Then Kerry shuddered and said, "Thank God you felt something was wrong. If you'd sat down in that chair . . ."

"Don't even think about it," I said.

# Souls Burning

*by Bill Pronzini*

Hotel Majestic, Sixth Street, downtown San Francisco. A hell of an address—a hell of a place for an ex-con not long out of Folsom to set up housekeeping. Sixth Street, south of Market—South of the Slot, it used to be called—is the heart of the city's Skid Road and has been for more than half a century.

Eddie Quinlan. A name and a voice out of the past, neither of which I'd recognized when he called that morning. Close to seven years since I had seen or spoken to him, six years since I'd even thought of him. Eddie Quinlan. Edgewalker, shadow-man with no real substance or purpose, drifting along the narrow catwalk that separates conventional society from the underworld. Information seller, gofer, small-time bagman, doer of any insignificant job, legitimate or otherwise, that would help keep him in food and shelter, liquor and cigarettes. The kind of man you looked at but never really saw: a modern-day Yehudi, the little man who wasn't there. Eddie Quinlan. Nobody, loser—fall guy. Drug bust in the Tenderloin one night six and a half years ago; one dealer setting up another, and Eddie Quinlan, small-time bagman, caught in the middle; hard-assed judge, five years in Folsom, goodbye Eddie Quinlan. And the drug dealers? They walked, of course. Both of them.

And now Eddie was out, had been out for six months. And after six months of freedom, he'd called me. Would I come to his room at the Hotel Majestic tonight around eight? He'd tell me why when he saw me. It was real important—would I come? All right, Eddie. But I couldn't figure it. I had bought information from him in the old days, bits and pieces for five or ten dollars; maybe he had something to sell now. Only I wasn't looking for anything and I hadn't put the word out, so why pick me to call?

If you're smart you don't park your car on the street at night, South of the Slot. I put mine in the Fifth and Mission Garage at 7:45 and walked over to Sixth. It had rained most of the day and the streets were still wet, but now the sky was cold and clear. The kind of night that is as hard as black glass, so that light seems to bounce off the dark instead of shining through it; lights and their colors so bright and sharp reflecting off the night and the wet surfaces that the glare is like splinters against your eyes.

Friday night, and Sixth Street was teeming. Sidewalks jammed— old men, young men, bag ladies, painted ladies, blacks, whites, Asians, addicts, pushers, muttering mental cases, drunks leaning against walls in tight little clusters while they shared paper-bagged bottles of sweet wine and cans of malt liquor; men and women in filthy rags, in smart new outfits topped off with sunglasses, carrying ghetto blasters and red-and-white canes, some of the canes in the hands of individuals who could see as well as I could, and a hidden array of guns and knives and other lethal instruments. Cheap hotels, greasy spoons, seedy taverns, and liquor stores complete with barred windows and cynical proprietors that stayed open well past midnight. Laughter, shouts, curses, threats; bickering and dickering. The stenches of urine and vomit and unwashed bodies and rotgut liquor, and over those like an umbrella, the subtle effluvium of despair. Predators and prey, half hidden in shadow, half revealed in the bright, sharp dazzle of fluorescent lights and bloody neon.

It was a mean street, Sixth, one of the meanest, and I walked it warily. I may be fifty-eight but I'm a big man and I walk hard too; and I look like what I am. Two winos tried to panhandle me and a fat hooker in an orange wig tried to sell me a piece of her tired body, but no one gave me any trouble.

The Majestic was five stories of old wood and plaster and dirty brick, just off Howard Street. In front of its narrow entrance, a crack dealer and one of his customers were haggling over the price of a baggie of rock cocaine; neither of them paid any attention to me as I moved past them. Drug deals go down in the open here, day and night. It's not that the cops don't care, or that they don't patrol Sixth regularly; it's just that the dealers outnumber them ten to one. On Skid Road any crime less severe than aggravated assault is strictly low priority.

Small, barren lobby: no furniture of any kind. The smell of ammonia hung in the air like swamp gas. Behind the cubbyhole desk was an old man with dead eyes that would never see anything they didn't want to see. I said, "Eddie Quinlan," and he said, "Two-oh-two" without moving his lips. There was an elevator but it had an OUT OF ORDER sign on it; dust speckled the sign. I went up the adjacent stairs.

The disinfectant smell permeated the second floor hallway as well. Room 202 was just off the stairs, fronting on Sixth; one of the metal 2s on the door had lost a screw and was hanging upside down. I used my knuckles just below it. Scraping noise inside, and a voice said, "Yeah?" I identified myself. A lock clicked, a chain rattled, the door wobbled open, and for the first time in nearly seven years I was looking at Eddie Quinlan.

He hadn't changed much. Little guy, about five-eight, and past forty now. Thin, nondescript features, pale eyes, hair the color of sand. The hair was thinner and the lines in his face were longer and deeper, almost like incisions where they bracketed his nose. Otherwise he was the same Eddie Quinlan.

"Hey," he said, "thanks for coming. I mean it, thanks."

"Sure, Eddie."

"Come on in."

The room made me think of a box—the inside of a huge rotting packing crate. Four bare walls with the scaly remnants of paper on them like psoriatic skin, bare uncarpeted floor, unshaded bulb hanging from the center of a bare ceiling. The bulb was dark; what light there was came from a low-wattage reading lamp and a wash of red-and-green neon from the hotel's sign that spilled in through a single window. Old iron-framed bed, unpainted nightstand, scarred dresser, straight-backed chair next to the bed and in front of the window, alcove with a sink and toilet and no door, closet that wouldn't be much larger than a coffin.

"Not much, is it," Eddie said.

I didn't say anything.

He shut the hall door, locked it. "Only place to sit is that chair there. Unless you want to sit on the bed? Sheets are clean. I try to keep things clean as I can."

"Chair's fine."

I went across to it; Eddie put himself on the bed. A room with a view, he'd said on the phone. Some view. Sitting here you could look down past Howard and up across Mission—almost two full blocks of the worst street in the city. It was so close you could hear the beat of its pulse, the ugly sounds of its living and its dying.

"So why did you ask me here, Eddie? If it's information for sale, I'm not buying right now."

"No, no, nothing like that. I ain't in the business any more."

"Is that right?"

480

"Prison taught me a lesson. I got rehabilitated." There was no sarcasm or irony in the words; he said them matter-of-factly.

"I'm glad to hear it."

"I been a good citizen ever since I got out. No lie. I haven't had a drink, ain't even been in a bar."

"What are you doing for money?"

"I got a job," he said. "Shipping department at a wholesale sporting goods outfit on Brannan. It don't pay much but it's honest work."

I nodded. "What is it you want, Eddie?"

"Somebody I can talk to, somebody who'll understand—that's all I want. You always treated me decent. Most of 'em, no matter who they were, they treated me like I wasn't even human. Like I was a turd or something."

"Understand what?"

"About what's happening down there."

"Where? Sixth Street?"

"Look at it," he said. He reached over and tapped the window; stared through it. "Look at the people . . . there, you see that guy in the wheelchair and the one pushing him? Across the street there?"

I leaned closer to the glass. The man in the wheelchair wore a military camouflage jacket, had a heavy wool blanket across his lap; the black man manipulating him along the crowded sidewalk was thick-bodied, with a shiny bald head. "I see them."

"White guy's name is Baxter," Eddie said. "Grenade blew up under him in 'Nam and now he's a paraplegic. Lives right here in the Majestic, on this floor down at the end. Deals crack and smack out of his room. Elroy, the black dude, is his bodyguard and roommate. Mean, both of 'em. Couple of months ago, Elroy killed a guy over on Minna that tried to stiff them. Busted his head with a brick. You believe it?"

"I believe it."

"And they ain't the worst on the street. Not the worst."

"I believe that too."

"Before I went to prison I lived and worked with people like that and I never saw what they were. I mean I just never saw it. Now I do, I see it clear—every day walking back and forth to work, every night from up here. It makes you sick after a while, the things you see when you see 'em clear."

"Why don't you move?"

"Where to? I can't afford no place better than this."

"No better room, maybe, but why not another neighborhood? You don't have to live on Sixth Street."

"Wouldn't be much better, any other neighborhood I could buy into. They're all over the city now, the ones like Baxter and Elroy. Used to be it was just Skid Road and the Tenderloin and the ghettos. Now they're everywhere, more and more every day. You know?"

"I know."

"Why? It don't have to be this way, does it?"

Hard times, bad times: alienation, poverty, corruption, too much government, not enough government, lack of social services, lack of caring, drugs like a cancer destroying society. Simplistic explanations that were no explanations at all and as dehumanizing as the ills they described. I was tired of hearing them and I didn't want to repeat them, to Eddie Quinlan or anybody else. So I said nothing.

He shook his head. "Souls burning everywhere you go," he said, and it was as if the words hurt his mouth coming out.

Souls burning. "You find religion at Folsom, Eddie?"

"Religion? I don't know, maybe a little. Chaplain we had there, I talked to him sometimes. He used to say that about the hard-timers, that their souls were burning and there wasn't nothing he could do to put out the fire. They were doomed, he said, and they'd doom others to burn with 'em."

I had nothing to say to that either. In the small silence a voice from outside said distinctly, "Dirty bastard, what you doin' with my pipe?" It was cold in there, with the hard bright night pressing against the window. Next to the door was a rusty steam radiator but it was cold too; the heat would not be on more than a few hours a day, even in the dead of winter, in the Hotel Majestic.

"That's the way it is in the city," Eddie said. "Souls burning. All day long, all night long, souls on fire."

"Don't let it get to you."

"Don't it get to *you*?"

". . . Yes. Sometimes."

He bobbed his head up and down. "You want to do something, you know? You want to try to fix it somehow, put out the fires. There has to be a way."

"I can't tell you what it is," I said.

He said, "If we all just did *something*. It ain't too late. You don't think it's too late?"

"No."

"Me neither. There's still hope."

"Hope, faith, blind optimism—sure."

"You got to believe," he said, nodding. "That's all, you just got to believe."

Angry voices rose suddenly from outside; a woman screamed, thin
482

and brittle. Eddie came off the bed, hauled up the window sash. Chill damp air and street noises came pouring in: shouts, cries, horns honking, cars whispering on the wet pavement, a Muni bus clattering along Mission; more shrieks. He leaned out, peering downward.

"Look," he said, "look."

I stretched forward and looked. On the sidewalk below, a hooker in a leopard-skin coat was running wildly toward Howard; she was the one doing the yelling. Chasing behind her, tight black skirt hiked up over the tops of net stockings and hairy thighs, was a hideously rouged transvestite waving a pocket knife. A group of winos began laughing and chanting "Rape! Rape!" as the hooker and the transvestite ran zig-zagging out of sight on Howard.

Eddie pulled his head back in. The flickery neon wash made his face seem surreal, like a hallucinogenic vision. "That's the way it is," he said sadly. "Night after night, day after day."

With the window open, the cold was intense; it penetrated my clothing and crawled on my skin. I'd had enough of it, and of this room and Eddie Quinlan and Sixth Street.

"Eddie, just what is it you want from me?"

"I already told you. Talk to somebody who understands how it is down there."

"Is that the only reason you asked me here?"

"Ain't it enough?"

"For you, maybe." I got to my feet. "I'll be going now."

He didn't argue. "Sure, you go ahead."

"Nothing else you want to say?"

"Nothing else." He walked to the door with me, unlocked it, and then put out his hand. "Thanks for coming. I appreciate it, I really do."

"Yeah. Good luck, Eddie."

"You too," he said. "Keep the faith."

I went out into the hall, and the door shut gently and the lock clicked behind me.

Downstairs, out of the Majestic, along the mean street and back to the garage where I'd left my car. And all the way I kept thinking: There's something else, something more he wanted from me . . . and I gave it to him by going there and listening to him. But what? What did he really want?

I found out later that night. It was all over the TV—special bulletins and then the eleven o'clock news.

Twenty minutes after I left him, Eddie Quinlan stood at the window of his room-with-a-view, and in less than a minute, using a high-

483

powered semiautomatic rifle he'd taken from the sporting goods outfit where he worked, he shot down fourteen people on the street below. Nine dead, five wounded, one of the wounded in critical condition and not expected to live. Six of the victims were known drug dealers; all of the others also had arrest records, for crimes ranging from prostitution to burglary. Two of the dead were Baxter, the paraplegic ex-Vietnam vet, and his bodyguard, Elroy.

By the time the cops showed up, Sixth Street was empty except for the dead and the dying. No more targets. And up in his room, Eddie Quinlan had sat on the bed and put the rifle's muzzle in his mouth and used his big toe to pull the trigger.

My first reaction was to blame myself. But how could I have known or even guessed? Eddie Quinlan. Nobody, loser, shadow-man without substance or purpose. How could anyone have figured him for a thing like that?

*Somebody I can talk to, somebody who'll understand—that's all I want.*

No. What he'd wanted was somebody to help him justify to himself what he was about to do. Somebody to record his verbal suicide note. Somebody he could trust to pass it on afterward, tell it right and true to the world.

*You want to do something, you know? You want to try to fix it somehow, put out the fires. There has to be a way.*

Nine dead, five wounded, one of the wounded in critical condition and not expected to live. Not that way.

*Souls burning. All day long, all night long, souls on fire.*

The soul that had burned tonight was Eddie Quinlan's.

# The Spell of the Black Siren
*by Dick Donovan*

It was towards the end of spring, some years ago, when Trill was suddenly called upon to investigate a case which had in it all the elements of a startling romance. The gentleman whose name figured so prominently in the story was very well known in London society, and was regarded as one of the brilliant band of young men whom the late Earl of Beaconsfield—then plain Mr. Disraeli—spoke of as 'the coming moulders of England's destiny.' This prediction has been somewhat falsified, although one or two of the band have certainly distinguished themselves.

At the period that the events I am about to relate occurred, the Hon. Richard Shaw Fenton was a confidential clerk in the War Office, where he was looked upon with very great favour by his superiors. He was the son of Lord Jeffery Fenton, who so greatly distinguished himself during the Crimean War, and was honoured by being presented with the freedom of his native town and a jewelled sword subscribed for by his fellow townsmen.

Young Fenton was a handsome man, endowed apparently with almost all those qualities which are calculated to endear men to men, and beget the love and admiration of women. He was unmarried, and consequently he was in much request by designing mammas; for although he had little to look forward to apart from his own efforts, it was confidently anticipated that he would rise to high position, as he had powerful friends at court. And this advantage, backed up by his own abilities and ambition, could not fail—so people said—to ultimately give him power and wealth.

One evening, about nine o'clock, he left the War Office in a hansom, bearing some very important documents, which he was charged to deliver personally to a distinguished General temporarily residing at Hyde Park Gate, where he was confined to his room by a severe attack of gout. It was during a period of excitement caused by strained relations between Great Britain and France. A territorial difficulty had arisen between the two countries, and there had been such a conflict of opinion that matters had reached an acute stage, and in both countries the shameless catch-penny representatives of the press had indulged in threats and recriminations, and had openly talked of war. There had been an unusual number of 'Meetings of the Cabinet.' The air was thick with rumours. The public mind was in that supersensitive condition when definiteness would have been hailed with joy as a relief from vagueness and suspense. The ignorant oracles of the halfpenny evening rags had produced a morbid tension of the nerves amongst the unthinking classes, and sensational innuendo had lost its effect. A real sensation was needed; a something that would divert attention for the moment from the one burning topic of conversation —the topic which had completely overshadowed that ever-fruitful one of the weather. People talked of war instead of the weather. Even the barber who shaved you forgot his stock theme, and questioned his victim as to what he thought the issue of it all would be.

The sensation so much needed came at last. In the early light of the spring morning, a policeman pacing his weary rounds in the neighborhood of Sloane Square noticed a hansom cab drawn up by the railings of the square. The horse, probably thinking he was on his accustomed rank, stood limp-legged and with drooped head. The reins were hanging loosely on his back. The driver was on his perch, but the upper half of his body was prone on the roof of the cab. Inside was a fare, a gentleman, well dressed, but with shirt front crumpled, his neckgear disarranged, and his highly polished hat lying at his feet. Like the driver he seemed sunk in profound slumber, and all the efforts of the policeman failed to produce the slightest arousing effect on either of them. Indeed it suddenly dawned upon the policeman, with the suddenness of a shock, that both men were dead. So he summoned aid, and the cab and its burden were taken to the nearest police station. There the two insensible men were hauled out, and for once the police inspector on duty proved that all members of the force do not hastily jump to the conclusion that because a man is speechless and helpless he is necessarily drunk, for he secured the assistance without loss of time of the divisional police surgeon. When that gentleman arrived, he pronounced the cab-driver *in extremis*, and that pronouncement was soon verified, for a ghastly pallor spread itself over his face and his heart ceased to beat. The fare still breathed stertorously, and vigorous means were taken to restore animation. Visiting cards which he had on his person proved that he was no other than the Hon. Richard Shaw Fenton of the War Office.

After about an hour's treatment the patient was so far reanimated that his removal with all speed to the hospital was decided on, and an ambulance having been secured, he was conveyed to St. George's Hospital, and a messenger was despatched to inform his friends.

Now here at once was a first-class mystery, but, as was subsequently proved, it was only the beginning. For the succeeding two or three days Fenton lay in a half-dazed state, and was incapable of answering rationally the questions put to him; but one thing—and a very important thing, too—was brought to light. The documents he was conveying from the War Office to the General had not reached the person to whom they were addressed; they had disappeared, and Mr. Fenton could give no information about them. His mind seemed a perfect blank.

The post-mortem examination, which was perforce made, of the remains of the unfortunate cabman, revealed the fact that he had fallen a victim to some powerful drug, which had acted as a heart-depressant, and his heart being constitutionally weak, he had succumbed. In Fenton's case his heart had managed to struggle against the effects of the drug, but it had been left in such a highly nervous and irritable state that it was considered advisable to keep him in a condition of absolute rest.

In the meantime Vincent Trill had been set to work. The missing documents were precious—indeed, of such vital importance that his instructions were that he must recover them, if possible, at all cost.

As may be supposed, there was a great deal more beneath the surface than appeared. The prying and inquisitive reporter got hold of the broad facts as given above, but he could get no more, for the friends of the Hon. Richard Shaw Fenton, and the authorities alike were desirous of hushing the matter up, for obvious reasons; so the reporter, with the monumental impudence for which he is framed, invented a highly plausible story one day, to contradict it and invent another the next.

In order to supply the necessary evidence at the adjourned inquest the viscera of the cabman had been subjected to analysis, and the report that was finally brought up was to the effect that the man had died from the administration of a very powerful narcotic, but what it was could not be determined. Mr. Fenton, who had so far recovered as to be able to give evidence at the adjourned inquest, stated that he hired the cab in Pall Mall; that on his way to Hyde Park he called at an hotel, where he met two friends, with whom he remained in conversation for nearly an hour. That previous to leaving the hotel he ordered some whisky and soda to be given to the cabman. He then got into the cab, and was driven off, and remembered nothing more.

This remarkable story was promptly investigated. It was proved to be true. The hotel was a highly respectable house. The two friends mentioned were well-known gentlemen, who swore that when Fenton left there was nothing whatever the matter with him; while the landlord of the house indignantly disputed the insinuation that the fatal drug had been administered at his house either wilfully or inadvertently. Trill's most searching investigation failed to disprove this assertion, so an open verdict was returned, and the mystery was as great a mystery as ever. It may be as well to state here at once that Vincent Trill came to the conclusion that for some terrible reason the Hon. Richard Shaw Fenton had lied, and, for reasons of his own, was concealing something which might have thrown light on the affair. It was only too evident that the drugging was done after the hotel was left; but as Fenton persisted in his statement, and nothing else could be dragged from him, there was no other course left but to endeavour to solve the mystery by such means as the clever detective was capable of commanding. There were three things that suggested themselves to Trill:

Firstly, Fenton had called somewhere else after leaving the hotel.

Secondly, it was known that he was the bearer of very important papers.

Thirdly, he had been drugged in order that the papers might be stolen.

This reasoning, however, although it seemed logical enough, did not suggest a rational theory as to why the cabman should have been drugged too. At least, at first it did not; but on pondering on the subject, it gradually dawned upon Trill that whoever had administered the drug intended that it should (and hoped that it would) prove fatal in each case, so that the mystery would remain a mystery for ever. It was very obvious that Mr. Fenton had strong reasons for concealing the truth, and that seemed to suggest—to Trill, at any rate, it did— that he had been where he ought not to have been, and the attraction that had drawn him there was, in all probability, a woman. That woman held the key to the problem, and unless she could be found the problem would go unsolved.

It has been stated that Fenton was a bachelor, and in much request at houses where there were marriageable daughters, and was very well known to a large number of ladies moving in good society in London. He occupied apartments in St. James's Street, and was regarded as a very reserved and secretive man, by no means given to making confidants. Although all Fenton's friends believed, or professed to believe, that no blame was attachable to him, the authorities took another view; and as the loss of the papers was not only a very serious thing in itself but proved that Fenton was not reliable, Trill did not abandon his quest.

When Fenton left the hospital he was still unwell, and remained so for some time, during which he kept to his rooms, and received no visitors save his most intimate friends. But three weeks after leaving the hospital he had so far recovered his health and spirits as to accept an invitation to be the guest of a lady of fashion who resided near Haslemere. This lady—a Mrs. Gerald Vandelour—was very wealthy. She was, or was supposed to be, the widow of a military officer; but those who partook of her hospitality—which was very lavish—did not allow any vagueness or uncertainty as to her past to stand as a barrier between them and her entertainments. Her house was a magnificent one; she kept quite an army of servants, and lived in a style that suggested that money was no object.

When Fenton arrived he found a large number of guests already assembled. On the following day there was to be a garden *fête* on a magnificent scale, and a huge marquee was in process of erection on the extensive lawn. Mrs. Gerald Vandelour was a very showy and seductive-looking woman, with a mass of fluffy fair hair, and a pink and white complexion—due in a large measure to art—and a figure that inclined to stoutness; but, nevertheless, she was graceful withal and lithe. She was particularly attentive to Fenton: indeed, she seemed to patronise him, took him under her wing, and treated him much as if he had been a great boy.

Amongst the guests was a singularly striking woman: a woman so dark that she might have passed for a Spanish gipsy. She had raven-black hair, intensely dark flashing eyes, an imperious bearing, and a commanding, haughty manner. She was a woman of marvellous beauty, and yet there was something—a something that was absolutely indescribable—about her that repelled rather than attracted. In age she was under thirty-five, but might have passed for thirty. She was known as 'Madame Revel.'

Fenton looked ill, haggard, and worn; and whenever Madame was near it seemed as if he tried to avoid her. And yet, when opportunity offered, she courted his society: she smiled on him sweetly, her white teeth gleamed, and her dark flashing eyes peered into his until his drooped and he turned from her.

The *fête* was a brilliant affair. Beauty and youth were strongly in evidence. Light, flowers, music, sweet scents, laughter, gaiety made it difficult to imagine that there was a heavy heart amongst that brilliant throng, or sorrow and suffering anywhere. It was a languid night. The air was heavy; the stars shone through a haze; a crescent moon sailed dreamily amongst filmy clouds. At eleven o'clock dancing and music ceased, in order that the guests might partake of supper in the great marquee, where an army of waiters were ready to minister to the wants of the (apparently) light-hearted people. But when the guests took their seats two persons were absent. They were Madame Revel and Fenton. A waiter was also absent—a mooning, clumsy sort of fellow, who had been rated several times during the evening for his stupidity. He was known as John Stokes, and when the supper was in full swing John Stokes was nowhere to be found. Not that it mattered very much, for there were plenty of attendants without him; but still, he ought to have done his duty. Instead of that he was lying at full length in the shadow of some beech trees in a secluded part of the grounds. But he wasn't asleep: oh, dear, no! With senses keenly alert, with eyes and ear strained, he was witnessing a scene as weird, as

489

startling and dramatic as even the most vivid imagination could conceive.

The night was not dark. The crescent moon and the stars shed a dreamy light over the scene. The trees were sharply outlined, and looked ghostly and grim. The light breeze that stirred the foliage somehow sounded like a human moan of pain; and the laughter and conversation of the revellers—subdued by distance—only seemed to accentuate the silence of the night that brooded like a spell of enchantment over the landscape. From his concealment in the shadow of the beeches, Stokes, the waiter, gazed on a lawn, in the centre of which was a very fine statue, by Canova, of Apollo stringing a lyre. Against the pedestal of the statue was a rustic seat, and two persons occupied it. They were the wonderfully handsome Madame Revel— who might have been the spirit of the scene, the goddess of night— and the Hon. Richard Shaw Fenton.

At such a time and under such circumstances, it might have been supposed that the man had led the lady to the seclusion, away from the fret of the throng, that he might pour into her ears an impassioned tale such as a man tells when he has fallen a prey to beauty's charms; but so far from this being the case Fenton had given evidence of being ill at ease.

The conversation between the twain was carried on in low tones, so that the strained ears of Stokes could catch no portion of it, but his keen vigilant eyes saw signs that even a fool would have found no difficulty in interpreting. At times Fenton would start up as if he intended to break from his companion; but then would she stretch forth a white jewelled hand which touched his and caused him to sink into the seat again. Two or three times he covered his face with his hands and sighed; and once while in this attitude the word 'Never, never!' repeated twice floated to the ears of the listener. It was like the soul-wrung exclamation from one who was suffering unbearable torture of mind. Almost immediately after he sprang to his feet as if under the influence of some stern resolution; but once more Madame stretched forth her hand, though this time she did not touch him. She made strange and mystic passes in the air, and as if she had put forth some subtle magic he stood motionless for a few moments, and then sank back like one whose volition had gone. She passed her hand over his head and down his face twice. He shuddered as if convulsed, but otherwise remained motionless and statue-like. The charmer then drew from her pocket a little book, and with a gold pencil began to write down something that he was saying.

This strange scene lasted for about ten minutes. Then Madame rose

490

and departed silently, save for the rustle of her silken skirts. For some time the man sat in a heap and motionless. He might have been frozen into the stony stillness of death; but at last the influence of the spell passed, and with another convulsive shudder and a muffled cry he fell on his face on the sward. Stokes emerged from his hiding-place, and kneeling down examined him, and as he seemed to be in a faint, Stokes hurried away, and procuring brandy returned to find Fenton partly revived and sitting up.

'I beg your pardon, sir,' said the man; 'but I found you lying here, and thinking you were ill I hurried for some brandy. Here it is.'

'Thank you, thank you,' answered Fenton, and seizing the glass with a nervous clutch he tossed the potent liquid down his throat. His face was of a ghastly pallor; but the moon rays falling on his eyes filled them with a strange, unnatural, unearthly light. He staggered to his feet and, pressing both his hands to his temples, murmured: 'God bless my life! How strange! how strange! Yes, I've been ill; I must have fainted. There, thank you, that will do! I am obliged for your attention. Please leave me; I wish to be alone.'

The waiter bowed and withdrew, but not far; and, still watching, he beheld Fenton sink into the seat once more and bury his face in his hands, though he did not maintain this attitude long, but, rising suddenly, he rejoined the company, where Madame Revel was the centre of an admiring group of friends. The hostess caught sight of him, and hurrying to him exclaimed:

'O you truant! wherever have you been to?' Then running her eyes hurriedly over her guests, she added: 'Now then, sir, confess! what pretty girl have you been flirting with?' But suddenly altering her tone from banter to alarm, she cried: 'Why, man, how ill you look! Your face is ashen. What's the matter with you?'

'O nothing,' he said, with a ghastly laugh; 'nothing, I assure you. Well, that is, not being very strong yet, I think I must have been overcome by the heat of the evening and—and fainted; well, I fancy so, for there is a blank I can't fill in.'

'Poor boy! poor boy!' murmured the hostess sympathetically. 'Come with me now, and I will give you some champagne cup—it will revive you;' and, taking his arm, she led him into the marquee, as the band was beginning the strains of a strange and dreamy waltz.

The following morning Stokes, the waiter, was summarily discharged as an 'incompetent, clumsy, and lazy fellow.' Fenton remained under the roof of his hostess for three or four days, for he was ill and she had to nurse him. In the meantime, Madame Revel had taken her departure, and returned to her town house in Sloane Street. The morning after her return a gentleman called at her residence and sent in his card, which bore the name 'Adolphe Coppé,' and in one corner of the card was this sign—***—that is, three stars. A few minutes later he was ushered into Madame Revel's presence. She received him in her boudoir, and stretched forth her white, delicate hand for him to touch. She was attired in an elegant and costly robe. In her raven hair was a tiny red rose. She looked singularly handsome, and her white teeth gleamed as she smiled graciously on her visitor.

'Your name is unknown to me,' she remarked prettily, 'but you are evidently one of us. You belong to the Brotherhood of the Three Stars?'

'You will see I have the sign on my card,' he answered evasively, though she did not seem to notice his evasion.

'You have business of importance?' she asked, with a shade of anxiety shedding itself over her handsome features.

'I have, madame. The president of the Brotherhood in Paris is pleased that you have succeeded in obtaining such valuable information from Mr. Fenton.'

'Monsieur le Président has received the papers then?' she remarked quickly.

A strange and gratified expression came into her visitor's face as he answered: 'It seems so.'

'Ah! that is good,' exclaimed the lady; 'but I have done even better. Fenton and I were guests the other night at the house of a mutual friend at Haslemere, and I placed him under a spell and extracted from him valuable secrets, which I intend to convey to the president myself.'

'Yourself?'

'Yes. I leave to-morrow evening by the Paris mail from Victoria.'

'You are a wonderfully clever woman,' said the guest. 'You seem to have made good use of Fenton.'

She smiled sarcastically as she answered: 'Poor fool—yes. He is my tool, my slave. I have bent him to my will—twisted him round my finger. My power over him is tremendous.'

Again the pleased and gratified expression spread itself over Coppé's features.

'Of that there is no doubt,' he answered. 'My object in calling on you was to say that your presence is earnestly desired in Paris; but you have already anticipated that by your resolve to leave to-morrow.'

'O yes. I had determined on that,' she answered.

'Then I need not trouble you further, and my mission ends.'

492

In a little while Coppé took his departure, after some hospitality dispensed graciously by Madame.

The following evening the lady duly drove up to Victoria Station and was superintending the registration of her luggage when a hand was laid upon her shoulder, and a stern voice said:

'Madame Revel, I hold a warrant for your arrest.'

She turned quickly, her eyes flashing like an enraged tigress'.

'A warrant for my arrest? What for?' she demanded haughtily.

'Firstly, on suspicion of causing the death of William Pritchard, a cabman; and, secondly, for having stolen Government papers.'

She staggered a little, as if from a shock, but quickly recovering, said with a sneer:

'You are mistaken. This is infamous. You shall pay dearly for this insult.'

'If I am mistaken, that is my affair, and I will accept the penalty; but I do not think I am mistaken. My name is Vincent Trill. I am a detective. As John Stokes, the waiter, I witnessed the scene on the lawn at Haslemere, when by your infamous designs and arts you deprived Fenton of his power of independent action.'

Madame looked very uneasy, and cast a momentary, nervous glance round about, as if contemplating some means of escape from the trap in which she had been so cleverly caught. But Trill again touched her, and indicating two men who stood beside him, he said:

'These are plain-clothes policemen. You would like, perhaps, to avoid a scene.'

She took the hint, merely remarking:

'I must yield to force; but, I repeat, you are mistaken.'

Trill and one of his men accompanied her to a cab, while the other man was left behind to take charge of her luggage. Trill had made a clever capture of one of the most daring and dangerous of a band of notorious conspirators in the pay of the French Secret Service, whose ramifications extended to every capital of Europe. He had come to suspect Madame by having closely shadowed Fenton, and found that he was in the habit of regularly visiting the lady, with whom he had become madly infatuated. On the night that he was ordered to convey the papers to the house of the General at Hyde Park, there is no doubt he called at Madame Revel's house on his way in compliance with a note he had received from her. There he and the cabman were dosed with some subtle drug. The unfortunate cabman was included, presumably because it was deemed advisable that he and his fare might fall into the hands of the police as 'drunk and incapable;' and in order to avoid a scandal, Fenton would necessarily have preserved silence as to his movements. In spite of Trill's cleverness, however, Madame Revel managed to checkmate him, but at a fearful cost. When she arrived at Bow Street it was found that she was suffering from illness, and before medical aid could be summoned she had lapsed into insensibility from which nothing could arouse her, and in four hours she had ceased to breathe. A daring and determined woman, she had played for high stakes, and finding herself on the losing side she had managed while in the cab to convey a deadly drug to her lips, and thus paid the penalty of her crimes with her life.

# The Stolen Cigar-Case

*by Bret Harte*

I found Hemlock Jones in the old Brook Street lodgings, musing before the fire. With the freedom of an old friend I at once threw myself in my old familiar attitude at his feet, and gently caressed his boot. I was induced to do this for two reasons; one that it enabled me to get a good look at his bent, concentrated face, and the other that it seemed to indicate my reverence for his superhuman insight. So absorbed was he, even then, in tracking some mysterious clue, that he did not seem to notice me. But therein I was wrong—as I always was in my attempt to understand that powerful intellect.

"It is raining," he said, without lifting his head.

"You have been out then?" I said quickly.

"No. But I see that your umbrella is wet, and that your overcoat, which you threw off on entering, has drops of water on it."

I sat aghast at his penetration. After a pause he said carelessly, as if dismissing the subject: "Besides, I hear the rain on the window. Listen."

I listened. I could scarcely credit my ears, but there was the soft pattering of drops on the pane. It was evident, there was no deceiving this man!

"Have you been busy lately?" I asked, changing the subject. "What new problem—given up by Scotland Yard as inscrutable—has occupied that gigantic intellect?"

He drew back his foot slightly, and seemed to hesitate ere he returned it to its original position. Then he answered wearily: "Mere trifles—nothing to speak of. The Prince Kopoli has been here to get my advice regarding the disappearance of certain rubies from the Kremlin; the Rajah of Pootibad, after vainly beheading his entire bodyguard, has been obliged to seek my assistance to recover a jewelled sword. The Grand Duchess of Pretzel-Brauntswig is desirous of discovering where her husband was on the night of the 14th of February, and last night"—he lowered his voice slightly—"a lodger in this very house, meeting me on the stairs, wanted to know 'Why they don't answer his bell.'"

I could not help smiling—until I saw a frown gathering on his inscrutable forehead.

"Pray to remember," he said coldly, "that it was through such an apparently trivial question that I found out, 'Why Paul Ferroll killed his Wife,' and 'What happened to Jones'!"

I became dumb at once. He paused for a moment, and then suddenly changing back to his usual pitiless, analytical style, he said: "When I say these are trifles—they are so in comparison to an affair that is now before me. A crime has been committed, and, singularly enough, against myself. You start," he said; "you wonder who would have dared to attempt it! So did I; nevertheless, it has been done. *I have been robbed!*"

"*You* robbed—you, Hemlock Jones, the Terror of Peculators!" I gasped in amazement, rising and gripping the table as I faced him.

"Yes; listen. I would confess it to no other. But *you* who have followed my career, who know my methods; yea, for whom I have partly lifted the veil that conceals my plans from ordinary humanity; you, who have for years rapturously accepted my confidences, passionately admired my inductions and inferences, placed yourself at my beck and call, become my slave, grovelled at my feet, given up your practice except those few unremunerative and rapidly-decreasing patients to whom, in moments of abstraction over *my* problems, you have administered strychnine for quinine and arsenic for Epsom salts; you, who have sacrificed everything and everybody to me—*you* I make my confidant!"

I rose and embraced him warmly, yet he was already so engrossed in thought that at the same moment he mechanically placed his hand upon his watch chain as if to consult the time. "Sit down," he said; "have a cigar?"

"I have given up cigar smoking," I said.

"Why?" he asked.

I hesitated, and perhaps coloured. I had really given it up because, with my diminished practice, it was too expensive. I could only afford a pipe. "I prefer a pipe," I said laughingly. "But tell me of this robbery. What have you lost?"

He rose, and planting himself before the fire with his hands under his coat tails, looked down upon me reflectively for a moment. "Do you remember the cigar-case presented to me by the Turkish Ambassador for discovering the missing favourite of the Grand Vizier in the fifth chorus girl at the Hilarity Theatre? It was that one. It was incrusted with diamonds. I mean the cigar-case."

"And the largest one had been supplanted by paste," I said.

"Ah," he said with a reflective smile, "you know that?"

"You told me yourself. I remember considering it a proof of your extraordinary perception. But, by Jove, you don't mean to say you have lost it."

He was silent for a moment. "No; it has been stolen, it is true, but I shall still find it. And by myself alone! In your profession, my dear fellow, when a member is severely ill he does not prescribe for himself, but calls in a brother doctor. Therein we differ. I shall take this matter in my own hands."

"And where could you find better?" I said enthusiastically. "I should say the cigar-case is as good as recovered already."

"I shall remind you of that again," he said lightly. "And now, to show you my confidence in your judgment, in spite of my determination to pursue this alone, I am willing to listen to any suggestions from you."

He drew a memorandum book from his pocket, and, with a grave smile, took up his pencil.

I could scarcely believe my reason. He, the great Hemlock Jones! accepting suggestions from a humble individual like myself! I kissed his hand reverently, and began in a joyous tone:

"First I should advertise, offering a reward; I should give the same intimation in handbills, distributed at the 'pubs' and the pastry-cooks. I should next visit the different pawnbrokers; I should give notice at the police station. I should examine the servants. I should thoroughly search the house and my own pockets. I speak relatively," I added with a laugh, "of course, I mean *your* own."

He gravely made an entry of these details.

"Perhaps," I added, "you have already done this?"

"Perhaps," he returned enigmatically. "Now, my dear friend," he continued, putting the note-book in his pocket, and rising—"would you excuse me for a few moments? Make yourself perfectly at home until I return; there may be some things," he added with a sweep of his hand towards his heterogeneously filled shelves, "that may interest you, and while away the time. There are pipes and tobacco in that corner and whiskey on the table." And nodding to me with the same inscrutable face, he left the room. I was too well accustomed to his methods to think much of his unceremonious withdrawal, and made no doubt he was off to investigate some clue which had suddenly occurred to his active intelligence.

Left to myself, I cast a cursory glance over his shelves. There were a number of small glass jars, containing earthy substances labeled "Pavement and road sweepings," from the principal thoroughfares and suburbs of London, with the sub-directions "For identifying foot tracks." There were several other jars labeled "Fluff from omnibus and road-car seats," "Cocoanut fibre and rope strands from mattings in public places," "Cigarette stumps and match ends from floor of Palace Theatre, Row A, 1 to 50." Everywhere were evidences of this wonderful man's system and perspicacity.

I was thus engaged when I heard the slight creaking of a door, and I looked up as a stranger entered. He was a rough-looking man, with a shabby overcoat, a still more disreputable muffler round his throat, and a cap on his head. Considerably annoyed at his intrusion I turned upon him rather sharply, when, with a mumbled, growling apology for mistaking the room, he shuffled out again and closed the door. I followed him quickly to the landing and saw that he disappeared down the stairs.

With my mind full of the robbery, the incident made a singular impression on me. I knew my friend's habits of hasty absences from his room in his moments of deep inspiration; it was only too probable that with his powerful intellect and magnificent perceptive genius concentrated on one subject, he should be careless of his own belongings, and, no doubt, even forget to take the ordinary precaution of locking up his drawers. I tried one or two and found that I was right—although for some reason I was unable to open one to its fullest extent. The handles were sticky, as if someone had opened them with dirty fingers. Knowing Hemlock's fastidious cleanliness, I resolved to inform him of this circumstance, but I forgot it, alas! until—but I am anticipating my story.

His absence was strangely prolonged. I at last seated myself by the fire, and lulled by warmth and the patter of the rain on the window, I fell asleep. I may have dreamt, for during my sleep I had a vague semi-consciousness as of hands being softly pressed on my pockets—no doubt induced by the story of the robbery. When I came fully to my senses, I found Hemlock Jones sitting on the other side of the hearth, his deeply concentrated gaze fixed on the fire.

"I found you so comfortably asleep that I could not bear to waken you," he said with a smile.

I rubbed my eyes. "And what news?" I asked. "How have you succeeded?"

"Better than I expected," he said, "and I think," he added, tapping his note-book—"I owe much to *you.*"

Deeply gratified, I awaited more. But in vain. I ought to have remembered that in his moods Hemlock Jones was reticence itself. I told him simply of the strange intrusion, but he only laughed.

Later, when I rose to go, he looked at me playfully. "If you were a married man," he said, "I would advise you not to go home until you had brushed your sleeve. There are a few short, brown seal-skin hairs on the inner side of the fore-arm—just where they would have adhered if your arm had encircled a seal-skin sacque with some pressure!"

"For once you are at fault," I said triumphantly, "the hair is my own as you will perceive; I have just had it cut at the hair-dressers, and no doubt this arm projected beyond the apron."

He frowned slightly, yet nevertheless, on my turning to go he embraced me warmly—a rare exhibition in that man of ice. He even helped me on with my overcoat and pulled out and smoothed down the flaps of my pockets. He was particular, too, in fitting my arm in my overcoat sleeve, shaking the sleeve down from the armhole to the cuff with his deft fingers. "Come again soon!" he said, clapping me on the back.

"At any and all times," I said enthusiastically. "I only ask ten minutes twice a day to eat a crust at my office and four hours' sleep at night, and the rest of my time is devoted to you always—as you know."

"It is, indeed," he said, with his impenetrable smile.

Nevertheless I did not find him at home when I next called. One afternoon, when nearing my own home I met him in one of his favourite disguises—a long, blue, swallow-tailed coat, striped cotton trousers, large turn-over collar, blacked face, and white hat, carrying a tambourine. Of course to others the disguise was perfect, although it was known to myself, and I passed him—according to an old understanding between us—without the slightest recognition, trusting to a later explanation. At another time, as I was making a professional visit to the wife of a publican at the East End, I saw him in the disguise of a broken-down artisan looking into the window of an adjacent pawn-

shop. I was delighted to see that he was evidently following my suggestions, and in my joy I ventured to tip him a wink; it was ab-
stractedly returned.

Two days later I received a note appointing a meeting at his lodgings that night. That meeting, alas! was the one memorable occur-
rence of my life, and the last meeting I ever had with Hemlock Jones!
I will try to set it down calmly, though my pulses still throb with the
recollection of it.

I found him standing before the fire with that look upon his face
which I had seen only once or twice in our acquaintance—a look
which I may call an absolute concatenation of inductive and deductive
ratiocination—from which all that was human, tender, or sympathetic,
was absolutely discharged. He was simply an icy, algebraic symbol!
Indeed his whole being was concentrated to that extent that his
clothes fitted loosely, and his head was absolutely so much reduced in
size by his mental compression that his hat tipped back from his forehead and literally hung on his massive ears.

After I had entered, he locked the doors, fastened the windows,
and even placed a chair before the chimney. As I watched those significant precautions with absorbing interest, he suddenly drew a revolver and presenting it to my temple, said in low, icy tones:

"Hand over that cigar-case!"

Even in my bewilderment, my reply was truthful, spontaneous, and
involuntary. "I haven't got it," I said.

He smiled bitterly, and threw down his revolver. "I expected that
reply! Then let me now confront you with something more awful,
more deadly, more relentless and convincing than that mere lethal
weapon—the damning inductive and deductive proofs of your guilt!"
He drew from his pocket a roll of paper and a note-book.

"But surely," I gasped, "you are joking! You could not for a moment
believe—"

"Silence!" he roared. "Sit down!"

I obeyed.

"You have condemned yourself," he went on pitilessly. "Condemned yourself on my processes—processes familiar to you, ap-
plauded by you, accepted by you for years! We will go back to the
time when you first saw the cigar-case. Your expressions," he said in
cold, deliberate tones, consulting his paper, "were: 'How beautiful! I
wish it were mine.' This was your first step in crime—and my first
indication. From 'I wish it were mine' to 'I will have it mine,' and the
mere detail, 'How can I make it mine,' the advance was obvious. Silence! But as in my methods, it was necessary that there should be an

499

overwhelming inducement to the crime, that unholy admiration of yours for the mere trinket itself was not enough. You are a smoker of cigars."

"But," I burst out passionately, "I told you I had given up smoking cigars."

"Fool!" he said coldly, "that is the *second* time you have committed yourself. Of course, you *told* me! what more natural than for you to blazon forth that prepared and unsolicited statement to *prevent* accusation. Yet, as I said before, even that wretched attempt to cover up your tracks was not enough. I still had to find that overwhelming, impelling motive necessary to affect a man like you. That motive I found in *passion*, the strongest of all impulses—love, I suppose you would call it," he added bitterly; "that night you called! You had brought the damning proofs of it in your sleeve."

"But," I almost screamed.

"Silence," he thundered. "I know what you would say. You would say that even if you had embraced some young person in a sealskin sacque what had that to do with the robbery. Let me tell you then, that that sealskin sacque represented the quality and character of your fatal entanglement! If you are at all conversant with light sporting literature you would know that a sealskin sacque indicates a love induced by sordid mercenary interests. You bartered your honour for it—that stolen cigar-case was the purchaser of the sealskin sacque! Without money, with a decreasing practice, it was the only way you could insure your passion being returned by that young person, whom, for your sake, I have not even pursued. Silence! Having thoroughly established your motive, I now proceed to the commission of the crime itself. Ordinary people would have begun with that—with an attempt to discover the whereabouts of the missing object. These are not my methods."

So overpowering was his penetration, that although I knew myself innocent, I licked my lips with avidity to hear the further details of this lucid exposition of my crime.

"You committed that theft the night I showed you the cigar-case and after I had carelessly thrown it in that drawer. You were sitting in that chair, and I had risen to take something from that shelf. In that instant you secured your booty without rising. Silence! Do you remember when I helped you on with your overcoat the other night? I was particular about fitting your arm in. While doing so I measured your arm with a spring tape measure from the shoulder to the cuff. A later visit to your tailor confirmed that measurement. It proved to be *the exact distance between your chair and that drawer!*"

500

I sat stunned.

"The rest are mere corroborative details! You were again tampering with the drawer when I discovered you doing so. Do not start! The stranger that blundered into the room with the muffler on—was myself. More, I had placed a little soap on the drawer handles when I purposely left you alone. The soap was on your hand when I shook it at parting. I softly felt your pockets when you were asleep for further developments. I embraced you when you left—that I might feel if you had the cigar-case, or any other articles, hidden on your body. This confirmed me in the belief that you had already disposed of it in the manner and for the purpose I have shown you. As I still believed you capable of remorse and confession, I allowed you to see I was on your track twice, once in the garb of an itinerant negro minstrel, and the second time as a workman looking in the window of the pawnshop where you pledged your booty."

"But," I burst out, "if you had asked the pawnbroker you would have seen how unjust—"

"Fool!" he hissed; "that was one of *your* suggestions to search the pawnshops. Do you suppose I followed any of your suggestions—the suggestions of the thief? On the contrary, they told me what to avoid."

"And I suppose," I said bitterly, "you have not even searched your drawer."

"No," he said calmly.

I was for the first time really vexed. I went to the nearest drawer and pulled it out sharply. It stuck as it had before, leaving a part of the drawer unopened. By working it, however, I discovered that it was impeded by some obstacle that had slipped to the upper part of the drawer, and held it firmly fast. Inserting my hand, I pulled out the impeding object. It was the missing cigar-case. I turned to him with a cry of joy.

But I was appalled at his expression. A look of contempt was now added to his acute, penetrating gaze. "I have been mistaken," he said slowly. "I had not allowed for your weakness and cowardice. I thought too highly of you even in your guilt; but I see now why you tampered with that drawer the other night. By some incredible means—possibly another theft—you took the cigar-case out of pawn, and like a whipped hound restored it to me in this feeble, clumsy fashion. You thought to deceive me, Hemlock Jones: more, you thought to destroy my infallibility. Go! I give you your liberty. I shall not summon the three policemen who wait in the adjoining room—but out of my sight for ever."

As I stood once more dazed and petrified, he took me firmly by the ear and led me into the hall, closing the door behind him. This reopened presently wide enough to permit him to thrust out my hat, overcoat, umbrella and overshoes, and then closed against me for ever!

I never saw him again. I am bound to say, however, that thereafter my business increased—I recovered much of my old practice—and a few of my patients recovered also. I became rich. I had a brougham and a house in the West End. But I often wondered, pondering on that wonderful man's penetration and insight, if, in some lapse of consciousness, I had not really stolen his cigar-case!

# Summer's End

*by William Manners*

Nature was playing the bully. A big bully of sun and endless heat; of flat-bottomed, mocking gray clouds. It wasn't picking on someone its size in Jim Schlieper, standing in his east corn field, fighting it with bent, straining body and a little hoe.

He straightened. His forearm moved mechanically across his wet forehead. The sun overhead was white, squashed out and quivering in its own heat. Jim looked at it, at the clouds crouched along the horizon. His eyes moved as his forearm had just moved, out of habit, a habit strengthened by endless repetitions.

He'd tell his brother to get out, he was thinking. To get out. A man can stand only so much. . . .

And then he marched down the rows of corn, their premature tassles at his knees. Down the yellow, clod-paved aisles. He was thinking of Bernice now. That laughing sparkle in her eyes. He'd seen it again that noon. He'd just washed up, and was drying himself, still standing there under the catalpa tree, when the truck pulled up the road. She'd been to Greeley; she'd come toward him with two big bags of groceries in her arms. It was then he saw her eyes. Big. Brown. Those of a youngster caught in a cooky jar. He was afraid. He turned his head and there was his brother, on the flagstone beside the pump.

His brother—Garrote McGee, Johnny Wilson, Abe Fineberg, Abe Fine, The Piecework Kid. . . .

502

All afternoon, working under the burning sun, he'd talked to himself, thinking of it. Words he'd say to his brother. He wouldn't let him do this to him. He wouldn't let him take Bernice. If there'd only have been a baby, if there'd only be money now, that would hold her. The same words over and over again to make his tongue strong, so that when the time came he'd be able to say them. Get out, he'd say. Get out.

He walked along the fence. Slid down the clay bank. Cut across the meadow. His heavy shoes were on the cinder road now, crunching loud in the stillness with each step. He held the hoe at his side like a rifle. He moved like a soldier advancing over No Man's Land. He'd waited long enough, he was thinking. Maybe too long. Clear out, he'd say.

Between the brown-weathered barns. Around the empty silo. Across the flagstones.

There was a steel scraper at the porch's edge. He ran the soles and heels of his shoes aimlessly over it. Noticing that he was still carrying the hoe, he leaned it against the trellised pillar of the porch. Then he went through the screen door and into the kitchen.

He stopped inside the door. The high-ceilinged kitchen, long and wide, with the giant, black coal stove, the varnished kitchen cabinet, the geraniums in the window that Bernice watered even though the cisterns were dry and the wells low.

The kitchen was too quiet. A fly buzzed through a sunbeam. The clock ticked loudly, importantly.

"Bernice," Jim called out with tentative restraint. He walked across the linoleum. "Bee . . . Bee . . . !" He stopped at the dining room door, turned and came back into the kitchen.

The milk bottle, empty and in the center of the kitchen table, caught his eye. There was a piece of paper under it.

Standing there, looking down, he read it. He read it as if he had read it many times before, as if he were obliged to read it. His eyes remained on the penciled lines after he had finished.

*Jim dear,*

*I've gone off with John. Forgive me for hurting you. It's the only way that's clear to me, to the happiness I've always wanted.*

His eyes moved down now to his wife's name signed at the bottom of the note, and John's name under it in bold, mocking, ribald scrawl.

Months ago, Jim might have let out an animal cry, gone racing in pursuit. But this was September. The sun had melted ferocity out of him. All that was left of him was a little dot in the fields, a little dot that scratched the earth in abject supplication and entreaty, day after day, day after day.

Jim picked up the sheet of paper and walked about the house holding it in his hand. He did not blame Bernice. She was a smart girl; she always knew what she was doing. You can't blame a person fleeing from a burning building—this house, these fields, his life, they were a burning building. Winter was running toward him, and his house with its bare shelves, its empty smokehouse, its barren cellar.

A burning building. The words obliterated time and space, spotlighted a night in his memory. It was the night the tenement on East Eleventh Street burned. His mother and father—his stepfather really —had been trapped in that fire. His stepfather, a bawling hulk with a fleshy face. He spoke German. When he was angry, however, and wanted to be certain that he was understood, he yelled in English.

John stayed on in New York after that. He hadn't taken it the way Jim had. John was hard; he was like his father. Jim was a male image of his mother, soft, easy going, kind. A Saint Bernard. John was a bulldog mixed with wolf and fox.

Jim landed in Greeley, Ohio, because he was walking across the country and was tired and the man who'd given him his last hitch also offered him a job. He worked in the general store for eight months. Then in the Challenge Gas Station. Then for old man Atkinson, in his abbatoir at the south end of town. And then he met Bernice.

For years, while he was yet a kid in New York, he'd said that some day he would be a farmer. And now that he'd met Bernice, and had saved every cent he possibly could out of his earnings, he bought this little farm . . . a house, outbuildings, scattered fruit trees, forty acres, ten in woodland. And a mortgage was thrown in as part of the transaction.

He never dreamed, let alone dared to hope, that Bernice would marry him. She was beautiful. He was fat, clumsy . . . a nobody trying to be a farmer. The talk around Greeley, that she was a wild one, didn't escape his ears. A hundred fellows were courting her, all at the same time. She danced at the Redmen's with strangers. All this merely made Jim all the more self-conscious, and all the more miserable because she was so far beyond him.

But his awkward, groping advances were miracles. Bernice fell in love with him and they were married. All the others had been goodtime fellows, unimportant episodes in her life. Jim was big and serious, the only man she could love, marry, and help build a home. That was the way she put it.

Now Jim walked about in the big, empty, silent house. The note from Bernice still in his hands. Walked as though the house was a part of Bernice, and being a part of her, he wanted to be near it, in every part of it.

When they had come up the hill together, and she had seen it for the first time, she cried out, her hands clasped in excitement: "What a huge place!" She laughed then. "What a huge family of kids it'll take to fill it." That sparkle, mischievous, bright as a morning star, was in her eyes when she had said that. It was the first time he had seen it. It hadn't frightened him that time.

But he saw it many times after that. The time she spoke of going to the World's Fair, forgetting the financial impossibility of such a trip. The evenings he'd look up from his paper to see her huddled over a detective story, her eyes wide, shining. She read thousands of them. The day the plane flying over their farm circled, its engine missing fire, and then seemingly getting out of its spasm, shooting away and out of sight. . . .

She's a wild one, the people in Greeley said. But he only laughed at them and their tepid standards. Bernice was vibrant with life, a robin with spring surging inside. Beside her, he was a gray clod of earth in the field. That was what made him afraid. How could she love him? Every day that she spent with him was a heavenly gift. Every day, every single day.

Cruelly his memory brought Jim to the present. The day, a week ago, his brother had come, come to stay awhile. Bernice was surprised, she didn't know that Jim had a brother. He covered his confusion with silence. And when she wanted to know what he did for a living, he lied to her, told her that he was a traveling salesman.

It didn't take the polished John, in his tailored clothes, a very long time. You could see he liked Bernice . . . in his way. And she—he didn't want to think about that. And then this noon, when she'd come back from Greeley, her eyes sparkling with joyous, excited fire. And the note . . .

This note. Jim looked at it, watched it as it dropped from his fingers, floated easily to the floor.

The shotgun, with the initials *J. S.* on its stock, rested on wooden pegs in the wall of the hallway. Long strides took Jim's hands to it. He walked out of the screen door with it. A hot dusk filled the back porch.

Tomorrow would be Sunday, he thought. Long, empty, painfully meaningless hours. Not Sunday alone, but all days. He'd go to Sunset Rock. Together they had watched many a day end there. It would be the right place—Sunset Rock. . . .

Shadows sprang out at him as he went down the road between the barns. The gun was wrenched out of his hands. "He's goin' rabbit huntin'," a voice laughed. "Rabbit hunting."

Jim struggled in the arms that were around him. They came off him. His heart pounded. He stood back, breathing hard. The three men were around him.

"Take it easy, brother," the man at his right said, impatience making a whine of his voice. "Easy. Easy. We want some information, that's all."

Jim looked at them. Between their heads he saw the hood of a car, its engine purring.

"We're looking for a certain party. We gotta get in touch with him. He's stayin' with you. Detroit's a long ways to come. Well . . . ?"

Jim said: "There's no one here. The house is empty."

The three men jostled past him. He stood there without moving. Lights blinked on, one after another, in all the windows of the house. He stood there looking at the windows, listening to the echoing tramp of feet moving across the floors inside.

Then the meaning of these three men broke through his daze, splashed cold reality into his face. Bernice was in danger! These men were killers! They were out hunting John! They wanted to kill him! Bullets would be flying everywhere! Bernice . . . !

The three men came out of the house. "We got a bum tip, mister. Excuse please." They went by him. They slid into the car, which backed, turned. Its headlight beams flashed over him. The car straightened, roared straight ahead.

There was no daze in Jim's mind now. It was cold and clear as a frosty morning. He had to get to Bernice. He had to take her away from John. Those were orders he gave himself. Greeley. The Redmen's Hall. This was Saturday night. Maybe . . . maybe. It was a long shot, but there was no other choice.

The truck tore over the two and a half miles to Greeley. Down Eastman Street, over to Main and the dance hall. The place was a noisy jam, with music blaring proudly, triumphantly above it all. Fellows and girls sat in the opened windows. They filled the hall and the stairs leading to the second floor.

Jim pushed his way in and up the stairs. A young girl giggled at his

506

set face. He moved along the bar, searching faces, out on the crowded dance floor, around its rim. The number finished with a double toot on the trombone signifying an intermission. Jim hurried to the stand. The musicians were putting their instruments down and standing up.

"Mrs. Schlieper!" he called out loudly. "Bernice! Bernice!"

Faces turned and looked up at him. Jim stood there, waiting.

He stepped down and across toward the door. The bartender called to him, finished putting a wine bottle on the shelf behind him. "Your missus was here earlier in the evenin'," he said. "Sport she was with said something 'bout goin' over to Elmwood, over to the Bordertown night club they got over there."

"Thanks, Ed," Jim said. "Thanks."

He turned, only to face the three who were out hunting John. They wore new clothes. They stood stiffly. "Say, Ed, what did this lady's boy friend look like?" one of them asked.

The bartender told them. He leaned on the bar and went into details.

One of the three, shorter than the others, a dent across the bridge of his nose, stepped up close to Jim. The bar was against Jim's back. He couldn't get away from the slap that caught him hard across the cheek and mouth. It came again, landing on the same place. Jim took it. The other two stood there, ready to back the play of the fellow with the banged-up nose, if Jim should be fool enough to make that necessary. That was plain. Satisfied, they turned and left.

Then Jim was racing down the stairs and into his truck. The shotgun was in the seat beside him. Though he knew following these men was hopeless, what else could he do? Perhaps John and Bernice hadn't stayed at the Bordertown. His prayer was made of that hope.

He pushed the truck to the limit, crossed the Pennsylvania state line and entered the village of Elmwood. He couldn't see the other car in the wide, empty street.

Then, as he crossed the double railroad tracks, he saw it. The car was coming back. It whizzed by. Jim's body chilled into a single piece of ice, for he knew what that meant. They had already seen John. Their murder visit was over. John was dead—killed. And Bernice. . . .

But then he saw the prowl cars ahead. They were a pure white. Lined along the curb, they reflected the glint of red and green and blue neon that ran up and down the gables of the Bordertown.

"Thank God!" Jim exclaimed. Those three hard men in new clothes who'd come to murder John . . . one look at the white cars of the law and they'd been frightened off. Or was that it? "Oh. God!"

507

Jim hurried out of the truck, ran across the walk and down the tree-bordered path that led to the night club. State troopers were at its double doors.

One of them stepped in his way. "Not so fast! What's the matter there, mister? Where yuh goin'?"

"My wife!" Jim gasped, out of breath. He could feel his heart pounding hollowly inside him. "My wife! She—she's in there."

"Jim!"

The trooper turned at the shrill shout behind him. Jim dashed past him into the amber light of the foyer and into Bernice's arms. Tears were running down his cheeks. He held Bernice with both arms tight about her.

Over her shoulder, he saw a police officer, gold braid on his coat. "She's a swell little lady," the officer said, nodding his head. "You got a swell little lady."

Beyond him, on the small rectangle of dance floor, was John. He was alive. He was bent forward in a straight-backed chair; his black hair, usually plastered into one solid piece, was mussed into wildness now. There was a circle of troopers about him.

The officer was rambling on: "Can you imagine her nabbing the Piecework Kid, and all by herself? Can you tie that? And him a guy that put the three McGovern boys to the wall up in Detroit, blastin' 'em down!"

"Let's get out of here," said Jim. "Let's get out of this place."

Bernice's tiny hand was on his arm. "But, Jim—wait a minute. I've got to see the officer. It's something about some money we get."

Jim was glad to get out of the Bordertown. Bernice stepped up beside him in the truck. Softly he put his fingers to the curve of her cheeks. She was here beside him. Alive. Real. Taking her into his arms, his lips met hers.

"I had to write that note, dear," she was saying. "It was the only way to trap him."

"Trap him? You mean, trap John?"

"I knew all about him the first night he came," she said excitedly. "He tried to kiss me. And I gave him a good stiff punch in the jaw. But he got ahold of me. Squeezed up against him. I felt the gun under his arm. I recognized him then. The Piecework Kid. I'd read lots about him in magazines. How he didn't like women. Or liquor. Said that in his business you had to leave them both alone."

"Darling," Jim said proudly, happily.

508

"Honestly, Jim, you didn't want to turn him in did you? You couldn't; he was your brother. But I knew what you thought."

"I don't know what I wanted to do. I just didn't want him around. I didn't want to have anything to do with it."

Bernice made a small-girl display of twisting her shoulders proudly. "May I brag?" she asked. "Thanks. Well, this woman-hater went wild about me. Said I wasn't a lot of chrome and blond upholstery like the other women he knew . . . those are his own words. So I eloped with him, and got him out here for a drink in my honor. A whiskey sour . . . then another one. I knew he couldn't take it, because he wasn't a drinker. Then he had a Tom Collins, I believe it was, on top of that. He asked for that one himself."

"He surely must have been drunk!"

"I told the waiter to phone for the state cop then. Of course I knew about the reward—that's really why I did it, that's why I had to do it. This morning when I was at Greeley. . . ."

"You're wonderful, darling," Jim said, putting his cheek to hers.

"Jim dear, will you listen to me? This morning when I was at Greeley, Doc Moorhead . . . Jim dear, we're going to have a little Jim."

Her eyes were sparkling in that way again.

# The Terrarium Principle

*by J. V. Drexel*

Andrea Parker was on the back porch, working on her latest project— the planting of seeds in a bottle terrarium—when she heard Jerry's car in the driveway. She took off her gloves, brushed flecks of potting soil off her gardening shirt, and went into the kitchen to meet him as he opened the garage door.

There was a preoccupied scowl on Jerry's face. He looked rumpled, the way Columbo used to look on television. Which was unusual; her husband may have been a police lieutenant attached to the Homicide Division, but he definitely was not the Peter Falk type.

He brushed his lips over hers—not much of a kiss, Andrea thought —and said, "I could use a drink." He went straight to the refrigerator and began tugging out one of the ice trays.

"Rough day?" she asked him.

"You can say that again. Except that the operative word is frustrating. One of the most frustrating days I've ever spent."

"Why?"

"Because a man named Harding committed murder in a locked room this morning and I can't prove it. *That's* why."

"Want to talk about it?"

He made a face. But he said, "I might as well. It's going to be on my mind all evening anyway. You can help me brood."

Andrea took the ice tray away from him, shooed him into the living room, and made drinks for both of them. When she brought them in, Jerry was sitting on the couch with his legs crossed, elbow resting on one knee and chin cupped in his palm. He really did look like Columbo tonight. All he needed, she thought, was a trench coat and a cigar.

She handed him his drink and sat down beside him. "So why can't you prove this man Harding committed murder? You did say it happened in a locked room, didn't you?"

"Well, more or less locked. And I can't prove it because we can't find the gun. Without it we just don't have a case."

"What exactly happened?"

"It's a pretty simple story, except for the missing gun. The classic kind of simple, I mean. Harding's uncle, Philip Granger, has—or had —a house out in Roehampton Estates; wealthy guy, made a lot of money in oil stocks over the years. Harding, on the other hand, is your typical black-sheep nephew—drinks too much, can't hold down a job, has a penchant for fast women and slow horses.

"This morning Harding went out to his uncle's house to see him. The housekeeper let him in. According to her, Harding seemed upset about something, angry. Granger's lawyer, Martin Sampson, happened to be there at the time, preparing some papers for Granger to sign, and he confirms the housekeeper's impression that Harding was upset.

"So Harding went into his uncle's study and either he or Granger locked the door. Fifteen minutes later both Sampson and the housekeeper heard a gunshot. They were sure it came from the study; they both ran straight for that door. But the door was locked, as I said. They pounded and shouted, and inside Harding yelled back that somebody had shot his uncle. Only he didn't open the door right away. It took him eight and one-half minutes by Sampson's watch to get around to it."

"Eight and a half minutes?" Andrea said. "What did he say he was doing all that time?"

510

"Looking out the window, first of all, for some sign of a phantom killer. Harding's claim is that window was open and Granger was shot through the window from outside; he says Sampson and the housekeeper must have been mistaken about where the shot came from. The rest of the time he was supposedly ministering to his uncle and didn't stop to open the door until the old man had died."

"But you think he spent that time hiding the gun somewhere in the room?"

"I *know* that's what he was doing," Jerry said. "His story is implausible and he'd had arguments with his uncle before, always over money and sometimes to the point of violence. He's guilty as sin—I'm sure of it!"

"Couldn't he have just thrown the gun out the window?"

"No. We searched the grounds; we'd have found the gun if it had been out there."

"Well, maybe he climbed out the window, took it away somewhere, and hid it."

"No chance," Jerry said. "Remember the rain we had last night? There's a flower bed outside the study window and the ground there was muddy from the rain; nobody could have walked through it without leaving footprints. And it's too wide to jump over from the windowsill. No, the gun is in that room. He managed to hide it somewhere during those eight and one-half minutes. His uncle's stereo unit was playing, fairly loud, and if he made any noise the music covered it —Sampson and the housekeeper didn't hear anything unusual."

"Didn't one of them go outdoors to look in through the study window?"

"Sampson did, yes. But Harding had drawn the drapes. In case the phantom killer came back, he said."

"What's the study like?" Andrea asked.

"Big room with masculine decor: hunting prints, a stag's head, a wall full of books, overstuffed leather furniture, a large fireplace—"

"I guess you looked up the fireplace chimney," Andrea said.

He gave her a wry smile. "First thing. Nothing but soot."

"What else was in the room?"

"A desk that we went over from top to bottom. And model airplanes, a clipper ship in a bottle, a miniature train layout—all kinds of model stuff scattered around."

"Oh?"

"Evidently Granger built models in his spare time, as a hobby. There was also a small workbench along one wall."

"I see."

"The only other thing in there was the stereo unit—radio, record player, tape deck. I thought Harding might have hidden the gun inside one of the speakers, but no soap."

Andrea was sitting very still, pondering. So still that Jerry frowned at her and then said, "What's the matter?"

"I just had an idea. Tell me, was there any strong glue on the workbench?"

"Glue?"

"Yes. The kind where you only need a few drops to make a bond and it dries instantly."

"I guess there was, sure. Why?"

"How about a glass cutter?"

"I suppose so. Andrea, what are you getting at?"

"I think I know what Harding was doing for those eight and a half minutes," she said. "And I think I know just where he hid the gun."

Jerry sat up straight. "Are you serious?"

"Of course I'm serious. Come on, I want to show you something." She led him out through the kitchen, onto the rear porch. "See that terrarium?"

"What about it?"

"Well, it's a big glass jar with a small opening at one end, right? Like a bottle. There's nothing in it now except soil seeds, but pretty soon there'll be flowers and plants growing inside and people who don't know anything about terrariums will look at it and say, 'Now how in the world did you get those plants through that little opening?' It doesn't occur to them that you *didn't* put plants in there; you put seeds and they grew into plants."

"I don't see what that has to do with Harding—"

"But there's also a way to build a bottle terrarium using full-grown plants," she went on, "that almost never occurs to anybody. All you have to do is slice off the bottom of the container with a glass cutter; then, when you've finished making your garden arrangement inside, you just glue the bottom back on. That's what some professional florists do. You can also heat the glass afterward, to smooth out the line so nobody can tell it's been cut, but that isn't really necessary. Hardly anyone looks that close."

A light was beginning to dawn in Jerry's eyes. "Like we didn't look close enough at a certain item in Granger's study."

"The ship in a bottle," Andrea said, nodding. "I'll bet you that's where Harding put the gun—inside the ship that's inside the bottle."

"No bet," Jerry said. "If you're right, I'll buy you the fanciest steak dinner in town."

He hurried inside, no longer looking like Columbo, and telephoned police headquarters. When he was through talking he told Andrea that they would have word within an hour. And they did — exactly fifty-six minutes had passed when the telephone rang. Jerry took it, listened, then grinned.

"You were right," he said when he'd hung up. "The bottom of the bottle had been cut and glued back, the ship inside had been hollowed out, and the missing gun was inside the ship. We overlooked it because we automatically assumed nobody could put a gun through a bottle neck that small. It never occurred to us that Harding didn't *have* to put it through the neck to get it inside."

Andrea smiled. "The terrarium principle," she said.

"I guess that's a pretty good name for it. Come on, get your coat; we'll go have that steak dinner right now."

"With champagne, maybe?"

"Sweetheart," he said, "with a whole magnum."

# Three Men and a Corpse

*by Victor K. Ray*

The black coupe slid along the dark street, and a gun spat flame. The explosions, three of them, punctuated the engine's high whine. I shoved Joey Sciortino sideways, fell beside him, listened to the echoes reverberate in the narrow canyon of the street. I twisted to look at the car, a black Ford. I saw part of the license number, 26 J 34—something.

Joey's hand had dug inside his coat as he fell, and when he raised up he had a .38. Then he put it back inside his coat. "What happened?" he gasped.

When I got my breath back, I said, "They missed."

The car had already turned the corner, the noise of its engine mixed and lost in the sounds of the city. The street was vacant, except for us. The light at the far end of the block cast long shadows in our direction.

Then we saw the alley mouth that had been only a few feet ahead of us. We hadn't even noticed it before. We looked down the alley at a crumpled figure which lay on the cement.

"Look, Steve!" said Joey. "They weren't shooting at us." Joey's voice sounded young and relieved, and I realized he was pretty inexperienced in this kind of thing, after all. He wasn't the kind of guy he was trying to be, the kind who usually packs a .38.

I moved down the alley to the figure. I shined my pen-light into the gray, thin face. He was dead.

Behind me, Joey said, "Steve, let's get out of here."

I said, "I know this guy, Joey."

"Let's get out of here—quick!" he said.

I turned out my light. "We ought to report this, Joey."

"Cops'll be swarming all over the place in three minutes." I could see Joey's face in the dimness. There was a film of sweat on it. He wheeled, moved back to the sidewalk, looked both ways.

I stood there for a minute thinking we ought to report this. Thinking you can't walk into a murder, and then walk out on it. Not when you're a private detective.

I was thinking about my friend Hamp Sprague, a detective on the force, and what he'd said this morning. He'd said, "Steve, you guys are always on the wrong side of the law. Murder's not very pleasant any way you take it, but when you're looking at it from the wrong side, it's worse. I wouldn't like your kind of work at all."

I stood there over the body in the alley, thinking maybe Hamp was right. I'd been in town twenty-four hours, and I was looking into the eyes of a dead man, and thinking about not reporting it.

Then I heard Joey's voice again, strained, tense. "Steve, I can't afford to be tied up with a thing like this." He started to move down the street.

I said, "Wait a minute, Joey. I'm coming."

I joined him, and we walked fast back in the direction from which we'd come, back toward the little bar one street over. I could hear his breathing.

"You in trouble with the police, Joey?"

"No." As we came to the corner, he looked back.

We turned the corner, and kept walking, faster and faster, with Joey a couple of steps ahead.

"I haven't got any trouble with the cops, Steve," he said. "But they're laying for me, I think."

"Not Hamp Sprague?"

"Yeah, Hamp. You wouldn't think Hamp would try to pin some-

514

thing on me, would you? Looks like he'd have better things to do with his time."

At the next corner, the lighted front of the little bar was visible, and we went down to it. Then, two or three blocks over, we heard a police siren split the air.

Joey let out his breath. "There it is," he said. "Let's have a drink. I could use one."

We went in. We both hoisted our first one fast.

Hamp Sprague had told me about Joey, that Joey was heading for trouble. When I'd finally asked Hamp to join my agency in San Francisco, he'd said no, and steered the conversation quickly onto Joey. Joey and Hamp and I had grown up together.

Of course, Joey was dead wrong about Hamp trying to pin something on him. Hamp could have been the best friend Joey Sciortino ever had. Joey had known that once, but he'd forgotten it.

Things had been pretty hot then, the last time I'd seen Joey. We hadn't been able to have a drink, mull over old times. We'd been on Iwo.

Joey had come home shortly after that. He'd been rehabilitated. But good. I hadn't come home. I'd stopped in San Francisco on the way, had set myself up as a private detective, was doing pretty well. But I needed help to run my business. And I wasn't having much luck finding guys I knew I could depend on.

Hamp hadn't even wanted to talk about it.

He'd said, "I hate to see Joey digging his grave, Steve. He's running with Shade Cantrell's outfit. It's just a matter of time before Joey's in too deep to pull out." Hamp had brushed his hand back through his thick, prematurely graying hair, his eyes troubled.

I'd said, "It's hard to protect a guy, when he doesn't want to be protected."

"The mortality rate is high," said Hamp. "It's just a matter of time till Joey gets it."

The picture was clear. Hamp wanted to do something for Joey before somebody else did it to him. Mostly, cops sit on their hands till it's too late. That gives you some idea of Hamp Sprague.

Hamp had said, "Just this morning we picked up a guy in a ditch at the edge of town, with four bullets in him. We don't even know who the guy was." He'd looked at me, and grinned. "Maybe he was a private detective. Anyway, it may take us three or four days to find out. Then any hope of running down his killer will be gone. That's the way Joey will end one of these days. In a ditch, or in an alley. The mortality rate is high."

515

Maybe contact with an old friend would snap Joey out of it, we'd said. When he'd first come back, Joey had talked about setting up as a private detective. Then he'd found it profitable to drop the idea for a job with Shade Cantrell. Well, I could take him back to San Francisco.

We'd met on the street. I'd made it look like an accident, because Joey was already getting touchy. We'd had our drinks, talked over old times. I'd made my offer. But I hadn't gotten to first base with him.

He'd said, "It's not for me, Steve." His tone of voice had said, "It's too tame. There's not enough money in it."

I'd sat thinking about my two friends. One of them thought private detecting was too dirty. The other thought it was too clean.

Joey and I had started walking a couple of blocks over to a joint owned by Shade Cantrell, the Crystal Club, and we'd run into the gunfire, and the body in the alley.

Now, back in the little bar, the drinks had their effect. I began to calm down. I'll never learn to like death in any form. I looked in the bar mirror at Joey beside me. His face was still pale, tight.

I finished my drink, set the glass down. "Drink up, Joey," I said.

It jarred him out of his reverie. He jumped a little, grinned. "Sure."

I motioned the bartender for another.

"Steve, who was that guy?" asked Joey suddenly. "You said you knew him."

"Nobody you'd know," I said. "He's from the coast."

Our drinks arrived. We raised our glasses. But some of our high spirits were gone.

"Did you know him well?" Joey pursued.

"He was just a guy mixed up in the rackets. I didn't know him very well."

Joey turned on his stool, went over to the juke box, and put a couple of nickels in. The music came up full and solid.

Joey came back. "What was that guy's name, Steve?"

"The guy back in the alley? Bruce Wardell. Something like that."

"I wonder why he got it," said Joey softly, his words almost lost in the music.

We listened. I could feel Joey's eyes turn on me every minute or two. I began getting an idea. The thing in the alley had shaken him up. It made me know again that he was pretty young in this kind of thing. That was good. There was still time. Hamp Sprague had been right.

When the two records were finished, I said, "Did you get a look at the guy in the alley?"

"No."

"He was a young guy. The last I saw of him was a couple of months ago. He was working his way up, carried a Russian automatic, I remember. I don't think he'd used it yet, but you couldn't be sure. Nobody could be sure. He was on his way up."

I spun around on my stool, went over to the juke box, played the first number over again. I said, "There's been quite a bit of hell raised in San Francisco lately. Everybody's trying to set himself up in some nice spot. This guy, Bruce Wardell, was going up fast. I don't think he'd bumped anybody off, but when somebody got bumped, Wardell was there to take his place." I waited to see how he took it.

Joey shifted nervously, lit a cigarette.

"It was just a question of time till he got it," I said. "Maybe they'll catch his killer, maybe they won't. One thing certain, it won't make any difference to Bruce Wardell."

Joey pulled at his collar, wiped his face with his handkerchief. "These drinks are hitting me, Steve. Let's get out in the air. I've got to show up at the Crystal Club."

We got off the stools, and started for the door. Joey stopped. "Steve, let's take a taxi over there." He was thinking of the two blocks of dark, narrow streets.

"Okay." I went over to the wall telephone and called one. When I turned, Joey was back at the bar. He wasn't drinking again, just sitting. He waved the bartender away. His face was pale, a line drawn down his jaw.

Suddenly he spun around on the stool, and yelled halfway across the bar, "Steve. I'll do it! I'll take your offer."

His voice was too loud, and he turned red, grinned. He got off the stool, and walked toward me. "San Francisco, here we come!" He was laughing. He stuck out his hand and I shook it. He was happy as a kid, and so was I.

Hamp had been right. He'd said there ought to be something you could do for a guy like Joey—and there was. The killing had done it.

The taxi arrived then. "128 West Grand," Joey told the driver.

I said, "I thought you had to show up at the Crystal Club."

"The hell with that, Steve. There's one guy I want to tell about taking you up on that job. I want to tell him right now."

128 West Grand was Hamp Sprague's address.

We got over there in about five minutes. Hamp had just gotten home. We told him the good news. His heavy face split from ear to ear. "By golly," he said softly. "By golly, that's wonderful."

It was a fine excuse to break out a bottle, and Hamp did.

I kept thinking about that body back in the alley, the thin gray face, the staring eyes. Bruce Wardell.

I had to report it. Maybe some private detectives take murder as casually as they take a drink of bourbon.

I could say, "By the way, Hamp, old man, we saw a killing tonight. Yeah, it happened right in front of us. I even knew the victim. Boy, we got out of there fast! Report it? Why—uh. . . ."

There is one magic time to report a homicide. That's the minute you find it.

Hamp poured drinks around for us again. Then he went into the kitchen to get more ice. I followed him.

In the kitchen, I said, "Joey and I saw a little trouble tonight, Hamp." I tried to say it calmly, but my voice wouldn't keep a level pitch.

Hamp said, "Yeah?" He pulled the ice tray out.

"We saw a murder."

"Yeah?"

"Did you hear what I said?"

He put the ice tray under the hot water faucet, let the cubes fall into a bowl.

"I said we saw a murder. . . . We didn't report it."

He refilled the ice tray with water, and went back to the ice box.

"I don't think you understand, Hamp." I felt like my voice might get away from me again. "We were walking down the street, a guy was shot in an alley about ten feet away from us. We thought they were shooting at us. I saw the car. License number, 26 J 34—something. You should be able to do something with that much of the number."

Hamp turned around, went back to the sink for the bowl of ice. "Yeah," he said.

I grabbed him by the arm. "What's the matter with you, Hamp? Are you drunk? I'm reporting a murder!"

"Okay, Steve. I don't guess this is the first murder you ever reported."

I said, "Wait a minute." I got a cigarette out, lit it. "Aren't you going to call headquarters and give them that license number?"

"Yeah," he said. "I'll call 'em." But he didn't make any move to do it. There was a funny look in Hamp's eyes.

The telephone was in the little hall just off the kitchen. I went to it. "I'm going to call headquarters," I said.

"What are you so worried about, Steve? We picked up the body already. A punk named Bruce Wardell. Four bullet holes in him. You probably knew him in San Francisco. He was in the rackets out there, working up too fast."

I turned around and picked up the telephone. I put my finger down on the dial. And then I stopped. I held the receiver in mid-air for a minute. Then I put it down slowly.

I turned around. "How many bullet holes did you say?"

"Four—er—maybe it was three."

"It was four, Hamp. You said four." I began to understand. He'd had me on the ropes for a few minutes. Watching Hamp Sprague shrug off a murder was like getting punched on the chin. I remembered the story he'd told me this morning.

I said, "You picked up Bruce Wardell, all right. But the first time you picked him up was this morning—in a ditch at the edge of town."

I thought of the way Hamp had talked this morning: *There ought to be some way to snap Joey out of it.*

I said, "You staged a 'killing' for Joey's benefit. You figured I'd know Wardell, because it's my business to know guys like him. You counted on me to be sure Joey got the parallel between Bruce Wardell and himself." I looked at Hamp standing there holding that bowl of ice.

He grinned.

I was thinking of that dark street, the high whine of an engine, the three shots.

I said, "That car, license number 26 J 34— That was yours."

"That's right, Steve."

Then I thought of the body. And it suddenly came to me. "The body," I said. "You had to steal the body of Bruce Wardell from the morgue."

Hamp looked at me with mock seriousness. "Steve! I wouldn't do a thing like that!"

"The hell you wouldn't. But what if I'd reported that 'killing' to headquarters?"

"The desk sergeant was working with me," said Hamp.

That gives you some idea of Hamp Sprague.

"I slipped," continued Hamp sadly. "When I said Wardell had four bullet holes in him. I should have known you'd count those shots, even if you thought hell was breaking loose. You'd remember that only three shots were fired. I had only three blank cartridges tonight."

"You slipped on that," I said. "But you slipped before that, by knowing too much about Bruce Wardell. If he'd actually been murdered tonight, you couldn't have found out this quick that he was from San Francisco, and mixed up in the rackets out there."

"Yeah, I guess that's right," he admitted. He laughed suddenly, and

I laughed, too. We both looked at that bowl of melting ice then, and thought of Joey in the other room, waiting. We were laughing so hard, I thought Joey would hear us, and come in.

Hamp winked. "I'm pretty smart, ain't I, kid?"

We went in where Joey was. He was sitting over by the radio with his ear glued to it, listening to the high wail of a trumpet.

He looked up, and said, "I thought you guys had found another bottle out there."

We filled our glasses again. We raised them. I looked at Joey. The lines of strain and tension had disappeared.

I looked at Hamp, and he winked, saying again with his look, "I'm pretty smart, ain't I, kid!"

I nodded.

I thought, yeah, you're pretty smart, Hamp. You're so smart we can't get along without you. The three of us are going to bust San Francisco wide open.

I thought, you're going back with us, if I have to try a little friendly blackmail. And I could do it, too. A detective on the force stealing a corpse from the morgue!

I winked back at him, and we drank.


# Today's Special—Poison!

*by V. E. Thiessen*


When Dermott Slade turned to murder he did so with the same relentless precision that had made him a successful confidence man.

Sitting in the one room that was his temporary quarters, Dermott lifted his head to stare out the window at the man he intended to kill. Rex Whitehall, a tall, grey-haired man, was walking down the street toward him. Dermott glanced at his watch. It was precisely seven in the fall evening, almost dark. As he glanced out the window, Dermott could see Whitehall turning into the entrance of the Vopopulous Grill, across the street. Dermott grinned. Whitehall was on schedule as usual. Dermott could set his watch by the punctual arrival of Whitehall at the grill.

That meant that Dermott had fifteen minutes to finish the murder.

520

He had one more menu to type. Dermott seized the printed blank, rolled it into his machine until the printed square marked TODAY'S SPE- CIAL was under his keys. He glanced at the stack of finished menus beside him. Today's special was the same as yesterday's, though some other items had changed. Dermott had only to type this final line: DELUXE HAMBURGERS—WITH FRENCH FRIES—25C

The thought occurred that Whitehall would be eating across the street, that he would be eating the day's special as was his invariable custom, and so, in a sense, this last might be considered as his obitu- ary. The thought amused Dermott, and he let his mind run over the murder plan, and grinned.

He jerked the menu from the machine, dropped it on the others and glanced at his watch. Thirteen minutes. He got up, opened a small cabinet and drew out a vial of chemical and a Roi-Tan cigar. Carefully he stripped the wrapper from the pierced end of the cigar. He rolled a bit of paper to a funnel shape and began to sift the chemi- cal until about a quarter of a gram had gone into the hole. He tapped the cigar, compacting the chemical somewhat, then carefully folded the cellophane wrapper back to its original condition.

When Whitehall put that cigar in his mouth and drew smoke he would also draw a few grains of potassium cyanide. Sure it would taste funny, but for a moment Whitehall would blame it on the sulphur in the match. Then it would be too late.

The acids of the stomach, working on the potassium cyanide, would have converted it to hydrocyanic acid—prussic acid—and death would be almost instantaneous.

Dermott put the rest of the vial back in a drawer, slipped the cigar in his side pocket, picked up the menus and went out of his room into the night. Going across the street he glanced at his watch. Eight min- utes. Whitehall would be eating his hamburger now.

The beauty of this plan was that it was perfect. In addition to the shrewd knowledge of human nature that is the tool of every confi- dence man, Dermott had a theory of crime, a theory on the simple art of murder.

The secret of successful crime, according to Dermott, lay in never being suspected. Modern police laboratories were so well equipped, routine so perfect, that once a criminal was suspected, the evidence to convict could be found.

If one were hanged for leaving a fingerprint, according to Dermott, the error was not in leaving the fingerprint, but in being suspected, for only then did they take the second print for the comparison.

There was no reason for the police to connect Dermott with Whitehall. Though Dermott had been watching Whitehall for two weeks, he had never spoken to the man, never been seen with him. The only possible connection was through Sam Watt, Dermott's erstwhile companion in confidence games, and Sam was dead.

Dermott pushed his way into the Vopopulous Grill. Nick Vopopulous grinned at him from the grill, and Nick's twelve-year-old kid beside him said, "Hi, Dermott."

"Hi." Dermott tousled the kid's hair, handed the menus to Popo. "Here's tomorrow's garbage list," he kidded.

"Thank you." Vopopulous dumped the menus in a drawer, then flipped hamburgers on the grill.

Dermott stood a moment, looking down the counter. Several customers were in the little place. That made it better. At the far end, Whitehall was finishing the last of his cup of coffee.

Any moment now, Dermott told himself. His hand was on the cigar in his pocket. He grinned at the Vopopulous kid. "Gimme one of those cigars," he said.

The kid held the box toward him. Dermott extended his hand, picked a cigar.

"I'll take one of those too," Whitehall said, behind him, at the front counter.

As the kids eyes flickered toward the sound of Whitehall's voice, Dermott dropped the palmed cigar. He struck a match to give him time while he watched Whitehall. If Whitehall changed his habits now, Dermott would have to act fast to get that cigar back.

Whitehall's routine was right in the groove. He took only one cigar, the handiest one, and thrust it in his upper coat pocket.

Dermott eased out his breath. The murder was done. He tousled the kid's hair again, called, "I'll get the new menu copy in the morning, Popo," and turning, walked out of the grill. In the street, Dermott stood a moment, considering, before he mounted the steps to his room.

Once inside the room he poured himself a quick, short drink. He took only one—Dermott was not the kind of man to hamper himself with too much alcohol. Besides, he had only twenty minutes; after that he had to go to the park to find Whitehall's body.

He sat down and began to think methodically over the entire chain of events, probing for any weak spots, for any link that might throw him under the fatal suspicion of the law.

His knowledge of Whitehall had begun with the death of Sam Watt, Dermott's partner. This death was in no wise due to an unsuccessful scheme, it was due to one of those quirks of mother nature. Sam Watt had died of pneumonia.

Sam Watt had been versatile. He had been involved in the notorious Gatesville jewel robbery. The last of the proceeds of that robbery, a huge perfect diamond, was at present reposing in the heel of Whitehall's shoe. According to Watt, half of that diamond was his, and this interest in illegal booty he had willed Dermott just before he died.

The more Dermott had considered the facts, the less it appeared he could demand the diamond, or that Whitehall would honor such a claim. Never one to plan without first determining the facts, Dermott had located Whitehall and watched him. The arrangement whereby he lived in this tiny room and typed menus for Popo, the Greek across the street, was merely a means to study the man, Whitehall, who ate there. When the fact had developed that Whitehall was entirely alone, without connections, living quietly on his bank account until conditions should be better to fence the stone, Dermott's mind first began to consider the direct method of getting the stone.

It appeared to be the perfect opportunity. His connection with Whitehall could never be traced. Though he had watched the man for weeks they had never met, never spoken.

And so Dermott Slade had decided. There had been only the problem of determining whether the stone still lay in its hiding place in Whitehall's shoe heel, or whether it had been fenced or concealed in some new place.

The matter had been determined to Dermott's satisfaction by the simple expedient of a wad of gum dropped under Whitehall's shoe. Whitehall's reaction to Popo's innocent offer to clean the shoe with a kitchen knife had been slight but revealing. Dermott was satisfied.

Dermott glanced at his watch. By now another step in the lonely pattern of Whitehall's habits would be complete. Whitehall would have gone to the park that lay nearby and would be sitting on one of the benches on the west side. He would sit there in the dark, quietly consuming a small bottle of whiskey, a lonely, thoughtful old man. When the whiskey was gone Whitehall would take from his pocket the cigar he had bought at supper and smoke that until it was the merest fragment of a butt. Then he would rise and go to his apartment and retire.

It must, Dermott thought, be a lonely sort of life, knowing that the wealth that lay in his heel was a thing that made friendships dangerous, made any publicity undesirable. Still, for a hundred thousand, a

523

man could stand a few months of the simple life. And at least White-hall had liquor and tobacco.

Dermott rose, shrugged into his coat, slipped a short screwdriver and a pair of gloves into his pocket. Then he went out of the room down the stairs into the night and began to walk slowly toward the park.

There was no problem with Dermott as to disposal of the stone. He knew a private collector who would pay more than a fence for the jewel, and the jewel would never again be seen in public.

Dermott could see the hundred thousand. He began thinking about a trip to Bermuda. It would be lovely there, and good hunting if he could pick up another helper as good as Sam Watt had been.

He pulled his thoughts up short. Trouble with you, Dermott, you think too much, he told himself. You start spending it before you get it, and you'll goof up somewhere.

By now the black night shape of willows that fringed the park was in his view, and he cut across the street and onto the grass of the park. On the other side of the willows, deep in shadow, was the soli-tary bench that Whitehall had established as his own.

When Dermott reached the fringe of trees he looked at his watch. By now Whitehall must be finishing the whiskey. Dermott crept slowly between the trees.

He could see Whitehall through the foliage, and for a moment he had the fear that he had mistimed it, that he was late. Then Whitehall moved and some object came hurtling toward Dermott. He ducked, and the hard glass of a whiskey bottle crashed against a willow. Whitehall had finished his pint. Now his dark bulk was fumbling in his pocket for matches.

Dermott tensed, turned his head this way and that. The crucial moment had arrived. If luck held there would be no wandering lovers.

His luck held. The match flared, and Whitehall drew on his cigar. The end of the cigar glowed for an instant. Then Whitehall took the cigar from his mouth, looked at it. He choked once, half rose from the park bench, then fell twisting onto it again. Dermott's heart ham-mered. The diamond—if only the diamond were still there.

By the time Dermott had slipped noiselessly beside him, Whitehall had stopped breathing. Dermott wasted no more than a single glance, dropped to one knee and began to use the screwdriver on the right heel of the dead man's shoe. A moment later the heel came away and a cool hard lump fell into Dermott's hand.

He gasped at the size of it, risked holding it momentarily under the moonlight that filtered through the trees. It glittered with the

524

thousand irridescent lights that perfect gems contain. Dermott thrust it into his coat pocket. He picked up the cigar. Might as well let Popo's hamburgers take the blame for the poisoning.

Then he put the heel back on and began an even, unhurried walk back to his room.

Once there, he set about the final steps of destroying evidence. The cigar was shredded, and cigar and remains of the potassium cyanide were washed down the drain, washed long and carefully, to clear the trap of poison. The poison itself would not be traced. Dermott had flown to California, visited an old school friend who taught analytic chemistry at the university. While looking at the laboratory, the cyanide had somehow found its way into Dermott's possession.

The police would check for poison sales within a radius of two hundred miles, Dermott figured. Unless he were suspected and his actions traced, there was nothing to lead the police to the California laboratories.

And there was nothing to connect him with the crime. Dermott filled the clean vial with aspirin and placed it in his desk drawer, now an innocent receptacle.

The diamond he placed in a small cardboard cylinder. He wrapped this carefully with tape and thrust a copper wire entirely through the cylinder thus developed. Then, opening the back of his radio and pulling the chassis out, he added this to the similar mass of odd condensers and resistors inside. The screwdriver was ordinary; he dropped it with other tools in a drawer.

The pattern was complete. Dermott smiled and began to prepare for bed. He slept as soundly as a baby.

When he arose, the pattern of the night before came back to him, and he checked it again, smiling at the neat perfection of the plan. He would have to show up for the menus, tell Popo he would be leaving at the end of the week. It wouldn't be wise to draw attention by leaving now.

When he reached the grill he found Popo in a dither. The boy was trying to comfort him.

"Hi, kid." Dermott tousled the kid's hair. "What's eatin' your pop?"

Vopopulous waved fat hands wildly. "Police," he shouted. "Police come here and drive all my trade away. It's in the morning paper." He pointed a pudgy, shaking finger at the paper.

Whitehall's body had been found by ten-thirty that night. With their customary vigor, the police had completed identification and a swift autopsy in time to make the final edition of the morning paper.

Dermott ordered coffee, read the article slowly and carefully. According to the analysis, the dead man's last meal had consisted of hamburger, french fries and cyanide. Dermott grinned.

At two o'clock in the afternoon two police detectives were at Dermott's door. He stared unbelievingly at them; then his mind began to click like a well-oiled machine. Certainly he had anticipated this. As a bare possibility, Popo or the kid had mentioned him, and the cops were merely making the routine check of anyone known to have eaten at the grill.

One of the detectives, a big, blond man, said, "Mr. Slade, we want to ask you some questions about a man named Whitehall. You knew him?"

Dermott's breath was tight in his chest. With a little care this would be the final questioning. After all, there was no link between the dead man and himself.

He said, "I didn't know Whitehall, never spoke to him."

"Just what connection did you have with the grill?"

"A slight one," Dermott explained. "I'm looking for a job, something in the advertising line. I don't have a lot of money, and the first time I ate across the street I noticed the greasy, handwritten menus. Popo can't write worth a darn, so I offered to type his menus for meals."

"When do you type these menus?"

"In the afternoon. Popo gives me the copy at breakfast. I go job-hunting the rest of the morning. Then after lunch I type the menus. I take them over to Popo's at supper time."

"Did you take these menus over last night, the night before Whitehall was killed?"

"Yes."

"Did you see Whitehall?"

Dermott considered. "Yes, come to think about it, I did."

"What did he eat?"

Dermott's mind was racing. Popo would have told him about Whitehall's always eating the day's special. That had been hamburger the last couple of days. Might be best not to let them know he had noticed such facts.

"I didn't notice," Dermott said. "The paper said hamburger and french fries. They were on special yesterday and today."

The blond man nodded at his companion. "I guess that does it," he said.

Dermott relaxed. Suspicion would never touch him.

526

The other man came up beside him and took his arm. "You'll have to come to Headquarters with us," he said.

Dermott pulled away, lifted amazed eyes. "But why?" he demanded.

The blond man said softly, "A lot of times when a man writes and is thinking about something else, he writes what he is thinking about without realizing it. I'm afraid you made that mistake. Your confession to Whitehall's murder is on one of those menus. If they were written after he was killed, then anyone might have made a mistake like yours. But you typed this menu before Whitehall ate his fatal meal."

His mind whirling, Dermott lifted his eyes to the menu that was thrust before him. The day's special was before his eyes, the typed letters as black as the maw of a dungeon. In the dim recesses of his mind, imagination flared fiercely, and he could see the tentacles of the law, reaching, plucking a fact here, a fact there, learning about the laboratory in California, finding the jewel after days of combing the room.

He was suddenly aware that sweat had started in the palms of his hands.

The menu read simply:

DELUXE HAMBURGER—
WITH CYANIDE—25c

# The Trailor Murder Mystery

### by Abraham Lincoln

In the year 1841, there resided, at different points in the State of Illinois, three brothers by the name of Trailor. Their Christian names were William, Henry and Archibald. Archibald resided at Springfield, then as now the seat of Government of the State. He was a sober, retiring, and industrious man, of about thirty years of age; a carpenter by trade, and a bachelor, boarding with his partner in business—a Mr. Myers. Henry, a year or two older, was a man of like retiring and industrious habits; had a family, and resided with it on a farm, at Clary's Grove, about twenty miles distant from Springfield in a north-westerly direction. —William, still older, and with similar habits, resided on a farm in Warren county, distant from Springfield something more than a hundred miles in the same North-westerly direction. He was a widower, with several children.

In the neighborhood of William's residence, there was, and had been for several years, a man by the name of Fisher, who was somewhat above the age of fifty; had no family, and no settled home; but who boarded and lodged a while here and a while there, with persons for whom he did little jobs of work. His habits were remarkably economical, so that an impression got about that he had accumulated a considerable amount of money.

In the latter part of May, in the year mentioned, William formed the purpose of visiting his brothers at Clary's Grove and Springfield; and Fisher, at the time having his temporary residence at his house, resolved to accompany him. They set out together in a buggy with a single horse. On Sunday evening they reached Henry's residence, and staid over night. On Monday morning, being the first Monday of June, they started on to Springfield, Henry accompanying them on horseback. They reached town about noon, met Archibald, went with him to his boarding house, and there took up their lodgings for the time they should remain.

After dinner, the three Trailors and Fisher left the boarding house in company, for the avowed purpose of spending the evening together in looking about the town. At supper, the Trailors had all returned, but Fisher was missing, and some inquiry was made about him. After supper, the Trailors went out professedly in search of him. One by one they returned, the last coming in after late tea time, and each stating that he had been unable to discover anything of Fisher.

The next day, both before and after breakfast, they went professedly in search again, and returned at noon, still unsuccessful. Dinner again being had, William and Henry expressed a determination to give up the search, and start for their homes. This was remonstrated against by some of the boarders about the house, on the ground that Fisher was somewhere in the vicinity, and would be left without any conveyance, as he and William had come in the same buggy. The remonstrance was disregarded, and they departed for their homes respectively.

Up to this time, the knowledge of Fisher's mysterious disappearance had spread very little beyond the few boarders at Myers', and excited no considerable interest. After the lapse of three or four days, Henry returned to Springfield, for the ostensible purpose of making further search for Fisher. Procuring some of the boarders, he, together
528

with them and Archibald, spent another day in ineffectual search, when it was again abandoned, and he returned home.

No general interest was yet excited.

On the Friday, week after Fisher's disappearance, the Postmaster at Springfield received a letter from the Postmaster nearest William's residence, in Warren county, stating that William had returned home without Fisher, and was saying, rather boastfully, that Fisher was dead, and had willed him his money, and that he had got about fifteen hundred dollars by it. The letter further stated that William's story and conduct seemed strange, and desired the Postmaster at Springfield to ascertain and write what was the truth in the matter.

The Postmaster at Springfield made the letter public, and at once, excitement became universal and intense. Springfield, at that time, had a population of about 3,500, with a city organization. The Attorney General of the State resided there. A purpose was forthwith formed to ferret out the mystery, in putting which into execution, the Mayor of the city and the Attorney General took the lead. To make search for, and, if possible, find the body of the man supposed to be murdered, was resolved on as the first step.

In pursuance of this, men were formed into large parties, and marched abreast, in all directions, so as to let no inch of ground in the vicinity remain unsearched. Examinations were made of cellars, wells, and pits of all descriptions, where it was thought possible the body might be concealed. All the fresh, or tolerably fresh graves in the graveyard, were pried into, and dead horses and dead dogs were disinterred, where, in some instances, they had been buried by their partial masters.

This search, as has appeared, commenced on Friday. It continued until Saturday afternoon without success, when it was determined to despatch officers to arrest William and Henry, at their residences, respectively. The officers started on Sunday morning, meanwhile, the search for the body was continued, and rumors got afloat of the Trailors having passed, at different times and places, several gold pieces, which were readily supposed to have belonged to Fisher.

On Monday, the officers sent for Henry, having arrested him, arrived with him. The Mayor and Attorney Gen'l took charge of him, and set their wits to work to elicit a discovery from him. He denied, and denied, and persisted in denying. They still plied him in every conceivable way, till Wednesday, when, protesting his own innocence, he stated that his brothers, William and Archibald, had murdered Fisher; that they had killed him, without his (Henry's) knowledge at the time, and made a temporary concealment of his body;

529

that, immediately preceding his and William's departure from Springfield for home, on Tuesday, the day after Fisher's disappearance, William and Archibald communicated the fact to him, and engaged his assistance in making a permanent concealment of the body; that, at the time he and William left professedly for home, they did not take the road directly, but, meandering their way through the streets, entered the woods at the North West of the city, two or three hundred yards to the right of where the road they should have travelled, entered them; that, penetrating the woods some few hundred yards, they halted and Archibald came a somewhat different route, on foot, and joined them; that William and Archibald then stationed him (Henry) on an old and disused road that ran near by, as a sentinel, to give warning of the approach of any intruder; that William and Archibald then removed the buggy to the edge of a dense brush thicket, about forty yards distant from his (Henry's) position, where, leaving the buggy, they entered the thicket, and in a few minutes returned with the body, and placed it in the buggy; that from his station he could and did distinctly see that the object placed in the buggy was a dead man, of the general appearance and size of Fisher; that William and Archibald then moved off with the buggy in the direction of Hickox's mill pond, and after an absence of half an hour, returned, saying they had put him in a safe place; that Archibald then left for town, and he and William found their way to the road, and made for their homes.

At this disclosure, all lingering credulity was broken down, and excitement rose to an almost inconceivable height. Up to this time, the well-known character of Archibald had repelled and put down all suspicions as to him. Till then, those who were ready to swear that a murder had been committed, were almost as confident that Archibald had had no part in it. But now, he was seized and thrown into jail; and indeed, his personal security rendered it by no means objectionable to him.

And now came the search for the brush thicket, and the search of the mill pond. The thicket was found, and the buggy tracks at the point indicated. At a point within the thicket, the signs of a struggle were discovered, and a trail from thence to the buggy track was traced. In attempting to follow the track of the buggy from the thicket, it was found to proceed in the direction of the mill pond, but could not be traced all the way. At the pond, however, it was found that a buggy had been backed down to, and partially into the water's edge.

Search was now to be made in the pond; and it was made in every imaginable way. Hundreds and hundreds were engaged in raking, fish-

530

ing, and draining. After much fruitless effort in this way, on Thursday morning the mill dam was cut down, and the water of the pond partially drawn off, and the same processes of search again gone through with.

About noon of this day, the officer sent for William, returned having him in custody; and a man calling himself Dr. Gilmore, came in company with them. It seems that the officer arrested William at his own house, early in the day on Tuesday, and started to Springfield with him; that after dark awhile, they reached Lewiston, in Fulton county, where they stopped for the night; that late in the night this Dr. Gilmore arrived, stating that Fisher was alive at his house, and that he had followed on to give the information, so that William might be released without further trouble; that the officer, distrusting Dr. Gilmore, refused to release William, but brought him on to Springfield, and the Dr. accompanied them.

On reaching Springfield, the Dr. re-asserted that Fisher was alive, and at his house. At this, the multitude for a time, were utterly confounded. Gilmore's story was communicated to Henry Trailor, who without faltering, reaffirmed his own story about Fisher's murder. Henry's adherence to his own story was communicated to the crowd, and at once the idea started, and became nearly, if not quite universal, that Gilmore was a confederate of the Trailors, and had invented the tale he was telling, to secure their release and escape.

Excitement was again at its zenith.

About three o'clock the same evening, Myers, Archibald's partner, started with a two-horse carriage, for the purpose of ascertaining whether Fisher was alive, as stated by Gilmore, and if so, of bringing him back to Springfield with him.

On Friday a legal examination was gone into before two Justices, on the charge of murder against William and Archibald. Henry was introduced as a witness by the prosecution, and on oath re-affirmed his statements, as heretofore detailed, and at the end of which he bore a thorough and rigid cross-examination without faltering or exposure. The prosecution also proved, by a respectable lady, that on the Monday evening of Fisher's disappearance, she saw Archibald, whom she well knew, and another man whom she did not then know, but whom she believed at the time of testifying to be William, (then present,) and still another, answering the description of Fisher, all enter the timber at the North West of town, (the point indicated by Henry,) and after one or two hours, saw William and Archibald return without Fisher.

Several other witnesses testified, that on Tuesday, at the time William and Henry professedly gave up the search for Fisher's body, and started for home, they did not take the road directly, but did go into the woods, as stated by Henry. By others, also, it was proved, that since Fisher's disappearance, William and Archibald had passed rather an unusual number of gold pieces. The statements heretofore made about the thicket, the signs of a struggle, the buggy tracks, &c., were fully proven by numerous witnesses.

At this the prosecution rested.

Dr. Gilmore was then introduced by the defendants. He stated that he resided in Warren county, about seven miles distant from William's residence; that on the morning of William's arrest, he was out from home, and heard of the arrest, and of its being on a charge of the murder of Fisher; that on returning to his own house, he found Fisher there; that Fisher was in very feeble health, and could give no rational account as to where he had been during his absence; that he (Gilmore) then started in pursuit of the officer, as before stated; and that he should have taken Fisher with him, only that the state of his health did not permit. Gilmore also stated that he had known Fisher for several years, and that he had understood he was subject to temporary derangement of mind, owing to an injury about his head received in early life.

There was about Dr. Gilmore so much of the air and manner of truth, that his statement prevailed in the minds of the audience and of the court, and the Trailors were discharged, although they attempted no explanation of the circumstances proven by the other witnesses.

On the next Monday, Myers arrived in Springfield, bringing with him the now famed Fisher, in full life and proper person.

Thus ended this strange affair and while it is readily conceived that a writer of novels could bring a story to a more perfect climax, it may well be doubted whether a stranger affair ever really occurred. Much of the matter remains in mystery to this day. The going into the woods with Fisher, and returning without him, by the Trailors; their going into the woods at the same place the next day, after they professed to have given up the search; the signs of a struggle in the thicket, the buggy tracks at the edge of it; and the location of the thicket, and the signs about it, corresponding precisely with Henry's story, are circumstances that have never been explained. William and Archibald have both died since—William in less than a year, and Archibald in about two years after the supposed murder. Henry is still living, but never speaks of the subject.

It is not the object of the writer of this to enter into the many curious speculations that might be indulged upon the facts of this narrative; yet he can scarcely forbear a remark upon what would, almost certainly, have been the fate of William and Archibald, had Fisher not been found alive. It seems he had wandered away in mental derangement, and, had he died in this condition, and his body been found in the vicinity, it is difficult to conceive what could have saved the Trailors from the consequence of having murdered him. Or, if he had died, and his body never found, the case against them would have been quite as bad, for, although it is a principle of law that a conviction for murder shall not be had, unless the body of the deceased be discovered, it is to be remembered, that Henry testified that he saw Fisher's dead body.

# A Tulip in the Snow

*by John McCurnin*

The yellow eyes of the big sedan shone brightly on the criss-cross puzzle of automobile tracks in the new fallen snow. Here and there, warmly lit windows blinked by through the branches of front lawn evergreens. Street lamps, getting farther apart now, stood like desolate sentinels against the low hanging horizon.

Behind the wheel, his face a sullen mask in the glow of the dash light, a man broke the speed of the big sedan around a sharp corner and then let it out across the city limits and out into the flat, snow-covered countryside.

At his side, another man hunched his red head deeper into his pulled-up coat collar and shifted two trench spades in his freckled hands to an easier riding position.

In the back seat two indistinct forms rode in silence, and in the flare of a match lighting a cigarette, a dapper young man in a leather jacket, derby hat, and white scarf cast a sharp, searching glance at the man on the seat beside him. Instantly, he recognized the sunken cheeks and high face bones of his older companion and his seeking eyes narrowed. It was Bleeker—lieutenant and Number One rod-man for Stoney Joe Hellman. Bleeker's presence meant something was underway, that Stoney Joe trusted only to Bleeker or to himself.

For only a moment the face of the younger man showed the expression of a trapped animal and then relaxed again into a practiced carelessness. He forced a laugh, an almost self-mocking laugh, and tried to sound casual. "So it's Bleeker—Big Gun Bleeker," he said nervously flippant. "Where are we going, Bleeker?"

Bleeker sucked in on his cigarette and let the smoke curl out. "To Joe's. Joe wants you," he said dryly. Each word was spoken so that it hung by itself, complete and alone.

The younger man grew silent and turning his sleek, thin face to the window, watched the telephone poles flashing by and the snow, like a great white sheet streaking away from the car. Nervously, his hands stole into his jacket pockets and for a moment he fingered the loose tulip bulbs he'd bought only an hour before. If only he'd stayed in the hideout tonight instead of going out for those bulbs. If he didn't have that crazy yen for red tulips, blood red tulips, he'd have stayed in and Joe would still be looking for him. Still, he had the yen and the bulbs had to be planted quick—should have been planted before now, before the first snow. And then, sooner or later Joe would have caught up with him. Joe was like that.

The big sedan swerved, half skidded, and the trench spades grated together as it straightened into a side road and rolled on. At the sight of the side road, a strange, ominous feeling whipped through him and he turned and gazed thoughtfully through the window at the endless stretch of flint-colored sky.

He knew, now, where they were and he knew how barren and deserted the river-end of Joe's country place was. He knew, because other times he had sat where Bleeker was now, ready to do the job Bleeker was going to handle. A shudder chilled through him at the thought of the lonely spot but quickly he tried to think of something else, tried to shake off the yellow streak that was creeping slowly down his back.

Then he saw the open maw of the river ahead and the car turned off the side road. Scrub brush scraped the fenders and the big sedan rolled and lurched over uneven ground. Then trees closed over them and they stopped. The driver cut off the lights and they waited.

He could hear the river, now, close by, muddy and full, rushing recklessly on with the load of the late fall rains. He strained his sleek, thin face toward the window and tried to see it but the small haw trees on the bank cut off his view.

Bleeker lit a cigarette and he could feel Bleeker's cold eyes on him through the darkness. "Why did you kill Joe's kid brother?" Bleeker finally asked.

534

The blunt question jolted him and he could feel the flush of hot blood in his face. But why blow up? Joe knew. Bleeker knew. They knew everything the cops didn't know. "Gimme a cigarette," he said, trying to settle down.

Bleeker handed him the pack and lit a match. "Why did you kill him?" he asked again.

The younger man pulled deeply on the cigarette. "I didn't intend to," he answered, letting the smoke out. "But he was cutting me out with Joe. I aimed low. Thought maybe I could scare him yellow so he wouldn't rate with Joe anymore."

"But you hit him clean. In the head."

"I didn't aim right."

"I wish I could aim wrong like that," Bleeker said. "Joe's been a kill-crazy maniac ever since the kid died."

A black form, straight and tall, crunched through the snow out of a pine thicket, stopped, flashed a light, and moved on toward the car. Even in the dim reflection light of the snow he could almost see Joe's ultra neat, expertly tailored figure, his smart homberg hat, and he could remember the feel of the expensive cloth Joe's clothes were made of. But that was Joe all over. Nothing too good for Joe. Strictly imported fabrics made strictly to his own design by only the best tailors. Even his buttons had to be just right—exclusive.

"Okay, Bleeker," Joe said, opening the door. "Let's go."

Bleeker pulled his feet back to let the younger man out first. The other doors opened and the trench spades grated together harshly as the red-headed man laid them on the ground. All the feeling had gone out of his legs now and he was conscious of a dull, violent silence. His breath stopped. So this was how it was—

"Joe!" he suddenly sputtered. "Listen, Joe. I didn't mean to kill the kid—"

"Ready, Bleeker?" Joe cut him off.

"Joe! Listen, Joe—" Desperately he grabbed the front of Joe's coat. Joe's powerful hands reached up and slowly he could feel his hold pried loose, his hands dragging down the front of Joe's heavy, exclusively tailored coat. One of his clutching hands clung to a button and the hand locked in a helpless grip. Roughly, an open hand uppercut caught him full on the chin and he reeled weakly backward.

"For a rod that could eat a steak a half hour after handling a job, you look pretty good, Guido," Joe sneered.

The uppercut blow and the caustic tone of Joe's voice stopped him and he groped for control. "Okay, Joe," he said thickly. "Where do I get it?"

"Go to the house," Joe commanded. Then to the driver and the red-headed man: "Stay here."

Bleeker flashed a light toward the path Joe's tracks had made and he started, his hands feeling the loose tulip bulbs in his pockets.

Joe and Bleeker followed, one on either side, Bleeker flashing the torch so he could pick his way.

They shot him in the back of the head just under the brim of his derby hat, right near the pine thicket, and for only a second his clenched hands shot upward; he lunged once to the right, once to the left, right again, and then crumpled.

And with each lunge, his head had spilled a bright red splotch over the white snow, brilliant, like the deep red of a Dutch tulip lying on a white tablecloth.

The driver and the red-headed man with the freckled hands buried him there in a shallow grave in the soggy wet earth under the snow and within an hour the spot was as lonely and deserted as it had been for months and years before.

April came and the swollen river almost overflowed its banks with the spring thaw. May came and the marsh grass turned to livid green. June came and a boy, barefooted, with overall pants rolled up to his knees, stopped and dropped his fishing line into the river just near the row of small haw trees along the banks.

And when his young eyes fell on a single, deep red tulip blooming near the pine thicket, he arose at once and wondered what his chances were of digging it up and transplanting it to his own front yard at home. With his bare hands, he dug carefully around the roots, and he kept digging until his eyes, horrified, glued themselves on a hand, a human hand, holding the bulb from which the deep red tulip had grown.

In the other hand, the police found one large, imported horn button and it was of such an exclusive design that they had very little trouble in tracing down the tailor that had sewn it on the coat of the ultra neat, well-tailored man who had ordered it—exclusively.

# The Umbrosa Burglary

*by R. C. Lehmann*

During one of my short summer holidays I happened to be spending a few days at the delightful riverside residence of my friend James Silver, the extent of whose hospitality is only to be measured by the excellence of the fare that he sets before his guests, or by the varied amusements that he provides for them. The beauties of Umbrosa (for that is the attractive name of his house) are known to all those who during the summer months pass up (or down) the winding reaches of the Upper Thames. It was there that I witnessed a series of startling events which threw the whole country into a temporary turmoil. Had it not been for the unparalleled coolness and sagacity of Picklock Holes the results might have been fraught with disaster to many distinguished families, but the acumen of Holes saved the situation and the family plate, and restored the peace of mind of one of the best fellows in the world.

The party at Umbrosa consisted of the various members of the Silver family, including, besides Mr. and Mrs. Silver, three high-spirited and unmarried youths and two charming girls. Picklock Holes was of course one of the guests. In fact, it had long since come to be an understood thing that wherever I went Holes should accompany me in the character of a professional detective on the look-out for business; and James Silver, though he may have at first resented the calm unmuscularity of my marvellous friend's immovable face, would have been the last man in the world to spoil any chance of sport or excitement by refraining from offering a cordial invitation to Holes. The party was completed by Peter Bowman, a lad of eighteen, who to an extraordinary capacity for mischief added an imperturbable cheerfulness of manner. He was generally known as Shockheaded Peter, in allusion to the brush-like appearance of his delicate auburn hair, but his intimate friends sometimes addressed him as Venus, a nickname which he thoroughly deserved by the almost classic irregularity of his Saxon features.

We were all sitting, I remember, on the riverbank, watching the countless craft go past, and enjoying that pleasant industrious indolence which is one of the chief charms of life on the Thames. A punt had just skimmed by, propelled by an athletic young fellow in boating costume. Suddenly Holes spoke.

"It is strange," he said, "that the man should be still at large."

"What man? Where? How?" we all exclaimed breathlessly.

"The young puntsman," said Holes, with an almost aggravating coolness. "He is a bigamist, and has murdered his great aunt."

"It cannot be," said Mr. Silver, with evident distress. "I know the lad well, and a better fellow never breathed."

"I speak the truth," said Holes, unemotionally. "The induction is perfect. He is wearing a red tie. That tie was not always red. It was, therefore, stained by something. Blood is red. It was, therefore, stained by blood. Now it is well known that the blood of great aunts is of a lighter shade, and the colour of that tie has a lighter shade. The blood that stained it was, therefore, the blood of his great aunt. As for the bigamy, you will have noticed that as he passed he blew two rings of cigarette smoke, and they both floated in the air *at the same time*. A ring is a symbol of matrimony. Two rings together mean bigamy. He is, therefore, a bigamist."

For a moment we were silent, struck with horror at this dreadful, this convincing revelation of criminal infamy. Then I broke out:

"Holes," I said, "you deserve the thanks of the whole community. You will of course communicate with the police."

"No," said Holes, "they are fools, and I do not care to mix myself up with them. Besides, I have other fish to fry."

Saying this, he led me to a secluded part of the grounds, and whispered in my ear.

"Not a word of what I am about to tell you. There will be a burglary here to-night."

"But Holes," I said, startled in spite of myself at the calm omniscience of my friend, "had we not better do something; arm the servants, warn the police, bolt the doors and bar the windows, and sit up with blunderbusses—anything would be better than this state of dreadful expectancy. May I not tell Mr. Silver?"

"Potson, you are amiable, but you will never learn my methods." And with that enigmatic reply I had to be content in the meantime.

The evening had passed as pleasantly as evenings at Umbrosa always pass. There had been music; the Umbrosa choir, composed of members of the family and guests, had performed in the drawing-room, and Peter had drawn tears from the eyes of every one by his touching rendering of the well-known songs of "The Dutiful Son" and

538

"The Cartridge-bearer." Shortly afterwards, the ladies retired to bed, and the gentlemen, after the customary interval in the smoking-room, followed. We were in high good-humour, and had made many plans for the morrow. Only Holes seemed preoccupied.

I had been sleeping for about an hour, when I was suddenly awakened with a start. In the passage outside I heard the voices of the youngest Silver boy and of Peter.

"Peter, old chap," said Johnny Silver, "I believe there's burglars in the house. Isn't it a lark?"

"Ripping," said Peter. "Have you told your people?"

"Oh, it's no use waking the governor and the mater; we'll do the job ourselves. I told the girls, and they've all locked themselves in and got under their beds, so they're safe. Are you ready?"

"Yes."

"Come on then."

With that they went along the passage and down the stairs. My mind was made up, and my trousers and boots were on in less time than it takes to tell it. I went to Holes's room and entered. He was lying on his bed, fully awake, dressed in his best detective suit, with his fingers meditatively extended, and touching one another.

"They're here," I said.

"Who?"

"The burglars."

"As I thought," said Holes, selecting his best basket-hilted life-preserver from a heap in the middle of the room. "Follow me silently."

I did so. No sooner had we reached the landing, however, than the silence was broken by a series of blood-curdling screams.

"Good heavens!" was all I could say.

"Hush," said Holes. I obeyed him. The screams subsided, and I heard the voices of my two young friends, evidently in great triumph.

"Lie still, you brute," said Peter, "or I'll punch your blooming head. Give the rope another twist, Johnny. That's it. Now you cut and tell your governor and old Holes that we've nabbed the beggar."

By this time the household was thoroughly roused. Agitated females and inquisitive males streamed downstairs. Lights were lit, and a remarkable sight met our eyes. In the middle of the drawing-room lay an undersized burglar, securely bound, with Peter sitting on his head.

"Johnny and I collared the beggar," said Peter, "and bowled him over. Thanks, I think I could do with a ginger-beer."

The man was of course tried and convicted, and Holes received the thanks of the County Council.

"That fellow," said the great detective to me, "was the best and cleverest of my tame team of country-house burglars. Through him and his associates I have fostered and foiled more thefts than I care to count. Those infernal boys nearly spoilt everything. Potson, take my advice, never attempt a master-stroke in a houseful of boys. They can't understand scientific induction. Had they not interfered I should have caught the fellow myself. He had wired to tell me where I should find him."

# Waiting

*Jim Knapp*

There was another murder last night.

I was powerless to stop it. I wanted to stop it, but I couldn't. It happened.

I had waited in the dark, empty house for hours. My mind was screaming "Another woman will not die tonight." But another woman had died.

You can read about it in today's newspaper. The article is very sketchy. The victim's name was withheld pending notification of family members, but you don't need to read the paper. I can tell you about the victim. She was middle-aged and financially affluent. And her husband is in the hospital. When she came home alone after visiting hours . . . well it didn't take long. The struggles are always brief and they really don't suffer much. A distraught, unsuspecting, middle-aged woman is no match for an attacker trained in martial arts.

After her struggles stopped and the doughy mound of lifeless flesh lay sprawled on the kitchen floor it was a simple matter to remove all the valuables. There was the whole night to remove cash and jewelry and . . . anything else.

Now I might as well say right here that the motive for these killings isn't robbery. The cops have figured out that much. I know a police detective and he tells me things. He probably tells me things he shouldn't, but we're friends. The police shrinks have done a psychological profile of the killer. They figure it's a male, in his thirties, with an intense hatred of his mother. She was probably wealthy and
540

she most likely rejected him. That's why his victims are always wealthy. It's also why they're in their sixties or seventies.

This was the eleventh killing. I hope it will be the last. I hope I can stop more from happening.

The first victim was Vivian Fairgate. She was murdered on June third, nineteen-ninety; that was thirteen months ago. The killer had waited in the still darkness until she returned home from the hospital. Then he snapped her neck.

I had to find out exactly what the police knew about last night's murder. Grabbing the phone I punched in the number to my cop buddy. He answered on the third ring. His voice had the mellow raspiness of a heavy cigarette smoker. "Homicide. Detective Newman."

"Hi, Eddie. Me. You on the Elwood case?"

"Yeah."

"Anything new?"

"You know, buddy, I think you're starting to take advantage of me. I've talked to you more than I should because we've been friends for a long time and because of, you know, what happened. But I keep this up I'm gonna end up with my ass in a jam."

There was too much at stake to allow him to put me off. "Anything new?" I asked again. I had to know.

"Jesus. You don't quit. O.K. Same M.O. They were pretty well off. Not servants and homes all over the world and invitations to the whitehouse rich, but they were very high into the upper-middle class. Nice home, cottage at the lake, winters in Florida kinda rich. Husband in the hospital. That goddamn rag of a newspaper won't quit printing hospital admissions. We asked nice, and we threatened nasty, but they say it's policy. Freaking policy littering the city with bodies! What crap!

"Anyway, no signs of forced entry. The dame walks in, the perp is waiting inside, and he snaps her neck. He steals enough stuff to simulate a robbery. No prints, no witnesses, no nothing. Not enough of a time pattern to project with any accuracy when he'll strike again. I guess it's just our bad fortune that we live in such an affluent burg. Not enough manpower to stake out every rich dame whose husband just died or was admitted to the hospital or whatever. We need a little luck."

"Thanks, Eddie. I guess I've got a morbid interest."

"Listen, buddy, take my advice. Think about something else. This doesn't concern you, it really doesn't. Let it lie. Take up fishing. One heart attack should be enough to make a guy your age wise up. Life's

541

too short. Learn to relax. If I had your money I'd take a nice long trip."

"Maybe you're right," I said. But of course I wouldn't be able to let it lie. It wasn't that simple. And I suspect he knew it, too.

Sure I had had a heart attack. Damn near cashed in. But that was over a year ago and I'm in better shape now than I was when I was forty. When I got out of the hospital I started walking. Then I worked my way up to jogging. Even took up Tai-Chi; an exercise regime and life-style that promotes good health and harmony with the world but is also a deadly Chinese form of the martial arts. There's another hobby, too, that Eddie doesn't know about; I took a mail order course. I'm a bonafide locksmith.

One month later the hospital admissions section of the newspaper reported that Elton L. Collier III had been taken by ambulance to St. Mary's Hospital, the victim of a severe stroke.

I paced most of the afternoon. I should leave town. I should get drunk. I should get this terrible pounding voice out of my head. Why couldn't I stop myself from doing what I knew I would do.

At three o'clock in the afternoon I clipped the phone line to the Collier residence, rendering the burglar alarm ineffective, and used my locksmith picks to let myself into the lovely, silent home.

Then I waited. Waited as I had waited in other elegant, lonely homes. Waited while the grandfather clock ticked and the air conditioner cycled on and off. Waited while the automatic ice maker dumped its load into the plastic bin. Watched as light reflected off the shimmering surface of the back-yard swimming pool. Waited with old hands sweating in rubber gloves. Waited while a grieving and terrified woman kept vigil by a hospital bed wondering if the man she shared her life with would ever return to her . . . would ever be the same.

Shadows grew longer as the sun dropped lower in the sky. A dog barked a few houses away as he welcomed his master home from work. A lawn sprinkler came on across the street. Still I waited.

Darkness came. It would be another two hours before visiting hours ended. Finally, there was a scrape at the kitchen door. Someone was coming in. I moved on rubber soled shoes and was waiting when the door opened.

He was in his mid-thirties. Just like the police psychologist said. He wore dark clothes and rubber gloves. No mask needed. He never left a witness.

Before he had time to react to my presence I buried a fist in his stomach, paralyzing his diaphragm. With practiced moves I snapped

542

his neck. I did it quickly and cleanly and with no remorse, only the faster beating of my heart. Hoisting his limp body to my shoulders I carried him to the second floor and dropped him—head first—off the balcony onto the apron of the swimming pool.

Then I carefully locked up, hauled my sixty-five-year-old frame to my own lonely home, and mixed a very dry martini in a heavy highball glass. Light from the crystal chandelier above rainbowed from the tumbler as I raised it in salute to the painting on the wall, the portrait of my deceased beloved, and I said aloud, "Well, Vivian, maybe we can both rest now."

The phone woke me the next morning. It was Eddie Newman. Detective-First. "I got some news, old buddy. It's over. The guy that killed your wife is dead. He was apparently trying to climb up to a balcony to gain entrance to an upper bedroom. He slipped and the fall broke his neck. I wish we'd nailed him and put him away forever; but we had the wrong house staked out again. Well, at least he's out of circulation."

"Yes," I said. "Thanks."

The waiting was over.


# While the Cat's Away—

*by Dorothy Dunn*


Bill Vogel was slumped over his kitchen table asleep. He looked just the way he'd looked last night when I left him—only messier, more bleary-eyed.

I waded across empty bottles and shook him. He flung out an arm, knocking a glass over. The last flat highball that he'd passed out on spilled out, soaking into the cloth.

"Come out of it, Bill! This is the third day. You're beginning to look like a good corner for spiders."

"Go away, Julien," he muttered. "You're always bothering me. Stop bothering people. Quit shaking me!"

"Look at this mess, Bill. Nine o'clock in the morning. The sun coming in on all this. It stinks."

"Damn the sun!"

"And you, Bill. Don't know which is worse, this smelly kitchen or you. Come on. At least take a shower and get into some clean clothes. Martha's coming home today."

"Have a drink, Julien. And if you don't like the odor around here, just scram."

"I will. But if you think I'm going to let Martha find you this way, you're nuts."

Bill gave me a sly look out of his puffy eyes.

"Whaddaya care how Martha finds me?"

"She's my sister, Bill."

"And my wife. I got the most say."

"Granted. Look, Bill, don't get the idea I'm interfering. I just know you wouldn't want her to find you this way. You'll thank me later."

"I'll thank you to mind your own business."

"I'm doing that. Martha is my . . ."

"Cut it out, Julien. You're a little ridiculous, you know." He fumbled toward the half-emptied bottle of bourbon and got it to his mouth with a trembling hand. "Brrr!" he shuddered, as it went down. "Hair of the dog . . ."

"What got you off on this bat?" I asked, now that he seemed fully awake. "Just because Martha took a little trip to see the folks is no reason for you to get blind."

"I'm not blind."

"Okay—so you're not blind. But you've certainly been on a bat."

"Not funny, Julien."

"Not meant to be," I said. "Look fella, this isn't at all like you. What started it, anyway?"

"Own business. Remember?"

He waved an imperious arm toward the door. I agreed with him. It was his own business if he wanted to stay drunk forever. But this was different. Martha was coming home today and she'd be sore as a new blister if she found Bill in this condition. She hated drinking so much that she might even be sore enough to leave him, and I didn't want that to happen.

She was arriving on the early afternoon train. I had just four hours to get Bill cleaned up and out of the mood. Four hours to do that and clean up the kitchen. I'd need a shovel for that, I thought.

After much protest, Bill gave in with a nasty smile. At two o'clock I was plenty tired, but we were ready for Martha. He looked quite decent in a blue flannel sport shirt and gabardine slacks fresh from the cleaners. The smell of shaving lotion didn't kill the alcohol odor, but what's a couple of beers among friends? I had a bottle beside me to back him up.

We were ready. I had scrubbed the linoleum, washed a mountain of dishes, and walked blocks to throw the empties in somebody else's ash pit.

"You think of everything, Julien," said Bill, as we sat there waiting. "One would think you were setting a stage. What a mind for details!"

"Ordinary," I told him.

"Maybe," he said, lighting a cigarette and holding it over the stained places on his hand. "But I'd say that it's more than ordinary. Tell me, why all the pains? What's it to you that you spend four hours of your pleasure-loving life to keep me out of the dog house? What's your angle?"

"Charity," I said, "begins at home."

"In a pig's eye."

"Martha's my sister. She hates drunks and she's not good at concealing her hates."

"No," said Bill, running a shaking hand across his face. "She's not good at concealing things, is she?"

Something about the way he said that frightened me. He looked bitter and harassed, as though the bottom had dropped out of his dream house.

"What's wrong, Bill? What's eating you that you break one of Martha's commandments? You've been a good boy for the two years you've been married to her. Why the sudden urge for a binge?"

He shook himself back to attention. God knows what he'd been thinking about. I doubt if he'd heard much of what I'd said until the last part.

"Good boy, Julien. Yes, indeed! I've been a model husband, wouldn't you say?"

"Martha thinks so, no doubt about that. That's why I . . ."

"Stuck your nose in this morning?"

"Skip it," I said, getting sore. "I should have let you wallow . . ."

"Yes," he said pointedly. "You should have. I feel like the devil now."

I tried to be sympathetic.

"Want something to eat?" He looked like he hadn't taken anything solid for days. His cheek bones seemed higher and his face was drawn. "I could fix you a sandwich."

He winced. "Have a heart, Julien. And stop banging your fingers on that table!"

"Sorry. But isn't that train late? She was due in at two. It's almost three now."

Bill just sat there, looking miserable. At last he said: "All right, Julien, you asked for it. You had to hang around and wait. You had to clean house and play nurse and now you've had your fun. The joke's on you. *Martha isn't coming back!*"

"You're kidding!" I said, getting to my feet angrily. "Martha called me the day she left and told me she'd be back on the fifteenth at two o'clock."

Bill grinned unpleasantly. "Why should I kid, Julien? She's not coming back—ever."

I didn't get it. I looked around at the house. All the stuff she'd accumulated through the two years of her marriage. The silver coffee service, the rosewood desk that she'd talked out of Grandma, the sewing basket with her crochet needle stuck through a ball of thread. If she'd been leaving Bill for good, she'd not have left any of the possessions she liked so much. Not Martha. She was as acquisitive as a squirrel and you could never pry her loose from so much as an empty candy box.

"Where is she?" I asked.

Bill just shrugged and that made me furious.

"Don't you even know whether or not she arrived safely in Peoria?" I asked. "Did you hear from her, or from the folks?"

"Not a thing, Julien. But they're your folks. Did you get any word?"

"No, but I'm on the black list with my family. You know that. Do you mean to say that your wife has been missing for a week and all you've done about it is soak your head in bourbon?"

"Something like that," said Bill.

"You don't care?"

"Why should I?"

He had me there. Martha is my sister, but I don't like her much. She's overbearing. However, I was anxious for her to get home and be on good terms with Bill. I wanted that desperately because I needed money again. Bill wouldn't let me have it, but Martha would draw it out of her personal account the minute I spoke the word. She'd have to do it. I'm probably the only person in the world who knows that she killed her first husband to collect his insurance.

I sat around for another hour, stewing.

"Aren't you worried, Bill?"

"Worried? Why should I be? Martha can take care of herself. She's quite a self-sufficient woman."

546

"Yes—she is."

Bill didn't know the half of that. Martha had plenty of money he didn't know anything about, and she'd got it all for herself. But I wanted to know where she was. I'd been banking on getting the five thousand I owed in gambling debts from her.

"Why don't you phone Peoria, Bill? Find out from the folks if she's there."

He gave me a silly, disinterested smile.

"Call them yourself, Julien. They're your folks and you're the one that's worried. I'm not."

I thought about the folks and decided against it. They were stiff-necked and grim. I didn't like them any better than I did Martha. But I needed money.

"How do you know she's not coming back, Bill?"

"Because I told her not to," he said, taking a shot of whiskey to chase down with his beer.

"You put up with Martha for two years and then decide that your marriage is a flop? Just like that? Why did you wait so long if you wanted a divorce?"

"She never tried to kill me before," said Bill calmly.

I gasped. If I hadn't known about Martha's first husband, I'd have thought Bill was pulling another one of his bum jokes. Like letting me clean up the house. But I could see my sister in the role too plainly. I knew her hunger for possessions, her passion for money. Nothing else counted with Martha. But I tried to act shocked.

"Are you sure, Bill?"

"Sure I'm sure! I hadn't intended to tell you, but if you're going to sit around here asking stupid questions, you might as well know. Cyanide, Julien. Lovely stuff, cyanide. Especially if you drop it into your husband's tea."

"Good Lord, Bill! Why, just a drop of that stuff . . ."

He took another drink.

"How right you are. Just a drop or two. I was just lucky. I saw her putting it into the cup with an eye dropper, and she didn't know I was standing at the door."

"Maybe you were mistaken," I said. "Maybe it wasn't cyanide at all."

"Oh, no, Julien, my boy. I was too smart for her. I told her if she'd get my check book I'd leave her a blank one for any shopping she wanted to do. As soon as she left the table, I poured the tea into an empty mayonnaise jar and slipped it into my coat pocket. When she came back, she thought I'd drunk it. That was very amusing, Julien!

You should have seen her face—the expectant gleam in her eyes as she waited for me to die. I believe she'd have told people I committed suicide. It was a lot of fun fooling her, Julien. You've no idea."

"You're getting drunk again," I cautioned.

"Sure. Sure I am! And why not? I had that little mayonnaise jar, remember? And I own a drug store. Also a diploma for pharmacy. It wasn't much of a trick for me to analyze a cup of tea! It was loaded with cyanide. So I told her to get out and stay out. Would you care for a drink, Julien?"

I poured some of his whiskey into a shot glass and drained it. Then at his insistence, I took another. There was a strange kind of excitement coming over me then. I decided to forget about Peoria and trying to find Martha to get my five thousand. Maybe I had a bird in the hand. Right here. Maybe I was going to get something on Bill that would be worth a little change.

"Terrible thing to have happened to you, Bill. I can't understand it. She must have gone out of her head to try a thing like that. I just can't imagine Martha attempting . . ."

"Can't you, Julien? Even if she was doing it for money?"

"Money? You don't have that kind of money," I said. "Not the kind people murder to get. Or do you?"

I wanted to know about Bill's money right then. How much he had, how deep I might be able to cut into him later on. I needed a permanent source.

He just laughed. "Insurance is money, Julien. Just like money to the beneficiary. I'm worth twenty thousand dollars on a slab. Imagine that? Martha placed a high value on her husband, didn't she?"

"Martha?"

"Yes. She said she believed in insurance and she talked me into taking the policy. Lovely girl, Martha. So practical about the future. Incidentally, Julien—"

"Yes?"

"Why don't you resent these accusations I'm making against your sister? You were certainly being solicitous about her feelings this morning."

I gulped down another shot before I answered, trying to get my angles figured out. I wondered vaguely if Bill had done away with Martha—if they'd had a violent quarrel and he'd killed her. It just didn't seem logical to me that she'd have left the house without taking her own belongings with her. Not sister Martha.

"Resent what you're saying, Bill? Why should I, if you're telling the truth?"

548

He gave me a steady stare.

"Why should I lie?"

I didn't know why he should lie, but there was a look about him that didn't quite ring true. I got up and paced the room nervously, wondering how far I could go with him. There was a huge oak chest in front of the windows, beautifully carved and as mellow as a museum piece. Martha counted it as her prize possession and would never sell it, although it was worth a lot of money. Something else she'd wormed out of Grandma. If she'd gone away of her own volition, she'd have taken that chest with her, I knew that.

I walked toward it, wondering what was kept inside. But Bill's voice made me freeze, my hand outstretched.

"Stay away from that window, Julien!" he yelled.

I had that funny feeling that stays in your system for a few minutes after you've been startled. But I had another feeling, too, as I went back to my chair and looked at Bill's face. His breathing was ragged and he looked white. He wasn't acting now. He'd been very much afraid that I'd open the chest.

"The window, Bill?" I teased. "You meant the chest, didn't you? You meant don't touch the chest. Right?"

He didn't answer. He just stared moodily into his glass. But I was sure I was right. The chest was about six feet long, I noticed. About three feet deep. I felt pretty confident all at once, pretty sure of myself.

"Interesting piece of furniture," I drawled. "Grandma used to tell wild tales about the way it came into her possession. It's out of a royal house in Spain, according to her. All hooked up with pirates and bloodshed. Martha was crazy about it."

"The bloodshed—or the chest?" he asked.

I smiled.

"The chest, Bill. She'd never have gone off for good without that chest."

He gave me a strange look.

"Something on your mind, Julien?"

I nodded, glad that the showdown was here.

"There's five thousand dollars on my mind," I told him. "I was very fond of Martha."

"And you'd be satisfied with money instead of justice?"

"Sometimes a man takes justice into his own hands," I said with a shrug. "If she tried to poison you—well, I can see your point. I'm the only person in town who would ever think of looking for Martha, or

549

reporting her disappearance to the police. You know how the folks are. They're glad when they don't hear from their ungrateful children. And if you'd like to pay me five thousand dollars for—well, for cleaning your house this morning . . ."

"Why five thousand, Julien? That's little enough for that type of work. Would you want more later?"

"No . . . no, indeed. But if I have five thousand, I can clear up a certain debt that's pressing."

I wished I'd made it ten thousand right off the bat. They always yelp when you ask for the second payment.

Bill filled two glasses and we raised them in a mock toast.

"You're a bright boy, Julien. You keep your eyes open."

"Or closed, according to the price." I was feeling pretty good. I'd just got another idea. "Incidentally, Bill, I believe I have another little item you'd be interested in buying for another five thousand. It would be very cheap at that price because it might insure your safety later."

"Safety insurance?" asked Bill.

"Yes. I have a little gadget that's real evidence against Martha— positive proof of her guilt in another matter."

Bill's eyes half-closed and he tensed in his chair.

"I see you're interested," I said.

"Depending on what the evidence is and what it proves."

"It's an eye-dropper with some cyanide left in it, with Martha's fingerprints on the glass part. It proves that Martha killed her first husband—Avery Chandler."

"That's very interesting," he said. "I'd heard that Chandler committed suicide. I suppose he had a lot of insurance?"

"Yes, he did have. But the insurance company couldn't prove Martha's guilt. They paid off. Now suppose you were ever arrested for killing your wife—just a supposition, of course—this evidence wouldn't exonerate you. But it would help sway the jury, lighten the sentence."

"I can see that it would," said Bill. "You know, my insurance policy has a suicide clause, too. I've forgotten what arguments Martha advanced to have it included, but I didn't suspect her at the time and let it go through. Later, I began to wonder about it."

"Lucky for you that you wondered, Bill. Do you think ten thousand is too much for my complete—uh—cooperation?"

"Not at all, Julien. I consider my life is worth that much. You see, I was in a very strange position. I couldn't have Martha locked up because I couldn't prove that she'd put the cyanide in my tea. My story would have sounded foolish if she had denied it. And I couldn't just let her go free, either, because I'm sure she'd have tried it again. At the moment, I couldn't accuse her of murder. No murder without a body, you know."

I looked at the carved chest pointedly, sure that Martha was there.

"But where you have a body," I said, "you have a very dangerous set-up. Will you write a check, Bill, or would you rather draw out the cash tomorrow?"

"Cash, I think. Unless you'd be able to get that evidence over here tonight?"

"Afraid I couldn't do that," I told him. "It's in my safe-deposit box and the bank's closed." I needed time to go out and buy an eye-dropper and there wasn't any point in looking too anxious.

"Tomorrow, then," said Bill, reaching out to shake hands.

I wasn't expecting it. He jerked me off my feet in a quick judo twist over his knee. Then he tied me to a straight chair and walked over to the chest behind my back. I could feel my scalp crawling as I heard the lid of the oak chest creaking. Surely, he wasn't going to kill me and dump me in there beside Martha to await a fool-proof method of disposal! But maybe he was. I'd been an idiot to tell him so much. He knew that the folks wouldn't bother to look for me, either. And he'd only been pretending to be drunk. I felt sure of that now.

My back was toward the chest and I couldn't jog my chair around. I could just hear the noise of the lid and the scraping footsteps around it.

Then Bill came over to the desk and took a gun from the side drawer. He flipped the chamber open, making sure it was loaded.

"Don't shoot me, Bill! I'll give you the evidence for nothing . . . I'll . . ."

"Stop whining, Julien. Of course you'll produce that evidence for nothing. You've probably bled Martha for years. I've always wondered how you managed to live without working."

"I'll give it to you, Bill! Only don't kill me the way you did Martha!"

He worked his jaw back and forth and then swung my chair around so that I could see the chest.

It took a little while for me to understand, for the panic to strike. The small man sitting on the lid had yellow-colored hair and looked a lot like Avery Chandler, Martha's first husband. But it wasn't Avery. I knew that. It was Tom Chandler, Avery's brother.

"I see that you recognize me, Julien," he said.

"Yes. But I don't understand . . ."

Tom Chandler's laugh was bitter.

"You don't? Then I'll tell you, Julien. When my brother died three years ago, I was sure he hadn't committed suicide, that Martha had murdered him. But I couldn't prove it. I decided to play a waiting game and spent a good bit of money having you watched. Finally, I realized that Martha was paying you blackmail and decided that you must be the one who had evidence."

I felt trapped and cheated. I turned to Bill.

"You were lying, weren't you? About Martha trying to kill you."

"No, Julien, I wasn't lying. I did see her load the tea with poison. The only difference in the story is this. I didn't say anything to her about it. I just encouraged her to take the trip to see her ailing grandmother. Then I did some checking with the insurance company. Through them, I got in touch with Tom Chandler and we decided to concentrate on you for what we wanted. I believe we have that now. The police can get an order to open your lock box at the bank."

"You had Chandler hidden in the chest to listen? Was that it?"

"To listen and record. There's a dictaphone in there, too. That's why I wanted you to keep away from the window. I was afraid you'd trip on the wires. But your type of mind has to jump at its own sneaking conclusions."

Then my senses returned and I realized they didn't have anything that would hurt me. It had been Martha that killed Avery Chandler— not me.

"Suppose you untie me, Bill, and stop being dramatic. I haven't killed anybody."

"Just sit still, Julien. Martha's due home any minute. She wired that she'd be here on the late train instead of two o'clock and asked especially that I have you wait for her."

Tom Chandler went to the phone and called the police. "We're ready now," he said. The two plain-clothes men got there just before Martha's cab drew up.

She came in with a big smile, telling the taxi driver to be careful with her bag.

"Greetings!" she called gaily. "I'm home at last."

I believe she was talking to the house and all the things she owned.

"We have company," said Bill in a grim voice.

She saw Tom Chandler then and turned as white as a funeral lily.

"What's the meaning of this?" she demanded. "Bill, you know I can't stand drinking parties, all those bottles, and what is Julien tied up for?"

"Julien has a key that we'd like to have," said Bill quietly.

Tom walked over to the chest and turned on the record for the detectives. He spoke to Martha for the first time. "I believe this will interest you, too."

When it was over, she gave me a look of hatred.

"Your lock-box key . . . ?" said one of the detectives.

"In my wallet," I told him.

He got it out of my pocket and Martha watched him tossing it in his palm.

"Shall we go?" he asked her.

"Never mind," she said. "I know what you'll find because I've paid a lot of money to keep it hidden. Sure, I killed Avery Chandler. But my brother helped me plan it. I believe you ought to take him along, too."

She flashed me a look of contempt and I felt a new crawling fear inside of me. I hadn't helped her! I'd found that eye-dropper by accident and guessed the rest. And now she was going to name me as an accessory!

"That's a lie, officer!" I had just been untied.

"Come along," he said in that same bored, quiet voice.

I got panicky then and tried to bolt, but Bill tripped me. The detective handcuffed my wrist to Martha's.

In the car, on the way to headquarters, I hissed in her ear: "You fool! You didn't need to confess. There isn't any evidence in my box at the bank! Look at the mess you've got us into."

"No evidence, Julien?" Her voice was shaking. "You told me you had the eye-dropper . . ."

"Well, I don't have it," I told her. "I found the thing that day and threw it into a sewer. I was just protecting you at first. It didn't occur to me until later that it was worth money."

"So all this time I've been paying you, there was no evidence?"

"No evidence," I said. "But you couldn't wait to confess! You were just too anxious to get even with me!"

Her laughter was high-pitched and eerie. I wondered if she was going to put on an act and plead insanity, or if she really was crazy.

Personally, I didn't care much. At the moment, I wasn't feeling any too bright myself.

# The Wire-Pullers

*by Morris Cooper*

*Barry is dead, silent, a stiffened mass of inert flesh on a cold grey slab in the city morgue, an ounce of lead in his heart, a red circle on his throat. . . .*

The words kept running endlessly through my head, repeating themselves like a cracked phonograph record. This must be part of a dream, a gag, and in another moment the lights would flash on and everybody would laugh and yell "Surprise!" and Barry's laughter would be the longest and the loudest and the happiest.

Only it wasn't a dream and I was already awake. Nick, the bartender at the Blue Parrot, laid a hand on my arm when I reached for the brandy bottle.

"Why don't you go home, Mr. Travis?" he said. "All this stuff ever does is make trouble look twice as big as it really is."

I shook my head dully and the face in the blue mirror stared at me stupidly.

"Barry's dead, Nick. Today was going to be his wedding day, but Barry's dead and pretty soon they're going to put him in a dark hole and pile dirt all over him."

"I know," Nick said. He tilted the bottle and two ounces of brandy filled a double-shot glass. An ounce for the bullet in Barry's heart, an ounce for the bullet in Barry's throat.

"To Barry Dillon." He let the brandy roll down his throat. In all the years I've known Nick, that was the only time I ever saw him take a drink.

I pushed myself away from the bar, and the muted tones of the juke box trumpet followed me into the rain-swept streets. Hard-driving sheets of water pelted against my bare face, mingled with the barber's tonic in my hair, ran down the back of my neck. Like a cold needle shower. Like twenty hours ago. . . .

"Wow!" Barry hopped out of the shower in the police locker room and toweled his reddened skin. He waved a wet hand in my direction

554

and I ducked the miniature spray. I slid down the bench, making room for him to get into his locker.

He was tying his shoelaces when I said, "I guess it must be true."

"What?" Barry lifted his face and I could see the tiny bridge of freckles that arched across his nose and disappeared into the dead-white scar that gave his left eye a sort of puckered-up, impish look.

"What must be true?" Barry repeated the question.

I lit a cigarette and my hand shook like a rookie making his first pinch. "The word is out that you and Orchid made a little trip to the city hall today."

Barry said, "You heard right. Two bucks for a license and tomorrow we'll be married. Even wangled a special dispensation on the three-day ruling." He stood up and got a polka-dot tie from his locker. "Judge Krantz is going to perform the ceremony. And, Ray, I want you to stand up with me."

I nodded my head and watched the red-tipped ash fall from my cigarette to the floor and die. "If that's the way you want it."

"That's the way I want it." Unconsciously he ran a thumb across the scar that puckered his left eye. I remembered the night he got that and the Silver Star. And along the line he managed to keep Uncle from paying off on my GI insurance.

"Take a ride with me," Barry said as we left police headquarters. "I want to show you something." I tried not to think as I followed him to the parking lot, but the thoughts hammered at my brain like tiny trapped goblins.

We rode in silence. I thought of Orchid and J. B. van Nostrand and Princess Dine von Konig-Hollerstein III. And I thought of 9:15 P.M.

At 9:15 P.M. Karl Melcig would sit in a chair and buckled straps would keep him from rising; witnesses would peer through the heavy-plated window in the little concrete chamber and a hand would pull a lever and a pellet would drop and the sovereign state would have exacted the penalty due it for the murder of one of its citizens.

Karl Melcig was going to die tonight because Barry was a good cop, and because Barry hadn't yet learned that you've got to let a couple of little fish get by while you wait for the big ones.

Barry didn't like the idea of kids going hungry because their old man couldn't stay away from the horses, and he went to the back room of Klymer's Cigar Store to tell him he didn't want him running a handbook in his district. He found Klymer, but Klymer was no longer interested in making book. And Karl Melcig still had the gun in his hand. As simple as that.

That's what you say. J. B. van Nostrand is a big man. He pays for his pew by the year and he hasn't missed a Sunday at church for thirty years. He's big business and people call him J. B. and he buys the first poppy on Armistice Day—with pictures in all the newspapers.

J. B. sells influence. But it didn't work with Barry. Not even when he was offered a job as chief security officer at a big plant a thousand miles away, and at five times the salary he was getting. There was only one requirement—poor vision.

But Barry wasn't buying any. I never found out what he told J. B., but they tell me that for the first time in his life the great man raised his voice in a fit of temper.

When the storm cooled off and while they were waiting for the trial, Orchid came into the picture. Orchid L'Morte. Some smart publicity boy had tagged her with that name when she first became a night club show girl, and it stuck. The Orchid of Death.

Whatever it was, Orchid had it. She wasn't beautiful, but when you looked into her eyes something stuck in your throat and you became the only man in the world and Orchid the only woman.

Orchid handled lots of payoff money for J. B.—coming and going. But Barry's vision was still 20-20 when Melcig came to trial. He got a message after the jury brought in a verdict of guilty:

*Melcig will wait for you. He'd be lonely if he had to make that trip by himself.*

I don't like death threats, but Barry only laughed and kept on stroking Princess Dine von Konig-Hollerstein III. I couldn't stand that snooty Pomeranian, but Barry went for anything that belonged to Orchid. And Princess was her "bay-bee."

So now Barry and Orchid had a marriage license and a judge. And Karl Melcig was waiting for 9:15 P.M. And J. B. van Nostrand was still selling influence, only it didn't look as if Melcig was going to get his money's worth. And a guy named Klymer, whom no one remembered, was dead and buried because he'd been too greedy to keep on paying a few bucks protection money to the syndicate. . . .

Barry nudged me. "Don't go to sleep on me now, Ray." We were parked in front of Tylo's Jewelry Store.

I followed Barry in and he showed me what he'd had made up. It was one of his metal Army identification tags attached to a tiny gold-plated padlock. I read the engraving on the back of the dog-tag: FROM ONE MUTT TO ANOTHER.

Barry grinned. "It's for Princess. Cute, eh?"

"Yeah." I grabbed Barry by the elbow. "C'mon and let's put on the feedbag and maybe I'll get drunk."

"Ray," he said, "I've got lots of time in front of me. I'm"—he hesitated—"I'm meeting Orchid at 9:30."

I had to say something. "Guess it must be tough for her."

Barry nodded agreement. "Orchid is saying good-bye to all the old things. Beginning tomorrow she's going to live on a policeman's salary."

"Don't forget the Princess," I said. "Probably won't eat if the meat doesn't come from a pedigreed cow."

Barry laughed and laughed and slapped me on the back. "It's a great world, Ray. A great world to be in love in."

They found the car parked under a giant elm. Barry was sitting behind the wheel, and his puckered left eye was still open, as if he were trying to get one last look. If the medical examiner was right, Karl Melcig didn't have to wait more than half an hour for company on that trip to the next world. But I've got a hunch that they didn't stay on the same road long.

Police routine is automatic but it can't always blast through a granite wall. J. B. was still selling influence and proving he could deliver. Influence is a thing that reaches far, sometimes far enough to touch some of the guys that wear a copper's badge and make them look the other way.

The rain was still running down my neck and I was in front of the apartment building where Orchid lived. The apartment that Orchid was going to give up for the love of a cop named Barry.

There was something familiar about the geezer who came out of the front entrance without seeing me. They'll never learn that turned-down brims and hunched-over scurrying makes a cop look twice. I pegged him as I was riding up in the elevator. John Santos. One of those holier-than-thou boys who had been elected controller on a reform wave. By the time the voters woke up, Santos was gone and so was a substantial portion of the city's treasury.

Any other time I would have made tracks after him, but not now. Hell, I wasn't born a cop.

Orchid opened the door and I couldn't be sure if the shadow on her face was sorrow or fear. She was wearing something long that was made of sheer silk and it clung to her body like water. I thought of the slave markets in the days of the Caliphs and of the king's ransom she would have brought.

"Come in, Ray." I followed her across a living room that was a fantasy of orchid-shaded hues. I could understand why some men might be willing to die for her, why some men *would* die because of her.

Princess jumped into my lap when I sat down. I remembered Barry had liked her, so I didn't shove her off. I fondled the engraved dog-tag Barry had shown me yesterday.

My clothes were sticking to me like wet plaster and Orchid started to mix a drink, but I shook my head. She sat down across from me and made a platform for her chin with the backs of her hands. I wondered if the devil ever bothered assuming the guise of a woman.

"It's hard to realize we'll never see him again." Orchid's voice was low. She rested her eyes on me and I felt vaguely uncomfortable—almost as though I were being false to Barry's memory.

I tried to be casual, but my voice sounded strangely loud in that room. I felt Barry's ghost somewhere near, watching, waiting. "Any idea who did it, Orchid?"

Her eyes widened slowly and then the lids dropped. "I haven't the faintest notion. Why would anyone want to kill Barry?"

Orchid was all things to many men, but the role of innocence she was attempting now was not becoming.

"Don't tell me," I said, "that you've forgotten the death threat Barry got." Princess ran a wet tongue over my hand at the mention of Barry's name.

"That." Orchid shook her head impatiently and long black hair tumbled across her shoulders. "Melcig was executed last night and I don't believe in ghosts who shoot people."

I spoke slowly, carefully. "I believe in J. B. A man in his position can't afford to let his prestige be shaken. Once that's gone he's got nothing left to sell. Barry defied him, and now he's cold meat in the morgue."

Orchid shuddered. "Don't be so morbid. And stop jumping to conclusions."

I laughed, but there was no mirth in it. "Don't play coy with me, Orchid. Barry believed what you said about making a clean break."

"And you?"

I shrugged my shoulders. "I asked Santa Claus for a pair of skates when I was five. I got them when I was seven because I saved up enough money selling newspapers."

Orchid took a deep breath and the thin silk across her bosom tightened. "Maybe Barry believed in Santa Claus."

558

"Maybe. And maybe," I added softly, "the guy was just plain in love."

She didn't answer and I went on: "It's a matter of principle with J. B. Having someone defy him is as bad as finding a squealer in his organization."

Orchid said, "That's going to take a lot of proving."

I felt the stone wall around me. "More proving than I'll ever be able to do. J. B. has long arms, but someone must have fingered Barry for him."

There was something like curiosity in Orchid's eyes, and then it was gone. Her voice was almost a purr and Princess perked up her ears.

"You don't honestly believe J. B. killed Barry?"

"What difference does it make whose finger was on the trigger?" I asked. "Barry was no one's fool, and despite all his joshing about that death threat, he would have stayed on guard at least a few days after Melcig's execution. But there wasn't the slightest sign that he'd been suspicious and done anything to defend himself."

"I wish I could help. Oh, how I wish I could help." She pressed her chin until the point was bloodless and white.

I could feel the stone wall getting higher and higher. "Didn't he say anything last night that might help?" I asked. "Maybe he mentioned where he was heading when he left you."

"Last night?" There was a puzzled note in Orchid's voice. "I didn't see Barry at all yesterday."

I kept on playing with Princess' padlocked dog-tag. "I thought he had a date with you last night?"

"He phoned and said something important had come up. He said he'd meet me today"—her voice broke—"and take me to city hall to be married."

"Just that? No other message—or maybe a note?"

"Just that," she answered. "My last memory of Barry will always be his voice over the phone saying good-night."

I felt as if I was going to be sick and I stood up. Princess gave an indignant yelp as she tumbled to the rug. It was an effort to move my lips. "I've got to go."

Orchid held out a hand and I pulled her to her feet. Her sharp nails dug into my palm and for a long moment her taut body swayed against mine and there was fire in my blood.

"Don't stay away too long, Ray," she whispered. "Don't stay away."

I shook myself free. I felt her eyes on me as I crossed the room to the foyer. I saw a pad on the telephone table and the scrawled number on the damp paper and then I was out of the apartment.

The rain was still falling and I walked for a long time. My clothes stuck to me like a shroud but the fire left my blood and my breathing became easier. I made a telephone call and then I went back to the Blue Parrot.

Nick was polishing glasses and I said to him, "Pour me a big one while I make a call." The room was full of shadows and the juke box was silent.

I went to a phone booth and closed the door after me.

The Blue Parrot was one of the places that came under J. B.'s influence and I knew that the phone wires were tapped and one of his boys listened in on everything that was said. It takes a lot of information to keep the selling value of influence at par.

I dialed precinct headquarters and when the desk sergeant answered I said, "This is Travis. Send a couple of boys out to 298 Fillmore and they can pick up John Santos."

The sergeant whistled. "That a straight tip?"

"The McCoy. I got it from his girl friend."

A scrawled number on a pad and a call to the chief operator. And Santos? Orchid was a big girl but she shouldn't have left phone numbers lying around—not on pads dampened by rain-wet fingers. It takes a lot of money for that intangible object called influence and Orchid was a beautiful girl to collect the long green. I wondered how much Santos had left in his pocket after he'd finished paying off.

I went back to the bar and to the drink that was waiting for me. The face in the mirror watched and I thought of tomorrow and of all the days that would come after. The ground over Barry's grave would harden, and grass would grow and die and grow again. I thought of a girl named Orchid and a guy who loved her. I thought of Barry and a dog-tag and a mutt who had gotten under his skin. And I thought of J. B. and what happened to a squealer.

A bell kept ringing in my head and then I heard Nick's voice. "There's a call for you, Mr. Travis." He pointed to the same booth I had used.

The sergeant was jubilant. "That was a hot tip, Ray. Nabbed Santos just as he was pulling out. He must have had a hunch we were coming."

"Yeah."

"Ray. There's something you ought to know. A call came in a few minutes ago—about Orchid."

I waited.

"Someone in her apartment building heard a couple of shots. When the prowl car got there Orchid was dead. Whoever did it got away. Tough."

I hung up and went back to the bar. A long time later Nick said, "I'm closing, Mr. Travis."

I dropped a nickel into the juke box and when the music was good and loud I went out into the street. It had stopped raining and the air was cold, and light was beginning to break the sky.